THE TRUTH ABOUT THE HARRY QUEBERT AFFAIR

FRANCE

"By the end you are exhausted and delighted by the relentless stream of literary adrenaline which the narrator has continuously injected into your veins"　　　　　MARC FUMAROLI, *Le Figaro*

"If you dip your toes into this major novel, you'll have had it; you won't be able to stop yourself racing through it to the last page. You'll be manipulated, thrown off course, flabbergasted, irritated and captivated by a story with manifold new developments, false trails and spectacular turns of events"　　　　　BERNARD PIVOT, *Le Journal du Dimanche*

"A masterstroke . . . a kind of crime novel with not one plot line but many, full of shifting rhythms, changes of course and multiple layers which, like a Russian doll, slot together beautifully"

MARIANNE PAYOT, *L'Express*

ITALY

"After *The Truth about the Harry Quebert Affair*, the contemporary novel will no longer be the same and nobody can pretend not to realize it. Verdict: Summa cum laude . . . At least 110 out of 10. A beautiful novel"

ANTONIO D'ORRICO, *Corriere della Sera*

"Narrative talent is about making an artwork out of life. Dicker has got it"　　　　　MASSIMO GRAMELLINI, *Vanity Fair*

SPAIN

"The furore inspired by the extremely young Dicker and his masterful novel is quite something: we have before us the great thriller that everyone has been waiting for since the Millennium Trilogy by Stieg Larsson"

LAURA FERNÁNDEZ, *El Cultural de El Mundo*

"This book will be celebrated and studied by future writers. It is a model thriller . . . Do read this book"

ENRIQUE DE HÉRIZ, *El Periódico de Catalunya*

"I have never wanted to recommend a book so highly . . . I was mesmerized and intrigued long after I had finished reading . . . A combination of echoes from 'Twin Peaks' and the 'Death on the Staircase' series, John Grisham, 'Psycho' and 'The Exorcist,' and *The Hotel New Hampshire* by John Irving"   SERGI PÀMIES, *La Vanguardia*

GERMANY

"Joël Dicker has written a novel that demonstrates just what can be achieved when a young writer has the courage to give absolutely everything to their work . . . Not only has he dared to take on the greats of his craft like Philip Roth or John Irving, but indeed he has often outdone them . . . This has all the ingredients of a global bestseller"

PEER TEUWSEN, *Die Ziet*

"Brilliantly narrated"   THOMAS BURMEISTER, *Stern*

THE NETHERLANDS

"Joël Dicker overwhelms his readers. Wonderful dialogue, colourful characters, breathtaking twists and a plot that allows no pause for breath . . . all is perfectly weaved together to create an irresistible story in which absolutely nothing is as it seems"   *Trouw*

"Dicker writes a story full of such intelligence and subtlety that you can only regret the fact it comes to an end. A novel that works on so many levels: a crime story, a love story, a comedy of manners, but equally an incisive critique of the art of the modern author"   *Elsevier*

ROMANIA

"It's a crime novel, noir fiction, a coming-of-age story, a romance, a burlesque, a novel within a novel within a novel, a postmodern novel"

Cărturești.ro

"It was said about this novel that it's a kind of Swiss Millennium Trilogy. Probably because it is not a slim work, but also because of the way in which this novel uses a social and political background that is indubitably real"   *HotNews.ro*

THE TRUTH ABOUT
THE HARRY QUEBERT
AFFAIR

JOËL DICKER

Translated from the French by
Sam Taylor

MACLEHOSE PRESS
QUERCUS · LONDON

First published in the French language as
La Vérité sur l'Affaire Harry Quebert
by Éditions de Fallois / L'Âge d'Homme, Paris, 2012
First published in Great Britain in 2014 by

MacLehose Press
an imprint of Quercus
55 Baker Street
7th Floor, South Block
London W1U 8EW

A CIP catalogue record for this book is available
from the British Library

ISBN (HB) 978 0 85705 309 1
ISBN (TPB) 978 0 85705 310 7
ISBN (Ebook) 978 1 84866 325 1

10 9 8 7 6 5 4 3 2 1
Designed and typeset in Minion by Libanus Press Ltd
Printed and bound in Great Britain by Clays Ltd, St Ives plc

To my parents

THE TRUTH ABOUT THE HARRY QUEBERT AFFAIR

The Day of the Disappearance

(Saturday, August 30, 1975)

"Somerset Police. What's your emergency?"

"Hello? My name is Deborah Cooper. I live on Side Creek Lane. I think I've just seen a man running after a girl in the woods."

"Could you tell me exactly what happened, ma'am?"

"I don't know! I was standing by the window. I looked over toward the woods, and I saw this girl running through the trees. There was a man behind her. I think she was trying to get away from him."

"Where are they now?"

"I can't see them anymore. They're in the forest."

"I'm sending a patrol over right now, ma'am."

The news story that would shock the town of Somerset, New Hampshire, began with this phone call. On that day, Nola Kellergan, a fifteen-year-old local girl, disappeared. No trace of her could be found.

PROLOGUE

October 2008
(thirty-three years after the disappearance)

My book was the talk of the town. I could no longer walk the streets of Manhattan in peace. I could no longer go jogging without passersby recognizing me and calling out, "Look, it's Goldman! It's that writer!" Some even started running after me so they could ask me the questions that were gnawing at them: "Is it true what you say in your book? Did Harry Quebert really do that?" In the café in the West Village where I was a regular, certain customers felt free to sit at my table and talk to me. "I'm reading your book right now, Mr Goldman. I can't put it down! The first one was good, of course, but this one . . . Did they really pay you two million bucks to write it? How old are you? I bet you're not even thirty. Twenty-eight! And you're already a multi-millionaire!" Even the door-man at my building, whose progress through my book I was able to note each time I came or went, cornered me for a long talk by the elevator once he had got to the end. "So that's what happened to Nola Kellergan? That poor girl! But how could it happen? How could such a thing be possible, Mr Goldman?"

All of New York, the entire country, in fact, was going crazy for my book. Only two weeks had passed since its publication, and it already promised to be the best-selling book of the year. Everyone wanted to know what had happened in Somerset in 1975. They were talking about it everywhere: on T.V., on the radio, in every newspaper, all over the Internet. In my late twenties, I had, with this book—only the second of my career—become the most famous writer in the country.

The case that had shocked the nation, and from which the core of my story was taken, had blown up several months earlier, at the beginning of summer, when the remains of a girl who had been missing for thirty-three years were discovered. So began the events described in this book, without which the rest of America would never even have heard of the little town of Somerset, New Hampshire.

PART ONE

Writers' Disease
(eight months before the book's publication)

31

In the Caverns of Memory

"The first chapter, Marcus, is essential. If the readers don't like it, they won't read the rest of your book. How do you plan to begin yours?"

"I don't know, Harry. Do you think I'll ever be able to do it?"

"Do what?"

"Write a book."

"I'm certain you will."

In early 2008, about a year and a half after my first novel had made me the new darling of American letters, I was seized by a terrible case of writer's block—a common affliction, I am told, for writers who have enjoyed sudden, meteoric success. My terror of the blank page did not hit me suddenly; it crept over me bit by bit, as if my brain were slowly freezing up. I had deliberately ignored the symptoms when they first appeared. I told myself that inspiration would return tomorrow, or the day after, or perhaps the day after that. But the days and weeks and months went by, and inspiration never returned.

My descent into Hell was divided into three stages. The first, necessary for all breakneck falls, was a blistering rise. My first novel sold one million copies, propelling me, in my twenties, into the upper echelons of the literary world. It was the fall of 2006, and within a few weeks I was a celebrity. I was everywhere: on T.V. screens, in newspapers, on the covers of magazines. My face smiled out from huge advertisements on the subway. Even the harshest critics on the East Coast agreed: Marcus Goldman was destined to become a great writer.

After only one book, the doors of a new life were opening to me. I left my parents' place in New Jersey and moved into a plush apartment in the Village. I swapped my old Ford for a brand new Range Rover with tinted windows. I started going out to expensive restaurants. I had taken on a literary agent who also managed my schedule and came to watch baseball with me on a giant screen in my new apartment. I rented an office close to Central Park, where a secretary named Denise, who was a little in love with me, opened my mail, made me coffee, and filed my important documents.

For the first six months after the publication of the book, I contented myself with enjoying the sweetness of my new existence. In the mornings I went by the office to leaf through any new articles about me, to surf the Internet, and to read the dozens of fan letters I received every day. Then, feeling pleased with myself and satisfied that I'd done enough work for the day, I would wander the streets of Manhattan, causing a stir when I passed by. I spent the rest of my days enjoying the new rights I'd been granted by celebrity: the right to buy anything I liked; the right to a V.I.P. box in Madison Square Garden to watch the Rangers; the right to share red carpets with pop stars whose albums I had bought when I was younger; the right to make every man in New York jealous by dating Lydia Gloor, the star of the country's top-rated T.V. show. Sure that my success would never end, I took no notice when my agent and my publisher fired off their first warnings about getting back to work and writing my second novel.

It was during the next six months when I realized the tide was turning. The flood of fan mail slowed to a trickle, and fewer people stopped me on the street. Soon, those who did recognize me started asking, "Mr Goldman, what's your next book about? And when's it coming out?" I understood that it was time to get started, and I did. I wrote down ideas on loose sheets of paper and made outlines on my laptop. But it was no good. So I thought of other ideas and made other outlines. Again, without success. Finally, I bought a new laptop, in the hope that it would come pre-loaded with good ideas. All in vain. Next, I tried changing my work habits: I made Denise stay in my office until late at night so she could take dictation of what I imagined were great sentences, wonderful one-liners, and the beginnings of remarkable novels. But when I looked at them the next day, the one-liners seemed dull, the sentences badly constructed, and the beginnings all dead ends. I was entering the second stage of my disease.

By the fall of 2007, a year after the publication of my first book, I had still not set down a single word of the next one. I began to understand that glory was a Gorgon who could turn you to stone if you failed to continue performing. My share of the public's attention had been taken over by the latest rising politicians, the stars of the hottest new reality T.V. show and a rock band that had just broken through. It was a ludicrously short time frame as far as I was concerned since my book had appeared, but on a global scale it was an eternity. During that same year, in the United States, more than four million babies had been born, almost two and a half million people had died, more than thirty thousand had been shot to death, half a million had started taking drugs, fifty thousand had become millionaires, and some forty thousand had died in automobile accidents. And I had written just one book.

Schmid & Hanson, the powerful New York publishers who had paid me a tidy sum to publish my first novel and who had great hopes for my future work, were pestering my agent, Douglas Claren—and he, in turn, was hounding me. He told me that time was running out, that it was imperative I produce a new manuscript. I tried to reassure him in order to reassure myself, telling him that my second novel was progressing well and that there was nothing to be worried about. But despite all the hours I spent in my office, the pages on my desk remained blank; inspiration had abandoned me without warning. At night, in bed, unable to sleep, I would torture myself by thinking that soon the great Marcus Goldman would no longer exist. That thought frightened me so much that I decided to go on vacation to clear my head. I treated myself to a month in a five-star hotel in Miami, supposedly to recharge my batteries, firmly convinced that relaxing beneath palm trees would enable me to rediscover my creative genius. But Florida was, of course, nothing but an attempt to escape. Two thousand years before me, the philosopher Seneca had experienced the same troublesome predicament: No matter where you go, your problems go with you. It was as if, having just arrived in Miami, a kind Cuban baggage handler had run after me as I left the airport and said:

"Are you Mr Goldman?"

"Yes."

"This belongs to you."

And he handed me an envelope containing a sheaf of papers.

"Are these my blank pages?"

"Yes, Mr Goldman. Surely you weren't going to leave New York without them?"

And so I spent that month in Florida alone with my demons in a luxury suite, wretched and disheartened. On my laptop, which I never shut down, the document I had named *new novel.doc* remained blank. It was after buying a margarita for the hotel pianist that I realized I had caught a disease sadly common in artistic circles. Sitting next to me at the bar, the pianist explained that he had written only one song in his entire life, but that it had been a massive hit. He had been so successful that he had never been able to write anything else, and now, penniless and miserable, he scraped out a living by playing other people's tunes for the hotel's guests. "I was touring all the time back then, performing in the biggest venues in the country," he told me while gripping my lapel. "Ten thousand people screaming my name . . . chicks fainting or throwing their panties at me. It was something else, man." And, having licked the salt from around his glass like a small dog, he added, "I swear to you it's the truth." That was the saddest thing: I knew he wasn't lying.

The third stage of my nightmare began when I returned to New York. On the plane home, I read an article about a young author who'd just published a novel to huge acclaim. Life was taunting me: Not only had I been forgotten, but now I was going to be replaced. A panicky Douglas met me at the airport: Schmid & Hanson had run out of patience and they wanted proof that the novel was progressing and that I would soon submit the manuscript.

"We're up shit creek," he told me in the car, as we drove back to Manhattan. "Please tell me your stay in Florida revived you, and that your book is almost finished! There's this new guy everyone's talking about . . . His book's going to be a bestseller this Christmas. And you, Marcus? What have you got to give us for Christmas?"

"I'm going to buckle down," I promised him, as fear gripped me. "I'll get there! We'll do a big promotional campaign! People loved the first book—they'll love the next one too!"

"Marc, you don't understand. We could have done that a few months ago. That was our strategy: ride the wave of your success. The public wanted Marcus Goldman, but as Marcus Goldman was busy chilling out in Florida, the readers bought a book by someone else instead. Books are interchangeable: People want a story that excites them, relaxes them, entertains them. And if you don't give them that, someone else will—and you'll be history."

Newly chastened, I went to work as never before: I began writing at six in the morning and didn't stop until nine or ten at night, carried away by the frenzy of despair. I strung words and sentences together, came up with dozens of story ideas. But, much to my frustration, I didn't produce anything worthwhile. Denise spent her days worrying about me. She had nothing else to do—no dictation to take, no letters to file. She paced up and down the hallway, and when she couldn't take it anymore, she pounded on my door.

"I'm begging you, Marcus," she said. "Please, *please* open the door! Come out of your office for a while, go for a walk in the park. You haven't eaten anything all day!"

I yelled in reply: "Not hungry! Not hungry! No book, no dinner!"

She was practically sobbing. "Don't say things like that, Marcus! I'm going to the deli at the corner to buy a roast beef sandwich, your favorite. I'll be quick!"

I heard her pick up her bag and run to the door, then clatter down the stairs as if her rushing might change anything. I had finally grasped the seriousness of my situation: Writing a book from scratch had seemed easy, but now that I was at the height of my fame, now that it was time to live up to my talent, to repeat the weary climb toward success that is the writing of a good novel, I no longer felt capable of it. I had been floored by the writers' disease, and there was no-one to help me to my feet. Everyone I talked to about it told me it was nothing to worry about, that it was probably very common, and that if I didn't write my book today, I would do it tomorrow. For two days, I tried writing in my old bedroom, at my parents' place in Montclair, the room where I had found the inspiration for my first novel. But that ended in pitiful failure. My mother was not altogether blameless for this, because she spent both of those days sitting next to me, squinting at the screen of my laptop and repeating, "It's very good, Markie."

Finally, I said, "Mom, I haven't written a single line."

"But I can tell it's going to be very good."

"Mom, if you'd just leave me alone . . ."

"Why do you need to be alone? Are you hungry? Do you want pancakes? Waffles? Some eggs, maybe?"

"I'm not hungry."

"So why do you want me to leave you alone? Are you saying it disturbs you to be with the woman who gave birth to you?"

"No, it doesn't disturb me, but . . ."

"But what?"

"Nothing, Mom."

"You need a girlfriend, Markie. Do you think I don't know you've split up with that T.V. actress? What's her name again?"

"Lydia Gloor. But we weren't really together in the first place. I mean, it was just a fling."

"'Just a fling'! That's how young people are nowadays. Nothing is ever more than 'just a fling,' and they end up bald and childless at fifty!"

"What does that have to do with being bald, Mom?"

"It doesn't have anything to do with being bald. But do you think it's right that I should find from a magazine that you're with this girl? What kind of son does that to his mother? And guess what? Just before you went to Florida, I go to Scheingetz's—the hairdresser's, not the butcher's—and everyone in the salon is looking at me strangely. I ask what's going on, and Mrs Berg, with her head under a dryer, shows me a magazine she's reading: There's a picture of you and that Lydia Gloor, standing in the street together, and the headline of the article says that you've separated. Everyone in the hairdresser's knew you'd split up, and I didn't even know you'd been dating this girl! Obviously, I didn't want to look like an idiot, so I said she was a charming girl and that she'd often had dinner with us at the house."

"I didn't tell you about her because it wasn't serious. She wasn't The One, you know?"

"But they're never The One! You never meet any of the right people, Markie! That's the problem. Do you really think T.V. actresses know how to keep a home? You know, I met Mrs Levey yesterday at the grocery store, and her daughter is single too. She'd be perfect for you. And she has very nice teeth. Should I ask her to come over now?"

"No, I'm trying to work."

And just then the bell rang.

"I think that's them," my mother said.

"What do you mean, 'that's them'?"

"Mrs Levey and her daughter. I asked them to come over for tea at four o'clock. It's four exactly. Punctuality is important in a woman. Don't you love her already?"

"You invited them over for tea? Get rid of them, Mom! I'm not here to have a tea party—I have a book to write!"

"Oh, Markie, you really need a girlfriend. A girlfriend you'll get engaged to and then marry. You think too much about books and not enough about getting married."

Nobody understood what was at stake. Soon after the start of the new year, in January 2008, Roy Barnaski, the head of Schmid & Hanson, summoned me to his office on the fifty-first floor of a skyscraper on Lexington Avenue to give me a serious talking-to. "So, Goldman, when will I have this new manuscript?" he barked. "We have a contract for two more books. You need to get to work, and be quick about it! This is a business! Did you see that guy whose book came out before Christmas? He's replaced you in the eyes of the public! His agent says his next novel is almost finished already. And yours? You're costing us money! So pull yourself together. You need to pull a rabbit out of your hat. Write me a great book, and you can still save your career. I'm giving you six months. You have until the end of June."

Six months to write a book, when I had been blocked for more than a year. Worse still, Barnaski had not informed me, when he gave me this deadline, of the consequences of failing to meet it. It was Douglas who did that, two weeks later. "Barnaski is going apeshit. Do you know what'll happen if you don't deliver in June? He'll sue the shit out of you. They'll take all your money, and you'll have to wave goodbye to this beautiful life of yours. This cool apartment, those fine Italian shoes, your Range Rover . . . they'll take it all."

Lesson number two: Not only is glory ephemeral, but it also comes at a price. The evening after Douglas delivered his warning, I picked up my phone and dialed the number of the only person I thought might be able to help me out of this quicksand: Harry Quebert, formerly my college professor, and above all one of the bestselling and most highly respected authors in the country. I had been close friends with him for more than a decade, since I'd been his student at Burrows College in Massachusetts.

It had been more than a year since I had spoken to him. I reached him at his house in Somerset, New Hampshire. When he heard my voice, he said mockingly:

"Oh, Marcus! Is it really you? Incredible. I haven't heard a word from you since you became a star. I tried calling you a month ago and was told by your secretary that you weren't coming to the phone for anyone."

"I'm in trouble, Harry," I answered bluntly. "I don't think I'm a writer anymore."

He immediately dropped the sarcasm. "What're you talking about?"

"I don't know what to write anymore. I'm finished. Totally blocked. It's been like this for months, maybe a year."

He laughed warmly, reassuringly. "It's just a mental hang-up, Marcus! Writer's block is as senseless as sexual impotence: It's just your genius panicking, the same way your libido makes you go soft when you're about to play hide-the-salami with one of your young admirers and all you can think about is how you're going to give her an orgasm that can be measured on the Richter scale. Don't worry about genius—just keep churning out the words. Genius comes naturally."

"You think?"

"I'm sure of it. But you might have to give up a few of your celebrity parties. Writing is a serious business. I thought I'd taught you that."

"But I am working hard! That's all I'm doing! And yet I'm not getting anywhere."

"Well, maybe you're in the wrong place, then. New York is a wonderful city, but there's too much noise. Why don't you come here, to my place, the way you did when you were my student?"

Leaving to find the inspiration for a new book in a seaside village, in the company of my old mentor—it was exactly what I needed. So it was that, one week later, in mid-February 2008, I went to visit Harry in Somerset, New Hampshire. This was a few months before the dramatic events I am about to narrate.

Before it provided the setting for a scandal that shook the nation in the summer of 2008, no-one had ever heard of Somerset. It is a small town by the ocean, about fifteen minutes from the Massachusetts border. On its main street you can find a movie theater—always showing films a month or two after the rest of the country—a few shops, a post office, a police station, and a handful of restaurants, including Clark's, the town's historic diner. Around this center, there were peaceful neighborhoods of painted wooden houses with porches and slate roofs, bordered by perfectly manicured lawns. It was like something from a mythical America, where no-one ever locks his door; one of those places frequently found in New England, so calm that you feel sheltered from all the world's storms.

I knew Somerset well, having visited Harry there as a student. Harry lived in a beautiful stone and solid-pine house—located outside town, on Shore Road in the direction of Maine—that overlooked a stretch of water identified on maps as Goose Cove. It was a writer's house, with an ocean view and a deck with a steep staircase that took you straight down to the beach. All around was a tranquil wilderness: the coastal forest, the shoreline of shells and boulders, the damp thickets of ferns and moss, a few walking trails that ran alongside the beach. If you didn't know civilization was only a few miles away, you might easily believe yourself to be at the end of the earth. It was also easy to imagine yourself an old writer here, producing masterpieces out on the deck, inspired by the tides and the light on the ocean.

I left New York on February 10, in the depths of my writer's block.

The country was already quaking from the first vibrations of the presidential election: Five days earlier, Super Tuesday (held in February, rather than the usual March, a hint that this was going to be an extraordinary year) had all but awarded the Republican nomination to Senator John McCain, while on the Democratic side the battle between Hillary Clinton and Barack Obama was still raging. I drove to Somerset without stopping. It had been a snowy winter, and the landscape that rushed past me was blanketed with white. I loved New England, I loved its tranquility, I loved its vast forests, I loved its ponds with water lilies where you could swim in summer and skate in winter, I liked that you didn't have to pay sales tax or income tax in New Hampshire. My memory is that when I arrived at Harry's house that day, on a cold and misty afternoon, I immediately experienced a feeling of inner peace. Harry was waiting for me on the porch, bundled up in a huge winter coat. I got out of the car and he came over to meet me, placing his hands on my shoulders and offering me a generous, reassuring smile.

"What's going on, Marcus?"

"I don't know, Harry."

"Come on, let's go in. You've always been oversensitive."

Even before I unpacked, the two of us sat down in his living room to chat for a while. He made coffee. A fire crackled in the hearth. It was warm inside. Through the large bay window, I saw the ocean roiled up by icy winds and sleet falling onto the rocks.

"I'd forgotten how beautiful it is here," I murmured.

He nodded.

"You'll see that I'm going to take good care of you. You're going to write a novel that will knock 'em all out. There's nothing to worry about—all great writers go through this."

He seemed as serene and confident as ever. I had never seen him show any self-doubt; his mere presence radiated natural authority. He was in his mid-sixties and he looked great, with his always impeccable silvered mane of hair, his wide shoulders, and a body still taut and powerful from long years spent boxing. In fact, it was through this sport, which I too practiced regularly, that we had first become friends at Burrows College.

The ties that bound me to Harry, which I will come back to later on in this story, were deep and strong. He had entered my life in 1998, when I arrived at Burrows. He was fifty-seven. He had spent the last thirteen years sprinkling his stardust on the English department of this modest rural school. Before this, I had known Harry Quebert the Great Author by name, like everyone else did. At Burrows, I met Just Harry, the man who would become one of my closest friends, in spite of the difference in our ages, and who would teach me to be a writer. His own apotheosis had come in the middle of the 1970s, when his second book, *The Origin of Evil*, had sold a million or more copies and won two of the country's most prestigious literary awards: The National Book Critics Circle Award and the National Book Award. Since then, he had published books on a regular basis and had a popular monthly column in the *Boston Globe*. I hoped that in the next few weeks he would be able to turn me into a writer again and teach me how to cross the chasm of the blank page. "Writers get blocked sometimes. It comes with the territory," he explained. "But if you get down to work, it will unblock itself—you'll see." He put me in his ground-floor office, where he himself had written most of his books, including *The Origin of Evil*. I spent long hours in there, trying to write, but most of the time all I did was stare out at the ocean and the snow. When he brought me coffee or something to eat, he would see the despair on my face and attempt to cheer me up. Eventually, one morning, he said, "Don't look like that, Marcus. Anyone would think you were dying."

"I'm not far off."

"Come on. It's fine to worry about what the world is coming to, but you shouldn't fret like this over a book."

"But you . . . have you ever had this problem?"

He laughed loudly.

"Writer's block? Are you kidding? More than you can even imagine!"

"My publisher says if I don't write a new book now, I'm finished."

"You know what a publisher is? He's a failed writer whose father was rich enough that he's able to appropriate other people's talents. You'll see, Marcus—everything will be O.K. You've got a great career ahead of you. Your first book was remarkable, and the second will be even better. Don't worry—I'm going to help you find your inspiration again."

I cannot say that my time in Somerset gave me back my inspiration, but it was undeniably good for me. For Harry too, whom, I knew, often felt lonely: He was a man with no family and with few distractions. Those were happy days. In fact, they were our last happy days together. We spent them taking long walks by the sea, listening to opera, hiking cross-country ski trails, attending local cultural events, stopping in at supermarkets in search of little cocktail sausages, the profits from which were donated to military veterans (Harry was crazy about those sausages; he thought they alone justified the war in Iraq). We also often went to Clark's, where we would eat lunch and laze around all afternoon drinking coffee and talking about life, just as we used to when I was his student. Everyone in Somerset knew and respected Harry, and soon everyone knew me too.

The two people I felt closest to were Jenny Dawn, who ran Clark's, and Ernie Pinkas, the unpaid municipal librarian, a good friend of Harry's who sometimes came to Goose Cove in the evenings for a glass of Scotch. I went to the library myself every morning to read the *New York Times*. On the first day, I noticed that Ernie Pinkas had put a copy of my book on prominent display. He showed it to me proudly and said, "You see, Marcus, your book has pride of place here. It's the library's most borrowed book. When's the next one coming out?"

Harry had been sitting in the same place at Clark's for thirty-three years: Table 17, which boasted a metal plaque put there by Jenny with the inscription:

IT WAS AT THIS TABLE, IN THE SUMMER OF 1975,
THAT HARRY QUEBERT WROTE HIS FAMOUS NOVEL,
"THE ORIGIN OF EVIL"

I had seen this plaque so many times, but I had never really paid it much attention. It was only during this stay that I began taking a keen interest in it, spending a long time contemplating it. Soon I was obsessed by those lines. Sitting at this ugly little wooden table, sticky with grease and maple syrup, in this small-town diner in New Hampshire, Harry had written his great masterpiece, the book that had made him a literary legend. Where had he found such inspiration? I wanted to sit at this table too, to write and be struck by genius. And in fact I did sit there, with pens and sheets of paper, for two afternoons straight, but it was no good. Finally, I asked Jenny: "So he just sat at this table and wrote?"

She nodded. "All day long, Marcus. The whole blessed day. He never stopped. It was the summer of 1975—I remember it well."

I felt a kind of fury boiling within me. I too wanted to write a master-piece; I too wanted to write a book to which all other books would be compared. These feelings came to the fore after I had been in Somerset for almost a month, and Harry discovered that I had still not written a single word. It was early March, in Harry's office at Goose Cove, where I was waiting for divine inspiration. Harry walked in, an apron tied around his waist, bringing me some doughnuts he'd just made.

"How's it going?" he asked.

"I'm writing something amazing," I replied, passing him a sheaf of papers like the Cuban baggage handler gave me three months earlier.

He put down his plate and looked at them excitedly, before realizing they were blank.

"You haven't written anything? You've been here more than three weeks and you haven't written anything at all?"

I lost my temper. "Nothing! Nothing! Nothing of any worth! Only scenarios for second-rate novels."

"But, dear God, Marcus, what do you want to write?"

I replied without thinking: "A masterpiece! I want to write a masterpiece!"

"A masterpiece?"

"Yes. I want to write a great novel, with great ideas! I want to write something unforgettable."

Harry looked at me for a moment and then burst out laughing. "Your hubris always did get on my nerves. I've been telling you that for years. You're going to become a very great writer—I know it. I've been sure of it since I first met you. But do you want to know what your problem is? You're in too much of a hurry! How old are you, exactly?"

"Twenty-eight."

"Twenty-eight years old! And you already expect to be a cross between Saul Bellow and Arthur Miller? Glory will come to you—don't be in such a hurry. I'm closing on seventy, and I'm terrified. Time flies by, you know, and each year that passes is another year I can't get back. What do you think's going to happen, Marcus? That you'll just produce another book, like a hen laying an egg? A career has to be built slowly. And as for writing a great novel, you don't need great ideas. Just be yourself and you'll get there, I have absolutely no doubt about that. I've been teaching literature for twenty-plus years—twenty-plus *long* years—and you're the most brilliant student I ever had."

"Thank you."

"Don't thank me. It's the simple truth. But don't come to me like a crybaby because you haven't received the Nobel Prize yet! For God's sake, you're twenty-eight years old! Jesus . . . stick your great novels up your ass! The Nobel Prize in Stupidity, that's what you deserve."

"But how did you do it, Harry? *The Origin of Evil.* That's a masterpiece! And it was only your second book. How did you do it? How *do* you write a masterpiece?"

He smiled sadly. "You don't write a masterpiece. It writes itself. And, you know, for lots of people, that is the only book I've ever written . . . I mean, none of the novels that came afterward had the same success. Whenever anyone mentions my name, the first thing they think about— almost the only thing they think about—is *The Origin of Evil*. And that's sad, because I think if I'd been told at your age that I'd already reached the summit of my career, I'd have drowned myself in the ocean. Don't be in so much of a hurry."

"Do you regret that book?"

"Maybe . . . a little bit . . . I don't know . . . I don't like to dwell on regrets. They tell you that you have not come to terms with what you've done."

"But what should I do, then?"

"Do what you've always done best: write. And if I can give you some advice, don't be like me. You and I are very similar in many ways, so I'm begging you: Don't repeat the mistakes I made."

"Like what?"

"In the summer I came here, in 1975, I too wanted desperately to write a great novel. I was obsessed by the desire to become a great writer."

"And you succeeded."

"You don't understand. Sure, I'm now a so-called 'great writer,' but I'm living on my own in this enormous house. My life is empty, Marcus. Don't be like me. Don't let yourself be eaten up by ambition. Otherwise, you'll be left with a lonely heart and a bunch of sad words. Why don't you have a girlfriend?"

"I haven't found anyone I really like."

"I think the problem is you fuck like you write: It's ecstasy or it's nothing. Find someone good, and give her a chance. Do the same with your book: Give yourself a chance too. Give your life a chance! You know what my main occupation is? Feeding the seagulls. I collect stale bread—in that tin in the kitchen with SOUVENIR OF ROCKLAND,

MAINE written on it—and I throw it to the seagulls. You shouldn't spend all your time writing."

Despite the wisdom Harry was lavishing upon me, I remained obsessed by this idea: How had he, at my age, found the key to unlocking the genius that had enabled him to write *The Origin of Evil*? This question circled my brain ever faster, and because Harry had let me have the run of his office, I decided I had the right to rummage around a bit. I had no idea what I was about to discover. It all began when I opened a drawer in search of a pen and found a notebook and some pages of working notes. I was very excited—it was an opportunity I hadn't dared hope for, a chance to understand how Harry worked, to find out if his papers were covered in cross-outs or if his genius flowed naturally from him. Insatiable, I began searching his library for other papers, hoping to find the manuscript of *The Origin of Evil*. I had to wait for Harry to leave the house, but as it happens, Thursday was the day he taught at Burrows, leaving early in the morning and generally not returning until evening. And on the afternoon of Thursday, March 6, 2008, I discovered something that I decided to forget immediately: In 1975 Harry had had an affair with a fifteen-year-old girl.

I uncovered his secret while rummaging furiously and shamelessly through the shelves of his office. Concealed behind the books, I found a large varnished wooden box with a hinged lid. This, I sensed, could be the Holy Grail: the manuscript of *The Origin of Evil*. I grabbed the box and opened it, but to my dismay there was no manuscript inside, just a series of photographs and newspaper articles. The photographs showed a young Harry—thirty-something, magnificent, elegant, proud—and by his side, a teenage girl. There were four or five pictures, and she was in all of them. In one of them, Harry was lying shirtless—tanned and muscular—on a beach, next to the smiling young girl, who wore sunglasses tucked into her long blond hair to hold them in place; he was holding her tightly to him and kissing her on the cheek. On the back of the photograph was an annotation: *Nola and me, Martha's*

Vineyard, late July. At that moment I was too caught up in my discovery to hear Harry return from campus much earlier than expected. I heard neither the crunch of his Corvette's tires on Goose Cove's gravel driveway, nor the sound of his voice as he entered the house. I didn't hear anything, because inside the box, underneath the photographs, I found a letter, undated. In a child's hand, on pretty writing paper, were these words:

> *Don't worry, Harry. Don't you worry about me. I'll find a way to meet you. Wait for me in Room 8. I like that number, it's my favorite. Wait for me there at 7 p.m. And then we'll go away forever.*
>
> *I love you so much.*
> *Hugs and kisses,*
> *Nola*

So who was this Nola? My heart pounding, I began skimming the newspaper clippings: articles that described the mysterious disappearance of a certain Nola Kellergan one August evening in 1975. And the Nola in the newspaper photographs was the same as the Nola in Harry's photographs. It was at that precise moment that Harry entered the office, carrying a tray with cups of coffee and a plate of cookies. Having pushed open the door with his foot, he dropped the tray, because he had found me crouched on the carpet with the contents of his secret box scattered before me.

"But . . . what are you doing?" he shouted. "Are you . . . spying on me, Marcus? I invite you to my home and you betray my trust by going through my private things? And you call yourself a friend!"

I muttered some pitiful excuses: "I just happened upon it, Harry. I found the box by chance. I shouldn't have opened it. I'm sorry."

"Damn right you shouldn't have opened it! How dare you! What the hell did you think you were doing?"

He snatched the photographs from my hands, quickly gathered up all the newspaper clippings, and shoved everything back haphazardly into the box. He then carried the box to his bedroom and closed the door. I had never seen him like this, and I couldn't tell whether the emotion that gripped him was panic or rage. Through the door, I repeated my excuses and thought up new ones, telling him that I hadn't meant to hurt him, that I'd found the box by chance, but nothing made any difference. It was two hours before he came out of his room again: He went downstairs to the living room and downed several whiskeys. When he seemed to have calmed down a bit, I finally dared approach him.

"Harry . . . who is that girl?" I asked gently.

He lowered his eyes. "Nola."

"Who is she?"

"Don't ask me who she is. Please."

"Harry, who is she?" I repeated.

He shook his head. "I loved her, Marcus. I loved her so much."

"But how come you never mentioned her to me?"

"It's complicated . . ."

"Nothing is complicated between friends."

He shrugged. "I guess I may as well tell you, now that you've seen those photographs. In 1975, when I arrived in Somerset, I fell in love with this fifteen-year-old girl. Her name was Nola and she was the love of my life."

There was a brief silence.

I finally asked: "What happened to her?"

"It's a sordid business. She disappeared. One night in late August, someone who lived nearby saw her, bleeding, and she was never seen again. I'm sure you saw the newspaper articles. She's never been found. No-one knows what happened to her."

"That's terrible."

He nodded. There was a long silence.

"Nola changed my life, you know. And I would have given up becoming the great Harry Quebert, the famous writer; I would have given up all the glory and the money and the fame if it meant I could have kept her. Nothing I've been able to do since she disappeared has given as much meaning to my life as the summer we spent together."

I had never seen Harry look so shaken before. After staring hard at me for a moment, he added: "Marcus, no-one knows about this. You are now the only one who does. And you must keep the secret."

"Of course."

"Give me your word!"

"I promise, Harry."

"If anyone in Somerset were to find out that I'd had an affair with Nola Kellergan, it could ruin me."

"You can trust me, Harry."

That was all I knew about Nola Kellergan. We did not speak about her again, nor about the box, and I decided to bury this episode forever in the caverns of my memory. It never crossed my mind that a few months later Nola's ghost would return to haunt us both.

I went back to New York at the end of March, after six weeks in Somerset. I was three months from Barnaski's deadline and knew I had no chance of saving my career. I had burned my wings, and now I was in free fall. I was the sorriest and least productive famous writer in New York. The weeks passed, and I spent most of my time fervently preparing for my defeat. I found a new job for Denise, contacted a legal firm that might prove useful when the time came for Schmid & Hanson to take me to court, and I made a list of objects to which I was most attached and needed to hide at my parents' place before the sheriffs started banging on my door. At the beginning of June—that fateful month, the month they would build my scaffold—I started marking off the days until my artistic death: There were thirty days left, then I would be summoned to Barnaski's office and executed. The countdown had begun.

30

Marcus the Magnificent

"Your second chapter is very important, Marcus. It has to be incisive, hard-hitting."

"Hard-hitting?"

"Yeah, like boxing. You're right-handed, but when you're in the guard position it's your left hand that hits first. A good, hard jab stuns your opponent, and you follow it with a powerful cross from your right to knock him out. That's what your second chapter has to be: a right-handed punch to the reader's jaw."

It was Thursday, June 12. I had spent the morning at home, reading in my living room. Outside, it was hot but wet: New York had been under a warm drizzle for the past three days. About one in the afternoon, my telephone rang. At first, it seemed there was no-one at the other end. Then I made out a stifled sob.

"Who's there?" I said.

"She . . . she's dead."

I recognized his voice immediately, though it was barely audible.

"Harry? Is that you?"

"She's dead, Marcus."

"Who?"

"Nola."

"What? What do you mean?"

"She's dead, and it's all my fault. What did I do? What did I do, for God's sake?"

He was crying.

"Harry, what are you talking about? What are you trying to tell me?"

He hung up. I called back right away, but there was no answer. I tried his cell phone without success. I tried again many times, leaving several messages on his answering machine. But I didn't hear back. At that point, I had no idea that Harry had called me from the state police headquarters in Concord. I understood nothing of what was going on until about 4 p.m., when Douglas called me.

"Jesus, Marc, have you heard?"

"Heard what?"

"My God, turn on the T.V.! It's about Harry Quebert! It's Quebert!"

I put on the news. To my amazement I saw the house at Goose Cove on the screen and heard the presenter say: "It was here, in his home in Somerset, New Hampshire, that author Harry Quebert was arrested today after police discovered human remains on his property. Initial inquiries suggest this may be the body of Nola Kellergan, a local girl who disappeared from her house at the age of fifteen in August 1975 and has never been seen since." The room began spinning around me, and I collapsed onto the couch in a daze. I couldn't hear anything clearly anymore—not the T.V., nor Douglas, at the other end of the line, bellowing, "Marcus? Are you there? Hello? He killed a girl? Quebert killed a girl?" In my head, everything blurred together like a bad dream.

So it was that I found out, at the same time as a stupefied America, what had happened a few hours earlier: That morning a landscaping company had arrived at Goose Cove, at Harry's request, to plant hydrangea bushes. When they dug up the earth, the gardeners found human bones buried three feet deep and had immediately informed the police. A whole skeleton had quickly been uncovered, and Harry had been arrested.

On the T.V. screen, it was all moving very fast. They cut between live broadcasts from the scene of the crime in Somerset and from Concord, the New Hampshire capital, located sixty miles to the northwest, where Harry was in police custody. Apparently a clue found close to the body strongly suggested that here were the remains of Nola Kellergan; a police spokesman had already indicated that if this information was confirmed, Harry Quebert would also be named as a suspect in the murder of one Deborah Cooper, the last person to have seen Nola alive on August 30, 1975. Cooper had been found murdered the same day, after calling the police. It was appalling. The rumble grew ever louder as the news crossed the country in real time, relayed by television, radio, the Internet, and social networks: Harry Quebert, sixty-seven, one of the greatest authors of the second half of the twentieth century, was a child predator.

It took me a long time to realize what was happening. Several hours, perhaps. At 8 p.m., when a worried Douglas came by to see how I was holding up, I was still convinced that the whole thing was a mistake.

"How can they accuse him of two murders when they're not even sure it's the body of this Nola?" I said.

"Well, there was a corpse buried in his yard, however you look at it."

"But why would he have brought people in to dig up the place where he'd supposedly buried a body? It makes no sense! I have to go there."

"Go where?"

"New Hampshire. I have to defend Harry."

Douglas replied with typical down-to-earth Midwestern sobriety: "Absolutely not, Marcus. Don't go there. You don't want to get involved in this mess."

"Harry called me . . ."

"When? Today?"

"About one this afternoon. I must have been the one telephone call he was allowed I have to go there and support him! It's very important."

"Important? What's important is your second book. I hope you haven't been taking me for a ride and that you really will have a manuscript ready by the end of the month. Barnaski is shitting bricks. Do you realize what's going to happen to Harry? Don't get mixed up in this, Marc. Don't screw up your career."

On the T.V., the state attorney general was giving a press conference. He listed the charges against Harry: kidnapping and two counts of murder. Harry was formally accused of having murdered Deborah Cooper and Nola Kellergan. And the punishment for these crimes, taken together, was death.

Harry's fall was only just beginning. Footage of the preliminary hearing, which was held the next day, was broadcast on T.V. We saw him arrive in the courtroom, tracked by dozens of cameras and illuminated by photographers' flashbulbs, handcuffed and surrounded by policemen. He looked as if he had been through hell: somber faced, unshaven, hair disheveled, shirt unbuttoned, eyes swollen. His lawyer, Benjamin Roth, stood next to him. Roth was a renowned attorney in Concord who had often advised Harry in the past. I knew him slightly, having met him a few times at Goose Cove.

The whole country was able to watch the hearing live, as Harry pleaded not guilty, and the judge ordered him remanded into custody in New Hampshire's State Prison for Men. But this was only the start of the storm. At that moment, I still had the naive hope that it would all be over soon, but one hour after the hearing, I received a call from Harry's lawyer.

"Harry gave me your number," Roth said. "He insisted I call. He wants you to know that he's innocent, that he didn't kill anybody."

"I know he's innocent," I said. "Tell me how he's doing?"

"Not too great, as you can imagine. The cops have been giving him a hard time. He admitted to having a fling with Nola the summer she disappeared."

"I knew about Nola. What about the rest?"

Roth hesitated a second before answering. "He denies it. But . . ."

"But what?" I demanded.

"Marcus, I'm not going to hide it from you. This is going to be difficult. The evidence is . . ."

"The evidence is *what*? Tell me, for God's sake!"

"This has to stay a secret. No-one can know."

"I won't say a word. You can trust me."

"Along with the girl's remains, the investigators found the manuscript of *The Origin of Evil*."

"What?"

"I'm telling you, the manuscript of that damn book was buried with her. Harry is in deep shit."

"What does Harry say?"

"He says he wrote that book for her. That she was always snooping around his home in Goose Cove, and that sometimes she would borrow his pages to read. He says that a few days before she disappeared, she took the manuscript home with her."

"What? He wrote that book for her?"

"Yes. But that can't get out, under any circumstances. You can imagine the scandal there'd be if the media found out that one of the bestselling books of the last fifty years is not a simple love story, like everyone thinks, but the fruit of an illicit affair between a guy of thirty-four and a girl of fifteen . . ."

"Can you get him released on bail?"

"Bail? You don't understand how serious this is. There's no question of bail when it comes to capital crimes. The punishment he risks is lethal injection. Ten days from now his case will be presented to a grand jury, which will decide whether to pursue charges and hold a trial. It's just a formality. There's no doubt there will be a trial."

"And in the meantime?"

"He'll stay in prison."

"But if he's innocent?"

"That's the law. I'm telling you—this is a very serious situation. He's accused of murdering two people."

I slumped back on the couch. I had to talk to Harry.

"Ask him to call me!" I said to Roth.

"I'll pass on your message."

"Tell him I absolutely have to talk to him, and that I'm waiting for his call."

Right after hanging up, I went to my bookshelves and found my copy of *The Origin of Evil*. Harry's inscription was on the first page:

> *To Marcus, my most brilliant student,*
> *Your friend,*
> *H. L. Quebert, May 1999*

I immersed myself once again in that book, which I hadn't opened in years. It was a love story, mixing a straight narrative with epistolary passages, the story of a man and woman who loved each other without really being allowed to love each other. So he had written this book for that mysterious girl about whom I still knew nothing. I finished rereading it in the middle of the night, and contemplated the title. And, for the first time, I wondered what it meant. Why *The Origin of Evil*? What kind of evil was Harry talking about?

Two days passed, during which the D.N.A. analyses and dental impressions confirmed that the skeleton discovered at Goose Cove was indeed that of Nola Kellergan. The investigators were able to determine that the skeleton was that of a fifteen-year-old child, indicating that Nola had died more or less at the time of her disappearance. But, most important, a fracture at the back of the skull provided the certainty, even after more than thirty years, that Nola Kellergan had died from at least one blow to the head.

I had no news of Harry. I tried to get in touch with him, through the state police, through the prison, and through Roth, but without success. I paced my apartment, tormented by thousands of questions, plagued by the memory of his weird call. By the end of the weekend, I couldn't take it anymore, and I decided that I had little choice but to go to see what was happening in New Hampshire.

At first light on Monday, June 16, 2008, I packed my suitcases and got in my Range Rover. I left Manhattan by Franklin Roosevelt Drive, which runs alongside the East River. New York sped past me—Harlem, the Bronx—and I joined the I-95 north. Only when I had gotten far enough from the city not to be tempted to give up my idea and go home like a good boy did I call my parents to tell them I was on my way to New Hampshire. My mother told me I was crazy:

"What are you doing, Markie? Surely you're not going to defend that sick criminal?"

"He's not a criminal, Mom. He's my friend."

"Well, then, your friends are criminals! Your father's right here—he says you're running away from New York because of your book."

"I'm not running away."

"Are you running away because of a woman?"

"I told you I'm not running away. I don't have a girlfriend."

"When will you have a girlfriend? I've been thinking again about that Natalia you introduced us to last year. She was such a sweet *shiksa*. Why don't you call her?"

"You hated her."

"And why aren't you writing books anymore? Everyone loved you when you were a great writer."

"I'm still a writer."

"Come home! I'll make you hot dogs and apple pie."

"Mom, I'm twenty-eight years old. I can make hot dogs myself if I want them."

"Did you know your father's not allowed to eat hot dogs anymore? The doctor told him." (I heard my father grumbling that he was actually allowed to eat one occasionally, and my mother repeating, "No more hot dogs for you, or any other junk food. The doctor says it clogs up your system!") "Markie, darling? Your father says you should write a book about that Quebert. That would get your career going again. Everyone's talking about Quebert, so everyone would talk about your book. Why don't you come and have dinner with us? We haven't seen you in so long. And you love my apple pie . . ."

I had crossed into Connecticut when, stupidly deciding to change the radio from my opera C.D. to the news, I learned that there had been a leak within the police department: The media now knew about the discovery of the manuscript of *The Origin of Evil* alongside Nola Kellergan's remains, and of Harry's confession that the book was inspired by his relationship with her. I stopped at a gas station to refuel and found the attendant inside, eyes glued to the T.V., which was replaying the news about Harry on a loop. I went up to him and asked him to turn up the volume. Seeing the look of horror on my face, he said, "What? You didn't know? It's been all over the news for hours. Where have you been, on Mars?"

"In my car."

"Heh. No radio?"

"I was listening to opera. It takes my mind off things."

He stared at me. "Don't I know you?"

"I don't think so."

"I've seen you before somewhere."

"I've got one of those faces."

"No, I'm sure I've seen you before. You one of them T.V. guys, is that it? Maybe an actor or something?"

"No."

"So what do you do?"

"I'm a writer."

"Yeah, that's it! I read your book last year. I remember now—your face was on the back. Wait, I have it here somewhere."

He disappeared for a moment, returning from the storeroom, triumphant, with a copy in hand.

"There you go—it's you! Look, it's your book. Marcus Goldman—that's your name. It's right here on the cover."

"If you say so."

"So, what's new, Mr Goldman?"

"Not much, to be honest."

"And where are you going today, if you don't mind my asking?"

"New Hampshire."

"Nice area, especially in summer. Going fishing?"

"You could say that."

"What kind of fishing? There are places up there just *swarming* with black bass."

"Fishing for trouble, I believe. I'm going to see a friend up there who's got problems. Serious problems."

"Well, at least his problems can't be as bad as Harry Quebert's!"

He burst out laughing and shook me warmly by the hand because "we don't get many celebrities around here." Then he offered me a cup of coffee for the road.

Public opinion was overwhelmingly against Harry. He was incriminated definitively not only by the fact of the manuscript's being found with Nola's skeleton, but above all by the revelation that his most famous book had been inspired by an affair with a fifteen-year-old girl. This had caused a deep sense of unease. Had America honored a homicidal pedophile by elevating Harry to the ranks of literary stardom? Journalists came up with various theories for why Harry might have murdered Nola. Was she threatening to unmask their relationship? Maybe she'd wanted to break up with him and he'd lost his head? All the way to New Hampshire, I kept turning these questions over in my mind. I tried to think about something else by switching from the news back to opera but every track made me think of Harry, and as soon as I thought of him, I thought again about that girl who'd been lying in the ground for more than thirty years next to that house where I had spent some of the happiest times of my life.

After a five-hour journey, I finally arrived at Goose Cove. I had driven there without really thinking: Why did I come here rather than Concord, where Harry and Roth were? Satellite transmission vans were parked on the side of Shore Road, and journalists hung around on the narrow gravel path that led to the house, reporting for several different T.V. stations. As I was about to turn onto the path, they all flocked to my car, blocking my way so they could see who it was. One of them recognized me and called out, "Look, it's that writer! It's Marcus Goldman!" The swarm buzzed excitedly, and camera lenses tapped my car's windows. "Do you believe Harry Quebert killed that girl?" "Did you know he wrote *The Origin of Evil* for her?" "Should the book be withdrawn from sale?" I kept my windows raised and sunglasses on. Local police officers, there to control the flood of journalists and gawkers, recognized me and succeeded in clearing a passage. I was able to disappear down the driveway, under groves of mulberries and tall pine trees. I could still hear a few journalists shouting: "Mr Goldman, why have you come to Somerset? What are you doing at Harry Quebert's house?"

Why was I here? Because it was Harry. Because, surprising as this might seem—and I didn't realize it myself until that very moment— Harry was the most treasured friend I had. In high school and college, I had been unable to forge strong friendships with people my own age, the kind of friendships that last forever. Harry was all I had in life, and, curiously, I didn't need to know if he was guilty or not; that fact would not in any way alter our deep bond of friendship. It was a strange feeling: I think I would have liked to hate him, to spit in his face while the nation watched; that would have been simpler. But these events did not affect the feelings I had for him in the slightest. At worst, I thought, he is a man, and men have demons. Everyone has demons. The question is simply to know up to what point those demons can be tolerated.

I parked on the gravel driveway. Harry's red Corvette was there, where he always left it, in the little outbuilding that he used as a garage. As if the master were at home and all were well in the world. I wanted to go inside, but the front door was locked. This was the first time I could remember it being locked. I walked around the house; there were no police here anymore, but the rear access to the property had been cordoned off with police tape. I settled for looking from afar at the wide area that had been marked off, reaching as far as the edge of the woods. You could just make out the gaping crater, evidence of the intensity of the police excavation, and next to it the discarded hydrangea bushes, which were drying out.

I must have lingered there for some time, because the next thing I knew I heard a car behind me. It was Roth, who had come from Concord. He had seen me on television and driven here immediately. His first words were: "So, you came?"

"Yes. Why?"

"Harry told me you'd come. He told me you were a stubborn son of a bitch and you'd come here to stick your nose in this business."

"Harry knows me well."

Roth put his hand in his jacket pocket and brought out a piece of paper.

"It's from him," he told me.

It was a handwritten note.

My dear Marcus,

If you are reading this, it's because you have come to New Hampshire to find out what's happened to your old friend.

You are a brave guy. I never doubted that. I swear to you that I am innocent of the crimes of which I am accused. Nevertheless, it seems likely I will be in prison for some time and you have better things to do than look after me. Concentrate on finishing the novel you're supposed to hand in at the end of the month. Your career is more important. Don't waste your time on me.

Kind regards,
Harry

P.S. If by chance you wish to stay awhile in New Hampshire in spite of this, or to come here from time to time, you know Goose Cove is your home. Stay as long as you like. All I ask of you is one favor: Feed the seagulls. Leave some bread for them on the deck. It's important to feed the seagulls.

"Don't give up on him," Roth said. "He needs you."

I nodded. "How's it looking for him?"

"Bad. You saw the news? Everyone knows about the book. It's a disaster. The more I learn about this, the more I wonder how I'm going to defend him."

"Where did the leak come from?"

"Straight from the prosecutor's office, in my opinion. They want to turn up the pressure on Harry by condemning him in the court of public opinion. They want a full confession. They know that in a case that's more than thirty years old, nothing is worth as much as a confession."

"When can I see him?"

"Tomorrow morning. The state prison is in Concord. Where are you going to stay?"

"Here, if I can."

He made a face.

"I doubt it," he said. "The police searched the house. It's a crime scene."

"Isn't the crime scene over there, where there's a hole?" I asked.

Roth went to inspect the front door, then quickly walked around the house. He was smiling when he came back.

"You'd make a good lawyer, Goldman. There's nothing sealing off the house."

"Does that mean I'm allowed to stay?"

"It means there is nothing prohibiting you from staying here."

"I'm not sure I follow you."

"That's the beauty of U.S. law, Goldman: When there is no law, you invent one. And if you get into trouble, you take it to the Supreme Court, which rules in your favor and publishes a judgment in your name— *Goldman v. the State of New Hampshire.* So go ahead and take possession of this place—there's nothing stopping you, and if the police have the nerve to come and hassle you about it, tell them there's a loophole in the law, mention the Supreme Court, and then threaten to sue them. That sometimes scares 'em off. On the other hand, I don't have the keys to the house."

I dug into my pocket and showed Roth what I had.

"Harry gave them to me a long time ago."

"You're a magician! But, please, don't cross any police lines—we'd get into trouble."

"I won't. So what did the search of the house turn up?"

"Nothing. That's why they haven't sealed it off."

Roth left, and I entered the vast, empty house. I locked the door behind me and went straight to the office, in search of the box I'd found. But it wasn't there anymore. What could Harry have done with it? I desperately wanted to get hold of it, and I began searching the bookshelves in the office and the living room. Then I decided to inspect each room in the house, in the hope of finding even the smallest clue that might help me understand what had happened here in 1975. Was it in one of these rooms that Nola had been murdered?

I ended up finding a few photo albums I had never noticed before. I opened them randomly and discovered pictures of Harry and me from when I was in college: in the classroom, in the boxing ring, on campus, in the diner where we would often meet. There were even pictures from my graduation. Another album was full of press clips about me and my book. Certain passages were circled in red or underlined. Apparently Harry had followed my career from the beginning. I even found a clipping from the Montclair newspaper in 2006, reporting on the ceremony organized in my honor by Felton High School. How had he gotten hold of that? I remembered the day well. It was just before Christmas. My first novel was on the bestseller lists and the principal of my old high school, carried away by the excitement, had decided to pay me what he considered a well-earned tribute.

The event took place amid great pomp one Saturday afternoon in the school's main hall, before a select audience of current and former students, and a few local journalists. Everyone had been crammed in on folding chairs in front of a large curtain, which, after a triumphant speech, the principal had raised to reveal an impressive glass cabinet, inscribed with the words: IN TRIBUTE TO MARCUS P. GOLDMAN, KNOWN AS MARCUS THE MAGNIFICENT, A PUPIL IN THIS SCHOOL BETWEEN 1994 AND 1998. Inside this cabinet was a display including a copy of my novel, my old school reports, a few photographs, and my volleyball and cross-country jerseys.

I smiled as I reread the article. My time at Felton High—a small public school in Montclair—had made such an impression on my classmates and teachers that they had nicknamed me Marcus the Magnificent. But on that day in December 2006, as they applauded that cabinet in my honor, what everybody failed to realize was that my status as Felton's undisputed star for four glorious years was, due to a series of misunderstandings, fortuitous to begin with and then deliberately orchestrated.

It all began in my freshman year, when I had to choose a sport. I had decided on either football or soccer, but the number of spots on those two teams was limited, and on the day we were supposed to register, I arrived very late at the registrar's office.

"We're closed," said the fat woman behind the desk.

"Please," I begged her, "I absolutely have to register, otherwise they'll fail me."

She sighed. "Name?"

"Goldman. Marcus Goldman."

"Which sport?"

"Football. Or soccer."

"They're both full. All that's left is acrobatic dance and volleyball."

Acrobatic dance and volleyball? It was like choosing between cholera and the plague. I knew that joining the dance team would have made me the butt of my classmates' jokes, so I chose volleyball. But Felton had not had a decent volleyball team in decades, and no-one went out for it. So the volleyball team was made up of the rejects from all the other sports, or of people who turned up late on registration day. And that is how I became part of a team that was clumsy and inept, but that would provide the foundations for my glory. Hoping to be picked up by the football team later in the season, I wanted to show such sporting prowess that I would get myself noticed. So I trained with a hunger I had never shown before, and by the end of the first two weeks, our coach saw in me the star he had been waiting years for. I was immediately made team captain, and I didn't have to make any great efforts in order to be considered the best volleyball player in the school's history. I easily beat the record for the number of kills made during the past twenty years— which was absolutely pathetic—and as reward for this, my name was listed in the school's Order of Merit, something that had never before happened to a freshman. This was enough to impress my classmates and win the attention of my teachers. From this I came to understand that in order to be magnificent, all that was needed was to distort the way others perceived me; in the end, everything was a question of appearances.

I learned fast. Obviously there was no longer any question of my leaving the volleyball team, because my now sole obsession was to become the best, by any means necessary, to hog the spotlight, no matter what the cost. Soon afterward there was a science fair, won by an annoying little nerd named Sally. I finished sixteenth. At the awards ceremony, in the school auditorium, I arranged it so that I could give a speech—and made up a spiel about the weekends I had worked as a volunteer helping mentally handicapped people. This had, I explained, taken valuable time away from my science project. But, eyes shining with tears, I concluded: "Winning first prize doesn't matter much to me, as long as I can provide my Down's syndrome friends with even a glimmer of happiness." Of course everyone was deeply moved by this, and I easily eclipsed Sally in the eyes of my teachers and classmates—and even in the eyes of Sally herself, who, having a severely handicapped little brother (something I was completely unaware of), refused her prize and demanded that it be given to me instead. This got my name displayed under the categories of Sport, Science and Good Citizenship on the Order of Merit, which—fully aware as I was of my duplicity—I had secretly renamed the Hoarder of Merit. But by now I was like someone possessed, and I couldn't stop myself. One week later, I beat the record for raffle-ticket sales by buying them myself with the money I had saved during two years spent picking up litter from the lawn at the local swimming pool. This was all it took for a rumor to start circulating around the high school: Marcus Goldman was an exceptional human being. It was this observation that led students and teachers alike to call me Marcus the Magnificent. It was like a trademark, a guarantee of absolute success, and soon my fame spread all over our corner of Montclair, filling my parents with immense pride.

This scam led me to practice the noble art of boxing. I'd always had a weakness for the sport, and I'd always been a pretty good slugger, but in going off to train in secret at a Brooklyn gym—an hour by train from my home—where nobody knew me and Marcus the Magnificent did not exist, what I was seeking was the ability to be weak; I was claiming the right to be beaten by someone stronger than I was, the right to lose face. This was the only way I could escape the monster of perfection I had created. In that boxing gym, Marcus the Magnificent could lose; he could be bad at something. And the real Marcus could exist. Because, little by little, my obsession with being number one was growing beyond imagining. The more I won, the more terrified I became of losing.

During my junior year, budget cuts forced the principal to get rid of the volleyball team. So, to my great dismay, I had to choose a new sport. Both the football and soccer teams were now making eyes at me, of course, but I knew that if I joined one of them, I would be confronted with players who were much more gifted and determined than my old volleyball teammates. If I did that, I risked being eclipsed, becoming anonymous again . . . or worse. What would people say when Marcus Goldman—Marcus the Magnificent, former volleyball captain and team record holder for the number of kills made in the past twenty years— found himself the football team's water boy? For two weeks I was in a state of anxiety, until I heard about the high school's little-known cross-country team, which consisted of two stumpy-legged fat kids and one scrawny wimp. Moreover, it turned out to be the only sports team at Felton that did not participate in any interscholastic competition. This ensured that I would never have to measure myself against anyone who might prove dangerous to me. It was, then, with relief and without the slightest hesitation, that I joined Felton's cross-country team, where— from the very first training session, under the infatuated gaze of the principal and a few groupies—I easily beat the times set by my teammates.

Everything might have gone swimmingly had not the principal, inspired by my results, come up with the absurd idea of organizing a major cross-country meet featuring all the schools of the region in order to boost Felton's image, confident that Marcus the Magnificent would win easily. Panicking at this news, I trained relentlessly for a whole month, but I knew there was nothing I could do against the other schools' race-hardened runners. I was nothing but a flimsy façade; I was going to make a fool of myself, and on home turf too.

The day of the race, all of Felton, along with half of my neighborhood, was there to cheer me on. The race began and, as I feared, I was immediately left in the wake of the other runners. This was the crucial moment; my reputation was at stake. It was a six-mile race. I was going to finish last, defeated and disgraced. I had to save Marcus the Magnificent at all costs. So I gathered all my strength, all my energy, and desperately launched myself into an insane sprint. Cheered on by a few supporters, I took the lead. It was at this point that I resorted to the Machiavellian plan I had devised. Leading the competition and sensing that I had reached my physical limit, I pretended to trip and threw myself to the ground, rolling spectacularly and howling as the crowd erupted. It turned out I had broken my leg, which had certainly not been my intention, but which—for the price of an operation and two weeks in the hospital—saved my reputation. The next week, the high school newspaper reported it this way:

During this historic race, Marcus "the Magnificent" Goldman was easily dominating his opponents on his way to what promised to be a crushing victory, when he became the unwitting victim of the poor quality of the track: He fell heavily and broke a leg.

This was the end of my running career and my sports career in general. Due to serious injury, I was exempted from sport during the rest of my time in high school. As a reward for my commitment and sacrifice, a plaque inscribed with my name was displayed on the Wall of Honor, alongside my volleyball jersey. The principal, cursing the poor quality of the facilities at Felton, had the entire track resurfaced at great cost, paying for it by draining the budget for school outings and thus depriving every student in the school of any kind of extracurricular activity the following year.

In the spring of my senior year, bedecked with perfect grades, certificates, awards and letters of recommendation, I had to make the fateful decision of where to go to college. So when one afternoon, lying on my bed and reading the three acceptance letters I'd received—one from

Harvard, another from Yale, and the third from Burrows, a small, little-known school in Massachusetts—I did not even hesitate; I chose Burrows. Entering a great university meant risking my reputation as Marcus the Magnificent. At Harvard or Yale the bar would have been set too high. I had no desire to face the nation's elite, who would insatiably monopolize the deans' lists. The dean's list at Burrows seemed much more accessible to me. Marcus the Magnificent did not want to burn his wings. Marcus the Magnificent wished to remain Magnificent. Burrows was perfect: a modest campus where I would be bound to shine. I had no trouble convincing my parents that the English department at Burrows was superior in every respect to that of Harvard and of Yale, and that is how, in the fall of 1998, I came to leave Montclair for the small industrial town in Massachusetts where I would make the acquaintance of Harry Quebert.

In the early evening, while I was still out on the deck, looking through photo albums and brooding over memories, I received a call from my panic-stricken agent.

"Marcus, for God's sake! I can't believe you went to New Hampshire without telling me! I've had journalists calling, asking what you were doing, and I didn't even know you were there. Come back to New York. Come back while there's still time. This case is completely beyond you! Quebert has an excellent lawyer. Let him do his job, and you concentrate on your book. You have to deliver your manuscript to Barnaski in two weeks."

"Harry needs a friend to stand by him," I said.

There was a silence and then Douglas began muttering, as if he had only now realized what he'd been missing for months. "You don't have a book, do you? You're two weeks from Barnaski's deadline and you haven't even bothered to write this goddamn book! Is that it, Marc? Are you there to help a friend, or are you escaping New York?"

"Shut up, Doug."

There was another long silence.

"Tell me you have an idea, at least. Tell me you have a plan and that there's a good reason you've gone to New Hampshire."

"Isn't friendship enough?"

"Jesus Christ, what do you owe this guy that you have to go there for him?"

"Everything. Absolutely everything."

"What do you mean, *everything*?"

"It's complicated, Douglas."

"For God's sake, what are you trying to say?"

"Doug, there was an episode of my life that I've never told you about. When I got out of high school, I might easily have taken a wrong turn. And then I met Harry. In some ways, he saved my life. Without him, I would never have become the writer I am now. It happened in Burrows, Massachusetts, in 1998. I owe him everything."

29

Is It Possible to Fall in Love with a Fifteen-Year-Old Girl?

"I would like to teach you writing, Marcus—not so that you know how to write, but so that you become a writer. Because writing books is no small feat. Everyone knows how to write, but not everyone is a writer."

"And how do you know when you're a writer, Harry?"

"Nobody knows he's a writer. It's other people who tell you."

Everyone who remembers Nola says she was a wonderful girl. One of those girls who leaves an impression on people: gentle and considerate, radiant and good at everything. Apparently, she had a unique joie de vivre that could light up even the dreariest days. She worked at Clark's on Saturdays; she would twirl lightly between the tables, her wavy blond hair dancing in the air. She always had a kind word for every customer. She was all you saw. Nola was a world in herself.

She was the only child of David and Louisa Kellergan, southern evangelicals from Jackson, Alabama, where she herself was born on April 12, 1960. The Kellergans moved to Somerset in the summer of 1969, after the father had been hired as pastor for the congregation of St James's

Church in Somerset. The church, located on the south side of town, was an impressive wooden building of which nothing remains today, because it was eventually merged with the main church in Montburry due to dwindling budgets and attendances. A McDonald's had been built in its place. Upon their arrival, the Kellergans moved into a nice one-story house belonging to the parish, located at 245 Terrace Avenue. It was, in all probability, through her bedroom window that Nola disappeared into the woods six years later, on August 30, 1975.

These details were among the first given to me by the regulars at Clark's, where I went the morning after my arrival in Somerset. I woke spontaneously at dawn, tormented by the unpleasant feeling that I was not really sure what I was doing here. After I went running on the beach, I fed the seagulls, and it was then that I wondered if I had really come all the way to New Hampshire just to give bread to seabirds. My meeting in Concord with Benjamin Roth, who would take me to visit Harry, was not until 11 a.m.; in the meantime, because I did not want to be alone, I went to eat pancakes at Clark's. Harry used to take me there early in the mornings when I was a student and staying with him. He would wake me before dawn, unceremoniously shaking me and explaining that it was time to put on my running gear. Then we would go down to the beach to run and box. When he got tired, he would coach me, interrupting what he was doing supposedly in order to correct my movements and positions, although it was really so he could catch his breath. Jogging and exercising, we would cover the few miles of beach that link Goose Cove to Somerset. Then we would climb up the rocks of Grand Beach and pass through the still-sleeping town. On the main street, which was still plunged in darkness, we would see from afar the bright light that poured through the bay window of the diner, the only place open at such an early hour. Inside, all was perfectly calm; the few customers were truck drivers or farm hands eating their breakfast in silence. In the background, we could hear the radio, always tuned to a news channel but with the volume turned so low that it was impossible to understand all the newscaster's words. On hot mornings, the ceiling fan creaked metallically as it beat the air, making dust motes dance around the lamps. We would sit at Table 17, and Jenny would appear instantly to serve us coffee. She always smiled at me with a gentleness that was almost maternal. She said, "Poor Marcus—is he making you get up at dawn? He's done that ever since I've known him." And we would laugh.

But on June 17, 2008, despite the early hour, Clark's was already bustling. Everyone was talking about the case, and when I entered, the regulars crowded around me to ask if it was true, if Harry had had an affair with Nola, and if he had killed her and Deborah Cooper. I avoided their questions and sat down at Table 17, which was still free. That was when I discovered that the plaque in honor of Harry had been removed. All that remained were two screw holes in the wood of the table and the shape where the metal had discolored the varnish.

Jenny came to serve me coffee and greeted me kindly. She looked sad.

"Are you staying at Harry's place?" she said.

"Yes. You took off the plaque?"

"Yes."

"Why?"

"He wrote the book for that girl, Marcus. For a fifteen-year-old girl. I can't leave the plaque there. That's not love—it's disgusting."

"I think it's a little more complicated than that," I said.

"And I think you should keep your nose out of this, Marcus. You should go back to New York and stay far away from all of this."

I ordered pancakes and sausage. A grease-stained copy of the *Somerset Star* was on the table. On the front page there was a large photograph of Harry at the peak of his fame, with that respectable air and profound, self-assured look. Just below was a picture of him entering the hearing room of the Concord courthouse, the fallen angel, handcuffed, his hair a mess, his face drawn and haggard. There were inset photographs of Nola and Deborah Cooper, and the headline read: WHAT HAS HARRY QUEBERT DONE?

Ernie Pinkas arrived just after I did and sat at my table with his cup of coffee.

"I saw you on T.V. last night," he said. "Have you moved here?"

"Yeah, maybe."

"Why?"

"I don't know. For Harry."

"He's innocent, huh? I can't believe he would have done such a thing. It's insane."

"I don't know anymore, Ernie."

At my request Pinkas recounted how, after the police had unearthed Nola's remains at Goose Cove, everyone in Somerset had been alerted by the sirens of the police cars that had converged from all over the county, from highway patrols to unmarked Investigative Services Bureau cars, and even a forensics van.

"When we learned that it was probably Nola Kellergan's body, it was a shock for everyone," Ernie Pinkas said. "None of us could believe it: After all this time, the poor girl was just there, under our noses. I mean, how many times have I been to Harry's place, and drunk a Scotch on that deck? Practically right next to her . . . Say, Marcus, did he really write that book for her? I can't believe there was anything between them. Do you know anything about it?"

To avoid having to reply, I stirred my spoon around inside my cup until I had created a kind of whirlpool. All I said was, "It's a big mess, Ernie."

Soon afterward Travis Dawn, Somerset's chief of police and Jenny's husband, sat at my table. He was a mild-mannered man in his sixties whose hair was going white, the kind of nice-guy country cop who had not scared anyone for a long time.

"I'm sorry, son," he said as he greeted me.

"Sorry for what?"

"This case that's blown up in your face. I know you're very close to Harry. It can't be easy for you."

Travis was the first person to show concern about how I might be feeling. I nodded, and asked him: "How come I'd never heard of Nola Kellergan before, in all the time I'd been coming here?"

"Because until we found her corpse at Goose Cove, it was ancient history. The kind of history people don't like to remember."

"So what happened on August 30, 1975? And what's the story with Deborah Cooper?"

"It's a nasty business, Marcus. A very nasty business. And I experienced it firsthand because I was working that day. I was just a junior police officer at the time. I was the one who took the call from the station. Deborah Cooper was a kind woman who'd been living alone, since the death of her husband, in a house on Side Creek Lane. You know where Side Creek is? That's where the huge forest begins, two miles beyond Goose Cove. I remember Mrs Cooper well. I hadn't been a police officer for long back then, but she called regularly. Especially at night, to report any suspicious noises near her house. She was scared stiff, living out there in that big house on the edge of the forest, and she needed someone to go over and reassure her from time to time. Each time, she would apologize for bothering us and would offer cake and coffee to the officers who went to check on her. And the next day she'd come to the station to bring us something. Just a kind woman, you know? The type you're always happy to serve. So anyway, on that day Mrs Cooper called the police and said she'd seen a girl being chased by a man in the forest. I was the only officer on patrol in Somerset and I went to her house immediately. This was the first time she'd called in the daytime. When I got there, she was waiting in front of her house. She told me, 'Travis, you're going to think I'm crazy, but I really did see something strange.' I went to look about at the edge of the forest, where she'd seen the girl, and I found a piece of red fabric. I immediately decided we had to take this thing seriously, so I called Chief Pratt, who was Somerset's chief of police at the time. He was off-duty, but he came right away. The forest is huge, even with two of us to look around it. We went deep into the woods. After a mile or so, we found traces of blood, blond hairs, and more scraps of red fabric. But we didn't have time to think this through any further, because at that moment we heard a gunshot from the direction of Deborah Cooper's house. We ran over there and found Mrs Cooper in her kitchen, lying in a pool of her own blood. Afterward we found out that she'd called the station again to tell them that the girl she'd seen earlier had come to her house to take refuge."

"The girl went back to the house?"

"Yes. While we were in the forest, she reappeared, covered in blood and asking for help. But when we got back there, apart from Mrs Cooper's corpse, there was nobody left in the house."

"And this girl, it was Nola?"

"Yes. We realized that pretty quickly. First, when her father called a little later to say she'd disappeared. And then when we found out that Deborah Cooper had identified her during her second call to the station."

"What happened next?"

"After that second call from Mrs Cooper, units from the area were on their way. When they reached the border of the forest, a sheriff's deputy saw a black Chevrolet Monte Carlo racing north. The car was pursued, but it got away from us in spite of the roadblocks. We spent the weeks that followed searching for Nola; we turned the whole area upside down. Who would have thought she'd be at Goose Cove, Harry Quebert's place? All the clues suggested she'd probably be found somewhere in that forest. We searched the woods endlessly. We never found the car and we never found the girl. We'd have dug up the whole country if we could, but the search was called off after three weeks because the bigwigs in the state police said it cost too much and there was no way of knowing if we'd ever find anything."

"Did you have a suspect at the time?"

He hesitated for a moment, and then told me: "This was never official, but there was Harry. We had our reasons. I mean, the Kellergan girl disappeared three months after his arrival. Strange coincidence, isn't it? Most of all there was the car he drove at the time: a black Chevrolet Monte Carlo. But there wasn't enough evidence against him. Basically that manuscript is the proof we were looking for thirty-three years ago."

"I don't believe it, not Harry. And anyway, why would he leave such compromising proof with the body? And why would he hire gardeners to dig up the very place where he'd buried a corpse? It doesn't make any sense."

Travis shrugged. "If I've learned one thing as a cop, it's this: You never know what people are capable of. Especially those you think you know well."

With these words, he stood up. "If I can do anything for you, don't hesitate to ask," he told me before leaving. Pinkas, who had followed the conversation without saying a word, now expressed his incredulity. "Can you believe it? I never knew the police suspected Harry."

I did not reply. I just tore off the front page of the newspaper and put it in my pocket. And, although it was still early, I left for Concord.

The New Hampshire State Prison for Men was at 281 North State Street, in northern Concord. Roth was waiting for me in the parking lot, smoking a cheap cigar. He looked unfazed. The only greeting he gave was a pat on the shoulder, as though we were old friends.

"First time in prison?" he asked me.

"Yes."

"Try to relax."

"What makes you think I'm not?"

There was a pack of journalists hanging around.

"They're everywhere," he told me. "Whatever you do, don't reply when they greet you. They're scavengers, Goldman. They'll harass you until you give them something. You have to be tough and stay silent. The slightest thing you say could be misinterpreted and turned against us and ruin my defense."

"What is your defense?"

He looked at me very seriously. "Deny everything."

"Deny everything?" I repeated.

"Everything. Their relationship, the kidnapping, the murders. We're going to plead not guilty, Harry will be acquitted, and I'm planning to get millions of dollars in damages from the state of New Hampshire."

"What about the manuscript the police found with the body? And Harry's confession about his relationship with Nola?"

"That manuscript doesn't prove anything! Writing is not killing. And anyway, Harry's already given a plausible explanation for that: Nola took the manuscript before she disappeared. As for their relationship, it was just a fling. You see, the prosecutor can't prove anything."

"I talked to Somerset's police chief, Travis Dawn. He says Harry was a suspect at the time."

"Bullshit!" Roth said, who resorted to foul language easily when he was annoyed.

"Apparently the suspect at the time drove a black Chevrolet Monte Carlo. Travis says that was the model Harry drove."

"More bullshit!" Roth said. "But useful to know. Good work, Goldman—that's the kind of information I need. You know all those hicks in Somerset, so question them to find out what kind of crap they'll tell the jury if they're called as witnesses. And try to find out who drinks too much and who beats his wife; a witness who drinks or beats his wife is not a credible witness."

"Kind of a despicable technique, isn't it?"

"War is war, Goldman. Bush lied to the nation in order to attack Iraq, but it was necessary. You see, we kicked Saddam's ass, we liberated the Iraqis, and the world has been a better place ever since."

"The majority of this country was opposed to that war. It was a total disaster."

"Oh no," he said. "I knew it . . ."

"What?"

"Are you voting Democrat, Goldman?"

"Of course I'm voting Democrat."

"You'll see—they're going to stick rich guys like you with stupendous tax hikes. Don't come crying to me afterward. You need balls to govern America. And elephants have bigger balls than donkeys. That's just how it is—it's genetic."

"It's edifying to talk with you, Roth. Anyway, the Democrats have already won the presidency. Your wonderful war was unpopular enough to tilt the balance in our favor."

His smile was mocking, almost incredulous. "Come on, don't tell me you really believe that! A woman and a black, Goldman! A woman and a black! Come on—you're an intelligent kid—let's be serious: Who is going to elect a woman or a black to be the head of our country? Write a book about it—a nice science fiction adventure. What will it be next time? A Puerto Rican lesbian and an Indian chief?"

At my request, after going through the usual formalities, Roth left me alone with Harry for a while in the room where he had been waiting for us. He was sitting at a plastic table, dressed in a prisoner's uniform, his face haggard. The moment I entered the room, his eyes lit up. He stood and we embraced for a long time, before silently taking our places on opposite sides of the table. Finally he said, "I'm scared, Marcus."

"We're going to get you out of here, Harry."

"I've got a T.V., you know. I see everything that's being said. I'm finished. My career is over. My life is over. This is the beginning of my fall. I believe I'm falling."

"You should never be afraid of falling, Harry."

He gave a faint, sad smile.

"Thank you for coming."

"That's what friends do. I've moved into Goose Cove. I've fed the seagulls."

"You know, I'll understand if you want to go back to New York."

"I'm not going anywhere. Roth is a strange bird, but I get the feeling he knows what he's doing, and he says you'll be acquitted. I'm going to stay here. I'm going to help you. I'll do whatever it takes to find out the truth and I will clear your name."

"What about your new novel? Your editor's expecting it at the end of the month, isn't he?"

I bowed my head.

"There is no novel. I have no more ideas."

"What do you mean, *no more ideas?*"

I didn't reply. Instead, I changed the subject by reaching into my pocket and pulling out the front page of the newspaper I'd taken from Clark's a few hours earlier.

"Harry, tell me. I need to understand. I need to know the truth. I can't stop thinking about that phone call you made to me the other day. You asked what you had done to Nola . . ."

"It was the emotion talking, Marcus. I'd just been arrested, I had the right to one phone call, and the only person I wanted to tell was you. Not to tell you I'd been arrested, but to tell you she was dead. Because you were the only one who knew about Nola and I needed to share my grief with someone. Through all those years, I hoped she was alive somewhere. But she'd been dead the whole time. She was dead and I felt responsible for it, for all sorts of reasons. Responsible because I wasn't able to protect her, I guess. But I never harmed her. I swear to you I am innocent; I didn't do anything I'm accused of doing."

"I believe you. What did you tell the police?"

"The truth. That I was innocent. Why would I have decided to plant bushes in that spot if I'd . . . it's utterly grotesque! I told them I didn't know how that manuscript came to be there, but that they should know I wrote that novel for and about Nola, before she disappeared. That Nola and I loved each other. That we'd had a love affair during the summer before her disappearance and that I'd written a novel about it, of which I possessed two manuscripts at the time: an original, handwritten; and a typed copy. Nola was very interested in what I was writing. She even helped me make a clean copy. And the typed version of the manuscript ... one day I couldn't find it anymore. It was late August, just before she disappeared. I thought that Nola had taken it to read—she did that sometimes. She read what I'd written and then told me what she thought. She took my pages without asking me. But this time I wasn't able to ask if she'd taken the manuscript because she disappeared. I still had the handwritten copy. You know all about the success it had a few months later."

"So you really wrote *The Origin of Evil* for Nola?"

"Yes. I saw on T.V. that they're talking about withdrawing it from stores."

"But what happened between you and Nola?"

"I told you—a love affair. I fell madly in love with her. And I think that was my downfall."

"What else do the police have against you?"

"I don't know."

"And the box? Where is that box with the letter and the photographs? I couldn't find it in your house."

He didn't have time to reply. The door to the room opened, and he gestured to me to keep quiet. It was Roth. He joined us at the table and, while he was sitting down, Harry discreetly picked up the notebook I'd placed in front of me and wrote a few words I was unable to read at that moment.

Roth began by giving a long description of how he expected the proceedings to unfold. Then, after a thirty-minute soliloquy, he asked Harry: "Is there anything you haven't yet told me about Nola? I have to know everything."

There was a silence. Harry stared at us for a long time, and then said, "Actually, there is something you should know. It's about the day she disappeared. That evening, she was supposed to meet me ..."

"Meet you?" Roth repeated.

"The police asked me what I was doing on the evening of August 30, and I told them I was out of town. I lied. That is the only point on which I did not tell the truth. That night I was close to Somerset, in a room of a motel next to Shore Road, on the way to Maine. The Sea Side Motel. It still exists. I was in Room 8, lying on the bed, waiting, wearing cologne like a teenager, holding a bouquet of blue hydrangeas, her favorite flowers. We were supposed to meet at 7 p.m., and I remember that I was waiting and she didn't come. At 9 p.m. she was still not there. Nola was never late. Never. I put the hydrangeas in the sink to soak, and I turned on the radio to distract myself. It was a humid, stormy night. I felt as if I were suffocating in my suit. I took her letter from my pocket and reread it ten times, maybe a hundred. That letter she'd written to me a few days earlier, that brief love letter I could never forget, it said she would meet me there in that room, at 7 p.m., and we would go away forever.

"I remember the radio announcer saying it was 10 p.m. Ten o'clock, and still no Nola. I ended up falling asleep fully clothed, stretched out on the bed. When I opened my eyes again, it was morning. The radio was still on, and I heard the seven o'clock news: '*Police issued a general alert in the Somerset region after the disappearance of fifteen-year-old Nola Kellergan yesterday evening, around 7 p.m. Police would like to hear from anyone with information about the girl's whereabouts. At the time she disappeared, Nola Kellergan was wearing a red dress . . .*' I leaped out of bed in panic. I quickly got rid of the flowers, then left right away for Somerset, with my clothes all creased and my hair a mess. The room had been paid for in advance.

"I had never seen so many police in Somerset. There were vehicles from all the surrounding counties. On Shore Road, a large roadblock was checking every car entering and leaving the town. I saw the chief of police, Gareth Pratt, holding a pump-action shotgun.

"'Chief, I just heard the news on the radio,' I said.

"'Filthy business,' he replied.

"'What happened?'

"'Nobody knows. Nola Kellergan disappeared from home. She was seen near Side Creek Lane last night, and since then, there hasn't been a trace of her. We've secured the whole area and we're searching the forest.'

"Her description was being broadcast over and over again on the radio: 'Young girl, white, five foot two, one hundred pounds, long blond hair, green eyes, a red dress. She is wearing a gold necklace with the name Nola engraved on it.' Red dress, red dress, red dress, the radio repeated. That red dress was her favorite. She'd put it on for me. So there you go—that's what I was doing on the night of August 30, 1975."

Roth and I were speechless.

"You really were going to elope?" I said.

"Yes."

"That's why you said it was your fault when you called me the other day? You arranged to meet her, and she disappeared on her way to your rendezvous . . ."

He nodded, appalled.

"Were it not for that meeting, she might still be alive today."

When we left the room, Roth told me that this story about the planned elopement was a disaster, and that it must not get out, under any circumstances. If the prosecution got hold of this, Harry was screwed. In the parking lot, we went our separate ways. I waited until I was in my car before opening my notebook and reading what Harry had written:

Marcus—on my desk there is a porcelain pot. Inside, you'll find a key. It's the key to my locker at the gym in Montburry. Number 201. Everything is there. Burn it all. I am in danger.

Montburry was about ten miles inland of Somerset. I went there that afternoon after stopping by Goose Cove and finding the key in the pot, hidden under paper clips. There was only one gym in Montburry, in a modern glass building on the town's main road. In the empty changing rooms, I found Locker 201 and opened it with the key. Inside was a sweat suit, some protein bars, a pair of weight-lifting gloves, and the wooden box I had discovered a few months earlier in Harry's office. It was all in there: the photographs, the articles, the handwritten note from Nola. I also found a thickly bound sheaf of yellowed pages. The cover page was blank; there was no title. I flipped through the other pages. It was a hand-written text, and as soon as I had read the opening lines, I understood that this was the manuscript of *The Origin of Evil*. So this manuscript that I had searched so long for a few months earlier had been hidden in a gym locker all that time. I sat down on a bench and took a moment to skim the pages, excited and amazed: The writing was perfect, with no cross-outs. Men entered the locker room to get changed, but I took no notice; I couldn't tear my eyes away from the manuscript. The masterpiece I had so desperately wanted to write . . . Harry had written it. He had sat at a table in a diner and written words of absolute genius, wonderful sentences that moved the whole country, taking care to hide within his work the story of his love affair with Nola Kellergan.

When I got back to Goose Cove, I obeyed Harry to the letter. I lit a fire in the living room hearth and threw the contents of the box into it: the letter, the photographs, the press clips, and, last, the manuscript. *I am in danger*, he had written to me. But what danger did he mean? The flames grew higher. Nola's letter turned to ashes, and the photographs burned from the inside out, disappearing completely in the heat. The manuscript caught fire in a huge orange flame and the pages disinte-grated into cinders. Sitting in front of the fireplace, I watched Harry and Nola's story disappear.

Tuesday, June 3, 1975

The weather was bad today. It was late afternoon and the beach was deserted. The sky was darker and more threatening than it had been since his arrival in Somerset. The wind whipped up the ocean, which foamed and raged. Soon it would rain. It was the bad weather that had drawn him out of the house: He had gone down the wooden staircase that led from the deck to the beach and had sat on the sand. With his notebook on his knees, he let his pen slide over the paper; the imminent storm inspired him with ideas for a great novel. In recent weeks he'd had several good ideas for his new book, but none of them had led anywhere.

The first drops fell from the sky, sporadically at first, and then suddenly it was a shower. He wanted to run and find shelter, but it was at that moment that he saw her: She was barefoot by the ocean, her sandals in her hand, dancing in the rain and skipping in the waves. He watched her, wonderstruck. She was following the pattern of the eddies, careful not to wet the hem of her dress. In a brief moment of inattention, she let the water rise up to her ankles and laughed with surprise. She waded a little deeper into the gray ocean, whirling around and offering herself to the immensity. It was as if the world belonged to her. The wind blew her blond hair, but a yellow clip in the shape of flowers prevented it from blowing into her face. Torrents of water were now pouring from the sky.

When she noticed his presence about thirty feet from her, she stopped in her tracks. Embarrassed that he had seen her, she called out, "Sorry . . . I didn't notice you there."

He felt his heart pound.

"Please don't apologize," he replied. "Continue. Please continue! It's the first time I've seen someone love rain so much."

She was radiant.

"You love it too?" she asked enthusiastically.

"Love what?"

"The rain."

"No . . . I . . . I hate it, in fact."

Her smile was glorious.

"How can you hate rain? I've never seen anything so beautiful. Look at it! Look!"

He lifted his head. Water was beading on his face. He watched those millions of dashes streaking the landscape, and he turned around in a circle. She did the same. They laughed. They were both soaked. They ended up taking refuge under the deck. From his pocket he took a pack of cigarettes that had been partly spared by the deluge, and lit one.

"Can I have one?" she asked.

He handed her the pack and she took one. He was captivated.

"You're the author, aren't you?" she asked.

"Yes."

"From New York . . ."

"Yes."

"I have a question for you: Why leave New York to come to this hole?"

He smiled. "I felt like a change of scenery."

"I would love to visit New York!" she said. "I'd walk around for hours, and I'd see all the shows on Broadway. I would love to be a star. A star in New York . . ."

"Excuse me," Harry said, "but do we know each other?"

She laughed again that delicious laugh.

"No. But everyone knows who you are. You're the author. Welcome to Somerset. My name is Nola. Nola Kellergan."

"Harry Quebert."

"I know. Everyone knows—I told you."

He held out his hand to shake hers, but instead she leaned on his arm and, standing on tiptoes, kissed him on the cheek.

"I have to go. Don't tell anyone that I smoke, O.K.?"

"O.K."

"Goodbye, Mr Author. I hope I'll see you again."

And she vanished into the pouring rain.

Who was this girl? His heart was racing. For a long time he stayed there under the deck, motionless; he stayed there until darkness fell. He was no longer aware of the rain, or the night. He wondered how old she could be. She was too young, he knew. But he was smitten. It felt as if she had set fire to his soul.

*

A call from Douglas brought me back to reality. Two hours had passed. Daylight was fading. Nothing remained in the hearth but embers.

"Everyone is talking about you," Douglas told me. "Nobody understands what you're doing in New Hampshire. Everyone says it's the biggest fuck-up of your life."

"Everyone knows that Harry is my friend. It's the least I can do."

"But this is different. There are those murders, that book. I don't think you realize the enormity of this thing. Barnaski is furious. He says you've gone to New Hampshire to hide. And he's right. Today is June 17. Thirteen days from now, you're finished."

"Jesus Christ, don't you think I know that? Is that why you're calling? To remind me of the mess I'm in?"

"No, I'm calling because I have an idea."

"An idea? Alright—I'm listening."

"Write a book about the Harry Quebert affair."

"What? No, it's out of the question. I'm not going to exploit Harry's troubles to relaunch my career."

"Why is that 'exploiting his troubles'? You told me you were going there to defend him. So, prove his innocence and write a book about it. Can you imagine how big it would be?"

"All that in two weeks?"

"I talked about it to Barnaski, to calm him down . . ."

"What? You—"

"Listen to me, Marc, before you get on your high horse. Barnaski thinks this is a golden opportunity! He says that Marcus Goldman writing about the Harry Quebert affair is a seven-figure deal! It could be the book of the year. He's prepared to renegotiate your contract. He's offering to wipe the slate clean: a new contract with him that would supersede the previous one, and with an advance of a million dollars. You know what that means?"

What it meant was that this book would be a surefire bestseller, a guaranteed success, and a mountain of cash in the bargain.

"Why would Barnaski do that for me?"

"He's not doing it for you; he's doing it for himself. You don't understand—everyone here is talking about this case. A book like that would be the deal of the century!"

"I don't think I'm capable of it. I don't know how to write anymore. I don't even know if I ever knew how to write. And investigating a crime . . . that's what the police are for. I don't know anything about that."

Douglas wouldn't let it go. "This is the chance of a lifetime."

"I'll think about it."

"When you say that, it means you won't think about it."

This observation made us both laugh. He knew me well.

"Do you think it's possible to fall in love with a fifteen-year-old girl?"

"No."

"How can you be so sure?"

"I'm not sure of anything."

"And what is love?"

"Marc, please, this is not the time for a philosophical conversation."

"But he loved her! Harry fell madly in love with this girl. He was on the beach, in front of his house. He saw her and he fell in love. Why her and not someone else?"

"I don't know. But I would be curious to know why you feel so bound to Quebert."

"Marcus the Magnificent," I replied.

"What?"

"Marcus the Magnificent. A young man who couldn't get ahead in life. Until he met Harry. It was Harry who taught me to be a writer. He taught me the importance of knowing how to fall."

"What are you talking about? Have you been drinking? You're a writer because you have talent."

"No, I'm not. You're not born a writer; you become one."

"Is that what happened at Burrows?"

"Yes. He passed on all his knowledge to me. I owe him everything."

"You want to tell me about it?"

"If you like."

So that evening I told Douglas the story of what tied me to Harry. After our conversation, I went down to the beach. I needed to get some fresh air. Thick clouds could be seen through the darkness. It was a humid night; a storm was brewing. Suddenly the wind whipped up: The trees began shaking furiously, as if the world itself were announcing the fall of the great Harry Quebert.

It was much later when I returned to the house. As I reached the front door I found a plain, unaddressed envelope, inside of which I found a typed message. It said:

Go home, Goldman.

28

The Importance of Knowing How to Fall
(Burrows College, Massachusetts, 1998–2002)

"Harry, if I could learn only one thing from you, what would it be?"

"I'd like to ask you the same question."

"For me, it's *the importance of knowing how to fall.*"

"I agree entirely. Life is a long drop down, Marcus. The most important thing is knowing how to fall."

As well as being the year of the great ice storm that paralyzed the northern United States and part of Canada, leaving millions of people in darkness for several days, 1998 was also the year I met Harry. That fall I moved to the Burrows College campus, a mix of prefabricated housing and Victorian buildings surrounded by vast and beautifully kept lawns. I was given a nice room in the east wing of dormitories, which I shared with a pleasant, skinny, bespectacled black kid from Minnesota named Jared, who had left his interfering family and, visibly terrified by his new freedom, kept asking if he was *allowed* to do things. "Am I allowed to buy a Coke? Am I allowed to get back to campus after 10 p.m.? Am I allowed to keep food in my room? Am I allowed to skip class if I'm sick?" I always replied that since the Thirteenth Amendment had abolished slavery, he was allowed to do whatever he liked, and he glowed with happiness.

Jared had two obsessions: studying, and calling his mother to tell her everything was fine. For my part, I had only one: becoming a famous writer. I spent my time writing short stories for the school literary magazine, but it published only about half of them, and always on the worst pages—the ones with the ads for local businesses that nobody was interested in: Lukas Printing, Forster Tire & Lube, Françoise Hair Salon, and Julie Hu Flowers. This seemed to me scandalous and unjust. In truth, from the time I arrived at Burrows, I had to face up to some extremely tough competition in the shape of Dominic Reinhartz, a junior with an exceptional talent for writing. His stories were always given pride of place in the magazine, and each time a new issue came out I would hear students talking admiringly about him in the library. The only unswerving support I received came from Jared, who read my short stories enthusiastically as they came off my printer and read them again when they appeared in the magazine. I always gave him a copy, but he insisted on paying the two dollars for it, two dollars that he worked so hard to earn as part of the cleaning staff at the school. His admiration for me seemed limitless. He would often say, "You're a brilliant man, Marcus . . . what are you doing in a place like Burrows, Massachusetts, huh?" One Indian-summer evening, we stretched out on the campus lawn to drink beer and watch the sky. First Jared had asked if we were allowed to drink beer on campus, then he had asked if we were allowed on the lawns at night. Finally he spotted a shooting star and cried out: "Make a wish, Marcus! Make a wish!"

And I thought that a shooting star, though it could be beautiful, was a star that was afraid of shining and was fleeing as far away as possible. A bit like me.

*

On Thursdays, Jared and I made sure we never missed the class given by one of the most important people at the college: the writer Harry Quebert. He called the shots at Burrows, and everyone listened to and respected his opinion, not only because he was Harry Quebert—*the* Harry Quebert, an American institution—but also because he was naturally impressive: tall, elegant, and with a speaking voice that could be both warm and thunderous. The students were all grateful that he gave his time to such a small institution, aware that a simple phone call was all it would take for him to be hired by the most prestigious schools in the country. He was also the only professor at Burrows who taught all his courses in the main amphitheater, which was usually reserved for graduation ceremonies and theatrical performances.

This was also the year of the Lewinsky affair: the year of the presidential blow job, when the country discovered, to its horror, that fellatio had infiltrated the highest echelons of public life. The affair was on everyone's lips, so to speak. On campus people talked of nothing else, and we all wondered what was going to become of President Clinton.

One Thursday morning in late October, Harry Quebert began his class with these words: "Ladies and gentlemen, we're all very excited by what's happening in Washington at the moment, aren't we? The Lewinsky affair . . . Consider this: In the entire history of the United States of America, two reasons have been identified for terminating a presidential term of office—being a notorious crook, like Richard Nixon, or dying. And up until today, nine presidents have had their term of office cut short for one of those two reasons. Nixon resigned, and the other eight died, half of them assassinated. But now a third reason may be added to that list: fellatio. Cock sucking, blow jobs, giving head, playing the skin flute. And everyone is wondering if our great president, due to having his pants around his knees, is still our great president. Because this is America's grand obsession: sex and morality. America is a pecker paradise. And you will see, a few years from now, that no-one will remember that Mr Clinton saved our failing economy, governed expertly with a Republican majority in the Senate, or made Rabin and Arafat shake hands. But everyone will remember the Lewinsky affair, because blow jobs, ladies and gentlemen, remain engraved in people's memories. But so what if our president likes to get sucked off occasionally? He's not exactly the only one. Who else in this room enjoys that?"

Harry scanned the auditorium. There was a long silence. Most of the students were staring at their shoes. Jared, sitting next to me, actually closed his eyes to avoid meeting Quebert's gaze. I raised my hand. I was sitting toward the back, and Harry, pointing at me, called out: "Stand up, my young friend. Stand up tall so we can see you, and tell us what's on your mind."

Proudly I stood on my chair.

"I like blow jobs a lot, Professor. My name is Marcus Goldman and I love getting my dick sucked. Just like the president."

Harry lowered his reading glasses and gave me an amused look.

"Tell us, young man, do you like being sucked off by boys or girls?"

"By girls, Professor Quebert. I am a heterosexual and a good American. God bless our president, sex, and America."

There was laughter from the stunned audience, and then applause. Harry was delighted. He explained to my fellow students:

"You see, nobody will see this poor boy the same way anymore. Everyone will think: He's the disgusting one who likes head. And irrespective of his talents, irrespective of his qualities, he will always be 'Mr Blow job.'" He turned toward me again. "Mr Blow job, could you explain to us now why you made such a confession while your fellow students all had the good sense to keep their mouths shut?"

"Because in pecker paradise, Professor Quebert, sex can cause your downfall, but it can also propel you to the top. And now that everyone's eyes are fixed on me, I have the pleasure to inform you that I write very good short stories that appear in the literary magazine, issues of which will be on sale for only five dollars when this class is over."

At the end of the class, Harry came to find me at the amphitheater exit. My classmates had almost exhausted my stock of magazines. Harry bought the last copy.

"How many did you sell?" he asked me.

"All I had. About fifty copies. And about a hundred people ordered a copy, paid in advance. I bought them for two dollars each and I sold them for five. And not only that, but one of the members of the magazine's staff just offered to make me editor. He said I'd given the magazine a huge publicity boost and he'd never seen anything like it. Oh yes, I almost forgot: About ten girls gave me their phone numbers. You're right: This really is pecker paradise. And it's up to each of us to use that fact wisely."

He smiled and offered me his hand.

"Harry Quebert," he said.

"I know who you are, sir. I am Marcus Goldman. I dream of becoming a great writer like you. I hope you like my short story."

We exchanged a solid handshake and he told me, "Dear Marcus, I have no doubt whatsoever that you will go far."

Truth be told, the farthest I went that day was to the office of the dean of humanities, Dustin Pergal, who summoned me there in a rage.

"Young man," he said in an excited, nasal voice, tightly gripping the armrests of his chair, "is it true you spoke words of a pornographic nature today in the college amphitheater?"

"Pornographic? No."

"Is it not true that in front of three hundred of your fellow students, you spoke out in praise of oral relations?"

"I talked about blow jobs, sir. Yes, indeed."

He lifted his eyes to the ceiling.

"Mr Goldman, do you admit using the words *God, bless, heterosexual,* and *America* in the same breath?"

"I don't recall my exact words, but, yes, it was something like that."

He attempted to remain calm and to articulate his words slowly:

"Mr Goldman, could you explain to me what kind of obscene statement could contain all of those words at the same time?"

"Oh, please don't worry, Dean—it wasn't obscene. It was simply a blessing of God, America, sex, and all practices arising from it. From the front, from behind, from the left, from the right . . . every which way, if you see what I mean."

He lifted his eyes to the ceiling again.

"Is it true that you then set up an unauthorized stand selling literary magazines?"

"Absolutely, sir. But it was a case of force majeure that I will gladly explain now. You see, I put a great deal of effort into writing short stories for the magazine, but the editors always publish me on the worst pages. So I needed some publicity—otherwise nobody would read me. Why write if nobody is reading?"

"Is it a short story of a pornographic nature?"

"No, sir."

"I would like to take a look at it."

"Sure. It's five dollars a copy."

Pergal exploded.

"Mr Goldman! I don't think you grasp the seriousness of the situation! People were shocked by what you said. Students have complained. It is a troublesome situation for you, for me, for everybody. Apparently, you declared"—he read from a page in front of him—"'I like blow jobs. I am a heterosexual and a good American. God bless our president, sex, and America.' What in God's name is this nonsense?"

"It's just the truth, Dean: I am a heterosexual and a good American."

"I don't want to know that! Your sexual orientation is of no interest to anybody! As for the disgusting practices involving your nether regions, they have nothing to do with your fellow students!"

"But all I did was answer Professor Quebert's questions."

When he heard this, Pergal almost choked.

"What . . . What did you say? Professor Quebert's questions?"

"Yes. He asked who liked being sucked off, and I raised my hand because I consider it rude not to reply when someone asks you a question. He asked whether I preferred being sucked off by boys or by girls. That's all."

"Professor Quebert asked you whether you liked . . ."

"Exactly. You see, Dean, it's President Clinton's fault. What the president does, everybody wants to do."

Pergal got up to look for a folder from among his hanging files. Then he sat down again and looked me straight in the eyes.

"Who are you, Mr Goldman? Tell me a little about yourself. I am curious to know where you're from."

I explained that I was born in Montclair, New Jersey, to a mother who worked in a department store and an engineer father. Only son. Happy childhood and adolescence despite an above-average intelligence. Felton High School. Marcus the Magnificent. Giants fan. Braces on at fourteen. Vacations spent with an aunt in Ohio, grandparents in Florida. All perfectly normal. No allergies, no serious illnesses. Food poisoning from chicken at a Boy Scout summer camp at age eight. Liked dogs but not cats. Sports practiced: volleyball, cross-country and boxing. Ambition: Become a famous writer. Nonsmoker because smoking gives you lung cancer and makes your breath smell. Favorite meal: steak with macaroni and cheese. Occasional consumption of seafood, particularly at Joe's Stone Crab in Florida, even if my mother says it brings bad luck due to our *affiliations*.

Pergal listened to my biography without batting an eyelid. When I had finished, he said simply: "Mr Goldman, stop this nonsense, will you? I have looked at your file. I made a few phone calls. I talked to the principal of Felton High School. He told me you were an extraordinary student who could have gone to any of the great universities. So tell me: What are you doing here?"

"I beg your pardon, Dean?"

"Mr Goldman, who chooses Burrows over Harvard and Yale?"

My star performance in the amphitheater would change my life completely, even if it almost cost me my place at Burrows. Pergal concluded our interview by telling me that he needed to consider my fate, but in the end, the incident did not have any consequences for me. I discovered years later that Pergal—who believed that a student who caused a problem once would cause problems always—had wanted to expel me, and that it was Harry who had insisted that I be allowed to remain at Burrows.

The day after this memorable episode, I was elected the new editor of the literary magazine, with a mandate to give it a new dynamic. In true Marcus the Magnificent style, I decided that this new dynamic would be to stop publishing the works of Reinhartz and to give myself the cover of each issue. The following Monday, I bumped into Harry at the campus boxing gym, where I had been going regularly since I arrived at Burrows. It was, however, the first time I had seen him there. The gym was normally empty; Burrows students did not box, and apart from me, the only regular was Jared, whom I had persuaded to box a few rounds with me every other Monday because I needed a partner—preferably a weak one, so I would be sure to win. And once every two weeks, I took a certain pleasure in beating him up: the pleasure of forever being Marcus the Magnificent.

The Monday that Harry came to the gym, I was busy working on my guard position in front of a mirror. He looked just as elegant in sweats as he did in his double-breasted suits. Entering the gym, he waved to me from afar and said simply, "I didn't know you liked boxing too, Mr Goldman." Then he trained with a bag in a corner of the gym. He was lively and quick, with very good movements. I was desperate to speak to him, to tell him how I'd been summoned by Pergal after his class to talk with him about blow jobs and freedom of expression; to inform him that I was the new editor of the literary magazine; and to say how much I admired him. But I was too intimidated.

He came back to the gym the next Monday, when he watched my biweekly battering of Jared. From ringside he looked on as I pitilessly and methodically taught my roommate a lesson, and after the fight he told me that he thought I was a good boxer, that he himself wanted to start boxing again seriously in order to keep fit, and that any advice I had would be welcome. He was more than fifty years old, but beneath his baggy T-shirt it was possible to discern a broad-shouldered, powerful body: He hit the speed bag skillfully; he was well balanced; his footwork had slowed somewhat, but it was stable; his guard and his reflexes were intact. So I suggested he work with the bag to begin with, and we spent the evening there.

He came back the following Monday, and he kept coming back. And in some ways I became his personal trainer. The connection between Harry and me began in this way, through training together. We often chatted for a while when training was over, sitting side by side on the wooden bench in the locker room, letting the sweat dry on our skin. After a few weeks, the moment I had been dreading arrived: Harry said he wanted to get in the ring with me for three rounds. I didn't dare hit him, of course, but he lost no time delivering a few jarring right-handers to my chin, knocking me to the canvas on several occasions. He laughed and said that it had been years since he'd done this and he'd forgotten how much fun it was. Having given me a good beating and called me a wimp, he suggested we get dinner. I took him to a seedy student dive on a lively street in Burrows, where we talked about books and writing while eating hamburgers oozing with grease.

"You're a good student," he told me. "You're well read."

"Thank you. Have you read my short story?"

"Not yet."

"I would really like to know what you think."

"All right, then, my friend, if it would make you happy, I promise I will take a look at it and tell you what I think."

"And whatever you do, don't hold back."

"You have my word."

He had called me his friend, and I was overwhelmed with excitement. I called my parents that very evening to give them the news: After only a few months at school, I was eating dinner with the great Harry Quebert. My mother was so thrilled, she called half of New Jersey to announce that her amazing Marcus—Marcus the Magnificent—had already made close contacts in the highest literary spheres. Marcus was going to become a great writer; there was no doubt about that.

Those dinners after boxing soon became part of the Monday night ritual, and they galvanized my feeling of being Marcus the Magnificent. I had a special relationship with Harry Quebert; now, when I spoke during his classes on Thursdays, while the other students had to make do with a simple "miss" or "sir," he called me "Marcus."

A few months later—it must have been January or February, just after the Christmas holidays—I insisted, during one of our Monday dinners, that Harry tell me what he thought of my short story, because he had still not given me his opinion. He hesitated, and then asked, "Do you really want to know, Marcus?"

"Absolutely. And be as critical as you like. I'm here to learn."

"You write well. You have a lot of talent."

I blushed with pleasure.

"What else?" I exclaimed impatiently.

"You're gifted—that's undeniable."

I felt elated.

"Is there anything I need to improve, in your opinion?"

"Oh, of course. You know, you have lots of potential, but essentially, what I read was bad. Very bad, in fact. Utterly worthless. And the same is true for all the other stories by you I've been able to read in the magazine. It's criminal, cutting down trees to print crap like that. There just aren't enough forests for the number of bad writers in this country. Something must be done."

My blood ran cold. I felt as if I had been sucker punched. So it turned out that Harry Quebert, the king of literature, was also the king of bastards.

"Are you always like this?" I said angrily.

He smiled with amusement, giving me a lordly stare, as if he were savoring the moment.

"How am I?" he said.

"Unbearable."

He laughed.

"You know, Marcus, I know exactly the type of person you are: a conceited little prick who thinks Montclair is the center of the world. A little like the Europeans thought of themselves in the Middle Ages, before they got on a ship and discovered that most of the civilizations across the oceans were more developed than theirs was, which they attempted to hide by massacring the inhabitants. What I mean, Marcus, is that you are a terrific guy, but there's a good chance you will just fizzle out if you don't get your ass in gear. Your writing is good. But you have to reevaluate yourself and work much harder. Your problem is that you don't work hard enough. You're too easily satisfied. You line the words up without choosing them carefully, and it shows. You think you're a genius, huh? You're wrong. Your work is sloppy, and consequently it's worthless. You're still at square one. Do you follow me?"

"Not really."

I was furious. How dare he, even if he was Harry Quebert? How dare he talk like this to Marcus the Magnificent?

He continued: "I'm going to give you a simple example. You're a good boxer. That's a fact. You know how to fight. But look at you—you only ever measure yourself against that pathetic, skinny kid whom you batter with such smugness that it makes me want to vomit. You fight him only because you know you're guaranteed to beat him. That makes you a weakling, Marcus. A chicken. A spineless ninny. A nothing, a zero, a bluffer, a waste of space. You're just a sham. And the worst thing is that you're perfectly happy with that. Measure yourself against a real opponent! Show some balls! Boxing never lies: Getting into a ring is a very reliable way of finding out your worth. You floor the other guy or he floors you, but either way you can't lie, to yourself or to others. You are what is known as an impostor. You know why the magazine ran your stories in their back pages? Because they were bad. That's all. And why were Reinhartz's stories so popular? Because they were very good. That might have made you want to surpass yourself, to work like crazy and produce a wonderful story, but it was so much simpler to put on your little performance, to get rid of Reinhartz and give yourself the magazine cover rather than judging yourself honestly. Let me guess, Marcus: You've acted like this all your life. Am I wrong?"

Enraged, I cried, "You know nothing, Harry! Everyone liked me in high school! I was Marcus the Magnificent!"

"Look at you. You don't know how to fall! You're afraid of falling. And that is why, if nothing changes, you will become an empty, boring person. Look at yourself in the mirror, for Christ's sake, and ask yourself what the hell you're doing at Burrows! I read your file! I talked to Pergal! He was *that* close to throwing you out, my little genius! You could have gone to Harvard, Yale, the whole Poison Ivy League if you'd wanted, but no, you had to come here, because the Lord God gave you a pair of balls so small that you didn't have the guts to measure yourself against real opponents. I also called Felton. I talked to the principal—that poor dupe—who was on the verge of tears as he told me about Marcus the Magnificent. By coming here, Marcus, you knew you would be that invincible character you created out of nothing, that character who is not equipped to face the real world. You knew in advance that here there was no risk of falling. And that, I think, is your problem: You have not yet grasped the importance of knowing how to fall. That's precisely what will cause your downfall if you don't pull yourself together."

After saying this, he scribbled an address in Lowell, Massachusetts (fifteen minutes by car from Burrows), on his napkin. He told me it was a boxing gym where, every Thursday, there were fights open to everyone. And then he was gone, leaving me to pay the bill.

The following Monday Quebert did not show up at the gym, and the same thing happened the Monday after that. In the amphitheater, he called me "sir" and acted disdainful. Finally I decided to go see him at the end of one of his classes.

"Aren't you coming to the gym anymore?" I asked.

"I like you, Marcus, but as I already told you, I think you're a pretentious little crybaby, and my time is too precious to waste it with you. You do not belong at Burrows and I have no reason to be in your company."

And so the following Thursday, I borrowed Jared's car and drove to the boxing gym Harry had told me about. It was a vast hangar in an industrial zone. A frightening place, crowded inside, the air stinking of sweat and blood. In the central ring, a particularly ferocious fight was taking place, and the numerous spectators massed close to the ropes were screaming like beasts. I was scared, and I wanted to run away, to admit defeat, but I never got the opportunity. A huge black guy, who I discovered was the gym's owner, appeared in front of me. "You here to box, whitey?" he asked. I said yes, and he sent me to change in the locker room. Fifteen minutes later, I was facing him in the ring for a two-round fight.

I will never forget the beating he gave me that evening. I thought I was going to die. I was massacred as the crowd cheered wildly, thrilled to see the nice little greenhorn student from New Jersey get his face smashed in. Despite the state I was in, I made it a point of honor to hold on until the end of the second round. It was a question of pride, waiting for the final bell before collapsing to the ground, a K.O. When I opened my eyes again, barely conscious but thanking God that I was not dead, I saw Harry leaning over me with a sponge and a bowl of water.

"Harry? What are you doing here?"

He dabbed at my face delicately with the sponge. He smiled.

"My dear Marcus, you have a pair of balls beyond belief. That guy must weigh sixty pounds more than you. You fought magnificently. I'm very proud of you."

I tried to get up, but he dissuaded me.

"Don't move like that. I think you've broken your nose. You're a good guy, Marcus. I suspected you were, but now you've proved it. The way you fought tonight, you've proved that the hopes I've had for you since our first meeting were not in vain. You've demonstrated that you're capable of surpassing yourself. From now on, we're going to be friends. I've been wanting to tell you: I have no doubt at all that you will be a great writer. And I'm going to help you."

So it was after this episode in Lowell that our friendship truly began, and that Harry Quebert, my literature professor by day, became Just Harry, my boxing partner on Monday nights, my friend, and my master on certain afternoons during the holidays when he taught me how to be a writer. The writing lessons generally took place on Saturdays. We met in a diner close to campus, and sitting at a large table where we could spread out our books and papers, he read through my work and gave me advice, always encouraging me to start over and to constantly rework my sentences. "A piece of writing is never good," he told me. "There is simply a moment when it is less bad than before." Between our meetings, I spent hours in my room working and reworking my stories. And that was how I, who had always skimmed through life with a certain ease, I who had always fooled the world, learned to face up to myself.

Not only did Harry teach me to write, but he also taught me to open my mind. He took me to the theater, to exhibitions, to the movies. To Symphony Hall in Boston too; he said that well-played music could make him cry. He believed that he and I were very similar, and he often told me about his past as a writer. He said that writing had changed his life, and that this had happened in the mid-1970s. I remember one day, when he'd taken me near Teenethridge to listen to a choir of old people, how he opened up the deep recesses of his memory to me. He was born in 1941 in Benton, New Jersey, the only son to a mother who was a secretary and a father who was a doctor. His story began in earnest in the late 1960s, when, having earned his Ph.D. in English at New York University, he was hired as an English teacher at a high school in Queens. But he always felt cramped in the classroom; his sole dream was, as it had always been, to write. He published his first novel in 1972. He had high hopes for it, but it sank without trace. So he decided to begin a new stage in his life. "One day," he explained to me, "I withdrew my savings from the bank and I went for it. I decided it was time to write a damn good book, and I began looking to rent a house by the ocean where I could spend a few months and work in peace. I found a house, in Somerset, and I immediately knew it was the right one. I left New York in late May 1975 and moved to New Hampshire, never to leave there again. Because the book I wrote that summer opened the gates of glory to me. Yes, Marcus, that was the year, moving to Somerset, that I wrote *The Origin of Evil*. I eventually bought the house with the advance I was paid for it, and I still live there. It's a stunning place—you'll see. You'll have to come and visit sometime . . ."

I went to Somerset for the first time in early January 2000, during the college's Christmas break. At the time, Harry and I had known each other for little over a year. I remember I arrived with wine for him and flowers for his wife. When Harry saw the huge bouquet, he gave me a funny look and said: "Flowers? That's interesting, Marcus. Is there something you'd like to share with me?"

"They're for your wife."

"My wife? But I'm not married."

I realized then that in all the time we had known each other, we had never spoken about his private life. There was no Mrs Harry Quebert. There was no Quebert family. There was only Quebert. Just Harry. A man who was so bored at home that he became friends with one of his students. I truly understood this when I saw his fridge. Just after my arrival, when we were sitting together in the living room—a beautiful room with wood-paneled walls and floor-to-ceiling bookshelves—Harry asked if I would like something to drink.

"Lemonade?" he suggested.

"Sure."

"There's a pitcher in the fridge, made just for you. So go help yourself, and bring me a large glass too, please."

When I opened the fridge, I saw that it was empty. Inside, there was only that pathetic pitcher of lemonade, carefully prepared, with star-shaped ice cubes, slices of lemon peel, and mint leaves. It was a single man's fridge.

"Your fridge is empty, Harry," I said, as I returned to the living room.

"Oh, I'll go grocery shopping later. I don't have many guests."

"You live alone here?"

"Of course. Who do you expect me to live with?"

"A girlfriend?"

He smiled sadly. "No girlfriend. No kids. Nobody."

That first stay in Somerset made me realize that the image I'd had of Harry had been incomplete: His house by the sea was immense but utterly empty. The revered Harry L. Quebert became Just Harry whenever he went home to his little New Hampshire town. A cornered man, sometimes a little sad, he enjoyed long walks on the beach just below his house and was devoted to feeding the seagulls with the stale bread he kept in a tin box. I wondered what could have happened in this man's life that he should have ended up this way.

Harry's solitude would not have bothered me, if our friendship hadn't begun, inevitably, to cause talk. The other students insinuated that we were having an affair. One Saturday morning I finally asked him straight out, "Harry, why are you always alone?"

He shook his head; I saw his eyes shine.

"You're asking me about love, Marcus, but love is complicated. It is at once the most extraordinary and the worst thing that can happen to you. You'll discover it for yourself one day. Love can hurt so much. All the same, you should not be afraid of falling, and especially not of falling in love, because love is also very beautiful. But like everything that's beautiful, it dazzles you and hurts your eyes."

From that day on, I began to visit Harry regularly in Somerset. Sometimes I came from Burrows just for the day; sometimes I spent the night. Harry taught me to be a writer, and I did what I could to make him feel less alone. And so it was in the years leading up to my graduation, I saw Harry Quebert the star writer whenever I was at Burrows, and in Somerset I hung out with Just Harry, the solitary man.

In the summer of 2002, after four years at Burrows, I received my degree. On graduation day, after the ceremony, when I gave the valedictory speech in the main amphitheater to an audience including my family and friends from Montclair, who were moved to find that I was still Marcus the Magnificent, I walked through campus with Harry for a little while. We strolled beneath the thick-trunked plane trees, and eventually found ourselves at the boxing gym. The sun was bright. It was a beautiful day. We made one final pilgrimage together among the punching bags and boxing rings.

"This is where it all began," Harry said. "What are you going to do now?"

"Go back to New Jersey. Write a book. Become a writer, just as you taught me. Write a great novel."

He smiled. "A great novel? Patience, Marcus—you've got your whole life to do that. Will you come here from time to time, you think?"

"Of course."

"You're always welcome in Somerset."

"I know, Harry. Thank you."

He looked at me, and took me by the shoulders. "It's been years since our first meeting. You've changed. You've become a man. I can't wait to read your first novel."

We stared into each other's eyes for a long time, and he added: "Why do you want to write, deep down?"

"I don't know."

"That's not an answer. Why do you write?"

"It's in my blood. When I wake up in the morning, it's the first thing I think about. That's all I can say. Why did you become a writer, Harry?"

"Because writing gave meaning to my life. In case you haven't noticed, life generally doesn't have any meaning—unless you strive, every God-given day, to provide it with some. You have talent, Marcus. Give meaning to your life, make the wind of victory blow in your name. To be a writer is to be alive."

"What if I don't manage it?"

"You'll manage it. It will be difficult, but you'll get there. The day writing gives meaning to your life, you will be a true writer. Until that happens, whatever you do, don't be afraid of falling."

It was the novel I wrote during the next two years that propelled me to the heights of fame. There was a bidding war among publishers, and finally, in 2005, I signed a contract for a nice sum with Schmid & Hanson. Roy Barnaski, a shrewd businessman, gave me a three-book contract. As soon as it appeared, in the fall of 2006, the book was a huge success. Felton High School's Marcus the Magnificent had become a famous novelist, and my life was turned upside down: I was twenty-six years old, rich, well known, and talented. I was far from imagining that Harry's lesson was just beginning.

27

Where the Hydrangeas Were Planted

"Harry, I have doubts about what I'm writing. I don't know if it's any good. If it's worth—"

"Put your shorts on, Marcus. And go for a run."

"Now? But it's pouring rain."

"Spare me your whining. Rain never hurt anyone. If you're not brave enough to run in the rain, you'll certainly never be brave enough to write a book."

"Is this another one of your famous maxims?"

"Yes. And this rule applies to all of the Marcuses inside you: the man, the boxer, and the writer. Anytime you have doubts about what you're doing, go outside and run. Run until you can't run anymore. Run until you feel that fierce desire to win being born within you. You know, Marcus, I used to hate rain too before . . ."

"What changed your mind?"

"Someone."

"Who?"

"Go. Leave now, and don't come back until you're exhausted."

"How am I supposed to learn if you never tell me anything?"

"You ask too many questions, Marcus. Have a good run."

He was a big man and he didn't exactly look easygoing: an African American with hands like bear paws, wearing a too-tight blazer that revealed his powerful, stocky build. The first time I saw him, he was pointing a revolver at me. He was the first person who had ever threatened me with a gun. He entered my life on June 18, 2008, the day I began my investigation into the murders of Nola Kellergan and Deborah Cooper. That morning, after almost forty-eight hours at Goose Cove, I decided it was time to go see the gaping hole that had been dug sixty feet from the house and that, up to this point, I had been content to observe from a distance. After slipping under the police tape, I spent a long time inspecting that area that I knew so well. Goose Cove was surrounded by beach and shore-side forest, and there were no barriers or signposts to mark the limits of the property. Anybody could come and go, and it wasn't unusual to see people walking along the beach or cutting through the woods. The trench was on a grassy plot overlooking the ocean. When I reached it, thousands of questions began buzzing in my head. In particular, I wondered how many hours I had spent on that deck, or in Harry's office, while the girl's corpse was rotting underground. I took photographs and even a few videos with my cell phone, trying to imagine the decomposed body, as found by the police. Fixated as I was upon the crime scene, I did not sense the threatening presence behind me. It was only when I turned around to film the distance to the deck that I saw a man, a few yards away, aiming a revolver at me.

"Don't shoot!" I cried. "Please don't shoot, for God's sake! I'm Marcus Goldman! Writer!"

Instantly he lowered his gun.

"You're Marcus Goldman?"

He slid the pistol into a holster hanging from his belt, and I noticed he was wearing a badge.

"You're a cop?" I asked him.

"Sergeant Perry Gahalowood. New Hampshire State Police, Investigative Services Bureau. What are you doing here? This is a crime scene."

"Do you do this a lot, hold people up with your gun? What if I'd been with the feds? You'd have looked pretty stupid then, wouldn't you? I'd have kicked you off the property right away."

He laughed.

"You? A cop? I've been watching you for ten minutes, walking around on tiptoes so you don't get your loafers dirty. And federal agents don't scream when they see a gun. They get theirs out and shoot everything that moves."

"I thought you were a criminal."

"Because I'm black?"

"No, because you look like a criminal. Is that a bolo tie you're wearing?"

"Yes."

"You know they're not cool anymore?"

"Are you going to tell me what the hell you're doing here?"

"I live here."

"What do you mean, you live here?"

"I'm a friend of Harry Quebert. He asked me to look after the house in his absence."

"Harry Quebert is accused of a double murder. His house has been searched and sealed off. I'm throwing you out, my friend."

"There are no seals on the house."

He looked puzzled for a moment, then replied, "I hadn't thought some wannabe writer would come here and squat."

"You should have thought. Even if that is difficult for a policeman."

"I'm going to throw you out anyway."

"Legal loophole!" I said. "No seals means access is not prohibited! I'm staying here. If you try to throw me out, I'll take you to the Supreme Court and sue you for threatening me with your gun. I will claim millions in damages. I've filmed everything."

"Roth is behind this, isn't he?" Gahalowood said with a sigh.

"Yes."

"That asshole. He'd send his own mother to the electric chair if it would get one of his clients off."

"Legal loophole, Sergeant. Legal loophole. I hope you're not mad at me."

"I am. But in any case, we're not interested in the house anymore. On the other hand, I am warning you now not to cross any more police tape. Can't you read? It says CRIME SCENE—DO NOT CROSS."

Having recovered my self-assurance, I dusted off my shirt and took a few steps toward the hole.

"The thing is, Sergeant, I'm running an investigation too," I told him very seriously. "Tell me what you know about the case."

He laughed again.

"I don't believe this. You're running an investigation? That's a new one. You owe me fifteen dollars, by the way."

"Why?"

"That's what I paid for your book. I read it last year. A very bad book. Probably the worst I've read in my entire life. I would like to be reimbursed."

I looked him straight in the eyes and said, "Fuck off, Sergeant."

And since I was walking without looking where I was going, I fell into the hole. I began screaming because I was in the place where Nola had died.

"You are unbelievable!" Gahalowood shouted from the edge of the hole.

He gave me his hand and helped me back up. We went to sit on the deck and I gave him his money. All I had was a fifty-dollar bill.

"Do you have any change?"

"No."

"Keep it, then."

"Thank you, writer."

"I'm not a writer anymore."

I would soon discover that Sergeant Gahalowood was a crabby and extremely stubborn man. Nevertheless, after I'd nagged him for a while, he told me he'd been on duty the day the discovery was made, and that he had been one of the first to see inside the hole.

"There were human remains, and a leather bag. The name *Nola Kellergan* was stitched on the inside of the bag, and there was a manuscript, in reasonably good condition. I imagine leather preserves paper."

"How did you know this manuscript was Harry Quebert's?"

"At the time, I didn't know. I showed it to him in the interview room and he acknowledged it right away. I checked the text afterward, of course. It corresponds word for word to his book, *The Origin of Evil.* Strange coincidence, don't you think?"

"Just because he wrote a book about Nola doesn't mean he killed her. He says that manuscript disappeared, and that Nola sometimes took his pages."

"We found the girl's corpse in his yard. With the manuscript of his book. Show me the proof of his innocence, writer, and maybe I'll change my mind."

"I'd like to see that manuscript."

"Out of the question. It's evidence."

"But I've told you: I'm investigating this too," I insisted.

"I'm not interested in your investigation, writer. You'll have access to the case files when Quebert goes before the grand jury."

I wanted to show him that I was not some hopeless amateur, and that I, too, had a certain knowledge of the case.

"I spoke with Travis Dawn, now Somerset's police chief. Apparently, at the time Nola disappeared, they had a suspect: the driver of a black Chevrolet Monte Carlo."

"I know all about it," Gahalowood said. "And guess what, Sherlock: Harry Quebert had a black Chevrolet Monte Carlo."

"How do you know about the car?"

"I read the report from back then."

I thought about this for a second, and then said, "Wait a minute,

Sergeant. If you're so clever, explain to me why Harry would have wanted bushes planted in the very place where he'd buried Nola."

"He didn't expect the gardeners to dig so deep."

"That makes no sense and you know it. Harry didn't kill Nola Kellergan."

"How can you be so sure?"

"He loved her."

"They all say that at their trials: 'I loved her too much, so I had to kill her.' When you love someone, you don't kill her."

With these words, Gahalowood got up from his chair.

"Are you leaving already, Sergeant? But our investigation has hardly even begun."

"Our investigation? Mine, you mean."

"When will we meet again?"

"Never, writer. Never."

And he left without further ado.

While Gahalowood did not take me seriously, the opposite was true for Travis Dawn, whom I went to see soon afterward at the police station in Somerset, to give him the anonymous message from the evening before.

"'Go home, Goldman'? When did you find this?"

"Last night. I went for a walk on the beach. When I came back, this message was jammed in the front door."

"And I suppose you didn't see anything . . ."

"Nothing."

"Is this the first time?"

"Yes. Then again, I've been here only two days . . ."

"I'm going to register a complaint in order to open a file. We have to be careful, Marcus."

"At first, I thought it might be my mother's doing."

"No, this is serious. Don't underestimate the emotional impact of this case. Can I keep this letter?"

"It's all yours."

"Thank you. Can I do anything else for you? I assume you didn't come to see me just to tell me about this piece of paper."

"I'd like you to come with me to Side Creek, if you have time. I want to see the place where it all happened."

Not only did Travis agree to take me to Side Creek, he even took me back thirty-three years. In his patrol car we retraced his steps when he responded to Deborah Cooper's first call. From Somerset, we headed toward Maine along Shore Road, which hugs the coastline. We passed Goose Cove and then, a few miles on, arrived at the intersection on the edge of the Side Creek forest. Deborah Cooper had lived at the end of this path. Travis turned off here and we parked in front of the house, a pretty wooden structure, facing the ocean and surrounded on three sides by woods. It was a beautiful but isolated place.

"It hasn't changed," Travis told me, while we walked around the house. "It's been repainted—the color is a little lighter than before—but everything else is the way it was then."

"Who lives here now?"

"A couple from Boston who come for the summer. They don't arrive until July and they leave at the end of August. The rest of the time it's empty." He showed me the back door, which led directly to the kitchen, and said: "The last time I saw Deborah Cooper alive, she was standing in front of this door. Chief Pratt had just arrived. He told her to stay where she was and not to worry, and we left to search the woods. Who could imagine that twenty minutes later she'd be killed by a bullet to the chest?"

As he was speaking, Travis was walking toward the woods. I realized that he was taking the path he'd walked with Chief Pratt thirty-three years earlier.

"What ever happened to Chief Pratt?" I said, following him.

"He's retired. He still lives in Somerset, on Mountain Drive. You've seen him around, I'm sure. A burly guy who always wears golf pants."

We entered the rows of trees. Through dense vegetation, we could see the beach, slightly below. After we had walked for a good fifteen minutes, Travis stopped dead in front of three very straight pine trees.

"It was here," he told me.

"What was here?"

"Where we found all that blood, tufts of blond hair, and a scrap of red fabric. It was horrible. I'll never forget this place. There's more moss on the rocks and the trees have grown taller, but for me, nothing has changed."

"What did you do then?"

"We realized something serious must have happened, but we didn't have time to hang around any longer because we heard that gunshot. It's crazy—we didn't see anything on our way here. I mean the girl or her murderer must have passed us at some point. I don't know how we could have missed them. I think they must have been hidden by the undergrowth, and that he must have been preventing her from making noise. The woods are huge; it's not difficult to go unseen. I imagine she must have escaped while her attacker was distracted for a moment, and that she must have run to the house to seek help. He came to find her in the house and took care of Mrs Cooper."

"So as soon as you heard the gunshot, you went back to the house . . ."

"Yeah."

We walked back along the path and returned to the house.

"It all happened in the kitchen," Travis told me. "Nola came out of the forest, calling for help; Mrs Cooper let her in, then went to the living room to call the police and tell them that the girl was with her. I know that the telephone was in the living room because I had used it myself to call Chief Pratt half an hour before. While she was on the phone, the attacker entered the kitchen to grab Nola, but at that moment Mrs Cooper reappeared and he shot her. Then he took Nola to his car."

"Where was this car?"

"By the side of Shore Road, where it passes this goddamn forest. Come with me—I'll show you."

From the house, Travis led me back into the woods, but in a different direction this time, guiding me confidently through the trees. We came out soon onto Shore Road.

"The black Chevy was here. At the time, the edges of the road weren't so well cleared, and it was concealed by the bushes."

"How do we know this is the path he took?"

"There were traces of blood going from the house to here."

"And the car?"

"Vanished. Like I told you, a deputy sheriff who was coming in as support happened to see it. There was a chase, and there were roadblocks all over the area, but he lost us."

"How did the murderer manage to escape through the holes in the dragnet?"

"I would love to know that, and I have to say that there are many things about this case that I'm still wondering about after thirty-three years. You know, there's not a day that passes without me getting in my police car and thinking how things might have been different if we'd caught that goddamn Chevy. Maybe we could have saved the girl . . ."

"You think she was in the car, then?"

"Now that we've found her body two miles from here, I'd say it's certain."

"And you also think it was Harry who was driving that black Chevy, huh?"

He shrugged.

"Let's just say that, given recent events, I don't see who else it could have been."

The former police chief, Gareth Pratt, whom I went to speak with that same day, seemed to share his former deputy's opinion regarding Harry's guilt. He received me on his porch, wearing golf pants. His wife, Amy, served us drinks and then pretended to tend to the potted plants on their porch so she could eavesdrop on our conversation—a fact she did not attempt to conceal, commenting from time to time on what her husband was saying.

"I've seen you before, haven't I?" Pratt said.

"Yes, I often come to Somerset."

"It's that nice young man who wrote that book," his wife said.

"You're not that guy who wrote a book?" he repeated.

"Yes," I replied. "One of those guys."

"Gareth, I just told you that," Amy cut in.

"Darling, please don't interrupt us. I'm the one he's come to see. So, Mr Goldman, how can I help you?"

"I'm trying to find out a few things about the murder of Nola Kellergan. I spoke to Travis Dawn, who told me that you already had suspicions about Harry at the time."

"That's true."

"On what basis?"

"Several things tipped us off. Particularly the way the car chase went: It suggested that the murderer was somebody local. He had to have known the area perfectly in order to disappear like that with every police car in the county on his tail. And then there was that black Monte Carlo. As you probably guessed, we made a list of all the people in the area owning that particular model. The only one not to have an alibi was Quebert."

"And yet, in the end, you didn't follow up your suspicions . . ."

"No, because apart from the description of the car, we had no real evidence against him. We very quickly removed him from our list of suspects. The discovery of that poor girl's body in his yard proves that we were wrong. It's crazy—I always thought he seemed like such a nice guy. Maybe, deep down, that skewed my judgment. He was always so charming, friendly . . . I mean, what about you, Mr Goldman? If I've understood correctly, he was a friend of yours. Now that you know about the girl in his yard, haven't you thought of anything he might once have said or done that could have aroused your suspicions?"

"No, Chief. Nothing comes to mind."

As I returned to Goose Cove, I noticed, beyond the police tape, the hydrangea bushes dying by the side of the trench, their roots exposed. I went to the garage and found a spade. Then, entering the forbidden zone, I dug a hole in a square of soft ground overlooking the ocean, and I planted the bushes.

August 30, 2002

"Harry?"

It was six in the morning. He was standing on the deck, holding a cup of coffee. He turned around.

"Marcus? You're sweating . . . don't tell me you've already been running?"

"Yeah. I've done my eight miles."

"What time did you get up?"

"Early. You remember, two years ago, when you forced me to get up at dawn? That became a habit. I get up early so that the world belongs to me. What about you—what are you doing outside?"

"I'm observing, Marcus."

"What are you observing?"

"You see that little grassy area between the pines, overlooking the beach? I've been meaning to do something with that for a long time. It's the only part of the property flat enough to be used as a garden. I would like to create a pretty niche for myself, with two benches, an iron table, and hydrangeas growing all around. Lots of hydrangeas."

"Why hydrangeas?"

"I knew someone who liked them. I would like to have flower beds filled with hydrangeas so that I can always remember her."

"Was she someone you loved?"

"Yes."

"You look sad, Harry."

"Pay no attention."

"Why don't you ever talk about your love life?"

"Because there's nothing to say. Just look—look carefully. Or, better yet, close your eyes! Yes, close your eyes tightly so that no light penetrates your eyelids. Can you see? There is that paved path going from the deck to the hydrangeas. And there are those two little benches, from which you can see both the ocean and the beautiful flowers. What could be better than seeing the ocean and the hydrangeas? There's even a little pool, with a fountain in the form of a statue in the middle. And if the pool is big enough, I'll put multicolored Japanese carp in it."

"Fish? They wouldn't last an hour. The seagulls would gobble them up."

He smiled.

"The seagulls can do what they like here, Marcus. But you're right: I won't put carp in the pool. Go take a hot shower before you catch a cold. I don't want your parents thinking I'm not looking after you. I'm going to make breakfast . . . Marcus—"

"Yes, Harry?"

"If I'd had a son—"

"I know, Harry. I know."

On the morning of Thursday, June 19, 2008, I went to the Sea Side Motel. It was very easy to find: From Side Creek Lane, you continued north straight along Shore Road for four miles, and you could not miss the huge wooden sign announcing:

SEA SIDE MOTEL & RESTAURANT
Since 1960

The place where Harry had waited for Nola was still there; I had undoubtedly passed it hundreds of times, never paying it the slightest attention. But then, why would I have, until now? It was a red-roofed wooden building surrounded by a rose garden; just behind it was the forest. All the first-floor rooms opened onto the parking lot; to reach the upstairs rooms, you took an outdoor staircase.

According to the front-desk clerk, the motel had barely changed since it was built. The rooms had been modernized and a restaurant had been added next to the main building, but that was all. He showed me the motel's fortieth-anniversary commemorative book, containing photographs that bore out what he said.

"Why are you so interested in this place?" he finally said.

"Because I'm looking for some important information."

"Go on."

"I would like to know if someone slept here, in Room 8, on the night of Saturday, August 30, 1975."

He laughed. "Nineteen seventy-five? Are you serious? Since we went digital, the farthest back we can go is two years. I could tell you who slept here on August 30, 2006, if you like. Well, theoretically I could. Obviously I don't have the right to reveal that kind of information."

"So there's no way of knowing?"

"Apart from the register, the only things we keep are e-mail addresses and our newsletter. Would you be interested in receiving our newsletter?"

"No, thank you. But I would like to see Room 8 if possible."

"I can't just show it to you. But it is vacant. Would you like to rent it for the night? It's a hundred dollars."

"Your sign says all the rooms are sixty-five dollars. You know what? I'm going to slip you twenty dollars, you're going to show me the room, and everyone will be happy."

"You drive a hard bargain. But O.K."

Room 8 was on the second floor. It was an ordinary motel room, with a bed, a minibar, a television, a small desk, and a bathroom.

"Why are you so interested in this room?" the clerk wanted to know.

"It's a long story. A friend told me he spent the night here, in 1975. If that's true, it means he's innocent."

"Innocent of what?"

I did not reply, but asked another question of my own. "Why do you call this place the Sea Side Motel? There isn't even a sea view."

"No, but a path goes through the forest to the beach. It's in the brochure. Our customers couldn't care less, though; the people who stop here don't go to the beach."

"So are you saying that you could, for example, walk along the beach from Somerset, come through the forest, and arrive here?"

"It's possible, yes."

I spent the rest of my day at the library, going through the archives and attempting to reconstruct the past. Ernie Pinkas was a big help to me in this regard; he was very generous with his time.

According to newspaper articles from the time, nobody noticed anything strange on the day of the disappearance: neither a fleeing Nola, nor a prowler near the house. Everyone regarded the disappearance as a total mystery, with Deborah Cooper's murder only compounding the puzzlement. Nevertheless, certain witnesses, mostly neighbors, reported hearing noises and shouts coming from the Kellergan house that day, while others stated that the noises were actually music, played at high volume by the Reverend David Kellergan, as was his wont. The *Somerset Star*'s investigations indicated that Mr Kellergan was doing odd jobs in his garage, and that he always listened to the same music when he was working. He turned the volume up enough to cover up the sounds of his tools, believing that good music, even when played too loud, was always preferable to the sound of hammering. But if his daughter had called out for help, he would not have heard her. According to Pinkas, Mr Kellergan always blamed himself for having played his music too loud: Afterward, he never left the family home on Terrace Avenue, living there as a hermit, playing the same record over and over again, loud enough to deafen himself, as a form of punishment. He was the only one of Nola's parents still alive. Nola's mother, Louisa, had died a long time before. Apparently, on the night Nola was identified, journalists assailed David Kellergan in his home. "It was such a sad scene," Pinkas told me. "He said something like, 'So she's dead . . . I've been saving up all this time so I could send her to college.' And guess what— the next day five fake Nolas appeared at his door. After the money. The poor guy was completely disoriented. What is the world coming to, Marcus? Some people have shit for hearts—that's what I think."

"And the father often did that, blasted music at high volume?"

"Yes, all the time. Actually, about Harry . . . I saw Mrs Quinn yesterday, in town . . ."

"Mrs Quinn?"

"Yeah, she's the former owner of Clark's. She's telling anyone who'll listen that she always knew Harry had designs on Nola. She says she had irrefutable proof at the time."

"What kind of proof?" I asked.

"No idea. Have you heard from Harry?"

"I'm going to see him tomorrow."

"Say hello for me."

"Go and see him, if you want . . . he'd like that."

"I'm not sure I want to."

Pinkas was seventy-five years old and used to work at a textile factory in Concord; he had never gone to college and regretted not having been able to find any outlet for his love of books beyond volunteering as a librarian. I knew he owed an eternal debt of gratitude to Harry, who had allowed him to take literature classes at Burrows College for free. So I had always considered him one of Harry's most faithful supporters. But now even he preferred to keep his distance.

"You know," he said, "Nola was such a special girl—unfailingly gentle and kind. Everyone here loved her! She was like a daughter to all of us.

So how could Harry have . . . I mean, even if he didn't kill her, he wrote that book about her! I mean, shit – she was fifteen years old! She was a kid! And he loved her so much he wrote a book about her? A love story! I've been married for fifty years, and I've never felt the need to write a book about my wife."

"But that book was a masterpiece."

"That book is the devil's work. It's perverted. I threw away all the copies we had here. People are too upset about this."

I sighed, but said nothing. I didn't want to have an argument with him. All I said was: "Ernie, can I have a package sent to you here, at the library?"

"A package? Of course. Why?"

"I asked my cleaning lady to pick up something important from my apartment and send it to me by FedEx. But I'd prefer it be delivered here, it's safer."

The mailbox at Goose Cove provided an accurate reflection of the state of Harry's reputation: The whole country, having admired him before, was now condemning him, sending him hate mail. This was the biggest scandal in the history of publishing. *The Origin of Evil* had already disappeared from the shelves of libraries and from school curricula, and the *Boston Globe* had dropped Harry's column from its pages; as for Burrows College's board of directors, they had decided to dismiss him, effective immediately. The newspapers had no qualms about describing him as a sexual predator; he was the subject of every debate and conversation. Roy Barnaski, scenting a surefire commercial opportunity, wanted a book on the scandal at any price. And since Douglas had not managed to persuade me, Barnaski ended up calling me himself to deliver a brief lesson on the market economy.

"The public wants this book," he explained. "Listen to this: You even have fans chanting your name outside our building."

He put me on speakerphone and signaled his assistants, who belted out: "Gold-man! Gold-man! Gold-man!"

"They're not fans, Roy—they're your staff. Hi, Marisa."

"Hi, Marcus," Marisa said.

Barnaski picked up the receiver again. "Listen, you need to think about this. We're bringing a book out in the fall. A guaranteed success! A month and a half to write it—does that sound fair to you?"

"A month and a half? It took me years to write my first book. And I don't even know what I would write. Nobody knows what happened yet."

"I can provide you with ghostwriters, you know, to speed the process along. And it doesn't have to be great literature—people just want to know what Quebert did with that girl. Just give us the facts—with some suspense and some sleazy details, and a little sex, of course."

"Sex?"

"Come on, Goldman, I don't have to teach you how to do your job. Who would want to buy this book if there weren't some indecent scenes between the old guy and the seven-year-old girl? That's what people want! We'll sell it by the bucket load, even if the book's no good. That's what matters, isn't it?"

"Harry was thirty-four years old, and Nola was fifteen!"

"Don't split hairs. If you write this book, as I told your agent, I'll tear up your previous contract and offer you a million-dollar advance as thanks for your cooperation."

I refused point blank, and Barnaski lost his temper: "Alright, if you want to play hardball, let's play hardball. I expect a manuscript from you in exactly eleven days. And if I don't get it, I will sue the shit out of you!"

He hung up on me. Soon afterward, while I was buying groceries in the general store in Somerset, I received a call from Douglas. Barnaski had undoubtedly been in touch with him. "Marc, you can't mess around with this," he said. "Let me remind you that Barnaski has you by the balls! Your previous contract is still valid and your only means of getting out of it is to accept his proposal. And this book would be a huge boost to your career. An advance of a million dollars—there are worse things in life, aren't there?"

"Barnaski wants me to do a hatchet job! It's out of the question. I don't want to write a book like that—a piece of garbage churned out in a few weeks. Good books take time."

"But this is the way it is today! Writers who hang around in a daydream waiting for inspiration to come . . . all that is in the past! Everyone wants your book, even without your having written a single word of it, because everybody wants to know the truth. And they want it now. There's a narrow window of opportunity. This fall, there's the election . . ."

"So why would any publisher want to risk publishing a book that's got nothing to do with the election?"

"That's Barnaski through and through. He's a fuckwit, a genius, an asshole, but he'll pull it off, you see. Believe me, only he could do it."

I couldn't believe in anything anymore. I paid for my groceries and returned to my car. That was where I found a piece of paper slipped under one of the windshield wipers. The same message, once again:

Go home, Goldman.

I looked around: There was nobody. A few people sitting at an outdoors table at a nearby restaurant, customers coming out of the general store. Who was following me? Who wanted me to give up my investigation into the death of Nola Kellergan?

The day after this latest incident—Friday, June 20—I went to see Harry in prison again. Before leaving Somerset, I stopped at the library, where my package had just been delivered.

"What is it?" Pinkas asked. He was curious, and was hoping I would open it in front of him.

"A tool that I need."

"What kind of tool?"

"A tool for work. Thank you for receiving it, Ernie."

"Wait—don't you want some coffee? I've just made some. Do you want a knife to open your package?"

"Thanks, Ernie, maybe next time. I have to go."

Arriving in Concord, I decided to swing by the state police headquarters in order to find Sergeant Gahalowood and present him with a few theories I'd put together since our brief first meeting.

The New Hampshire Division of State Police headquarters, where the criminal division—known as the Investigative Services Bureau—had its offices, was a large red-brick building: 33 Hazen Drive, in the center of Concord. It was almost 1 p.m.; I was told that Gahalowood had left for his lunch, and was asked to wait in a corridor, near a table where there were magazines and a coffee machine. When he arrived an hour later, he looked angry.

"You!" he exploded when he saw me. "They called me and they said, 'Perry, hurry up—there's a guy here who's been waiting for you for an hour,' and I interrupt my meal to come see what's happening because it might be important, and what do I find? The writer!"

"Don't be mad. I thought we got off on the wrong foot, and that maybe—"

"I hate you, writer. I'm warning you now. My wife read your book— she thought you were good-looking and intelligent. Your face, on the back cover, has been smiling out from her nightstand for weeks. You've been living in our bedroom! You've slept with us! You've had dinner with us! You've been on vacation with us! You've taken baths with my wife! You've made all her friends cluck like hens! You have ruined my life!"

"You're married, Sergeant? That's funny. You're so disagreeable, I would have bet anything you didn't have a family."

He sank his face into his double chin. "In the name of God, what do you want?" he barked.

"To understand."

"That's pretty ambitious for a guy like you."

"I know."

"Let the police do their job, will you?"

"I need information, Sergeant. I have a pathological desire to know everything. I'm a control freak, you see—I have to control everything."

"Really? Then control yourself!"

"Could we go to your office?"

"No."

"Just tell me if Nola really did die at fifteen years old."

"Yes. The bone scan confirmed it."

"So she was abducted and killed at the same time?"

"Yes."

"But that bag . . . why was she buried with that bag?"

"I have no idea."

"And if she had a bag with her, couldn't that lead us to think she was running away?"

"If you're packing a bag to run away, you fill it with clothes, don't you?"

"Exactly."

"Because the only thing in her bag was that book."

"One point for you," I said. "Your insight blows me away. But that bag—"

He interrupted: "I should never have mentioned that bag the other day. I don't know what got into me."

"Me neither."

"Pity, I guess. Yes, that's it: You made me feel sorry for you, with your bewildered look and your muddy shoes."

"Thank you. And just to continue: What could I learn from the autopsy? Actually, do you say *autopsy* when it's just a skeleton?"

"I don't know."

"Would *forensic examination* be a more appropriate term?"

"I don't give a damn about the exact term. What I can tell you is that she had her skull smashed! Smashed! Bang! Bang!"

As he accompanied these words with gestures, miming someone hitting with a bat, I asked him: "So it was done with a bat?"

"I don't know, you son of a bitch!"

"A man? A woman?"

"What?"

"Couldn't a woman have carried out the attack? Why is it necessarily a man?"

"Because the eyewitness, Deborah Cooper, expressly identified a man. Anyway, this conversation is over, writer. You're getting on my nerves."

"But what do you think of this case?"

He took a family photograph out of his wallet. "I have two daughters, writer. Fourteen and seventeen. I can't imagine going through what Mr Kellergan has gone through. I want the truth. I want justice. Justice does not mean merely adding up the various facts; it is much more complex than that. So I am going to carry out my investigation. If I discover proof that Quebert is innocent, believe me, he will be freed. But if he's guilty, you can be sure I will not let Roth grandstand the jury into acquitting a criminal. Because that is not justice either."

Beneath his bull-like aggression, Gahalowood had a philosophy that I liked.

"You're a good guy, Sergeant. How about I buy you a doughnut and we continue our little chat?"

"I don't want a doughnut. I want you to get the hell out of here. I've got work to do."

"But you have to explain to me how an investigation works. I don't know how to do it."

"Goodbye, writer. I've seen enough of you to last me the rest of the month. Maybe the rest of my life."

I was disappointed not to be taken seriously, but I didn't insist. I held out my hand. He crushed my fingers in his powerful grip, and

I left. But out in the parking lot, I heard him calling me: "Hey, writer!" I turned around and saw his hefty form jogging toward me.

"Writer," he said breathlessly when he'd caught up with me. "Good cops don't focus on the killer . . . they focus on the victim. You need to find out about the victim. And you have to start at the beginning, before the murder. Not at the end. You're making a mistake by concentrating on the murder. You have to find out who the victim was. Find out who Nola Kellergan was . . ."

"And Deborah Cooper?"

"If you want my opinion, it's all linked to Nola. Deborah Cooper was just a collateral victim. Find out who Nola was—you'll discover her killer and Deborah Cooper's at the same time."

Who was Nola Kellergan? That was the question I intended to ask Harry when I saw him at the state prison. He didn't look good. He seemed highly preoccupied by the contents of his gym locker.

"Did you find everything?" he asked, before he even greeted me.

"Yes."

"And you burned it all?"

"Yes."

"The manuscript too?"

"The manuscript too."

"Why didn't you tell me you'd done it? I was worried sick. And where have you been for the last two days?"

"I was carrying out my investigation. Harry, why was that box in a gym locker?"

"I know that seems weird to you. After your visit in March, I became afraid that someone else would find it. It seemed to me that anyone might discover it: an inconsiderate visitor, the cleaning lady. I decided it was prudent to hide my mementos somewhere else."

"You hid them? But that makes you look guilty. And that manuscript . . . it was *The Origin of Evil*?"

"Yes. The very first draft."

"I recognized the text. There was no title on the cover page . . ."

"The title came to me afterward."

"After Nola's disappearance, you mean?"

"Yes. But let's not talk about that manuscript, Marcus. It was cursed. It brought only evil into my life. Now Nola is dead and I'm in prison."

We looked at each other for a moment. I put a plastic bag on the table, inside of which were the contents of the package I had received.

"What is it?" Harry asked.

Without replying, I took out a minidisc player with a microphone connected to it. I set it up in front of Harry.

"Marcus, what the hell are you up to? Don't tell me you kept that damn thing . . ."

"Of course, Harry. I took good care of it."

"Put it away, please."

"Don't be like that, Harry."

"What the hell do you plan to do with it?"

"I want you to tell me about Nola, about Somerset, about everything. About the summer of 1975, about your book. I need to know. And, Harry, I'd be grateful if you would tell me the truth."

He smiled sadly. I pressed RECORD and let him talk. It was a nice scene: Here in this prison visiting room, where husbands were reunited with their wives, fathers with their children, I was reunited with my old mentor, who told me his story.

I ate early that evening, on the way back to Somerset. Afterward, because I had no desire to go straight to Goose Cove, where I would be alone in that immense house, I drove along the coast for a while. The sun was setting, the ocean sparkling: It was all so beautiful. I passed the Sea Side Motel, the Side Creek forest, Side Creek Lane and Goose Cove; I went through Somerset and ended up at Grand Beach. I walked up to the water's edge, then sat down on the shells to watch night fall. The distant lights of Somerset danced on the surface of the waves; the seagulls shrieked loudly, mockingbirds sang in the surrounding bushes, and I heard the lighthouse foghorns. I pressed PLAY on the recorder, and Harry's voice rang out in the darkness:

You know Grand Beach, Marcus? It's the first beach you see if you're coming to Somerset from Massachusetts. I sometimes go there at dusk and look out at the town's lights. And I think over everything that happened there thirty-three years ago. That beach is where I stopped on the day I first arrived in Somerset. It was May 20, 1975. I was thirty-four years old. I was coming from New York, where I'd made a decision to take responsibility for my own future. I had ditched everything: I'd quit my job as an English teacher, I'd gathered up my savings, and I'd decided to make a go of it as a writer. I was going to hole myself up in New England and write the novel of my dreams.

To begin with, I had thought about renting a house in Maine, but a Boston real estate agent persuaded me to choose Somerset. He'd told me about a house that corresponded exactly to what I was looking for—it was Goose Cove. The moment I saw it, I fell in love with it. It was exactly the place I needed: a calm, rustic retreat, but not altogether isolated, because Somerset was not many miles away. I liked the town a lot too. Life seemed gentle there: Children played in the streets; crime was nonexistent. It was like a picture-postcard town. The house at Goose Cove was well beyond my means, but the real estate agent allowed me to pay the rent in installments, and I calculated that if I didn't spend too much money, I could just about make ends meet. And I had a feeling that I was making a good choice. I was right too, because that decision changed my life: The book I wrote that summer would make me rich and famous.

I think what I liked so much about Somerset was the status I soon began to enjoy there. In New York, I was just a high school teacher who moonlighted as a writer, but in Somerset I was Harry Quebert, a writer who had come from New York to write his next novel. You know, Marcus, that thing with your being Marcus the Magnificent in high school, when you contented yourself with distorting the way you appeared to others in order to shine? That's exactly what happened to me when I came here. I was young, self-confident, good-looking, athletic, and cultivated, and not only that, but I lived in the beautiful Goose Cove house. The people in the town, even if they'd never heard of me before, assumed I was successful because of the way I acted and the place where I lived. That was all it took for the locals to imagine that I was a big celebrity in New York. So, overnight, I became someone. The respected writer I couldn't be in New York, I was in Somerset. I had provided the local library with a few copies of my first book, and guess what? That pathetic pile of pages, cold-shouldered by New York, provoked great excitement here in Somerset. It was 1975 in a small New Hampshire town that was looking for a raison d'être, long before the Internet and all that, and in me it found the local star it had always dreamed of having.

It was about 11 p.m. when I got back to Goose Cove. As I drove down the narrow gravel driveway, my headlights illuminated a masked figure, who instantly fled into the woods. I hit the brakes and leaped out of the car, yelling, ready to pursue the intruder. That was when my eye was caught by a bright glow: Something was burning near the house. I ran over to see what was happening. Harry's Corvette was on fire. The flames had already taken hold, and a plume of acrid smoke was rising toward the sky. I called for help, but there was nobody to hear me. All that surrounded me was the woods. The Corvette's windows exploded in the heat, the car itself began to melt, and the flames grew higher, licking the garage walls. There was nothing I could do. It was all going to burn.

26

N-O-L-A

(Somerset, New Hampshire, Saturday, June 14, 1975)

"The reason writers are such fragile beings, Marcus, is that they suffer from two sorts of emotional pain, which is twice as much as a normal human being: the heartache of love and the heartache of books. Writing a book is like loving someone. It can be very painful."

STAFF MEMO

You will have noticed that Harry Quebert has come to eat lunch in our restaurant every day for the past week. Mr Quebert is a famous New York writer and we should pay him special attention. His needs must be met with the greatest discretion. No-one should bother him.

Table 17 is reserved for him until further notice. It must always be free in case he arrives.

Tamara Quinn

The tray was unbalanced by the weight of the maple syrup bottle. As soon as she placed it there, it tipped over; in attempting to catch it, she lost her balance and, with a mighty crash, she and the tray both fell to the ground.

Harry leaned over the counter.

"Nola? Are you alright?"

She got to her feet, a little dazed.

"Yes, yes, I . . ."

The two of them assessed the damage for a moment, before bursting into laughter.

"You shouldn't laugh, Harry," Nola gently reprimanded him. "If Mrs Quinn finds out I've dropped another plate, I'll lose my job."

He went behind the counter and crouched down to help her pick up the pieces of broken glass that lay in a sticky mass of mustard, mayonnaise, ketchup, maple syrup, butter, sugar, and salt and pepper.

"My God," he said, "can someone explain to me why for the past week every time I order something, my server brings me all these condiments at the same time?"

"It's because of the memo," Nola replied.

"The memo?"

She pointed at a piece of paper stuck behind the counter. Harry stood up and reached for it.

"Harry, no! What are you doing? If Mrs Quinn finds out—"

"Don't worry—there's nobody here."

It was 7 a.m., and Clark's was still empty.

"What is this about?"

"Mrs Quinn gave us orders."

Some customers came in, interrupting their conversation. Instantly Harry returned to his table and Nola rushed back to her station.

"I'll bring you some more toast right away, Mr Quebert," she solemnly declared, before disappearing into the kitchen.

Behind the swinging doors, she hesitated dreamily for a moment, smiling to herself. She loved him. She had loved him since their first meeting, two weeks earlier on the beach; since that glorious rainy day when, by chance, she had gone walking near Goose Cove. She was sure of it. It was an unmistakable feeling; there was nothing else like it. She felt different, happier; the days seemed more splendid. And most of all, whenever he was there, she felt her heart beat faster.

He had begun coming to Clark's every day to write, causing Tamara Quinn, the restaurant's owner, to call an urgent meeting of all her "girls," as she called her waitresses. It was on this occasion that she had showed them her memo. "You will have noticed, girls," Tamara said to her employees, who were lined up in military fashion, "that for the past week, the famous New York writer Harry Quebert has been coming here every day, which shows that he finds in our restaurant the standards of refinement and quality found in the very best establishments on the East Coast. Clark's is a restaurant of high standing: We must show we can meet the expectations of our most demanding customers. As some of you have brains that are smaller than peas, I have written a memo to remind you of how Mr Quebert must be treated. You must read it, reread it, and learn it by heart! I will be conducting random tests. It will be displayed in the kitchen and behind the counter." Tamara had then reiterated her orders: Do not disturb Mr Quebert, because he needs calm and concentration. Work to ensure that he feels at home here. His previous visits to Clark's indicate that he always orders black coffee. Serve him coffee when he arrives, and nothing else. If he wants anything else—if Mr Quebert is hungry—he will ask for it himself. Do not bother him by suggesting he order food, as you must do for all our other customers. If he orders food, bring him all the condiments and extras we have, so he doesn't have to ask for them: mustard, ketchup, mayonnaise, pepper, salt, butter, sugar, and maple syrup. Famous writers should not have to ask for what they want; their minds must be free so that they can create in peace. Maybe what he is writing—the notes he is taking while he sits in the same place, for hours on end—is the beginning of a great masterpiece, and one day soon Clark's will be known all over the country.

And Tamara Quinn dreamed that with the money she would earn thanks to the book she would open a second branch in Concord, then one in Boston, and New York, and all the major cities on the East Coast, all the way down to Florida.

"But Mrs Quinn," Mindy, one of the waitresses, asked. "How can we be sure that Mr Quebert only wants black coffee?"

"Because I know it. Period. In the best restaurants, important customers do not have to order: The staff knows their habits. Is this one of the best restaurants?"

"Yes, Mrs Quinn," the waitresses replied. "Yes, Mom," bellowed Jenny, because she was Mrs Quinn's daughter.

"Don't call me Mom here," Tamara ordered. "This is not some country inn."

"What should I call you then?" Jenny asked.

"Don't call me anything. You listen to my orders and you obey them. There's no need to speak at all. Understood?"

Jenny nodded.

"Have you understood or not?" her mother repeated.

"Well, yeah, I have understood, Mom. I was nodding, I—"

"Very good, darling. You see how quickly you learn. Alright then, girls, I want to see you all acting servile . . . Good! And now, nod. Yes, just like that . . . from the top to the bottom . . . Excellent. Anyone would think they were at the Chateau Marmont."

The waitresses applauded each other in the wake of this ringing endorsement.

"Now let's do a test!" Tamara said, making no attempt to hide her excitement. "I'm going to sit at the table. Pretend I'm him."

Tamara sat at Table 17 and nonchalantly snapped her fingers. Mindy rushed to the table in such a panic that she almost tripped over her feet.

"Yes, Mr Kew-burrrt?" she called.

"Mindy, for God's sake! He's a famous writer, not a farmer! It's pronounced *Kuh-bear*. Like in French. You know why? Because he is a refined gentleman! *Kuh-bear.* Repeat after me: *Kuh-bear.* It should be pronounced with grace and delicacy. *Kuh-bear.* As if he were the King of France. Alright girls, go ahead . . ."

The chorus of waitresses croaked like frogs: "*Kuh-bear. Kuh-bear. Kuh-bear.*"

Tamara, nodding, congratulated her obedient employees:

"Very good, girls. You see—you *can* do it when you put your minds to it."

Tamara Quinn was not the only one thrown into a state of excitement by the presence of Harry Quebert in Somerset; the whole town was abuzz. Some people said he was famous in New York, and others agreed with this so as not to seem uncultivated. Ernie Pinkas, who had made several copies of Harry's first novel available in the library, said he had never heard of him, but nobody paid heed to a factory worker who knew nothing about New York high society. And, above all, everyone agreed that not just anybody could have moved into the magnificent house at Goose Cove, which had not been rented for years.

Harry Quebert also aroused great excitement among young women of marriageable age, and sometimes even their parents. Because Harry Quebert was single. He was a man in search of love, and his reputation, his intellectual capacities, his wealth, and his physical attributes made him a catch. At Clark's, the entire staff quickly understood that Jenny Quinn—a pretty, sexy blonde, and a former cheerleader and prom queen at Somerset High School—had a crush on Harry. Jenny, who worked at Clark's every weekday, was the only waitress to disobey the memo brazenly; she flirted with Harry, talked to him constantly, interrupted his work, and never brought all his condiments to him at one time. Jenny didn't work weekends; on Saturdays Nola filled in.

The chef rang the service bell, tearing Nola from her thoughts. Harry's toast was ready. She put the plate on her tray; before going back out, she fiddled with the yellow clip that held her hair in place, then proudly pushed the door open. She had been in love for two weeks.

She took Harry's order to him. Clark's was slowly filling up.

"Enjoy your meal, Mr Quebert," she said.

"Call me Harry . . ."

"Not here," she whispered. "Mrs Quinn doesn't want us to."

"She's not here. No-one will know . . ."

She indicated the other customers with her eyes, then went on with her work.

Harry took a bite of his toast and scribbled a few lines in his notebook. He wrote the date: Saturday, June 14, 1975. He filled up the pages without really being aware of what he was writing. During the three and a half weeks he'd been here, he had not managed to begin his novel. The ideas that had come to him had not led anywhere, and the harder he tried, the less he succeeded. He felt as if he were slowly sinking, suffering from the worst affliction imaginable for people of his kind: He had contracted the writers' disease. Each day, his fear of the blank page grew stronger, to the point where he doubted the merits of having moved here. He was sacrificing all his savings to rent that impressive beach house until September—the writer's house he had always dreamed of—but what good was that if he didn't know how to write? When he had signed the rental contract, his plan had seemed infallible to him: write a damn good novel, enough of which he would have completed by September to submit to major New York publishing houses, who would all be so dazzled by it that they would enter into a bidding war. They would pay him a significant advance to finish the book, his financial future would be guaranteed, and he would become the famous author he had always imagined himself to be. But already his dream was turning to ashes: He had not yet written a single line. At this rate, he would have to return to New York in the fall, penniless and bookless, and beg the principal of the high school where he had taught to take him back, and forget his hopes of glory forever. He might also have to work as a night watchman so he could put a little money aside.

He watched Nola chatting with the other customers. She was radiant. He heard her laugh, and he wrote:

Nola. Nola. Nola. Nola. Nola.
N-O-L-A. N-O-L-A.

N-O-L-A. Four letters that had turned his world upside down. Nola, the sweet girl who had made his head spin from the moment he first saw her. N-O-L-A. Two days after he had met her on the beach, he had seen her again in front of the general store; together, they had walked down the main street to the marina.

"Everyone says you've come to Somerset to write a book," she said.

"That's true."

"Oh, that's so exciting! You're the first author I've ever met! There are so many questions I'd like to ask you."

"Like what?"

"How do writers write?"

"It's something that just happens. Ideas swirl around your head until they become sentences that gush out onto paper."

"It must be wonderful to be a writer!"

He had looked at her, and he had fallen head over heels in love.

N-O-L-A. She had told him she worked at Clark's on Saturdays, and the following Saturday, at first light, he was there. He had spent the day there, watching her, admiring her every gesture. Then he remembered that she was only fifteen years old, and he felt ashamed. If anyone in the town came to suspect what he felt for the little waitress at Clark's, he would be in serious trouble. He might even end up in prison. So, to soothe their suspicions, he started eating lunch at Clark's every day. It was now a week that he had been a Clark's regular, coming in every day to work, feigning indifference, pretending that there was nothing to his being there. Nobody must know that on Saturdays his heart beat faster. And every day, wherever he worked—on the deck at Goose Cove, at

Clark's—all he was ever able to write was her name. Whole pages that he tore out and burned in his metal trash can. If anyone ever saw what he was writing, he would be finished.

Around noon, Nola was relieved by Mindy in the middle of the lunchtime rush, which was unusual. She approached Harry's table, accompanied by a man who had arrived late in the morning and had ordered an iced tea at the counter.

"Goodbye, Mr Quebert," Nola said. "I'm finished for today. I just wanted to introduce you to my father, Reverend David Kellergan."

Harry stood up and the two men exchanged a friendly handshake.

"So you're the famous writer," Kellergan smiled.

"And you must be the pastor I've heard so much about," Harry said.

David Kellergan looked amused. "Don't pay any attention to what folks say. They always exaggerate."

Nola took a leaflet from her pocket and handed it to Harry.

"It's the end-of-year high school show today, Mr Quebert. That's why I have to leave early. It's at five o'clock. Would you like to come?"

"Nola, leave poor Mr Quebert in peace," her father gently chided her. "Why would he want to see the high school show?"

Harry thanked Nola for her invitation and said goodbye. Through the window, he watched her disappear around the corner, then he went back to Goose Cove to lose himself once more in his mess of papers.

It was 2 p.m. He had been sitting at his desk for two hours, and had written nothing. His eyes were riveted to his watch. He should absolutely not go to the high school. But no walls or fears of prison could stop his wanting to be with her; Harry's body was enclosed in Goose Cove, but his mind danced on the beach with Nola. Three o'clock came. And then four. He clung to his pen to prevent himself from leaving his office. She was fifteen years old.

At 4.50 p.m., Harry, elegant in a dark suit, entered the high school auditorium. The room was packed; the whole town was there. As he moved past the rows of seats, he had the feeling that everybody was whispering about him, that the parents whose eyes he met were saying: *I know why you're here.* Randomly choosing a row, he sank deep down into a seat so that nobody could see him.

The show began. There was a god-awful choir, and then a jazz ensemble that had no swing. There were dancers with no rhythm, a soulless duet, and soloists who couldn't sing. Then the lights went out, and the only thing that could be seen in the darkness was the halo of a spotlight on the stage. And she walked into it, dressed in a blue sequined dress that made her sparkle and shine. There was a hushed silence; she sat on a stool, checked her hair clip, and adjusted the microphone that had been placed in front of her. She then smiled dazzlingly at the audience, picked up a guitar, and burst into a rendition of "Can't Help Falling in Love" in a version she had arranged.

The audience watched and listened, openmouthed, and in that moment Harry realized that by sending him to Somerset, fate had propelled him toward Nola Kellergan. Perhaps his destiny was not to be a writer, but to be loved by this amazing young woman? He couldn't imagine a more wonderful fate. He was so overcome that, when the show ended, he stood up amid the applauding spectators and fled. He went straight back to Goose Cove, sat on the deck, and—swallowing large shots of whiskey—began frenetically writing her name. He no longer knew what he should do. Leave Somerset? But to go where? Back to the noise and chaos of New York? He had made a commitment to rent this house for four months, and had already paid half of the money. He had come here to write a book; he could not just give up. He had to get a grip on himself and behave like a writer.

When he had written so much that his wrist hurt and drunk so much whiskey that his head spun, he went miserably down to the beach and slumped against a large rock to contemplate the horizon. Suddenly he heard sounds behind him.

"Harry? Harry, what's happened to you?"

It was Nola, in her blue dress. She ran toward him and knelt on the sand.

"What is it? Are you in pain?"

"What . . . what are you doing here?" was all the response he could muster.

"I waited for you after the show. I saw you get up during the ovation, and I couldn't find you afterward. Why did you leave so suddenly?"

"You can't stay here, Nola."

"Why?"

"Because I've been drinking. I mean, I'm a bit drunk. I regret it now. If I'd known you were coming, I would've stayed sober."

"Why were you drinking? You look sad . . ."

She nestled against him, and her bright eyes penetrated his.

"The solitude is killing me, Nola."

"I'm going to keep you company, then."

"You can't . . ."

"I want to. Unless I'm bothering you."

"You could never bother me."

"Harry, why are writers such lonely people? Hemingway, Melville . . . they're the loneliest men in the world!"

"I don't know whether it's that writers are lonely or whether it's loneliness that makes them write . . ."

"And why do all writers commit suicide?"

"Not all writers commit suicide. Only writers whose books aren't read."

"I read your book. I borrowed it from the library, and I read it in a single night! I loved it! You are a truly great writer, Harry! Harry . . . this afternoon, I sang for you. That song, it was for you."

He smiled and looked at her. She stroked his hair tenderly and repeated: "You are a truly great writer, Harry. Don't feel lonely. I'm here."

25

About Nola

"How does one become a writer, Harry?"

"By never giving up. You know, Marcus, that freedom—the desire for freedom—is a war in itself. We live in a society of defeated office workers, and to get ourselves out of this fix, we must fight—against ourselves and against the whole world. Freedom is a constant battle of which we are barely even aware. I will never give up."

The drawback to small, isolated towns is that all they have are volunteer fire departments, which are slower to react than professional ones. On the evening of June 20, while I watched the flames roar from the Corvette and spread to the detached garage, quite a long time passed between the moment when I called 911 and the arrival of the fire trucks. So it was something of a miracle that the house itself was not touched, although for the fire chief, the miracle came down to the fact that the garage was a separate building, enabling the firefighters to quickly contain the fire.

Travis Dawn arrived just as they were finishing up.

"You're not hurt, are you, Marcus?" he asked as he ran toward me.

"No, I'm fine, except that the entire house almost burned down."

"What happened?"

"I came back from Grand Beach and as I turned in to the driveway, I saw someone running away into the forest. Then I saw the flames."

"Would you be able to identify the person you saw?"

"No. It all happened too fast."

At that moment we were called over by a policeman who had arrived at the same time as the firefighters, and who was searching the house's exterior. He had found a message, stuck in the doorway, which read:

Go home, Goldman.

"Jesus! I got another one of those yesterday," I said.

"Another?" Travis asked. "Where?"

"On my car. I stopped for ten minutes at the general store on my way home, and found that same message under a windshield wiper."

"Seems like somebody isn't happy about your presence in Somerset. Everyone knows you've been asking lots of questions."

"So you think it's someone who's afraid of what I might discover about Nola?"

"Maybe. I don't like it, in any case. This whole case is explosive. I'm going to leave a patrol car here for the night, just in case."

"There's no need for that. If this guy is after me, let him come. He'll find me."

"Calm down, Marcus. There'll be a patrol car here tonight, whether you like it or not. If this is a warning, as I think it is, it means there'll be more to come."

I went to the state prison early the next day to report this incident to Harry.

"'Go home, Goldman'?" he repeated, after I told him about the message.

"Yup. Typed on a computer."

"What are the police doing?"

"Travis Dawn came. He took the letter and said he'd have it analyzed. He thinks it's a warning. Maybe someone who doesn't want me digging into this thing. Someone who sees you as the perfect guilty party and who doesn't want me interfering."

"The person who murdered Nola and Deborah Cooper?"

"Maybe."

Harry looked serious.

"Roth told me I'm going in front of the grand jury next Tuesday. A handful of good citizens who are going to study my case and decide if the accusations have any merit. Apparently the grand jury always does what the prosecutor wants. It's a nightmare, Marcus. With each passing day, I feel as if I'm sinking ever deeper, as if I'm losing control. First they arrest me, and I think it's just a mistake, that I'll be free in a few hours, and then I find myself locked up here until the trial, which will take place God knows when, and facing the death penalty. Capital punishment, Marcus! I think about it all the time."

I could clearly see that Harry was wasting away. He had been in prison barely a week, and it was obvious that he would not last a month.

"We're going to get you out of here, Harry. We'll find out the truth. Roth is a very good lawyer—don't lose faith in him. And you should keep telling me your story. Tell me about Nola. Take up where you left off. What happened afterward?"

"After what?"

"After the episode on the beach. When Nola came to see you that Saturday, after the high school show, and she told you that you shouldn't feel lonely."

As I was speaking, I put my minidisc player on the table and pressed RECORD. Harry smiled faintly.

"You're a good guy, Marcus. Because you're right—this is what matters: Nola coming to the beach and telling me not to feel lonely, that she was there for me . . . Deep down, I've always been a bit of a loner, and suddenly that changed. With Nola, I felt part of a whole, an entity that the two of us formed together. Whenever she wasn't with me, there was an emptiness inside me, a feeling that something was missing, which I had never experienced before—as if, once she had entered my life, the world could no longer turn properly without her. But I also knew that the relationship between us was going to be complicated. That Saturday, we stayed together for a moment on the beach, then I told her it was late, that she ought to go home before her parents started worrying. I watched her walk along the beach and disappear into the distance, hoping she would turn around, just once, to wave at me. I absolutely had to get her out of my head. So during the entire next week, I forced myself to become closer to Jenny in order to forget Nola—that same Jenny who is now the manager of Clark's."

"Hang on . . . Are you telling me that the Jenny you're talking about, the waitress at Clark's in 1975, is Jenny Dawn, Travis's wife, who now runs Clark's?"

"The very same. Only thirty-three years older. Back then, she was a very pretty woman. She still is a beautiful woman, in fact. You know, she could have tried her luck as an actress in Hollywood. She often talked about it. Leaving Somerset and going off to live the dream in California. But she never did anything about it. She stayed here, she took over the restaurant from her mother, and now she is going to spend the rest of her life selling hamburgers. That's her fault. We live the life we choose, Marcus. And I know what I'm talking about."

"Why do you say that?"

"It doesn't matter . . . I'm rambling, and now I've lost my place. Oh, yes, about Jenny. So, at twenty-four years old, she was a very beautiful woman: a high school prom queen, the kind of voluptuous blonde who would turn any man's head. Everyone had his eye on Jenny back then. I spent my days at Clark's in her company. I had a tab there and I put everything on it. I hardly took any notice of what I was spending, even though I'd blown my savings on renting the house and my budget was very tight."

Wednesday, June 18, 1975

Since Harry Quebert had arrived in Somerset, it was taking Jenny Quinn a good hour longer to get ready in the mornings. She had fallen in love with him the first day she saw him. She had never felt like this before; he was the man of her dreams, she was certain. Each time she saw him, she imagined their life together: their triumphant wedding and their New York home. Goose Cove would become their summer house, where he could read over his manuscripts in peace while she visited her parents. He would take her far away from Somerset; she would no longer have to wipe grease-covered tables or clean the toilets in this hick restaurant. She would have a career on Broadway, she would make movies in California. Magazines would run features about the two of them.

She wasn't making this up. It was obvious that something was happening between her and Harry. He loved her too—there was no doubt. Why else would he come to Clark's every day? Every day! And the conversations they had at the counter! She loved it so much when he came to sit across from her so they could chat awhile. He was different from all the men she had met before, far more sophisticated. Her mother, Tamara, had given orders that the employees must not distract him or talk to him, and she sometimes argued with Jenny at home because she believed her daughter's behavior with him was inappropriate. But her mother didn't understand anything. She didn't understand that Harry loved her so much, he was writing a book about her.

It was several days ago now that she had wondered about the book, but that morning she felt certain. Harry arrived at Clark's with the sun, about 6.30 a.m., just after it opened. It was rare that he turned up so early; normally the only customers at that time were truck drivers and traveling salesmen. He had hardly even sat at his usual table before he began frantically scribbling, almost bent over the page, as if afraid that someone would see what he was writing. Occasionally he stopped, and gave her long, lingering looks; she pretended not to notice, but she knew he was staring hungrily at her. At first she had not understood the reason for these insistent looks. It was just before noon when she realized he was writing a book about her. Yes, she—Jenny Quinn—was the main character in Harry Quebert's new masterpiece. That was why he did not want anyone to see his words. As soon as she realized, she was overcome with excitement. She took the opportunity offered by the lunch hour to give him a menu and chat with him a little bit.

He had spent the morning writing the four letters of her first name: *N-O-L-A*. Sometimes he would close his eyes so he could picture her, and then, in an attempt to cure himself, would force himself to look at Jenny. Jenny was a very beautiful woman; why couldn't he love her?

When, just before noon, he saw Jenny coming toward him with coffee and a menu, he covered up the page with a blank sheet, as he did every time someone approached.

"It's time to eat something, Harry," she ordered in an overly maternal voice. "You haven't swallowed a thing all day, apart from a half-gallon of coffee. You'll get heartburn if you try to get by on an empty stomach."

He made himself smile politely and partake in a brief conversation. He noticed that his forehead was sweating, and wiped it quickly with the back of his hand.

"You're hot, Harry. You work too hard!"

"That's possible."

"Are you inspired?"

"Sure. Things are going pretty well at the moment."

"You haven't lifted your head from the page all morning."

"That's true."

Jenny gave him a smile of complicity.

"Harry . . . I know this is forward of me, but could I read it? Just a few pages? I'm curious to see what you're writing. It must be wonderful."

"It's not ready yet."

"I'm sure it's already magnificent."

"We'll see later."

She smiled again.

"Let me bring you a lemonade to cool you down. Would you like something to eat?"

"I'll take bacon and eggs."

Jenny went straight into the kitchen and sang out: "Bacon and eggs for the grrrreat writer!"

Her mother, who had seen her talking to him in the dining room, scolded her. "Jenny, I want you to stop bothering Mr Quebert!"

"Bothering him? Oh, Mom, you have no idea. I'm his inspiration."

Tamara Quinn gave her daughter a skeptical look. Jenny was a nice girl, but far too naive.

"Who's been filling your head with such nonsense?"

"I know Harry has a crush on me, Mom. And I'm pretty sure I'm a big part of his new book. No, Mom, your daughter will not be serving bacon and coffee all her life. Your daughter is going to become someone."

"What are you talking about?"

Jenny exaggerated a little so that her mother would understand.

"Harry and me—it will soon be official."

And, smirking triumphantly, she swanned out of the kitchen.

Tamara Quinn could not suppress a smile: If her daughter succeeded in getting her hooks into Quebert, Clark's would be famous all over the country. Who knows—maybe the wedding could even take place here; she would find a way to persuade Harry. A fenced-off area, large white tents on the street, a hand-picked guest list; half of New York's crème de la crème, dozens of journalists to cover the event, and flashbulbs endlessly popping. Harry Quebert was heaven-sent.

Harry left Clark's in a rush at 4 p.m. that day, as if he had lost track of the time. He dived into his car, which was parked in front of the restaurant, and sped off. He didn't want to be late; he didn't want to miss her. Soon after his departure, a Somerset police car parked in the space he had vacated. Nervously gripping his steering wheel, Officer Travis Dawn discreetly scanned the inside of the restaurant. Deciding that there were still too many people around, he did not dare enter. Instead he remained in his car and rehearsed the line he had prepared. Just one line—he could manage that. He looked at himself in the rearview mirror and recited: "Jello, Henny. I was thinking we could go to the movies together on Saturday . . ." He cursed himself: He had messed it up again! Just one simple line, not even twenty-five words, and he couldn't get it right! He unfolded the piece of paper and reread what he had written:

Hello, Jenny. I was thinking, if you were free, that we could go to the movie theater in Montburry on Saturday night.

That really wasn't so difficult, was it? He had to walk into Clark's, smile, sit at the counter, and ask for coffee. While she filled his cup, he had to say it. He checked his hair, then pretended to talk into the car's radio microphone so that, if someone saw him, he would appear to be busy. He waited two minutes. Four customers left Clark's together. The coast was clear. His heart was pounding; he could feel it reverberate inside his rib cage, in the veins of his hands, in his head . . . even his fingertips seemed to react to each heartbeat. He got out of his car, the piece of paper scrunched up in his fist. He loved her. He had loved her since high school. She was the reason he had stayed in Somerset. When he went to the police academy, they'd recognized his abilities and had suggested he might want to aim higher than his local police force. They had talked about the state police, even the feds. A guy from Washington, D.C., had told him: "Son, don't waste your time in some hick town. The F.B.I. is recruiting. The F.B.I., son!" Yes, they had suggested he apply to the F.B.I. He might even have asked to join the Secret Service. But there was this young woman who waitressed at Clark's, in Somerset, this woman he had always hoped would finally notice him: Jenny Quinn. So he had asked to be assigned to the Somerset police. Without Jenny, his life had no meaning. Standing in front of the restaurant's entrance, he took a deep breath and then went in.

She thought about Harry while mechanically rubbing a towel over cups that were already dry. Recently he had been leaving every day at about 4 p.m.; she wondered where he went. Was he meeting someone? And, if so, who? A customer sat down at the counter, dragging her from her daydreams.

"Hello, Jenny."

It was Travis, a nice guy she'd known in high school who had become a policeman.

"Hi, Travis. Can I get you coffee?"

"Sure."

He closed his eyes for a moment in order to concentrate. She placed a cup in front of him and filled it. Now was the time to do it.

"Jenny . . . I wanted to tell you . . ."

"Yes?"

She fixed her large bright eyes on his, and he was completely unnerved. What was the next part of the line?

"The movie theater," he said.

"What about the movie theater?"

"I . . . there's been a robbery at the movie theater in Manchester."

"Oh, really? A robbery in a movie theater? How strange."

"I mean, at the post office in Manchester."

Why the hell was he talking about that robbery? The movies! He was supposed to be talking about the movies!

"At the post office or the movie theater?"

The movie theater. The movie theater. The movie theater. The movie theater. Talk about the movie theater! He felt as if his heart were about to burst. He said, "Jenny . . . I wanted to . . . I mean, I was wondering maybe if . . . I mean, if you wanted to . . ."

At that moment Tamara called her daughter from the kitchen.

"Excuse me, Travis, I have to go. Mom's been in a foul mood recently."

She disappeared through the swinging doors without giving the young policeman a chance to finish. He sighed and muttered under his breath: "I was thinking, if you were free, that we could go to the movie theater in Montburry on Saturday night." Then he left a five-dollar bill for a 50-cent coffee that he had not even drunk and walked out of Clark's, sad and disappointed.

"Where did you go at four o'clock every day, Harry?" I asked.

He did not answer immediately. He looked through the nearest window, and I thought I saw a smile on his face. Finally he said, "I needed to see her . . ."

"Nola?"

"Yes. You know, Jenny was a great girl, but she wasn't Nola. When I was with Nola, I felt truly alive. I don't know how else to explain it to you. Each second I spent with her was a second of life lived as fully as possible. That's what love is, I think. That laugh . . . I have heard it in my head every day for the last thirty-three years. That extraordinary look in her eyes . . . I can still see it, right in front of me. The way she put her hair back in place, the way she chewed her lips. Her voice still echoes inside me. When I walk down Main Street, to the marina, to the general store, I see her again, talking to me about life and books. In June 1975, she had been in my life less than a month, yet I had the impression she had always been part of it. And when she wasn't there, nothing seemed to have any meaning: A day without Nola was a day wasted. I needed to see her so much that I couldn't wait until the following Saturday. So I began going to the high school gates to wait for her. That's what I did when I left Clark's at four o'clock. I took my car and I went to the high school in Somerset. I parked in the teachers' parking lot, just in front of the main entrance, and, hidden in my car, I waited until she left. As soon as she appeared, I felt so much more alive, so much stronger. All I needed was the joy of seeing her. I watched her until she got on the school bus, and I waited there until the bus drove off. Was I crazy, Marcus?"

"No, I don't think so."

"All I know is that Nola lived inside me. Literally. And then it was Saturday again, and that Saturday was a beautiful day. Clark's was empty—everyone was at the beach—and Nola and I had long conversations. When she finished work, about 6 p.m., I offered her a ride home. I dropped her off a block from her house, on a deserted street, where no-one could see. She asked if I would like to walk with her some of the way, but I explained that it was complicated, that people would talk if they saw us walking together. I remember she said to me, 'Walking together isn't a crime, Harry . . .'

"'I know, Nola. But I think people would start asking questions.'

"She frowned. 'I love being with you so much, Harry. You're an extraordinary person. It'd be nice if we could be together a little bit without having to hide.'"

Saturday, June 28, 1975

It was 1 p.m. Jenny Quinn was busying herself behind the counter at Clark's. She jumped each time the door of the restaurant opened, hoping it would be him. But it never was. She was crabby and irritable, but she was wearing a beautiful cream-colored ensemble that was only for special occasions. The door slammed again, and again it was not Harry. It was her mother.

"Darling, what are you doing, dressed like that?" Tamara asked. "Where's your apron?"

"Maybe I don't want to wear your horrible aprons anymore. I'm allowed to look pretty from time to time, aren't I? Do you think I enjoy serving hamburgers all day long?"

Jenny had tears in her eyes.

"Alright, tell me what's going on," her mother said.

"It's Saturday and I'm not supposed to be working! I never work on weekends!"

"But you were the one who insisted on replacing Nola when she asked for the day off today."

"Yeah. Maybe. I don't know anymore. Oh, Mom, I'm so miserable!"

Jenny was nervously fiddling with a bottle of ketchup, clumsily dropped it. It slipped out of her hands and smashed, and her immaculate white sneakers were splattered red. She burst into tears.

"My darling, what's happened to you?" her mother asked.

"I'm waiting for Harry, Mom! He always comes on Saturday . . . So why isn't he here? Oh, Mom, I'm so stupid! How could I have believed that he loved me? A man like Harry would never want a common diner waitress like me! I'm such an idiot!"

"Come on, don't be like that," Tamara said soothingly, taking her daughter in her arms. "Take the day off, go and have some fun. I'll fill in for you. I don't want you to cry. You're a wonderful girl, and I'm sure that Harry has a crush on you."

"Then why isn't he here?"

Mrs Quinn thought for a moment. "Did he know you were working today? You never work Saturdays. You know what I think, darling? Harry must be very sad on Saturdays. It's the day he doesn't get to see you."

Jenny's face lit up.

"Oh, Mom, why didn't I think of that?"

"You should go to his house. I'm sure he'd be very happy to see you."

What a wonderful idea! She would go find Harry at Goose Cove and take him a nice picnic lunch. The poor guy was probably working so hard he'd forgotten to eat. She rushed to the kitchen to stock up.

At that very moment, 130 miles away, in the little town of Rockland, Maine, Harry and Nola were picnicking on a seaside boardwalk.

Nola was throwing pieces of bread to the huge, screeching seagulls.

"I love seagulls!" she shouted. "They're my favorite birds. Maybe because I love the ocean, and wherever there are seagulls, you'll find the ocean. It's true, even when the horizon is blocked by trees, you can look up in the sky and see seagulls and know that the ocean is close. Will there be seagulls in your book, Harry?"

"If you want. I'll put anything you want in this book."

"What's it about?"

"I'd like to tell you, but I can't."

"Is it a love story?"

"Kind of."

He looked at her, amused. He was holding a notebook, and was attempting to draw the scene in pencil.

"What are you doing?" she asked.

"Making a sketch."

"You draw too? Show me—I want to see it!"

She came close.

"That's so beautiful, Harry!"

She cuddled up to him in a rush of tenderness, but he pushed her away, almost by reflex, and looked around to make sure nobody had seen.

"Why did you do that?" Nola asked. "Are you ashamed of me?"

"Nola, you're fifteen . . . and I'm thirty-four. People would be shocked."

"People are stupid!"

He laughed, and sketched her furious expression in a few lines. She pressed herself to him again, and he let her. Together, they watched the seagulls fighting over the scraps of bread.

They had decided a few days earlier to make this getaway. He had waited for her near her house, after school. Close to the bus stop.

"Harry? What are you doing here?" she had said.

"I don't really know, to be honest. But I wanted to see you. I . . . Nola, I've been thinking about your idea again . . ."

"About being alone together?"

"Yes. I was thinking we could go away this weekend. Not far. To Maine, for example. Someplace where nobody knows us. So we can feel more free. Only if you want to, of course."

"Oh, that would be wonderful! But it will have to be Saturday. I can't miss the Sunday service."

"Then let's make it Saturday. Can you get off work?"

"Of course! I'll ask Mrs Quinn for the day off. And I know what to tell my parents. Don't worry about it."

I know what to tell my parents. As soon as he heard these words, he wondered what had got into him, falling for an adolescent girl. And here on the beach in Rockland, the thought returned to him.

"What are you thinking about?" Nola asked, still pressed against him.

"About what we're doing."

"What's wrong with what we're doing?"

"You know perfectly well what's wrong with it. Or maybe you don't. What did you tell your parents?"

"They think I'm with my friend Nancy Hattaway, and that we left very early to spend the day on her boyfriend Teddy's father's boat."

"And where is Nancy?"

"On the boat with Teddy. Alone. She said I was with them so Teddy's parents would let them take the boat."

"So her mother thinks she's with you, and your mother thinks you're with Nancy. So if they call each other, the stories will hold up."

"Exactly. It's a foolproof plan. I have to be home by eight. Will we have time to go dancing? I really want to dance with you."

It was 3 p.m. when Jenny arrived at Goose Cove. As she parked her car in front of the house, she noticed that the black Chevrolet was not there. She rang the doorbell anyway, but there was no reply. She walked around the house to check that he was not out on the deck. He must have gone out to clear his head, she thought. He had been working very hard; he needed to take breaks. He would undoubtedly be very happy to find a nice snack on his table when he returned: roast beef sandwiches, hard-boiled eggs, cheese, raw vegetables with an herb dip that she had made herself, a slice of pie, and some fruit.

Jenny had never before seen the inside of the house at Goose Cove. She thought it was beautiful. The place was vast and tastefully decorated. There were exposed beams on the ceilings, large bookcases against the walls, varnished wooden floorboards, and wide bay windows offering a clear view of the ocean. She could not help imagining herself living here with Harry: summer breakfasts on the deck, cozy winters spent by the fireplace, with Harry reading to her from his new novel. Why yearn for New York? Even here, together, they would be so happy. They would not need anything but each other. She set her meal on the dining room table and then sat in a chair and waited. She was going to surprise him.

She waited for an hour. What could he be doing? Bored, she decided to wander around the house. The first room she entered was the office. It was somewhat cramped but nicely furnished, with a closet, an antique ebony writing desk, shelves on the wall, and a wide wooden desk cluttered with pens and papers. This was where Harry worked. She did not want to snoop or betray his trust; she simply wanted to see what he spent all day writing about her. And nobody would ever know. Convinced she was within her rights, she took the first sheet from the top of the pile and read it, her heart pounding. The opening lines were crossed out in black felt tip, so she could not read any of the words. But below that she could read quite clearly:

I go to Clark's only to see her. I go there only to be close to her. She is everything I have ever dreamed of. I am possessed. I am haunted. She is forbidden. I should not. I should not go there. I should not even stay in this miserable town. I should leave, run away, never come back. I am not allowed to love her. It is forbidden. Am I crazy?

Aglow with happiness, Jenny hugged the sheet to her chest. Then she did a little dance and cried out: "Harry, my love, you're not crazy! I love you too, and you can do anything you want with me. Don't run away! I love you so much!" Excited by her discovery, she quickly put the sheet back on the desk, fearing that she might get caught, and walked back into the living room. She lay down on the couch, lifted the hem of her skirt so her thighs were showing, and unbuttoned her blouse to reveal the tops of her breasts. Nobody had ever written anything so beautiful about her. She would give herself to him as soon as he returned. She would offer him her virginity.

At that very moment David Kellergan walked into Clark's and sat at the counter where, as always, he ordered a large glass of iced tea.

"Your daughter isn't here today, Reverend," Tamara Quinn told him as she brought him his iced tea. "She took the day off."

"I know, Mrs Quinn. She's out sailing, with friends. She left at dawn. I offered to drive her, but she wouldn't have it. She told me to rest, to stay in bed. She's such a kind girl."

"She certainly is, Reverend. I'm very happy with her."

David Kellergan smiled, and Tamara thought for a moment about this jolly, gentle-faced man in round spectacles. He had to be fifty, and he was thin and rather frail, but he radiated great strength. He never raised his voice, which was calm and composed. She liked his sermons, in spite of his strong southern accent. His daughter was a lot like him: gentle, friendly, obliging, affable. David and Nola Kellergan were good people, good Americans and good Christians. They were well liked in Somerset.

"How long have you been living here now, Reverend?" Tamara Quinn asked. "I feel like you've been here forever."

"Nearly six years, six wonderful years."

The pastor glanced at the other customers and, a regular himself, noticed that Table 17 was free.

"Hey, the writer isn't here," he said.

"Not today. He's a charming man, you know."

"I know. I met him here. He kindly came to see the end-of-year high school show. I would very much like to make him a member of the congregation. We need people like him to take this town forward."

Tamara thought of her daughter then and, smiling, could not stop herself from sharing the big news. "Don't tell anyone, Reverend, but he and my Jenny are maybe an item."

David Kellergan smiled and took a long drink of iced tea.

Rockland, 6 p.m. On a deck overlooking the harbor, drenched in late-day sunlight, Harry and Nola sipped glasses of fruit juice. Nola wanted Harry to tell her about his life in New York. "Tell me everything," she said. "Tell me what it's like to be a celebrity there." He knew she was imagining a life of cocktails and canapés, so what could he tell her? That he bore no resemblance to the version of him they had dreamed up in Somerset? That his first book had vanished without a trace? He might lose her. So he decided to invent, to play to the full his role as a gifted, respected artist, weary of red carpets and the excitements of New York, come to find the breathing space necessary for his genius in a small New Hampshire town.

"You're so lucky," she said when she heard his story. "What an exciting life you lead! Sometimes I wish I could run away, far from Somerset. I feel like I'm suffocating here, you know. My parents are difficult people. My father is a good man, but he's religious: He has some strange ideas. My mother is so hard on me! You'd think she had never been young. And it's so boring, having to go to church every Sunday! I don't know if I believe in God. Do you believe in God? If you believe in Him, I will too."

"I don't know. I don't know anymore."

"My mother says we have to believe in God, or He will punish us very severely. Sometimes I think that if there's any doubt the safest thing is to be very good."

"Ultimately," Harry retorted, "the only one who knows whether or not God exists is God Himself."

She laughed. A simple, innocent laugh. She held his hand tenderly and asked, "Is it O.K. not to love your mother?"

"I think so. Love is not an obligation."

"But it's in the Ten Commandments. Love your parents. It's the fourth one, or the fifth. I can't remember. Then again, the First Commandment is to believe in God. So if I don't believe in God, that means I don't have to love my mother, doesn't it? My mother's so harsh. Sometimes she locks me in my bedroom. She says I've been corrupted. I'm not corrupted, though—I just want to be free. I want to be able to dream a little. Oh, my God, it's six o'clock already! I wish I could stop time! I have to go home now, and we didn't even have time to dance."

"We'll dance, Nola. We'll dance one day. We have our whole lives for dancing."

At 8 p.m. Jenny woke up with a start. She had fallen asleep waiting for him. The sun was setting; it was evening. She was sprawled on the couch, a thread of drool hanging from the corner of her mouth. She had bad breath. She pulled up her panties, buttoned her breasts away, quickly packed up the picnic and fled Goose Cove in a cloud of shame.

They reached Somerset a few minutes later. Harry stopped in a back street near the marina, so that Nola could meet up with her friend Nancy and they could go home together. They stayed in the car for a moment. The street was deserted; the day was ending. Nola took a package from her bag.

"What's that?" Harry asked.

"Open it. It's a gift for you. I found it in a little store in the center of town, near where we had those fruit juices. It's a souvenir, so you never forget this wonderful day."

He unwrapped it. It was a blue painted tin emblazoned with the words SOUVENIR OF ROCKLAND, MAINE.

"It's for putting dry bread in," Nola said. "So you can feed the seagulls at your house. You have to feed the seagulls—it's important."

"Thank you. I promise I'll always feed the seagulls."

"Now say something sweet to me, Harry. Tell me I'm your darling Nola."

"Darling Nola . . ."

She smiled, and moved her face close to his for a kiss. He pulled back suddenly.

"Nola," he said abruptly. "We can't do this."

"Why not?"

"You and me—it's too complicated."

"What's complicated about it?"

"All of it. You should go meet your friend now—it's getting late. I . . . I don't think we should see each other again."

He got out of the car quickly then, to open the door for her. She had to leave now. It was so difficult not to tell her how much he loved her.

"So that's the breadbox in your kitchen?" I said.

"Yes. I feed the seagulls because Nola asked me to."

"What happened after Rockland?"

"That day was so wonderful that I became afraid. It was wonderful but too complicated. So I decided I had to distance myself from Nola and make do with another girl."

"Jenny?"

"You got it."

"So?"

"I'll tell you another time, Marcus. We've done a lot of talking, and I'm tired."

"Of course—I understand."

I turned off the recorder.

24

Memories of Independence Day

"Get in the guard position, Marcus."

"The guard position?"

"Yes. Go on! Raise your fists, place your feet, get ready to fight. What do you feel?"

"I . . . I feel ready for anything."

"That's good. You see, boxing and writing are very similar. You get in the guard position, you decide to throw yourself into battle, you lift your fists, and you hurl yourself at your opponent. A book is more or less the same. A book is a battle."

"You have to stop this investigation, Marcus."

These were the first words Jenny spoke to me when I went to Clark's to ask her about her relationship with Harry in 1975. The fire at Goose Cove had been reported on television, and news of it was gradually spreading.

"Why would I stop?" I said.

"Because I'm worried about you. I don't like this kind of thing." Her voice had a mother's tenderness. "It starts with a fire and who knows how it will end."

"I'm not going to leave this town until I've understood what happened thirty-three years ago."

"You're unbelievable! You're stubborn as a mule, just like Harry!"

"I take that as a compliment."

She smiled.

"Alright, what can I do for you?"

"I'd like to have a talk with you. We could go for a walk outside, if you like."

She left Clark's in the hands of one of her employees and we went down to the marina. We sat on a bench, facing the sea, and I looked at this woman, who, according to my calculations, must be fifty-seven years old. Life had left its mark on her: Her body was too thin, her face lined, her eyes sunken. I tried to imagine her the way Harry had described her to me: a pretty young blonde with a voluptuous body, a prom queen during her high school years. Out of nowhere she asked: "What's it like?"

"What's what like?"

"Fame."

"It's painful. It can be enjoyable, but it often hurts too."

"I remember when you were a student and you used to come to Clark's with Harry to work on your writing. He made you work like a dog. You spent hours there, at his table, rereading, scribbling, starting over. I remember seeing you and Harry running at dawn with that iron discipline. You know, he looked so happy when you came. He wasn't the same person. And we knew whenever you were coming, because he would tell everyone, days in advance. He would repeat, 'Did I tell you Marcus is coming to visit me next week? What an extraordinary kid he is. He'll go far—I'm sure of it.' We all knew how lonely Harry was in his big house. The day you came into his life, everything changed. He was reborn. As if the lonely old man had finally succeeded in being loved by someone. Your visits did him so much good. After you left, he would go on and on about you: Marcus this and Marcus that. He was so proud of you. Proud like a father is proud of his son. You were the son he never had. He talked about you all the time—you never left Somerset. And then one day, we saw you in the newspaper. The big new author, Marcus Goldman. A great writer was born. Harry bought all the newspapers in the general store, he bought rounds of drinks in Clark's. Three cheers for Marcus! And we saw you on T.V., we heard you on the radio . . . people around here talked about nothing but you and your book. Harry bought dozens of copies and gave them to everyone. And we asked him how you were doing and when we were going to see you again. And he replied that he was sure you were doing very well, but that he hadn't heard from you. That you must be very busy. You stopped calling him overnight, Marc. You were so busy being famous that you dropped Harry like a stone. He was so proud of you, just waiting for a little sign from you, but it never came. You had succeeded, you had found fame, so you didn't need him anymore."

"That's not true!" I protested. "I did get carried away by success, but I still thought about him. Every day. I didn't have a second to myself."

"Not even a second to call him?"

"Of course I called him!"

"You called him when you were up shit creek, sure. Because, having sold I don't know how many millions of books, Marcus the Great Author got scared and couldn't remember how to write anymore. We got the news about that as it happened too. How do you think I know all this? Harry sat at the counter of Clark's, worrying because he'd had a phone call from you, saying that you were depressed, that you didn't know what to write for your next book, that your publisher was going to take all his money back. And suddenly, there you were again, in Somerset, with your sad puppy-dog eyes, and Harry doing everything he could to raise your spirits. Poor sad little writer, what on earth can you find to write about? And then . . . a miracle, two weeks ago: The story breaks, it's a big scandal, and who turns up? Harry's good friend Marcus. What the hell are you doing in Somerset, Marcus? Looking for inspiration for your next book?"

At first, somewhat stunned, I made no reply. Then I said, "My publisher wants me to write about it. But I won't do it."

"But that's the point: You can't not do it! Because a book is probably the only way to prove to the world that Harry is not a monster. He didn't do anything—I'm sure of it. Deep down inside, I know. You can't abandon him—you're the only one he has. You're famous. People will listen to you. You have to write a book about Harry, about your years together. Tell everyone what an amazing man he is."

"You love him, don't you?" I whispered.

She lowered her eyes. "I don't think I know what *love* means."

"I think you do. It's obvious from the way you talk about him, despite all your efforts to hate him."

She smiled sadly, and in a broken voice said, "I've thought about him every day for more than thirty years. Seeing him so lonely, when I would have loved to make him happy. And as for me . . . look at me, Marcus. I dreamed of being a movie star, but all I am is a queen of french fries. I have not had the life I wanted."

I sensed she was ready to confide in me, so I said, "Jenny, tell me about Nola, if you would . . ."

She smiled sadly.

"She was a very sweet girl. My mother really liked her, and that annoyed me. Because, until Nola, I had always been the pretty little princess of this town, the one all the men looked at. She was nine years old when she moved here. At that point, of course, nobody cared. And then, one summer, as often happens to girls when they reach puberty, all the men noticed that Nola had become a pretty young woman, with beautiful legs, full breasts, and the face of an angel. And this new Nola, in her swimsuit, stirred up a lot of desire."

"Were you jealous of her?"

She reflected for a moment.

"Oh, what the hell, it doesn't matter now, so I may as well be honest:

Yes, I was a little jealous. Men looked at her, and a woman notices that."

"But she was only fifteen."

"She didn't look like a little girl—believe me. She was a woman. A beautiful woman."

"Did you suspect anything between her and Harry?"

"Not in the slightest! Nobody here imagined anything of the kind. Not with Harry or with anyone else. She was beautiful, but she was fifteen years old—everyone knew that. And she was the pastor's daughter."

"So there was no rivalry between you for Harry?"

"God, no!"

"And was there anything between you and Harry?"

"Not really. We went out a few times. He was very popular with the women here. I mean, a celebrity from New York turning up in a place like this . . ."

"Jenny, I have a question that may surprise you, but . . . did you know that when he arrived here, Harry was a nobody? Just a high school teacher who'd spent all his savings to rent the house at Goose Cove?"

"What do you mean? He was a writer, though—"

"He had written a novel, but it wasn't a success at all. I think there was a misunderstanding about how famous he was, and he used that so that he could be in Somerset what he had wanted to be in New York. And because he then published *The Origin of Evil*, which really did make him famous, the illusion was perfect."

She laughed, almost amused.

"Well! I never would have guessed. Good old Harry . . . I remember our first real date. I was so excited that day. It was the Fourth of July."

I quickly made the calculations in my head: July 4 was six days after the trip to Rockland. That was when Harry had decided to get Nola out of his head. I encouraged Jenny to continue her story: "Tell me about the Fourth of July."

She closed her eyes, as if transported back in time. "It was a beautiful day. Harry had come to Clark's and asked me to go see the fireworks in Concord. He said he would come and fetch me at 6 p.m. My shift normally ended at 6.30, but I told him that would be fine. And Mom let me leave early so I could get ready."

Friday, July 4, 1975

The Quinn family house was in an uproar. It was 5.45 p.m. and Jenny was not ready. She ran up and down the stairs like a Fury in her underwear, each time holding up a different dress.

"What about this one, Mom? What do you think?" she asked, entering the living room for the seventh time.

"No, not that one," Tamara said harshly. "It makes your butt look big. You don't want Harry to think you've been stuffing yourself, do you? Try another one!"

Jenny hurried back up to her bedroom, sobbing that she was a hideous girl, that she had nothing to wear, and that she was going to remain single and ugly until the end of her life.

Tamara was nervous—her daughter had to be at her best. Harry Quebert was in a whole other league from the people of Somerset, and she couldn't afford to make a mistake. As soon as her daughter had told her about her date, she had ordered her to leave Clark's. It was the lunch-hour rush, and the restaurant was packed, but she didn't want her Jenny to stay a single second longer amid the greasy smells that could soak into her hair and her skin. Tamara had sent her to a hairdresser and given her a manicure, and then she had cleaned the house from top to bottom and prepared a "sophisticated" aperitif in case Harry Quebert wanted a snack while he was there. So her Jenny had not been wrong: Harry really was wooing her. Tamara was very excited, and could not stop thinking about marriage. Her daughter would finally get hitched. She heard the front door bang. Her husband, Robert, who worked as an engineer in a Concord glove company, had been called out for an emergency at the factory and here he was, just come home. Her eyes widened in horror.

Robert noticed immediately that the first floor had been thoroughly cleaned and spruced up. There was a bouquet of irises in the entrance hall, where he had never seen flowers before.

"What's going on here, honey bunny?" he asked as he went into the living room, where a little table had been laid with petits fours, savory snacks, a bottle of champagne, and some flutes.

"Oh, Bobby, my Bobbo," Tamara replied, feeling irritated but forcing herself to be kind, "this is not a good time. I really don't need you getting under my feet. I left a message for you at the factory."

"I didn't get it. What did it say?"

"That you should not, under any circumstances, come home before seven o'clock."

"Oh. Why?"

"Because—would you believe it?—Harry Quebert has invited Jenny to see the fireworks in Concord this evening."

"Who's Harry Quebert?"

"Oh, Bobbo, you should keep up with things more! He's the famous writer who moved here at the end of May."

"Oh. And why shouldn't I enter the house?"

"'*Oh*'? That's all you have to say—'oh'? A great writer is wooing our daughter, and all you can say is 'oh'? Well, that proves my point: I do not want you in the house because you are incapable of conducting an intelligent conversation. For your information, Harry Quebert is not just anybody—he has moved into the house at Goose Cove."

"The house at Goose Cove? Holy cow!"

"That might seem expensive and impressive to you, but for a man like him, renting the house at Goose Cove is just a spit in the ocean. He is a star in New York!"

"A spit in the ocean? I don't know that expression."

"Oh, Bobbo, you really don't know anything."

Frowning, Robert moved closer to the buffet that his wife had prepared.

"Do not touch, Bobbo!"

"What are these things?"

"They're not things. It is a sophisticated aperitif. It's very chic."

"But you told me we were going to the neighbors' barbecue tonight! Are we still going? It's the Fourth of July!"

"Yes, we're going. But later. And whatever you do, don't tell Harry Quebert that we're going to eat hamburgers like ordinary people."

"But we are ordinary people. I like hamburgers. You run a burger joint."

"You don't understand anything, Bobbo! It's not the same. And I have big plans for us."

"I didn't know that. You never told me."

"I don't tell you everything."

"Why don't you tell me everything? I tell you everything. Actually, I had a stomachache all afternoon. I had terrible gas. It hurt so bad, I even had to lock myself in my office and get down on all fours to fart. You see how I tell you everything?"

"That's enough, Bobbo! You're ruining my concentration!"

Jenny reappeared with another dress.

"Too dressy," Tamara barked. "You need to be elegant but relaxed."

Robert Quinn took advantage of his wife's momentary inattention to sit in his favorite chair and pour himself a glass of Scotch.

"No sitting!" Tamara shouted. "You'll get everything dirty. Do you know how long I spent cleaning this room? Go get changed."

"Changed?"

"Wear a suit. You can't receive Harry Quebert in your slippers!"

"Why have you taken out the bottle of champagne we were keeping for a special occasion?"

"This *is* a special occasion! Don't you want our daughter to marry well? Now stop quibbling and go get changed. He'll be here soon."

To make sure he obeyed her, Tamara escorted her husband as far as the staircase. At that moment, Jenny came down in tears, wearing nothing but panties and a bra, explaining between sobs that she was going to have to cancel the whole thing because it was too much for her. Robert whined in turn that he wanted to read his newspaper rather than having to partake in a serious discussion with this great writer and that, in any case, he never read books because they put him to sleep, and that he wouldn't know what to say to him. It was 5.50, ten minutes before Harry was due. All three of them were arguing in the entrance hall when suddenly the doorbell rang. Tamara thought she was going to have a heart attack. He was here. The great writer was early.

The doorbell rang. Harry walked toward the door. He was wearing a linen suit and a light hat, ready to go out with Jenny. He opened the door; it was Nola.

"Nola? What are you doing here?"

"You mean 'hello'? It's polite to say 'hello' when you see someone, not 'what are you doing here?'"

He smiled. "Hello, Nola. I'm sorry—it's just that I wasn't expecting you."

"What's going on? I haven't heard from you since our day in Rockland. Not a word all week! Did I do something wrong? Didn't you enjoy it? Oh, Harry, I loved our day in Rockland so much. It was magical!"

"You didn't do anything wrong. And I really liked our day in Rockland too," Harry said.

"So why haven't you been in touch?"

"It's because of my book. I've had a lot of work."

"I would like to be with you every day. For the rest of my life."

"You're an angel."

"We can be together every day now," Nola said. "I don't have school anymore."

"What do you mean?"

"School's over, it's summer vacation. Did you really not know?"

"No."

"It will be wonderful, won't it?" Nola said happily. "I've been thinking, and I've decided that I could look after you here. You would find it easier to work in this house than in Clark's, with so many people and so much noise. You could write on your deck. The ocean is so beautiful, I'm sure it would inspire you! And I'd take care of you. I'll make you a happy man! Please let me make you a happy man, Harry."

He noticed that she had brought a basket with her.

"It's a picnic," she said. "For us, this evening. I even have a bottle of wine. I was thinking we could have a picnic on the beach. It would be so romantic."

He didn't want a romantic picnic. He didn't want to be near her. He didn't want her, period: He had to forget her. He regretted the Saturday they had spent in Rockland. He had taken a fifteen-year-old girl to another state, without her parents' knowledge. Had the police stopped them, they might even have believed he had kidnapped her. This girl was going to ruin him. He had to remove her from his life.

All he said was, "I can't, Nola."

She looked utterly dejected. "Why not?"

He had to tell her that he had a date with someone else. It would be hard for her to hear, but she had to understand that any relationship between them was impossible. He couldn't bring himself do it, however, so once again he lied. "I have to go to Concord. I'm seeing my publisher, who's coming for the Fourth of July. It will be very boring. I would rather have done something with you."

"Can I come with you?"

"No. I mean, you'd be bored."

"You're very handsome in that shirt, Harry."

"Thank you."

"Harry . . . I'm in love with you. Ever since that rainy day when I saw you on the beach, I've been madly in love with you. I want to be with you for the rest of my life!"

"Stop—don't say that."

"Why not? It's the truth! I can't bear not being with you, even for one day! Each time I see you, my life seems so much more beautiful . . . You hate me, don't you, Harry?"

"What? No! Of course not!"

"Yes, you do, I know it. You think I'm ugly. And you were bored by me in Rockland. That's why you haven't been in touch. You think I'm a stupid, boring, ugly little girl."

"Don't talk nonsense. Come on, I'll take you home."

"Call me 'Darling Nola' . . . Say it to me again."

"I can't, Nola."

"Please!"

"I can't. Those words are forbidden."

"But why? Why, for God's sake? Why can't we love each other if we love each other?"

"Come on, I'm going to drive you home," he repeated.

"But, Harry, what's the point of living if we're not allowed to love?"

He did not reply. He led her to the black Chevrolet. She was crying.

It was not Harry Quebert at the door, but Amy Pratt, the wife of Somerset's police chief. She was the organizer of the summer gala, one of the town's biggest annual events, which would take place that year on Saturday, July 19. When the doorbell rang, Tamara had sent her half-naked daughter and her husband upstairs, before discovering that it was not their famous visitor at the door. Amy Pratt was selling tickets for the raffle that would be held at the gala. That year first prize was a weeklong vacation at a luxury hotel on Martha's Vineyard, famous as a summer residence for many noted writers, actors, and politicians. Tamara's eyes shone when she heard about the first prize. She bought two books of tickets, and then—even though decorum dictated that she should offer a cold drink to her visitor, who was moreover a woman she liked—she showed her to the door without any qualms because it was now 5.55.

Jenny, who had calmed down, appeared in a little green summer dress that suited her beautifully, followed by her father, who was wearing a three-piece suit.

"It wasn't Harry—it was Amy Pratt," Tamara said casually. "I knew it wasn't him. You should have seen yourselves scurrying off like rabbits. Ha! I knew perfectly well it wasn't him, because he's a sophisticated man, and sophisticated people are never early. It's even more impolite than being late. Remember that, Bobbo, the next time you're worrying about being late for a meeting."

The living room clock chimed six times, and the Quinn family stood in line behind the front door.

"Please, just be natural!" Jenny begged.

"We are very natural," her mother said. "Aren't we, Bobbo?"

"Yes, honey bunny. But I think I've got gas again. I feel like a bomb that's about to explode."

A few minutes later, Harry rang the doorbell at the Quinns' house. He had just dropped Nola at a street near her house so they would not be seen together. He had left her in tears.

Jenny told me how wonderful that Fourth of July date had been for her. In a reverie, she described the carnival, their dinner, the fireworks over Concord.

From the way she spoke about Harry, it was clear that she had never stopped loving him, and that the aversion she felt toward him now was, above all, the expression of the pain she felt at having been passed over for Nola. Before I left, I asked her, "Jenny, who do you think can tell me the most about Nola?"

"About Nola? Her father, obviously."

Her father. Obviously.

23

Those Who Knew Her Well

"And the characters? Where do you get inspiration for your characters?"

"From everyone. A friend, the cleaning lady, the bank clerk. But be careful: It's not the people themselves who provide your inspiration, but what they do. The way they act makes you think of what one of the characters in your novel might do. Writers who say they are not inspired by anyone are lying, but they are right to do so; they spare themselves a great deal of trouble that way."

"What do you mean?"

"It is a writer's privilege, Marcus, to be able to settle his scores with his friends and enemies through the intermediary of his book. The only rule is that he must not mention them by name, because that means opening the door to lawsuits and headaches. What number have we reached on the list?"

"Twenty-three."

"So this is the twenty-third rule, Marcus: Only write fiction. Anything else will just bring you trouble."

On Sunday, June 22, 2008, I met the Reverend David Kellergan for the first time. It was one of those grayish summer days that you find in New England, when the ocean mist is so thick that it remains stuck to the tree-tops and the roofs. The Kellergan house was in the center of an attractive residential area. It appeared not to have changed since their arrival in Somerset. The walls were the same color and the same bushes were planted all around. The roses that had been planted then had grown to fill the flower beds, but the cherry tree that now stood in front of the house, I learned, had ten years ago replaced an earlier one after it died.

Deafeningly loud music was reverberating from the house when I arrived. I rang the doorbell several times, but there was no reply. Finally a neighbor shouted to me, "If you're looking for Mr Kellergan, there's no point in ringing the doorbell. He's in the garage." I went to knock on the door of the garage, which was, indeed, where the music was coming from. I had to keep knocking for a long time, but eventually the door opened and I found myself standing before a fragile little old man with gray hair and gray skin, wearing overalls and goggles. It was David Kellergan, age eighty-five.

"What is it?" he shouted politely enough above the music, which was so loud as to be almost unbearable.

I had to cup my hands around my mouth to make myself heard.

"My name is Marcus Goldman. You don't know me, but I'm investigating Nola's death."

"Are you from the police?"

"No, I'm a writer. Could you turn the music off or lower the volume a little?"

"Sorry. I never turn off the music. But we can go into the living room if you like."

He led me through the garage. It had been entirely transformed into a workshop, with pride of place given to a Harley-Davidson. In one corner, an old record player connected to a stereo system blasted out jazz standards.

I had been prepared for a cold reception. I had imagined that, after being harassed by journalists, Mr Kellergan would be desperate for some peace, but in fact he was very friendly. Despite all the time I had spent in Somerset, I had never seen him before. He clearly had no idea about my friendship with Harry, and I decided not to mention it. He made us two glasses of iced tea and we sat down together in the living room. He still had the goggles strapped to his forehead, as if he had to be ready to return to his motorcycle at any moment, and that deafening music was still audible in the background. I tried to imagine this man thirty-three years earlier, when he was the dynamic pastor at St James's Church.

He stared at me curiously, and then asked, "What brings you here, Mr Goldman? A book?"

"I'm not entirely sure, Reverend. I really just want to know what happened to Nola."

"Don't call me Reverend. I'm not a pastor anymore."

"I'm sorry about your daughter, sir."

He gave me a surprisingly warm smile.

"Thank you. You're the first person to offer condolences, Mr Goldman. The whole town has been talking about my daughter for two weeks. They all rush to read the latest developments in the newspapers, but not one of them has come here to find out how I'm doing. The only people who knock at my door, apart from journalists, are neighbors complaining about the noise. But grieving fathers are allowed to listen to music, don't you think?"

"Absolutely, sir."

"So you're writing a book?"

"I don't know if I'm capable of writing anymore. It's so difficult to write well. My publisher wants me to write a book about Nola. He says it will relaunch my career. Would you be opposed to the idea of a book about your daughter?"

He shrugged. "No. it might help other parents. You know, my daughter was in her bedroom the day she disappeared. I was working in the garage, with my music on. I didn't hear a thing. When I went to see her, she was no longer in the house. Her bedroom window was open. It was as if she had vanished into thin air. I didn't watch over my daughter properly. Write a book for parents, Mr Goldman. Parents should take better care of their children."

"What were you doing in the garage that day?"

"I was working on that motorcycle. The Harley you saw."

"It's a beautiful machine."

"Thank you. I got it from an auto-body mechanic in Montburry who told me he'd stripped everything he could from it. He gave it to me for a song. So that's what I've been doing since my daughter disappeared: working on that lousy motorcycle."

"Do you live alone?"

"Yes. My wife died a long time ago . . ."

He got up and brought me a photo album. He showed me little Nola, and his wife, Louisa. They looked happy. I was surprised by how easily he trusted me, when he really didn't know me at all. I think, deep down, he wanted to bring his daughter back to life a little bit. He told me that they had arrived in Somerset in the summer of 1969 from Jackson, Alabama. He had had a growing congregation there, but the call of the sea had been too strong: St James's congregation was looking for a new pastor, and he was hired. The main reason for leaving Alabama was to find a peaceful place to raise Nola. The country was on fire back then with political conflicts, racial segregation, and the Vietnam war. The events of the 1960s in the South—police brutality, the Klan, the burning of black churches, rioting after the deaths of Martin Luther King Jr. and Bobby Kennedy— pushed them to begin searching for a place that was sheltered from all this unrest. So when his broken-down little car, before beginning the descent toward Somerset and worn out by the weight of the trailer it pulled, arrived on outskirts of Montburry, with its large ponds covered with water lilies, David Kellergan congratulated himself on his choice when he saw the beautiful, peaceful little town in the distance. How could he have imagined that it would be here, six years later, that his only child would disappear?

"I drove past your former church," I said. "It's been turned into a McDonald's."

"The whole world is being turned into a McDonald's, Mr Goldman."

"But what happened?"

"It all went so well for years. Then my Nola disappeared, and everything changed. Well, one thing changed: I stopped believing in God. If God really existed, children would not disappear. I started acting strangely, but nobody dared show me the door. Little by little the community broke up. Fifteen years ago the congregation of Somerset merged with that of Montburry, for financial reasons. They sold the building. Nowadays the faithful go to Montburry on Sundays. I was never able to work after the disappearance, even though it was not until six years later that I officially resigned. The parish still pays me a pension. And it sold me the house for a nominal sum."

David Kellergan then told me about his earlier, carefree, happy years in Somerset—the best years of his life, according to him. He reminisced about those summer evenings when he would allow Nola to stay up so she could read on the porch—how he wished those summers could have gone on forever. He also told me how his daughter conscientiously put aside the money she earned at Clark's every Saturday; she said she was going to use it to travel to California and become an actress. He was so proud when he went to Clark's and heard how pleased the customers and Mrs Quinn were with her. For a long time after her disappearance, he wondered if she had gone to California.

"You mean if she had run away?"

"Run away?" he said indignantly. "Why would she run away?"

"What about Harry Quebert? How well do you know him?"

"Hardly at all. I met him a few times."

"You hardly know him?" I said, surprised. "But you've been living in the same town for more than thirty years."

"I don't know everyone, Mr Goldman. And, you know, I live a fairly solitary life. Is it true, about Harry Quebert and Nola? Did he really write that book for her? What does that book mean, Mr Goldman?"

"I'll be honest with you—I think your daughter loved Harry, and that her feelings were reciprocated. That book tells the story of an impossible love affair between two people who are not from the same social class."

"I know," he shouted. "I know! So what did Quebert do? Replace *perversion* with *social class* to give himself a little dignity and sell millions of books. A book that describes the obscene things he did with Nola— with my little Nola—which the whole country read and glorified for thirty years!"

These last words had been spoken with a violent anger I would never have suspected possible in such an apparently frail man. He was silent for a moment, pacing furiously around the room. I could still hear music howling in the background.

"Harry Quebert did not kill Nola," I said.

"How can you be so sure?"

"We can never be sure of anything. That's why life is so complicated sometimes."

He frowned. "What do you want to know, Mr Goldman? If you've come here, it must be because you have questions to ask me."

"I'm trying to understand what could have happened. You didn't hear anything the evening your daughter disappeared?"

"Nothing."

"Some of the neighbors said at the time that they heard shouting."

"Shouting? There wasn't any shouting. There was never any shouting in this house. Why would there have been? I was busy in the garage that day. For the whole afternoon. At 7 p.m., I began making dinner. I went to get Nola from her bedroom so she could help me, but she wasn't there. At first I thought she'd maybe gone for a walk. I waited for a while and then, as I was beginning to worry, I walked around the neighbor-hood. I had not gone a hundred yards when I came upon a crowd of people. The neighbors were all talking about how a young woman had been seen at Side Creek, covered in blood, and that police cars from all over the area were coming into town and sealing off the exits. I ran to the nearest house to call the police, to warn them that it might be Nola. Her bedroom was on the ground floor. I have spent more than thirty years wondering what could have happened to my daughter. And I have often thought that if I'd had other children, I would have made them sleep in the attic. But there were no other children."

"Did you notice your daughter behaving strangely the summer she disappeared?"

"No. I don't know. I don't think so. That's another question I often ask myself, and I have no answer."

He did recall, however, that when the summer vacation began that year, Nola had sometimes seemed sad. He'd put that down to adolescence. I asked him if I could see his daughter's bedroom; he led me there like a museum guard, warning me sternly not to touch anything. He had left the room exactly as it was, he said. Everything was there: the bed, the shelf filled with dolls, the little bookcase, and the desk scattered with pens, a long metal ruler, and sheets of yellowed paper. It was writing paper—the very same paper on which the note to Harry had been written.

"She found that paper in a stationery store in Montburry," her father explained to me when he saw I was interested in it. "She adored it. She always had some on her. She used it for writing letters, leaving notes. That paper *was* Nola. She always had several spare pads."

There was also a portable Remington typewriter in a corner of the room.

"Was this hers?" I asked.

"Mine. But she used it too. The summer she disappeared, she used it a lot. She said she had important documents to type. In fact, she often took it with her away from the house. I offered to give her a ride, but she never accepted. She went on foot, carrying the typewriter in her arms."

"So this room is just as it was the day your daughter disappeared?"

"Everything was exactly where it is now. When I came to get her for dinner, the window was open and the curtains were moving in the breeze."

"Do you think someone came into her room that evening and took her away by force?"

"I don't know what to tell you. I never heard anything. And the police never found any signs of a struggle."

"The police found a bag with her. A bag with her name stitched inside it."

"Yes, they even asked me to identify it. It was the present I gave her for her fifteenth birthday. She saw that bag in Montburry one day when we were there together. I still remember the store, on the main street. I went back the next day to buy it. And I paid the store to stitch her name inside it."

I was trying to back up a theory. "But if it was her bag, that means she took it with her. And if she took it, that means she was going somewhere, doesn't it? Mr Kellergan, I know this is hard to imagine, but do you think Nola could have been running away?"

"I don't know anymore. The police asked me that question thirty-three years ago, and they asked me again a few days ago. But she never lacked for anything here. Clothes, money—she had what she wanted. Look, her money box is there, on her shelf, still full." He took a metal box from one of the higher shelves. "Look, there's a hundred and twenty dollars here! A hundred and twenty dollars! Why would she have left that here if she was running away? The police said that damn book was in her bag. Is that true?"

"Yes."

Questions continued to buzz around my head: Why would Nola run away without taking any clothes or money? Why would she have taken nothing but that manuscript?

In the garage, the record had finished playing its final track, and Nola's father rushed off to reset the needle. I did not want to disturb him any longer, so I said goodbye and left, taking a photograph of the Harley-Davidson on my way out.

When I got back to Goose Cove, I went down to the beach to do some boxing. To my great surprise, I was soon joined by Sergeant Gahalowood, who had come to the house. I was wearing earphones and did not notice him until he tapped me on the shoulder.

"You're a fit guy," he said, looking at my bare chest and wiping his hand, covered in my sweat, on his pant leg.

"I try to stay in shape."

I took the recorder from my pocket to turn it off.

"A minidisc player?" he said in his usual unpleasant tone. "Did you somehow miss the fact that Apple revolutionized the world and that you can now store an almost unlimited amount of music on a portable hard drive called an iPod?"

"I'm not listening to music, Sergeant."

"So what do you listen to while you're exercising?"

"Doesn't matter. Why don't you tell me instead to what I owe the honor of your visit? And on a Sunday too."

"I received a call from Chief Dawn about the fire on Friday evening. He's worried, and I have to admit I think he has a point. I don't like it when things take this kind of turn."

"Are you telling me you're worried for my safety?"

"Not in the slightest. I simply want to make sure this doesn't degenerate any further. We know that crimes against children always cause a big stir among the public. I can assure you that every time the dead girl is mentioned on T.V., there are thousands more perfectly civilized fathers out there who are ready to cut off Quebert's balls."

"Except that, in this case, I was the one who was targeted."

"That's precisely why I'm here. Why didn't you tell me you'd received an anonymous letter?"

"Because you threw me out of your office."

"True."

"Can I get you a beer, Sergeant?"

He hesitated for a moment, then accepted. We walked up to the house together and I went to fetch two bottles which we drank on the deck. I told him how, coming back from Grand Beach two nights before, I had seen the arsonist.

"He was wearing some sort of mask. All I saw was his outline. And the message was the same as before: 'Go home, Goldman.' That's the third."

"Chief Dawn told me. Who else knows that you're running your own investigation?"

"Everyone. I mean, I spend my days questioning everyone I see. It could be anybody. What are you thinking? You think it's someone who doesn't want me to dig into this story?"

"Someone who doesn't want you to discover the truth about Nola. How's your investigation going, by the way?"

"My investigation? So you're interested in it now?"

"Maybe. Let's just say that your credibility has skyrocketed since someone started threatening you."

"I talked to David Kellergan. He's a good guy. He showed me Nola's bedroom. I imagine you've been to see it too."

"Yes."

"So if she was running away, how do you explain the fact that she didn't take anything with her? No clothes, no money, nothing."

"Because she wasn't running away," Gahalowood said.

"But if she was kidnapped, why weren't there any signs of a struggle? And why would she take that bag containing the manuscript with her?"

"That could be explained by her knowing her murderer. Maybe they were even having an affair. In that case, he might have appeared at her window, as he sometimes did, and persuaded her to go with him. Maybe just for a walk."

"You're talking about Harry."

"Yes."

"So what happens? She takes the manuscript and escapes through the window?"

"Who says she took the manuscript? Who says she ever had the manuscript? That's Quebert's explanation, his way of justifying the presence of his manuscript with Nola's corpse."

For a fraction of a second I thought about telling him what I knew about Harry and Nola: that they had arranged to meet at the Sea Side Motel and elope. But I preferred not to mention it for the moment because I didn't want to harm Harry's case. Instead I asked, "So what is your theory?"

"Quebert killed the girl and buried the manuscript with her body. Maybe because he was feeling remorse. It was a book about their love, and their love had killed her."

"What makes you say that?"

"There's an inscription on the manuscript."

"An inscription? What does it say?"

"I can't tell you that. Confidential."

"Oh, cut the crap, Sergeant! You've told me either too much or not enough. You can't hide behind confidentiality just when it suits you."

He sighed with resignation. "Fine. It says: *Goodbye, darling Nola.*"

"What are you going to do with that note?" I asked.

"It's being examined by a handwriting expert. Hopefully we can get something from it."

I was deeply disturbed by this "darling Nola." Those were the exact words spoken by Harry himself, words I had recorded.

I spent part of my evening thinking this over, with no idea what I should do. At 9 p.m., I received a call from my mother.

"For God's sake, Markie," she said. "It's two days that I can't reach you. Are you going to die trying to save that Prince of Darkness?" Apparently, news of the fire had appeared on T.V.

"Relax, Mom. Relax."

"Everyone is talking about you here, and it's not all flattering, if you know what I mean. In the neighborhood everyone's asking questions. They wonder why you insist on staying with that Harry."

"Without Harry I would never have become the Great Goldman, Mom."

"You're right: Without that guy, you would have become the Very Great Goldman. As soon as you started hanging around with that man in college, you changed. You're Marcus the Magnificent, remember? Even old Mrs Lang, the supermarket cashier, still asks me, 'How is Marcus the Magnificent?'"

"Mom, there never was a Marcus the Magnificent."

"Never was a Marcus the Magnificent?" I heard her call my father over. "Nelson, come here, will you? Markie says there never was a Marcus the Magnificent." My father mumbled something indistinct in the background. "You see, your father says the same thing: In high school, you were Marcus the Magnificent. I bumped into your former principal yesterday. He told me he had such memories of you . . . I thought he was going to cry, he was so emotional. And afterward he told me, 'Oh, Mrs Goldman, I don't know what kind of trouble your son has gotten mixed up in now.' You see how bad things are? Even your old principal is asking questions. And what about us? Why do you rush to take care of an old teacher instead of looking for a wife? You're nearly thirty years old and you still haven't married anyone! Do you want us to die without seeing you married?"

"You're fifty-two, Mom. We still have a little time."

"Stop splitting hairs! Who taught you to do that, huh? Something else we can thank that damn Quebert for. Why don't you concentrate on bringing us home a nice young woman? Why? Aren't you going to say anything?"

"I haven't met anyone I like recently. Between my book, my publicity tour, the next book—"

"Excuses! Those are nothing but excuses! And the next book? What is that going to be about? Sexual perversion? I don't know you anymore, Markie . . . Markie, darling, listen: I have to ask you. Are you in love with this Harry? Are you homosexualizing with him?"

"No! Not at all!"

I heard her say to my father: "He says no. That means yes." Then, in a whisper, she asked me, "Do you have the disease? Your mother will love you even if you're sick."

"What? What disease are you talking about?"

"The disease that men who are allergic to women get."

"Are you asking me if I'm homosexual? No! And even if I was, there's nothing wrong with that. But I like women, Mom."

"Women? What do you mean, *women*? Can't you just concentrate on loving one woman and marrying her? Women! Aren't you capable of being faithful? Is that what you're trying to tell me? Are you one of those sex addicts, Markie? Do you want to go to a psychiatrical doctor to get some mental work done?"

Finally I hung up, dejected. I felt very alone. I sat in Harry's office, started up the recorder, and listened to his voice again. I needed new evidence, some tangible proof that would change the course of the investigation, something that would shine a new light on this mind-numbing puzzle I was attempting to solve, which at the moment went no further than Harry, a manuscript, and a dead girl. As I thought about it, I was overcome by a feeling I had not experienced for a long time: the desire to write. I wanted to write about what I was going through, what I was feeling. Soon my head was overflowing with ideas. It was more than a mere desire; I needed to write. This had not happened to me in more than a year and a half. I felt like a volcano suddenly waking and preparing to erupt. I rushed to my laptop and, after wondering for a moment how I could begin, I typed the opening lines of what would become my next book:

In the spring of 2008, about a year and a half after I had become the new star of American literature, something happened that I decided to bury deep in my memory: I discovered that my college professor Harry Quebert—sixty-seven years old and one of the most respected writers in the country—had been romantically involved with a fifteen-year-old girl when he was thirty-four. This happened during the summer of 1975.

On Tuesday, June 24, 2008, a grand jury confirmed the legitimacy of the accusations made by the D.A. and formally indicted Harry for kidnapping and murder. When Roth told me of the jury's decision, I shouted into the telephone: "You've apparently studied law—can you explain to me on what basis they are going through with this bullshit?"

The answer was simple: on the basis of the police file. And Harry's indictment would allow us, as the defense team, access to that file. The morning I spent with Roth studying the evidence was somewhat tense, not least because, as he went through the documents, he kept repeating, "Oh shit, that is not good. That is not good at all."

"It's not getting anyone anywhere to keep saying it's not good," I said. "You're the one who's supposed to be good, aren't you?" He replied only with a bewildered expression that didn't inspire much confidence.

The file contained photographs, witness accounts, and forensic reports. Some of the photographs were from 1975: pictures of Deborah Cooper's house, then her body lying on her blood-covered kitchen floor, and finally the place in the forest where traces of blood, human hair, and scraps of clothing had been found. We then zoomed forward thirty-three years to photographs of Goose Cove, where we could see, lying at the bottom of the hole dug by the police, a skeleton in the fetal position. In places there were still scraps of flesh clinging to the bones and there were a few sparse hairs on top of the skull; the skeleton was wearing a half-rotted dress, and next to it was that much-discussed leather bag. I retched.

"That's Nola?"

"That's her. And Harry's manuscript was found in that bag. There was nothing else, just the manuscript. The prosecutor's argument is that a girl who's running away does not go empty-handed."

The autopsy report revealed a major skull fracture. Nola had been beaten with incredible violence, her occipital bone smashed. The forensic examiner believed that the murderer had used a very heavy stick or a similar object such as a bat.

Next we read various statements: from the gardeners, from Harry, and one in particular, signed by Tamara Quinn, in which she claimed to Sergeant Gahalowood that she had discovered at the time that Harry was infatuated with Nola, but that the proof of this, which had been in her possession, had later disappeared, and consequently nobody had believed her.

"Is her testimony credible?" I asked.

"With a jury, yeah," Roth replied. "And we don't have anything we can counter with. Harry himself admitted during the interrogation that he'd had a relationship with Nola."

"Goddamn it! Is there anything in this file that doesn't condemn him?"

On that point Roth had his own ideas. He rummaged through the documents and handed me a thick sheaf of papers bound by sticky tape.

"A copy of the famous manuscript," he told me.

The cover page had no title, but in the center three handwritten words could be clearly read:

Goodbye, darling Nola

Roth launched into an explanation. He believed that using this manuscript as the main evidence against Harry was a serious mistake by the prosecutor's office: The handwriting analysis was under way, and as soon as the results were known—he was convinced they would prove

Harry's innocence—the whole case would collapse like a house of cards.

"This is the centerpiece of my defense," he told me triumphantly. "With a little luck, we might not even have to go to trial."

"But what if the writing is authenticated as Harry's?" I asked.

Roth gave me a strange look.

"Why the hell should it be?"

"There's something important you should know: Harry told me he spent a day in Rockland with Nola, and that she asked him to call her 'darling Nola.'"

Roth went pale. "You do understand," he said, "that if, one way or another, he wrote this note"—and without even finishing his sentence, he gathered his things and took me to the state prison. He was beside himself.

Roth had barely set foot in the visiting room before he was brandishing the manuscript under Harry's nose and yelling, "She told you to call her 'darling Nola'?"

"Yes," Harry replied, bowing his head.

"Can you see what's written here? On the first page of this goddamn manuscript! When were you planning to tell me, for fuck's sake?"

"I can assure you it's not my writing. I didn't kill her! I did not kill Nola! For God's sake, you do know that, don't you? You know I'm not a child killer!"

Roth calmed down and took a seat.

"We know it, Harry," he said. "But all these coincidences are disturbing. The elopement, this note . . . And I have to defend your ass to a jury of good citizens who are going to want to condemn you to death before the trial even begins."

Harry stood up and began pacing the small concrete room.

"The whole country is rising up against me. Everyone wants me dead. People are calling me a pedophile, a pervert, a psycho. They're burning my books. But you have to know, and I will say this again for the last time: I am not some kind of madman. Nola was the only woman I ever loved, and, unfortunately for me, she was only fifteen. But it was love, for God's sake—you can't control love!"

"But we're talking about a fifteen-year-old girl!" Roth said.

Despairingly, Harry turned toward me.

"Do you feel the same way, Marcus?"

"What bothers me is that you never told me about any of this," I said. "We've been friends for ten years, and you never mentioned Nola. I thought we were close."

"But what could I have told you, for Christ's sake? 'Oh, Marcus, by the way, I never told you this before, but in 1975, when I came to Somerset, I fell in love with a fifteen-year-old girl, who changed my life and disappeared three months later, and I've never really gotten over it'?"

He kicked a plastic chair and sent it hurtling toward the wall.

"Harry," Roth said, "if you didn't write that note—and I believe you when you say that—do you have any idea who did?"

"No."

"Who knew about you and Nola? Tamara Quinn claims she suspected it all along."

"I don't know! Maybe Nola told some of her friends about us . . ."

"But do you think it probable that someone knew about it?" Roth said.

There was a silence. Harry looked so sad and broken that it wrung my heart.

"Come on," Roth insisted, attempting to make Harry talk. "I can sense you're not telling me everything. How can you expect me to defend you if you hide things?"

"There were . . . There were those anonymous letters."

"What anonymous letters?"

"Just after Nola disappeared, I began receiving anonymous letters. I would find them in my front doorway when I came home. I was scared stiff at the time. It meant that someone was spying on me, keeping watch over when I was coming and going. At one point, I was so scared that I would call the police after I received one, and would tell them I thought I'd seen a prowler. They would send a patrol car, which calmed me down. Of course I couldn't mention the real reason I was so worried."

"But who could have sent you those letters?" Roth asked. "Who knew about you and Nola?"

"I don't have the faintest idea. In any case, it went on for maybe four or more months. And after that, nothing."

"Did you keep them?"

"Yes. They're in my house. Hidden between the pages of an encyclopedia in my office. I assume the police didn't find them because nobody has mentioned them to me."

As soon as I got back to Goose Cove, I picked up the encyclopedia he had mentioned. Concealed between its pages I found an envelope containing about ten small pieces of paper. Letters, on yellowed paper, each with the same typewritten message:

> *I know what you've done with that 15-year-old girl.*
> *And soon the whole town will know.*

So someone did know about Harry and Nola. Someone who had kept silent about it for thirty-three years.

During the next two days, I tried to question everyone who might have known Nola in any way whatsoever. Ernie Pinkas was, again, very helpful in this regard: Having found the 1975 Somerset High School yearbook in the library, and using the telephone book and the Internet, he provided me with the current contact information for most of Nola's former classmates who still lived in the area. Unfortunately, this angle of attack did not prove very fruitful. Though these people were now in their forties, all they could give me were childhood memories that did not have much bearing on the investigation. Until I realized that one of the names on the list was not unknown to me: Nancy Hattaway, the girl Harry told me had provided Nola with her alibi for the trip to Rockland.

According to the information provided by Pinkas, Nancy Hattaway ran a clothing and quilt store located in a strip mall on Shore Road, just south of town. I went there for the first time on June 26. It was an attractive, colorful storefront sandwiched between a café and a hardware store. The only person I found inside was a woman in her late forties with short gray hair and wearing reading glasses. She was seated at a desk, and after she greeted me politely, I asked her, "Are you Nancy Hattaway?"

"That's me," she replied, getting to her feet. "Do I know you? Your face seems familiar."

"My name is Marcus Goldman. I'm—"

"The writer," she interrupted. "It's come back to me now. I've heard you're asking lots of questions about Nola." She seemed defensive. Immediately afterward, she added: "I assume you're not here for my quilts?"

"That's true. And it's also true that I'm interested in the death of Nola Kellergan."

"What does that have to do with me?"

"If you really are who I think you are, you knew Nola very well. When you were fifteen."

"Who told you that?"

"Harry Quebert."

She moved away from her chair and strode purposefully toward the door. I thought she was going to ask me to leave, but instead she turned the CLOSED sign so it was facing out, and bolted the door. Then she turned in my direction. "How do you like your coffee, Mr Goldman?"

We spent more than an hour in the back room of her store. She was indeed the same Nancy that Harry had mentioned to me. She had never married.

"You never left Somerset?" I said.

"Never. I'm much too fond of this town to leave. So, what exactly would you like to know, Mr Goldman?"

"Call me Marcus. I need someone to tell me about Nola."

She smiled.

"Nola and I were in the same class at school. We'd been friends ever since she arrived in Somerset. We lived almost next door to each other, on Terrace Avenue, and she often came to our house. She said she liked coming there because I had a *normal* family."

"Normal? What do you mean?"

"I assume you've met her father?"

"Yes."

"He's a very strict man. It's hard to imagine how he could have had a daughter like Nola: intelligent, sweet, kind, friendly."

"I'm surprised by your comments about Mr Kellergan. I met him a few days ago, and he seemed like quite a gentle man."

"He can come across that way. In public, at least. He'd been re-cruited to save St James's, which had fallen into neglect, after apparently performing miracles in Alabama. And it's true that soon after he took it over, the church was full every Sunday. But apart from that, no-one really knows what went on in the Kellergan house."

"What do you mean?"

"Nola used to get beaten."

"What?"

According to my calculations, the incident that Nancy Hattaway then told me about took place on Monday, July 7, 1975, during the period when Harry was keeping his distance from Nola.

Monday, July 7, 1975

It was summer. The weather was absolutely glorious, and Nancy had come to get Nola at her house so they could go to the beach together. As they walked along Terrace Avenue, Nola suddenly said, "Hey, Nancy, do you think I'm a wicked girl?"

"A wicked girl? No, of course not!"

"Because at home, I've been told I'm a wicked girl."

"Why would anyone say such a thing?"

"It doesn't matter. Where are we going to go swimming?"

"At Grand Beach. But, Nola, why would anyone say that to you?"

"Maybe it's true," Nola said. "Maybe it's because of what happened when we were in Alabama."

"What happened in Alabama?"

"It doesn't matter."

"You look unhappy."

"I am."

"But it's summer! How can you be unhappy when it's summer?"

"It's complicated, Nancy."

"Are you in trouble? If you're in trouble, you should tell me!"

"I'm in love with someone who doesn't love me."

"Who?"

"I don't want to talk about it."

"Is it Cody? I saw him flirting with you. I was sure you had a crush on him! What's it like, going out with a junior? But he's a jerk, isn't he? He's a total jerk! You know, just because he's on the basketball team doesn't mean he's a nice guy. Is that who you went out with last Saturday?"

"No."

"So who is it? Oh, come on, tell me. Have you slept together? Have you already slept with a guy?"

"No! What's wrong with you? I'm saving myself for the love of my life."

"I wish you would tell me who you were with on Saturday."

"It doesn't matter. He'll never love me, anyway. Nobody will ever love me."

They arrived at Grand Beach. It was not a very pretty beach, but they could have it all to themselves because it was always deserted. Best of all, the tides left behind natural pools in the large hollow rocks that were then warmed up by the sun. They enjoyed lounging in these pools, the water temperature much warmer than that of the ocean. Because there was nobody else on the beach, they did not have to hide in order to put on their bathing suits, and Nancy noticed that Nola had bruises on her breasts.

"Nola, that's horrible! What is that?"

Nola covered up her chest.

"Don't look!"

"But I already saw! You've got marks—"

"It's nothing."

"It's not nothing! What is it?"

"It was Mom. She hit me on Saturday."

"What? Don't be ridiculous—"

"It's true! She's the one who says I'm a wicked girl."

"That's crazy! What are you talking about?"

"It's true! Why doesn't anybody ever believe me?"

Not daring to ask any more questions, Nancy changed the subject. After their swim, they went to the Hattaways' house. Nancy took some ointment from her mother's bathroom and gave it to Nola to rub on her bruised breasts.

"Nola," she said. "About your mother . . . I think you should talk to someone. Maybe the nurse at the high school . . ."

"Let's forget it, Nancy. Please . . ."

When she recalled her final summer with Nola, Nancy had tears in her eyes.

"What happened in Alabama?" I asked.

"I have no idea. I never found out. Nola never told me."

"Did it have anything to do with their moving here?"

"I don't know. I'd like to help you, but I just don't know."

"And her heartache, do you know who that was caused by?"

"No," Nancy said.

I was fairly certain it was Harry, but I needed to know whether Nancy knew this.

"But you were aware that she was seeing someone," I said. "You provided each other with alibis when you went out with boys."

She smiled.

"The first few times, we did it so we could spend the day in Concord. For us, Concord was a big adventure; there was always something to do there. We felt like grown-ups. Afterward we used the alibis again, me because I wanted to go on my boyfriend's boat, just the two of us, and her for . . . You know, I had a feeling back then that Nola was seeing an older man. She'd dropped hints about it."

"So you knew about her and Harry Quebert . . ."

"My God, no!" she said instantly.

"You just told me that Nola was seeing an older man."

There was an awkward silence. I realized that Nancy had certain information that she had no desire to share.

"Who was that man?" I demanded. "It wasn't Harry Quebert, right? Nancy, I realize you don't know me, that I've turned up out of the blue and I'm forcing you to dig deep in your memories. If I had more time, I would do things in a better way. But time is running out—Harry Quebert is rotting in prison, and I am convinced he didn't kill Nola. So if you know anything that might help me, you have to tell me."

"I don't know anything about Harry," she admitted. "Nola never told me. I found out about it from the T.V. this summer, like everybody else. But she did tell me about a man. Yes, I knew she had a relationship with a much older man. But that man was not Harry Quebert."

I was dumbfounded.

"When was this?" I asked.

"I don't remember the story in any detail—it's been a long time—but I can assure you that in 1975, the summer that Harry Quebert arrived here, Nola had a relationship with a man in his forties."

"In his forties? Do you remember his name?"

"There is no way I'd forget that. It was Elijah Stern, probably one of the richest men in New Hampshire."

"Elijah Stern?"

"Yes. She told me she had to strip naked for him, to obey his wishes. She had to go to his house in Concord. Stern sent his chauffeur to come and get her. A strange guy—Luther Caleb was his name. He came to get her in Somerset and took her to Stern's place. I know that because I saw it happen with my own eyes."

22

Police Investigation

"Harry, how can you be sure you always have the strength to write books?"

"Some people have it, some don't. You will have it, Marcus. I know you will."

"How can you be so certain?"

"Because it's in you. Like a disease. Because the writers' disease isn't an inability to write anymore, it's being incapable of stopping."

EXTRACT FROM *THE HARRY QUEBERT AFFAIR*
Friday, June 27, 2008, 7.30 a.m. I am waiting for Sergeant Perry Gahalowood. This case began only about ten days ago, but it feels as if it's been going on for months. I think the little town of Somerset is hiding some strange secrets, that people are telling much less than they actually know. What I need to find out is why everybody is keeping silent. I found the same message again last night: *Go home, Goldman.* Someone is trying to scare me.

I wonder what Gahalowood will say when I tell him what I've

discovered about Elijah Stern. I Googled him: He is the last heir to a financial empire and its principal manager. He was born in 1933 in Concord, where he still lives. He is now seventy-five years old.

I wrote that while I waited outside Gahalowood's office. I was interrupted by the sergeant's expressionless voice:

"What are you doing here, writer?"

"I've made some surprising discoveries, Sergeant."

He opened the door to his office, placed his foam coffee cup on a side table, threw his jacket over a chair, and raised the blinds. And then, still busying himself in the office, he said to me, "You could have phoned. That's what civilized people do—arrange a meeting and come here at a time that suits both parties. Do things right, you know?"

In a single breath, I blurted out: "Nola had a lover besides Harry. Harry received anonymous letters back then about his relationship with Nola, so somebody knew about it."

He stared at me, wide-eyed.

"How the hell do you know all that?"

"I told you, I'm running my own investigation."

He instantly looked grumpy again.

"You're pissing me off, writer. You're messing up my investigation."

"Are you in a bad mood, Sergeant?"

"Yes. Because it's 7 a.m. and you're already waving your arms around in my office."

I asked him if he had something I could write on. With a resigned expression, he led me to an adjacent room. Photographs of Side Creek and Somerset had been pinned to a corkboard on the wall. He indicated a whiteboard next to this and handed me a dry-erase marker.

"Go ahead," he said with a sigh. "I'm listening."

I wrote Nola's name on the board and drew arrows connecting it to the other people involved. First was Elijah Stern, then Nancy Hattaway.

"Maybe Nola Kellergan was not quite the perfect little girl described by everyone," I said. "We know she was in a relationship with Harry. We now know she had another relationship, during the same period, with a certain Elijah Stern."

"The businessman?"

"The very same."

"Who's been feeding you this crap?"

"Nola's best friend at the time, Nancy Hattaway."

"How did you find her?"

"The 1975 Somerset High School yearbook."

"Alright. And what are you trying to tell me, writer?"

"That Nola was not a happy kid. At the beginning of the summer, her affair with Harry started going bad. He rejected her and she became depressed. Her mother, meanwhile, was beating the living daylights out of her. Sergeant, the more I think about it, the more obvious it seems to me that her disappearance was the result of strange events that took place that summer, although nobody wants to admit that."

"Go on."

"Well, I think other people knew about Harry and Nola. Maybe Nancy Hattaway, although I'm not sure about that—she says she didn't know about it and she seems sincere. In any case, someone was writing Harry anonymous letters—"

"About Nola?"

"Yes. Look—I found this in his house." I showed him one of the letters I had brought with me.

"In his house? But we searched it."

"Never mind that. Don't you see? This means someone knew about them all along."

He read the message out loud: "'I know what you've done with that 15-year-old girl. And soon the whole town will know.' When did Quebert receive these letters?"

"Just after Nola's disappearance."

"Does he have any idea who might have written them?"

"None at all, unfortunately."

I turned toward the corkboard. "Is this your investigation, Sergeant?"

"Absolutely. Let's go back to the beginning, if you don't mind. Nola Kellergan disappeared on the evening of August 30, 1975. The Somerset police report at the time states that it can't be determined for sure whether she was kidnapped or whether she was running away and it all went wrong. There were no signs of a struggle, and no witnesses. Nevertheless, looking at the facts today, we are leaning heavily toward the kidnapping theory—in particular because she took no money or clothes with her."

"I think she ran away," I said.

"Alright—let's go with that theory, then," Gahalowood said. "She climbs out of the window and runs away. Where does she go?"

It was time to reveal what I knew.

"She was going to meet Harry," I replied.

"You think?"

"I know. He told me. I haven't mentioned it to you until now because I was afraid it would compromise him, but I think it's time to put our cards on the table. On the evening she disappeared, Nola was supposed to meet Harry in a motel on Shore Road. They were going to elope."

"Elope? Where?"

"That I don't know. But I intend to find out. Anyway, on that fateful evening, Harry was waiting for Nola in a motel room. She'd sent him a letter saying she'd meet him there. He waited all night for her. She never came."

"Which motel? And where is that letter?"

"The Sea Side Motel. Several miles north of Side Creek. I went there—it still exists. As for the letter . . . I burned it. To protect Harry."

"You burned it? Are you fucking crazy? What got into you? Do you want to go to prison for destroying evidence?"

"I shouldn't have done it. I regret it, Sergeant."

Still cursing me, Gahalowood took out a map of the Somerset region and spread it out on a table. He showed me the center of town, pointed to Shore Road, which ran along the coast, then Goose Cove, then the Side Creek forest. Thinking out loud, he said, "If I were a girl running away and I didn't want to be seen, I would go to the nearest beach and walk along it until I reached Shore Road. In other words, either toward Goose Cove or toward—"

"Side Creek," I said. "There's a footpath through the woods connecting the ocean to the motel."

"Bingo!" Gahalowood shouted. "So it wouldn't be too much of a leap to imagine that the girl ran away from home. Terrace Avenue is there and the nearest beach is . . . Grand Beach! So she went to the beach and walked along it until she reached the woods. But what could have happened to her there in that damn forest?"

"Someone might have seen her on her way through the woods. A maniac, who tried to rape her, and then grabbed a heavy stick and murdered her."

"Maybe, writer, but you're leaving out a detail that poses some serious questions: the manuscript. And that handwritten note: *Goodbye, darling Nola.* That means whoever killed and buried Nola knew her, and that he had feelings for her. And if we assume that this person was not Harry, you'll have to explain to me how she ended up in possession of his manuscript."

"Nola had it with her. That's certain. Even though she was running away, she didn't want to take any baggage with her; that would run the risk of drawing unwanted attention, particularly if her parents saw her as she was leaving. And she didn't need anything anyway: She imagined that Harry was rich, that he would buy them everything they needed for their new life. So what was the one thing she took with her? The sole object that could not be replaced: the manuscript of the book that Harry had just written and that she had taken with her to read, as she often did. She knew this manuscript was important to Harry. She put it in her bag and ran away from home."

Gahalowood thought about my theory for a moment.

"So according to you," he said, "the murderer buried the bag and the manuscript with her to get rid of evidence?"

"Exactly."

"But that doesn't explain why there was that note written on the manuscript."

"That's a good point," I admitted. "Maybe it's proof that Nola's murderer loved her. Could this be a crime of passion? A moment of madness that, once it was over, made the murderer want to write that note so that her grave was not anonymous? Someone who loved Nola and could not bear her relationship with Harry? Someone who knew she was running away and who, unable to dissuade her, preferred to kill her rather than lose her? That theory has legs, don't you think?"

"It has legs, writer, but as you say, it's only a theory. Now we have to verify it. As with all theories. Welcome to the difficult and meticulous world of being a cop."

"What do you suggest, Sergeant?"

"We've done the handwriting analysis on Quebert, but we'll have to wait a while before we get the results. But another point needs to be cleared up. Why bury Nola at Goose Cove? It's next to Side Creek, so why bother moving a body just to bury it two miles away?"

"No body, no murder," I suggested.

"That's what I was thinking too. Maybe the killer felt surrounded by the police. He had to make do with burying it somewhere nearby."

We contemplated the whiteboard on which I had finished writing my list of names:

Harry QUEBERT		*Tamara* QUINN
Nancy HATTAWAY	**NOLA**	*David and Louisa* KELLERGAN
Elijah STERN		*Luther* CALEB

"All these people have a probable link with Nola or with the case," I said. "It could even be a list of potential suspects."

"It's a list that gives me a headache, I can tell you that," Gahalowood said.

I ignored him and went on to review the names on the list.

"Nancy was only fifteen years old in 1975 and had no motive. I think we can eliminate her. Tamara Quinn is telling anybody who'll listen that she knew all about Harry and Nola . . . perhaps she wrote the anonymous letters to Harry."

"A woman?" Gahalowood interrupted. "I don't know about that. It takes a huge amount of strength to smash someone's skull like that. I think a man is far more likely. Particularly because Deborah Cooper clearly identified Nola's pursuer as a man."

"What about Nola's parents? The mother beat her daughter—"

"Beating your daughter is nothing to be proud of, but it's a long way from the savage attack that Nola suffered."

"I read on the Internet that when children disappear, the culprit is often a member of the family."

Gahalowood rolled his eyes.

"I read on the Internet that you're a great writer. So clearly the Internet is just a pack of lies."

"Let's not forget Elijah Stern. I think we should interrogate him as soon as possible. Nancy Hattaway said that he sent his chauffeur, Luther Caleb, to bring Nola to his home in Concord."

"Calm down, writer. Elijah Stern is an influential man from a very rich family. He is immensely powerful. The kind of man the D.A. is not going to want to cross swords with unless there is overwhelming evidence to back up the case. What do you have against him, apart from your witness, who was just a girl when this happened? Her testimony is pretty much worthless now. We need evidence, solid proof. I've been through the Somerset police reports. There is no mention of Harry, Stern, or this Luther Caleb."

"But Nancy Hattaway seems like a reliable witness to me."

"I'm not saying she's not. I just don't trust memories of something that happened more than thirty years ago. I'm going to try to find out more about that story, but I'll need more evidence before I take Stern seriously as a suspect. I'm not going to risk my career by interrogating a guy who plays golf with the governor unless I have at least some evidence against him."

"There's also the fact that the Kellergans came to Somerset from Alabama for a specific reason that nobody seems to be altogether sure of. David Kellergan told me they came here for the fresh air, but Nancy Hattaway told me that Nola had mentioned an event that took place while the family was living in Jackson."

"Hmm. You need to look into that, writer."

I decided not to say anything to Harry about Elijah Stern until I had more solid evidence. On the other hand, I did tell Roth because it seemed to me that this evidence could prove crucial for Harry's defense.

"Nola Kellergan was having an affair with Elijah Stern?" he gasped into the telephone.

"Yup. And my source is reliable."

"Good work, Marcus. We'll subpoena Stern, we'll bury him in court, and we'll turn the situation upside down. Imagine the jurors' faces when Stern, having solemnly sworn on the Holy Bible, gives them all the juicy details of his bedtime adventures with the Kellergan girl."

"Don't say anything to Harry yet. I want to wait until I know more about Stern."

I went to the prison that same afternoon, where Harry corroborated what Nancy Hattaway had said about Nola's situation at home.

"Those beatings . . . it was horrible."

"She also told me that at the beginning of summer, Nola seemed unhappy."

Harry nodded miserably.

"I made Nola very unhappy when I pulled away from her, and the results were disastrous. After I'd gone to Concord with Jenny on the Fourth, I was completely overwhelmed by my feelings for Nola. I desperately needed to distance myself from her. So the next day, Saturday, I decided not to go to Clark's."

As I recorded Harry's voice telling me about the nightmarish weekend of July 5–6, 1975, I began to see how accurately *The Origin of Evil* had traced his affair with Nola, mixing the story with actual extracts from their correspondence. So, in fact, Harry had never hidden their relationship; from the beginning, he had confessed his impossible love affair to the entire world. In the end I had to interrupt him to say, "But Harry, all of this is in your book!"

"All of it, Marcus, all of it. But nobody ever tried to understand. So many people have analyzed that novel, talking about allegories, symbols, and literary devices that I have never even mastered, when, in reality, all I did was write a book about Nola and me."

Saturday, July 5, 1975

It was 4.30 a.m. The streets of the town were deserted, and the rhythm of his footsteps was all that could be heard. Since he had made the decision not to see her anymore, he hadn't been able to sleep. He would wake up involuntarily before dawn and wouldn't be able to fall back asleep. So he would put on his shorts and go running on the beach, chasing seagulls and imitating the way they flew. He would run until he reached Somerset. It was six miles from Goose Cove; he practically sprinted that distance. Normally, having run all the way across town, he would take the Massachusetts road, as if he were leaving town altogether, then stop at Grand Beach, where he would watch the sun rise. But that morning, when he got as far as Terrace Avenue, he stopped to catch his breath and walked for a while between the rows of houses, soaked with sweat, his pulse beating in his temples.

He walked past the Quinns' house. The previous evening, which he'd spent with Jenny, had unquestionably been the most boring of his life. Jenny was a great girl, but she didn't make him laugh and she didn't inspire him. The only one who did was Nola. He walked on down the road until he arrived at the forbidden house: the Kellergans', where, the previous evening, he had left Nola in tears. He'd had to force himself to act coldly so that she would understand. But she hadn't understood anything. She'd said, "Why are you doing this to me, Harry? Why are you being so mean?" He'd thought about her throughout the evening. During the meal in Concord, he had even left the table for a moment to make a call from a telephone booth. He had asked the operator to put him through to Mr Kellergan in Somerset, and then as soon as it had begun ringing, he'd hung up. When he returned to the table, Jenny had asked him if he felt unwell.

Now, standing motionless on the sidewalk, he stared at the windows. He tried to imagine which room she was sleeping in. He stayed like that for a long time. Suddenly, he thought he heard a noise; in his desperation to get away, he ran into some metal trash cans, which clattered and crashed as they tipped over. A light went on in the house, and Harry sprinted away.

Back at Goose Cove he sat in his office to write. It was the beginning of July, and he had still not begun his great novel. What would happen if he couldn't manage to write? He would return to his miserable life. He would never be a writer. He would never be anything. For the first time, he considered suicide. Around seven in the morning, he fell asleep at his desk, his head resting on ripped-up pages covered with cross-outs.

At twelve-thirty, in the employees' bathroom at Clark's, Nola splashed water onto her face, hoping to remove the red marks around her eyes. She had been crying all morning. It was Saturday and Harry hadn't come to the restaurant. He didn't want to see her anymore. Saturdays at Clark's had been when they met; this was the first time he'd failed to show up. She'd been full of hope when she woke that morning: She imagined he would come to tell her how sorry he was for being beastly to her, and she, of course, would forgive him. The idea of seeing him again had put her in a wonderful mood; when she was getting ready, she'd even put some rouge on her cheeks. But her mother had reprimanded her severely at the breakfast table: "Nola, what are you hiding from me? I want to know."

"I'm not hiding anything."

"Don't lie to me! Don't you think I've noticed? Do you think I'm an idiot?"

"Oh no—I would never think that!"

"You think I haven't noticed how happy you are, that you're out all the time, that you put makeup on your face?"

"I'm not doing anything wrong—I promise."

"You think I don't know you went to Concord with that little slut Nancy Hattaway? You're a wicked girl, Nola! You make me ashamed of you!"

Her father had left the kitchen to lock himself in the garage. He always did that when there were arguments at home; he didn't want anything to do with them. And he'd turn on his record player in order not to hear the beating.

"I promise I'm not doing anything wrong," Nola repeated.

Louisa Kellergan stared at her daughter with a mixture of disgust and contempt. Then she sneered, "Nothing wrong? You know why we left Alabama . . . You know why, don't you? Do you want me to refresh your memory? Come here!"

She grabbed her by the arm and dragged her into the bedroom. She forced her to undress in front of her, then watched as the girl trembled in her underwear.

"Why do you wear brassieres?" Louisa Kellergan demanded.

"Because I have breasts."

"You should not have breasts! You're too young! Take off that brassiere and come here!"

Nola stripped naked and moved closer to her mother, who grabbed a metal ruler from her daughter's desk. First she looked her daughter up and down, and then, lifting the ruler, she smacked the girl's breasts. She smacked very hard, over and over again, and when her daughter curled up in pain, she ordered her to stand up and remain calm or she would get even more. And the whole time she was beating her daughter, Louisa repeated: "You must not lie to your mother. You must not be a wicked girl. Do you understand? Stop treating me like an idiot!" Jazz blasted at full volume from the garage.

The only reason Nola had found the strength to work her shift at Clark's was that she knew she would see Harry there. He was the only one who gave her the strength to keep going, and she wanted to keep going for him. But he hadn't come today. She looked at herself in the bathroom mirror, lifting her blouse and examining her breasts, which were covered in bruises. Her mother was right, she thought: She was wicked and ugly, and that was why Harry no longer wanted her.

Suddenly there was a knock at the door.

"Nola, what are you doing?" she heard Jenny say. "The restaurant is packed! You have to come out and serve!"

Nola opened the door in a panic, thinking that Jenny must have been phoned by another employee, angry that Nola had spent so much time in the bathroom. But Jenny had come to Clark's by chance. Or, rather, in the hope of seeing Harry. On arriving, she had noticed that nobody was waiting on the customers.

"Have you been crying?" Jenny asked when she saw Nola's face.

"I . . . I don't feel well."

"Splash some water on your face and join me out there. I'll help you during the rush. They're going crazy in the kitchen."

When the lunch hour was over and everything had calmed down, Jenny poured Nola a lemonade.

"Drink that," she said kindly. "You'll feel better."

"Thank you. Are you going to tell your mom that I screwed up today?"

"Don't worry—I won't breathe a word. Everyone gets down sometimes. What happened to you?"

"I've had my heart broken."

Jenny smiled. "Come on, you're still so young! You'll meet the right guy someday."

"I don't know . . ."

"Come on, look on the bright side! You know, not so long ago, I was in the same situation. I felt lonely and miserable. And then Harry arrived in town . . ."

"Harry? Harry Quebert?"

"Yes! He's so wonderful! Listen . . . it's not official yet and I shouldn't really be telling you this, but you and I are kind of friends, right? And I'm so happy to be able to tell someone: Harry loves me. He loves me! He's writing a book about me. Last night, he took me to Concord for the fireworks. It was so romantic."

"Last night?"

"Yes, we watched the fireworks above the river. It was beautiful!"

"So, Harry and you . . . Are you . . . You're together?"

"Yes! Oh, Nola, aren't you happy for me? Whatever you do, don't tell a soul. I don't want everyone to know. You know how people are: They get jealous so easily."

Nola felt her heart contract. So Harry loved someone else. He loved Jenny Quinn. It was all over—he didn't want her anymore. He had even replaced her. In her head, everything was spinning.

At 6 p.m., having finished her shift, Nola stopped off quickly at home, then went to Goose Cove. Harry's car was not there. Where could he be? With Jenny? The mere thought of that made her feel even worse; she forced herself to hold back her tears. She climbed the few steps that led to the porch door, took from her pocket the envelope she had addressed to him, and wedged it in the doorway. Inside the envelope were two photographs, both taken in Rockland. One showed a flock of seagulls by the sea. The second was a picture of the two of them taken during their picnic. There was also a short letter, a few lines written on her favorite paper:

Darling Harry,

I know that you don't love me, but I will love you forever.

I am giving you a photo of the birds that you draw so beautifully, and a photo of us so you will never forget me.

I know you don't want to see me anymore. But please write to me, at least. Just once. Just a few words, so I have something to remember you by.

I will never forget you. You are the most amazing person I have ever met.

I love you forever.

She ran away as fast as she could. She went down to the beach, took off her sandals, and ran into the water, just as she had the day she met him.

EXTRACTS FROM *THE ORIGIN OF EVIL,*
BY HARRY L. QUEBERT

The letters had begun when she left a note on the door of the house. A love letter, expressing all she felt for him.

> *My darling,*
> *I know that you don't love me, but I will love you forever.*
> *I am giving you a photo of the birds that you draw so beautifully, and a photo of us so you will never forget me.*
> *I know you don't want to see me anymore. But please write to me, at least. Just once. Just a few words, so I have something to remember you by.*
> *I will never forget you. You are the most amazing person I have ever met.*
> *I love you forever.*

He had replied a few days later, when he found the courage to write to her. Writing was hard enough anyway. Writing to her was an epic feat.

My darling,
How can you say that I don't love you? Here, for you, is a message of love, an eternal message mined from the most profound depths of my heart. A message to let you know that I think about you every morning when I awake and every evening when I fall asleep. Your face is etched upon my memory: When I close my eyes, you are right there with me.

Today, I came to your house at dawn. I have to confess,
I often do this. I kept watch over your window. There
were no lights on. I imagined you, sleeping like an angel.
Later on, I saw you, I admired you in your pretty dress. A
flowered dress that suits you so well. You look a little sad.
Why are you so sad? Tell me and I will be sad with you.
P.S.: Send me your letters by mail—it's safer.
I love you so much. Every day, and every night.

My darling,
I have just read your letter, and I'm replying right
away. To tell the truth, I read it ten times, maybe a
hundred! You write so well. Each word of yours is a wonder.
You have so much talent.
Why don't you want to come see me? Why do you
stay hidden? Why don't you talk to me? Why come all the
way to my window if you are not coming to meet me?
Show yourself, I beg you. I have been sad ever since
you stopped talking to me.
Write to me quickly. I can't wait for your next letter.

He knew that, from now on, writing to her would be his way
of loving her, since he could not be physically close to her. They
would kiss the paper the way they burned to kiss each other.
They would wait for the mailman like lovers waiting at a railway
platform.

Sometimes, in absolute secrecy, he would hide at the corner of
her street and wait for the mailman to pass. He watched her rush
out of the house and throw herself upon the mailbox to seize the
precious letter. She lived only for these love letters. It was, at once,
a beautiful and a tragic scene: Love was their greatest treasure,
but they were denied it.

My sweet darling,

I can't show myself to you because that would cause us too much harm. We are not from the same world; people would never understand.

How I suffer from my low birth! Why must we live according to other people's rules? Why can't we simply love each other in spite of our differences? This is the world today: a world where two beings who love one another cannot hold hands. This is the world today: full of codes and rules. But they are dark rules that tarnish and imprison people's souls. But our souls are pure; they can't be imprisoned.

My love for you is infinite and eternal, and it has been since the very first day.

My love,

Thank you for your last letter. Never stop writing: It is so beautiful.

My mother wants to know who is writing to me so often. She is suspicious that I am constantly hanging around the mailbox. To calm her down, I told her it was a friend I met at summer camp last year. I don't like lying, but it's simpler this way. We cannot tell anyone. I know you are right: People would make trouble for us. Even if it hurts me so much to send you letters when we are so close.

21

On the Difficulties of Love

"Marcus, do you know what is the only way to know how much you love someone?"

"No."

"By losing them."

On the road to Montburry there is a small lake, known throughout the region, and on cloudless summer days it is invaded by families and children's summer camps. The banks of the lake are covered with beach towels and sun umbrellas, parents lying slumped beneath them while their children splash noisily in the green, lukewarm water. Trash from picnics, dropped in the water and carried away by the current, piles up in parts of the lake, turning the water to foam. The Montburry local government has endeavored to clean up the shores of the lake ever since the regrettable incident, two years earlier, when a child stepped on a used syringe. Picnic tables and barbecue pits have been provided to avoid the many open fires that made the lawn look like a lunar landscape; the number of trash cans has been doubled; toilets have been installed in prefabricated buildings; the parking lot, which adjoins the edge of the lake, has been enlarged and paved over; and, from June to August, a maintenance team comes every day to clear trash, used condoms, and dog shit from the shore.

The day I went to the lake, for the purposes of my book, some children had caught a frog—probably the last one alive in this body of water—and were trying to dismember it by pulling on its two hind legs.

Ernie Pinkas says that this lake is a good illustration of the decline of humanity. Thirty-three years earlier, the lake was unspoiled. It was difficult to reach: You had to leave your car on the roadside, cross a patch of woodland, and then walk for a good half-mile through tall grass and wild rosebushes. But all the effort was worth it in the end: The lake was beautiful, covered in pink water lilies and overhung by immense weeping willows. Through the clear water, you could see the trails left by shoals of golden perch, which were hunted by herons that waited amid the roses. At one end of the lake, there was even a small beach of gray sand.

It was to this lakeside that Harry came to hide from Nola. He was here on Saturday, July 5, while she was leaving her first letter at the door of his house.

Saturday, July 5, 1975

It was late morning when he arrived at the lake. Ernie Pinkas was already there, lounging on the bank.

Pinkas laughed when he saw him. "So you finally came. It's a shock to see you anywhere other than Clark's."

Harry smiled.

"You've told me so much about this lake that I couldn't not come."

"Nice, isn't it?"

"Beautiful."

"This is New England. It's protected, and that's what I like about it. Everywhere else in the country they're building and concreting all over the place. But here it's different; I can guarantee you that, thirty years from now, this place will still be unspoiled."

They cooled down in the water together, then dried themselves and talked about literature.

"On the subject of books," Pinkas said, "how is yours coming along?"

Harry shrugged.

"Don't be like that. I'm sure it's very good."

"No, I think it's very bad."

"Let me read it. I'll give you an objective opinion—I promise. What don't you like about it?"

"Everything. I have no inspiration. I don't know how to begin. I'm not even sure I know what my subject is."

"What kind of story is it?"

"A love story."

"Ah, love . . ." Pinkas sighed. "Are you in love?"

"Yes."

"Well, that's a good start. I was wondering—don't you miss your life in New York a little?"

"No. I'm happy here. I needed some tranquility."

"But what do you do in New York, exactly?"

"I . . . I'm a writer."

Pinkas hesitated to contradict him. "Harry . . . don't take this the wrong way, but I talked to one of my friends who lives in New York . . ."

"And?"

"He says he's never heard of you."

"Not everybody knows me. Do you know how many people live in New York?"

Pinkas smiled to show that there was no malice in what he was saying.

"I don't think anyone knows you. I contacted the publisher who put out your book—I wanted to order more copies. I hadn't heard of that publisher, but I thought that was just my own ignorance until I found out it was actually a print shop in Brooklyn. I called them, Harry. You paid a print shop to publish your book."

Ashamed, Harry lowered his head.

"So you know the truth," he muttered.

"I know the truth about what?"

"That I'm an impostor."

Pinkas placed a friendly hand on his shoulder.

"An impostor? Come on, don't be ridiculous! I loved your book! That's why I wanted to order more copies. You don't have to be a famous writer to be a good writer. You have a huge amount of talent, and I am sure you will soon be successful. Who knows? Maybe the book you're writing now will be a masterpiece."

"What if I don't write it?"

"You will. I know you will."

"Thank you, Ernie."

"Don't thank me. It's just the truth. And don't worry—I won't tell a soul. All of this will remain between us."

Sunday, July 6, 1975

At exactly 3 p.m., Tamara Quinn positioned her husband on the porch. He was wearing a suit and holding a glass of champagne, a cigar in his mouth.

"Don't move a muscle," she ordered.

"But my shirt is making me itch, honey bunny."

"Shut up, Bobbo! Those shirts are expensive, and expensive clothes don't make you itch."

Honey bunny had bought the new shirts in a fashionable Concord store.

"Why can't I wear my other shirts?"

"I already told you: I don't want you wearing your disgusting old rags when a great writer is coming over!"

"And I don't like the taste of cigars . . ."

"Other way around, numbskull! You put it in your mouth the wrong way. Can't you see that the band shows where your mouth goes?"

"I thought it was a lid."

"Don't you know anything about chicness?"

"Chicness?"

"It means chic things."

"I didn't know chicness was a word."

"That's because you don't know anything! Harry will be here in fifteen minutes. Please try to behave as if you're worthy of him. And try to impress him."

"How?"

"Smoke your cigar thoughtfully. Like a great businessman. And when he talks to you, act superior."

"How do you act superior?"

"Very good question. Since you're stupid and don't know anything about anything, you'll have to make do with being evasive. Answer his questions with questions. If he asks you, 'Are you for or against the war in Vietnam?' you reply, 'If you're asking me that question, obviously you have a very clear view on the subject?' And there you go, boom! You serve the champagne! That is what is called a 'diversion tactic.'"

"Yes, honey bunny."

"And don't disappoint me."

"No, honey bunny."

Tamara went back into the house and Robert sat down in a wicker chair, feeling dejected. He hated Harry Quebert, who was supposedly a great writer but seemed more like a great stuffed shirt to him. And he hated seeing his wife put on these elaborate courtship dances for him. He was doing what she asked only because she had promised he could be her Naughty Bobbo this evening and that he could even sleep in her room. The Quinns had separate bedrooms. In general, once every three or four months, she would agree to have sex, usually after a long period of pleading, but it had been a long time since he had been allowed to spend the whole night with her.

Upstairs, Jenny was ready: She was wearing a long evening dress, wide skirted with puffed shoulders, fake jewelry, too much lipstick, and too many rings on her fingers. Tamara arranged her daughter's dress and smiled at her.

"You're beautiful, my darling. Quebert is going to fall head over heels in love with you when he sees you!"

"Thanks, Mom. But you don't think it's too much?"

"Too much? No, it's perfect."

"But we're only going to the movie theater!"

"And afterward? What if you go to a chic restaurant? Did you think about that?"

"There aren't any chic restaurants in Somerset."

"Well, maybe Harry has reservations at a very chic restaurant in Concord for his fiancée."

"Mom, we're not engaged yet."

"But you will be soon, darling, I'm sure. Have you kissed?"

"Not yet."

"In any case, if he feels you up, for God's sake let him do it!"

"Yes, Mom."

"And what a charming idea it was of his to suggest you go to the movies!"

"Actually, that was my suggestion. I got my nerve up, called him, and said, 'You're working too hard, Harry! Let's go see a movie this afternoon.'"

"And he said yes . . ."

"Right away! Without a second's hesitation!"

"You see—it's just as if it had been his idea."

"I always feel guilty about disturbing him while he's working, because he's writing about me. I know—I saw something that he wrote. He said that he only came to Clark's to see me."

"Oh, darling! That's so exciting."

Tamara took a makeup box and touched up her daughter's face while continuing to daydream. He was writing a book for her. Soon, in New York, everyone would be talking about Clark's, and about Jenny. There would probably be a movie too. What an enticing prospect! By sending them Quebert, God had answered all her prayers. She was so glad they had been good Christians—here was their reward. Her thoughts sped on: She absolutely had to organize a garden party next Sunday to make this thing official. It would be short notice, but the Saturday after that was the summer gala, and the whole town, shocked and envious, would see her Jenny in the arms of the great writer. Her friends had to see her daughter and Harry together before then, so that the rumor would have time to go around town; that way, they would be the evening's star attraction. Oh, what joy! She had been so worried about her daughter; she might have ended up with a truck driver. Or, worse, with a socialist. Or, worse still, a black! She shuddered at the thought: her Jenny with a black man. She was instantly gripped with anxiety: Many great writers were Jews; what if Quebert was a Jew? Maybe even a socialist Jew! It was too bad that Jews could look white, because that made them invisible. At least blacks had the honesty to be black, so they could be easily identified. But Jews were sly. Her stomach was in knots; she could feel the muscles cramping. Ever since the Rosenbergs, she had been terrified of Jews. They had given the atomic bomb to the Russians, after all. How could she find out if Quebert was Jewish? Suddenly she had an idea. She looked at her watch. She had just enough time to go to the general store before he arrived. She went off in a hurry.

At 3.20 p.m., a black Chevrolet Monte Carlo parked in front of the Quinns' house. Robert Quinn was surprised to see Harry Quebert get out of it; it was a model Robert particularly liked. He also noted that the Great Writer was dressed very casually. In spite of this, he greeted him formally and immediately offered him a drink of great chicness, just as his wife had told him to.

"Champagne?" he said.

"Um, to be honest, I'm not really a champagne kind of guy," Harry said. "Maybe just a beer, if you have one."

"Of course!" Robert said, suddenly informal and enthusiastic.

He knew about beer. He even had a book about all the beers made in America. He ran to grab two cold bottles from the fridge and, in passing, announced to the ladies upstairs that the not-so-grand-as-all-that Harry Quebert had arrived. Sitting on the porch, shirtsleeves rolled up, the two men toasted the day by clinking their bottles together and talking about cars.

"Why the Monte Carlo?" Robert said. "I mean, given your situation, you could have chosen any model you liked."

"It's sporty and practical. And I like its style."

"Me too! I came close to buying one last year."

"You should've gone for it."

"My wife didn't want me to."

"You should've bought the car first and asked her opinion afterward."

Robert laughed; in fact, this Quebert was a simple, friendly, and likeable guy. At that moment, Tamara burst out, carrying what she had gotten from the general store: a plate of miniature ham sandwiches. "Hello, Mr Quebert! Welcome! Would you like a ham sandwich?" Greeting her, Harry helped himself to a sandwich. Seeing her guest eat, Tamara felt a sweet wave of relief wash over her. He was the perfect man: neither a black nor a Jew.

Regaining her composure, she noticed that Robert had taken off his tie and that the two men were drinking beer from the bottle.

"What are you doing? You're not drinking champagne? And you, Robert, why are you half undressed?"

"It's hot!" Robert complained.

"I prefer beer," Harry said.

And then Jenny arrived, overdressed but beautiful in her evening gown.

At the same time, at 245 Terrace Avenue, David Kellergan found his daughter in tears in her bedroom.

"What's the matter, Nola?"

"Oh, I'm so upset . . ."

"Why?"

"It's because of Mom . . ."

"Don't say that . . ."

Nola was sitting on the floor, her face contorted. The pastor felt so sorry for her.

"Why don't we go to the movies?" he suggested. "You, me, and a bucket of popcorn! The movie starts at four—we still have time."

"My Jenny is a very special girl," Tamara explained, while Robert took advantage of his wife's divided attention to stuff his face with ham. "Did you know that at only ten years old, she had already won all the beauty contests in the area? Do you remember, Jenny darling?"

"Yes, Mom," Jenny said with a sigh, ill at ease.

"How about we look at the old photo albums!" Robert suggested, his mouth full, reciting the line his wife had made him learn.

"Oh, yes!" Tamara said. "The photo albums!"

She hurried to fetch a pile of albums that documented all twenty-four years of Jenny's existence. Turning the pages, she cried out, "But who is this beautiful girl?" And she and Robert would chorus: "It's Jenny!"

After the photographs, Tamara ordered her husband to fill the champagne flutes, then she talked about the garden party she was planning for the following Sunday.

"If you're free, come and have lunch with us next Sunday, Mr Quebert."

"I'd like that," he replied.

"Don't worry—it won't be anything fussy. I mean, I do realize that you came here to escape the pressures of New York society. It will just be a country lunch with a few nice people."

At ten minutes to four, while the black Chevrolet Monte Carlo was parking in front, Nola and her father entered the lobby.

"Go find us a couple seats," David Kellergan suggested to his daughter. "I'll get the popcorn."

Nola went into the theater the very moment that Harry and Jenny were entering the lobby.

"I'll meet you inside," Jenny said to Harry. "I'm just going to visit the restroom."

Harry went into the theater and, suddenly, amid the crush of people, found himself face-to-face with Nola.

As soon as he saw her, he felt his heart explode. He missed her so much.

As soon as she saw him, she felt her heart explode. She had to speak to him. If he was dating Jenny, she needed to hear it from him.

"Harry," she said, "I—"

"Nola—"

At that instant Jenny moved through the crowd toward them. Nola saw her and realized she had come with Harry, so she fled.

"Everything O.K., Harry?" Jenny asked. She had not seen Nola. "You look a little strange."

"Yes . . . I . . . I'll be back. You can find us some seats. I'm going to buy popcorn."

"Oh yes! Popcorn! Ask for lots of butter."

Harry went out through the swinging doors. He saw Nola cross the lobby and climb up to the mezzanine, which was closed to the public. He rushed up the stairs to catch her.

The second floor was deserted; he caught up with her, grabbed her hand, and held her against a wall.

212

"Let me go," she said. "Let me go or I'll scream!"

"Nola! Nola, don't be mad at me."

"Why are you avoiding me? Why don't you come to Clark's anymore?"

"I'm sorry . . ."

"Why didn't you tell me you were involved with Jenny Quinn? You don't find me attractive—is that it?"

"What? I'm not involved with her. Who told you that?"

She released a huge sigh of relief. "Jenny and you—you're not together?"

"No! I'm telling you we're not."

"So you don't think I'm ugly?"

"Ugly? Nola, what are you talking about? You're so beautiful."

"Really? I've been so upset . . . I thought you didn't want me. I thought about jumping out of the window."

"Don't say things like that."

"So tell me again that you think I'm pretty . . ."

"You're very pretty. I'm sorry I upset you."

She smiled. This whole thing was nothing but a misunderstanding! "Let's not talk about this anymore," she whispered. "Hold me tight. I think you're so wonderful, so handsome, so . . ."

"I can't, Nola . . ."

"Why not? If you really found me beautiful, you wouldn't reject me!"

"I find you very beautiful. But you're a child."

"I'm not a child!"

"Nola . . . you and me, it's impossible."

"Why are you so beastly to me?"

"Nola, I . . ."

"Leave me alone. Leave me alone, and don't talk to me anymore. Don't talk to me anymore or I'll tell everyone that you're a pervert. Go back to your little darling! She told me you were together. I know every-thing! I know everything and I hate you, Harry! Go away! Go away!"

She pushed him away, hurtled downstairs, and ran out of the building. Harry gloomily returned to the theater. As he pushed open the door, he bumped into David Kellergan.

"Hello, Harry."

"Reverend!"

"I'm looking for my daughter. Have you seen her? I had asked her to find seats for us, but she seems to have disappeared."

"I . . . I think I saw her leaving."

"Leaving? But the movie's about to start."

When the movie was over, they went to eat pizza in Montburry. Driving back to Somerset, Jenny was aglow: It had been a wonderful evening. She wanted to spend all her evenings—her whole life—with this man.

"Harry, don't take me home right away," she begged him. "It's all been so perfect. I'd like to make this night last a little longer. We could go to the beach."

"The beach? Why the beach?"

"Because it's so romantic! Park near Grand Beach—there's never anyone there. We could flirt like students, lying on the hood of the car. We could look at the stars and enjoy the night. Please . . ."

He wanted to refuse, but she insisted. So he suggested the forest instead of the beach; the beach was for Nola. He parked near Side Creek Lane, and as soon as he turned off the engine, Jenny threw herself at him, kissing him full on the mouth. She held his head and stuck her tongue down his throat. Her hands touched him all over. She made a loathsome groaning noise. In the cramped confines of the car, she climbed on top of him, and he felt her nipples hard against his chest. She was a beautiful woman. She would have made a perfect wife. He could have married her the next day without hesitation: Lots of men would have killed for a woman like Jenny. But another's name was already engraved on his heart. Four letters that left no space for any others: N-O-L-A.

"You're the man I've always dreamed of," Jenny said.

"Thank you."

"Are you happy with me?"

He did not reply, but merely pushed her gently away.

"We should go back, Jenny. I didn't realize it was so late."

He started the car and headed toward Somerset.

When he dropped her off at her house, he didn't notice that she was crying. Why had he not answered her? Didn't he love her? She wasn't asking for all that much, after all. All she wanted was a nice man who would love and protect her, give her flowers occasionally, and take her out to eat. Even for hot dogs if he didn't have much money. What did Hollywood matter, in the end, if she could find someone she loved and who loved her in return? Standing on the porch, she watched the black Chevrolet disappear into the night, then she broke into sobs. She put her hands to her face so her parents would not hear her. Particularly her mother—she didn't want to have to tell her what had happened. She was waiting for the lights upstairs to go out before she entered the house, when suddenly she heard the sound of an engine, and she lifted her head, hoping it would be Harry, coming back to hold her tight and console her. But it was a police car, stopping in front of the house. She recognized Travis Dawn, brought here by chance during his patrol.

"Jenny? Everything O.K.?" he asked through the car's open window.

She shrugged. He cut the engine and opened his door. Before getting out of the vehicle, he unfolded a piece of paper that had been in his pocket and quickly reread the words written on it:

ME: *Hi, Jenny. How are you?*

HER: *Hi, Travis! What's up?*

ME: *I just happened to be passing by.* ~~*You are beautiful.*~~ *You're looking well. I was wondering if you had a partner for the summer gala. I was thinking we could go together.*

— *IMPROVISE* —

Suggest a walk and/or going for a milkshake.

He joined her on the porch and sat next to her.

"What's the matter?" he asked.

"Nothing," Jenny said, wiping her tears.

"It's not nothing. I can see you've been crying."

"Someone is hurting me."

"Who? You can tell me everything . . . I'll take care of him for you!"

She smiled sadly and rested her head on his shoulder.

"It doesn't matter. But thank you, Travis—you're a nice guy. I'm glad you dropped by."

He dared to place a comforting arm around her shoulders.

"You know," Jenny said, "I got a letter from Emily Cunningham, remember, from high school? She's living in New York now. She found a good job and she's pregnant with her first child. Sometimes it seems like everyone's left this place. Everyone except me. And you. Why did we stay in Somerset?"

"I don't know. It depends . . ."

"But you . . . why did you stay?"

"I wanted to stay close to someone I like a lot."

"Who? Do I know her?"

"Well, actually, you know, Jenny, I wanted to . . . I wanted to ask you . . . I mean, if you . . . What I mean is . . ."

He crunched up the piece of paper in his pocket and tried to relax. But at that moment the front door crashed open. It was Tamara, in bathrobe and curlers.

"Jenny, darling, what are you doing out here? I thought I heard voices . . . Oh, but it's you, Travis. How are you?"

"Hello, Mrs Quinn."

"Jenny, you're just in time. Come in and help me, would you? I need to take these things out of my hair, and your father is useless. You'd think the good Lord had given him feet instead of hands."

Jenny stood up and waved goodbye to Travis, then disappeared into the house. Travis sat alone on the porch for a long time afterward.

That same evening, at midnight, Nola climbed out of her bedroom window and left her house to go see Harry. She had to know why he didn't want her anymore. Why had he not even replied to her letter? Why didn't he write to her? It took her a good half-hour to walk to Goose Cove. She saw a figure on the deck, light from the house illuminating him. Harry was sitting at his big wooden table, looking out at the ocean. He jumped when she called his name.

"Jesus, Nola! You scared me!"

"That's how I make you feel? Scared?" She started to weep. "I don't understand . . . I love you so much. I've never felt like this . . ."

"Did you slip away from home?"

"Yes. I love you, Harry. Do you hear me? I love you as I have never loved anyone and as I will never love anyone again."

"Don't say that, Nola . . ."

"Why not?"

His stomach was in knots. The pages he was hiding in front of him contained the first chapter of his novel. He had finally managed to start it. It was a book about her. He was writing her a book. He loved her so much, he was writing her a book. He did not dare tell her that, however. He was too scared of what might happen.

"I can't love you," he said, pretending to be emotionless.

She let the tears run down her cheeks.

"You're lying! You're a bastard and a liar! Why take me to Rockland, then? What was the point of all that?"

He forced himself to be cruel.

"It was a mistake."

"No! No! It was special, you and me! Is it because of Jenny? Do you love her? What does she have that I don't?"

And Harry, incapable of uttering a single word, watched Nola flee, in tears, into the night.

"That was a horrible night," Harry told me in the visiting room of the state prison. "What Nola and I felt for each other was so powerful. The kind of love you feel only once in your life. I can still see her running away that night, on the beach. And I was wondering what to do. Should I run after her? Or should I stay holed up at Goose Cove? Would I have the courage to leave this town? I spent the next few days at the lake in Montburry, just so I wouldn't be at home, where she could come and find me. As for my book—the reason I had to come to Somerset, the reason I had spent all my savings—it was not progressing. Worse than that, in fact: I had written the opening pages, but now I was blocked again. It was a book about Nola, but how could I write without her? How could I write a love story that was doomed to failure? I spent hours and hours staring at those pages, hours and hours to produce just a few words. Three lines. Three bad lines. The most banal platitudes. I was in that pitiful stage when you begin to hate everything connected to books and writing because all of it seems better than yours—even a restaurant menu strikes you as being composed with extraordinary talent. 'T-bone steak: eight dollars.' How skillfully put! I should have thought of that! It was horrifying, Marcus: I was miserable, and because of me, Nola was miserable too. For almost a whole week, I avoided her as much as I could. But, on several evenings, she came to Goose Cove, bringing wildflowers that she had picked for me. She knocked at the door. And I just played dead. I heard her collapse against the door. I heard her knocks continue while she sobbed. And I stayed on the other side, without moving. I waited. She sometimes stayed like that for more than an hour. Then she would leave the flowers by the door and I would hear her walk away. I would rush to the kitchen window and watch her go up the driveway. I loved her so much, I wanted to rip my heart out. But she was fifteen! So I would go outside to pick up the flowers and, as with all the other bouquets she brought me, I put them in a vase in the living room. I would stare at those flowers for a long, long time. And then, that Sunday—July 13, 1975—something terrible happened."

Sunday, July 13, 1975

A dense crowd stood in front of 245 Terrace Avenue. The news had already spread through town. It had come from Chief Pratt—or rather from his wife, Amy, after her husband had received an emergency call from David Kellergan. Amy Pratt had immediately told her neighbor, who had called a friend, who had called her sister, whose children, mounting their bicycles, had gone off to ring the doorbells of their friends' houses: Something bad had happened. In front of the Kellergans' house, there were two police cars and an ambulance; Officer Travis Dawn was holding back the gawkers on the sidewalk. Music could be heard blaring from the garage.

It was Ernie Pinkas who told Harry, at ten that morning. He banged on the door, and realized he had woken him when Harry opened it in his bathrobe, his hair a mess.

"I came just so you could hear the news."

"What news?"

"It's Nola Kellergan."

"What about her?"

"She tried to kill herself."

20

The Day of the Garden Party

"Harry, is there an order to what you're telling me?"

"Yes, absolutely."

"What is it?"

"Well, now that you ask me . . . maybe there isn't, actually."

"Harry! This is important! I'm not going to make it if you don't help me!"

"Listen, my order doesn't really matter. What counts in the end is your order. So what number are we up to? Nineteen?"

"Twenty."

"Alright. So, twenty: Victory is within you. All you need is to want to let it out."

On the morning of Saturday, June 28, Roy Barnaski called.

"Goldman," he said, "do you know what date Monday is?"

"June 30."

"June 30. Yes, indeed! Crazy how time flies. *Il tempo è passato,* Goldman. And what happens on June 30?"

"It's National Meteor Day," I said. "I just read an article about it."

"On June 30 your deadline expires, that is what happens on that day. I've just spoken with your agent. He says he doesn't call you anymore because you're out of control. 'Goldman has lost it' were his exact words. We're trying to give you a helping hand here, to work out an arrangement, but it seems you'd rather drive your career straight into a brick wall."

"A helping hand? You want me to contrive some kind of pornographic story about Nola Kellergan."

"Get off your high horse, Marcus. I just want to entertain the public. Make them want to buy books. People are buying fewer and fewer books, except when they contain squalid stories that correspond to their own worst urges."

"I am not going to churn out trash for you or anybody."

"As you wish. Then this is what will happen on Monday: Marisa, my secretary, whom you know well, will come to my office for our weekly 10.30 meeting where we go over what manuscripts are due. She will tell me: 'Marcus Goldman had until today to deliver his manuscript. We haven't received anything.' I'll nod somberly. I'll probably give you the rest of the day, postponing my unenviable duty, and then, around 5.30 p.m., with a very heavy heart, I'll call Richardson, the head of our legal department, to inform him of the situation. I'll tell him we're going to begin legal proceedings against you for breach of contract, and that we're going to claim ten million dollars in damages."

"Ten million dollars? You're being ridiculous, Barnaski."

"Damn right. Fifteen million!"

"You're a jerk, Barnaski."

"You see, that's exactly where you're wrong, Goldman. You're the jerk! You want to play with the big boys, but you're not playing by the rules. You want to play for the championship, but you're refusing to take part in the playoffs, and that's not how it works. And you know what? With the money we'll get from you, I'll pay an ambitious young writer to tell the story of Marcus Goldman, or how a talented young man with an overactive conscience sabotaged his career and future. He'll go to interview you in the seedy little hut in Florida where you'll be living, getting wasted every morning so you don't have to think about the past. See you soon, Goldman—in court."

He hung up.

Soon after this edifying telephone call, I went to Clark's to get lunch. By chance I bumped into the Quinns. Tamara was sitting at the counter, scolding her daughter because she was doing everything wrong, and Robert was hidden away at a far table, eating scrambled eggs and reading the sports section of the *Concord Herald*. I sat next to Tamara, opened a newspaper, and pretended to read it so I could listen to her grumbling that the kitchen was filthy, the service too slow, the coffee cold, the syrup bottles sticky, the sugar bowls empty, the tables dirty, that it was too hot in the restaurant, her toast was burnt and she wouldn't pay a single cent for it, and two dollars for this coffee was outright theft. She said she would never have sold this restaurant to her daughter had she known she was going to turn it into a second-rate greasy spoon. She'd had such ambitions for this place, and back in her day people came from all over for her hamburgers, which everyone said were the best in the state. Then she turned to me with a contemptuous look and said, "Hey, you—why are you eavesdropping?"

I put on a butter-wouldn't-melt expression and turned to face her.

"Me? I wasn't eavesdropping, ma'am."

"You obviously were, or you wouldn't have replied! Where are you from?"

"New York."

She softened instantly, as if the words 'New York' had a tranquilizing effect. "What is such a handsome young New Yorker doing in Somerset?" she asked.

"I'm writing a book."

Her face darkened again, and she started bellowing. "A book? You're a writer? I hate writers! They're all lazy good-for-nothing liars. What do you live on? Government handouts? My daughter owns this restaurant, and I'm warning you now—you won't get credit here! So if you're not going to pay, then get the hell out of here. Get out before I call the cops. The chief of police is my son-in-law."

Behind the counter, Jenny looked embarrassed.

"Mom, this is Marcus Goldman. He's a well-known writer."

Mrs Quinn almost spat out her coffee.

"You're that little son of a bitch who was always hanging around Quebert?"

"Yes, ma'am."

"You've grown since I last saw you. In fact, you're not bad looking now. You want to know what I think of Quebert?"

"No, thank you, ma'am."

"Well, I'm gonna tell you anyway. I think he's a goddamn piece of shit and he deserves to fry!"

"Mom!" Jenny protested.

"It's the truth!"

"Mom, stop!"

"Shut your mouth, kiddo. I'm talking, not you. Write this down, Mr Asshole Writer. If you have an ounce of honesty, write the truth about Harry Quebert: He is the lowest of the low, a pervert and a murderer. He killed poor Nola, nice Mrs Cooper, and in some ways he killed my Jenny too."

Jenny ran into the kitchen. I think she was crying. Sitting iron backed on her stool, eyes bright with fury, and finger jabbing at the air, Tamara Quinn told me the reason for her wrath, and how Harry Quebert had dishonored her good name. Sunday, July 13, 1975, should have been a proud day for the Quinn family, who were hosting a garden party—from noon onward (as specified on the invitations, which had been sent to a dozen guests)—on the freshly mown lawn behind their house.

*

July 13, 1975

It was an important event, and Tamara Quinn had spared no expense: There was a big tent in the yard; silverware and white napkins on the long table; a buffet lunch ordered from a caterer in Concord, with an array of savory appetizers, lobsters, scallops, steamed clams, and a Waldorf salad; even a waiter to serve the cold drinks and Italian wine. It was going to be a social gathering of the first order, and everything had to be perfect. Jenny was officially introducing her new boyfriend to a few select members of Somerset's social scene.

It was ten minutes to twelve. Tamara looked out over the backyard: Everything was ready. Because of the heat, she would wait until the last minute to bring out the dishes. How delighted everyone would be to nibble scallops, clams, and lobster while listening to Harry Quebert's scintillating conversation and admiring, at his side, her ravishing Jenny. The Quinns were on the verge of greatness, and Tamara shivered with pleasure as she imagined the scene. She admired her arrangements once more, then went over the seating plan she had written on a sheet of her best writing paper, which she was trying to learn by heart. Everything was perfect. The only things missing now were her guests.

Tamara had invited four of her friends and their husbands. She had spent a long time thinking over the number of guests. It was a difficult choice. Too few, and people might think that the party was a failure; too many, and her exquisite country lunch might resemble a church picnic. In the end she had decided to invite some of the biggest rumor-mongers in town. Soon everybody would be saying that Tamara Quinn was organizing highly select, chic events now that her future son-in-law was the rising star of American letters. So there was Amy Pratt, because she was in charge of the summer gala; Belle Carlton, who considered herself the local arbiter of good taste because her husband got a new car every year; Cindy Tirsten, who ran several women's clubs; and Donna Mitchell, an annoying woman who talked too much and constantly boasted about how successful her children were. Tamara was getting ready to wow them all. Each had called her when they received the invitation to find out what the occasion was. But she had kept them in suspense: "I have some important news to announce." She couldn't wait to see their faces when they caught an eyeful of her Jenny and the great Quebert, together for life.

Preoccupied as she was with her garden party, Tamara was one of the few Somerset residents not currently crowding in front of the Kellergans' house. She had heard the news, like everyone else, early that morning, and she had been worried about how it might affect her party. But, thank God, Nola's suicide attempt had been a failure, and now Tamara felt doubly lucky: first of all because, had Nola died, she would have had to cancel the party altogether, for it would not have been appropriate to celebrate in such circumstances; and second, it was a blessing that today was Sunday, rather than Saturday, because if Nola had tried to kill herself on Saturday, Tamara would have had to replace her at Clark's and that would have been very complicated. Nola, she thought, was a very good girl to have attempted suicide on a Sunday *and* to have failed in the attempt.

Satisfied with the arrangements outside, Tamara went into the house to monitor what was happening there. She found Jenny at her post in the entrance hall, ready to welcome the guests. But she did have to scold Robert, who was wearing a shirt and tie but had not yet put on his pants—because on Sundays he was allowed to read the newspaper in his underwear in the living room; he liked it when the draft from the open windows blew inside his underpants because that cooled him down, particularly his hairy parts, and he found that very pleasant.

"Enough parading around naked, Bobbo!" his wife rebuked him. "All that is over now. Do you really imagine you're going to walk around in your underwear when the great Harry Quebert is our son-in-law?"

"You know," Bobbo replied, "I don't think he's like everyone thinks. He's actually a very simple guy. He likes car engines and cold beer, and

I don't think he would be offended to see me in my Sunday attire. I'll ask him."

"You will not ask him anything of the kind! I don't want to hear any of your nonsense during this meal! In fact, I don't want to hear you at all. Oh, my poor Bobbo, if only it were legal, I would sew your lips shut. Every time you open your mouth, you sound like an imbecile. From now on, you wear a shirt and pants on Sundays. Period. I don't want to see you hanging around the house in your underpants anymore. We're very important people now."

While she was speaking, she noticed that her husband had scribbled something on a card that was in front of him on the coffee table.

"What's that?" she barked.

"It's . . . something."

"Show me!"

"No," he said daringly, and grabbed the card.

"Bobbo, I want to see it!"

"It's a personal letter."

"Oh, Sir is writing personal letters now! Show me! Am I the one who makes the decisions in this house or not?"

She tore the card from her husband's hands as he tried to hide it under his newspaper. The picture on the front was of a puppy. In a sarcastic voice, she read out loud:

Dearest Nola,

We wish you a quick recovery
and hope to see you at Clark's very soon.
We're sending you candy to put some
sweetness back in your life.

Kind regards,
The Quinn family

"What is this crap?" Tamara yelled.

"It's a card for Nola. I'm going to buy her some candy to go with it. She'll like that, don't you think?"

"You're ridiculous, Bobbo! This card with a puppy on the front is ridiculous. What you've written is ridiculous. 'We hope to see you at Clark's very soon.' She's just tried to off herself—do you really think she feels like going back to work? And candy? What do you want her to do with candy?"

"Eat it. I think she'll be pleased. You see, you ruin everything—that's why I didn't want to show you."

"Oh, stop whining," Tamara snapped, tearing the card into pieces. "I'll send her flowers from a nice store in Montburry—not your supermarket candy. And I'll write the note myself, on a tasteful blank card. I will write, in elegant handwriting: 'Wishing you a full recovery. From the Quinn family and Harry Quebert.' Now put your pants on. My guests will be here soon."

Donna Mitchell and her husband rang the doorbell at exactly noon, quickly followed by Amy and Chief Pratt. Tamara signaled to the waiter to bring the welcome cocktails, which they drank in the backyard, where Chief Pratt told them how he had been dragged out of bed by the telephone.

"The Kellergan girl tried to swallow a bunch of pills. I think she swallowed anything and everything, including a few sleeping pills. But nothing too serious. She was taken to the hospital in Montburry to have her stomach pumped. It was her father who found her, in the bathroom. He says she had a fever, and she accidentally took the wrong medicine. I don't know about that, but . . . anyway, the important thing is the kid is O.K."

"It's lucky it happened in the morning and not at noon," Tamara said. "It would have been a shame if you'd not been able to come."

"Speaking of which," Donna said, unable to contain herself any longer, "what is this important news you have to announce?"

Tamara smiled broadly and replied that she would prefer to wait until all the guests had arrived. The Tirstens showed up soon afterward, and the Carltons at 12.20, blaming their tardiness on a steering problem in their new car. Now everyone was there. Everyone except Harry Quebert. Tamara suggested a second welcome cocktail.

"Who are we waiting for?" Donna asked.

"You'll see," Tamara replied.

Jenny smiled; it was going to be a wonderful day.

At 12.40, Harry still hadn't arrived. A third welcome cocktail was served. Then a fourth, at 12.58.

"Another welcome cocktail?" Amy Pratt complained.

"It's because you are very, very welcome," declared Tamara, who was beginning to really worry.

The sun was beating down. Robert groaned that he was hungry, then received a magisterial smack on the back of his neck for his pains. At 1.15, there was still no sign of Harry. Tamara started to feel nauseated.

"We hung around waiting," Tamara told me at the counter at Clark's. "My God, did we hang around! And it was unbearably hot. All the guests were sweating like pigs."

"I'd never been so thirsty in my life," called out Robert, attempting to join the conversation.

"Shut your mouth! I'm the one being questioned, not you. Great writers like Mr Goldman are not interested in jackasses like you."

She threw a fork at him and then turned back to me. "So, anyway, we waited until 1.30."

Tamara was hoping his car had broken down or even that he'd been in an accident. Anything, as long as he wasn't standing them up. Under the pretext of having things to do in the kitchen, she went several times to call the house at Goose Cove, but there was no reply. So she listened to the news on the radio, but there was no mention of any accident, or of any famous writers dying in New Hampshire. Twice, she heard the sound of a car in front of the house, and each time her heart leaped. It was him! But, no, it was just her stupid neighbors.

Eventually the guests could take it no more. Overcome by the heat, they took shelter in the tent, where it was cooler, and then sat in their assigned places amid a deathly silence. "This better be big news," Donna said finally.

"If I drink any more of these cocktails, I think I'm going to throw up," Amy said.

After a while, Tamara asked the waiter to put out the buffet dishes and suggested to her guests that they begin lunch.

By two o'clock the meal was well under way, and still there was no news of Harry. Jenny was too anxious to eat. She was trying not to cry in front of everyone. Tamara was trembling with fury. Two hours late! Clearly he wasn't coming. How the hell could he have done such a thing? What kind of gentleman behaved in such a way? And if that weren't enough, Donna started nagging her to announce this oh-so-important news. Tamara remained mute. Poor Robert, wishing to save the situation and his wife's honor, got up from his chair, solemnly lifted his glass, and declared proudly to the assembled guests: "My dear friends, we would like to announce that we have a new television." There was a long, uncomprehending silence. Tamara, unable to bear the inanity, stood up in turn and announced: "Robert has cancer. He's going to die." Everyone was deeply moved, including Robert himself, who had no idea he was dying and wondered when the doctor had called and why his wife had not told him. Suddenly Robert began to cry, because he would miss being alive. His family, his hometown—he would miss all of it. And they all hugged him, promising that they would visit him in the hospital until his final breath and that they would never forget him.

Harry did not turn up at Tamara Quinn's garden party because he was at Nola's bedside. As soon as Pinkas told him the news, he went straight to the hospital in Montburry. For several hours he stayed in the parking lot, behind the wheel of his car, unsure what to do. He felt guilty: If she had wanted to die, it was because of him. That thought made him also want to kill himself. Overwhelmed, he was now beginning to understand just how deep his feelings were for Nola. When she had been there, close to him, he had been able to convince himself that there was nothing serious between them, and that he had to distance himself from her, but now that he had almost lost her, he could no longer imagine living without her.

It was 5 p.m. when he finally dared enter the hospital. He was hoping he would not see anyone, but in the main lobby he bumped into David Kellergan, his eyes red from crying.

"Reverend . . . I heard about Nola. I am truly sorry."

"Thank you for coming, Harry. You probably heard that Nola tried to commit suicide, but that's just a miserable lie. She had a headache and she picked up the wrong medicine. She often gets distracted, as all children do."

"Of course," Harry replied. "Damn medicines. Which room is Nola in? I'd like to say hi."

"That's good of you, but it's best that she not have too many visitors right now. You don't want to tire her out. I'm sure you understand."

The pastor did, however, have a little notebook with him, which visitors could sign. Having written, *Get well soon. H. L. Quebert*, Harry went back outside to hide in the Chevrolet. He waited another hour, and when he saw Kellergan walking across the parking lot to his car, he returned discreetly to the hospital's main building and asked for directions to Nola's room. Room 26, second floor. He knocked at the door, his heart racing. No reply. He quietly opened the door: Nola was alone, sitting on the edge of the bed. She turned her head. Her eyes lit up at first, and then she looked angry.

"Leave me alone, Harry. Leave me alone, or I'll call the nurse."

"Nola, I can't leave you alone—"

"You've been so horrible. I don't want to see you. It was because of you that I wanted to die."

"Forgive me, Nola."

"I'll forgive you if you want me. Otherwise, leave me in peace."

She stared at him; he looked so sad and guilty that she couldn't help smiling.

"Oh, Harry darling, don't put on that puppy face! Do you promise you won't be horrible anymore?"

"I promise."

"Ask my forgiveness for all those times you left me alone on your porch and wouldn't open the door."

"Please forgive me, Nola."

"Get down on your knees. Kneel down and ask me to forgive you."

He knelt down, not thinking anymore, and placed his head on her bare knees. She leaned over him and caressed his face.

In Somerset the garden party had been over for several hours, and Jenny, locked in her bedroom, was weeping. Robert had tried to comfort her, but she had refused to open the door. Tamara had left the house in a rage, on her way to Harry's house, where she intended to make him answer for his absence. Less than ten minutes after her departure, the Quinns' doorbell rang. It was Robert who opened the door and found Travis Dawn, eyes closed, in uniform, offering him a bunch of roses and breathlessly reciting: "Jenny-would-you-like-to-accompany-me-to-the-summer-gala-please-thank-you."

Robert burst out laughing.

"Hello, Travis. I'm guessing you'd like to speak to Jenny?"

Travis opened his eyes wide and stifled a cry.

"Mr Quinn? I . . . I'm sorry. I'm so pathetic! It's just that I wanted to . . . Well, would you allow me to take your daughter to the gala? If she wants to, of course. Although maybe she already has a date. Is she seeing someone? Oh, I knew it! I'm such an idiot!"

Robert gave Travis a friendly tap on the shoulder.

"Don't despair, son. In fact, your timing could hardly be better. Come in."

He showed the young police officer into the kitchen and took a beer from the fridge.

"Thank you," said Travis, placing his flowers on the countertop.

"No, this is for me. You need something much stronger."

Robert grabbed a bottle of whiskey and poured a double over a few ice cubes.

"Drink that straight down."

Travis obeyed.

"Travis, you look so nervous," Robert observed. "You have to relax. Girls don't like nervous guys. Believe me, I know what I'm talking about."

"I'm usually shy, but when I see Jenny, it's as if my brain freezes. I don't know what's—"

"That's love, son."

"You think?"

"No doubt about it."

"Your daughter is a wonderful girl, Mr Quinn. So gentle, and intelligent, and so beautiful! I don't know if I should tell you this, but sometimes I drive past Clark's just so I can see her through the window. When I look at her . . . when I look at her, my heart feels like it's going to burst out of my chest . . . I feel like my uniform is suffocating me. So . . . that's love?"

"Absolutely."

"And when that happens, I want to get out of the car, walk into Clark's, and ask her how she's doing and if she might, by any chance, like to go to the movies when her shift is over. But I never do it. Is that love too?"

"No, that's just goddamn stupid. That's how you end up not getting the girl you love. You can't be shy. You're young, good-looking. You've got everything you need."

"So what should I do?"

Robert poured him another whiskey.

"I'd like to bring Jenny down, but she's had a difficult afternoon. If you want my advice, drink that and go home. Take off your uniform and put on an ordinary shirt. Then call here and ask Jenny out to dinner. Tell her you feel like having a hamburger at the Denny's in Montburry. She loves it there. You see, your timing is perfect. And on your date, when things are relaxed, suggest going for a walk. You'll sit on a bench together, look up at the stars. You'll show her the constellations . . ."

"The constellations?" Travis said hopelessly. "But I don't know any."

"Just show her the Big Dipper."

"I don't know how to recognize the Big Dipper! Oh, God, I'm screwed!"

"Look, just show her any light in the sky and give it a name. Any name. Women always find it romantic when a guy knows the night sky. Just try not to mix up a shooting star with an airplane. After that, you can ask her if she'd like to be your date at the gala."

"You think she'll agree?"

"I'm sure she will."

"Oh, thank you, Mr Quinn! Thank you so much!"

Having sent Travis home, Robert coaxed Jenny out of her bedroom. They ate ice cream together in the kitchen.

"Now who will I go to the gala with?" Jenny asked miserably. "I'm going to be alone and everyone will make fun of me."

"Jenny, I'm sure there's a whole bunch of guys who would love to take you."

Jenny ate a huge spoonful of ice cream.

"Like who?" she said with her mouth full. "I don't know any."

At that moment, the telephone rang. Robert let his daughter answer it, and heard her say: "Oh, hi, Travis . . . Yes? . . . Yes, I'd love to . . . In thirty minutes? That's perfect. See you then." She hung up and eagerly told her father that her friend Travis had just called to ask her out to dinner in Montburry.

Robert feigned surprise. "You see," he said, "what did I tell you? No way would a girl like you have to go to the gala on her own."

At that moment, in Goose Cove, Tamara was nosing around. She had pounded on the door for a long time, with no response. If Harry was hiding, she was determined to find him, but there was nobody home, and she decided to carry out an inspection of the premises. She began with the living room, then the bedrooms, and, last, Harry's office. She rummaged through the papers on the desk until she found something he had just written:

My Nola, darling Nola, Nola my love. What have you done? Why did you want to die? Is it because of me? I love you. I love you more than anything. Don't leave me. If you die, I die. You are all that matters in my life, Nola.

Tamara put the note in her pocket, determined to destroy Harry Quebert.

19

The Harry Quebert Affair

"Writers who spend all night writing, addicted to caffeine and smoking hand-rolled cigarettes, are a myth, Marcus. You have to be disciplined. It's exactly the same as training to be a boxer. There are exercises to be repeated, at certain times of day. You have to be persistent, you have to maintain a certain rhythm, and your life has to be perfectly ordered. These are the three heads of Cerberus that will protect you from the writer's worst enemy."

"Which is what?"

"The deadline. Do you know what a deadline really means?"

"Tell me."

"It means that your brain, which is capricious by nature, must produce something within a period of time decided by someone else. Just as if you were a deliveryman and your boss demanded that you be at such-and-such address by such-and-such a time, you have to be there, and it doesn't matter if there are traffic jams or if you blow a tire. If you're late, you're fucked. It's exactly the same for the deadlines imposed by your editor. Your editor is both your wife and your boss. Without him, you are nothing, but you can't help hating him. You have to make your deadlines, Marcus. But if you can afford the luxury, ask for an extension. That's so much more fun."

It was Tamara Quinn herself who told me she had stolen the note from Harry's house. She told me the day after our conversation at Clark's. What she told me had piqued my curiosity, so I sought her out at home in order to hear more. She received me in the living room, excited by my interest in her. Mentioning the statement she had made to the police two weeks earlier, I asked how she had known about Harry's relationship with Nola. That was when she told me about her visit to Goose Cove after the garden party.

"That note I found on his desk," she said. "It made me want to throw up."

I realized she had never considered the possibility of a love affair between Harry and Nola.

"Did it ever cross your mind that they might have loved each other?" I asked.

"Loved each other? Come on—don't be ridiculous. Quebert is a pervert, period. I can't imagine for a second Nola would have responded to his advances. God knows he made her suffer for it . . . poor kid."

"So what did you do with the note?"

"I took it with me."

"Why?"

"To destroy Quebert. I wanted him to go to prison."

"Did you tell anyone about it?"

"Of course!"

"Who?"

"Chief Pratt. A couple of days after I found it."

"Only him?"

"I told more people about it when Nola disappeared. Quebert was someone the police needed to investigate."

"So if I understand correctly, you discover that Harry Quebert is infatuated with Nola, and you don't tell anyone but Chief Pratt about it until she disappears, nearly two months later?"

"That's right."

"Mrs Quinn," I said, "from the little I know about you, I find it hard to believe you didn't use what you discovered to hurt Harry as soon as you got the chance, considering how badly you thought he had behaved by not coming to your party. I mean, with all due respect, you seem more the type of person who would photocopy that note and plaster it all over town or put it in your neighbors' mailboxes."

She lowered her eyes.

"You don't understand. I was humiliated. Harry Quebert, the great writer from New York, had rejected my daughter for a fifteen-year-old girl. My daughter! How do you think that made me feel? I had spread the rumor that Harry and Jenny were an item, so imagine what people would have said. And Jenny was in love with him. She would have died, if she'd known. Obviously I decided to keep it to myself. You should have seen my Jenny's face the night of the summer gala. She looked so sad, even though Travis was with her."

"And Chief Pratt? What did he say when you told him?"

"He said he'd look into it. I talked to him again when Nola disappeared. He said it could be something they'd investigate. The problem was that, somewhere in there, the sheet of paper had vanished."

"*Vanished*? How?"

"I kept it in the safe at Clark's. I was the only one with access to it. But then, one day in early August, the page mysteriously vanished. And the evidence against Harry vanished with it."

"Who could have taken it?"

"I have no idea! It's a complete mystery. It was in a huge cast-iron safe, and I had the only key. All the restaurant accounts were inside that safe, along with the money to pay wages and some extra cash for orders. One morning I noticed the note was not there anymore. There was no sign of a break-in. Everything else was there except for that damn piece of paper. I don't have the faintest idea what could have happened."

This was becoming more and more interesting.

"Between you and me, Mrs Quinn," I said, "when you discovered Harry's feelings for Nola, how did you feel?"

"Disgusted. Angry."

"Would you have tried to get vengeance on Harry by sending him anonymous letters?"

"Anonymous letters? Do I look like the kind of person who would do something as pathetic as that?"

I let it go, and went on with my questioning.

"Do you think Nola might have had a relationship with any other men in Somerset?"

She almost spat out her iced tea.

"What is wrong with you? Seriously! She was a nice young girl, really sweet, hardworking, intelligent, always ready to help out. Why would you imagine she was bedding half the town at the age of fifteen?"

"It was just a simple question. Do you know someone named Elijah Stern?"

"Of course," she replied, as though it were obvious. Then she added: "He was the owner before Harry."

"The owner of what?" I asked.

"The house at Goose Cove. It belonged to Elijah Stern, and he used to stay there regularly. It was his family's house, I think. There was a time when we would see him quite often in Somerset. But once he took over his father's affairs in Concord, he no longer had time to come here, so he rented out Goose Cove, before eventually selling it to Harry."

I could not believe it.

"Goose Cove belonged to Elijah Stern?"

"Well, yes. What's the matter with you, Mr Bigshot New Yorker? You suddenly look pale."

At 10.30 a.m. on Monday, June 30, 2008, on the fifty-first floor of the Schmid & Hanson building on Lexington Avenue in New York, Roy Barnaski began his weekly manuscript meeting with Marisa.

"Marcus Goldman had until today to send you his manuscript," she recited.

"I assume you haven't received anything."

"Nothing, Mr Barnaski."

"I figured. I talked to him on Saturday. He is one stubborn son of a bitch. What a waste."

"What should I do?"

"Inform Richardson of the situation. Tell him we're going to take legal action."

Just then Marisa's assistant interrupted the meeting by knocking on the office door. She was holding a piece of paper.

"I know you're in a meeting, Mr Barnaski," she said, "but you've just received an e-mail and I think it's important."

"Who's it from?" Barnaski demanded, visibly annoyed.

"Marcus Goldman."

"Goldman? Give that to me!"

From: m.goldman@nobooks.com
Date: Monday, June 30, 2008—10:24

Dear Roy,
It is not a trashy book that will exploit the scandal in order to sell copies.
It is not a book because you are demanding it.
It is a book because I am a writer. It is a book that will tell a story.
It is a book that will recount the life of someone to whom I owe everything.
Please find attached the opening pages.
If you like it, call me.
If you don't like it, call Richardson, and I'll see you in court.
Have a good meeting with Marisa. Send her my regards.
Marcus Goldman

"Did you print out the attachment?"

"No, Mr Barnaski."

"Go print it now!"

"Yes, Mr Barnaski."

THE HARRY QUEBERT AFFAIR (provisional title)

by Marcus Goldman

In the spring of 2008, about a year and a half after I had become the new star of American literature, something happened that I decided to bury deep in my memory: I discovered that my college professor, Harry Quebert—sixty-seven years old and one of the most respected writers in the country—had been romantically involved with a fifteen-year-old girl when he was thirty-four. This happened during the summer of 1975.

I made this discovery one day in March, while I was staying in Harry's house in Somerset, New Hampshire. While looking through his bookshelves, I came across a letter and some photographs. I had no idea that this would be the prelude to what would become one of the biggest news stories of 2008.

[. . .]

The line of inquiry regarding Elijah Stern was suggested to me by a former classmate of Nola's: Nancy Hattaway, who still lives in Somerset. At the time, Nola admitted to her that she was in a relationship with a businessman from Concord, Elijah Stern, who would send his chauffeur—a certain Luther Caleb—to Somerset to bring her back to his house.

I have no information about Luther Caleb. As for Stern, Sergeant Gahalowood refuses to interrogate him. He believes there is nothing to justify mixing him up in the investigation at this point. So I am going to pay him a visit on my own. Some basic online research tells me that he went to Harvard and that he is still involved with the alumni association. He seems to be an art enthusiast, and is, apparently, well known as a collector. He is clearly a highly respected man. One particularly disturbing coincidence: The house at Goose Cove, where Harry lives, used to belong to Stern.

Those were the first paragraphs I wrote about Elijah Stern. I had just finished writing them when I added them to the rest of the document I sent to Roy Barnaski that morning. I left for Concord immediately afterward, determined to meet Stern and find out what linked him to Nola. I had been driving for thirty minutes when my cell phone rang.

"Hello?"

"Marcus? It's Roy Barnaski."

"Roy! Well, well . . . Did you get my e-mail?"

"Your draft is magnificent, Goldman! I absolutely love it; we're going to do it! I can't wait to find out what happens next."

"I'd be quite interested to know how the story develops myself."

"Write this book, Goldman, and we'll tear up the previous contract."

"I'll do this book, but in my own way. I don't want to hear your squalid suggestions. I don't want any of your ideas and I don't want to be censored."

"Do what you think is right. But this book has to come out in the fall. Since Obama clinched the nomination, his two books have been flying off the shelves. So we have to publish a book on this case as soon as possible, before we're drowned out by election fever. I need your manuscript by the end of August."

"The end of August? That leaves me barely two months."

"Exactly."

"That's not much time."

"So write fast. This is gonna be the biggest book of the fall. Does Quebert know?"

"No. Not yet."

"I'd advise you to tell him. And keep me up to date on your progress."

I was about to hang up when he shouted, "Goldman, wait!"

"What?"

"One thing. What changed your mind?"

"I got threatening letters. Quite a few of them. Someone seems very nervous about what I might discover. So it seemed to me that the truth might be worth writing a book about. For Harry, and for Nola. That's part of a writer's job, isn't it?"

But Barnaski was no longer listening. He was still stuck on what I had said.

"Threatening letters?" he said. "That's great! That'll really help sell the book. Imagine if someone tries to kill you—you could add another zero to the sales figures right away. Two if you actually die!"

"As long as I die after finishing the book."

"That goes without saying. Where are you? The connection is bad."

"I'm on the interstate. I'm going to see Elijah Stern."

"So you really think he's mixed up in this?"

"That's exactly what I'm hoping to find out."

"You're totally crazy, Goldman. That's what I like about you."

Elijah Stern lived in a manor on a hill above Concord. The entrance gates were open, and I drove onto the property. A paved driveway led to a large stone house, surrounded by spectacular flower beds, in front of which—in a courtyard with a fountain of a bronze lion—a uniformed chauffeur was waxing a luxury sedan.

I left my car in the middle of the courtyard, waved casually at the chauffeur as if I knew him well, and went to ring the doorbell in good spirits. A maid opened the door. I gave her my name and asked to see Stern.

"Do you have an appointment?"

"No."

"Then I'm afraid that won't be possible. Mr Stern does not see visitors who don't have an appointment. Who let you come this far?"

"The gates were open. How do I make an appointment?"

"Mr Stern is the one who makes appointments."

"Let me see him for a few minutes. It won't take long."

"That is not possible."

"Tell him I've come on behalf of Nola Kellergan. I think that name will mean something to him."

The maid asked me to wait outside, then quickly returned. "Mr Stern will see you," she said. "You must be someone really important." She led me through the first floor until we reached a wood-paneled office. An elegant man, seated at a desk, looked me up and down with a severe expression.

"My name is Marcus Goldman," I told him. "Thank you for seeing me."

"Goldman the writer?"

"Yes."

"To what do I owe the honor of this unannounced visit?"

"I'm investigating the Kellergan case."

"I didn't know there was anything left to investigate."

"Let's just say there are some unresolved issues."

"Isn't that the work of the police?"

"I'm a friend of Harry Quebert's."

"What does this have to do with me?"

"I heard that you lived in Somerset. That the house at Goose Cove, where Harry lives today, used to belong to you. I wanted to check that that was true."

He motioned for me to sit down.

"You have been informed correctly," he said. "I sold him the house in 1976, just before he became successful."

"So you know Harry?"

"Not well. I met him a few times when he first moved to Somerset. We didn't keep in touch."

"May I ask what your ties are with Somerset?"

He gave me a disagreeable look.

"Is this an interrogation, Mr Goldman?"

"Not at all. I was just curious why someone like you owned a house in a small town like Somerset."

"Someone like me? You mean very rich?"

"Yes. Compared with other towns on the shore, Somerset is not particularly exciting."

"It was my father who had that house built. He wanted somewhere by the ocean that was close to Concord. Somerset is a pretty little town. As a child, I spent many pleasant summers there."

"Why did you sell it?"

"When my father died, my family business became all-consuming. I no longer had time to enjoy the house. So I decided to rent it out, and did so for almost ten years. But there were not many tenants. The house was empty too often. So when Harry Quebert offered to buy it, I accepted right away. I sold it to him for a reasonable price too—I wasn't doing it for the money; I was just happy that it would continue to be lived in. I've always liked Somerset. I used to do a lot of business in Boston, and I would occasionally stop there. I supported their summer gala for many years. And Clark's serves the best hamburgers in the area. Or they did back then, at least."

"What about Nola Kellergan? Did you know her?"

"Vaguely. Everyone in the state heard about her when she disappeared. It's a horrible story. And now they've found her body at Goose Cove. And that book that Quebert wrote for her . . . it's so sordid. Do I regret selling it to him? Yes, of course. But how could I have known?"

"But, technically, when Nola disappeared, you still owned Goose Cove . . ."

"What are you insinuating? That I was mixed up in her death? You know, for the last ten days I've been wondering if Harry Quebert didn't buy that house just so he could be sure that nobody would discover the body buried in the yard."

Stern said he knew Nola vaguely; should I reveal to him that I had a witness who claimed he had been in a relationship with her? I decided to keep that card up my sleeve for now. Nevertheless, in order to provoke him a little, I did mention the name of his former chauffeur.

"What about Luther Caleb?" I said.

"What *about* Luther Caleb?"

"Do you know someone by that name?"

"If you're asking me that, you must already be aware that he was my chauffeur for many years. What kind of game are you playing, Mr Goldman?"

"A witness saw Nola getting into his car several times during the summer she disappeared."

He pointed a finger at me threateningly.

"Don't speak ill of the dead, Mr Goldman. Luther was an honorable, brave, and honest man. I will not allow his name to be sullied when he is no longer here to defend himself."

"He's dead?"

"Yes. He died a long time ago. You will certainly have heard that he was often in Somerset, and that is true: He took care of Goose Cove for me when I was renting it out. He made sure it stayed in perfect condition. He was a good-hearted man, and I will not allow you to insult his memory. Some small-minded rumor-mongers in Somerset will also tell you that he was strange, and it is true that he was different from most people. In every way. His face was badly disfigured, and his jaws did not fit together properly, which made him difficult to understand when he spoke. But he did have a good heart, and he was a very sensitive man."

"You don't think he could have been involved in Nola's disappearance?"

"No. Categorically not. I thought Harry Quebert was guilty. Isn't he in prison right now?"

"I am not convinced of his guilt. That's why I'm here."

"Oh, please—they found that girl buried in his yard and the

manuscript of one of his books with the body. A book he wrote for her . . . what more do you want?"

"Writing is not killing, sir."

"Your investigation must really be getting nowhere if you've come here to ask about my background and about Luther. This interview is over, Mr Goldman."

He summoned the maid to accompany me out.

I left Stern's office with the feeling that the interview had been of no use whatsoever. I wished I could have confronted him with Nancy Hattaway's accusations, but I did not have enough evidence yet. Gahalowood had warned me about this: One witness was not enough, because it was her word against Stern's. I needed some tangible proof. Which made me think I ought to take a quick look around the house.

When we reached the vestibule, I asked the maid if I could use the bathroom. She ushered me to the guest bathroom on the first floor, and indicated that she would wait for me by the front door. As soon as she had gone, I rushed down the corridor to explore the wing of the house in which I found myself. I did not know what I was looking for, but I knew I did not have much time. This was my only chance to find some evidence linking Stern to Nola. Heart pounding, I opened a few doors, praying that the rooms would not be occupied. But the whole place was empty: There was nothing but a series of richly decorated reception rooms. The windows looked out over the beautiful grounds. Listening for the faintest sound, I continued my search. Another door opened onto a small office. I quickly entered, and began opening cabinets. There were files inside, and piles of documents. The ones I looked through were of no interest. I was looking for something . . . but what? Thirty-three years after the murder, what could I hope to stumble upon in this house that would help me? I was running out of time; the maid would undoubtedly go looking for me in the bathroom if I didn't return soon. I finally came to a second corridor and entered that. It led to only one door, which I ventured to open: It gave onto a large veranda surrounded by a jungle of climbing plants that protected it from view. Here I found easels, a few unfinished canvases, paintbrushes scattered on a desk. It was a painter's studio. A series of pictures were hung on the wall, all very good. One of them caught my eye: I immediately recognized the suspension bridge by the sea, just before Somerset. That was when I realized that all these pictures were of Somerset. There was Grand Beach, the main street, even Clark's. The paintings were strikingly authentic. They were all signed L.C., and the dates did not go beyond 1975. And then I noticed another picture, larger than the rest, hung in a corner; there was a chair in front of it, and it was the only one to have its own light. It was a portrait of a young woman. Nothing was shown below the tops of her breasts, but it was clear that she was naked. I moved closer; her face was not unknown to me. I looked at the painting for a moment longer before I suddenly understood, with a quiver of shock. It was a portrait of Nola, no doubt about it. I took a few photographs with my cell phone and then quickly left the room. The maid was shuffling her feet by the front door. I said goodbye to her politely and left, trembling and soaked in sweat.

A half-hour after my discovery, I was in Gahalowood's office. He was furious, of course, that I had gone to see Stern without consulting him.

"You're out of control, writer. Out of control!"

"All I did was pay him a visit," I explained. "I rang the bell, I asked to see him, and he agreed. I don't see what harm was done."

"I'd told you to wait!"

"Wait for what, Sergeant? Your holy blessing? Evidence to fall from the sky? You complained that you didn't want to get on the wrong side of him, so I acted. You complain, I act! And look what I found in his house!"

I showed him the photographs on my cell.

"A painting?" he said disdainfully.

"Look at it more closely."

"My God . . . it looks like . . ."

"Nola! There is a painting of Nola Kellergan in Elijah Stern's house."

I e-mailed the photographs to Gahalowood, who blew them up and printed them.

"It really is her," he said when he had compared the painting with the photographs of her in the case file.

"So there is definitely a link between Stern and Nola," I said. "Nancy Hattaway states that Nola was in a relationship with Stern, and now we've found a portrait of Nola in his studio. And that's not all: Harry's house belonged to Elijah Stern until 1976. Technically Stern was the owner of Goose Cove at the time of Nola's disappearance. Amazing coincidence, huh? So get a warrant and call in the cavalry: We're going to search Stern's house and arrest him."

"A search warrant? Are you nuts? On what grounds? Your photographs? They're illegal. This evidence is inadmissible; you searched a house without authorization. I'm stuck. We need something else to be able go after Stern, and by the time we find anything, he'll surely have gotten rid of the painting."

"Except he doesn't know I've seen it. I asked him about Luther Caleb, and he lost his temper. As for Nola, he claimed to know her only vaguely when in fact there is a half-nude painting of her in his possession. I don't know who painted that picture, but there are others like it in the studio that are signed *L.C.* Luther Caleb, surely?"

"I don't like the direction this investigation is taking, writer. If I go after Stern and I'm wrong, I'm screwed."

"I know."

"Go talk to Harry about Stern. Try to find out more. I'm going to look more closely at Luther Caleb's story. We need solid evidence."

Listening to the car radio on the way from the police headquarters to the prison, I learned that all of Harry's books had been withdrawn from school libraries throughout most of the country. This was the lowest blow so far. In less than two weeks, Harry had lost everything. He was now censored as an author, spurned as a professor, demonized by an entire nation. Irrespective of the outcome of the investigation and the trial, his name was now sullied forever; no-one would ever be able to talk about his works without mentioning the huge controversy surrounding the summer he spent with Nola. This was the intelligentsia's version of a lethal injection.

And, worst of all, Harry was fully aware of the situation. As soon as I entered the visiting room, his first words to me were:

"What if they kill me?"

"Nobody's going to kill you, Harry."

"But I'm already dead, aren't I?"

"No. You're not dead! You're the great Harry Quebert! The importance of knowing how to fall, remember? The important thing is not the fall, because falling is inevitable. The important thing is knowing how to get up again. And we'll get up again."

"You're a good guy, Marcus. But friendship is blinding you to the truth. Ultimately the issue is not whether I killed Nola, or Deborah Cooper, or even John F. Kennedy. It's that I had a relationship with a kid, and that's unforgivable. And that book . . . why the hell did I write that book?"

"We'll get up again," I repeated. "You'll see. You remember that massive beating I took in Lowell, in that boxing ring in the hangar? I never felt better than when I got up from that."

He tried to smile, then asked, "What about you? Have you received any more threatening letters?"

"Let's just say that every time I go back to Goose Cove, I wonder what will be waiting for me."

"Find out who's doing it. Find him and give him the beating of his life. I can't stand the idea that someone is threatening you."

"Don't worry about me."

"What about your investigation?"

"I'm making progress. Harry, I've started writing a book."

"That's fantastic!"

"It's a book about you. I'll write about you, about Burrows. And I'll write about you and Nola. It'll be a love story. I believe in your love story."

"That would be a wonderful tribute."

"So you'll give me your blessing?"

"Of course. You know, you were probably one of my closest friends. I'm flattered to be the subject of your next book."

"Why are you using the past tense? Why did you say I *was* one of your closest friends? We still are, aren't we?"

He looked at me sadly. "I just said it like that."

I grabbed him by the shoulders. "We will always be friends! I won't abandon you. This book is the proof of my unfailing friendship."

"Thank you, Marcus. I'm touched. But friendship shouldn't be the motive behind this book."

"What do you mean?"

"You remember our conversation the day you graduated?"

"Yes. We went for a long walk across campus, then ended up at the boxing gym. You asked what I was planning to do now, and I said I was going to write a book. And then you asked why I wrote. I answered that I wrote because I liked it, and you said . . ."

"Yes, what did I say?"

"That life had very little meaning. And that writing gave life meaning."

"That's it exactly. And that's the mistake you made a few months ago, when Barnaski was demanding a new manuscript. You started writing because you had to write a book, not because you wanted to give your life meaning. Doing something just for the sake of doing it never works. So it isn't surprising that you were incapable of writing a single line. The gift of being able to write is a gift not because you write well, but because you're able to give your life meaning. Every day people are born and others die. Every day, hordes of anonymous workers come and go in tall gray buildings. And then there are writers. Writers live life more intensely than other people, I think. Don't write in the name of our friendship, Marcus. Write because it's the only way to make this tiny, insignificant thing we call *life* into a legitimate and rewarding experience."

I stared at him for a long time. I had the impression I was listening to the master's final lesson, and that was unbearable.

Finally he said: "She loved opera, Marcus. Put that in your book. Her favorite was 'Madame Butterfly.' She said the most beautiful operas were tragic love stories."

"Who? Nola?"

"Yes. This little fifteen-year-old kid was crazy about opera. After her suicide attempt, she spent about two weeks at Charlotte's Hill, which was a psychiatric hospital. I went to visit her secretly. I took her opera recordings that we played on a portable record player. She was moved to tears. She said that if she didn't become a Hollywood actress, she would be a singer on Broadway. You know, Marcus, I think Nola Kellergan could have made her mark on this country."

"Do you think her parents might have killed her?" I said.

"No, that seems unlikely to me. And then the manuscript, and that note in it. Anyway, I find it hard to imagine David Kellergan murdering his daughter."

"But she did have those bruises . . ."

"Those bruises . . . That was a strange story."

"And Alabama? Did Nola talk to you about Alabama?"

"Alabama? That's right—the Kellergans came from Alabama."

"No, there's something else. I think something happened in Alabama, something probably related to their move here. But I don't know what. And I don't know who could tell me."

"I'm sorry, Marcus. I get the impression that the deeper you dig into this case, the more mysteries you discover."

"That's not just an impression. Oh, and I found out that Tamara Quinn knew about you and Nola. She told me that she went to your house the day Nola attempted suicide. She was mad because you didn't show up at her garden party. But you weren't home, so she searched your office. She found a note you'd just written about Nola."

"Now that you mention it, I remember that one of my pages did disappear. I spent a long time searching for it. I thought I'd lost it, which really surprised me at the time because I'd always been so organized. What did she do with it?"

"She said she lost it."

"Was she the one sending the anonymous letters?"

"I doubt it. She never even imagined there was anything between you and Nola. She thought you were just fantasizing about her. Speaking of which, did Chief Pratt question you about Nola's disappearance during the investigation?"

"Chief Pratt? No, never."

This was strange. Why had Chief Pratt never questioned Harry? Tamara said she had told him what she knew.

Next, without mentioning Nola or the painting, I decided to bring up Elijah Stern.

"Stern?" Harry said. "Yes, I know him. He used to own Goose Cove. I bought it from him after I sold *The Origin of Evil*."

"How well do you know him?"

"Not well. I met him a couple of times that summer. The first time was at the gala. We were sitting at the same table. He was a likeable man. I saw him a few times afterward. He was generous. He believed in me. He did a lot for culture. He's a good man."

"When was the last time you saw him?"

"The last time? That must have been at the closing for the house. But why on earth are you asking about him all of a sudden?"

"No reason. By the way, Harry, the gala you're talking about—is that the one that Tamara Quinn was hoping you'd take her daughter to?"

"Yes. I went on my own in the end. What a night that was—I won first prize in the raffle: a weeklong vacation on Martha's Vineyard."

"Did you go?"

"Of course."

That evening, when I got back to Goose Cove, I found an e-mail from Roy Barnaski.

From: rbarnaski@schmidandhanson.com
Date: Monday, June 30, 2008—17:54

Dear Marcus,

The book is great. Further to our phone conversation this morning, please find attached a draft of a contract that I don't think you'll be able to refuse.

Send me more as soon as possible. As I told you, I intend to publish this fall. I think it will be a huge success. I am sure of it, in fact. Warner Brothers has already expressed interest in adapting it into a movie. The movie rights to be negotiated with you, of course.

In the contract, he promised me an advance of two million dollars.

I was awake for a long time that night, my head swirling with all kinds of thoughts. At 10.30 p.m., I got a call from my mother. There was a lot of background noise, and she was whispering.

"Markie! Markie, you'll never guess who I'm with."

"Dad?"

"Yes. But that's not what I mean! Listen: Your father and I decided to go to the city tonight, and we went to an Italian restaurant in Columbus Circle. And who do you think we bumped into in front of the restaurant? Denise! Your secretary!"

"Wow, really?"

"Don't play the innocent! Do you think I don't know what you've done? She told me everything! Everything!"

"Everything about what?"

"About how you sent her packing!"

"I didn't send her packing, Mom. I set her up at Schmid & Hanson. I didn't have anything else to offer her: no more books, no more projects, nothing. I had to help her plan for her future, didn't I? I found her a plum job in the marketing department."

"Oh, Markie, we had a big hug together. She says she misses you."

"Please, Mom . . ."

She whispered some more. I could barely hear her.

"I have an idea, Markie."

"What?"

"You know Solzhenitsyn?"

"The writer? Yes. What does that have to do with me?"

"I saw a documentary about him last night. And what an amazing coincidence that I did! Guess what? He married his secretary. His secretary! And who should I bump into today? Your secretary! It's a sign, Markie! She's not ugly, and, more important, she's full of estrogen! I can tell—women can smell that kind of thing. She's fertile, docile . . . she'd give you a child every nine months! I'll teach her how to raise the children, and that way they'll all be the way I want them to be! Isn't that wonderful?"

"Forget it, Mom. She's not my type—she's too old for me. And in any case she already has a boyfriend. And nobody marries their secretary."

"But Solzhenitsyn did. That means it's O.K.! She was there with a guy, I know, but he's a drip! He smells like supermarket cologne. You're a great writer, Markie. You're Marcus the Magnificent!"

"Marcus the Magnificent was knocked out by Marcus Goldman, Mom. And it was in that moment that I started to live."

"What do you mean?"

"Never mind. But please let Denise eat her dinner in peace."

An hour later, a patrol car stopped by to make sure everything was O.K. There were two cops—very likeable, about my age. I offered them some coffee, and they told me they were going to stay awhile in front of the house. It was a warm night, and I heard them chatting and joking through the open window, sitting on the hood of their car, smoking cigarettes. Listening to them, I suddenly felt very lonely, cut off from the world. I had just been offered a massive amount of money for the publication of a book that would undoubtedly put me back at the forefront of the literary scene; I was leading an existence that was the envy of millions of Americans. But there was something I didn't have: a real life. I had spent the first twenty-eight years of my life fulfilling my ambitions, and I was beginning the next part by attempting to keep those ambitions afloat. Now that I thought about it, I wondered when exactly I would decide just to live. I went on Facebook and scrolled down the list of my thousands of virtual friends; there was not a single one I could call to go for a beer with. I wanted a group of friends whom I could follow the hockey season with and go camping with on weekends; I wanted a girlfriend who could make me laugh and inspire me. I didn't want to be alone anymore.

In Harry's office, I spent a long time looking at the photographs I had taken of the painting; Gahalowood had given me a couple of enlarged prints. Who was the painter? Caleb? Stern? It was a very good painting, in any case. I turned on my minidisc player and listened again to that day's conversation with Harry.

"Thank you, Marcus. I'm touched. But friendship shouldn't be the motive behind this book."

"What do you mean?"

"You remember our conversation the day you graduated?"

"Yes. We went for a long walk across campus, then ended up at the boxing gym. You asked what I was planning to do now, and I said I was going to write a book. And then you asked why I wrote. I answered that I wrote because I liked it, and you said . . ."

"Yes, what did I say?"

"That life had very little meaning. And that writing gave life meaning."

Following Harry's advice, I sat at my computer to write.

Goose Cove, midnight. A light sea breeze enters the room through the open office window. It smells of vacation. Outside, the bright moon illuminates everything.

The investigation is progressing. Or at least Sergeant Gahalowood and I are gradually discovering the extent of our task. I think there's much more to this than a tale of forbidden love, or a sordid case of a runaway girl abducted by a prowler. There are still too many unanswered questions:

- In 1969, the Kellergans leave Jackson, Alabama, where David, the father, has a flourishing congregation. Why?
- Summer 1975: Nola has an affair with Harry Quebert, which will inspire him to write *The Origin of Evil*. But Nola also has a relationship with Elijah Stern, who asks her to pose nude for a painting. Who is she, really? A sort of muse?
- What is the role played by Luther Caleb, who Nancy Hattaway told me used to pick up Nola in Somerset in order to drive her to Concord?
- Apart from Tamara Quinn, who knew about Nola and Harry? Who could have sent Harry those anonymous letters?
- Why did Chief Pratt, who was leading the investigation into Nola's disappearance, not question Harry after hearing Tamara Quinn's revelations? Did he question Stern?
- Who the hell killed Deborah Cooper and Nola Kellergan?
- And who is that elusive shadow attempting to prevent me from telling this story?

EXTRACTS FROM *THE ORIGIN OF EVIL* BY HARRY L. QUEBERT

The tragedy had occurred on a Sunday. She was miserable, and she had tried to kill herself.

Her heart no longer had the strength to keep beating if it was not beating for him. To live, she needed him. Because he had understood that, he came to the hospital every day, in secret, to see her. How could someone so pretty have wanted to kill herself? He blamed himself. It was as if he were the one who had harmed her.

Every day he sat on a bench in the park adjoining the hospital, and secretly waited for the moment when she would come outside to enjoy the sunshine. Then he took advantage of her absence from her room to slip a letter under her pillow.

> *My sweet darling,*
> *You must never die. Angels never die.*
> *See how I am never far from you. Dry your tears, I beg you. I can't bear knowing that you are sad.*
> *I send you kisses to soothe your pain.*

Dear love,

What a surprise to find your note as I went to bed! I am writing to you in secret: We are not allowed to stay up after curfew, and the nurses here are real bitches. But I had to reply as soon as I read your letter. Just to tell you that I love you.

I dream of dancing with you. I would like you to ask me to the summer gala, but I know you don't want to. You say that if they see us together, then that would be the end. I don't think I will be out of here by then, in any case. But

*why live, if we can't love each other? That was the question
that tormented me when I did what I did.*

Eternally yours . . .

My wonderful angel,
*We'll dance together one day. I promise. A day will
come when love will triumph and we'll be able to love each
other openly. And we'll dance, we'll dance on the beach.
Just as we did on the day we first met.*

Dear love,
Dancing on the beach. That is all I dream about.
*Tell me we will dance on the beach one day, just you
and me . . .*

18

Martha's Vineyard
(Massachusetts, Late July, 1975)

"In our society, Marcus, the most admired men are those who build bridges, skyscrapers, and empires. But in reality, the proudest and most admirable are those who manage to build love. Because there is no greater or more difficult undertaking."

She danced on the beach. She played in the waves and ran on the sand, the wind blowing her hair. She laughed. She was so happy to be alive. From the hotel balcony, Harry watched her for a moment, then went back to the pages that covered the table. He had written forty or fifty pages since they had gotten here. He was writing fast, and well. It was thanks to her, to Nola, darling Nola. Finally he was writing his great novel. A love story.

"Harry," she called up to him, "take a break! Let's go swimming!" Deciding he could interrupt his work, he went up to their room, where he put away the pages in his briefcase and put on his bathing suit. He joined her on the beach, and they walked along the shore away from the hotel and the other guests. They crossed a line of rocks and found themselves in a remote cove. He held her and she clung tightly to his neck. Then they dived into the ocean and splashed around happily before drying themselves in the sun, stretched out on the large white hotel towels. She placed her head on his chest.

"This is the most wonderful vacation of my life," Harry said.

Nola's face lit up.

"Let's take a picture! That way, we'll never forget! Did you bring your camera?"

He took the camera from his bag and handed it to her. She squeezed against him, held the camera out at arm's length and, just before pressing the button, she gave him a lingering kiss on the cheek. They laughed.

"I think this will be a beautiful picture," she said. "You must keep it with you all your life."

"All my life. It will always be with me."

They had been there for four days.

Two weeks earlier

It was the third Saturday in July, the traditional day of the summer gala. For the third consecutive year, it took place not in Somerset but at the Montburry Country Club, the only venue worthy of hosting such an event, in the opinion of Amy Pratt, who—since taking the helm—had strived to make it an evening of great standing. She had stopped using Somerset High School's gymnasium, dropped the buffet in favor of a sit-down dinner with assigned seating, made it mandatory for men to wear ties, and introduced a raffle between the end of dinner and the beginning of dancing as a way to liven up the atmosphere.

In the months leading up to the gala, Amy Pratt could be seen around town selling her raffle tickets at top dollar; nobody refused to buy them, for fear of being given a bad table. According to some, the considerable proceeds from the ticket sales went straight into her pocket, but no-one dared to speak openly of this; it was essential to remain on good terms with her. Apparently one year she had deliberately neglected to designate a seat to a woman with whom she had had a disagreement. When it came time to eat, the lady found herself standing in the middle of the room.

Harry had decided not to go to the gala. He had bought his ticket a few weeks earlier, but now he was no longer in the mood to go out; Nola was still in the hospital, and he was miserable. He wanted to be alone. But on the morning of the gala, Amy Pratt came over and hammered at his door. It had been days since she had seen him in town; he no longer went to Clark's. She wanted to make sure he was not going to leave her in the lurch. He absolutely had to be at the gala—she had told everyone he would be there. This was the first time that a major New York luminary was going to attend, and—who knew?—perhaps next year Harry would return with the cream of show business. And, a few years from now, all of Hollywood and Broadway would come to New Hampshire to be seen at what would have become one of the most sought-after events on the East Coast. "You are coming tonight, Harry, aren't you? You will be there, won't you?" she had whined, while wriggling her body on his front porch. She had begged him, and he had finally agreed to go—mainly because he didn't know how to say no—and she had even managed to palm off fifty dollars' worth of raffle tickets on him.

Later that day he went to see Nola. On the way, he stopped off at a store in Montburry to buy more opera records. He couldn't help himself; he knew that music made her so happy. But he was spending too much money, and he couldn't go on like this. He didn't dare imagine the state of his bank account; his savings were going up in smoke, and at this rate he would soon not have enough money to pay the rent on the house for the rest of the summer.

At the hospital, the two of them took a walk on the grounds, and, hidden in a copse of trees, they embraced.

"Harry, I want to leave."

"The doctors say you can get out of here in a few days."

"You don't understand: I want to leave Somerset. With you. We will never be happy here."

"One day," he replied.

"One day, what?"

"We'll leave together one day."

Her face brightened.

"Really? Harry, are you serious? Will you take me far from here?"

"A long, long way. And we'll be happy."

"We'll be so happy!"

She held him tightly.

"Tonight's the gala," she said.

"Yes."

"Are you going?"

"I don't know. I promised Amy Pratt, but I'm not in the mood."

"Oh, please go! I've always dreamed of going. Ever since we moved here, I've dreamed that someone would take me. But I will never go . . . Mom won't let me."

"What would I do at the gala on my own?"

"You won't be alone, Harry. I'll be there with you, inside your head. We'll dance together! No matter what happens, I'll always be inside your head."

Upon hearing those words, he became angry.

"What do you mean, 'No matter what happens'? What are you implying?"

"Nothing—don't get angry with me. All I meant was that I'll always love you."

So for the sake of Nola's love, he grudgingly went to the gala. He had barely arrived before he regretted his decision: He felt ill at ease amid the crowds of people. To give himself a semblance of composure, he sat at the bar and ordered a martini, and then another, while watching the guests arrive. The room filled quickly, and the hubbub of conversation grew louder. He felt sure that everyone was staring at him, as if they all knew he loved a fifteen-year-old girl. Feeling shaky, he went to the bathroom, where he splashed water on his face and then locked himself in a stall and sat on the toilet to collect himself. He took a deep breath. He had to stay calm. Nobody could know about him and Nola. They had always been so careful and discreet. There was no reason to worry. Just act naturally. He felt his guts untwist. He opened the stall door, and it was at that moment that he discovered these words scrawled in red lipstick on the mirror above the sink:

PEDOPHILE SCUM

Panic-stricken, he gasped, looked all around him, and pushed at all the stall doors: nobody. The bathroom was deserted. He hurriedly grabbed a paper towel, soaked it with water, and rubbed at the lipstick words, which were transformed into a long, greasy red smear on the mirror. Then he sneaked out of the bathroom, afraid of being seen. Battling nausea, his forehead coated with sweat and his pulse beating in his temples, he went back to the ballroom, trying to act as if nothing had happened. Who knew about him and Nola?

Dinner had been announced, and the guests were heading toward their tables. A hand gripped his shoulder, and he jumped. It was Amy Pratt. He was sweating profusely.

"Is everything O.K., Harry?" she asked.

"Yes . . . Yes . . . I'm just a little hot."

"I put you at the head table. Come with me—it's just over here."

She guided him to a large table decorated with flowers, where a man in his forties was already seated, looking bored.

"Harry Quebert," declared Amy Pratt ceremoniously, "allow me to present Elijah Stern, who generously funds this gala. It is thanks to him that the raffle tickets are so cheap. He is also the owner of the house you're renting at Goose Cove."

Elijah Stern offered his hand with a smile, and Harry laughed. "So you're my landlord, Mr Stern?"

"Call me Elijah. It's a pleasure to meet you."

When the main course was over, the two men went outside to smoke a cigarette and take a short walk around the grounds.

"Are you happy with the house?" Stern asked.

"Extremely happy. It's a beautiful place."

His cigarette butt glowing red, Stern grew nostalgic as he told Harry how the house at Goose Cove had been his family's vacation home for many years. His father had ordered its construction because his mother suffered from migraines and the doctor told her that the ocean air would help.

"When my father saw this plot of land by the ocean, he fell in love with it immediately. He bought it without a second's thought, with the intention of building a house on it. He drew up the plans himself. We spent so many great summers there. But time goes by, and now my father is dead, my mother has moved to California, and there's no-one left to live at Goose Cove. I love that house; I even had it renovated a few years ago. But I'm not married, I don't have children, and I hardly ever have time to enjoy it; it's too big for me anyway. So I decided to rent it out. I couldn't bear the idea of its being unoccupied and falling into disrepair. I'm happy that someone like you is living there."

Stern explained how as a child he had attended his first dances and experienced his first loves in Somerset. Ever since then, he had made a point of coming back here once a year—for the gala—in memory of those years.

They each lit another cigarette and sat together on a stone bench.

"So what are you working on at the moment, Harry?"

"A novel. A love story. Well, I'm trying to work on it anyway. You know, everyone here seems to think I'm some sort of famous writer, but that's just a misunderstanding." Harry knew Stern was not the kind of man to be easily fooled.

"People here are very impressionable," Stern said. "You only have to look at the turn for the worse this gala has taken. So . . . a love story?"

"Yes."

"How far have you gotten?"

"I'm just beginning. To tell the truth, I'm not managing to write anything."

"That's unfortunate for a writer. Is something bothering you?"

"You could say that."

"Are you in love?"

"Why do you ask?"

"Out of curiosity. I was wondering if you had to be in love in order to write a love story. Anyway, I am always very impressed by writers. Perhaps because I would have liked to be a writer myself. Or an artist of any kind. I have an unconditional love for painting. But unfortunately I have very little artistic talent. What's the title of your book?"

"I don't have one yet."

"And what kind of love story is it?"

"A story of forbidden love."

"That sounds really interesting," Stern said. "We'll have to meet up again sometime."

At 9.30 p.m., after dessert, Amy Pratt announced the drawing of the raffle, presided over, as always, by her husband. Chief Pratt read out the winning numbers one by one, his mouth too close to the microphone. All the prizes, most provided by local businesses, were fairly cheap and unappealing—except for the top prize, the drawing of which provoked a great deal of excitement: It was an all-expenses-paid one-week stay for two people at a luxury hotel on Martha's Vineyard. "Your attention, please," bellowed Chief Pratt. "The winner of the first prize is . . . listen carefully . . . ticket number one-three-eight-five!" There was a brief silence, and then Harry, realizing he had the winning ticket, stood up in surprise. There was a roar of applause, and several guests came up to congratulate him. He was the center of attention for the rest of the evening: Nobody had eyes for anyone but him. But he had eyes for nobody, because the center of his attention was sleeping, at that moment, in a small hospital room fifteen miles away.

As Harry was leaving, he ran into Elijah Stern in the cloakroom.

Stern smiled. "First prize in the raffle. Seems like you're a naturally lucky guy."

"Yeah. And to think I almost didn't buy a ticket."

"Do you need me to take you somewhere?" Stern asked.

"Thank you, Elijah, but I have my car."

They walked to the parking lot together. A black sedan was waiting for Stern, with a man standing beside it, smoking a cigarette. Stern indicated him and said, "Harry, I'd like you to meet my right-hand man. Actually, unless you would rather I didn't, I was planning on sending him to Goose Cove to take care of the rosebushes. It'll be time to prune them soon, and he's a talented gardener, unlike the idiots sent by the rental agency who let all my plants die last year."

"That's fine, Elijah. Please do whatever you like."

As he approached the man, Harry noticed his dreadful appearance: His body was huge and muscular, his face twisted and scarred. He greeted him with a handshake.

"I'm Harry Quebert."

"Good evening, Mifter Quebert," the man replied, his speech halting and difficult to follow. "My name iv Lufer Caleb."

Speculation swept Somerset the day after the gala: Who would Harry Quebert take with him to Martha's Vineyard? Nobody had ever seen him with a woman. Did he have a girlfriend in New York? A movie star, perhaps? Or would he take a young woman from Somerset? Had he already made a conquest here, so discreetly that no-one had noticed? Would her name and picture appear in one of those celebrity magazines?

The only person not thinking about the vacation was Harry himself. On Monday morning, July 21, he was at home, sick with worry. Who knew about him and Nola? Who had followed him into the bathroom? Who had dared besmear the mirror with those vile words? In lipstick . . . so it was definitely a woman. But who? To distract himself, he sat at his desk and concentrated on putting his pages in order. For the past week, his pages had been accumulating in a jumble on his desk, but he always numbered them, according to a very precise chronological code, so that he could file them afterward. Having put them in order, he realized that one of them was missing. He recalled it clearly: It was a page about Nola, written the day of her suicide attempt. He went through his papers twice and emptied his satchel, but it was nowhere to be found. It was impossible. He had always made sure to check that he left nothing on the table at Clark's. At Goose Cove, he mostly wrote in his office, and if he sat on the deck, he always brought back to his office whatever he had written. There was no way he could have lost that page . . . so where was it? Having searched the house in vain, he began to wonder whether someone had come in search of compromising evidence against him. The same person who had written those words on the bathroom mirror? The thought made him feel so ill that he almost threw up.

Nola was able to leave Charlotte's Hill that day. She went to Goose Cove to see Harry almost immediately after returning home. He was on the beach, with his tin box of stale bread. As soon as she saw him, she threw herself into his arms. He lifted her in the air and swung her around.

"Oh, Harry! I missed it so much, being here with you!"

He held her as tightly as he dared.

"Nancy told me you won first prize at the raffle."

"Yes! Can you believe it?"

"A vacation for two on Martha's Vineyard! When is it for?"

"I can choose the dates. All I have to do is call the hotel to make a reservation."

"Will you take me with you? Oh, Harry, take me with you so we can be happy together without having to hide!"

He didn't reply. They walked a little farther along the beach, watching the waves crash onto the sand.

"Where do the waves come from?"

"From far away," Harry said. "They come a long way to see the shores of America, and then they die."

He stared at Nola and, suddenly overcome by anger, took her face in his hands.

"For God's sake, Nola! Why did you want to die?"

"It's not about wanting to die. It's about not being able to live anymore."

"But don't you remember that day on the beach, after your school show, when you told me not to worry because you were there? How will you watch over me if you kill yourself?"

"I know, Harry. I'm sorry. Please forgive me."

And on that beach where they met and fell in love, she got down on her knees to beg for forgiveness. And again, she said: "Take me with you, Harry. Take me to Martha's Vineyard." In the euphoria of the moment, he promised he would. But, later, when he watched her heading home along the path that led from Goose Cove, he realized he could not take her with him. It was impossible. Someone already knew about them; if they went off together, the whole town would know. He would go to prison. If she asked him again, he would postpone the trip. He would postpone it indefinitely.

The next day he went back to Clark's for the first time in a long time. Jenny was serving, as usual. Her eyes lit up when she saw Harry: He had returned. Was it because of the gala? Had he been jealous to see her with Travis? Did he want to take her to Martha's Vineyard? If he went there without her then that would mean he did not love her. This question was so urgent in her mind that she asked him before she even took his order: "Who are you going to take to Martha's Vineyard, Harry?"

"I don't know," he replied. "Maybe no-one. Maybe I'll make use of the time to work on my book."

She frowned. "It would be a waste to go to such a beautiful place alone."

She was secretly hoping he would reply, "You're right, Jenny, my love. Let's go together and kiss beneath the setting sun." But all he said was: "Can I get some coffee, please?" And Jenny, the slave, obeyed. At that moment, Tamara Quinn emerged from her office in the back of the restaurant, where she had been doing the accounts. Seeing Harry seated at his usual table, she rushed over to him and, without even a hello, told him in a voice full of rage and bitterness: "I've just been looking over the accounts. We're not going to offer you any more credit, Mr Quebert."

"I understand," Harry said, wishing to avoid a scene. "I'm sorry about your invitation last Sunday . . . I—"

"I am not interested in your excuses. I received your flowers, which went straight into the garbage. I would like you to pay what you owe here before the end of the week."

"Of course. Please give me the bill. I'll pay you immediately."

She brought him the itemized bill and he almost choked when he saw it. He owed Clark's more than five hundred dollars. He had been spending without counting: five hundred dollars in food and drinks, thrown away, just so he could be with Nola. In addition to this bill, he also received, the next morning, a letter from the rental agency. He had already paid the first half of his stay at Goose Cove, which took him until the end of July. The letter informed him that there was still a thousand dollars to pay for the use of the house until September. But he didn't have a thousand dollars. He had hardly any money at all. Once he had paid Clark's, he would be completely broke. What should he do? Call Elijah Stern and explain the situation to him? But what was the point? He had not written the great novel he had dreamed of writing. He was nothing but a phony.

Having given it some thought, he called the hotel on Martha's Vineyard. He knew what he was going to do: give up the house, put an end to this masquerade. He would leave for a week with Nola so they could be together one last time, and afterward he would disappear. The desk clerk told him there was one room available for the week of July 28 to August 3. That was what he had to do.

Having made the reservation, he called the rental agency. He explained that he had received their letter but, due to a stroke of misfortune, he had no choice but to go back to New York. So he asked them to terminate the rental contract starting August 1, and he managed with the greatest difficulty to persuade the rental agent—citing practical reasons—to let him have the house until Monday, August 4, at which date he would return the keys directly to the agency's Boston branch, on his way to New York. As he spoke on the telephone, he felt the sobs rising in his throat. So this was how his tale was ending, with the supposedly great novelist Harry Quebert incapable of writing three lines of the masterpiece he had once dreamed of creating. He was on the verge of breaking down, but before hanging up he managed to say, "That's perfect. I will drop off the keys at your office on August 4, on my way back to New York." Then, having replaced the receiver, he jumped when he heard a hoarse voice behind him say, "You're leaving, Harry?" It was Nola. She had come into the house unannounced. There were tears in her eyes.

"You're leaving?" she said again. "What's going on?"

"Nola . . . I have problems."

She hurried over to him.

"What problems? You can't leave! Harry, you can't leave!"

"Nola . . . I have to tell you something. I'm not a famous writer. I lied about everything. About myself, about my career. I don't have any money left. I can't afford to stay in this house any longer. I can't stay here."

"We'll find a solution! I know you're going to become a famous writer. You're going to make lots of money! Your first book was wonderful, and this book that you're working so hard on—it will be a huge success; I'm sure of it!"

"This book is a monstrosity, Nola. It's full of horrible words."

"What horrible words?"

"Words I shouldn't have written. But it's because of the love I feel."

"Then make them beautiful! Work on them! Write beautiful words!"

She took him by the hand and sat him down on the deck. She brought him his papers, his notebooks, his pens. She made coffee, put on an opera record, and opened the living room windows so he would hear it properly. She knew that music helped him concentrate. Obediently he pulled himself together and set to work, starting all over again; he was going to write as if his relationship with Nola were a possibility. He wrote for two hours, the words coming unprompted, perfectly formed sentences pouring naturally from his pen as it danced upon the paper. For the first time since he had been in Somerset, he felt as if his novel were truly being born.

When he lifted his eyes from the page, he noticed that Nola—sitting in a wicker chair, set back so as not to disturb him—had fallen asleep. The sunlight was glorious, the air hot. And suddenly it seemed to him, with this novel, with Nola, with this house by the sea, that his life was a wonder. It even seemed to him that leaving Somerset was not a bad thing: He would finish his novel in New York, he would become a great writer, and he would wait for Nola. Leaving did not mean he had to lose her. Quite the opposite, perhaps. Once she had finished high school, she could go to college in New York. And they would be together. Until then they would write to each other, and see each other during the holidays. The years would pass, and soon their love would no longer be forbidden. Gently, he woke Nola. She smiled at him and stretched.

"How's your writing going?"

"Really well."

"That's wonderful, Harry! Can I read it?"

"Soon. I promise."

A flock of seagulls flew over the water.

"Don't forget the seagulls. You have to put seagulls in your novel."

"There'll be seagulls on every page, Nola. What would you think about coming to Martha's Vineyard with me? There's a room available next week."

She beamed.

"Yes! Let's go! Let's go together."

"But what will you tell your parents?"

"Don't worry about that, darling Harry. I'll take care of my parents. You just concentrate on your writing. So, are you going to stay?"

"No, Nola. I have to leave at the end of the month. I can't pay for this house anymore."

"The end of the month? But that's now."

"I know."

Her eyes welled up with tears.

"New York isn't far. You can come and visit me. We'll write to each other. We'll talk on the phone. And why not go to college there? You told me you had dreamed of seeing New York."

"College? But that's three years away!"

"Don't worry. The time will pass quickly. Time flies when you're in love."

"Don't leave me, Harry. I don't want Martha's Vineyard to be our farewell trip."

"Nola, I don't have any more money. I can't stay here."

"Please—we'll find a solution. Do you love me?"

"Yes."

"So there you go. If we love each other, we'll find a way. People who love each other always find a way to go on loving each other. Promise to at least think about it."

"Alright, I promise."

They went away one week later, at dawn on Monday, July 28, without ever having talked again about the departure that, in Harry's mind, was inevitable. Harry blamed himself for getting swept away by his dreams of greatness. How could he have been so naive as to expect to write a great novel in the space of a single summer?

They met at four in the morning, in the marina parking lot. Somerset was sleeping. They drove as far as Boston, making good time. There they ate breakfast. Then they continued directly to Falmouth, where they took the ferry. It was mid-morning when they arrived on Martha's Vineyard. From then on, they lived as if in a dream, in that beautiful hotel by the ocean. They swam, they walked, they ate together in the hotel's large dining room, and nobody looked at them or asked them any questions. On Martha's Vineyard, they were able to live.

They had been there for four days. Stretched out on the hot sand, in their cove, sheltered from the world, they thought of nothing but the happiness they felt at being together. She played around with the camera, and he thought about his book.

She'd told Harry that her parents believed she was at a friend's house, but she'd lied. She'd run away. It would have been too complicated to justify a whole week's absence, so she'd escaped through her bedroom window at dawn. And while she and Harry were relaxing on the beach, David Kellergan was agonizing in Somerset. On Monday morning he'd found her bedroom empty. He hadn't notified the police. First she'd attempted suicide, and now she'd run away; if he told the police, everyone would know. He decided to give himself seven days to find her. Seven days, as the Lord had made the week. He spent them in his car, crisscrossing the area. He feared the worst. After seven days, he would leave it to the authorities.

Harry didn't suspect a thing. He was blinded by love. Perhaps that was also why, the morning they left for Martha's Vineyard, when Nola met him at dawn in the marina parking lot, he didn't see the figure lurking in the darkness, watching them.

They returned to Somerset on the afternoon of Sunday, August 3. As they crossed the border between Massachusetts and New Hampshire, Nola began to cry. "Don't go, Harry. Don't leave me here." She told him that he'd worked so well on his book in the past few days that he couldn't risk losing his inspiration. "I'll look after you," she said, "and you won't have to do anything but concentrate on your writing. You're writing a wonderful novel—it would be wrong of you to ruin everything." And she was right: She was his muse, his inspiration, the reason he was able to write so well. But it was too late; he no longer had enough money to pay for the house. He had to leave.

He dropped Nola a few blocks from her house, and they kissed one last time. Her cheeks were covered in tears. She held on to him tightly to stop him from leaving.

"Tell me you'll still be here in the morning!"

"Nola, I . . ."

"I'll bring you warm bread, I'll make you coffee. I'll take care of everything. I will be your wife, and you will be a great writer. Tell me you'll be here . . ."

"I'll be here."

Her expression was suddenly radiant.

"Really?"

"I'll be here. I promise."

"Promising is not enough, Harry. Swear it! Swear in the name of our love that you won't leave me."

"I swear it, Nola."

He lied because it was too difficult. As soon as she disappeared around the corner, he drove quickly back to Goose Cove. He had to move fast; he didn't want to risk her coming to see him and catching him in the act of escaping. By that evening he would be in Boston. Once inside he hurriedly gathered his belongings. He crammed his suitcases into the trunk of his car and threw everything else he had in the backseat. Then he closed the shutters and turned off the lights. And he ran away. He ran away from love.

He wanted to leave her a message. He scrawled a few lines—*Darling Nola, I had to leave. I will write to you. I love you forever*—on a scrap of paper he jammed in the door frame, and then removed, out of fear that someone else might find it. So, no message—that was safer. He locked the door behind him, got in his car, and drove off. He fled as fast as he could. Goodbye, Goose Cove. Goodbye, New Hampshire. Goodbye, Nola.

It was over, forever.

17

Escape Attempt

"You should prepare for your writing as you prepare for a boxing match, Marcus: In the days leading up to the fight, you should be training at only seventy per cent so the rage that explodes on the day of the match has been allowed to slowly simmer and rise within you."

"What does that mean?"

"That when you have an idea, rather than immediately turning it into one of your unreadable stories and publishing it on the first page of your magazine. You should not let it out. You should nurture it inside you to allow it to ripen until you feel it's the right moment. This will be number—where are we now?"

"Eighteen."

"No, we're at seventeen."

"So why ask me, if you already know?"

"To see if you're paying attention."

"Alright: number seventeen, Harry. Turn your ideas . . ."

" . . . into illuminations."

In the visitors' room of the New Hampshire state prison on Tuesday, July 1, 2008, I listened, rapt, as Harry told me that on the evening of August 3, 1975, as he was about to leave Somerset, just as he got onto Shore Road, he passed a car coming the other way, and it instantly did a U-turn and sped after him.

Sunday evening—August 3, 1975

For a moment he thought it was a police car, but it had no siren or flashing light. A car was hot on his heels, honking its horn, and he had no idea why. Suddenly he was afraid he was going to be held up. He stepped on the gas, but his pursuer managed to pass him and force him to come to a stop on the shoulder by swerving in front of him. Harry leaped out of his car, ready to fight, before recognizing Stern's chauffeur, Luther Caleb, as he got out of the other car.

"You're out of your mind!" Harry yelled.

"Pleave excuve me, Mifter Quebert. I didn't mean to fcare you. But Mifter Ftern defperately wantf to fee you. I've been fearching for you for feveral dayv now."

"What does Mr Stern want?"

Harry was trembling, his blood pumping furiously through his veins.

"I have no idea, fir," Luther said. "But he faid it wav important. He've waiting for you at hiv houfe."

Harry grudgingly agreed to follow Luther to Concord. Night was falling. They drove until they reached Stern's vast property, where Caleb, without a word, guided Harry through the house to a wide terrace. Stern was sitting at a table, wearing a light bathrobe and drinking lemonade. As soon as he saw Harry, he stood up to greet him, visibly relieved.

"I was starting to think I would never manage to find you! Thank you for coming here at such a late hour. I called you at the house, I sent Luther to look for you every day. But there was no sign of you. Where on earth were you hiding?"

"I was out of town. What's so important?"

"I know everything! And you wanted to keep me in the dark?"

Harry felt himself weaken. So Stern knew about Nola.

"Wh—what are you talking about?" he stammered, playing for time.

"The house at Goose Cove, of course! Why didn't you tell me you were going to have to give it up? The agency told me you were returning the keys tomorrow, so you can understand why it was so urgent that I speak to you. I think it's such a shame that you're leaving. I don't need the money from renting out the house, and I would like to support your writing. I want you to stay at Goose Cove while you finish your novel. What do you think? You told me the place inspired you, so why leave? I've already arranged everything with the agency. If you enjoy being in that house, then stay a few months longer. I would be very proud to have contributed to the creation of a great novel. Please don't refuse. I don't know many writers . . . I have my heart set on helping you."

Harry sighed with relief and collapsed into a chair. He instantly accepted Elijah Stern's offer. It was an unhoped-for opportunity: being able to stay in the house for a few more months, being able to finish his novel with Nola's inspiration. If he lived frugally, he should be able to make ends meet. He stayed with Stern for a while on the terrace, talking literature. He felt obligated to be polite to his benefactor, but all he wanted was to drive back immediately to Somerset so he could find Nola and tell her he had found a solution. Then he worried that maybe she had already paid an impromptu visit to Goose Cove. Had she found the door locked? Had she discovered that he had run away, that he had been ready to abandon her? The thought made him anxious, and after allowing a decent amount of time to pass, he made his excuses and left, driving at top speed back to Goose Cove. He hurriedly unlocked the house, opened the shutters, turned on the lights, put all his belongings back in their place, and covered up all traces of his escape attempt. Nola must never know.

*

"So that's how I was able to remain at Goose Cove and finish my novel," Harry told me. "And in the weeks that followed, that's all I did: write. I wrote like a madman, I wrote in a fever, I wrote so much that I lost all sense of morning and evening, of hunger and thirst. I wrote without stopping, I wrote until my eyes hurt, until my wrists and head hurt, until everything hurt. I wrote until I wanted to throw up. For three weeks I wrote night and day. And that whole time, Nola looked after me. She came to check that I was O.K., made sure I was eating, made sure I was sleeping, and whenever she saw that I couldn't write anymore, she took me out for a walk. She was discreet, invisible, omnipresent. Thanks to her, everything was possible. And best of all, she typed up my hand-written pages on a portable Remington. She often took a section of the manuscript home with her. Without asking me. The next day, she would tell me what she thought. She often went into rhapsodies. She told me it was a magnificent novel, that it was the greatest thing she had ever read. With her wide eyes full of love, she made me feel ten feet tall."

"What did you say to her about the house?" I asked.

"That I loved her more than anything, that I wanted to stay near her, and that I had come to an arrangement with my bank that enabled me to continue renting Goose Cove. It was thanks to her that I was able to write that book, Marcus. I no longer went to Clark's; I was hardly ever seen in town. She looked after me and took care of everything. She even told me I couldn't go shopping on my own because I didn't know what I needed, so we went shopping together in supermarkets far from Somerset, where nobody would bother us. Whenever she discovered that I had skipped a meal or eaten a bar of chocolate for dinner, she would be angry with me. I loved it when she was angry . . . I wish she could have gone on being sweetly angry with me throughout all my books, all my life."

"So you really did write *The Origin of Evil* in a few weeks?"

"Yes. I was possessed by a kind of creative fever that I have never experienced since. Was it powered by love? Undoubtedly. I think that when Nola disappeared, part of my talent disappeared with her. Now you understand why I beg you not to worry when you feel uninspired."

A guard came in and told us that time was almost up.

"So you said Nola took the manuscript with her?" I said quickly, trying not to lose the thread of our conversation.

"She took home the parts she had typed up. She reread them and gave me her opinion. Marcus, that month—August, 1975—was paradise. I was so happy. We were so happy. But in spite of that, I remained haunted by the idea that someone knew about us. Someone who was capable of scrawling obscenities on a mirror. That same someone might easily spy on us from the woods and see everything. The thought made me sick."

"Is that why the two of you wanted to leave? I mean, when you arranged to elope, the night of August 30—why did you do that?"

"That was because something awful happened. Are you recording this?"

"Yes."

"I'm going to tell you about a very serious incident, so that you'll understand. But no-one else can know about it."

"You can trust me."

"You know, for our week on Martha's Vineyard, instead of saying she was with a friend, Nola had simply run away. She left without saying a word to anyone. When I saw her again the day after our return, she was terribly upset. She told me her mother had beaten her, and indeed her body was covered in bruises. That day, she told me her mother often punished her for nothing. That she hit her with a metal ruler, and also did a really terrible thing: She filled a bowl with water, took her daughter by her hair, and forced her head underwater. Just like they do to terrorist suspects. She said it was to deliver her."

"Deliver her?"

"Deliver her from evil. A kind of baptism, I imagine. Jesus in the Jordan River, or something like that. At first I couldn't believe it, but the evidence was there. So I asked her why her father didn't intervene, and she said he locked himself in the garage and played music very loud whenever her mother punished her. He didn't want to hear, she said. Nola couldn't take it anymore—she'd had enough. I wanted to go see the Kellergans, to deal with this problem, to put an end to it, but Nola begged me not to. She told me she would get in terrible trouble, that her parents would move away, and that we would never see each other again. But still, this couldn't be allowed to continue. So toward the end of August— around the twentieth—we decided we had to leave. Soon. And secretly, of course. We were going to go to British Columbia, maybe, and live in a cabin. Have a simple life by the edge of a lake. Nobody would ever have known."

"So that's why you decided to elope?"

"Yes."

"But why don't you want anyone to know this?"

"That's only the beginning of the story. Soon afterward I made a terrible discovery about Nola's mother—"

At that moment we were interrupted by the guard again. The visit was over.

"Let's finish this conversation next time, Marcus," Harry said, standing up. "But in the meantime, keep it to yourself."

"Sure. But just tell me this: What would you have done with the book if you'd eloped?"

"I would have been a writer in exile. Or not a writer at all. At that point, it no longer mattered. Only Nola mattered. Nola was my world. Nothing else was important."

I was dumbstruck. So that was the insane plan Harry had devised thirty-three years earlier: eloping to Canada with this girl he had fallen madly in love with. Leaving with Nola, and living a secret life by the edge of a lake, never suspecting that on the night they had arranged to flee, Nola would disappear and be murdered, nor that the book he had written in record time, and was prepared to give up, would go on to be one of the greatest publishing successes of the last fifty years.

In a second interview Nancy Hattaway gave me her version of the week on Martha's Vineyard. She told me that in the week following Nola's return from Charlotte's Hill, they had gone swimming together every day at Grand Beach, and that on several occasions Nola had stayed with Nancy's family for dinner. But the following Monday, when she rang the doorbell at 245 Terrace Avenue to meet Nola for the beach, as she had on the previous days, she was told that Nola was not feeling well.

"All week," Nancy told me, "it was the same old tune: 'Nola is sick. She can't have visitors.' Even my mother, who—intrigued—went there to find out what was going on, wasn't allowed into the house. And that's when anyone answered at all. It drove me crazy. I knew something was up. And it was just as I'd thought: Nola had disappeared."

"What made you think that? She could have been bedridden."

"It was my mom who noticed this one detail: There was no more music. For the whole week, there was no music at all."

I played devil's advocate: "Maybe they just didn't want to disturb her because she was ill."

"This was the first time in a long time that there had not been any music coming from that house. It was very unusual. I wanted to know for certain, so after I'd been told for the umpteenth time that Nola was sick and in bed, I sneaked around to the back of the house and looked through Nola's window. Her room was empty, and the bed had not been slept in. One thing was sure: Nola wasn't there. And then on Sunday evening, there was music again. That damn jazz music echoed from the garage once more, and the next day Nola reappeared. You think that's a coincidence? She came to my house that evening, and we went to the central square, on the main street. There I dragged it out of her, all the more determined because of the marks I saw on her back. Behind some trees, I made her lift up her shirt, and I saw that she had been badly beaten. I demanded to know what had happened, and she ended up admitting that she had been punished because she had run away for a whole week. She'd gone with a man, an older man. Stern, I'm sure. She told me it was wonderful and that it had been worth the beating."

I didn't tell Nancy that Nola had spent the week with Harry, not Elijah Stern. In any case, she didn't seem to know much more about Nola's relationship with Stern.

"I think there was something sordid about her relationship with him," she continued. "Especially now when I think about it again. Luther Caleb came to Somerset to get her in his car, a blue Mustang. I know he drove her to see Stern. It was all done in secret, of course, but I did see it happen once. At the time, Nola told me: 'Don't mention this to anyone! Swear it, on our friendship. We would both get in trouble if you did.' And I said, 'But, Nola, why are you seeing that old guy?' And she replied, 'For love.'"

"But when did that begin?" I asked.

"I don't know what to tell you. I learned about it during the summer, but I can't remember exactly when. So many things happened that summer. Maybe that affair had been going on for much longer. Maybe even years . . . who knows?"

"But you did tell someone about it in the end, didn't you? When Nola disappeared."

"Of course! I talked to Chief Pratt about it. I told him everything I knew—everything I've told you. He told me not to worry about it, and that he would get to the bottom of the whole case."

"Are you prepared to repeat all of this in court?"

"Of course—if it's necessary."

I wanted to interview David Kellergan again, with Gahalowood present. I called the sergeant to suggest this.

"You want the two of us to interrogate Mr Kellergan? You must have something specific in mind."

"Yes and no. I would like to discuss the new evidence with him: his daughter's relationships and the beatings she received."

283

"You want me to ask the minister if his daughter was, by any chance, a slut?"

"Come on, Sergeant, you know perfectly well that the evidence we're uncovering is important. In the past week, all the things you were so certain about have been swept away. Could you tell me, right now, who Nola Kellergan really was?"

"Alright, writer, you've convinced me. I'll come to Somerset tomorrow. You know Clark's?"

"Of course. Why?"

"Let's meet there at ten. I'll explain why."

The next morning I went to Clark's a bit early so I could talk to Jenny a little about the past. I mentioned the 1975 summer gala, and she told me about one of her worst memories of the ball—when Harry won first prize in the raffle. She had secretly hoped she would be the chosen one, that Harry would come and pick her up one morning and take her for a week of love in the sun.

"I had hopes," she told me, "that he would choose me. I waited for him every day. Then, at the end of July, he disappeared for a week, and I realized he'd probably gone to Martha's Vineyard without me. I don't know who he went with . . ."

I lied in order to protect her. "Nobody," I said. "He went alone."

She smiled, as if relieved. Then she said: "Ever since I've known about Harry and Nola, since I found out he wrote that book for her . . . why did he choose her?"

"You don't choose that kind of thing. Didn't you ever have any suspicions about Harry and Nola?"

"Well, who could have imagined something like that?"

"Your mother? She says she was always aware of it. Didn't she ever talk to you about it?"

"She never mentioned a relationship between them. But it's true that when Nola disappeared, she said she suspected Harry. I remember that Travis, who was courting me at the time, would come to our house for lunch on Sundays, and that Mom would constantly repeat: 'I'm sure Harry is involved in Nola's disappearance!' And Travis would reply: 'We need evidence, Mrs Quinn, or else we'll never make it stick.' And my mother would say again: 'I had evidence. Irrefutable evidence. But I lost it.' I never believed it, though. The main reason Mom wanted him dead was because of her garden party."

Gahalowood arrived at Clark's at exactly 10 a.m. By then, Jenny was back in the kitchen, supervising the cook.

"You've struck gold, writer," he said, sitting down next to me at the counter.

"Why do you say that?"

"I've been doing some research on Luther Caleb. It hasn't been easy, but this is what I've found: He was born in 1945, in Portland, Maine. I don't know what brought him to this area, but between 1970 and 1975 he was monitored by the police in Concord, Montburry, and Somerset for inappropriate behavior toward women. He hung around in the streets, approaching women. There was even a complaint filed against him by a certain Jenny Quinn, now Jenny Dawn. She runs this restaurant. It was a complaint for harassment, filed in August 1975. That's why I wanted to meet you here."

"Jenny filed a complaint against Luther Caleb?"

"You know her?"

"Of course."

"Find her, will you?"

I asked one of the waitresses to get Jenny from the kitchen. Gahalowood introduced himself and asked her to tell him about Luther.

She shrugged. "Not much to say, really. He was a nice boy. Very sweet, in spite of the way he looked. He came to Clark's occasionally. I served him coffee and a sandwich. I never charged him, the poor guy. I felt bad for him."

"And yet you filed a complaint against him," Gahalowood said.

She looked surprised. "I see you're well informed, Sergeant. That was a long time ago. It was Travis who urged me to file a complaint. He said that Luther was dangerous and that he needed to be kept at a distance."

"Why dangerous?"

"He hung around Somerset a lot that summer. Sometimes he acted aggressively toward me."

"Why did Luther Caleb become violent?"

"Violent is a strong word. Let's just say aggressive. He insisted that I . . . Look, this is going to seem ridiculous."

"Please tell us, ma'am. This could be an important detail."

"He insisted that I sit for him. So he could paint me."

"Paint you?"

"Yes. He said that I was a beautiful woman, and that all he wanted was to be able to paint me."

"What happened to him?" I asked.

"One day we just never saw him anymore," Jenny replied. "Apparently, he was killed in a car accident. You should ask Travis—I'm sure he would know."

Gahalowood confirmed that Luther Caleb died in an automobile accident. On September 26, 1975—four weeks after Nola's disappearance—his car was discovered at the bottom of a cliff, near Sagamore, Massachusetts, about 120 miles from Somerset. Furthermore, Luther had attended a fine arts college in Portland, and Gahalowood said it was looking more and more likely that he was responsible for painting the portrait of Nola.

"That Luther seems like a strange guy," he said. "Could he have tried to attack Nola? Could he have been hanging around in the Side Creek forest? He kills her in a fit of violence, then gets rid of her body before escaping to Massachusetts. Plagued by guilt, knowing he's being hunted, he drives his car off the edge of a cliff. He has a sister in Portland. I tried to get hold of her but didn't get anywhere. I'll try again."

"Why didn't the police make the connection with him back then?"

"To make the connection, you would have to consider Caleb a

suspect. But none of the evidence in the original case file pointed to him."

"Can we go back to interrogate Stern? Officially? Maybe even search his house?"

Gahalowood frowned. "He's very powerful. Right now, until we find something more solid, the D.A. won't get involved. We need more tangible proof. Evidence, writer—we need evidence."

"What about the painting?"

"We can't use that. How many times do I have to tell you? Anyway, why don't you tell me what you're planning to do at Kellergan's house?"

"I need clarification on a few points. The more I learn about him and his wife, the more questions I have."

I mentioned Harry and Nola's trip to Martha's Vineyard, her mother's repeated beatings, the father hiding in the garage. It seemed there was a deep layer of mystery surrounding Nola, a girl who was both luminous and melancholy, whom everyone found radiant but who had attempted suicide. We ate breakfast and then we went off to find David Kellergan.

The front door of the house on Terrace Avenue was open, but Kellergan was not there; no music came from the garage. We waited for him on the porch. About a half-hour later he arrived on a sputtering motorcycle: the Harley-Davidson he had spent thirty-three years restoring. He rode it without a helmet, with earphones in his ears connected to a portable C.D. player. He bellowed his hello at us, because of the volume of the music, which he finally turned off after he had put on the record player in the garage, filling the whole house with sound.

"The police had to come here several times because of the volume of the music," he told us. "All the neighbors complained. Chief Travis Dawn came in person to try to persuade me to give up my music. 'How can I do that?' I said to him. 'The music is my punishment.' So he bought me a portable player and a C.D. of the record I play all the time. He said that, this way, I could make my own eardrums explode without making the police switchboard explode due to all the calls from neighbors."

"How's the motorcycle?" I asked.

"I finally finished it. Beautiful, isn't it?"

Now that he knew what had happened to his daughter, he had finally been able to complete his work on it.

David Kellergan showed us into his kitchen and served us iced tea.

"When will I get my daughter's body back, Sergeant?" he asked Gahalowood. "I have to give her a proper burial."

"Soon, sir. I know it's difficult."

Mr Kellergan fiddled with his glass.

"She liked iced tea," he told us. "Often, on summer evenings, we would take a big bottle of it down to the beach and watch the sun set and the seagulls dance in the sky. She loved seagulls. Did you know that?"

I nodded. Then I said, "Mr Kellergan, there are some gray areas in the case file. That's why Sergeant Gahalowood and I are here."

"Gray areas? I'm sure there are. My daughter was murdered and buried in a yard. Do you have any news?"

"Mr Kellergan, do you know a certain Elijah Stern?" Gahalowood asked.

"Not personally. I met him a few times in Somerset, but that was a long time ago. He's a very rich guy."

"And his chauffeur? Luther Caleb?"

"Luther Caleb . . . the name doesn't ring a bell, though I might have forgotten. So much time has passed, and my memory is starting to go. Why these questions?"

"Everything leads us to believe that Nola was linked to these two people."

"Linked?" repeated David Kellergan, who was not stupid. "What does *linked* mean in your diplomatic police language?"

"We think Nola was in a relationship with Mr Stern. I'm sorry to tell you this in such a blunt way."

Mr Kellergan's face turned red.

"Nola? What are you trying to insinuate? That my daughter was a whore? My daughter was the victim of that bastard Harry Quebert, a notorious pedophile who will soon be on death row! Go take care of him and stop speaking ill of the dead, Sergeant! This conversation is over. Goodbye, gentlemen."

Gahalowood stood up obediently, but there were still a few points I wanted to clear up.

"Your wife beat her, didn't she?" I said.

"I beg your pardon?" Kellergan choked.

"Your wife liked to give Nola a good hiding. Correct or not?"

"You're completely insane!"

I went on, regardless: "Nola ran away from home in late July 1975. She ran away, and you didn't tell anyone. Am I wrong? Why didn't you say anything? Were you ashamed? Why didn't you call the police when she ran away?"

He began to explain. "She was going to come back ... And one week later she did!"

"A week! You waited a week! And yet the night of August 30, when she disappeared, you called the police only one hour after you noticed she wasn't there. Why?"

Mr Kellergan's voice rose. "Because, that evening, when I went to search the area, I heard about a girl who'd been seen covered in blood on Side Creek Lane, and I instantly made the connection! What do you want from me, Mr Goldman? I have no family left, I have nothing! Why do you come here and open up these old wounds? Get the hell out of here! Get out right now!"

I refused to let him intimidate me.

"What happened in Alabama, Mr Kellergan? Why did you come to Somerset? And what happened here in 1975? Answer me, for God's sake! You owe that to your daughter!"

Kellergan got up and, as if possessed, threw himself at me, grabbing my throat with a strength I would never have guessed he had. "Get the hell out of my house!" he screamed, shoving me backward. I would probably have fallen over had not Gahalowood taken hold of me and dragged me outside.

"Are you insane, writer?" he said when we got back to the car. "Or are you just unusually stupid? Do you want to antagonize all our witnesses?"

"You have to admit there's something fishy about it."

"Something fishy? We just implied that his daughter was a slut, and he got mad. Seems pretty normal to me. On the other hand, he almost gave you a good beating. Pretty impressive for an old man. I'd never have thought he had it in him."

"I'm sorry—I don't know what got into me."

"And what's this stuff about Alabama?" he asked.

"I told you about it: The Kellergans left Alabama to come here. And I'm still pretty sure there was a good reason for their departure."

"I'll find out. If you promise to behave from now on."

"We'll get there, won't we, Sergeant? We're going to prove Harry's innocence, aren't we?"

Gahalowood stared at me.

"What worries me, writer, is you. I'm doing my job: I'm investigating two murders. But you seem obsessed by the need to prove Quebert innocent, as if you wanted to tell the rest of the country: See, he didn't do it, what do you have against this good man, this great writer? But what we have against him, Goldman, is that he was in love with a fifteen-year-old girl!"

"I know that! I think about it all the time, believe it or not. I came here as soon as the news broke, without thinking twice. My only concern was for my friend, my blood brother, Harry. If things had gone normally, I would have stayed only two or three days—long enough to ease my conscience—and I would have gone back to New York as quickly as possible."

"So why are you still here to piss me off?"

"Because Harry Quebert is the only friend I have. I'm twenty-eight years old, and he's my only friend. He taught me everything. He's been my only human connection for the last ten years. Apart from him, I have no-one."

I think Gahalowood must have felt sorry for me then, because he invited me to eat dinner at his house. "Come tonight, writer. We'll take stock of the investigation, have a bite to eat. You can meet my wife too." And as if it were killing him to be nice to me, he then added in his most disagreeable voice: "Well, my wife will be happy, anyway. She's been pestering me to invite you over ever since I mentioned you. She dreams of meeting you. Some dream!"

The Gahalowood family lived in a cute little house in a residential area west of Concord. Helen, the sergeant's wife, was elegant and extremely pleasant—the exact opposite of her husband. "I loved your book so much," she told me. "So are you really investigating with Perry?" Her husband grumbled that I was not investigating anything, that he was the boss, and that I had just been sent to ruin his life. His two daughters— two clearly well-adjusted teenagers—came to greet me politely before disappearing into their rooms.

"So you're the only one in the house who doesn't like me," I said to Gahalowood.

He smiled.

"Shut it, writer. Shut your mouth and come outside and have a nice cold beer. It's a beautiful evening."

We spent a long time on the deck, sitting comfortably in rattan chairs and consuming the contents of a plastic cooler. Gahalowood was wearing a suit, but he had put on a pair of old slippers. It was a hot evening, and we could hear children playing in the street. The air smelled of summer.

"You have a beautiful family," I told him.

"Thank you. How about you? Wife? Kids?"

"No, nothing."

"Dog?"

"Nope."

"Not even a dog? You must really be lonely, writer. Let me guess: You live in an apartment that's much too big for you in a trendy part of New York. A big apartment that's always empty."

I didn't even try to deny it.

"My agent used to come over to watch baseball with me. We had nachos with cheese. It was nice. But after everything that's happened, I don't know if he'll want to come to my apartment anymore. I haven't heard from him in weeks."

"So you're scared, huh?"

"I am. But the worst thing is I don't even know what it is I'm afraid of. I'm writing my new book about this case. It's going to earn me at least two million dollars, and I'm sure it'll be a bestseller. And yet, deep down, I'm unhappy. What do you think I should do?"

He looked at me, almost surprised.

"You're asking advice from a guy who earns seventy thousand dollars a year?"

"Yes."

"I don't know what to tell you, writer."

"If I were your son, what would you say?"

"You? My son? Just give me a minute to throw up. Why don't you go see a therapist? You know, I have a son. Younger than you—he's twenty."

"I didn't know."

He rummaged in his pocket and came up with a small photograph he had glued to a piece of card to maintain its shape. It showed a young man in uniform.

"Your son is in the military?"

"Second Infantry Division, deployed in Iraq. I remember the day he signed up. There was a mobile recruitment station in the mall parking lot. It was an obvious choice for him. He came home and told me he'd made his decision: He was giving up college and going off to fight in the war. Because of the images of 9/11 that kept racing through his head. So

I got out a map of the world and asked him, 'Where's Iraq?' He replied, 'Iraq is where we have to be.' What do you think of that, Marcus?" (This was the first time he had ever called me by my first name.) "Was he right or wrong?"

"I don't know."

"Me neither. All I know is that life is a series of choices, and that you have to keep making them."

That was a nice evening. It had been a long time since I had felt so surrounded by good feeling. After the meal, I went back out on the deck while Gahalowood helped his wife clean up. Night had fallen; the sky was the color of ink. I saw the Big Dipper glinting. All was calm. The children were no longer out in the street, and the only sound was the soothing *chirp chirp* of the crickets. Gahalowood came out to join me, and together we went over the investigation. I told him how Stern had generously allowed Harry to stay at Goose Cove.

"The same Stern who was in a relationship with Nola?" he said. "This whole thing is very strange."

"You're not kidding, Sergeant. And I can confirm that someone did know, back then, about Harry and Nola. Harry told me that at the summer gala, someone scrawled PEDOPHILE SCUM on the bathroom mirror while he was in one of the stalls. Speaking of which, where are we with the inscription on the manuscript? When will you have the handwriting analysis?"

"Sometime next week, theoretically."

"So we'll know soon."

"I've been through the police report on Nola's disappearance," Gahalowood told me. "The one written by Chief Pratt. I can confirm that there is no mention in there of Stern or of Harry."

"That's strange, because Nancy Hattaway and Tamara Quinn both told me they had informed Chief Pratt of their suspicions about Harry and Stern at the time of Nola's disappearance."

293

"But the report is signed by Pratt himself. So he knew and didn't do anything?"

"What can all this mean?" I asked.

Gahalowood looked somber.

"That he too might have had a relationship with Nola Kellergan."

"You think that . . . Jesus Christ! Chief Pratt and Nola?"

"The first thing we will do tomorrow, writer, is go and ask him."

On the morning of Thursday, July 3, Gahalowood came to pick me up at Goose Cove, and we went to see Chief Pratt in his Mountain Drive house. It was Pratt himself who opened the door. At first he saw just me, and his greeting was friendly.

"Mr Goldman, what brings you here? I've been hearing that you're leading your own investigation . . ."

I heard Amy asking who it was from inside the house, and Pratt replied, "It's Goldman, the writer." Then he noticed Gahalowood, a few steps behind me, and said, "Oh, so this is an official visit . . ."

Gahalowood nodded.

"Just a few questions, Chief," he said. "The investigation is getting bogged down and there are parts of the story that seem to be missing. I'm sure you understand."

We sat in the living room. Amy Pratt came in to greet us. Her husband suggested that she go outside to do some gardening, and without further ado she put on a hat and went out to tend to her rosebushes. It might have been funny were it not for the fact that, for reasons I could not yet explain, the atmosphere in the Pratts' living room had suddenly become very tense.

I let Gahalowood ask the questions. Despite his latent aggressiveness, he was a very good cop, with a strong grasp of psychology. He asked a few questions to begin with, nothing out of the ordinary. He asked Pratt to give a brief rundown of events leading up to the disappearance of Nola Kellergan. But Pratt quickly lost his patience: He said he had already made his report in 1975, and that all we had to do was read it.

It was at this point that Gahalowood replied: "Well, to be perfectly honest, I read your report, and I'm not convinced by it. For instance, I know that Mrs Quinn told you what she knew regarding Harry and Nola, and yet that is not even mentioned in the case file."

Pratt did not get flustered. "Mrs Quinn came to see me—that's true. She told me she knew everything, that Harry was fantasizing about Nola. But she had no evidence, and neither did I."

"You're lying," I said. "She showed you a page containing Harry's handwriting that clearly compromised him."

"She showed it to me once. Then that page disappeared. She had nothing. What could I have done?"

"What about Elijah Stern?" Gahalowood said, softening his tone. "What do you know about Stern?"

"Stern?" Pratt repeated. "Elijah Stern? What does he have to do with this?"

Gahalowood held the whip hand now. In a calm voice that brooked no argument, he said: "Cut the crap, Pratt. I know what's going on. I know you didn't carry out your investigation the way you should have. I know that when the girl disappeared, Tamara Quinn told you her suspicions about Quebert, and Nancy Hattaway informed you that Nola had been in a sexual relationship with Elijah Stern. You should at least have questioned them, searched their houses, clarified this story, and written it up in your report. That's standard procedure. But you didn't do any of that. Why? You had a murdered woman and a missing girl on your hands!"

I sensed Pratt's composure slipping. He raised his voice. "I combed the whole area for weeks," he said, "even on my days off! I went all out to find that girl! So don't come here—to my home—to insult me and question my work! Cops don't do that to other cops!"

"Sure, you carried out a huge search," Gahalowood said, "but you knew perfectly well there were people you should have questioned, and you didn't do it! Why, for God's sake? What were you covering up?"

There was a long silence. Gahalowood stared at Pratt with an icy calm.

"What were you covering up?" he asked again. "What happened with that girl?"

Pratt looked away. He stood up and went to the window, where he could avoid our eyes. For a moment he watched his wife out in the yard, clearing the weeds around her rosebushes.

"It was at the beginning of August," he said, his voice barely audible, "of that cursed summer. This is what happened, whether you believe me or not: One afternoon the girl came to see me in my office at the police station. There was a knock at the door, and Nola Kellergan came in, without waiting for me to answer. I was sitting at my desk, reading a case file. I was surprised to see her. I said hi, and asked what was going on. There was something strange about her. She didn't say a word. She closed the door and locked it behind her, then came toward me. Toward the desk, and . . ."

Pratt broke off. He was visibly shaken. He could no longer find the words. Gahalowood showed no sympathy whatsoever. Coldly, he asked: "And *what*, Chief Pratt?"

"This is the truth, Sergeant—I don't care if you believe me. She crawled under my desk, and . . . she . . . she unzipped my pants, and she took me in her mouth."

I jumped to my feet. "What the hell are you saying?"

"I'm telling you the truth. She sucked me off, and I let her do it. She told me, 'Let yourself go, Chief.' And when it was all over, she wiped her mouth and said, 'Now you're a criminal.'"

We were dumbstruck. So that was why Pratt hadn't interrogated Stern or Harry. Because he was directly involved in this case, just as they were.

Now that he had begun to clear his conscience, Pratt needed to go all the way. He told us there was another blow job afterward. But while the first had been initiated by Nola, the second was forced on her by him. He told us about an incident when, while out on patrol alone, he had found Nola walking home along Shore Road. She was close to Goose Cove, and she was carrying her typewriter. He offered to accompany her, but instead of heading toward Somerset, he took her into the woods at Side Creek.

"It was a few weeks before her disappearance," he told us. "I parked on the edge of the forest. There was nobody around. And I took her hand and made her touch me, and I asked her to do again what she'd done to me before. I unzipped my pants, I grabbed her by the back of her neck . . . I don't know what got hold of me. This has been haunting me for more than thirty years! I can't bear it anymore! Arrest me, Sergeant. I want to be questioned, I want be judged, I want to be forgiven. Forgive me, Nola! Forgive me!"

When Amy Pratt saw her husband being led from the house in handcuffs, she screamed so loudly that the whole neighborhood was alerted. The more curious came out onto their lawns to see what was happening, and I heard a woman call her husband so that he wouldn't miss the show: "The police are arresting Gareth Pratt!"

Gahalowood took Pratt in his car and drove, sirens wailing, to the state police headquarters in Concord. I remained on the Pratts' lawn. Amy was crying, on her knees in front of the rosebushes, and the neighbors—and the neighbors' neighbors, and the whole street, and the whole district, and soon half of Somerset—congregated in front of the house on Mountain Drive.

Stunned by what I had just learned, I ended up sitting on a fire hydrant and calling Roth to tell him what had happened. I did not have the courage to face Harry; I did not want to be the one to tell him. The television took care of that in the hours that followed. The media hype began all over again: Gareth Pratt, former chief of police in Somerset, has admitted to performing sexual acts on Nola Kellergan and is now a suspect in her murder. Harry called me collect from the prison in the early afternoon. He was in tears. He asked me to come to see him. He could not believe that all of this was true.

In the prison visiting room, I told him about our interview with Chief Pratt. He was a mess. At last I said, "That's not all . . . I think it's time you knew . . ."

"Knew what? You're scaring me, Marcus."

"The reason I mentioned Stern to you the other day is that I went to his house."

"And?"

"I found a painting of Nola there."

"A painting?"

"Stern has a nude painting of Nola in his house."

I had brought with me one of the blown-up photographs of the painting, and I showed it to Harry.

"It's her!" he cried. "It's Nola! It's Nola! What does this mean?"

A guard poked his head in to warn him to cool it.

"Try not to lose your temper," I said.

"But what does Stern have to do with all this?"

"I don't know . . . Did Nola ever mention him to you?"

"Never! Never!"

"Harry, as far as I'm aware, Nola had a relationship with Elijah Stern during that same summer you did."

"I don't believe that . . ."

"At least, from what I understand . . . Harry, you might have to accept that maybe you were not the only man in Nola's life."

Springing to his feet, he threw his plastic chair against the wall and screamed: "Impossible! Impossible! I was the one she loved! Do you hear me? She loved *me*!"

Guards rushed into the room and took him away. As he left, I heard him screaming: "Why are you doing this, Marcus? Why are you screwing everything up? Go to hell! You, Pratt, and Stern!"

It was after this episode that I began to write the story of Nola Kellergan, the fifteen-year-old girl who had captivated an entire New England town.

16

The Origin of Evil
(Somerset, New Hampshire, August 11–20, 1975)

"Harry, how long does it take to write a book?"
"That depends."
"On what?"
"On everything."

August 11, 1975

"Harry!"

Nola ran into the house. It was early morning, not even nine o'clock. Harry was in his office, reorganizing piles of papers. She appeared at the door, brandishing the satchel that contained the manuscript.

"Where was it?" Harry said, clearly annoyed. "Where the hell was that manuscript?"

"I'm sorry, Harry. Don't be mad at me. I took it last night. You were sleeping, and I took it so I could read it at home. I shouldn't have. But it's so wonderful! It's incredible! What a beautiful book."

Smiling, she handed it to him.

"So you liked it?"

"Did I like it?" she said. "I adored it! It's the most beautiful thing I've ever read. You're going to be famous, Harry. I mean it!"

As she said these words, she began to dance. She danced in the hallway; she danced into the living room; she danced on the deck. Wiping away the dew on the deck table she covered it with a tablecloth and set up his work space, arranging his pens, his notebooks, his pages, and some carefully chosen stones from the beach to act as paperweights. Then she brought him coffee, waffles, and fruit, and she put a cushion on his chair. She made sure everything was perfect so that he could work under the best possible conditions. Once he was seated at the table, she turned her attention to the house. She cleaned up, and made lunch; she took care of everything so that all he had to do was concentrate on his writing. As he wrote pages by hand, she read them, made a few corrections, and then typed them up on her Remington, like the most passionate, devoted secretary imaginable. Only when she had accomplished all of her tasks did she allow herself to sit close to Harry—although not too close, in order not to disturb him—and to watch him write. She was the writer's wife.

That day she left just after lunch. As always, she left him with a set of instructions: "I've made sandwiches for you. They're in the kitchen. And there's iced tea in the fridge. You must eat properly—and take a rest. Otherwise you'll get a headache. And you know what happens when you work too hard, Harry: You get those migraines that make you so cranky."

She hugged him.

"Are you coming back later?" Harry asked.

"No, I'm busy."

"Busy doing what? Why are you leaving so early?"

"Just busy. Women must remain mysterious. I read that in a magazine."

He smiled.

"Nola . . ."

"Yes?"

"Thank you."

"For what?"

"For everything. If it weren't for you, I would never have been able to write this book."

"That's what I want to do with my life: take care of you, be there for you, help you with your books . . . have a family with you. Think how happy we'll be! How many children do you want?"

"At least three!"

"Yes! How about four? Two boys and two girls, so there won't be too many arguments. I want to be Mrs Nola Quebert! Prouder of her husband than any other woman in the world!"

She left and walked up the driveway toward Shore Road. As before, she did not notice the figure crouched in the undergrowth.

It took her half an hour to reach Somerset on foot. She made this trip twice a day. When she got to town, she took the main street and continued until she reached the park, where, as arranged, Nancy Hattaway was waiting for her.

"Why here instead of the beach?" Nancy complained when she saw Nola. "It's so hot!"

"I'm meeting someone this afternoon . . ."

"What? Don't tell me you're seeing Stern again!"

"Don't say his name!"

"You're using me as an alibi again?"

"Please cover for me! I'm begging you!"

"I cover for you all the time!"

"Just once more. Please."

"Don't go!" Nancy pleaded. "You have to stop seeing this guy! I'm scared for you. What do you do together? Are you having sex with him?"

Nola's expression was gentle and soothing. "Don't worry, Nancy.

Please don't worry. You'll cover for me, won't you? Please say you'll cover for me: You know what happens if I'm caught lying. You know what happens to me at home ..."

Nancy heaved a sigh of resignation. "Alright. I'll stay here until you come back. But no later than 6.30 or my mother will give me hell."

"Of course. And if anyone asks, what did we do?"

"We spent the whole afternoon here, talking," Nancy repeated like a puppet. "But I'm sick of lying for you! Why do you do this?"

"Because I love him! I love him so much! I would do anything for him!"

"Ugh—I think it's disgusting. I don't even want to think about it."

A blue Mustang came down one of the streets bordering the park and stopped at the curb. "Time for me to go," Nola said. "See you later, Nancy. Thank you—you're a true friend."

She walked quickly toward the car and scrambled inside. "Hello, Luther," she said to the chauffeur, and the car disappeared, without anyone—apart from Nancy—having noticed anything strange.

An hour later the Mustang arrived in the courtyard of Elijah Stern's manor. Luther led the young girl inside. She knew the way to the room.

"Get undreffed," Luther told her gently. "I'm going to tell Mifter Ftern vat you have arrived."

August 12, 1975

As on every morning since the trip to Martha's Vineyard, when he had rediscovered his inspiration, Harry got up at dawn and went running before starting work.

As on every morning, he ran as far as Somerset. And as on every morning, he stopped at the marina to do push-ups. It was not yet six o'clock. The town was sleeping. He had avoided going by Clark's. It was opening time there, and he did not want to risk seeing Jenny. She was a great girl; she did not deserve to be treated like this. He spent a moment contemplating the ocean, which shone with all the improbable colors of the sunrise.

When she spoke his name, he jumped.

"Harry? So it's true? You really do wake up this early to go running?"

He turned around. It was Jenny, wearing her Clark's uniform. She moved closer and clumsily attempted to embrace him.

"I just like watching the sunrise," he said.

She smiled. If he was coming all this way, she thought, it must mean he did love her a little bit.

"Would you like to come to Clark's for coffee?" she asked.

"Thanks. But I don't want to break my rhythm."

She tried to conceal her disappointment.

"Let's at least sit together for a minute."

"I don't want to stop for long."

She frowned. "But I haven't heard from you recently. You don't come to Clark's anymore."

"I'm sorry. I've been busy with my book."

"There's more to life than books, you know. Come see me now and then. I'd like that. Mom won't yell at you, I promise. She shouldn't have made you pay your tab all at once."

"That doesn't matter."

"I should go and start my shift—we open at six. Are you sure you don't want some coffee?"

"I'm sure. Thanks."

"Maybe you could come over later?"

"No, I don't think so."

"If you come here every morning, I could wait for you at the marina . . . I mean, if you don't mind. Just to say hi."

"That's not necessary."

"Alright. Anyway, I'll be working until three this afternoon. If you want to come over to write . . . I won't disturb you, I promise. I hope you're not mad that I went to the gala with Travis. I don't love him, you know. He's just a friend. I . . . there's something I wanted to tell you, Harry. I love you. I love you like I've never loved anyone before."

"Don't say that, Jenny . . ."

The town hall bell rang six times; she was late. She kissed him on the cheek and ran. She should not have told him that she loved him; she regretted it already. She was such a fool. Heading up the street toward Clark's, she turned around to wave, but he had gone. If he comes to Clark's, she thought, that means he loves me a little bit, that all is not lost. She hurried on, but just before she reached the top of the hill, a large, malformed shadow appeared from behind a fence. In her surprise, Jenny couldn't help crying out. Then she recognized Luther.

"Luther! You scared me!"

A streetlamp illuminated the twisted face and powerful body.

"What dove . . . What dove he want from you?"

"Nothing, Luther."

He grabbed her arm and held it tightly.

"Doe . . . doe . . . doe . . . don't make fun of me! What dove he want from you?"

"He's a friend. Leave me alone now, Luther! You're hurting me! Leave me alone or I'll tell!"

He loosened his grip and said, "Have you thought about my propoval?"

"The answer is no, Luther. I don't want you to paint me. Now let me past! Or I'll say you've been hanging around, and you'll get in trouble."

As soon as she threatened this, Luther disappeared, running into the dawn like a frightened animal. Beginning to cry, she hurried to the restaurant. Before entering, she quickly wiped her eyes so that her mother would not notice her tears.

Harry was running again, crossing the town from one end to the other in order to reach Shore Road and follow it back to Goose Cove. He was thinking about Jenny. He must not give her false hope. He felt so bad for her. When he reached the crossroads, his legs gave way; his muscles had gone cold during his stop at the marina. He could feel himself cramping up, and he was alone by the side of an empty road. He regretted having gone to Somerset. He did not see how he would be able to run back to Goose Cove. At that moment a blue Mustang pulled up next to him. The driver lowered the window and Harry recognized Luther Caleb.

"Need fum help?"

"I overdid it . . . I think I've pulled something."

"Get in. I'll take you to your houfe."

"Lucky you happened by," Harry said, getting into the passenger seat. "What are you doing in Somerset so early?"

Caleb did not reply; they rode to Goose Cove without either of them saying another word. Having dropped Harry at home, Luther went back up the driveway, but instead of heading to Concord, he took a left turn, back toward Somerset, and parked in a little dead end in the forest. Luther left his car in the shade of the pines and then deftly made his way through the trees and crouched in the undergrowth close to the house. It was 6.15 a.m. He leaned against a tree trunk and waited.

At about nine o'clock, Nola arrived at Goose Cove to take care of her beloved.

August 13, 1975

"You see, Dr Ashcroft, I always do that, and afterward I feel angry with myself."

"How does it happen?"

"I don't know. It's as if it comes out of me against my will. It's like an urge, but it makes me miserable. Oh, it makes me so miserable! But I can't stop myself."

Dr Ashcroft looked closely at Tamara Quinn for a moment, then asked her, "Are you capable of telling people how you feel about them?"

"I . . . No. I never tell them."

"Why not?"

"Because they know."

"Are you sure?"

"Of course!"

"How would they know if you never tell them?"

She shrugged. "I don't know, Doctor."

"Does your family know you're coming to see me?"

"No. No! I . . . This is none of their business."

He nodded. "I think, Mrs Quinn, that you ought to try writing down what you feel. Writing things down can be soothing."

"I do. I record it all. Ever since I started coming here, I've been keeping a notebook that I always keep safe."

"And does that help?"

"I don't know. Yes, a little. I think."

"We'll talk again next week. It's time for my next patient."

August 14, 1975

It was around 11 a.m. Nola had been sitting on the deck at Goose Cove since early that morning, assiduously typing up handwritten drafts on the Remington, while across from her Harry was busy writing. "It's good!" Nola said excitedly as she read his words. "It's really good!" Harry smiled in response. He was filled with inspiration.

It was hot. Nola, noticing that Harry's glass was empty, left the deck for a moment to make iced tea in the kitchen. She had barely gone inside when a visitor appeared on the deck: Elijah Stern.

"Harry, you're working too hard!" Stern roared. Harry was startled, and then immediately overcome by panic: No-one could see Nola here.

"Elijah Stern!" Harry said, yet more loudly, so that Nola would hear him and stay inside.

"Harry Quebert!" Stern repeated, having no idea why Harry was shouting. "I rang the doorbell, but no-one answered. But I saw your car, and I thought maybe you were out on the deck, so I decided I'd take a look."

"And I'm very glad you did!" Harry shouted at the top of his voice.

Stern noticed the rough drafts, then the Remington at the other side of the table. "You write and type at the same time?" he asked.

"Yes. I . . . I write several pages simultaneously."

Stern collapsed into a chair. He was covered in sweat.

"Several pages at the same time? You must be a genius, Harry. So I was in the area, and I thought I'd stop by Somerset. What a beautiful town. I left my car on the main street and went for a walk. And ended up walking here. Old habits die hard, I guess."

"This house, Elijah . . . it's wonderful. Such a glorious setting."

"I'm so happy you were able to stay on."

"Thank you for your generosity. I owe you everything."

"Please don't thank me. You don't owe me anything."

"One day I'll have money, and maybe I'll buy this house."

"That would be great, Harry. I couldn't wish anything more for you. I would be glad to see the house come back to life. But, if you'll excuse my rudeness, I'm sweating like a pig and dying of thirst here."

Harry glanced nervously toward the kitchen, hoping that Nola had heard them and that she would not reveal herself.

"Unfortunately, I have nothing here to offer you other than water."

Stern laughed. "That's alright—no need to feel guilty. I had a feeling you might not have anything to eat or drink here. In fact, that's exactly what worries me—it's good to write, but you have to make sure you don't waste away! You should get married, so you have someone to look after you. But I'll tell you what—give me a ride into town, and I'll take you out to lunch. That'll give us the chance to talk. Only if you'd like to."

"I'd love to," said Harry, with relief. "Let me find my car keys."

He walked into the house. Passing the kitchen, he found Nola hiding under the table. She gave him a beautiful smile of complicity, her finger to her lips. He smiled back and joined Stern outside.

They took the Chevrolet and drove to Clark's, where they sat outside and ordered eggs, toast, and pancakes. Jenny's eyes shone when she saw Harry. It had been so long since he'd been to the restaurant.

"It's funny," Stern said. "I really did intend to go for just a short walk, and before I knew it I found myself at Goose Cove. It was as if the landscape lured me there."

"The coast between Somerset and Goose Cove is incredibly beautiful," Harry said. "I can't get enough of it."

"Do you often go that way?"

"Nearly every morning. I run. It's a great way to start the day. I get up at dawn and run as the sun rises. It's an amazing feeling."

"Sounds like you're a real athlete. I wish I had your discipline."

"An athlete? I'm not so sure about that. The day before yesterday, for instance, as I was coming back to Goose Cove, my legs cramped up. I couldn't even walk. Fortunately, your chauffeur saw me and very kindly took me to the house."

Stern smiled tensely. "Luther was here the day before yesterday?" he asked.

Their conversation was interrupted by Jenny, who brought them coffee and then moved away.

"Yes," Harry replied. "I was pretty surprised myself, actually, to see him in Somerset so early in the morning. Does he live near here?"

Stern seemed embarrassed.

"No, he lives on my property. I have an outbuilding for my staff. But he likes this area. It must be said that Somerset is beautiful at dawn."

"Didn't you say he was going to check on the rosebushes at Goose Cove? Because I've never seen him."

"But the plants are thriving, aren't they? So he must have stopped by."

"Still, I'm at the house most of the time—all the time, practically."

"Luther is a very discreet person."

"I was wondering: What happened to him? The way he speaks is so strange."

"He had an accident. A long time ago. He can appear a little frightening sometimes, but inside he's a wonderful man."

"I'm sure he is."

Jenny came back to top up our coffee cups, which were still full. She rearranged the napkin holder, refilled the salt shaker, and changed the bottle of ketchup. She smiled at Stern and nodded at Harry before disappearing inside.

"How's your book going?" Stern said.

"It's going very well. Thank you once again for letting me have the house. I feel very inspired."

"You're probably inspired by that girl, more than anything," Stern said with a smile.

"I beg your pardon?" Harry said, choking.

"Don't be embarrassed. There's nothing wrong with it. Jenny, the waitress—you're screwing her, aren't you? Because the way she's been acting since we arrived, she's certainly being screwed by one of us. And I know it's not me. So my assumption is that it must be you. Ha-ha—I don't blame you! She's a good-looking girl."

Relieved, Harry forced a laugh.

"Jenny and I are not together," he said. "Let's just say we flirted for a while. She's a nice girl, but—between you and me—I find her a little dull. I would like to find someone I'm really in love with, someone special. Someone different . . ."

"Well, don't worry about that. You'll find that rare pearl eventually—the girl who'll make you happy."

While Harry and Stern were eating lunch, Nola was walking home, carrying her typewriter along Shore Road as the sun beat down on her. A car came up from behind and pulled up next to her. It was a police car; Chief Pratt was at the wheel.

"Where are you going with that typewriter?" he said, laughing.

"I'm going home, Chief."

"On foot? Where on earth are you coming from? Never mind. Get in—I'll drive you home."

"Thank you, Chief Pratt, but I'd rather walk."

"Don't be silly. It's baking out here."

"No, thank you, Chief."

Chief Pratt's voice suddenly became aggressive. "Why don't you want me to take you home? I told you to get in the car! Now get in!"

Intimidated, Nola gave in, and Pratt made her sit in the passenger seat, next to him. But instead of continuing toward town, he did a U-turn and set off in the opposite direction.

"Where are we going? Somerset is the other way."

"Don't worry about it, kiddo. I just want to show you something. You're not scared, are you? I want to show you the forest—it's a beautiful place. You'd like to see a beautiful place, wouldn't you?"

Nola did not reply. Pratt drove to Side Creek, where he took a dirt road and parked in a clearing among the trees. There, he undid his seat belt, and then his zipper, and—grabbing Nola by the back of her neck—told her to do to him what she had done so perfectly in his office.

August 15, 1975

At 8 a.m., Louisa Kellergan went to see her daughter in her bedroom. Nola was waiting for her, sitting on the bed in her underwear. Today was the day. She knew. Louisa smiled tenderly at her daughter.

"You know why I'm doing this, Nola . . ."

"Yes, Mom."

"It's for your own good. So you'll go to Heaven. You want to be an angel, don't you?"

"I don't know if I want to be an angel, Mom."

"Now, now, don't talk nonsense. Come here, my darling."

Nola got up and followed her mother into the bathroom. The large basin was ready, filled with water. Nola looked at her mother. She was a pretty woman, with beautiful blond, wavy hair. Everyone said how alike they looked.

"I love you, Mom," said Nola.

"I love you too, my darling."

"I'm sorry I'm a wicked girl."

"You're not a wicked girl."

Nola knelt in front of the basin; her mother grabbed her hair and shoved her head underwater. She counted to twenty, slowly and harshly, then pulled Nola's head from the ice-cold water. Her daughter let loose a cry of panic. "Come on, my girl, this is your penance. And now, again . . ." And she held her daughter's head down once more.

In the garage, David Kellergan listened to his music.

He was horrified by what he had just heard.

"Your mother drowns you?" Harry repeated, still in shock.

It was noon. Nola had just arrived at Goose Cove. She had spent the whole morning crying, and despite her attempts to dry her reddened eyes when she reached his house, Harry had immediately noticed that something was wrong.

"She shoves my head in the basin," Nola explained. "The water is so cold! She shoves my head underwater and holds it there. Every time I feel like I'm going to die. I can't take it anymore, Harry. Help me."

She pressed herself against him. Harry suggested they go down to the beach—that always cheered her up. He picked up the box with SOUVENIR OF ROCKLAND, MAINE written on it, and they went to feed the seagulls. Then they sat on the sand and contemplated the horizon.

"I want to leave, Harry!" Nola exclaimed. "I want you to take me far away from here."

"Leave?"

"You and me, far from here. You said we would leave one day. I want to get away. Wouldn't you like to go with me? Please, I'm begging you, let's leave. Let's leave at the end of this horrible month. Let's say the thirtieth—that would give us two weeks to get ready."

"The thirtieth? Are you crazy?"

"No! What's crazy is continuing to live in this miserable town! What's crazy is loving each other the way we do and not being allowed to show it! What's crazy is having to hide, as if we were some weird animals! I can't take it anymore, Harry! I'm going to leave. The night of August 30. I can't stay here any longer. So please, come with me. Don't let me go on my own."

"What if they arrest us?"

"Who'll arrest us? We could be in Canada in three hours. And why would they arrest us? It's not a crime to leave. To leave is to be free, and who can stop us from being free? This is the land of the free, isn't it? Freedom is written into the Constitution. I'm going to leave—that's all there is to it. In two weeks, on the night of August 30, I'm leaving this horrible town. Will you come with me?"

Without thinking he said: "Yes! Of course! I can't imagine life without you, Nola. On August 30, we'll leave together."

"Oh, darling Harry, I'm so happy! What about your book?"

"It's almost finished."

"That's wonderful! You've made such quick progress."

"The book doesn't matter anymore. If I run away with you, I don't think I'll be able to be a writer. But who cares? All that matters is you. All that matters is us. All that matters is being happy."

"Of course you'll still be a writer! We'll send the manuscript to New York. I love your new novel, and I believe in you. So the thirtieth? In two weeks' time. Two weeks from now we'll go away. In three hours, we'll be in Canada. We'll be so happy—you'll see, Harry.

August 18, 1975

Sitting behind the wheel of his patrol car, he stared through the window of Clark's. They had hardly spoken since the gala; she was distancing herself from him, and that made him sad. She'd seemed especially unhappy for some time now. He wondered if this had something to do with him, and then he remembered that time he had found her in tears on the porch of her house and how she had said that someone was hurting her. What had she meant by *hurting*? Was she in some kind of trouble? Was someone physically harming her? Who? He decided to bite the bullet and go talk to her. As always, he waited for the diner to empty out a little before he dared go in. When he did finally enter, Jenny was busy clearing a table.

"Hi, Jenny," he said, his heart pounding.

"Hi, Travis."

"We haven't had much chance to talk since the gala," he said.

"I've been really busy here."

"I wanted to say how happy I was to go out with you that night."

"Thank you."

She seemed preoccupied.

"Jenny, you've seemed distant lately."

"No, Travis, it has nothing to do with you."

She was thinking about Harry. She thought about him day and night. Why was he rejecting her? Several days earlier he had come here with Elijah Stern, and he had barely even spoken to her. She had even seen the two men sniggering about her.

"Jenny, if you're upset about something, you know you can tell me anything."

"You're so good to me, Travis. But I have to finish clearing up now."

She headed toward the kitchen.

"Wait," Travis said.

He took her wrist to hold her back. He barely touched her, but Jenny cried out and dropped the plates, which shattered on the floor. He had accidentally pressed on the bruise covering her right wrist, where Luther had grabbed her, and which, despite the heat, she attempted to hide by wearing long sleeves.

"I'm really sorry," Travis said, kneeling to pick up the broken pieces. "It's not you."

He went with her into the kitchen and got a broom to clean up the mess. When he brought the broom back into the kitchen she was washing her hands, and because she had rolled up her sleeves, he was able to see the bluish marks on her wrist.

"What is that?" he asked.

"Oh, it's nothing. I banged it on the swinging doors the other day."

"Banged it? Don't lie to me!" Travis said. "Who did this to you?"

"It doesn't matter."

"Of course it matters! Tell me, Jenny. I'm not leaving here until I know his name."

"It was . . . it was Luther Caleb. Stern's chauffeur. It happened the other day. He was angry. He grabbed my wrist. But he didn't mean to hurt me. He doesn't know his own strength."

"This is serious, Jenny! This is very serious. I want you to let me know immediately if he ever comes back here."

August 20, 1975

She sang as she walked down the path to Goose Cove. A feeling of joy swept over her. In ten days they would leave together. In ten days she would finally start living. She spotted the house at the end of the driveway and began walking faster. She did not notice the figure hidden in the bushes. She entered the house through the front door, without ringing the doorbell, as she always did now.

"Harry, darling!" she called out.

There was no reply. The house seemed empty. She called out again. Silence. She went through the dining room and the living room, but didn't find him. He wasn't in his office or out on the deck. She went down the stairs to the beach and called his name. Maybe he'd gone swimming? He did that sometimes when he'd been working too hard. But there was

315

no-one on the beach. She began to panic: Where could he be? She went back to the house, called his name again. Nothing. She checked all the rooms on the first floor again, then went upstairs. Opening the door to his bedroom, she found him sitting on his bed, reading a stack of papers.

"Harry? Were you here all along? I've spent the last ten minutes looking all over for you."

Her voice had startled him.

"Sorry, Nola, I was reading. I didn't hear you."

He got up, shuffled the papers in his hands, and put them in his bureau.

She smiled. "So what was so fascinating that you didn't hear me yelling your name all over the house?"

"Nothing important."

"Is it the next part of your novel? Show me!"

"No, it's nothing important. I'll show you some other time."

She looked at him curiously. "Are you sure everything's O.K., Harry?"

He laughed. "Everything's fine, Nola."

They went out to the beach. She wanted to see the seagulls. She opened her arms wide as if they were wings, and ran in wide circles on the sand.

"I'd love to be able to fly, Harry! Only ten days! In ten days we'll fly away together! We'll leave this miserable town forever!"

Neither Harry nor Nola had any idea that Luther Caleb was watching them from the forest above the rocks. He waited until they had gone back into the house before emerging from his hiding place. Then he ran along the path from Goose Cove until he reached his Mustang. He drove to Somerset and left his car in front of Clark's. He rushed inside; he needed to speak to Jenny. Someone had to know. He had a bad feeling about this. But Jenny didn't want to see him.

"Luther? You shouldn't be here," she said, when he appeared at the counter.

"Jenny, I'm forry for ve other morning. I wav wrong to grab your arm ve way I did."

"I have a bruise."

"I'm forry."

"You have to leave now."

"No, wait . . ."

"I've filed a complaint against you, Luther. Travis says that if you come back to town, I should call him—and you'll have to deal with the police. You really ought to leave before he sees you here."

He looked upset. "You filed a complaint againft me?"

"Yes. You really scared me the other day."

"But I have to fpeak to you about fomefing important."

"Nothing is important, Luther. Please go away."

"It'f about Harry Quebert."

"Harry?"

"Yef. Tell me what you fink about Harry Quebert."

"Why are you asking me about him?"

"Do you truft him?"

"Trust him? Yes, of course. Why are you asking me that?"

"I have to tell you fomefing . . ."

"Tell me something? What?"

Just as Luther was about to reply, a police car appeared outside Clark's.

"It's Travis!" Jenny said. "Run, Luther, run! I don't want you to get in trouble."

Caleb was gone like a shot. Jenny saw him get back in his car and speed off. A few moments later, Travis Dawn rushed inside.

"Did I just see Luther Caleb?" he demanded.

"Yes," Jenny replied. "But he wasn't bothering me. He's a nice guy. I wish I hadn't filed that complaint against him."

"I told you to let me know. Nobody has the right to raise a hand to you! Nobody!"

Travis headed back to his car. Jenny rushed after him and stopped him on the sidewalk.

"Please, Travis, I'm begging you—don't make a big deal out of this! I think he's got the message now."

Travis looked at her and suddenly realized what it was he had been failing to understand. So that was why she had been so distant with him lately.

"No, Jenny, don't tell me you—"

"What?"

"Do you have a crush on that nutcase?"

"Huh? What are you talking about?"

"Jesus Christ! How could I have been so stupid?"

"No, Travis, I don't know what you're talking about."

He was no longer listening. He got in his car and set off, siren blaring and blue light flashing.

On Shore Road, just before Side Creek Lane, Luther saw the police car in his rearview mirror, and he pulled over. Travis got out of his car. He was furious. How could Jenny be attracted to this monster? How could she prefer Luther to him? He did everything for her, he'd even stayed in Somerset to be close to her, and now he'd been supplanted by this creep. He ordered Luther to get out of his vehicle, then looked him up and down.

"You goddamn retard, what have you been doing to Jenny?"

"Nofing, Travif. I fwear, it'f not what you fink."

"I saw the bruises on her wrist."

"I never meant to hurt her, I fwear. I regret it finferely. I don't want any trouble wiv ve polife."

"Don't want any trouble? But you're the one causing trouble! Are you fucking her?"

"What?"

"You and Jenny, do you fuck?"

"No! No!"

"I do everything I can to make her happy and you're the one who fucks her? For God's sake, what is wrong with this world?"

"Travif . . . it'f not what you fink at all."

"Shut your mouth!" Travis shouted, grabbing Luther by the collar, then throwing him to the ground.

He did not know what he should do. He thought of Jenny's rejection of him, and he felt humiliated and miserable. But he felt angry too. He'd had enough of being trampled on; it was time he started to act like a man. So he unsheathed his nightstick, held it high in the air, and began savagely beating Luther.

15

Before the Storm

"What do you think?"

"It's not bad. But I think you're placing too much importance on the words."

"On the words? But they're kind of important when you're writing, aren't they?"

"Yes and no. The meaning of the word is more important than the word itself."

"What do you mean?"

"Well, words are words and everyone can use them. All you need to do is open a dictionary and choose one. It is at this moment that it becomes interesting: Will you be capable of giving a particular meaning to that word?"

"I still don't understand."

"Take a word, and use it in one of your books at every opportunity. Choose a word randomly: seagull, for example. People will start to say of you: 'You know Marcus Goldman? He's the one who writes about seagulls.' And then a time will come when those same people, when they see a seagull, will think only of you. They'll watch those screeching birds and they'll think: 'I wonder what Goldman would make of them?' Then soon they'll start associating the words 'seagull' and 'Goldman.' And each time they see seagulls, they will think about your book, about all of your books. They will no longer see those seagulls in the same way. It is at this point that you know you are writing something. Words are for everybody, until you prove that you are capable of appropriating them. That's what defines a writer. You see, Marcus, some people would like you to believe that a book consists of relationships between words, but that's not true: It is in fact about relationships between people."

Monday, July 7, 2008, Boston, Massachusetts

Four days after the arrest of Chief Pratt, I met Barnaski in his suite at the Park Plaza in Boston to sign a two-million-dollar contract for my book on the Harry Quebert case. Douglas was there too; he was clearly relieved.

"What a turnaround!" Barnaski said. "The great Goldman is finally back to work, to everyone's delight."

I said nothing in reply, but simply took a stack of papers from my satchel and handed them to him. He grinned.

"So these are your opening fifty pages . . ."

"Yes."

"Can I take a minute to look at them?"

"Of course."

Douglas and I left the room so that Barnaski could read in peace, and we went down to the hotel bar, where we ordered dark draft beers.

"How are things, Marc?"

"O.K. The last four days have been crazy . . ."

He nodded. "This whole story is unbelievable! You have no idea how huge your book is going to be. Barnaski knows—that's why he offered you so much money. Two million bucks is nothing compared with what he might make from it. In New York, this case is all anyone talks about. The Hollywood studios are already talking about making it into a movie; all the other publishers want to bring out books on Quebert. But everyone knows that the only person who can really write about it is you. You're the only one who knows Harry, the only one who can write about Somerset from the inside. Barnaski says that if they are the first ones to bring out a book on this, Nola Kellergan could become a registered trademark for them."

"And what do you think?" I asked.

"That it's an exciting adventure for a writer. And a good way of countering all the disgraceful things that have been said about Quebert. The reason you went to Somerset in the first place was to defend him, wasn't it?"

I nodded, then glanced up above us, toward the building's upper floors, where Barnaski was reading the beginning of my story, expanded considerably in the light of recent events.

July 3, 2008, four days before the signing of the contract

A few hours had elapsed since Chief Pratt's arrest. I went back to Goose Cove from the state prison, where Harry had lost his head and I had come close to being smashed in the face by a flying chair. I parked in front of the house and, as I got out of the car, my eye was immediately caught by the piece of paper jammed in the front doorway: yet another letter. And this time, the message had changed:

Last warning, Goldman

First warning, last warning . . . what difference did it make? I threw the letter in the kitchen trash can and turned on the television. Chief Pratt's arrest was all over the news. Some commentators were calling into question the investigation he had led at the time, speculating that perhaps he had been deliberately negligent.

The sun was setting, and it promised to be a warm, dry night, the kind of summer evening that ought to be spent with friends, barbecuing huge steaks and drinking beer. I did not have any friends, but I thought I had steaks and beer. The fridge was empty, though; I had forgotten to buy groceries. I had forgotten myself. I realized that my fridge was like Harry's: a single man's fridge. I ordered a pizza and ate it on the deck. At least I had the deck and the ocean. All I was missing was a barbecue, some friends, and a girlfriend to make this the perfect evening. It was at that moment that I received a telephone call from one of my few friends, someone I hadn't heard from in quite some time: Douglas.

"Hey, Marc, what's up?"

"*What's up?* It's been weeks since I've heard from you. Where were you? You're supposed to be my agent, for Christ's sake!"

"I know—I'm sorry. We've been through a difficult time. You and me, I mean. But if you still want me as your agent, I would be honored to continue our collaboration."

"Of course I still want you. On one condition: that you continue coming to my apartment to watch baseball."

He laughed.

"Fine with me. You take care of the beer, I'll get the nachos."

"Barnaski offered me a contract," I said.

"I know. He told me. Are you going to sign it?"

"I think so, yeah."

"Barnaski wants to see you as soon as possible."

"Why?"

"To sign the contract."

"Already?"

"Yes. I think he wants to make sure you've actually started work on the book. The deadline is short—you'll have to write quickly. He's totally obsessed by the presidential campaign. Are you ready?"

"Yes—I've already started writing again. But I don't know what I ought to be writing, exactly. Should I tell everything I know? Should I say that Harry had intended to elope with the girl? This story is insane, Doug. I don't think you even realize."

"You just need to tell the truth, Marc. Tell the truth about Nola Kellergan."

"What if the truth harms Harry?"

"You have to tell the truth, anyway. It's your responsibility as a writer. No matter how difficult it is. That's my advice as a friend."

"What about your advice as an agent?"

"Cover your ass. Try not to end up with as many lawsuits as there are people in New Hampshire. For example, you told me the girl was beaten by her parents?"

"By her mother, yes."

"So just write that Nola was 'an unhappy mistreated girl.' Everyone will understand that her parents are responsible for the mistreatment, without it being made explicit. So no-one will be able to take you to court."

"But the mother plays an important part in this story."

"My advice as an agent: You need concrete proof if you're going to accuse people. Otherwise, you're going to spend the rest of your life in court. And I think you've probably had enough of that kind of hassle recently. Find a reliable witness who will tell you that the mother was an evil bitch and that she beat the living daylights out of the girl—and if you can't, then stick to 'unhappy and mistreated girl.' We also want to avoid an injunction on book sales due to libel problems. Where Pratt is concerned, on the other hand, now that everyone knows what he did, you can go into the sordid details. That'll boost sales."

Barnaski suggested we meet on Monday, July 7, in Boston, a city that had the advantage of being one hour from New York by plane and about the same from Somerset by car, and I agreed. That left me four days to work flat out on the book, so I would have a few chapters to show him.

"Call me if you need anything," Douglas told me again before hanging up.

"I will, thanks. Oh, Doug, wait . . ." I hesitated. "Remember when you used to make mojitos?"

I knew he was smiling.

"Of course I remember."

"Those were good times, weren't they?"

"These are still good times, Marc. We have wonderful lives, even if we go through more difficult periods now and then."

December 1, 2006, New York City

"Hey, Doug, can you make more mojitos?"

Standing behind the counter in my kitchen, Douglas—wearing an apron depicting a naked woman's body—howled like a wolf, grabbed a bottle of rum, and emptied it into a pitcher filled with crushed ice.

It was three months after the publication of my first book; my fame was at its peak. For the fifth time in the three weeks since I had moved into my apartment in the Village, I was hosting a party. There were dozens of people crammed into my living room, and I knew barely a quarter of them. But I loved that. Douglas was in charge of keeping the mojitos coming, and I was taking care of the White Russians, the only cocktail I had ever found drinkable.

"What a party!" Douglas said. "Is that your doorman dancing in your living room?"

"Yes. I invited him."

"And Lydia Gloor is here! Holy crap, can you believe it? Lydia Gloor is in your apartment!"

"Who's Lydia Gloor?"

"You've got to be kidding me. She's the actress of the moment. She's on that show that everyone's watching . . . well, everyone except you, obviously. How did you manage to get her here?"

"I have no idea. People ring the doorbell, and I let them in. *Mi casa es tu casa!*"

I went back into the living room carrying a tray of canapés and cocktail shakers. I saw through the window that it was snowing outside, and I felt a sudden desire to get some fresh air. I went onto the balcony without a coat; the air was icy. I contemplated the millions of lights around me, and I yelled at the top of my voice: "I am Marcus Goldman!" Just then, I heard a voice behind me. I turned around and saw a pretty blonde my own age whom I had never seen before in my life.

"Marcus Goldman, your friend Douglas says your phone is ringing."

Her face was familiar.

"Have I seen you somewhere before?" I asked.

"On T.V., probably."

"You're Lydia Gloor."

"Yes."

"Wow."

I asked if she would wait for me on the balcony, and rushed to the kitchen to answer the phone.

"Hello?"

"Marcus? It's Harry."

"Harry! It's great to hear your voice! How are you?"

"I'm O.K. I just thought I'd see how you were doing. It's kind of noisy there. Are you having a party? Maybe this is a bad time . . ."

"Just a small party. In my new apartment."

"You've left Montclair?"

"Yes, I bought an apartment in the Village. I live in New York now! You have to come see this place—the view is amazing."

"I'm sure it is. Anyway, it sounds like you're having fun. I'm happy for you, Marcus. You must have a lot of friends."

"I do! And not only that, but there is an incredibly hot actress waiting for me on my balcony! Ha-ha—this is just unbelievable! Life is sweet, Harry. And how about you? What are you up to tonight?"

"I . . . I just have friends over for steaks and beer. Who could ask for more? We're having a good time. All that's missing is you. But I just heard my doorbell, Marcus. Other guests arriving. I need to let you go. I don't know if we're all going to fit here—and God knows it's a big house!"

"Have a great night, Harry. I'll call you."

I went back onto the balcony. That was the evening I began going out with Lydia Gloor—the girl my mother would refer to as "that T.V. actress." At Goose Cove, Harry would open the door to the pizza delivery man. He would take his pizza and eat it in front of the television.

I did call Harry, as promised, after that night. But more than a year went by between those two calls. It was now February 2008.

"Hello?"

"Harry, it's Marcus."

"Oh, Marcus! Is it really you? Incredible. I haven't heard a word from you since you became a star. I tried calling you a month ago and was told by your secretary that you weren't coming to the phone for anyone."

"I'm in trouble, Harry," I answered bluntly. "I don't think I'm a writer anymore."

He immediately dropped the sarcasm. "What're you talking about?"

"I don't know what to write anymore. I'm finished. Totally blocked. It's been like this for months, maybe a year."

He laughed warmly, reassuringly. "It's just a mental hang-up, Marcus! Writer's block is as senseless as sexual impotence: It's just your genius panicking, the same way your libido makes you go soft when you're about to play hide-the-salami with one of your young admirers and all you can think about is how you're going to give her an orgasm that can be measured on the Richter scale. Don't worry about genius—just keep churning out the words. Genius comes naturally."

"You think?"

"I'm sure of it. But you might have to give up a few of your celebrity parties. Writing is a serious business. I thought I'd taught you that."

"But I am working hard! That's all I'm doing! And yet I'm not getting anywhere."

"Well, maybe you're in the wrong place, then. New York is a wonderful city, but there's too much noise. Why don't you come here, to my place, like you did when you were my student?"

July 4–6, 2008

In the days preceding the meeting with Barnaski in Boston, the investigation moved forward in spectacular style.

First, Chief Pratt was charged with engaging in sexual acts with a minor, and released on bail the day after his arrest. He moved temporarily to a motel in Montburry, while Amy went to stay with her sister, who lived out of state. Pratt's interview by the state police criminal division confirmed not only that Tamara Quinn had showed him the note about Nola that she had found in Harry's house, but also that Nancy Hattaway had told him what she knew about Elijah Stern. The reason Pratt had deliberately ignored these two avenues of investigation was that he feared Nola had told one of them about the incident in the police car, and he didn't want to risk compromising himself by interrogating them. He did, however, swear that he had nothing to do with the deaths of Nola and Deborah Cooper, and that the search he had carried out for Nola's body was beyond reproach.

On the basis of these statements, Gahalowood persuaded the prosecutor's office to issue a search warrant for Stern's home. The search took place on the morning of Friday, July 4. The painting of Nola was found in the studio and removed. Stern was taken to the state police headquarters to be interviewed, but he was not charged. Nevertheless this latest development ratcheted up public curiosity about the case even higher. First the famous writer Harry Quebert was arrested, then the former police chief Gareth Pratt, and now the richest man in New Hampshire was apparently mixed up in the death of young Nola Kellergan.

Gahalowood described Stern's interview to me in detail. "He's an impressive guy. Totally calm. He even told his army of lawyers to wait out in the hallway. That presence, those steel-blue eyes—he made me feel almost ill at ease during the examination, and God knows I've had plenty of experience with that kind of thing. I showed him the painting, and he acknowledged that it was of Nola."

"Why did you have this painting in your house?" Gahalowood had asked him.

Stern had replied, as if the answer were obvious, "Because it's mine. Is there a law in this state against hanging paintings on one's walls?"

"No. But this painting is of a young girl who was murdered."

"If I had a painting of John Lennon, would I be suspected of his murder?"

"You know perfectly well what I mean, Mr Stern. Where did you get this painting?"

"One of my former employees painted it. Luther Caleb."

"Why did he paint this picture?"

"He loved painting."

"When was this painting done?"

"Summer 1975. July or August, if my memory serves me."

"Just before the girl disappeared."

"Yes."

"How did it come to be painted?"

"With a paintbrush, I imagine."

"Cut the wisecracks, please, Mr Stern. How did he know Nola?"

"Everyone in Somerset knew Nola. The painting was inspired by her."

"Didn't it bother you to own a painting of a girl who'd disappeared?"

"No. It's a beautiful picture. We call this art. And true art is disturbing. Anything else is merely the result of the degeneration of a world corrupted by political correctness."

"Are you aware that the possession of a picture showing a naked fifteen-year-old girl could cause problems for you, Mr Stern?"

"Naked? Neither her breasts nor her genitalia are shown."

"But it's obvious that she's naked."

"Are you ready to defend your point of view in court, Sergeant? Because you would lose, and you know that as well as I do."

"I would just like to know why Luther Caleb painted Nola Kellergan."

"I told you: He loved painting."

"Did you know Nola Kellergan?"

"Slightly. Like everyone in Somerset did."

"Only slightly?"

"Only slightly."

"You're lying, Mr Stern. I have witnesses who will state that you were in a relationship with her. That you had her brought to your house."

Stern laughed. "Do you have any proof for what you're claiming? I doubt it, because it's not true. I never touched that young girl. Clearly, Sergeant, your investigation is going nowhere and you're struggling to find the right questions. So I'm going to help you: Nola Kellergan came to find me. She came to my house one day and told me she needed money. She agreed to pose for a painting."

"You paid her to pose?"

"Yes. Luther had great talent as a painter. Unbelievable talent. He had already painted some wonderful pictures for me—views of the New Hampshire coast, scenes of daily life—and I was thrilled by them. Luther had the potential to be one of the century's greatest painters, and I believed he might produce something magnificent if he painted that beautiful girl. And I was right: Were I to sell this picture today, with all the hype surrounding this case, I would undoubtedly make at least a million dollars, maybe two. Do you know many contemporary painters whose work sells for that much?"

Stern then stated that he had wasted enough time already and that the interview was over, and he left, followed by his army of lawyers, leaving Gahalowood speechless and adding yet another mystery to the investigation.

"Did you fully grasp that, writer?" Gahalowood asked me after he had finished his report on Stern's interrogation. "One day the girl goes to Stern's house and offers to pose for a painting in exchange for money. Can you believe it?"

"It's crazy. Why would she need money? To elope with Harry?"

"Maybe. And yet she didn't even take her savings with her. There's a tin box in her bedroom containing a hundred and twenty dollars."

"Where's the painting?" I asked.

"We're holding on to it for the moment. It's evidence."

"Evidence for what? I thought Stern hadn't been charged."

"Evidence against Caleb."

"Is he really a suspect?"

"I don't know. Stern wanted a painting of Nola, and Pratt wanted her to suck his cock, but what motive did they have for killing her?"

"Fear that she would talk?" I suggested. "She might have threatened to tell all, and in a moment of panic one of them might have hit her so hard that she died."

"But then why leave that note on the manuscript? *Goodbye, darling Nola.* This is someone who loved her. And the only one who loved her is Quebert. Everything brings us back to Quebert. What if Quebert, having learned about Pratt and Stern, lost his head and killed Nola? This might very well be a crime of passion. That was your theory at one point, if you remember."

"Harry, and a crime of passion? That makes no sense. When will we ever get the results from that damn handwriting analysis?"

"Soon. It's only a matter of days now, I think. Marcus, I have to tell you something: The D.A. is going to offer Quebert a deal. They'll drop the kidnap charge if he pleads guilty to a crime of passion. Twenty years in jail. He'd be out in fifteen if he behaved well. No death penalty."

"Why would Harry want a deal? He didn't do anything wrong."

I sensed there was something we were failing to see, a detail that would explain everything. I went back over Nola's final days, but nothing noteworthy seemed to have happened until that fateful evening of August 30. In fact after my conversations with Jenny Dawn, Tamara Quinn, and a few others from Somerset, it seemed to me that Nola Kellergan's last three weeks of life had been happy. On the other hand, Harry had depicted those torture scenes, Pratt had described how he had forced Nola to perform fellatio on him, and Nancy had told me about sordid meetings with Luther Caleb. Yet Jenny's and Tamara's testimonies were very different. According to them, there was nothing to suggest that Nola was unhappy or mistreated. Tamara even told me that Nola had asked to start waitressing again at Clark's once school started, which she had agreed to. I was so surprised by this that I twice asked her to confirm it. Why would Nola have taken steps to ensure she still had a job if she was planning to run away? Robert Quinn told me that he had seen her occasionally carry a typewriter, but that she sang and looked cheerful as she carted it along with her. From the sounds of it, Somerset in August 1975 was a kind of heaven on earth. I began to wonder if Nola had indeed intended to leave town. Then I was seized by a horrifying thought: How could I be sure that Harry was telling me the truth? How could I know whether Nola had really asked him to elope with her? What if it was just a ploy to get himself off the hook for her murder? What if Gahalowood had been right all along?

I saw Harry again on the afternoon of July 5, in prison. His expression was dreadful, his skin gray-hued. Lines I had never seen before had appeared on his forehead.

"The D.A. wants to offer you a deal," I said.

"I know. Roth already talked to me about it. A crime of passion. I could be out in fifteen years."

I understood from his tone that he was considering this option.

"Don't tell me you're going to accept that!" I said angrily.

"I don't know. It's a way of avoiding the death penalty."

"Avoiding the death penalty? What's that supposed to mean? That you're guilty?"

"No! But everything seems to condemn me. And I have no desire to play a hand of poker with jurors who've already decided I'm guilty. Fifteen years in prison: It's better than a life sentence, or death row."

"Harry, I'm going to ask you this one last time: Did you kill Nola?"

"Of course not! For Christ's sake, how many times do I have to tell you?"

"Then let's prove it."

I took out my minidisc recorder and placed it on the table.

"No, please! Not that thing again."

"I have to understand what happened."

"I don't want you to record me anymore. Please."

"Alright. I'll take notes instead."

I took out a notebook and a pen.

"I would like us to go back to our previous discussion about your elopement on August 30. Correct me if I'm wrong, but at the time the two of you decided to leave, your book was practically finished."

"I finished it a few days before we were supposed to leave. I wrote it very fast. I felt I was in a trance. Everything was so wonderful: Nola being there all the time, rereading my words, correcting them, typing them up. This may seem mawkish to you, but it was magical. The book was finished on August 27. I remember it well because that was the last time I saw Nola. We had agreed that I should leave town two or three days before her, so that people didn't become suspicious. So August 27 was our last day together. I had finished the novel in a month. It was wild. I was so proud of myself. I remember those two manuscripts stacked up impressively on the deck table: the handwritten original and the version that Nola had worked so hard to type up. We went down to the beach, to where we had first met three months earlier. We walked for a long time. Nola held my hand and said, 'Meeting you changed my life, Harry. See how happy we are together.' We walked on. Our plan was in place: I was

to leave the next morning, August 28, stopping by at Clark's so people would see me and so I could tell them that I would be away for a week or two due to urgent business in Boston. I would take a hotel room in Boston, keeping my receipts so that it would all fit together if the police questioned me. And then, on August 30, I would come back and take a room at the Sea Side Motel. Nola told me to reserve Room 8, because she liked that number. I asked her how she would manage to reach that motel, which was some miles from Somerset, and she told me not to worry, that she was a fast walker and knew a shortcut via the beach. She would meet me at the motel that night at 7 p.m. Then we would have to leave right away, cross the border into Canada, and find a place to hole up—an apartment we could rent. I would go back to Somerset a few days later, as if nothing had happened. The police would be bound to search for Nola and I had to stay calm. If they questioned me, I would say I had been in Boston and show them the hotel receipts. I would then spend the next week in Somerset in order to quell suspicions, while Nola stayed in our apartment and waited for me. After that, I would give back the keys to Goose Cove and leave Somerset for good, explaining that my novel was finished and that I now had to take care of getting it published. Then I would return to Nola and send the manuscript to publishing houses in New York, and from then on I would travel between New York and our hideaway in Canada until the book was published."

"And what would Nola do?"

"We were going to get her a fake I.D., so she could finish high school and then go to college. We would have waited until she was eighteen, and then she would have become Mrs Harry Quebert."

"Fake I.D.? But that's crazy!"

"I know."

"So what happened next?"

"That day—August 27—we rehearsed the plan several times on the beach, then went back to the house. We sat on the old couch in the living room—which wasn't old at the time but has become so because I could never bear to get rid of it—and we had our last conversation. These were her last words to me, Marcus. I'll never forget them. She said, 'We'll be so happy, Harry. I'll become your wife. You'll be a great writer. And a university professor. I always dreamed of marrying a university professor. And we'll have a big, sun-colored dog, a Labrador we'll name Storm. You'll wait for me, won't you? Please wait for me!' And I replied: 'I'll wait my whole life for you, Nola, if I have to.' Those were her last words, Marcus. After that I nodded off, and when I woke up the sun was setting and Nola was gone. The ocean was aglow with that pink light, and the sky was full of screeching seagulls. Those damn seagulls she loved so much. There was now only one manuscript on the deck table: the handwritten original. And next to it was that note, the one you found in the box. I know those sentences by heart. It said: 'Don't worry, Harry. Don't you worry about me. I'll find a way to meet you. Wait for me in Room 8. I like that number, it's my favorite. Wait for me there at 7 p.m. And then we'll go away forever.' I didn't look for the manuscript; I realized she had taken it so she could read it one more time. Or maybe to make sure I would meet her at the motel on the thirtieth. She took that damn manuscript with her, Marcus, as she did sometimes. And the next day I left town, just as we had planned. I stopped by at Clark's to have coffee, so that people would see me and I could tell them I was going away. Jenny was there, as she was every morning. I told her I had to go to Boston, that my book was almost finished and I had some important meetings there. And then I left. I left, never suspecting for a second that I had seen Nola for the last time."

I put down my pen. Harry was crying.

July 7, 2008

Roy Barnaski gave himself a half-hour to read through the fifty-odd pages I had given him before he called us back to see him.

"So?" I asked, as I entered the room.

"It's just brilliant, Goldman! Brilliant! I knew you were the man of the hour."

"Just to warn you: Those pages are essentially my notes. There are things in there that can't be published."

"Of course, of course. You'll get the final say."

He ordered champagne, spread the contracts out on the table, and went over the main points again: "Delivery of the manuscript at the end of August. The jacket art will be ready by then. The book will be edited and typeset in two weeks, and printing will take place in September. Publication is set for the final week of September, at the latest. What perfect timing! Just before the presidential election, and more or less exactly during Quebert's trial! It's marketing genius!"

"And what if the investigation is still ongoing?" I asked. "How am I supposed to finish the book?"

Barnaski had his response all ready and rubber-stamped by his legal department. "If the investigation is finished, it's a true story. If not, we leave it open, you suggest the ending, and it's a novel. Legally they can't touch us, and for readers it makes no difference. And in fact, it's even better if the investigation isn't over, because we could do a sequel. What a godsend!"

He gave me a knowing look. An employee brought in the champagne, and Barnaski insisted on opening it himself. I signed the contract while he popped the cork, spilling champagne everywhere, and filled two glasses. He gave one to Douglas and the other to me.

"Aren't you having any?" I asked.

Grimacing with distaste, he wiped his hands on a cushion. "I can't stand the stuff. Champagne is just for show. But appearances matter, Goldman."

And he was called out to take a telephone call from Warner Brothers about the movie rights.

*

On the way back to Somerset later that afternoon, I got a call from Roth.

"We've got the results, Goldman! The handwriting isn't Harry's! He didn't write that note on the manuscript!"

I whooped.

"So what does that mean, in concrete terms?" I said.

"I don't know yet. But if it's not his writing, that proves he did not have the manuscript when Nola was killed. And the manuscript is one of the main pieces of evidence against him. The judge has ordered a new hearing for this Thursday at 2 p.m. With it coming so fast, that has to be good news for Harry!"

I was thrilled: Harry would soon be free. So he had been telling the truth all along; he was innocent. I couldn't wait for Thursday. But the day before, on Wednesday, July 9, disaster struck. At about 5 p.m., I was in Harry's office at Goose Cove, going through my notes about Nola, when I received a call on my cell from Barnaski. His voice was shaking.

"Marcus, I have terrible news," he told me straight out.

"What's happened?"

"There's been a robbery . . ."

"What do you mean, a robbery?"

"Your pages . . . the ones you gave me in Boston."

"What? How is that possible?"

"They were in a drawer of my desk. Yesterday morning I couldn't find them . . . At first I thought Marisa must have put them in the safe; she does that sometimes. But when I asked her, she said she hadn't touched them. I spent all day yesterday searching for them, but without success."

My heart was pounding. I sensed there was worse to come.

"But what makes you think they were stolen?" I asked.

There was a long silence, and then he replied: "I've been getting phone calls all afternoon. From the *Globe*, *USA Today*, the *New York Times* . . . Someone sent copies of your pages to all the major newspapers, and they're about to print them. Tomorrow the whole country will be aware of what's going to be in your book."

PART TWO

Writers' Cure
(Writing the Book)

14

August 30, 1975

"You see, Marcus, the way it works in our society, we are constantly having to choose between reason and passion. Reason never helps anyone and passion is often destructive. So, don't ask me to help you choose."

"Why do you say that?"

"Just because. Life is a rip-off."

"Are you going to finish your fries?"

"No. Help yourself."

"Thank you, Harry."

"You're really not interested in what I have to say, are you?"

"Yes, I am. Very interested. I'm listening carefully to everything you say. Number Fourteen: Life is a rip-off."

"For God's sake, Marcus, you haven't understood anything. Sometimes I get the feeling I'm talking to a moron."

4 p.m.

It had been a beautiful day: one of those late-summer, sun-soaked Saturdays when Somerset seemed so peaceful. In the center of town, people were strolling around, stopping in front of store windows, enjoying the last days of summer. The streets of the residential areas, free of cars, had been taken over by the children, who organized bicycle and roller-skate races while their parents sipped lemonade and read newspapers on shady porches.

For the third time in less than an hour, Travis Dawn drove down Terrace Avenue in his patrol car, passing the Quinn family's house. The afternoon had been totally calm; not a single call had been made to the station. He had stopped a few cars to keep himself busy, but his mind was elsewhere: He could not think of anything but Jenny. There she was, sitting on the porch with her father. They had spent the whole afternoon doing crosswords, while Tamara pruned the bushes in anticipation of fall. As he approached the house, Travis slowed down to a crawl; he was hoping she would notice him, that she would lift her head and see him, that she would wave, encouraging him to stop for a moment and to say hello to her through his open window. Maybe she would even offer him a glass of iced tea and they would chat for a while. But she did not lift her head; she did not see him. She was laughing with her father. She seemed happy. He kept driving, and stopped about a hundred feet farther on, out of sight. He looked at the bouquet of flowers on the passenger seat and picked up the piece of paper that lay next to it, on which he had scribbled what he wanted to say to her:

Hello, Jenny. What a beautiful day. If you're free this evening, I was thinking we could go for a walk on the beach. Maybe we could even go see a movie? They have some new movies opening in Montburry. (Give her the flowers.)

It was easy enough, suggesting they go for a walk and catch a movie. But he did not dare get out of his car. He quickly started the car again and drove on, following the same patrol route that would bring him back in front of the Quinns' house within twenty minutes. He put the flowers under the seat so that no-one would see them. They were wild roses, picked near Montburry, by the side of a little lake that Ernie Pinkas had told him about. At first sight they were not as pretty as cultivated roses, but their colors were much more vibrant. He had often wanted to take Jenny there; he had even come up with a special plan. He would blindfold her and lead her to the rose beds, and only when she was standing right in front of them would he untie the blindfold, so the colors would explode before her eyes like fireworks. Afterward they would have a picnic by the lake. But he had never been brave enough to ask her. He was driving down Terrace Avenue now, passing the Kellergans' house. Not that he noticed—his attention was elsewhere.

Despite the beautiful weather, the Reverend David Kellergan had spent the whole afternoon shut up in his garage, fiddling with an old Harley-Davidson he hoped one day to get working again. According to the Somerset police report, he left his workshop only to get himself a drink from the kitchen, and each time he did so, he found Nola peacefully reading in the living room.

5.30 p.m.

As the afternoon wound down, the streets in the center of town slowly emptied, while in the residential areas the children returned home for dinner, and there was nothing to be seen on the porches but empty chairs and abandoned newspapers.

The police chief, Gareth Pratt, who was off duty, went home with his wife, Amy, after the two of them had spent part of the day out of town, visiting friends. Meanwhile the Hattaway family—Nancy, her two brothers, and their parents—were arriving back at their house on Terrace Avenue, after spending the afternoon at Grand Beach. It says in the police report that Mrs Hattaway, Nancy's mother, noticed ear-splitting music coming from the Kellergan house.

*

Harry arrived at the Sea Side Motel. He registered for Room 8 under an assumed name and paid cash in order to avoid having to show I.D. On his way there he had filled up his gas tank and bought flowers. Everything was ready. Only an hour and a half to wait, if that. When Nola arrived, they would celebrate being together again and then take off immediately. By 10 p.m. they would be in Canada. They would be together at last. She would never be unhappy again.

6 p.m.

Deborah Cooper, who had, since the death of her husband, been living alone in a house on the edge of the Side Creek forest, sat down at her kitchen table to make an apple pie. After peeling and slicing the fruit, she tossed a few pieces through the window for the raccoons and stayed by the window to watch them come. That was how she came to glimpse a figure running through the trees. Looking more carefully, she could see quite distinctly a young girl in a red dress pursued by a man, before the two of them disappeared into the trees. She rushed to the living room, where the telephone was, so she could call 911. The police report indicates that the call was made to the station at 6.21 p.m. It lasted twenty-seven seconds. This is the transcript:

> "Somerset Police. What's your emergency?"
> "Hello? My name is Deborah Cooper. I live on Side Creek Lane. I think I've just seen a man running after a girl in the woods."
> "Could you tell me exactly what happened, ma'am?"
> "I don't know! I was standing by the window. I looked over toward the woods, and I saw this girl running through the trees. There was a man behind her. I think she was trying to get away from him."
> "Where are they now?"
> "I can't see them anymore. They're in the forest."

"I'm sending a patrol over right now, ma'am."
"Thank you. Come quick!"

After hanging up, Mrs Cooper returned immediately to her kitchen window. She could no longer see anything. She wondered if her eyes had been deceiving her, but it was better to be safe than sorry. She left the house to wait for the patrol car.

The report indicates that the police station sent the information to the police in Somerset. The only officer on duty that day was Travis Dawn. He reached Side Creek Lane about four minutes after the call.

After quickly appraising the situation, Officer Dawn began an initial search of the forest. He walked through the woods for about a hundred feet, then found a scrap of red fabric. Judging that the situation might be serious, he decided to inform Chief Pratt, even though he was off duty. Dawn called him at home, from Mrs Cooper's house. It was 6.45 p.m.

7 p.m.

Chief Pratt decided that the situation was sufficiently serious that he should come in person to assess things: Only under the most exceptional circumstances would Travis Dawn have disturbed him at home.

Upon his arrival at Side Creek Lane, Chief Pratt told Mrs Cooper to lock herself in the house while he and Travis undertook a more extensive search of the forest. They followed the path that runs parallel to the beach, in the direction the girl in the red dress seemed to have gone. According to the police report, after the two policemen had walked just over a mile, they discovered traces of blood and some blond hairs in a clearing in the forest close to the ocean. It was 7.30 p.m.

It is likely that Mrs Cooper remained by her kitchen window to keep watch. The two policeman had already vanished from the path for quite some time when she saw a young woman appear from the forest, her dress torn and her face covered with blood, and heard her shout for help as she ran toward the house. In a panic, Mrs Cooper unlocked the kitchen door to let her in and rushed to the living room to call the police again.

The police report indicates that the second call from Mrs Cooper came in at 7.33 and lasted a little more than forty seconds:

"Police. What's your emergency?"

"Hello? This is Deborah Cooper. I . . . I called earlier to . . . to report a young girl who was being chased in the woods, and now she's here! She's in my kitchen!"

"Calm down, ma'am. Can you tell me what happened?"

"I don't know! She came from the forest. There are two policemen in the forest at the moment, but I don't think they saw her. I let her into my kitchen. I . . . I think it's the pastor's daughter . . . The girl who works at Clark's . . . I think it's her . . ."

"What is your address?"

"Deborah Cooper, Side Creek Lane, Somerset. I called you before! The girl is here—do you understand? Her face is covered in blood! Come quick!"

"Don't move, ma'am. I'm sending backup immediately."

The two policemen were inspecting the traces of blood when they heard the gunshot from the direction of the house. Without a second's thought, they ran back along the path, firearms at the ready.

At the same moment, the police station operator, unable to get hold of either Officer Travis Dawn or Chief Pratt on their car radios, and deciding that the situation was serious, issued a general alert to the sheriff's office and the state police, and sent all available units to Side Creek Lane.

*

7.45 p.m.

Officer Dawn and Chief Pratt arrived at the house, out of breath. They went through the back door, which opened into the kitchen, where they found Deborah Cooper dead, lying on the tiles in a pool of her own blood, with a gunshot wound to the chest. Having quickly searched the first floor of the house and found nothing, Chief Pratt ran to his car to inform the station and ask for backup. This is the transcript of his conversation with the police operator:

"This is Chief Pratt, Somerset Police. Urgent request for backup at Side Creek Lane at the Shore Road intersection. We have a woman dead from a bullet wound and probably a missing kid."

"Chief Pratt, we already received a distress call from a Mrs Deborah Cooper, of Side Creek Lane, at 7.33, informing us that a young girl had taken refuge at her house. Are the two cases connected?"

"What? Deborah Cooper is the dead woman. And there's no-one left in the house. Send all available units! There's some nasty shit going down here!"

"Units are on their way, Chief. I'll send you more backup."

Even before the conversation was over, Pratt heard a siren—the backup was already there. He had barely had time to inform Travis of the situation, and in particular to tell him to search the house again, when the radio crackled to life: There was a chase on Shore Road, a few hundred yards from there, between a sheriff's car and a suspicious vehicle that had been spotted by the edge of the forest. The deputy sheriff, Paul Summond, the first of the reinforcements to reach Somerset, had seen a black Chevrolet Monte Carlo, license plates unreadable, coming out of the woods and speeding away in defiance of his orders. It was headed north.

Chief Pratt jumped into his car and went to help Summond. He took a forest road that ran parallel to Shore Road, hoping to cut in front of the fugitive farther up. He burst onto the highway three miles beyond Side Creek Lane, just failing to intercept the black Chevrolet.

The cars were going at crazy speeds. The Chevrolet was following Shore Road northward. Chief Pratt sent a radio call to all available units to form roadblocks, and asked for a helicopter to be sent. Soon the Chevrolet, changing direction suddenly, turned onto a minor road, and then onto another. It was going very fast; the police vehicles were struggling to keep up. Pratt yelled into his car radio that they were losing the suspect.

The pursuit continued on narrow roads. The driver seemed to know exactly where he was going, and was gradually able to leave the police behind. Coming to an intersection, the Chevrolet just avoided crashing into a vehicle coming the other way, which stopped dead in the middle of the road. Pratt was able to get around the obstacle by driving over the grass, but Summond, just behind him, couldn't avoid colliding with the car. Fortunately nobody was seriously hurt. Pratt, now the only one with the Chevrolet in his sights, guided the backup as best he could. He lost visual contact with the car for a moment but spotted it again on the Montburry road before being left behind for good. He realized the suspect's vehicle had escaped them when he saw patrol cars coming toward him from the opposite direction. He immediately ordered more roadblocks on every road, a general search of the area, and the intervention of the state police. Back at Side Creek Lane, Travis Dawn was unequivocal: There was not the slightest trace of the girl in the red dress—not in the house or on the property surrounding it.

8 p.m.

In a panic, the Reverend David Kellergan called 911 and reported that his daughter, Nola, was nowhere to be found. A county sheriff's deputy, sent as backup, was the first to arrive at 245 Terrace Avenue, closely followed by Travis Dawn. At 8.15, Chief Pratt arrived. The conversation between Deborah Cooper and the police station operator left them in no doubt: Nola Kellergan was the girl who had been seen on Side Creek Lane.

At 8.25, Chief Pratt issued a new general alert confirming the disappearance of Nola Kellergan, fifteen years old, seen for the last time one hour earlier on Side Creek Lane. He ordered a missing-person appeal to be broadcast, stating that the police were searching for a young white girl, five foot two, one hundred pounds, long blond hair, green eyes, wearing a red dress and a gold necklace with the name NOLA engraved on it.

Police reinforcements came from all over the county. While an initial search of the forest and the beach was conducted in the hope of finding Nola Kellergan before nightfall, patrol cars roamed the area in search of the black Chevrolet, all traces of which had, for the moment, disappeared.

9 p.m.

State police units arrived at Side Creek Lane, commanded by Captain Neil Rodik. Forensics teams were also sent to Deborah Cooper's house and into the forest, where the traces of blood had been found. Powerful halogen lamps were used to illuminate the area; they found clumps of blond hair, broken fragments of teeth, and scraps of red fabric.

Rodik and Pratt, observing from a distance, took stock of the situation.

"Looks pretty violent," Pratt said.

Rodik nodded, then asked: "You think she's still in the forest?"

"Either she disappeared in that car or she's in the forest. We've already carried out a thorough search of the beach."

"I am asking myself," Rodik said, "has she been taken far away from here? Or is she lying hidden in the woods?"

Pratt sighed. "All I want is to find this girl alive, as quickly as possible."

"I know, Chief. But with all the blood she's lost, if she is still alive somewhere in the woods, she is going to be in a terrible state. You wonder how she found the strength to get as far as that house. Pure desperation, I guess."

"Yeah, probably."

"No news on the car?" Rodik said.

"Nothing. It's a real mystery. And there are roadblocks everywhere, in every possible direction."

When police discovered traces of blood leading from Deborah Cooper's house to the place near the woods where the black Chevrolet had been, Rodik's expression was resigned.

"I don't want to be a prophet of doom," he said, "but either she crawled somewhere to die or she ended up in the trunk of that car."

At 9.45, with the sun no more than a halo above the horizon, Rodik asked Pratt to call off the search for the night.

"You can't be serious," Pratt protested. "What if she's around here somewhere, still alive, waiting for help? Come on, we can't abandon her now! If she's in the forest, we'll find her, even if it takes all night."

Rodik was an experienced officer. He knew that local police were sometimes naive, and part of his job was to persuade them to face reality when the situation demanded.

"Chief Pratt, you have to call off the search. These woods are huge, and it's too dark to see. Searching at night is pointless. The best-case scenario is that you'll use up your resources, and you'll have to start all over again tomorrow. The worst-case scenario is that you might lose cops, and then you'd have to search for them too. You already have enough to worry about."

"But we have to find her!"

"Chief, trust my experience: Spending the night outside is a useless exercise. If the girl's alive, even if she's injured, we'll find her tomorrow."

The people of Somerset were beside themselves. Hundreds of gawkers surrounded the Kellergans' house, held back by lines of police. Everyone wanted to know what had happened. When Chief Pratt returned there, he had no choice but to confirm the rumors: Deborah Cooper was dead, and Nola had vanished. People cried out in fear; mothers took their children home and barricaded them inside, while fathers took out their old rifles and organized themselves into citizen militias to watch over the area. Chief Pratt's task became more complicated: He had to prevent the town from succumbing to panic. To reassure people, patrol cars roamed the streets while state police officers went door to door collecting witness statements from the Kellergans' neighbors.

11 p.m.

In the staff room of the Somerset police station, Chief Pratt and Captain Rodik reviewed the situation. There had been no evidence of a break-in or a struggle in Nola's bedroom. Nothing but the wide open window.

"Did the girl take anything with her?" Rodik asked.

"No. No clothes, no money. Her piggy bank hasn't been touched: There's a hundred and twenty dollars inside."

"Sounds like she was abducted."

"And none of the neighbors noticed anything."

"I'm not surprised. Someone must have persuaded the girl to go with him."

"Through the window?"

"Maybe. Or maybe not. It's August—everyone keeps their windows open. Maybe she just went out for a walk and encountered the wrong person."

"Apparently one witness, Gregory Stark, says he heard raised voices at the Kellergan house while he was out walking his dog. That was around 5 p.m., but he's not sure about it."

"What do you mean, he's not sure?" Rodik demanded.

"He says there was music blaring out from the Kellergans'. Very loud music."

"We've got nothing," Rodik grumbled. "Not a clue, not a trace. It's like a ghost came in and took her. All we have is a brief sighting of the girl covered in blood and screaming for help."

"What do you think we should do now?" Pratt asked.

"You've done everything you can for tonight, believe me. We need to think about tomorrow. Send everyone home to get some rest, but keep the roadblocks up. Prepare a search plan for the forest. We need to start again at dawn. You're the only one who can lead that search: You know the forest by heart. You should also send an alert to all police forces. Provide every detail about Nola: that piece of jewelry she was wearing and the dress. Physical details will make her stand out and allow witnesses to identify her. I'll pass on that information to the F.B.I., to neighboring state police forces, and to the border police. I'm going to ask for a helicopter for tomorrow and reinforcements with dogs. Try to get some sleep if you can. And pray. I like my job, Chief, but when children get abducted . . . it's more than I can bear."

Police cars came and went, and people gathered and gawked at the house on Terrace Avenue. Some wanted to go into the woods. Others turned up at the police station, offering to take part in the search. Panic took hold of the town.

Sunday, August 31, 1975

A cool rain fell hard all over the region, as a thick mist moved in from the ocean. At 5 a.m., close to Mrs Cooper's house, Chief Pratt and Captain Rodik stood under a hastily constructed tent and gave orders to the first groups of police and volunteers. On a map, the forest had been divided into sectors, each one assigned to a different team. Reinforcements of search-and-rescue teams and forest rangers were expected later that morning, enabling the search to be extended and exhausted team members to be replaced. The request for a helicopter had been canceled for now, due to poor visibility.

At 7 a.m., in Room 8 of the Sea Side Motel, Harry woke up with a start. He had slept in his clothes. The radio was still on, and a newsflash was being broadcast: "General alert in the Somerset region after the disappearance of a teenage girl. Nola Kellergan, aged fifteen, vanished last night, around 7 p.m. Police are seeking anyone with information. At the time of her disappearance, Nola Kellergan was wearing a red dress . . ."

Nola! They had fallen asleep and forgotten to leave. He leaped out of bed and called her name. For a fraction of a second, he really believed she was in the room with him. Then he remembered that she had not showed up at the motel. Why had she abandoned him? The radio mentioned her disappearance, so she must have left home as they had planned. But why would she leave without him? Had something gone wrong? Had she gone to seek refuge at Goose Cove? Their elopement was turning into a disaster.

Still not aware of how serious the situation was, he threw away the flowers and left the room in a hurry, his hair uncombed and his tie untied. He threw his bags in the trunk of the car and sped back toward Goose Cove. After barely two miles, he came upon a major police roadblock.

Chief Gareth Pratt had come to check on things. He was carrying a shotgun. Everyone was on edge. He recognized Harry's car in the line of vehicles and went over to see him.

"Chief, I just heard about Nola on the radio," Harry said, his window lowered. "What's going on?"

"Nobody knows. Nola disappeared from home. She was seen near Side Creek Lane last night, and since then there hasn't been a trace of her. We've secured the whole area and we're searching the woods."

Harry thought his heart was going to stop beating. Side Creek Lane was on the way to the motel. Had something happened to her on the way to their meeting? Had she feared, once she had been seen on Side Creek Lane, that the police would go to the motel and find them there together? So where was she hiding?

The chief noticed the horrified expression on Harry's face and the backseat of his car filled with luggage.

"Are you coming back from somewhere?" he said.

Harry decided he ought to stick to the cover story he had agreed on with Nola.

"I was in Boston. For my book."

"Boston?" Pratt said, surprised. "But you're coming from the north..."

"I . . . I know," Harry stammered. "I had to go to Concord before coming home."

The chief looked at him suspiciously. Harry was driving a black Chevrolet Monte Carlo. Pratt told him to turn off his engine.

"Is there a problem?" Harry said.

"We're searching for a car like yours that may be involved in this case.

"A Monte Carlo?"

"Yes."

Two officers searched the car and the luggage. They found nothing suspicious, and Chief Pratt allowed Harry to move on. As Harry was leaving, the chief said to him: "I would ask you not to leave the area. Just a precaution, of course." The car radio kept repeating Nola's description. "A young white girl, five foot two, one hundred pounds, long blond hair, green eyes, wearing a red dress and a gold necklace with the name NOLA engraved on it."

She was not at Goose Cove: not inside the house, on the deck, or on the beach. She was nowhere to be found. He called her name. He didn't care if anyone heard him. He paced up and down the beach, out of his mind. He searched the house for a letter, a note. But there was nothing. He began to panic. Why had she left home, if not to meet him?

354

No longer knowing what to do, he went to Clark's. That was where he learned that Mrs Cooper had seen Nola covered in blood before being found dead herself. He could not believe it. Why had he allowed her to walk to the motel on her own? He should have gone to meet her in Somerset. He walked across town until he reached the Kellergans' house, which was surrounded by police cars, and listened to people's conversations in an attempt to understand. When he got back to Goose Cove later that morning, he sat on the deck with a pair of binoculars and bread for the seagulls. And waited. She had got lost. She would come back. He surveyed the beach through the binoculars. He kept on waiting. Until nightfall.

13

The Storm

"The danger of books, Marcus, is that sometimes you lose control of them. When you are published, the thing that you have written in such solitary fashion suddenly escapes from your hands and enters the public realm. This is a moment of great danger; you must keep control of the situation at all times. It is disastrous to lose control of your own book."

EXTRACTS FROM THE MAJOR EAST COAST NEWSPAPERS
July 10, 2008

From the *New York Times*

MARCUS GOLDMAN PREPARES TO LIFT THE VEIL ON THE HARRY QUEBERT CASE
The rumor that writer Marcus Goldman was preparing a book on Harry Quebert has been widespread for a few days among publishing circles in New York City. Now it has been confirmed by

actual pages from the work in question, which were sent to major national newspapers last night. The book recounts Mr Goldman's own methodical investigation into the events that led to the murder of fifteen-year-old Nola Kellergan, who disappeared on August 30, 1975, in Somerset, New Hampshire, and whose body was found buried on the property of Harry Quebert near Somerset on June 12, 2008.

The rights to Mr Goldman's book were acquired for $2 million by the New York publishing house Schmid & Hanson. The firm's C.E.O., Roy Barnaski, who refused to comment, nevertheless revealed that the book is to be published this fall under the title *The Harry Quebert Affair*. [...]

From the *Concord Herald*

THE REVELATIONS OF MARCUS GOLDMAN

[...] Goldman, a close friend of Harry Quebert's, who was his professor at Burrows College, describes recent events in Somerset from the inside. His account begins with discovery of the relationship between Quebert and the young Nola Kellergan, aged fifteen at the time.

"In the spring of 2008, about a year and a half after I had become the new star of American literature, something happened that I decided to bury deep in my memory: I discovered that my college professor Harry Quebert—sixty-seven years old and one of the most respected writers in the country—had been romantically involved with a fifteen-year-old girl when he was thirty-four. This happened during the summer of 1975."

From the *Washington Post*

MARCUS GOLDMAN'S BOMBSHELL

[…] As his investigation proceeds, Goldman seems to go from discovery to discovery. He notes in particular that Nola Kellergan was repeatedly beaten. Her friendship and closeness with Harry Quebert gave her a stability she had never known before, allowing her to dream of a better life. […]

From the *Boston Globe*

THE SCANDALOUS LIFE OF YOUNG NOLA KELLERGAN

Marcus Goldman uncovers evidence that, until now, was unknown to the press.

She was a sex object for E.S., a powerful businessman from Concord, who sent his chauffeur to fetch her as if she were fresh meat. Half-woman, half-child, at the mercies of the fantasies of the men of Somerset, she also became the prey of the local police chief, who forced her to perform fellatio on him—that same police chief whose responsibility it would be to lead the search for her after she disappeared. […]

And that is how I lost control of a book that did not even exist yet.

In the early hours of the morning on Thursday, July 10, I discovered the sensational headlines in the press. Snippets of what I had written were spread over the front pages of all the national newspapers, but with the sentences abridged and taken out of context. My theories had become despicable assertions; my suppositions, proven facts; my reflections, vile value judgments. My work had been dismembered, my ideas pillaged, my thoughts violated. Goldman, a writer in remission struggling to find his way back from the terror of the blank page, had been killed.

As the town of Somerset slowly awoke in a state of shock, its inhabitants read and reread the articles in the newspapers. The house landline rang constantly, while some angry people came to knock at my door in search of explanations. I had to choose between facing up to them or hiding: I decided to face up to them. At ten o'clock, I downed two double whiskeys and went to Clark's.

As I walked past the restaurant's main window, I felt the eyes of the regulars staring daggers at me. I sat at Table 17, heart pounding, and Jenny, looking furious, rushed over to tell me that I was the lowest of the low. I thought she was going to throw the contents of the coffeepot in my face.

"So you came here just to make money out of our suffering?" she exploded. "Just so you could write filth about us?"

She had tears in her eyes. I tried to calm her: "Jenny, you know that's not true. Those notes should never have been published."

"But did you really write that crap?"

"I admit that those phrases, taken out of context, seem appalling."

"But did you write them?"

"Yes, but—"

"There is no *but*, Marcus!"

"I can promise you I never meant to cause any harm to anyone."

"You didn't mean to cause any harm? Shall I quote your masterpiece to you?" She unfolded a newspaper. "Look, here it is: 'Jenny Quinn, the waitress at Clark's, fell in love with Harry at first sight . . .' Is that how you define me? As a waitress, as a slutty serving wench drooling with lust every time she thinks about Harry?"

"You know that's not true."

"But that's what you wrote, for God's sake! It's printed in every newspaper in this goddamn country! Everybody is going to read that! My friends, my family, my husband."

Jenny was screaming. The other customers watched in silence. To let things cool down, I decided to leave, so I went to the library, hoping to find an ally in Ernie Pinkas, as he was the most likely to understand how words badly used could end in disaster. But he was not particularly happy to see me either.

"So, it's the great Goldman," he said when he saw me. "Have you come to look for more insults to write about our town?"

"I'm appalled by this leak, Ernie."

"Appalled? Give me a break. Everyone is talking about your book. You're the number one news item. You should be happy. Anyway, I hope you did well with all the information I gave you. Marcus Goldman, the omnipotent god of Somerset—Marcus, who turns up here and says to me: 'I need to know this, I need to know that.' Never a word of thanks, as if this were all perfectly normal, as if I were just the servant of the great Marcus Goldman. You know what I did this weekend? I'm seventy-five years old, and every other Sunday I have to work at the supermarket in Montburry to make ends meet. I collect carts from the parking lot, and I return them to the entrance of the store. I know there's no glory in it, I know I'm not famous like you, but I deserve a crumb of respect, don't you think?"

"I'm sorry."

"Sorry? Bullshit. You're not sorry at all. You didn't know because you're not interested. You've never shown any interest in anyone in Somerset. All you've ever cared about is being famous. But fame has a downside!"

"I am genuinely sorry, Ernie. Why don't we go get some lunch?"

"I don't want lunch! I want you to leave me in peace! I have books to put away. Books are important. You are nothing."

I went back to Goose Cove to hide out. Marcus Goldman, adopted son of Somerset, had, without meaning to, betrayed his own family. I called Douglas and asked him to publish a denial.

"A denial of what? All the newspapers did was summarize what you wrote. It'll be published in two months anyway."

"The newspapers twisted everything! Nothing they printed corresponds to my book."

"Come on—don't make a big deal of this. You need to concentrate on your writing. That's what matters. You don't have much time. I hope you haven't forgotten that three days ago you signed a two-million-dollar contract to write a book in seven weeks."

"I know! I know! But that doesn't mean it has to be garbage."

"A book written in a few weeks is a book written in a few weeks."

"That's how long it took Harry to write *The Origin of Evil.*"

"Harry is Harry, if you know what I mean."

"No, I don't know."

"He's a truly great writer."

"Oh, thanks very much. And what am I?"

"You know that's not what I meant. You are a—how can I put this?— a *modern* writer. People like you because you're young and dynamic. And hip. That's what you are—a hip writer. Nobody expects you to win the Pulitzer Prize; they like your books because they're cool, they're entertaining, and there's nothing wrong with that."

"Is that really what you think? That I'm an *entertaining* writer?"

"That's not what I said, Marc. But you must be aware that some of your popularity comes from you being young and good-looking."

"Good-looking? Are you serious?"

"Come on, Marc, you convey a certain image. As I told you, you're cool. Everybody likes you. You're like a good friend, a mysterious lover, the ideal son-in-law, all wrapped up in one friendly package. That's why *The Harry Quebert Affair* will be such a big success. Think about how crazy this is—your book doesn't even exist yet, but people are fighting over it already. I've never seen anything like this."

"*The Harry Quebert Affair?*"

"That's the title of the book."

"What do you mean?"

"You wrote it yourself in your notes."

"It was a provisional title. I made that perfectly clear: provisional title. *Pro-vi-sion-al.* Ever heard of it? It's an adjective meaning not definitive, temporary."

"Didn't Barnaski tell you? The marketing department thinks the title is perfect. They decided that last night. There was an emergency meeting due to the leak. They decided they ought to use it as a marketing tool and they launched the advertising campaign this morning. I thought you knew. Go look online."

"You *thought* I knew? For fuck's sake, Doug, you're my agent! You shouldn't think, you should act. You should make sure I know everything that's happening with my book, goddamn it!"

I hung up in a rage, and went to check my computer. The first page of the Schmid & Hanson website was devoted to my book. There was a big color photograph of me and some black-and-white pictures of Somerset, along with these words:

THE HARRY QUEBERT AFFAIR
Marcus Goldman's account of the
disappearance of Nola Kellergan
Coming this fall
Pre-order your copy now!

The hearing ordered by the judge following the results of the handwriting analysis was scheduled for two o'clock that afternoon. Journalists had taken over the steps of the courthouse in Concord, while television newscasters, covering the event live, rehashed the latest revelations. There was now talk of charges being dropped.

One hour before the hearing, I called Roth to tell him I would not be at the courthouse.

"Are you hiding, Marcus?" he taunted. "Come on, don't be shy. This book is a blessing for everyone: Harry'll be acquitted, your career'll be on the upswing, and mine will get a huge boost. I'll no longer just be Roth from Concord, I'll be the Roth who's mentioned in your bestseller! This book is perfectly timed, especially for you. What is it, two years since you last wrote anything?"

"Shut up, Roth! You don't know what you're talking about."

"Oh, cut the crap. You know as well as I do that your book's going to be a huge hit. You're going to tell the whole country that Harry's a pervert. You were lacking inspiration, you didn't know what to write, and now you're writing a book that is a surefire success."

"Those pages should never have reached the newspapers."

"But you wrote those pages. Don't feel guilty, though: Thanks to you, I expect to get Harry out of prison today. No doubt the judge reads the papers, so I shouldn't have any trouble convincing him that Nola was a slut who consented fully to what she did with Harry."

"Don't you dare, Roth!" I shouted.

"Why not?"

"Because that's not what she was. And he loved her. He loved her!"

But he had already hung up. I saw him soon afterward on my T.V. screen, climbing the courthouse steps with a triumphant grin plastered all over his face. Reporters thrust their microphones at him, asking if what had been written in the press was true: Had Nola Kellergan been having affairs with all the men in town? Was the investigation back to square one? He cheerfully answered yes to every question that was thrown at him.

This was the hearing that would give Harry his freedom. In barely twenty minutes the judge rattled off the flaws in the prosecution's case, and the whole thing fell like a bad soufflé. The main piece of evidence—the manuscript—was completely undermined as soon as it was established that the message *Goodbye, darling Nola* had not been written by Harry. The remaining pieces of evidence were blown away like feathers: Tamara Quinn's accusations could not be backed up by any material proof, while the black Chevrolet Monte Carlo had not even been considered incriminating during the original inquiry. The investigation was nothing but a big mess, and the judge decided that, in light of new evidence, he would release Harry Quebert on half a million dollars bail. The door was now open for charges to be dropped completely.

This spectacular twist provoked hysteria among the journalists. Now the D.A.'s motives in arresting Harry were widely questioned. Had he merely been seeking a publicity boost by throwing the famous writer to the lions of public opinion? In front of the courthouse, the cameras followed the parties as they descended the steps. First came Roth, jubilantly proclaiming that by tomorrow—the deadline for posting bail—Harry would be a free man. Then came the D.A., who attempted in vain to explain the logic of his investigations.

When I'd had enough of watching these developments on television, I went out for a run. I needed to run far, to challenge my body. I needed to feel alive. I ran until I reached the small lake in Montburry, which was swarming with children and families. On the way back, not far from Goose Cove, I was passed by a fire truck, immediately followed by another and by a police car. That was when I noticed the thick, bitter smoke billowing from the tops of the pines, and I understood at once: The house was on fire. The anonymous letter writer had finally carried out his threat.

I ran faster than I had ever run before, desperately hoping to save the house that I loved so much. The firefighters were hard at work, but the huge flames were devouring the front of the house. Everything was burning. A hundred feet from the blaze, by the path, a policeman was inspecting the words painted in red on the hood of my car: *Burn, Goldman, burn.*

At 10 a.m. the next day, the house was still smoldering. Most of it had been destroyed. State police forensics experts were examining the ruins, while a team of firefighters was on hand to ensure that the blaze did not start up again. The size and intensity of the flames suggested that gasoline or something similarly flammable had been poured over the porch. The fire had spread immediately. The deck and the living room had been completely destroyed, as had the kitchen. The second floor had escaped the worst of the flames, but the smoke and particularly the water had caused irreparable damage.

I felt like a ghost, still dressed in sweat pants, sitting on the grass and contemplating the devastation. I had spent the night there. At my feet was a bag that the firefighters had managed to rescue from my bedroom: Inside were a few clothes and my laptop.

I heard a car arrive, and a murmur among the crowd of ghouls behind me. It was Harry. He had just been freed. I had called Roth, and I knew he had told Harry about the fire. He walked toward me in silence, then sat on the grass and said, "What got into you, Marcus?"

"I don't know what to tell you."

"Don't say anything. Look what you've done. There's no need for words."

"Harry, I . . ."

He noticed the writing scrawled on the hood of my Range Rover.

"Your car's not damaged?"

"No."

"Good. Because I want you to climb in it and get the hell out of here."

"Harry . . ."

"She loved me, Marcus! She loved me. And I loved her in a way I have never loved anyone else. Why did you write all that shit? Huh? You know what your problem is? You've never been loved. You want to write love stories, but you don't know anything about love. I want you to leave right now. Goodbye."

"I never described or imagined Nola the way she was depicted in the press. They twisted my words, Harry!"

"But why the hell did you let Barnaski send that crap to the press in the first place?"

"It was stolen!"

He laughed cynically.

"Stolen? Don't tell me you're so naive that you believe whatever bullshit Barnaski is feeding you. I can assure you that he copied and sent those damn pages out himself."

"What? But—"

"Marcus, I think it would have been better if I'd never met you. Leave now. You're on my property and you're no longer welcome here."

There was a long silence. The firefighters and policemen were watching us. I picked up my bag, got in my car, and drove away. I called Barnaski right away.

"It's good to hear from you, Goldman," he said. "I've just seen the news about Quebert's house. It's all over the T.V. I'm glad you didn't get hurt. I can't talk for long—I have a meeting with the heads of Warner Brothers. They're already considering various screenwriters to write a movie of *The Affair* based on your first pages. They love it. I think we'll be able to sell them the rights for a small fortune."

I interrupted him. "There will be no book, Roy."

"What the hell are you talking about?"

"It was you, wasn't it? You sent my pages to the press! You've fucked everything up."

"You're fickle, Goldman. Worse than that, you're a diva, and I can't stand divas! You make a big deal of playing detective, and then, on a whim, you give it up. You know what? I'm going to put this down to the bad night you've just had and forget all about this phone call. There will be no book? For Christ's sake, who do you think you are?"

"A real writer. To write is to be free."

He forced a laugh.

"Bullshit! Who's been putting that crap in your head? You're a slave to your career, your ideas, and your success. You're a slave to your condition. To write is to be dependent. Not only on the people who read your books, but on those who don't. Freedom is complete bullshit. Nobody's free. I hold part of your freedom in my hands, just as the company's shareholders hold part of mine in theirs. Such is life, Goldman. Nobody's free. If people were free, they would be happy. How many genuinely happy people do you know?" I didn't reply, so he went on: "Freedom is an interesting concept. I knew a guy who was a trader on Wall Street, one of those golden boys, you know, rolling in money. One of those guys on whom fortune always seems to smile. One day he decided he wanted to be a free man. He saw a T.V. documentary about Alaska, and he decided he was going to be a hunter, happy and free, living in the open air. He quit his job, sold his apartment, and moved to southern Alaska. And guess what? This guy, who had always been successful at everything he'd done, was successful in this too; he became a genuinely free man. No attachments, no family, no house—just a few dogs and a tent. He was the only truly free man I ever knew."

"Was?"

"Yes, was. The poor bastard was free for four months, from June to October. And then when winter came, he ended up dying of exposure, having first eaten all of his dogs to stave off starvation. Nobody's free,

Goldman, not even hunters in Alaska. We're prisoners of other people and of ourselves."

While Barnaski was talking, I heard a siren behind me: I was being chased by an unmarked police car. I hung up and pulled over to the shoulder, thinking that I was about to be arrested for using my cell phone while driving. But it was Sergeant Gahalowood who got out of the car.

He came to my window. "Don't tell me you're going back to New York, writer," he said.

"What gave you that idea?"

"You were heading in that direction."

"I was just driving without thinking."

"Hmm. Survival instinct?"

"That's more true than you could imagine. How did you find me?"

"In case you hadn't noticed, your name is painted in red letters on the hood of your car. This is not the right time to go home, writer."

"Harry's house burned down."

"I know. That's why I came. You can't go back to New York."

"Why not?"

"Because you're not a quitter. I have rarely seen anyone so tenacious in my whole career."

"They pillaged my book."

"But you haven't written that book yet. Your fate is still in your own hands. You can still do anything you want. You have a gift for creativity. So get to work and write a masterpiece. You're a fighter, and you know it. You're a fighter, and you've got a book to write. And if you don't mind my bringing this up, you've got me up to my neck in shit. The D.A. is responsible for this, and so am I. I was the one who told him he had to arrest Harry quickly. I thought that thirty-three years after the murder, a surprise arrest would show confidence. A rookie mistake. And then you turn up, with your patent-leather shoes that would cost me a month's salary. I don't want to turn this into a love fest, here on the side of the road, but . . . don't go. We have to finish this investigation."

"I have nowhere to sleep now. The house burned down."

"You've just pocketed two million dollars, writer. I saw it in the newspaper. Just rent a suite at a hotel in Concord. I'll put my lunches on your tab. Speaking of which, I'm starving. Let's get going. We've got work to do."

During the week that followed, I avoided Somerset. I moved into a suite in a hotel in the center of Concord, and spent my days there working hard on both the investigation and my book. The only news I had of Harry came via Roth, who told me that he had moved into Room 8 of the Sea Side Motel, and that he didn't want to see me anymore because I had sullied Nola's name. Then he added: "So, just out of curiosity, why did you tell the press that Nola was a depressed little whore?"

"I didn't tell them anything at all! I had written a few notes, and I gave them to Barnaski, so he could see that my work was progressing. He faked a robbery and leaked them."

"If you say so . . ."

"For fuck's sake, I'm telling the truth!"

"In any case, bravo! I couldn't have done it better myself."

"What's that supposed to mean?"

"Turning the victim into a culprit. That's the surest way of dealing with an accusation."

"Harry was freed because of the handwriting analysis. You know that as well as I do."

"Come off it, Marcus. As I told you before, judges are just human beings. What's the first thing they do when they drink their coffee in the morning? They read the papers, like everyone else."

Roth was very down-to-earth, but not necessarily unpleasant, and he tried to comfort me by explaining that Harry was undoubtedly upset by the loss of Goose Cove, and that he would begin to feel better once the police had arrested the perpetrator. And there was a lead on this: The day after the fire, having methodically searched the property, they discovered a can of gasoline hidden in the undergrowth—and had managed to get a fingerprint from it. Unfortunately the print did not match any that the police had on file, and Gahalowood believed that, without more evidence, it would be difficult to catch the culprit. According to him, it was probably someone with no previous police record. Nevertheless he thought we could narrow down the search to locals— someone from Somerset who, having committed the crime in broad daylight, had hastily gotten rid of the incriminating evidence out of fear that he or she might be recognized by a passerby.

I had six weeks to turn the tide and make my book great. It was time to fight, and to become the writer I had always wanted to be. Every morning I devoted myself to the book, and in the afternoon I worked on the case with Gahalowood, who had transformed my suite into an extension of his office, using the hotel bellboys to cart around boxes containing witness reports, newspaper clippings, photographs and forensic reports.

We started the whole investigation over again, rereading the police reports, examining the interviews with all the witnesses at the time. We drew a map of Somerset and its environs, and we calculated all the distances: from the Kellergans' house to Goose Cove, and from Goose Cove to Side Creek Lane. Gahalowood personally verified all the traveling times, on foot and by car, and even the response time of the local police back then, which turned out to be very fast.

"It is difficult to criticize Chief Pratt's work," he told me. "The search was carried out with great professionalism."

"There's another thing," I said. "We know that Harry didn't write that message on the manuscript. So why was Nola buried at Goose Cove?"

"Because no-one was there, I guess. You told me that Harry had been telling everyone he was going away for a while."

"That's true. So you think the murderer knew that Harry wasn't home?"

"It's possible. But you have to acknowledge that it's kind of surprising that, when Harry came back, he didn't notice that someone had dug a hole on his property."

"He wasn't in a normal state of mind," I said. "He was devastated. He spent all his time waiting for Nola. That would be enough to distract him from a small pile of overturned earth. Especially at Goose Cove: As soon as it rains there, the ground turns to mud."

"Alright, so the murderer knows that no-one will disturb him there. And if the body is ever found, who will be accused?"

"Harry."

"Exactly."

"But then why write that message?" I asked. "Why write *Goodbye, darling Nola?*"

"That's the million-dollar question, writer. Well, it is for you, anyway."

Our main problem was that there were so many divergent clues. Several important questions remained unanswered, and Gahalowood wrote them on large sheets of paper.

Elijah Stern
- *Why did he pay Nola to pose for a painting?*
- *What motive did he have for killing her?*

Luther Caleb
- *Why did he paint Nola? Why did he hang around Somerset? What motive did he have for killing Nola?*

David and Louisa Kellergan
- *Did they beat their daughter to death?*
- *Why did they hide Nola's suicide attempt and the fact that she ran away for a week?*

Harry Quebert
- *Guilty?*

Chief Gareth Pratt
- *Why did Nola initiate a relationship with him?*
- *Motive: Did she threaten to talk?*
- *Tamara Quinn states that the page she stole from Harry's house disappeared. Who took it from the safe at Clark's?*
- *Who wrote the anonymous letters to Harry? Who knew about him and Nola for thirty-three years and never said anything?*
- *Who set fire to Goose Cove? Who wants to prevent us from finding out the truth?*

When Gahalowood had tacked these papers to a wall in my suite, he gave a long, despairing sigh.

"The more we find out, the murkier this gets," he said. "I think there is some central piece of evidence that would connect all these people and these events. That's the key to this investigation! If we find the link, we'll find the murderer."

He collapsed into an armchair. It was 7 p.m. and he was too tired to think anymore. As I had done every evening for the past several days, I got ready to box. I had found a boxing gym a fifteen-minute drive away—the hotel concierge, who went there himself, had recommended it—and had decided to make my return to the ring.

"Where are you going?" Gahalowood said.

"Boxing. You want to come?"

"Absolutely not."

I threw my things in a bag and waved goodbye. "Stay as long as you like. Just close the door behind you."

"Don't worry, I got them to give me another key for the room. Are you really going boxing?"

"Yes."

He hesitated, and then, as I crossed the threshold, I heard him call out.

"Hang on, writer. Maybe I'll come with you, after all."

"What changed your mind?"

"The temptation of beating you up."

On Thursday, July 17, we went to visit Neil Rodik, the police captain who had been jointly in charge of the 1975 investigation with Chief Pratt. He was now eighty-five years old and wheelchair bound, and he lived in a nursing home by the ocean. He still remembered the search for Nola; he said it was the biggest case of his career.

"That girl who disappeared . . . what a crazy story!" he told us. "What surprised me most was the part about the father playing music. That always bothered me. I always wondered how he could fail to notice that his daughter had been abducted."

"So you think she was abducted?" Gahalowood asked.

"It's difficult to say. No proof either way. Could the girl have gone for a walk outside and been picked up by a maniac in a van? Yeah, sure."

"Do you, by any chance, remember what the weather was like while you were searching for her?"

"It was terrible. It was raining, very misty. Why do you ask?"

"We were wondering how Harry Quebert could have failed to notice that someone had been digging in his yard."

"It's not impossible. It's a huge property. Do you have a yard, Sergeant?"

"Yes."

"How big is it?"

"Small."

"Do you think it would be possible for someone to dig a small hole while you were away that you wouldn't notice when you got back?"

"Actually, I guess it's possible."

On the way back to Concord, Gahalowood asked what I thought.

"The manuscript proves to me that Nola was not abducted from her home," I replied. "She went to meet Harry. They had arranged to meet at that motel. She left home discreetly, taking with her the only thing that mattered, Harry's book, which she had kept with her. She must have been abducted on the way to the motel."

Gahalowood smiled. "I think I'm beginning to like that theory," he said. "She runs away from home, which explains why no-one heard anything. She walks along Shore Road to reach the Sea Side Motel. And it is here that she's abducted. Or picked up by someone she trusted. The murderer wrote 'darling Nola.' So he knew her. He offers to give her a ride. And then he starts to touch her. Maybe he pulls over to the side of the road and puts his hand up her dress. She puts up a fight. He hits her, and tells her to stop struggling. But he hasn't locked the car doors, and she manages to escape. She wants to hide in the forest, but who lives close to Shore Road and the Side Creek forest?"

"Deborah Cooper."

"Exactly. The assailant runs after Nola, leaving his car by the side of the road. Deborah Cooper sees them and calls the police. While that's happening, the assailant catches Nola in the spot where her blood and hair is later found; she defends herself, and he beats her severely. Perhaps he even rapes her. But that's when the police arrive. Officer Dawn and Chief Pratt start searching the forest and gradually move closer to him. So he drags Nola into the depths of the forest, but she manages to escape again and gets back to Deborah Cooper's house, where she takes refuge. Dawn and Pratt continue searching the forest. They are too far away to realize what's happening. Deborah Cooper lets Nola into the kitchen and rushes to the living room to call the police. When she comes back, the assailant is there; he has entered the house to get Nola back. He shoots Cooper in the heart and takes Nola with him. He takes her to his car and throws her in the trunk. She is maybe still alive, but probably unconscious: She has lost a lot of blood. It is at this point that he passes the deputy sheriff's car. A chase begins. Having eluded his pursuers, he goes to hide out at Goose Cove. He knows the house is empty; that nobody will disturb him there. The police are searching for him farther away, on the Montburry road. He leaves his car in Goose Cove, with Nola inside; maybe he even hides it in the garage. Then he goes down to the beach and walks back to Somerset. Yes, I'm sure he lives in Somerset: He knows all the roads, he knows the forest, he knows Harry is away. He knows everything. He goes home without anyone noticing him. He showers, changes his clothes, and then, when the police arrive at the Kellergan house, where Nola's father has just announced her disappearance, he mingles with the crowd of onlookers on Terrace Avenue. That's why the murderer was never found: because, when everyone was searching for him in the area around Somerset, he was actually in Somerset, in the center of the action."

"Goddamn it," I said. "So he was there?"

"Yes. I think he's been there all this time. All he would have to do is return to Goose Cove in the middle of the night, getting there via the beach. By this point, I think, Nola must have been dead. So he buries her on the property, at the edge of the forest, where nobody will notice that the ground has been dug up. Then he picks up his car and parks it in his own garage, where he leaves it for quite a while so as not to awaken suspicions. The perfect crime."

I was blown away.

"What does that suggest about our suspect?" I said.

"A single man. Someone who was able to act without anyone asking questions, without anyone wondering why he no longer took his car out of the garage. Someone with a black Chevrolet Monte Carlo."

I let myself get carried away. "All we have to do is find out who in Somerset had a black Chevy at the time, and we'll have our man!"

Gahalowood instantly calmed me down.

"Pratt thought of that back then. Pratt thought of everything. His report includes a list of people who owned Monte Carlos in and around Somerset. He went to visit each of them, and they all had solid alibis. All but one: Harry Quebert."

Harry again. It always came back to Harry. We kept coming up with new criteria to uncover the murderer, and he kept being the common denominator.

"What about Luther Caleb?" I asked. "What kind of car did he have?"

"A blue Mustang."

I sighed. "What do you think we should do now, Sergeant?"

"Well, there's Caleb's sister. We still haven't questioned her. I think maybe it's time to pay her a visit. It's the only line of inquiry we haven't really explored yet."

That evening, after boxing, I decided to bite the bullet and go to the Sea Side Motel. It was about 9.30 p.m. Harry was sitting in a plastic chair in front of Room 8, enjoying the warm evening and drinking a can of soda. He said nothing when he saw me; for the first time I felt uncomfortable in his presence.

"I needed to see you, Harry. To tell you how sorry I am about all of this."

He nodded for me to sit down in the chair next to his.

"Soda?" he asked.

"Sure."

"The machine is at the end of the corridor."

I smiled and went to buy a Diet Coke. When I came back I said: "That's what you said to me the first time I went to Goose Cove. I was a junior. You'd made lemonade. You asked me if I wanted any, I said yes, and you told me to go to the fridge and help myself."

"Those were good times."

"Yeah."

"What changed, Marcus?"

"Nothing. Everything changed, but nothing changed. We all changed, the world changed. The World Trade Center collapsed, we went to war. But the way I look at you has not changed. You're still my master. You're still Harry."

"What changed, Marcus, is this fight between the master and the pupil."

"We're not fighting."

"And yet we are. I taught you how to write books, and look what your book has done to me. Look what harm it's caused me."

"I never wanted to cause you harm, Harry. We'll find whoever it was who burned Goose Cove, I promise."

"But will that give me back the thirty years of memories I've lost? My whole life went up in flames! Why did you write those things about Nola?"

I didn't reply. We sat in silence for a moment. In spite of the weak light from the wall lanterns, he noticed the cuts on my hands.

"Your hands," he said. "Have you started boxing again?"

"Yes."

"Your punches are badly placed. That was always your flaw. You hit well, but the first phalanx of your middle finger always stuck out too far, so it was grazed on impact."

"Let's box," I suggested.

"If you like."

We went into the parking lot together. There was no-one around. We took off our shirts. Harry was very thin. He looked at me.

"You're good-looking, Marcus. Go get married, for God's sake! Go and live!"

"I have to finish this investigation first."

"To hell with your investigation!"

We squared up to each other and exchanged punches; one of us hit, while the other kept his guard position to protect himself. Harry hit hard.

"Don't you want to know who killed Nola?" I asked.

He stopped dead. "Do you know?"

"No. But we're getting closer. Sergeant Gahalowood and I are going to see Luther Caleb's sister tomorrow, in Portland. And we still have people to question in Somerset."

He sighed. "Somerset . . . I haven't seen anyone since I got out of prison. The other day I stood outside my burned house for a while. A firefighter told me I could go inside. I retrieved up a few things and walked over here. Since then I haven't moved. Roth is taking care of the insurance and all that. I can't go to Somerset anymore. I can't look those people in the face and tell them I loved Nola and wrote a book for her. I can't even look myself in the face anymore. Roth said your book is going to be called *The Harry Quebert Affair*."

"That's true. It's a book about how great your book is. I love *The Origin of Evil*. It's the book that inspired me to become a writer."

"Don't say that."

"It's the truth. It's probably the most beautiful book I've ever read. You're my favorite writer."

"Oh, please shut up, for the love of God!"

"I want to write a book that will defend yours, Harry. When I first found out that you wrote it for Nola, I was shocked—I admit it. But then I read it again. You say it all in that book. Especially the ending. You describe the grief that will always be with you. I can't let people attack that book—it made me what I am. You know, the day I opened your fridge to get the lemonade, on my first visit to you, and saw how empty the fridge was, I understood your solitude. And that day I realized: *The Origin of Evil* is a novel about solitude. You wrote brilliantly about it."

"Please stop," Harry said.

"The ending is so beautiful. You give up Nola: She has disappeared forever, and you know it, and yet you wait for her in spite of everything. I have only one question, now that I have come to truly understand your book, and that concerns the title. Why did you give such a dark title to such a beautiful book?"

"It's complicated, Marcus."

"But I need to under—"

"It's too complicated . . ."

We looked at each other, face to face, both in the guard position, like two warriors. Finally he said, "I don't know if I'll be able to forgive you, Marcus."

"Forgive me? But I'll rebuild Goose Cove. I'll pay for everything. With the money I'm getting for this book, we'll reconstruct the whole house. You can't just end our friendship like that!"

He began to cry.

"You don't understand. It's not because of you. None of this is your fault, and yet I can't forgive you."

"Forgive me for what?"

"I can't tell you. You wouldn't understand."

"Harry, please, no more riddles! What the hell is going on?"

He wiped the tears from his face with the back of his hand.

"Do you remember my advice?" he asked. "When you were my student, I told you one day never to write a book if you don't know how it will end."

"Yes, I remember. I will always remember that."

"What's the ending to your book like?"

"It's a beautiful ending."

"But she dies at the end!"

"No, it doesn't end with the death of the heroine. Some good things happen afterward."

"Like what?"

"The man who spent more than thirty years waiting for her begins to live again."

EXTRACT FROM *THE ORIGIN OF EVIL* (final page)

When he understood that nothing would ever be possible and that his hopes were merely lies, he wrote to her for the final time. After all the love letters, now it was time for a letter of sadness. He had to accept the truth. From now on, he would do nothing but wait for her. He would spend his whole life waiting for her. But he knew perfectly well that she would never return. He knew he would never see her again, never hear her again, never find her again.

> *My darling,*
>
> *This is my final letter. These are my last words. I am writing you to say goodbye.*
>
> *From today on there will be no more "us."*
> *Lovers separate and never find each other again, and that is how love stories end.*
>
> *I will miss you, my darling. I will miss you so much.*
> *I am crying. Inside, I am burning.*
> *We will never see each other again. I will miss you so much.*
>
> *I hope you will be happy.*
>
> *You and me: That was a dream, I think. And now we must wake up.*
>
> *I will miss you all my life.*
>
> *Goodbye. I love you as I will never love anyone again.*

12

The Man Who Painted Pictures

"Learn to love your failures, Marcus, because it is your failures that will make you who you are. It is your failures that will give meaning to your victories."

The weather was glorious on Friday, July 18, the day we went to visit Sylla Caleb Mitchell, Luther's sister, in Portland, Maine. The Mitchell family lived in an elegant house in a residential neighborhood close to the center of town. Sylla received us in the kitchen; she had already set out on the table two steaming cups of coffee and a stack of photo albums.

Gahalowood had managed to get hold of her the day before. On the drive from Concord to Portland, he told me how, when he spoke to her on the phone, he had the feeling she'd been waiting for his call. "I introduced myself as a policeman, and I told her I was investigating the murders of Deborah Cooper and Nola Kellergan and that I wanted to meet to ask her a few questions. Usually people become nervous when they hear the words *state police*: They ask what it's about. But Sylla Mitchell just said: 'Come tomorrow whenever you like. I'll be here. It's important that we speak.'"

She sat across from us. She was attractive: a sophisticated-looking mother of two, who wore her fifty-something years well. Her husband stood farther back from the table, as if he did not wish to intrude.

"So is it all true?" she asked.

"Is what all true?" Gahalowood said.

"Everything I've read in the papers, all those dreadful things about that poor girl in Somerset."

"Yes. The press twisted things slightly, but the basic facts are true. Mrs Mitchell, you didn't seem very surprised when I called you."

She looked sad.

"As I told you yesterday on the phone," she said, "the newspaper did not name names, but I understood that 'E.S.' was Elijah Stern. And that his chauffeur was Luther." She picked up a newspaper and read aloud from it, as if to help her understand: "'E.S., one of the richest men in New Hampshire, sent his chauffeur to bring Nola from the center of town to his house in Concord. Thirty-three years later, one of Nola's friends, who was only a child at the time, said she was once present at one of these meetings with the chauffeur, and that Nola left as if she were going off to her death. This young witness described the chauffeur as a frightening man, with a powerful body and a deformed face.' With a description like that, it could only be my brother."

She stopped talking and looked at us. Gahalowood put our cards on the table: "We found a portrait of Nola Kellergan, more or less naked, in Elijah Stern's house," he said. "Apparently Nola agreed to pose for the painting in return for money. Luther went to get her in Somerset, and he took her to see Stern in Concord. We don't really know what happened there, but we do know that Luther painted a picture of her."

"He painted a lot!" Sylla said. "He was very talented. He could have made a career out of it. Do you . . . do you suspect him of having killed that girl?"

"Let's just say he's on our list of suspects," Gahalowood replied.

A tear rolled down Sylla's cheek.

"I remember the day he died. It was a Friday at the end of September. I had just turned twenty-one. We received a call from the police, who informed us that Luther had died in a car accident. I vividly remember the telephone ringing, and my mother picking it up. My father and I were standing close to her. Mom answered, and then whispered to us: 'It's the police.' She listened intently and then said, 'O.K.' I will never forget that moment. After that she hung up, looked at us, and said, 'He's dead.'"

"What happened?" Gahalowood said.

"The car went over some seaside cliffs in Sagamore, Massachusetts, and fell a hundred feet. Apparently he was drunk."

"How old was he?"

"Thirty . . . he was thirty. My brother was a good man, but . . . You know, I'm glad you're here. There's something I have to tell you. Something we should have said thirty-three years ago."

And, her voice trembling, Sylla told us about an incident that occurred about a month before the accident. It was Saturday, August 30, 1975.

August 30, 1975, Portland, Maine

The Caleb family had planned to have dinner that evening at Sylla's favorite restaurant, the Horseshoe, to celebrate her twenty-first birthday, which was two days later. Her father, Jay Caleb, had reserved the private room on the second floor for a surprise party. He had invited all her friends and a few relatives: thirty-odd people in all, including Luther.

The Calebs—Sylla; her father, Jay; and her mother, Nadia—arrived at the restaurant at 6 p.m. The other guests were already waiting for Sylla, and everyone cheered when she entered the room. There was music and champagne. Luther had not yet arrived. His father thought at first that he must have been held up in traffic. But by 7.30 p.m., when dinner was served, his son was still not there. Luther was not the type of person to be late, and his father began to worry. He tried calling Luther at his room on Elijah Stern's property, but there was no answer.

Luther missed dinner, dessert, and the dancing. At 1.30 a.m., the Calebs went home, worrying silently. They knew Luther wouldn't have missed his sister's birthday celebration for anything in the world. Back at home, Jay unthinkingly turned on the radio in the living room. One of the news items was about a major police operation in Somerset, following the disappearance of a fifteen-year-old girl. Somerset was a name they recognized. Luther had told them that he went there regularly to take care of the rosebushes on the grounds of a beautiful house near the ocean that Elijah Stern owned. Jay Caleb thought this was a coincidence. He listened attentively to the rest of the news, then to several other stations, to find out if maybe there had been a car accident in the area, but nothing was mentioned. He stayed up half the night, worrying, unsure whether to call the police or the hospitals, or just to wait at home, or to get in his car and search the road that led to Concord. He eventually fell asleep on the couch in the living room.

Early the next morning, still not having heard anything, he called Elijah Stern to ask if he had seen his son. "Luther?" Stern replied. "He's not here. He went on vacation. Didn't he tell you?" This whole thing was very strange. Why would Luther have gone away without telling them, especially when it meant missing his sister's birthday? And so, no longer content just to wait, Jay Caleb went out to look for his son.

Sylla Mitchell began to tremble. She got up abruptly from her chair and made some more coffee.

"That day," she said, "while my father went to Concord and my mother stayed at home in case Luther showed up, I was with friends. It was late when I got home. My parents were in the living room, and I heard my father say to my mother: 'I'm afraid Luther has done something terrible.' I asked him what was going on, and he told me not to tell anyone about Luther's disappearance, particularly not the police. He said he was

384

going to try to find Luther himself. He searched in vain for nearly a month. Until the accident."

A sob escaped her.

"What happened, Mrs Mitchell?" Gahalowood asked in a soothing voice. "Why did your father think Luther had done something wrong? Why didn't he want to call the police?"

"It's complicated, Sergeant. Everything is so complicated . . ."

She opened the photograph albums and began telling us about the Caleb family: about Jay, their kind father; about Nadia, their mother, a former Miss Maine who had passed on her love of art to her children. Luther was the firstborn; he was nine years older than she was. They were both born in Portland.

She showed us photographs from her childhood. The family home; vacations in Colorado, where she and Luther had spent their summers; the huge warehouse belonging to her father's company. There was a series of photographs of the family taken in Yosemite in 1963. Luther was eighteen years old, a handsome young man, slim and elegant. Then we came to a picture from the fall of 1974: Sylla's twentieth birthday party. The people in the photograph had all aged. Jay, the proud father, was now a pot-bellied sixty-something. The mother's face was wrinkled. Luther was nearly thirty, and his face was deformed.

Sylla looked at this picture for a long time.

"We were a great family, before," she said. "We were so happy, before."

"Before what?" Gahalowood asked.

She replied as if the answer were obvious: "Before the attack."

"What attack?" Gahalowood said. "I don't know anything about this."

Sylla placed the two photographs of her brother side by side.

"It happened in the fall after our vacation in Yosemite. Look at this photograph. See how handsome he was? Luther was a very special young man. He loved art. He had graduated from high school and been accepted to the Maine College of Art, here in Portland. Everyone said he could become a great painter, that he had a gift. He was happy too. But the Vietnam war had begun and he had just been called up by the army. He said that when he got back, he would go to art school and marry his fiancée, Eleanore Smith. She was his high school sweetheart. As I said, he was happy. Until that evening in September 1964."

"What happened?"

"Have you ever heard of the Field Goals Gang, Sergeant?"

"No, never."

"That's the name the police gave to a group of thugs who were running wild in the area back then."

September 1964

It was about 10 p.m. Luther had spent the evening with Eleanore, and he was walking back to his parents' house. He had to leave the next morning for boot camp. He and Eleanore had just decided that they would marry when he returned; they had sworn to stay faithful to each other, and they had made love for the first time, in Eleanore's childhood bed, while downstairs in the kitchen her unsuspecting mother made cookies for them.

When Luther left the Smiths' house, he turned around to look at it several times. On the porch, illuminated by streetlights, he could see Eleanore waving goodbye. After that he walked along Lincoln Road, a poorly lit street that was usually deserted at that time of night. It was the shortest route home; he had a three-mile walk ahead of him. A car passed, the beam of its headlights illuminating the road ahead. Soon afterward a second vehicle passed by at high speed. Its occupants yelled through the open window to frighten him. Luther did not react, and the car stopped dead in the middle of the street, about fifty feet ahead of him. He kept walking—what else could he do? Should he have crossed to the other side of the road? When he went past the car, the driver called out to him: "Hey, you! You from around here?"

"Yes," Luther replied.

They threw beer in his face.

"Fucking redneck!" the driver yelled.

The passengers shouted at him too. There were four of them in all but in the darkness, Luther couldn't make out their faces. He guessed they were young—between twenty-five and thirty—and they were clearly drunk and aggressive. He kept walking, his heart pounding. He wasn't a fighter. He didn't want any trouble.

"Hey, redneck!" the driver yelled again. "Where're you going?"

Luther sped up.

"Hey, come back! Come back here, and we'll show you how we deal with little shits like you."

Luther heard the car doors open and the driver shout: "Gentlemen, let the redneck hunt begin! A hundred dollars for whoever catches him." Luther started running as fast as he could, praying that another car would pass. But there was no-one to save him. One of his pursuers caught him and threw him to the ground, yelling to the others: "I've got him! I've got him! The hundred dollars is mine!" They all rushed up to Luther and began beating him. While he was stretched out on the ground, one of his attackers said, "Who wants to play some football? I suggest we practice field goals!" The others cheered and lined up, one by one, to kick his head with incredible force. When everyone had taken his turn, they left him for dead on the roadside. Forty minutes later he was found by a passing motorcyclist, who called for an ambulance.

"After a few days in a coma, Luther woke up with his face completely smashed up," Sylla explained. "He went through several operations to reconstruct his face, but the plastic surgeons never managed to give him back his former appearance. He was in the hospital for two months. When he came out he was condemned to live with a twisted face and a severe speech impediment. He didn't go to Vietnam, of course, but he no longer did anything else either. He stayed in the house all day long, in

387

a deep depression. He didn't paint; he had no plans. After six months, Eleanore broke off their engagement. She even left Portland. And who could blame her? She was eighteen years old, and she had no desire to sacrifice her life so she could look after Luther, who had become a miserable shadow of his former self."

"What about his attackers?" Gahalowood asked.

"They were never found. Apparently they had done the same thing to others in the area. But Luther was in a more serious condition than their other victims: He almost died. It was all over the press, and the police were after them. So after that they must have given up on their hobby. I imagine they were afraid of being caught."

"And what happened to your brother afterward?"

"Luther haunted the family home for two years. He was like a ghost. He didn't do anything anymore. My father stayed in his warehouse as late as possible each day, and my mother spent all her days out of the house. Those two years were really hard. And then, one day in 1966, someone rang our doorbell."

1966

He hesitated before unlocking the front door; he hated other people seeing him. But he was the only one home, and it might be important. He opened the door and found, standing in front of him, a very elegant-looking man in his thirties.

"Hello," the man said. "I'm sorry to disturb you like this, but my car has broken down. You don't happen to know a mechanic, do you?"

"Vat dependv," Luther replied.

"It's nothing serious. Just a flat tire. But I can't get my jack to work."

Luther agreed to take a look. The car was a luxury coupe, parked on the roadside three hundred feet from the house. A nail had pierced the front right tire. The jack was sticking because it needed grease, but Luther was able to get it working and change the tire.

"I'm impressed," the man said. "I was lucky to find you. What's your line of work? Are you a mechanic?"

"No. I don't do anyfing. I ufed to paint. But I had an acfident."

"So how do you make a living?"

"I don't make a living."

The man looked at Luther and offered his hand.

"My name is Elijah Stern."

"Lufer Caleb."

"Delighted to make your acquaintance, Luther. I owe you a debt of gratitude."

The two men looked at each other for a moment. Finally Stern asked the question that had been nagging at him ever since Luther had opened the door of the house.

"What happened to your face?" he asked.

"Have you heard of ve Field Goalv Gang?"

"No."

"Some guyv who ufed to attack people for pleavure. Vey kicked veir victimv in ve head av if it wav a football."

"Oh, my God, that's horrible. I'm so sorry."

Luther shrugged, fatalistic.

"My advice is not to give up on life," Stern said, smiling. "How would you like a job? I'm looking for someone to look after my cars and to be my chauffeur. I like you, Luther. If you'd be willing to work for me, the job is yours."

One week later, Luther moved to Concord.

Sylla thought that Stern had been heaven-sent.

"Thanks to Elijah Stern, Luther became someone again," she told us. "He had a job, he was earning money. It put some meaning back into his life. And best of all, he started painting again. He and Stern got along very well; Luther was not only his chauffeur, but also his right-hand man. Almost a friend, in fact. Stern had just taken over his father's business; he was living alone in a house that was much too big for him. I think he was glad to have Luther's company. They were very close. Luther stayed in his service for the next nine years. Until he died."

"Mrs Mitchell," said Gahalowood, "how was your relationship with your brother?"

She smiled. "He was such a special person. He was so gentle! He loved flowers, he loved art. He should never have ended up a limousine driver. Not that I have anything against chauffeurs, but Luther was very special. He often came to have lunch with us on Sundays. He would arrive in the morning, spend the day with us, and go back to Concord in the evening. I loved those Sundays, particularly when he started painting again. His old room was transformed into a studio. He had great talent. As soon as he started drawing, this incredible beauty seemed to radiate from him. I used to sit in a chair behind him and watch him work. I watched him draw lines that initially seemed chaotic but that gradually formed scenes of staggering realism. At first it would look like he was just scribbling, and then suddenly an image would appear among all those lines until finally every line became part of a whole. It was incredible, watching that happen. I told him he had to keep drawing, that he should think again about going to art school, that he should exhibit his paintings. But he didn't want to do that anymore. Because of his face, because of the way he spoke. Because of everything. Before the attack he used to say he painted because it was inside him. When he finally started painting again, after the attack, he said he did it to feel less lonely."

"Can we see some of his paintings?" Gahalowood said.

"Yes, of course. My father put together a sort of collection, made up of all the paintings left in Portland and those taken after Luther's death from his room on Stern's property. He said that one day we could give them to a museum. But all he did in the end was keep them in crates. I have them all now that my parents are dead."

Sylla led us to the basement, where one room was filled with large wooden crates. There were several large paintings as well as sketches and drawings piled up between the frames. The sheer number of pictures was impressive.

"Sorry it's such a mess," she said. "There's no order to the pictures, but they all remind me of Luther, so I haven't thrown anything away."

Rummaging through the pictures, Gahalowood uncovered a painting of a young blond girl.

"That's Eleanore," Sylla said. "Those paintings are from before the attack. He loved to paint her. He said he could paint her all his life."

Eleanore was a pretty young blonde with one intriguing detail: She looked strikingly similar to Nola. There were many other portraits of different women, all blondes, and all painted after the attack.

"Who are all these other women?" Gahalowood asked.

"I don't know," Sylla said. "They probably just came from Luther's imagination."

It was then that we came upon a series of charcoal sketches. In one of them I thought I recognized the inside of Clark's, with a beautiful but sad young woman standing at the counter. The resemblance to Jenny was stunning, but I thought it was a coincidence. Until, turning over the sketch, I found an inscription: *Jenny Quinn, 1974.*

"Why was your brother obsessed with painting all these blond women?" I asked.

"I don't know," Sylla said. "Honestly."

Gahalowood gave her a gentle, serious look, and said, "Mrs Mitchell, it's time you told us why, on the evening of August 31, 1975, your father said he thought Luther had done 'something terrible.'"

She nodded.

August 31, 1975

At nine that morning, as Jay Caleb hung up the telephone, he realized that something was terribly wrong. Elijah Stern had just told him that Luther was on vacation for an indeterminate length of time.

"What did he tell you exactly?" he'd asked Stern.

"He said he would probably have to stop working for me. That was two days ago."

"Stop working for you? But why?"

"I don't know. I thought you would know."

Jay now picked up the phone again so he could call the police. But he never dialed the number, feeling a strange foreboding.

Nadia, his wife, burst into the office. "What did Stern say?" she said.

"That Luther resigned on Friday."

"*Resigned?* Why on earth would he do that?"

Jay sighed. He was exhausted after his largely sleepless night.

"I have no idea," he replied. "I don't understand what's going on. I don't understand anything . . . I need to go look for him."

"Where, though?"

He shrugged. He didn't have the faintest idea.

"Stay here," he told Nadia, "in case he shows up. I'll call you as often as I can to check in."

He grabbed the keys to his pickup truck and set off, without even knowing where to begin. He finally decided to go to Concord. He hardly knew the town, and crisscrossed it blindly; he felt lost. Several times he drove past a police station. He would have liked to stop there and ask for help, but each time he considered this, something held him back. In the end he went to see Elijah Stern. But Stern was away, and it was one of the housekeeping staff who led Jay to his son's room. Jay had been hoping that Luther had left a message, but he found nothing. The room looked normal in every way: There was no clue to why he'd suddenly taken off.

"Did Luther say anything to you?" Jay asked the maid.

"No. I haven't been here for the last few days, but I've heard that Luther isn't coming back for a while."

"What does that mean? Has he resigned or just taken some vacation time?"

"I don't know what to tell you, sir."

It was strange, all this confusion surrounding Luther. Jay was now convinced that something serious must have happened to make his son disappear like this. He left Stern's estate and went back to town. He stopped at a restaurant for a sandwich and to call his wife. Nadia told him that there was no news. He skimmed the newspaper while he ate. The biggest story was the incident with the young girl in Somerset.

"What's this about a disappearance?" he asked the restaurant manager.

"Bad news . . . It happened in a little town about an hour from here. Some poor woman was murdered and a fifteen-year-old girl was kidnapped. Police all over the state are searching for her."

"How do I get to Somerset from here?"

"Take Route 4 east. When you get to the ocean, follow Shore Road south, and you'll be there."

Jay Caleb headed to Somerset. On Shore Road he was stopped twice by police roadblocks. Then, reaching the Side Creek forest, he was able to see the scale of the search: dozens of emergency vehicles, policemen everywhere, dogs barking, people shouting. He drove into the center of town, and just after the marina he stopped in front of a diner on the main street. The place was packed. He went in and sat at the counter. A beautiful young blond woman served him coffee. For a fraction of a second he thought he knew her. But how was that possible? This was the first time in his life he'd ever been there. He looked at her, she smiled, and then he noticed her name badge. And suddenly he understood: The woman Luther's charcoal sketch that he loved so much . . . it was her! He remembered the inscription on the back of the sketch: *Jenny Quinn, 1974.*

"Can I help you, sir?" Jenny asked. "You look a little lost."

"I . . . It's terrible, what happened here."

"Tell me about it! They still don't know what's happened to the girl. And she's so young! Only fifteen. I know her pretty well—she works here on Saturdays. Her name is Nola Kellergan."

"What . . . what did you say?" Jay stammered, hoping he had misheard.

"Nola. Nola Kellergan."

Hearing that name for the second time, he felt shaky. He thought he was going to puke. He had to get away from here. Far away. He left a bill on the counter and fled.

As soon as he entered the house, Nadia could see that her husband was upset. She moved toward him, and he practically collapsed into her arms.

"My God, Jay, what is it?"

"Remember when Luther and I went fishing a few weeks ago?"

"Yes. You caught those black bass that turned out to be inedible. Why?"

It was August 10. Luther had arrived in Portland the evening before, and they had agreed to go fishing early the next morning at a small lake. It was a beautiful day, the fish were biting, and they had chosen a particularly quiet area with no-one around to disturb them. The two men had drunk beer and talked about their lives.

"Vere'v fomefing I have to tell you, Dad," Luther had said. "I've met an amaving woman."

"Really?"

"I mean it. She've not like anyone elfe I've ever known. I'm in love wiv her, and she lovef me too. She told me fo. I'll introdufe you to her one day. I'm fertain you'll really like her."

Jay had smiled.

"Does this young lady have a name?"

"Nola, Dad. Her name iv Nola Kellergan."

Recalling that day now, Jay Caleb explained to his wife: "Nola Kellergan is the name of the girl from Somerset who disappeared. I'm afraid Luther has done something terrible."

Sylla came home just at that moment. She heard what her father said. "What does that mean?" she demanded. "What has Luther done?"

Her father explained the situation to her, then ordered her not to tell anyone. No-one must make the connection between Luther and Nola. Jay spent the whole next week searching for his son: He roamed all over Maine, then up and down the coast from Canada to Massachusetts. He checked out the kind of places—lakes and cabins—that his son loved. He thought perhaps he had panicked and gone into hiding in one of those out of the way spots, hunted like an animal by police from all over the country. But he found no trace of him. Every night he waited for him, listening for the faintest sound. When the police called to announce Luther's death, Jay seemed almost relieved. He insisted that his wife and daughter never speak of it again, so that the memory of his son would remain unsullied.

When Sylla had finished her account, Gahalowood asked: "Are you telling us you think your brother had something to do with Nola's abduction?"

"Let's just say he behaved strangely with women. He loved to paint them. Especially blondes. I know he sometimes drew them without their knowledge, hiding while he observed them. I never understood why he did that. So yes, I think something might have happened between my brother and that girl. My father thought Luther must have lost control of himself, that she rejected him and he killed her. When the police called to tell us he was dead, my father wept for a long time. But through his tears I heard him say: 'It's better this way. If I'd found him, I think I might have killed him, so he wouldn't end up on death row.'"

Gahalowood glanced around again at Luther's belongings and noticed a notebook. He opened it.

"Is this your brother's handwriting?"

"Yes. Those are instructions for pruning roses. He took care of the roses at Stern's place. I don't know why I kept this notebook."

"Can I take it?" Gahalowood asked.

"Yes, of course. But I doubt it will help much with your investigation. I've looked through it: It's all about gardening."

Gahalowood nodded. "I'm going to have to get a handwriting analysis done," he said.

11

Waiting for Nola

"Hit this bag, Marcus. Hit it as if your life depended on it. You should box like you write and write like you box: You should give everything you have because each match, like each book, might be your last."

The summer of 2008 was unusually calm. The battle for the presidential nominations was over by June, when Barack Obama was able to secure enough votes to lock up the Democratic nomination, while John McCain had become the presumptive Republican nominee in March. It was now time for the two parties to gather their forces; the conventions would not take place until the end of the summer.

This relative calm, prior to the media storm that would culminate on Election Day on November 4, left the Harry Quebert case as the country's number one news item. There were now "pro-Queberts" and "anti-Queberts": those who believed in the conspiracy theory and those who thought his release on bail was due only to a financial deal with David Kellergan. Ever since the publication of my notes in the press, my book had been on everyone's lips; the talk was all of the "new Goldman that will come out this fall." Elijah Stern, despite the fact that his name was not directly mentioned in the notes, had sued for defamation, hoping to prevent the book's publication. David Kellergan had also made clear his intention to go to court in order to defend himself from allegations that he had mistreated his daughter. And amid all this hype, two people were particularly happy: Roy Barnaski and Benjamin Roth.

Barnaski, who had sent his army of New York lawyers to New Hampshire to prepare for any legal imbroglio likely to delay the book's publication, was ecstatic. The leaks to the press—and there was now no doubt whatsoever that he was responsible for them—had guaranteed him extraordinary early orders from bookstores and enabled him to dominate the airwaves.

As far as the legal battle was concerned, there was now little doubt that the criminal case was about to collapse. Benjamin Roth was well on his way to making himself the most famous lawyer in the country. He accepted all requests for interviews and spent most of his time in local television and radio studios. The only condition he set was that they had to talk about him. "Think about it, Goldman," he told me. "I can charge a thousand dollars an hour now. And each time my name appears in a newspaper, I add another ten dollars to my hourly rate for future clients. It doesn't matter what the newspapers say about you; what matters is that you're in them. People remember having seen your photograph in the *New York Times*; they never remember the story." Roth had waited his whole career for the case of the century to fall into his lap, and now it had. He hogged the spotlight, telling the press everything it wanted to hear: He told them about Chief Pratt and Elijah Stern, he constantly repeated his opinion that Nola was a manipulative seductress and that Harry was, in fact, the real victim. In order to titillate his audience, he even began hinting—with made-up details to support his point—that half the men in Somerset had been intimately involved with Nola. This eventually became so unbearable that I was forced to call him.

"You need to give your pornographic fantasies a rest, Benjamin. You're dragging everyone's name through the mud."

"But that's exactly the point, Marcus. Ultimately my job is not to clear Harry's name but to show how filthy and disgusting everyone else is. And if there has to be a trial, I'll summon Pratt, I'll summon Stern, I'll call every man in Somerset to the stand so they can publicly atone for their carnal sins with the Kellergan girl. And when it came down to it I will prove that the only thing Harry did wrong was to allow himself to be seduced by that perverted young woman, like so many others before him."

"What are you talking about?" I said angrily. "That's not true at all!"

"Oh, come on—let's call a spade a spade. That girl was a slut."

"You're despicable," I said.

"Despicable? All I'm doing is summarizing what you yourself wrote in your book."

"No you're not, and you know that perfectly well. There was nothing flashy or provocative about Nola. She loved Harry, and he loved her."

"Love, love, always love! But what is love? It doesn't mean anything! Love is just a trick invented by men so they don't have to do their own laundry!"

The D.A. had been crucified by the press, and this affected the mood in the headquarters of the Investigative Services Bureau of the state police. The rumor was that the governor himself had ordered the police to solve the case as quickly as possible. Since the interview with Sylla Mitchell, Gahalowood had a clearer vision of the case; all the evidence pointed to Luther, and the sergeant was nervously awaiting the results of the handwriting analysis to confirm this. In the meantime he needed to find out more, particularly regarding Luther's presence in Somerset. And so on July 20 we met with Travis Dawn so he could tell us what he knew.

Because I still did not feel ready to return to Somerset, Travis agreed to meet us in a roadside diner near Montburry. I expected a hostile reception, due to what I had written about Jenny, but he was very polite.

"I'm sorry about those leaks," I told him. "They were personal notes. They should never have been published."

"I can't blame you, Marc—"

"You could—"

"All you did was tell the truth. I'm well aware that Jenny had a crush on Quebert. I could see the way she looked at him back then. In fact I think your theories are pretty solid, at least as far as I've seen. Anyway, what's the latest on the investigation?"

It was Gahalowood who replied. "The latest is that we have very strong suspicions regarding Luther Caleb."

"Luther Caleb—that nutcase? So the painting thing is true, then?"

"Yes. Apparently the girl went to see Stern quite often. Did you know about Chief Pratt and Nola?"

"No! I was shocked when I found out. You know, while I admit he got out of control, I have to say he was always a good cop. I don't think we should be calling into question his whole investigation, as the papers seem to be doing."

"What do you think of the suspicions back then about Stern and Quebert?"

"I think you're making too big a deal of them. Tamara Quinn says she told the chief about Quebert. But I think we need to put that in perspective. She claimed she knew everything, but she didn't really know anything at all. She had no proof of what she was saying. All she could say was that she'd *had* concrete proof, but that it had mysteriously disappeared. Nothing credible. You know yourself, Sergeant, how cautiously unsubstantiated accusations must be treated. The only evidence we had against Quebert was the black Monte Carlo. And that wasn't enough— far from it."

"One of Nola's friends told us she informed Pratt about what was going on with Stern."

"Pratt never told me about that."

"It's hard not to think that he botched the investigation, then, isn't it?" Gahalowood said.

"Don't put words into my mouth, Sergeant."

"What about Luther Caleb? What can you tell us about him?"

"Luther was a strange guy. He used to harass women. I even encouraged Jenny to file a complaint against him because he was aggressive toward her."

"Was he never a suspect?"

"Not really. His name was mentioned, and we checked what vehicle he was driving: a blue Mustang, I seem to remember. Anyway, it seemed unlikely that he would be our man."

"Why?"

"Just before Nola disappeared, I made sure he would never come back to Somerset."

"What do you mean?"

Travis suddenly looked uncomfortable.

"Well . . . I saw him at Clark's . . . This was mid-August, just after I had persuaded Jenny to file a complaint against him. He'd grabbed her and she'd been left with a huge bruise on her arm. I mean, it was pretty serious. He drove away when he saw me arrive. I chased him in my car, and I caught him on Shore Road. And . . . you know, Somerset is a peaceful town. I didn't want him coming here and roaming around—"

"What did you do?"

"I gave him a beating. I'm not proud of it. And—"

"And *what*, Chief Dawn?"

"I stuck my gun in his privates. I beat the shit out of him, and when he was bent double on the ground, I held him down, took out my Colt, loaded it, and pressed the barrel to his balls. I told him I never wanted to see him again in my life. He was moaning. He said he would never come back, and he begged me to let him go. I know it wasn't right, but I wanted to make sure we never saw him again in Somerset."

"And you think he obeyed?"

"Without a doubt."

"So you were the last person to see him in Somerset?"

"Yes. I passed on the order to my colleagues, with a description of his car. He never showed himself again. We found out that he had died in Massachusetts a month or so later."

"How did he die?"

"He went straight at a bend, I think. I don't know much more about it. To be honest I wasn't really interested. At that time we had more important things deal with."

When we came out of the diner, Gahalowood said, "I think that car is the key to the mystery. We have to find out who could have been driving a black Monte Carlo. Or rather, we should ask ourselves: Could Luther Caleb have been at the wheel of a black Chevrolet Monte Carlo on August 30, 1975?"

The next day I went back to Goose Cove for the first time since the fire. I went inside, ignoring the police tape marking off the porch. The house was in ruins. In the kitchen I found the box with the words SOUVENIR OF ROCKLAND, MAINE, still intact. I emptied out the stale bread inside and filled it with a few objects I found in other rooms. In the living room I discovered a small photo album that had miraculously escaped the flames. I took it outside and sat under a tall birch tree opposite the house to look through it. It was at that moment that Ernie Pinkas turned up. He said to me simply: "I saw your car in the driveway."

He sat next to me.

"Are those photographs of Harry?" he asked, nodding at the album.

"Yeah. I found it in the house."

There was a long silence. I turned the pages. The pictures dated from the early 1980s, I guessed. There was a yellow Labrador in several of them.

"Whose dog is that?" I said.

"Harry's."

"I didn't know he used to have a dog."

"His name was Storm. He must have lived twelve or thirteen years."

Storm. The name was not unknown to me, but I couldn't remember why.

"Marcus," Pinkas said, "I didn't mean to be cruel the other day. I'm sorry if I hurt you."

"It's O.K."

"No, it's not. I didn't realize you'd received threats. Was that because of your book?"

"Probably."

"But who did that?" he said angrily, pointing to what was left of the house.

"No-one knows. The police say an accelerant was used, like gasoline. An empty can was found near the house, but they couldn't match the fingerprints they took from it."

"So you received threats but you stayed anyway?"

"Yes."

"Why?"

"Why should I have left? Out of fear? You can't give in to fear."

Pinkas told me I was an exceptional person, and that he too would have liked to become an exceptional person, to be somebody in life. His wife had always believed in him. She had died a few years before, of cancer. On her deathbed she had told him, as if he were a young man with his whole life ahead of him: "Ernie, you will do something great with your life. I believe in you."

"I'm too old . . . My life is behind me," he'd replied.

"It's never too late, Ernie. Where there's life, there's hope."

But all Ernie had managed to do since his wife's death was land a job at the supermarket in Montburry so he could pay off her chemotherapy bills and maintain her headstone.

"I collect carts, Marcus. I walk around the parking lot, I hunt down the lonely, abandoned carts, I take them with me, I comfort them, and I put them away with all their cart friends in the cart station, for the next customers. The carts are never alone. Or, at least, not for long. Because in every supermarket in the world, there is an Ernie who comes to collect them and return them to their family. But who comes to collect Ernie and return him to *his* family? Why do we take better care of supermarket carts than we do of people?"

"You're right, Ernie. What can I do for you?"

"I would like to be listed in the Acknowledgments of your book. I would like you to mention my name on the last page, the way writers often do. And I would like it to be the first one. In big letters. Because I did help you get information, didn't I? Do you think that would be possible? My wife would be proud of me. Her husband would have contributed to the huge success of Marcus Goldman, the famous writer."

"You can count on me, Ernie," I told him.

"I'll read your book to her, Marc. Every day I'll sit next to her grave, and I'll read her your book."

"Our book, Ernie. Our book."

Suddenly we heard footsteps behind us. It was Jenny.

"I saw your car in the driveway, Marcus," she said.

Hearing those words, Ernie and I exchanged a smile. I stood up, and Jenny embraced me like a mother. Then she looked at the house and began to cry.

On my way back to Concord that day, I stopped by the Sea Side Motel to see Harry. He was standing in front of the door to his room, stripped to the waist, practicing boxing moves. When he saw me, he called out, "Come and box, Marcus."

"I've come to talk."

"We can talk while we box."

I handed him the SOUVENIR OF ROCKLAND, MAINE box that I had found in the house.

"I brought you this," I said. "A lot of your belongings are still in the house. Why don't you go see what you can salvage?"

"What is there to salvage?"

"Memories?"

He frowned. "Memories only make you sad. Just looking at this box, I feel like crying."

He held the box in his hands and pressed it to him.

"When she disappeared, I didn't take part in the search," he told me. "You know what I did?"

"No . . ."

"I waited for her. Searching for her would have meant she wasn't there anymore. So I waited for her, convinced she would come back to me one day. And when that day came, I wanted her to be proud of me. I spent thirty-three years preparing for her return. For thirty-three years I bought chocolate and flowers for her. I knew she was the only person I would ever love. And love, Marcus, comes only once in a lifetime. And if you don't believe me, that means you have never loved. In the evenings I lay on my couch and watched out for her, thinking she would appear the way she always used to. When I started traveling all over the country to give speeches, I would leave a note on my door: *Giving a speech in Seattle. Back next Tuesday.* In case she returned while I was away. And I always left my door unlocked. Always! I never once locked it, in thirty-three years. People said I was crazy, that I would come back one day and find the house had been robbed, but nobody robs anybody in Somerset, New Hampshire. Do you know why I spent so many years on the road, accepting every invitation I was offered? Because I thought I might find her that way. I roamed all over this country, from east to west and north to south, in big cities and little towns, and each time I made sure that the local papers announced my arrival. Sometimes I even bought an ad myself. And why did I do all that? For her. So that we could find each other again. And during each speech I scanned the audience, looking for young blond women of her age, searching for anyone who resembled her. Each time I thought maybe she'll be here. And after my speech, I would answer every question, agree to every request, hoping she might come to me. I spent years searching for her, looking first for fifteen-year-old girls, then sixteen-year-olds, then twenty-year-olds, then twenty-five-year-olds. The reason I stayed in Somerset is that I was waiting for Nola. And then, a month and a half ago, they found her, dead. Buried in my yard! I had been waiting for her all that time, and she was right there, next to me. In the place where I had always wanted to plant hydrangeas—for her! My heart's been breaking ever since they found her, Marcus. Because I lost the love of my life, and because if I hadn't arranged to meet her in this goddamn motel, maybe she would still be alive. So don't come here with your memories, because those memories are tearing out my heart. Stop, I'm begging you, please stop."

He walked toward the stairs.

"Where are you going, Harry?"

"To box. That's all I have left—boxing."

He went down to the parking lot and began making warlike movements under the worried gaze of customers in the neighboring restaurant. I followed him and stood opposite him in the guard position. He tried a flurry of punches, but even when boxing, he was no longer the same.

"Why did you come here, really?" he asked between two right-hand attacks.

"To see you."

"And why do you want to see me so badly?"

"Because we're friends!"

"But that's the point. You don't seem to understand this, but we can't be friends anymore."

"Why?"

"I love you like a son. And I will always love you. But we can no longer be friends."

"Because of the house? I'll pay for it, I told you. I'll pay for it all!"

"You still don't understand. It's not because of the house."

I lowered my guard for an instant, and he hit me with a series of punches to my right shoulder.

"Don't let your guard down, Marcus! If that had been your head, you'd have been knocked out."

"Fuck my guard! I want to know! Tell me what the hell you're getting at with all these riddles."

"They're not riddles. The day you understand, you'll have solved this whole case."

I stopped dead.

"For God's sake, what exactly are you trying to tell me? Are you hiding something from me? You haven't told me the whole truth?"

"I've told you everything. The truth is in your hands."

"I don't understand."

"I know. But when you do understand, everything will be different. You're going through a crucial phase of your life."

Pissed off, I sat down on the asphalt.

"Get up! Get up!" he shouted. "We're practicing the noble art of boxing!"

But I'd had enough of his noble art of boxing.

"Boxing only means something to me because of you, Harry. You remember the boxing championship of 2002?"

"Of course I remember. How could I forget?"

"So why can't we be friends anymore?"

"Because of books. Books brought us together, and now they're driving us apart. It was written."

"It was written? What's that supposed to mean?"

"It's all in the books. I knew this moment would come the day I first saw you."

"What moment?"

"It's because of the book you're writing now."

"This book? But I'll stop writing it, if that's what you want. Do you want me to give it up? Alright then, I'll give it up! No more book. No more nothing."

"Unfortunately that would make no difference. If it's not this one, it will be another."

"What are you trying to tell me? I don't understand."

"You are going to write this book, Marcus, and it will be wonderful. I'm very happy about that; don't get me wrong. But the time has come for us to separate. One writer leaves, and another is born. You're going to carry the torch. You're going to become a great writer. You've sold the rights to your manuscript for two million dollars! Three million! You're going to become someone very important. I always knew it."

"For God's sake, what are you trying to say?"

"Marcus, the key is in the books. It's right there in front of you. Look for it—look closely. Can you see where we are?"

"We're in a motel parking lot!"

"No! No, Marcus. This is the origin of evil. I have been dreading this moment for more than thirty years."

The boxing gym on the Burrows College campus, February 2002

"Your punches are badly placed, Marcus. You hit well, but the first phalanx of your middle finger sticks out too far, so it's grazed on impact."

"I don't feel it when I wear gloves."

"You should know how to box with bare hands. The gloves are only there so you don't kill your opponent. You would know it if you hit anything other than this bag."

"Harry . . . Why do you think I always box alone?"

"Ask yourself that question."

"I think it's because I'm afraid. I'm afraid of failing."

"But when you went to that gym in Lowell, on my advice, and you got smashed to pieces by that big black guy, how did you feel?"

"Proud. After the fight I felt proud. The next day, when I looked at my bruises I liked them. I had surpassed myself. I had shown balls. I had dared to fight."

"So you felt like you'd won?"

"Yes, I did. Even if, technically, I lost the match, I felt as if I had won."

"Well, there's your answer: It doesn't matter if you win or lose. What matters is how you fight between the first bell and the last one. The result of the match is just a piece of news for the public. Who can say you lost if you feel like you've won? Life is like a foot race, Marcus: There will always be people who are faster than you, and there will always be those who are slower than you. What matters, in the end, is how you ran your race."

"Harry, I found this poster on a wall . . ."

"The university boxing championship?"

"Yes, all the best universities will be represented—Harvard, Yale—I . . . I want to take part."

"Then I'll help you."

"Really?"

"Of course. You can always count on me, Marcus. Never forget that. We're a team, you and I. For life."

10

In Search of a Fifteen-Year-Old Girl
(Somerset, New Hampshire, September 1–18, 1975)

"Harry, how can you communicate emotions that you have not felt yourself?"

"That's your job as a writer. Writing means being able to feel things more strongly than other people do and to communicate those feelings. Writing means allowing your readers to see things they sometimes can't see. If only orphans wrote books about orphans, we'd never get anywhere. That would mean you'd never be able to write about a mother, a father, a dog, an airplane pilot, or the Russian Revolution unless you happened to be a mother, a father, a dog, an airplane pilot, or a witness to the Russian Revolution. You are only Marcus Goldman. And if every writer had to limit his writing to his own experiences, literature would be impoverished and would lose all its meaning. We're allowed to write about anything that affects us. And no-one can judge us for that. We're writers because we do one thing differently, one thing that everyone around us knows how to do: write. All the nuances reside there."

At one time or another, everyone thought he or she had seen Nola somewhere. In the general store of a neighboring town, at a bus stop, at the counter of a restaurant. One week after her disappearance, while the search continued, the police were having to deal with a vast array of erroneous witness statements. In Cheshire County a movie was interrupted after one of the moviegoers thought she had recognized Nola Kellergan in the third row. Near Manchester, a father accompanying his (blond, fifteen-year-old) daughter to a carnival was taken to the police station so their identities could be verified.

The search was intense but in vain. People from all over the region had joined in, but still no traces of the girl were found. F.B.I. specialists came to optimize the police work by pointing out the places that ought to be searched first, on the basis of experience and statistics: streams and rivers, the edges of forests near parking lots, garbage dumps where putrid waste rotted. The case seemed so complex that they even enlisted the aid of a medium, who had proved her abilities with two murder cases in Oregon, but she was unsuccessful this time.

The town of Somerset was in turmoil, invaded by onlookers and journalists. On the main street, the police station was a hive of activity. The search was being coordinated from there, and all information regarding the case was routed there to be sorted. The telephone lines were overloaded: The telephone rang constantly, often for nothing, and each call required attention. Teams with dogs had been sent to Maine and Massachusetts, again without success. The press conference given twice daily by Chief Pratt and Captain Rodik in front of the police station came to seem increasingly like a confession of helplessness.

Without anyone's realizing it, Somerset was being closely watched: Hidden among the reporters who had descended from all over the region, federal agents observed the neighborhood around the Kellergan house and listened in on the Kellergans' telephone calls. If this was an abduction, the kidnapper would soon show himself. He would call or, perhaps out of perversity, join the onlookers who thronged outside 245 Terrace Avenue to leave messages of support. And if this was not a case of someone's seeking a ransom but—as many feared—the work of a psychopath, then the killer had to be identified as quickly as possible, before he struck again.

The people of Somerset stood shoulder to shoulder. The men spent hours sweeping fields and forests, searching the banks of rivers and streams. Robert Quinn took two days off work to help with the search. Ernie Pinkas, with the approval of his foreman, left the factory one hour early so he could join the search teams from late afternoon until sunset. In the kitchen at Clark's, Tamara Quinn, Amy Pratt, and other volunteers prepared food for the searchers. The investigation was all they talked about:

"I have information!" Tamara Quinn repeated. "I have important information!"

"What? What? Tell us!" chorused the others, while buttering bread for sandwiches.

"I can't tell you . . . it's too serious."

And everyone began gossiping. They'd suspected for a long time that something not quite right was going on at 245 Terrace Avenue, and it was no surprise that it was ending badly. Mrs Phillips, whose son had been in the same high school class as Nola, said that during one lunch period, one of the kids had lifted up Nola's shirt as a joke, and everyone had seen that she had bruises on her body. Mrs Hattaway told how her daughter Nancy had been good friends with Nola and that, one week during the summer, Nola had seemingly disappeared and the Kellergans' home had been closed to all visitors. "And that music!" Mrs Hattaway added. "Every day I heard that music blaring from the garage, and I wondered why on earth anyone would need to deafen the whole neighborhood. I should have complained, but I never dared. I thought, well, it is the pastor, after all."

*

Monday, September 8, 1975

It was around noon.

Harry was waiting at Goose Cove. The same questions whirled constantly around his head: What had happened to Nola? Where could she be? How was it possible that the police had found no trace of her? He had been locked in his house, waiting, for a week now. He slept on the living room couch, listening for the faintest noise. He no longer ate. He felt as if he were going crazy. The more he thought about it, the more the idea came back to him: What if Nola had wanted to create a smoke-screen? What if she had faked an attack? Ketchup on her face and screams to make people believe she was being abducted, and then, while the police searched for her around Somerset, she would have all the time in the world to disappear far away, to go deep into the heart of Canada. Maybe soon they would think she was dead and no-one would search for her anymore. Had Nola planned this whole charade so the two of them could live in peace forever afterward? But if that was true, then why hadn't she met him at the motel? Had the police arrived too quickly? Had she been forced to hide in the woods? And what had happened at Deborah Cooper's house? Was there a connection between the two incidents, or was it simply a coincidence? If Nola had not been kidnapped, then why didn't she give him a sign that she was alive? Why hadn't she come to take refuge here, at Goose Cove? He forced himself to think: Where could she be? Somewhere only they knew about. Martha's Vineyard? It was too far. The tin box in the kitchen reminded him of their trip to Maine, at the start of their relationship. Was she hiding in Rockland? As soon as he had this thought, he grabbed his car keys and rushed outside. Opening the front door, he found himself face to face with Jenny, who was about to ring the doorbell. She had come to see if he was O.K.: It had been days since she had seen him, and she was worried. She thought his face looked dreadful. He had lost weight. He was wearing the same suit he had been wearing the last time she saw him, at Clark's a week ago.

"Harry, what's wrong?" she asked.

"I'm waiting."

"Waiting for what?"

"Nola."

She didn't understand. "Oh yes, it's so awful!" she said. "Everyone in town is horrified. It's been a week already and still not a single clue. Harry . . . you look unhappy. I'm worried about you. Have you eaten recently? I'm going to run you a bath and make you something to eat."

He didn't have time to deal with Jenny. He had to find out where Nola was hiding. Somewhat abruptly, he pushed her away, ran down the few wooden steps that led to the gravel driveway, and got in his car.

"I don't want anything," he said from his open window. "I'm very busy. I can't be disturbed."

"Busy doing what?" Jenny asked.

"Waiting."

His car disappeared behind a row of pine trees. She sat on the porch steps and started to cry. The more she loved him, the more unhappy she felt.

At that same moment, Travis Dawn was entering Clark's, holding roses. He hadn't seen her in many days, not since Nola's disappearance. He had spent the morning in the forest with the search teams, and then, getting back into his patrol car, he had seen the flowers under the seat. They were half dried up and strangely twisted, but he had felt a sudden desire to take them to Jenny, right then. As if life were too short. He took a break from work, long enough to find her at Clark's, but she was not there.

He sat at the counter, and Tamara Quinn approached immediately, as she did whenever she saw a man in uniform.

"How's the search going?" she asked, like a worried mother.

"We haven't found anything, Mrs Quinn. Nothing at all."

She sighed and contemplated the tired lines around the young policeman's eyes.

"Have you eaten, son?"

"Uh . . . no, Mrs Quinn. In fact, I came to see Jenny."

"She left for a bit."

She poured him a glass of iced tea and put a paper placemat and silverware in front of him. She noticed the flowers. "Are they for her?"

"Yes. I wanted to make sure she was O.K. After everything that's happened the last week or so . . ."

"She shouldn't be long. I asked her to be back before the lunch hour rush, but obviously she's late. She's losing her head over that guy."

"What guy?" asked Travis, feeling his heart contract.

"Harry Quebert."

"Harry Quebert?"

"I'm sure she's gone to his house. I don't know why she insists on trying to win over that little bastard. Anyway, you don't want to hear about that. The special today is cod with fried potatoes . . ."

"That's perfect, Mrs Quinn. Thank you."

She put a friendly hand on his shoulder.

"You're a good boy, Travis. I would be very happy for my Jenny to be with someone like you."

She went into the kitchen, and Travis glumly took a few swallows of iced tea.

Jenny arrived a few minutes later; she had hastily reapplied her makeup so it wouldn't be obvious she had been crying. She went behind the counter, put on her apron, and then noticed Travis. He smiled at her and handed her the bouquet of wilted flowers.

"I'm afraid they're past their prime," he apologized, "but I've been meaning to give them to you for a while now. I figured it was the thought that counted."

"Thank you, Travis."

"They're wild roses. I know a place near Montburry where there are hundreds of them. I'll take you there, if you like. Are you O.K., Jenny? You don't look too good . . ."

"I'm O.K."

"This terrible business getting you down, huh? Are you afraid? Don't worry—there're policemen everywhere now. And I'm sure we'll find Nola."

"I'm not afraid. It's something else."

"What?"

"Nothing important."

"Is it because of Harry Quebert? Your mother said you really like him."

"Maybe. Never mind, Travis, it doesn't matter. I . . . I have to go to the kitchen. I'm late, and Mom will be mad at me again."

Jenny disappeared behind the swinging doors and found her mother preparing food.

"You're late again, Jenny! You left me alone here to look after everyone!"

"Sorry, Mom."

Tamara handed her a plate of cod and fried potatoes.

"Take this to Travis, will you?"

"Yes, Mom."

"He's a nice boy, you know."

"I know . . ."

"Invite him to have lunch with us on Sunday."

"Eat lunch with us? No, Mom—I don't want to. He's not my type at all. I'd just get his hopes up. It wouldn't be fair."

"I'm not going to argue about it! You weren't so picky when you had no-one to take you to the gala and he came over to ask you. He likes you a lot—that's obvious—and he could make you a very nice husband. Forget Quebert, for God's sake! Nothing will ever happen with him—get that into your head! Quebert is not a nice man. You should be happy that a nice boy is courting you when you spend all day in an apron!"

"Mom!"

In a high-pitched voice, imitating a child's moans, Tamara mocked: "Mom! Mom! Stop being such a crybaby. You're almost twenty-five years old! Do you want to end up an old maid? All your school friends are married. What about you? You were the prom queen! What happened, for Christ's sake? Oh, I'm so disappointed in you. We'll have lunch with Travis on Sunday, and that's that. You're going to take that plate to him now, and you're going to invite him. And after that, you're going to wipe down the tables in the back because they're filthy. That'll teach you to be late all the time."

Wednesday, September 10, 1975

"You see, Doctor, there's this charming young policeman who's been flirting with her. I told her to invite him to lunch on Sunday. She didn't want to, but I forced her."

"Why?"

Tamara shrugged and rested her head on the armrest of the couch. She thought about it for a moment.

"Because . . . because I don't want her to end up alone."

"So you're afraid your daughter will be alone for the rest of her life?"

"Yes! Exactly! For the rest of her life!"

"What about you? Are you afraid of solitude?"

"Solitude is death."

"Are you afraid of dying?"

"I'm terrified of death, Doctor."

Sunday, September 14, 1975

At lunch with the Quinns, Travis was bombarded with questions. Tamara wanted to know everything about the investigation, which was not progressing. Robert had a few interesting things to say, but on the rare occasions that he tried to speak, his wife interrupted him, saying:

"Don't talk, Bobbo. It's not good for your cancer." Jenny looked miserable and barely touched her food. While serving the apple pie, Jenny finally dared ask, "So, Travis, do you have a list of suspects?"

"Not really. To be honest, we're kind of floundering at the moment. It's crazy—there's not a single clue."

"Is Harry Quebert a suspect?" Tamara demanded suddenly.

Jenny gasped. "Mom!"

"What? I have good reasons for mentioning his name: He's a pervert, Travis. A pervert! It wouldn't surprise me at all if he were involved in that poor girl's disappearance."

"That's a serious accusation, Mrs Quinn," Travis replied. "You can't say that kind of thing without proof."

"But I had proof!" she bellowed "I had it! I had a highly compromising note written by him locked in my safe at the restaurant! And I'm the only one with a key! And you know where I keep that key? Around my neck. I never take it off. Never! And when I went to get that piece of paper so I could hand it over to Chief Pratt, it had vanished! It wasn't there! How is that possible? I have no idea. It must be witchcraft."

"Maybe you just put it somewhere else," Jenny suggested.

"Shut your mouth, my girl. Are you trying to imply that I'm crazy? Bobbo, am I crazy?"

Robert moved his head in a gesture that indicated neither yes nor no, which made his wife even more irritable.

"Bobbo, why don't you answer when I ask you a question?"

"Because of my cancer," he finally replied.

"Alright then, no pie for you. It was the doctor who said it: Desserts could kill you, just like that."

"I never heard the doctor say that!" Robert protested.

"There you go—the cancer is making you deaf. Two months from now, you'll be with the angels, my poor Bobbo."

Travis attempted to ease the tension by going back to the original topic of conversation. "Well, I'm afraid if you don't have any proof, it won't stick. Police investigations have to be precise and scientific. And I know what I'm talking about: I finished first in my class at the police academy."

The mere idea of having lost the piece of paper that could have caused Harry's downfall sent Tamara into a frenzy. To calm herself, she grabbed the pie cutter and brutally chopped out a few slices of pie, while Bobbo sobbed because he really didn't want to die.

Wednesday, September 17, 1975

Tamara Quinn was obsessed with the missing piece of paper. She had spent two days searching her house, her car, and even the garage, where she never went. She found nothing. That morning, after the early break-fast rush at Clark's, she went into her office and emptied out the contents of her safe on the floor. No-one else had access to the safe; it was impossible that the paper had disappeared. It had to be there. She checked the contents again, but no luck. Vexed, she put her belongings back. Poking her head into the office, Jenny, found her mother reaching deep inside the huge steel box.

"Mom? What are you doing?"

"I'm busy."

"Don't tell me you're still looking for that stupid piece of paper!"

"Mind your own business, my girl, if you wouldn't mind! What time is it?"

Jenny looked at her watch. "Almost eight-thirty."

"Goddamn it! I'm late."

"For what?"

"I have a meeting."

"But you have to be here to sign off on the beverage delivery. Last Wednesday you—"

"You're a big girl, aren't you?" her mother broke in coldly. "You have two arms. You know where the stock is kept. You don't need a degree from Harvard to stack crates of Coca-Cola. I'm sure you'll do a fine job. And don't go making doe eyes at the deliveryman so he'll do it for you!

Without another look at her daughter, Tamara picked up her car keys and left. Thirty minutes later, a large truck parked behind Clark's. The deliveryman dumped a heavy pallet filled with crates of Coca-Cola in front of the service entrance.

"Need a hand?" he asked Jenny, after she signed for it.

"No, sir. My mother wants me to do it myself."

"As you like, ma'am. Have a good day."

The truck drove away, and Jenny began lifting the heavy crates one by one and carrying them into the stockroom. She felt like crying. Just then Travis drove past in his patrol car and spotted her. He immediately parked and got out of the car.

"Need some help?" he asked.

"I'm O.K. I'm sure you have better things to do," she said, without pausing from her work.

He grabbed a crate and tried to make conversation.

"Apparently the recipe for Coca-Cola is a secret. They keep it in a safe in Atlanta."

"I didn't know that."

He followed Jenny into the stockroom, and they stacked the crates. She didn't say anything, so he kept talking.

"I also heard that Coke is good for the morale of our troops, so ever since World War Two the government has been sending crates of the stuff to American soldiers stationed abroad. I read that in a book about Coke. But, I mean, I do read serious books too . . ."

They came out into the parking lot. She looked deep into his eyes.

"Travis . . ."

"Yes, Jenny?"

"Hold me. Take me in your arms and hold me tight! I feel so lonely!

I feel so miserable! I feel cold to the depths of my soul."

He took her in his arms and hugged her as tightly as he could.

"My daughter is starting to ask questions, Doctor. Just now she asked where I was going every Wednesday."

"What did you say to her?"

"That it was none of her business! And that she could take care of the Coke delivery. I don't see what it has to do with her, where I go."

"I sense from your tone of voice that you're angry."

"Yes! Yes! Of course, I'm angry, Dr Ashcroft!"

"Angry with whom?"

"With . . . with myself."

"Why?"

"Because I yelled at her again. You know, when you have children, you want them to be the happiest kids in the world. And then life gets in the way . . ."

"Tell me what you mean by that?"

"She always asks my advice, about everything! She's always trailing after me, saying: 'Mom, how do you do this? Mom, where does that go? Mom this and Mom that! Mom! Mom! Mom!' But I won't always be there for her. One day I won't be there to look after her anymore. And when I think about that, I feel it here, in my belly. As if my whole stomach is tied up in knots. It's physically painful, and it ruins my appetite."

"Are you saying you suffer from anxiety, Mrs Quinn?"

"Yes! Yes! Anxiety. Terrible anxiety. We try to do everything right; we try to always do our best for our children. But what will our children do when we are no longer here? What will they do? How can we be sure they'll be happy and that nothing will happen to them? It's like with that poor girl, Dr Ashcroft. That poor Nola—what happened to her? Where could she be?"

*

Where could she be? She was not in Rockland. She was not on any of the beaches or in any of the restaurants or stores. He called the hotel on Martha's Vineyard to find out whether anyone had seen a young blond girl, but the receptionist he spoke to thought he must be a madman. So he waited, every day and every night. He waited frantically and hopefully. She would come back, and they would go away together. They would be happy. She was the only person who had ever given any meaning to his life. Let all the books and houses burn, to hell with all music and all men—nothing mattered as long as she was with him. He loved her, and loving meant that, with her beside him, he didn't fear death or adversity. So he waited for her. And when night fell, he swore to the stars that he would wait forever.

While Harry refused to lose hope, Captain Rodik could not help noticing the total failure of the police operations in spite of the scale of the resources deployed. During a meeting with the F.B.I. and Chief Pratt, Rodik remarked bitterly: "The dogs aren't finding anything. The men aren't finding anything. I don't think we're going to find her."

"I'm largely in agreement with you," said the F.B.I. officer. "Generally, in cases like this, you either find the victim right away, dead or alive, or you receive a ransom demand. And if that doesn't happen, then the case joins the ever-growing list of unresolved missing-persons cases . Last week, as it happens, the F.B.I. received five reports of missing children nationwide. We can't deal with everything."

"But what could have happened to this kid?" asked Pratt, who could not face the idea of simply giving up. "Did she run away?"

"No. If she ran away, then why was she seen covered in blood and screaming?"

Rodik shrugged, and the F.B.I. man suggested they go for a beer.

At the final joint press conference the next day, the evening of September 18, Chief Pratt and Captain Rodik announced that the search for Nola

Kellergan was being called off. In nearly three weeks they had found no evidence at all, not even the smallest clue.

Volunteers, led by Chief Pratt, continued searching for several weeks after this, all the way out to the state borders. But she was never found. It was as if Nola Kellergan had flown away.

9

A Black Monte Carlo

"The words are good, Marcus. But don't write in order to be read; write in order to be heard."

My book was progressing. Little by little, the hours spent writing were producing results, and I began to feel once more the indescribable sensation that I had believed was lost forever. It was as if I had at last recovered a vital sense that, when it had failed, had made my entire being dysfunctional, as if someone had pressed a button in my brain, and suddenly it had started working again. It was as if I had come back to life. It was the feeling of being a writer.

My days began before dawn: I went running from one end of Concord to the other, while listening to my minidisc recorder. Back in my hotel room, I ordered a pot of coffee and got to work. I was aided once again by Denise, whom I had taken back from Schmid & Hanson; she had agreed to start work again in my office near Central Park. I sent her my pages by e-mail as I wrote them, and she corrected them. When a chapter was finished, I sent it to Douglas to get his opinion. It was funny to see how completely he was throwing himself into this book; I know for a fact that he sat by his computer all day, waiting for my chapters. Nor did he fail to remind me of my rapidly approaching deadline, telling me over and over: "If we don't get this done in time, we're screwed!" He said "we," though, theoretically, he was not at any risk himself. But he felt just as involved in the book as I did.

I think Douglas was taking a lot of heat from Barnaski and trying to protect me from it: Barnaski feared I would not be able to meet my deadline without outside help. He had already called me several times to say this himself.

"You have to use ghostwriters to get this done," he told me. "I have teams of them ready to work for you. Just give them the gist, and they'll write it for you."

"Never," I replied. "It's my responsibility to write this book. Nobody is going to do it for me."

"Oh, Goldman, I'm so sick of all your morals and lofty principles. Everybody gets their books written by other people these days. Untel, for example: He never refuses help from my teams."

"Untel doesn't write his own books?"

He gave his usual snigger. "Of course not! How the hell could he write that quickly? The readers don't want to know how Untel writes his books, or even who writes them. All they want, each summer, is to have a new Untel to read on their vacation. So we give it to them. It's called business."

"It's called cheating the public," I said.

"'Cheating the public'—Jesus, you're such a drama queen!"

I made him understand that it was out of the question that my book be written by anyone else but me. He had lost his patience.

"Goldman, I paid you two million dollars for this fucking book, so it would be nice if you could be a little more cooperative. If I think you need help from my writers, just fucking use them!"

"Calm down, Roy. You'll have the book by the deadline. At least you will if you stop calling me all the time."

"For fuck's sake, Goldman, I hope you're aware that I have my balls on the goddamn chopping block with. My balls! On the goddamn chopping block! I've invested a huge amount of money in this book, and the credibility of one of America's biggest publishing companies is on the line. So if you fuck this up—if there's no book because of you and your morals or God knows what other bullshit—and I have to walk the plank, you'd better know that you'll be walking it with me. And I'll make damn sure the sharks eat you first, you fucker!"

"O.K., I think I've got that, Roy, thanks."

For all his failings as a human being, Barnaski had an innate talent for marketing: My book was already the biggest sensation of the year, despite the fact that its promotional campaign was only just beginning. Soon after the house at Goose Cove had burned down, he had made a solemn declaration. "There is, hidden somewhere in America," he said, "a writer who is determined to tell the truth about what happened in Somerset in 1975. And because the truth sometimes hurts, there is somebody ready to do whatever it takes in order to keep him quiet." The next day an article appeared in the *New York Times* under the headline: WHO WANTS MARCUS GOLDMAN DEAD? My mother read it, of course, and called me right away.

"For the love of God, Markie, where are you?"

"I'm in my hotel suite in Concord. Room number—"

"Stop!" she yelled. "Don't tell me! I don't want to know."

"But you asked—"

"If you tell me, I won't be able to resist telling the butcher, who will tell his assistant, who will tell his mother, who is none other than the cousin of the registrar at Felton High School and who will of course tell him, and that devil will tell the principal, who will talk about it in the teachers' lounge, and soon all of Montclair will know exactly where my son is, and the guy who wants you dead will sneak up and strangle you in your sleep. Why are you staying in a suite, anyway? Do you have a girlfriend? Are you planning to get married?"

She then called my father over. I heard her shouting: "Nelson, come and listen. Markie's on the phone, and he's going to get married!"

"Mom, I'm not getting married. I'm on my own in the suite."

Gahalowood, who was in my room and had just eaten a very large breakfast on my tab, then amused himself by calling out: "Hey, what about me? I'm here!"

"Who is that?" my mother demanded.

"No-one."

"Don't lie to your mother! I heard a man's voice. Marcus, I'm going to ask you an extremely important medical question, and you have to be honest with the woman who carried you in her belly for nine months: Is there a homosexual man secretly hidden in your room?"

"No, Mom. It's just Sergeant Gahalowood. He's a policeman. We're investigating this case together, and he's also trying to add a couple of zeroes to my hotel bill."

"Is he naked?"

"What? Of course not! He's a policeman, Mom. We're working together."

"A policeman . . . I wasn't born yesterday, you know. I've seen that musical group, those men who sing together: a motorcyclist in leather, a plumber, an Indian, and a policeman . . ."

"Mom, this is a real policeman."

"Markie, in the name of your ancestors who fled the pogroms and for the love of your sweet mother, chase that naked man out of your room."

"I'm not going to chase anyone."

"Oh, Markie, why call me at all if you just want to make me suffer?"

"You called me, Mom."

"Yes, because your father and I are frightened about that criminal maniac who's after you."

"No-one is after me. The media just exaggerates."

"I check the mailbox every morning and every evening."

"Why?"

"Why? Why? He asks his mother why! For a bomb, of course!"

"I don't think anyone's going to put a bomb in your mailbox, Mom."

"We'll be killed by a bomb! And without ever having known the joy of being grandparents. Are you pleased with yourself? Just the other day, your father was followed by a big black car all the way home. Daddy ran inside, and the car parked in the street, right next to his."

"Did you call the police?"

"Of course. Two cars turned up, sirens screaming."

"And?"

"It was the neighbors. They'd gone and bought a new car! Without even telling us. A new car—can you imagine? When everyone is talking about how there's going to be a huge financial crisis, they go buy a new car. Don't you think that's suspicious? I think the husband must be involved in drug dealing or something like that."

"Mom, please stop talking shit about the neighbors."

"I know what I'm talking about. And don't talk like that to your poor mother, who might be killed at any moment by a bomb! How's your book?"

"It's going very well. I should have it finished in time."

"And how will it end? Maybe the man who killed the girl is trying to kill you."

"That's my only problem. I still don't know how the book will end."

On Monday afternoon, July 21, Gahalowood arrived at my suite as I was writing the chapter in which Nola and Harry decide to leave for Canada. He had news. He grabbed a himself bottle of beer from the minibar.

"I was just at Elijah Stern's house," he said.

"You went there without me?"

"Let me remind you that Stern has filed an injunction against your book. Anyway, I came here to tell you about it . . ."

Gahalowood explained that he had gone to see Stern unannounced in order to keep his visit unofficial, and that it was Stern's lawyer, Bo

Sylford, of Boston, who opened the door, drenched in sweat and wearing only sweatpants. "Give me five minutes, Sergeant," Sylford told him. "I'm going to take a quick shower, and then I'll be all yours."

"A shower?"

"As I said, writer, this Sylford guy was walking around half-naked. I waited in a little room, then he came back, wearing a suit, accompanied by Stern, who said to me: 'So, Sergeant, I see you have met my partner.'"

"His partner?" I repeated. "Are you telling me Stern is—"

"Gay. Which means it's unlikely he ever felt remotely attracted to Nola Kellergan."

"So what was going on with him and Nola?"

"That is the very question I asked him. He was fairly open about it."

Stern was apparently very annoyed by my book; in his opinion, I had no idea what I was talking about. So Gahalowood had seized the opportunity and asked him to clarify a few things relating to the case.

"Mr Stern," he said. "In light of what you have just told me about your . . . sexual orientation, could you please tell me what kind of relationship existed between yourself and Nola?"

"I told you from the beginning," Stern replied, without blinking. "A working relationship."

"A working relationship?"

"It's when someone does something for you and you pay her for it, Sergeant. In this case, she posed."

"So Nola Kellergan really did come here to pose for you?"

"Yes, but not for me."

"For who, then? Luther Caleb?"

"Yes, Luther. That's how he got his kicks."

The scene that Stern went on to describe took place one evening in July 1975. Stern did not recall the exact date, but it was toward the end of the month. Through cross-checking, I was able to establish that it must have occurred just before Nola and Harry went to Martha's Vineyard.

Concord. Late July, 1975

It was quite late already. Stern and Luther were alone in the house, playing chess on the terrace. The front doorbell rang, and the two men wondered who it could be at that hour. Luther went to open the door. He returned to the terrace accompanied by a beautiful young blond girl, her eyes reddened by tears. Nola.

"Good evening, Mr Stern," she said shyly. "I'm sorry to come here unannounced. My name is Nola Kellergan and I am the daughter of the pastor in Somerset."

"Somerset? You've come all the way from Somerset?" he asked. "How did you get here?"

"I hitchhiked. I had to speak to you."

"Do we know each other?"

"No, sir. But I have a very important request to make."

Stern contemplated this young lady, with her sparkling but sad eyes. He bade her sit down, and Caleb brought her a glass of lemonade and a plate of cookies.

She drank her lemonade thirstily, and almost amused by the scene, Stern told her: "I'm listening. What is it you have to ask me that is so important?"

"Once again, Mr Stern, please accept my apologies for disturbing you at such a late hour. But I had no choice. I have come to see you confidentially so that . . . I could ask you to hire me."

"Hire you? As what?"

"As whatever you like, sir. I would do anything for you."

"Hire you?" Stern repeated, not understanding. "But why? Do you need money?"

"In exchange, I would like you to allow Harry Quebert to stay at Goose Cove."

"Harry Quebert is leaving Goose Cove?"

"He can't afford to stay. He's already contacted the rental agency.

He can't pay next month's rent. But he has to stay! Because there is this book he has barely begun writing that I feel certain is going to be wonderful. If he has to leave, he'll never finish it. His career will be over. What a waste that would be! And then . . . there's me and Harry. I love him, Mr Stern. I love him as I have never loved anyone in my life. I know this will seem ridiculous to you, that you will say I'm only fifteen years old and know nothing about life. Well, maybe I do know nothing about life, Mr Stern, but I know my heart. Without Harry, I would be nothing."

She put her hands together as if praying, and Stern asked:

"What do you want from me?"

"I have no money. Which means I can't pay the rent of the house. But you could hire me! I would be your employee, and I would work for you as long as it took to pay you back for a few extra months in the house."

"I have enough employees already."

"I can do anything you want. Anything! Or let me pay the rent in installments: I already have a hundred and twenty dollars." She took some cash from her pocket. "This is all my savings. I work at Clark's on Saturdays; I'll keep working until I've paid you back."

"How much do you earn?"

She replied proudly: "Two dollars an hour. Plus tips!"

Stern smiled, touched by this request. He looked tenderly at Nola. He had no need for the income from Goose Cove; he could easily let Quebert stay there for a few months longer. But it was at this point that Luther asked to speak to him privately. They went to the room next door.

"Eli," said Caleb. "Pleave, I would like to paint her. Could I, pleave?"

"No, Luther. Not that. Not again . . ."

"Oh, pleave, let me paint her! It'f been fo long!"

"But why her?"

"Becaufe she lookf like Eleanore."

"Eleanore again? No, that's enough. You have to stop this now!"

But Caleb kept insisting, and in the end Stern gave in. He went back to see Nola, who was nibbling a cookie.

"Nola, I've given this some thought," he said. "I'm prepared to let Harry Quebert stay in the house for as long as he wishes."

She jumped up and hugged him around the neck.

"Oh, thank you! Thank you, Mr Stern!"

"But there's one condition . . ."

"Of course! Anything you want!"

"You will act as a model. For a painting. Luther is going to paint you. You will be nude, and he will paint you."

"Nude?" she choked. "You want me to take all my clothes off?"

"Yes. But only to act as a model. Nobody will touch you."

"But, sir, it's so embarrassing, being naked . . . I mean . . ." She started to sob. "I thought I could work in your garden, maybe, or shelve books in your library. I didn't think I would have to . . . I wasn't thinking of that."

She wiped the tears from her cheeks. Stern looked at this sweet little girl whom he was forcing to pose nude. He wished he could take her in his arms to comfort her, but he knew he must not let his feelings get the better of him.

"That's my price," he said coldly. "You pose nude, and Quebert keeps the house."

She nodded.

"I'll do it, Mr Stern. I'll do anything you want. I'm yours now."

Thirty-three years after this scene, haunted by remorse and as if seeking atonement, Stern had led Gahalowood to the terrace of his house.

"So that's how Nola entered my life," he said. "The day after her arrival, I attempted to contact Quebert to tell him he could stay at Goose Cove, but it was impossible to get hold of him. For a week I couldn't find him. I even sent Luther to wait around outside the house. He finally caught up with him as he was on his way out of town."

Gahalowood had then asked: "But didn't Nola's request seem strange to you? This was a fifteen-year-old girl having a relationship with a man in his thirties, and coming to you to ask a favor on his behalf."

"She spoke so well about love, Sergeant. I could never have phrased it like that. And I loved men; do you know how homosexuality was regarded back then? Even now, in fact . . . the proof being that I still hide my sexuality. Even when Marcus Goldman wrote that I was an old sadist and implied that I had abused Nola, I didn't dare respond with the truth. Instead I sent my lawyers to deal with it: I filed a lawsuit, hoping to block publication of the book. All I had to do was tell America that I belonged to the other side. But our fellow citizens are still very prudish, and I have a reputation to protect."

Gahalowood brought the conversation back to his main concern.

"Your arrangement with Nola—how did it work?"

"Luther went to get her in Somerset. I told him I did not want to know anything about all of that. I insisted he take his own car, rather than mine. As soon as I saw him leave for Somerset, I sent the staff out. I didn't want anyone to be there. I was too ashamed. So much so that I didn't want it to happen on the veranda that Luther generally used as a studio; I was afraid someone would see them there. So he took Nola to a small room next to my office. I greeted her when she arrived and said goodbye when she left. That was a condition I had imposed on Luther: I wanted to make sure everything went well. Or not badly, at least. The first time, I remember, she was on a couch that was draped with a white sheet. She was already naked, trembling, uncomfortable, frightened. I shook her hand, and it was ice cold. I never stayed in the room, but I always remained close, so I could be certain he wasn't hurting her in any way. In fact I even hid an intercom in the room. I would put it on before she arrived, that way, I could hear what was happening."

"And?"

"Nothing. Luther didn't say a word. He generally didn't speak much, because of his injuries. He painted her—that's all."

"So he didn't touch her?"

"Never! I'm telling you, I would not have allowed it."

"How many times did Nola come here?"

"I don't know. Maybe about ten."

"And how many pictures did he paint?"

"Only one."

"The one we took?"

"Yes."

So it was purely because of Nola that Harry had been able to stay in Somerset. But why exactly had Luther Caleb felt the need to paint her? And why had Stern—who, according to his own testimony, had been ready to let Harry stay in the house for free— given in to Caleb's request and forced Nola to pose nude? Gahalowood had not received any responses to these questions.

"I asked him," he told me. "I said to him, 'Mr Stern, there's one thing I still don't understand: Why did Luther want to paint Nola? You said earlier that this was how he got his kicks. Do you mean that painting provided him with a form of sexual pleasure?' But he said the subject was closed. It was a complicated story, he said, and I knew everything I needed to know; the rest belonged to the past. And he terminated the interview. I was there unofficially, so I couldn't force him to respond."

"Jenny told us that Luther wanted to paint her too," I reminded Gahalowood.

"So what are we talking about? Some kind of psycho with a paintbrush?"

"I have no idea. Do you think Stern might have agreed to Caleb's request because he was attracted to him?"

"That did cross my mind, and I asked Stern if there had been anything between him and Caleb. He replied very calmly that there had been nothing at all. 'I have been the faithful partner of Mr Sylford since the early seventies,' he told me. 'All I ever felt for Luther Caleb was pity, which is why I hired him in the first place. He had been seriously disfigured after a brutal beating. A life senselessly ruined. He was a skilled mechanic, and I needed someone to take care of my fleet of cars and be my chauffeur. We quickly built a bond of friendship. He was a nice guy, you know. I'm happy to say that we were friends.' But what nags at me, writer, is that bond he mentioned. He said it was a bond of friendship, but I have a feeling there was more to it than that. And I don't mean that it was sexual. I'm sure Stern was telling the truth when he said he felt no attraction for Caleb. No, I think the bond must have been more . . . unhealthy. That's the impression I had when Stern described how he gave in to Caleb's request and asked Nola to pose nude. That made him uncomfortable and ashamed, and yet he did it anyway, as if Caleb had some sort of power over him. Sylford must have sensed it too. Up to that point in the story, he had not said a word, he'd just listened, but when Stern told how he would greet Nola before the painting sessions, and how terrified she looked, lying there naked, he said: 'But, Eli, how could you? What is this all about? Why did you never tell me?'"

"What about Luther's disappearance?" I asked. "Did you talk to Stern about that?"

"Patience, writer. I saved the best part for last. Sylford, without meaning to, put Stern under pressure. He was upset, and he lost his lawyerly instincts. He started bellowing: 'For God's sake, Eli, explain yourself! Why did you never tell me? Why did you stay silent all these years?' Stern, as you can imagine, was rather abashed, and he replied: 'I stayed silent, yes, but I never forgot. I kept that painting for thirty-three years. Every day I would go into the studio, sit on the couch, and look at it. I had to withstand her gaze, her presence. And she would stare at me with those ghost eyes. That was my punishment!'"

Gahalowood, of course, asked Stern what punishment he was referring to.

"My punishment for having killed her a little bit!" Stern cried. "I think that by letting Luther paint her naked, I awoke some terrifying demons in him . . . I . . . I had told that young girl she had to pose nude for Luther, and I created a sort of bond between the two of them. I think I may be indirectly responsible for the death of that sweet girl!"

"What happened, Mr Stern?"

At first Stern remained silent. He paced around, visibly unsure whether he should tell what he knew. Then he made up his mind to talk.

"I quickly realized that Luther was in love with Nola, and that he wanted to understand why Nola was in love with Harry. That sickened him. And he became completely obsessed by Quebert, to the point that he would hide in the woods around Goose Cove to spy on him. I noticed that he was going to Somerset much more often than before, and I knew he would sometimes spend whole days there. I felt I was losing control of the situation, so one day I followed him. I found his car parked in the woods near Goose Cove. I left mine farther away, where no-one would see it, and I searched the woods. That was how I came to see him, without his seeing me. He was concealed in the undergrowth, spying on the house. I didn't show myself to him, but I wanted to teach him a lesson, to make him feel as if he'd just dodged a bullet. So I decided to go to Goose Cove, as if I were paying an impromptu visit to Harry. I walked down the driveway as if nothing were up. I went straight to the deck, making plenty of noise. 'Hello! Hello, Harry!' I shouted, to make sure that Luther would hear me. Harry must have thought I was crazy. I remember he started shouting his head off too. I let him believe I had left my car in Somerset and asked him for a ride into town in return for my buying him lunch. He agreed, and off we went together. I thought that would give Luther time to get away, and that he would think he'd had a close call. Harry and I went to Clark's. There Harry told me that a couple of days before, at dawn, Luther had given him a ride from Somerset to Goose Cove after he had cramped up while running. Harry asked me what Luther was doing in Somerset at that time of day. I changed the subject, but I was very worried: This had to stop. That evening I ordered Luther to stay away from Somerset, and told him he would be in trouble if he kept going. But he continued, in spite of everything. So a couple of weeks later I told him I didn't want him to paint Nola anymore. We had a terrible argument. This was Friday, August 29. He told me he could no longer work for me, and he left, slamming the door behind him. I thought he was just saying that in the heat of the moment, and that he would return. The next day, the fateful August 30, I left early for some private meetings. But when I got back, at the end of the day, and saw that Luther still hadn't returned, I had a strange foreboding. I went to search for him. I took the road to Somerset; it must have been about 8 p.m. I was passed on the way by a line of police cars. When I arrived in Somerset, I found the town in turmoil. People were saying that Nola had disappeared. I asked someone for the Kellergans' address, although in fact all I had to do was follow the crowds of onlookers and the emergency vehicles that were headed there. I stayed in front of their house for a while, surrounded by gossiping neighbors, incredulously contemplating the place where that sweet girl lived, that peaceful little white wooden house, with a swing hanging from the branch of an old cherry tree in the yard. I went back to Concord at nightfall and checked Luther's room to see if he was there. But of course he wasn't. The painting of Nola was, though, and it was finished. I took it with me and hung it in the studio. I never moved it from there. I stayed up all night waiting for Luther, but he never came. The next day his father telephoned me. He was searching for him too. I told him his son had left two days before, but I gave no further details. In fact I didn't tell anyone. I kept silent. Because to accept that Luther was guilty of kidnapping Nola Kellergan would mean accepting that I was a little guilty myself. I spent a month searching for Luther; I looked for him every day. Until his father called to tell me that he had died in a car accident."

"Are you telling me you think Luther Caleb killed Nola?" Gahalowood demanded.

Stern nodded. "Yes. I have thought that for thirty-three years."

This information left me speechless. I went to fetch us two more beers from the minibar and plugged in my recorder.

"You have to repeat all of that, Sergeant," I told him. "I have to record you, for my book."

He accepted with good grace. "If you like, writer."

I turned on the recorder. It was then that Gahalowood's cell phone rang. He answered, and I have his words on tape: "Are you sure?" he said. "You've checked everything? This is completely nuts!" He asked me for a pen and a piece of paper; he wrote down the information and hung up. Then he looked at me strangely and said: "That was an intern at the police station . . . I'd asked him to find me Luther Caleb's accident report."

"And?"

"According to the report, Luther Caleb was found in a black Chevrolet Monte Carlo registered to Stern's company."

Friday, September 26, 1975

It was a misty day. The sun had risen a few hours earlier, but the light was still gray and the landscape clouded by opaque smears. It was 8 a.m. when George Trent, a lobsterman, left the harbor of Plymouth, Massachusetts, by boat, accompanied by his son. His fishing zone was concentrated largely along the coast, but he was one of the few lobstermen to also leave traps in certain inlets neglected by others, since they were generally considered difficult to access or too dependent on the whims of the tide to be profitable. It was to one of these inlets that George Trent was headed that day, to pick up two traps. As he maneuvered his boat toward Ellisville Harbor, his son was suddenly distracted by a flash of light. A ray of sunlight had escaped through a gap in the clouds and reflected off something. This had lasted only a fraction of a second, but it had been so bright that the young man was intrigued. So he got out a pair of binoculars and scanned the coastline.

"What's up?" his father asked.

"There's something over there on the shore. I don't know what it is, but I saw something shining."

Gauging the level of the ocean in relation to the rocks, Trent decided that the water was deep enough to approach the shore. He moved the boat very slowly through the shallows.

"Tell me again what you saw," he said to his son.

"A reflection, definitely. But it must have been reflected off something unusual, like metal or glass."

They moved farther forward, and, on the rocks in front of them, they suddenly saw what it was that had grabbed their attention. "Jesus Christ!" said George Trent, wide-eyed. He rushed to the onboard radio to call the Coast Guard.

At 8.47 a.m., the Sagamore police were informed by the Coast Guard that a car had gone off the road that hugs the hills overlooking Ellisville Harbor and crashed onto the rocks below. Officer Darren Wanslow went to take a look. He knew the place well: a narrow road perched above steep sand dunes, offering a spectacular view. A small parking area had even been built on the end point to allow tourists to admire the vista. It was a beautiful place, but Officer Wanslow had always thought it dangerous because there was no guard rail. He had asked the county authorities to erect one on several occasions, but without success, in spite of the heavy traffic here on summer evenings. All they had put up was a warning notice.

As he neared the parking area, Wanslow saw a forest ranger's pickup truck, so he knew this must be where the accident had occurred. He turned off the car's siren and parked. Two rangers were looking out at the scene below: A Coast Guard boat was busy near the rocks, using an articulated arm.

"They say there's a car down there," one of the rangers told Wanslow. "But you can't see shit."

The policeman approached the edge. The slope was steep and covered in brambles, tall grass, and folds of rock. The ranger was right: It was impossible to make anything out.

"You think the car is just below?" he asked.

"That's what they said on the emergency channel. Given where the Coast Guard's boat is, I'd say the car was parked and then, for whatever reason, hurtled down the slope. I hope it wasn't teenagers coming to make out at night who forgot to put the hand brake on."

"Jesus, yeah," Wanslow whispered. "It'd be terrible if there were kids down there."

He inspected the part of the parking area closest to the dunes. There was a long grassy strip between where the asphalt ended and the slope began. He searched for signs of the car's path: weeds and brambles that might have been torn out as the vehicle hurtled down the slope.

"You think the car went straight over?" Wanslow asked the forest ranger.

"Probably. How long have we been saying that we need guard rails here? It's kids, I'm telling you. They probably drank one beer too many and drove straight over. Because if you haven't had too much to drink, you'd need a damn good reason not to stop after reaching the end of the parking area."

Down below, the boat performed a maneuver and moved away from the shore. The three men were then able to see a car swinging on the end of the articulated arm. Wanslow returned to his car and radioed the Coast Guard.

"What kind of car is it?" he asked.

"It's a Chevrolet Monte Carlo," came the answer. "Black."

"A black Monte Carlo? Can you confirm that it's a black Monte Carlo?"

"Affirmative. New Hampshire registration. There's a stiff inside. Doesn't look too good."

We had been driving for nearly two hours in Gahalowood's police car, a dusty Chrysler.

"You want me to drive, Sergeant?"

"Certainly not."

"You drive too slowly."

"I drive carefully."

"Your car is a trash can, Sergeant."

"It's a state police vehicle. Kindly show some respect."

"Alright, then it's a state trash can. How about we put some music on?"

"Forget it, writer. We're conducting an investigation—we're not on a day trip."

"I'll put it in my book, you know—that you drive like an old lady."

"Put some music on, writer. And turn up the volume. I don't want to hear you again until we're there."

I laughed.

"So remind me who this guy is," I said. "Darren . . ."

"Wanslow. He was a police officer in Sagamore. He was the one called to the scene when the lobstermen found Luther's car."

"This is crazy! Why didn't anyone make the connection?"

"No idea. That's what we need to find out."

"What is this Wanslow guy doing now?"

"He retired from the force a few years ago. He runs a garage now, with his cousin. Are you recording this?"

"Yes. What did you say to Wanslow on the phone yesterday?"

"Not much. He seemed surprised by my call. He said we'd find him in his garage during the day."

"Why didn't you just question him over the phone?"

"Nothing beats a face-to-face meeting, writer. The telephone is too impersonal. It's for pussies like you."

The garage was located on the way into Sagamore. Wanslow, when we found him, had his head under the hood of an old Buick. Inviting us inside, he kicked his cousin out of the office, cleared piles of binders full of accounts off the chairs so we could sit, spent a long time washing his hands at the sink, then poured us some coffee.

"So what brings New Hampshire State Police down here?" he asked.

"As I told you yesterday, we're investigating the death of Nola Kellergan," Gahalowood replied. "And in particular a car accident that happened here on September 26, 1975."

"The black Monte Carlo, huh?"

"Exactly. How did you know that's what we're interested in?"

"You're investigating the Kellergan case. I thought there must have been a link to it back then."

"Really?"

"Oh yeah. That's why I remember it. I mean, over the years, there are cases you forget and others that remain engraved in your memory. That accident was one of the memorable cases."

"Why?"

"When you're a cop in a small town like this, car accidents are among the bigger cases you have to deal with. I mean, the only dead bodies I saw, in my whole career, were due to car accidents. But this one was different. For weeks before this, we'd all been alerted to the kidnapping in New Hampshire. The feds were actively searching for a black Chevrolet Monte Carlo and they'd told us to keep an eye out. I remember spending those weeks looking for Chevys similar to that model, in all different colors, and flagging them down so I could check them out. I figured it would be pretty easy to repaint a car. Anyway, I felt involved in that case, like every other cop in the area. We desperately wanted to find that girl. And then, one morning, while I was in the station, the Coast Guard told us they were recovering a crashed car from the dunes at Ellisville Harbor. And guess what model it was . . ."

"A black Monte Carlo."

"Bull's-eye. With a New Hampshire registration and a corpse inside. I still remember inspecting that car. It had been completely crushed in the fall, and there was a guy inside, smashed to a pulp. We found his papers on him: Luther Caleb. I remember that clearly. The car was registered in the name of a big company in Concord—Stern Limited. We made a really careful search of the interior. There wasn't much; the water had caused a lot of damage. We did find the remains of some bottles of alcohol, smashed into a thousand pieces, but there was nothing in the trunk except a bag with a few clothes.

"You mean like a suitcase?"

"Yeah, that's it. Like a small suitcase."

"What did you do next?" Gahalowood asked.

"My job. I spent the rest of the day investigating. I wanted to know who this guy was, what he was doing there, and when the crash had occurred. I did some research on this Caleb, and guess what I found?"

"That a harassment complaint had been filed against him with the police in Somerset," Gahalowood said, almost casually.

"Exactly! How did you know?"

"That's my job."

"At that point I figured it couldn't be a coincidence. So the first thing I wanted to find out was if anyone had reported him missing. I mean, in my experience, when there's a car accident, there are usually loved ones worried about the victims; that's often what allows us to make an identification. But no-one had reported this guy missing. Strange, huh? So I called Stern Limited to find out more. I told them I had found one of their vehicles, and I was put on hold for a moment. Before I knew it I found myself talking to Mr Elijah Stern himself, the heir to the Stern family fortune. I explained the situation to him; I asked if one of his vehicles had disappeared, and he said no. I told him about the black Chevrolet, and he explained that it was the vehicle generally used by his chauffeur when he was off duty. I then asked him when he'd last seen his chauffeur, and he told me that he had gone on vacation. 'How long has he been on vacation?' I asked. 'Several weeks,' he replied. 'And where did he go?' He said he had no idea. I thought that was very strange."

"So what did you do?" Gahalowood asked.

"As far as I was concerned, we had found the number one suspect in the abduction of the Kellergan girl. So I immediately called the chief of police in Somerset."

"You called Chief Pratt?"

"Yes. I informed him of my discovery."

"And?"

"He came that day. He thanked me and carefully studied the case file. He was very friendly. He inspected the car and said that unfortunately it did not match the model he had seen during the pursuit, and now he was wondering if it really had been a Monte Carlo he had seen, or maybe it was something similar like a Nova, and that he would check this out with the sheriff's office. He added that he had already investigated this Caleb guy and that there had been enough exculpatory evidence to rule him out. He told me to send him the report anyway, though, which I did."

"So you told Chief Pratt about this, and he decided not to investigate it any further?"

"Yes. He assured me I was wrong. He seemed convinced, and he was the one running the investigation. He knew what he was doing. He concluded it was just a normal car accident, and that is what I put in my report."

"And that didn't seem strange to you?"

"At the time, no. I figured I must have gotten carried away. But even so, I didn't leave it there. I sent the corpse to forensics because I wanted to understand what could have happened, and to find out if the accident might have been caused by alcohol consumption—because of the bottles we found. Unfortunately the body had been so damaged by the violence of the fall and then by seawater that we weren't able to confirm anything. As I said, the guy was really smashed up. The only thing forensics could tell me was that the body had probably been there for several weeks before we found it. And God knows how much longer it might have stayed there if it weren't for that lobsterman. After that, the body was returned to the family, and that was the end of the story. As I said, everything led me to believe it was just a regular car accident. Obviously, now, with everything we've learned, especially about Pratt and the girl, I'm no longer sure about anything."

The scene as described by Darren Wanslow was indeed intriguing. When our interview was over, Gahalowood and I went to the marina in Sagamore to get a bite to eat. There was a tiny dock, with a general store and a postcard seller. It was a beautiful day: The colors were bright and the ocean seemed to go on forever. Around us, we could make out a few pretty-colored houses, some of them right on the beach, bordered by small, well-kept gardens. We had hamburgers and beer in a little restaurant that had a deck perched on stilts over the ocean. Gahalowood looked thoughtful as he chewed.

"What are you thinking?" I asked.

"That everything seems to point to Luther. He had a suitcase with him. He had prepared to run away, maybe taking Nola with him. But his plans went awry: Nola got away from him; he had to kill Deborah Cooper; and afterward he beat Nola so badly that she died."

"You think it's him?"

"I think so. But there are still unanswered questions. I don't understand why Stern didn't mention the black Chevy when he talked to us. That's a pretty important detail. Luther disappeared with a company car, and he didn't worry? And why the hell didn't Pratt pursue this lead?"

"You think Chief Pratt was involved in Nola's disappearance?"

"Let's just say I'd like to ask him why he gave up investigating Caleb in spite of Wanslow's report. I mean, he's given a prime suspect on a plate, in a black Monte Carlo, and he decides there's no connection. Don't you think that's strange? And if there really had been any doubt about the model of the car, if it was a Nova rather than a Monte Carlo, he should have made that known. Whereas in the report, the only car mentioned is a Monte Carlo."

*

We went to Montburry that afternoon, to the small motel where Chief Pratt was staying. It was a single-story building, with about a dozen rooms and a parking space in front of each door. The place was not exactly packed: There were only two vehicles parked out front, one of them presumably his. Gahalowood knocked on the door. No response. He knocked again. Still nothing. A maid went past and Gahalowood asked her to open the door for us.

"I can't," she replied.

"Yes, you can," Gahalowood said irritably, showing his badge.

"I've already tried several times today so I could clean the room," she explained. "I thought the guest must have gone out without my seeing him, but he left his key in the lock on the inside. It's impossible to get it open. That means he's in there. Unless he left and closed the door with the key still in the lock. That happens sometimes, with guests in a rush. But his car is here."

Gahalowood frowned. He banged hard on the door and ordered Pratt to open up. He tried looking through the window, but the curtain was drawn and he couldn't see anything. So he decided to force the door open. The lock gave way after his third try.

Chief Pratt lay stretched out on the floor, blood all around him.

8

The Identity of Anonymous

"Who dares, wins. Think about that motto, Marcus, whenever you are faced with a difficult choice. Who dares, wins."

EXTRACT FROM *THE HARRY QUEBERT AFFAIR*

On Tuesday, July 22, 2008, it was the small town of Montburry's turn to undergo the same kind of turmoil that just weeks earlier had seized Somerset, upon the discovery of Nola's body. Police cars came from all over the region, converging on a motel near the town's industrial zone. The rumor was that there had been a murder, and that the victim was the former police chief of Somerset.

Sergeant Gahalowood stood calmly in front of the door to the room. Several forensics officers were busy at the crime scene, but the sergeant was content to watch. I wondered what he was thinking. Finally he turned around and noticed me watching him, sitting on the hood of a police car. He gave me his enraged-bull look and came toward me.

"What are you doing with that recorder, writer?"

"Dictating the scene for my book."

"You realize you're sitting on the hood of a police car?"

"What are you doing with that recorder, writer?"

"Dictating the scene for my book."

"You realize you're sitting on the hood of a police car?"

"Oh, sorry, Sergeant. So what do we have?"

"Turn off the recorder, please."

I did what he told me.

"The initial evidence suggests that Chief Pratt was hit on the back of the head. Once, or more than once, with a heavy object."

"Like Nola?"

"Same kind of thing, yeah. He's been dead for more than twelve hours. Which takes us back to last night. I think he knew his murderer. Especially if he left the key in the door. He probably opened the door to him; maybe he was expecting him. The blows were to the back of the head, which means he had probably turned around. In all likelihood he did not suspect anything, and his visitor took advantage of that to deliver the fatal blow. We haven't found the murder weapon. The murderer almost certainly took it with him. It could have been an iron bar or something like that, which suggests it was probably not a disagreement that degenerated into a fight but a premeditated act. Someone came here to kill Pratt."

"Any witnesses?"

"None at all. The motel is practically deserted. Nobody saw anything, nobody heard anything. The front desk closes at 10 p.m. Then there's a night watchman who works right through till morning, but he was watching T.V. and he couldn't tell us anything. No security cameras, of course."

"Who could have done this, do you think?" I asked. "The same person who set fire to Goose Cove?"

"Maybe. In any case it was probably someone who'd been protected by Pratt and who was afraid that now he would talk. Maybe Pratt knew the identity of Nola's murderer all along."

"So you already have a theory, Sergeant?"

"Well, who is connected to Goose Cove and the black Chevrolet apart from Harry Quebert?"

"Elijah Stern?"

"Elijah Stern. I've been thinking about him for a while, and I thought about him again when I saw Pratt's corpse. I don't know if Elijah Stern murdered Nola, but I do think it's possible he's been covering for Caleb for the past thirty-three years. There's the mysterious vacation Caleb took, and the company car that Stern failed to report missing . . ."

"What are you thinking, Sergeant?"

"That Caleb is guilty, and Stern is somehow mixed up in this case. I think that after Caleb was spotted at Side Creek Lane in the black Monte Carlo, and after he had managed to lose Pratt in the car chase, he must have taken refuge at Goose Cove. The whole region is swarming with police, so he knows he has no chance of getting away, but on the other hand he also knows that nobody will come to Goose Cove to look for him. Nobody except Stern. It's likely that on August 30, 1975, Stern really did spend his day in private meetings, as he told me. But that evening, when he gets home and sees that Luther still hasn't returned—and, worse, that he has left with one of the company's cars, more discreet than his blue Mustang—I find it hard to imagine that Stern just stays home twiddling his thumbs. Logic suggests he would have gone looking for Luther to try to prevent him from doing something terrible. And I think that's what he did. But when he gets to Somerset, he is too late. There are police cars everywhere, and the tragedy he feared has already occurred. He has to find Caleb at any cost, and where is the first place he would look for him, writer?"

"Goose Cove."

"Exactly. It's his house and he knows that Luther feels safe there. It's possible Luther even had a spare key. Anyway, Stern goes to see what's happening at Goose Cove, and he finds Luther there."

August 30, 1975, according to Gahalowood's Theory

Stern found the Chevrolet in front of the garage. Luther was bending over the open trunk.

"Luther!" Stern yelled as he got out of his car. "What have you done?"

Luther was in a state of panic.

"We . . . we had an argument, Mifter Ftern . . . I didn't mean to hurt her."

Stern approached the car and discovered Nola lying in the trunk next to a leather shoulder bag; her body was twisted and she was not moving.

"But . . . you've killed her . . ."

Stern vomited.

"She would have called ve polife if I hadn't . . ."

"Luther! What have you done? Oh, God, what have you done?"

"Help me, Eli. Pleave help me."

"You have to get away, Luther. If the police catch you, you'll get the death penalty."

"No! Pleave!"

It was then that Stern noticed the butt of a pistol protruding from Luther's belt.

"What is that?"

"Ve old lady . . . She faw everyfing."

"What old lady?"

"In ve houfe, over vere . . ."

"Oh, my God, someone saw you?"

"Nola and I had an argument, Eli . . . She didn't want to let me . . . I wav forfed to hurt her—I had no choife. But she got away. She ran. She went into vat houfe. I went in vere too. I fought ve houfe wav empty. But vere wav an old lady, watching uv . . . I had to kill her, I had no choife. Eli, pleave help me—I'm begging you!"

They had to get rid of the body. Stern grabbed a shovel from the garage and began digging a hole. He chose to dig by the edge of the forest, where the soil was loose and where no-one—particularly Quebert— would notice the disturbed earth. He quickly dug a deep hole. He called Caleb to help him move the body, but he did not see him. He finally found him kneeling in front of the car, looking at a pile of papers.

"Luther? What the hell are you doing?"

He was crying.

"It'f Quebert'f book. Nola told me about it. He wrote a book for her. It'f fo beautiful."

"Bring that over here. I dug a hole."

"Wait!"

"Why?"

"I want to tell her vat I love her."

"What?"

"Let me write fomefing for her. Juft a few wordv. Pleave, may I borrow your pen? Afterward we'll bury her, and I will difappear forever."

Stern cursed at this, but he took a pen from the pocket of his jacket and handed it to Caleb, who wrote *Goodbye, darling Nola* on the first page. Then he ceremoniously placed the manuscript inside the bag, and he carried Nola's body over to the hole. He laid her inside, and the two men filled up the hole with earth and then scattered pine needles, broken branches and bits of moss over the fresh soil so that the illusion would be perfect.

"And after that?" I asked.

"After that," Gahalowood replied, "Stern needs to find a way to protect Luther. And that way is Pratt."

"Pratt?"

"Yes. I think Stern knew what Pratt had done to Nola. We know that Caleb hung around Goose Cove all the time, that he spied on Harry and Nola. He might have seen Pratt pick up Nola—obviously against her will—by the side of the road. And Luther would have told Stern. So, that evening, Stern leaves Luther at Goose Cove and goes to see Pratt at the police station. He waits until late at night, maybe until after 11 p.m., when the search ends. He wants to be alone with Pratt, and he bargains with him: He tells him to let Luther leave, making sure he gets through all the roadblocks, in return for his silence about Nola. And Pratt agrees. Otherwise, how likely is it that Caleb would have been able to drive as far as Massachusetts? But Caleb feels cornered. He has nowhere to go; he is lost. He buys some alcohol and drinks it. He wants to end it all. He drives off the parking area at Ellisville Harbor. A few weeks later, when the car is found, Pratt goes to Sagamore to hush things up. He ensures that Caleb does not become a suspect."

"But why would he want to deflect suspicions from Caleb once he's dead?"

"Because of Stern. Stern knew about him. By exonerating Caleb, Pratt was protecting himself."

"So Pratt and Stern knew the truth all along?"

"Yes. They buried this case deep in their memories. They never saw each other again. Stern got rid of the house at Goose Cove by selling it to Harry, and he never set foot in Somerset again. And for thirty-three years, it seemed like this case would never be solved."

"Until Nola's remains were discovered."

"And until a certain stubborn writer starts stirring things up. A writer who must be threatened so that he'll give up his search for the truth."

"So Pratt and Stern wanted to hush things up," I said. "But who killed Pratt, then? Stern, having seen that Pratt is about to crack and reveal the truth?"

"That's something we still have to find out. But not a word about any of this," Gahalowood warned me. "Don't write anything yet. I don't want another leak to the newspapers. I'm going to look into Stern's past. This will be a difficult theory to prove. In any case, there's one common denominator in all these scenarios: Luther Caleb. And if he really did kill Nola Kellergan, that will be confirmed—"

"By the handwriting analysis," I cut in.

"Exactly."

"One last question, Sergeant: Why would Stern be so determined to protect Caleb?"

"That's something I would very much like to know too."

The inquiry into Pratt's death promised to be complex; the police did not have any solid evidence or even the smallest clue. A little over a week after Pratt's murder, on Wednesday, July 30, Nola's body was finally buried, having been returned to her father. The ceremony took place at the cemetery in Somerset in the early afternoon, under unexpected drizzle and before a sparse gathering of mourners. David Kellergan rode his motorcycle all the way to the grave, but nobody there dared say anything. He was listening to music on his earphones, and apparently his only words were: "Why did we dig her up if we're just going to bury her again?" He did not cry.

I didn't go to the funeral because just when it was starting, I was doing something that seemed important to me: I was keeping Harry company. He was sitting in the parking lot, shirtless under the warm rain.

"Come in and dry off, Harry," I told him.

"They're burying her, aren't they?"

"Yes."

"They're burying her and I'm not even there."

"It's better this way. It's better that you're not there . . . because of everything that's happened."

"To hell with *what would people say*! They're burying Nola and I'm not even there to say goodbye to her, to see her one last time. To be with her. I've spent thirty-three years waiting to see her again, even if only for one last time. Do you know where I would like to be?"

"At the funeral?"

"No. In writers' heaven."

He stretched out on the asphalt and didn't move a muscle. I lay down next to him. The rain fell on both of us.

"Marcus, I wish I were dead."

"I know."

"How do you know?"

"Friends can sense that kind of thing."

There was a long silence. Finally, I said: "The other day, you said we couldn't be friends anymore."

"It's true. We're slowly saying goodbye to each other, Marcus. It's as if you knew I was going to die soon and you had a few weeks to make your farewells. It's the cancer of friendship."

He closed his eyes and held out his arms as if he were on a cross. I imitated him. And we stayed like that, stretched out on the asphalt, for a long time.

Later that day, I went to Clark's, hoping to talk to someone who had attended Nola's funeral. The place was practically empty; there was only one employee there, halfheartedly polishing the counter. He managed to gather enough strength to pour me a draft beer. That was when I noticed Robert Quinn, sitting at the back of the room, eating peanuts and filling in crossword puzzles in the old newspapers that lay on the tables. He was hiding from his wife. I went over to him. I offered him a pint; he accepted, and made room for me to sit next to him. It was a touching gesture: I could easily have sat opposite him, or on one of the fifty-odd empty chairs in the place. But he moved over so I could sit next to him.

"Were you at Nola's funeral?" I asked.

"Yes."

"How was it?"

"Horrible. Like this whole story. There were more journalists than loved ones."

We said nothing for a moment, and then, to make conversation, he said: "How's your book going?"

"It's progressing. But I reread it yesterday and realized I still have some gray areas I need to make clearer. Particularly regarding your wife. She told me she had a compromising note, written by Harry Quebert, which mysteriously disappeared. I don't suppose you know what happened to it, do you?"

He took a long swallow of beer and even ate a few peanuts before replying.

"It burned," he said. "That's what happened to that cursed piece of paper."

"What?" I said, stunned. "How do you know that?"

"Because I'm the one who burned it."

"Are you serious? Why? And why did you never say anything?"

He shrugged. "No-one ever asked me," he replied pragmatically. "My wife has been talking about that note for thirty-three years. She screams, she yells, she says, 'But it was there! In the safe! There!' She never said: 'Robert, darling, did you ever happen to see that note?' She never asked me, so I never told her."

I tried to hide my astonishment so he would continue talking. "So what happened?"

"It all began one Sunday afternoon. My wife organized a ridiculous garden party for Quebert, but Quebert didn't come. She was so mad, she decided to go see him at his house. I remember that day clearly: it was July 13, 1975. The same day Nola tried to kill herself."

Sunday, July 13, 1975

"Robert! Roooobert!"

Tamara burst into the house like a Fury, frantically waving a sheet of paper. She went through every room on the first floor before finding her husband reading the newspaper in the living room.

"Robert, for goodness' sake! Why don't you answer me when I call you? Are you going deaf? Look! Look at this! See how awful it is!"

She handed him the piece of paper she had stolen from Harry's house, and he read it.

My Nola, darling Nola, Nola my love. What have you done? Why did you want to die? Is it because of me? I love you. I love you more than anything. Don't leave me. If you die, I die. You are all that matters in my life, Nola.

"Where did you find this?" Robert asked.

"At that son of a bitch Harry Quebert's house!"

"You stole it from his house?"

"I didn't *steal* anything; I took it. I knew it! He's a disgusting pervert who's fantasizing about a fifteen-year-old girl. This makes me sick. I want to throw up! I want to throw up, Bobbo—do you hear me? Harry Quebert is in love with a little girl! It's illegal. He's a pig! A pig! And he spends all his time at Clark's just so he can ogle her. He comes to my restaurant just to leer at a girl's ass!"

Robert read the note several times. There was little doubt about it: Harry had written a love letter. A love letter to a fifteen-year-old girl.

"What are you going to do with this?" he asked his wife.

"I don't know."

"Are you going to call the police?"

"The police? No, Bobbo. Not just yet. I don't want everyone to know that Quebert the pervert prefers a little girl to our beautiful Jenny. Where is she, by the way? In her room?"

"Actually, that nice young man Travis Dawn came here just after you left, to invite her to the summer gala. They went to have dinner in

Montburry So Jenny has already found another date for the gala—isn't that great?"

"Oh, Bobbo, just shut up! And now get the hell out of here. I need to hide this note somewhere, and I don't want anyone to know where."

Robert obeyed, shuffling off to finish his newspaper on the porch. But he couldn't read a thing; he was too preoccupied by what his wife had discovered. So Harry, the great writer, was writing love letters to a girl half his age. Sweet little Nola. It was so disturbing. Should he warn Nola? Tell her that this Harry was driven by strange urges, and that he might even be dangerous? Shouldn't he call the police, so Harry could get professional help?

The summer gala was the following weekend. Robert and Tamara Quinn were standing in a corner of the room, sipping virgin cocktails, when Tamara spotted Harry Quebert. "Look, Bobbo," Tamara hissed. "There's the pervert!" They watched him for a long time, while a flood of insults poured from Tamara's mouth, loud enough to be heard only by Robert.

"What are you going to do with that note?" Robert finally asked.

"I don't know. But I do know that the first thing I'm going to do is make him pay what he owes me. He has five hundred dollars on the restaurant's tab!"

Harry seemed ill at ease. He got a beer from the bar for appearances' sake, then headed toward the restroom.

"There he is, going to the bathroom," Tamara said. "Look, look, Bobbo! You know what he's going to do?"

"A number one?"

"No, he's going to jerk off while thinking about that little girl!"

"What?"

"Oh, shut up, Bobbo. You talk too much. I don't want to hear you anymore. Stay here, will you?"

"Where are you going?"

"Don't move. Just watch and learn."

Tamara placed her glass on a high table and walked surreptitiously toward the bathroom that Harry Quebert had just entered. She followed him in, then came back out a few moments later, hurrying over to her husband.

"What did you do?" Robert demanded.

"Shut up—I told you already!" his wife scolded him as she picked up her drink. "Shut your mouth or you'll give us away."

Amy Pratt told her guests that they could now proceed to dinner, and a crowd of people converged slowly on the tables. Harry came out of the bathroom. He was sweating, in a panic. He joined the crowd.

"Look at him, bolting like a rabbit," Tamara whispered. "He's scared."

"Tell me what you did," Robert insisted.

Tamara smiled. Under the table, she played discreetly with the lipstick she had used to write on the bathroom mirror.

"Let's just say I left him a message he won't forget."

Sitting in the back of Clark's, I listened, entranced, to Robert Quinn's story.

"So it was your wife who wrote the message on the mirror?"

"Yup. She became obsessed with Harry Quebert. All she ever talked about was that note. She said she was going to use it to bring him down forever. She said that soon the newspapers would all announce: THE GREAT WRITER IS A BIG PERVERT. In the end, she told Chief Pratt about it. About two weeks after the gala. She told him everything."

"How do you know?" I asked.

He hesitated for a second before replying. "I know because . . . it was Nola who told me."

Tuesday, August 5, 1975

It was 6 p.m. when Robert got home from the glove factory. As always he parked his old Chrysler in the driveway, then, having turned off the engine, he adjusted his hat in the rearview mirror and made the look that the actor Robert Stack used to make when his character Eliot Ness was getting ready to beat the crap out of some mobsters. He often procrastinated like this before getting out of the car; for a long time now, he had not looked forward to entering his own house. Sometimes he took a detour on the way home; sometimes he stopped to buy ice cream. When he had finally managed to drag himself out of the vehicle, he seemed to hear a voice calling him from behind the bushes. He turned, looked around, and then noticed Nola, hidden among the rhododendrons.

"Nola?" Robert said. "Hey, sweetie, how are you?"

"I have to talk to you, Mr Quinn," she whispered. "It's very important."

"Come in then," he said, his voice still at a normal volume. "I'll make you some nice cold lemonade."

She shushed him, then said, "No, we need to find somewhere to talk. Could we get in your car and drive for a while? How about we go to the hot dog stand on the Montburry road. No-one would bother us there."

Although surprised by this, Robert did not refuse. They got into the car and drove toward Montburry, stopping after a few miles, in front of the hot dog stand. Robert bought fries and a soda for Nola, a hot dog and a nonalcoholic beer for himself. They sat at one of the picnic tables on the grass.

"So what's up, kiddo?" Robert asked. "What can be so serious that you can't even come in the house to talk about it over a glass of lemonade?"

"I need your help, Mr Quinn. I know this is going to seem strange to you, but . . . something happened at Clark's today, and you're the only person who can help me."

Nola then described the scene she had witnessed, by chance, two hours earlier. She had gone to see Mrs Quinn at Clark's to pick up her pay for the Saturdays she had worked before her suicide attempt. It was Mrs Quinn herself who had told Nola she could come any time she liked.

The only people in the restaurant were a few customers eating in silence and Jenny, who was busy putting away dishes and who told Nola that her mother was in her office, without thinking to make it clear that she was not alone. The office was the place where Tamara Quinn did her accounts, put the day's take into her safe, shouted into the telephone at suppliers who were late with their deliveries, or simply locked herself in with made-up excuses whenever she wanted some peace. It was a small room, the door to which was nearly always closed, and was marked PRIVATE. To get to it you went down the service corridor that led from the back room to the employees' bathroom.

As she reached the door and prepared to knock, Nola heard voices. There was someone in the room with Tamara. She could tell it was a man. She put her ear close to the door and heard a snippet of conversation.

"He's a criminal," Tamara said. "Maybe even a sexual predator. You have to do something."

"Are you sure it was Harry Quebert who wrote this note?"

Nola recognized Chief Pratt's voice.

"Absolutely certain," Tamara replied. "Written in his own hand. He has designs on the young Kellergan girl, and he's writing pornographic filth about her. You have to do something."

"O.K. You did the right thing by contacting me about this. But you entered his house illegally, and you stole this piece of paper. I can't do anything about it for the moment."

"So you're just going to wait until that maniac hurts the girl?"

"I said nothing of the sort. I'm going to keep an eye on Quebert. In the meantime, keep this note safe. I can't take it. I could get in trouble."

"I'll keep it in this safe," Tamara said. "No-one else has access to it. It will be perfectly secure. But please, Chief, you have to do something. That Quebert's a criminal and a piece of shit!"

"Don't worry. You'll see how we deal with guys like that around here."

Nola heard footsteps and instantly fled the restaurant.

*

Poor little girl, Robert thought, upon hearing Nola's account. It must have come as a shock to learn that Harry had these fantasies about her. She had needed to confide in someone, so she came to find him; he had to prove himself worthy of her trust and explain things to her, tell her that men were strange creatures, Harry Quebert in particular, and that she must keep her distance from him and call the police if she ever felt afraid he was going to hurt her. But what if he had already hurt her? Did she need to tell him that she had been abused? Was he up to dealing with such a revelation—he who, according to his wife, did not even know how to set the dinner table properly? Chewing his hot dog, he tried to come up with some comforting words, but just as he was preparing to speak, Nola told him:

"Mr Quinn, you have to help me get ahold of that piece of paper."

He almost choked.

"You can imagine how I felt," Robert Quinn said to me in Clark's. "I could hardly believe my ears. She wanted me to get that damn note for her. Would you like another beer?"

"That would be great, thanks. By the way, would you mind if I recorded this?"

"You want to record me? Go ahead. That's no more strange than the idea that anyone would have any interest in what I have to say."

He hailed the waiter and ordered two more beers. I took the recorder out of my pocket and pressed RECORD.

"So you were sitting outside the hot dog stand and she asked you for help," I prompted him.

"Yes. Apparently my wife was willing to do anything to destroy Harry Quebert. And Nola was willing to do anything to protect him. That conversation came as such a shock to me. That was how I learned there really was something between Nola and Harry. I remember the sparkle in her eyes when she told me. I said, 'What do you mean, *get ahold of that piece of paper?*' 'I love him,' she replied. 'I don't want him to get in trouble.

He only wrote that note because I attempted suicide. It's all my fault—I should never have tried to kill myself. I love him. He's everything I have, everything I could ever dream of having.' And we had this conversation about love. 'So, you mean that you and Harry Quebert, you . . .' 'We love each other!' 'Love? What are you talking about? You can't love him!' 'Why not?' 'Because he's too old for you.' 'Age doesn't matter.' 'Of course it matters!' 'Well, it shouldn't.' 'Look, this is just how it is: A young girl of your age should have nothing to do with a guy of his age.' 'I love him!' 'Stop saying that. Eat your fries.' 'But, Mr Quinn, if I lose him, I lose everything!' It was incredible: That girl was madly in love with Harry. What she felt for him was something I had never felt myself, or I couldn't remember ever having felt, for my own wife. And it was at that moment that I realized, thanks to a fifteen-year-old girl, that I had probably never been in love. That lots of people have never been in love. That they make do with good intentions; that they hide away in the comfort of a crummy existence and shy away from that amazing feeling that is probably the only thing that justifies being alive. A cousin of mine, who lives in Boston, works in finance. He earns a fortune, he's married, three kids, beautiful wife, beautiful car. The perfect life, right? One day, he goes home and tells his wife he's leaving—he's fallen in love with a Harvard student he met at a conference, a girl young enough to be his daughter. Everyone said he'd lost his mind, that he was having a midlife crisis, but I think he simply found love. People think they love each other, so they get married. And then one day they discover real love, without meaning to or even realizing it. It hits them right between the eyes. It's like hydrogen coming into contact with air: There's a huge explosion and everything gets destroyed. Thirty years of frustrated marriage blown to pieces in a single second, as if a gigantic septic tank, brought to boiling point, explodes, splattering filth all around it. The midlife crisis, the seven-year itch—call it what you want. For me, those are just people who grasp the scale of true love too late, and their life is overturned as a result."

"So what did you do?" I asked.

"For Nola? I refused. I told her I didn't want to get mixed up in this thing, and that I couldn't do anything even if I wanted to. I told her the letter was in the safe, and that the only key that opened it hung on a chain around my wife's neck, day and night. There was nothing to be done. She begged me; she said that if the police got their hands on that note, Harry would get into serious trouble, that his career would be wrecked, that he would maybe even go to prison, when he hadn't done anything wrong. I remember the fire in her eyes, the way she spoke, her body language . . . the passion she felt for him was so intense. I remember she said to me: 'They're going to ruin everything, Mr Quinn! The people of this town are completely crazy! It reminds me of that play we read in school by Arthur Miller, "The Crucible." Have you read it?' Her eyes became wet with tiny tears, about to overflow and stream down her cheeks. I had read that play. I remember the fuss when it opened on Broadway, right in the middle of the Rosenberg affair. It gave me shivers at the time because the Rosenbergs had young kids too, and I remember wondering what would happen to Jenny if I were executed. I felt so relieved that I wasn't a Communist."

"Why did Nola come to you about this?"

"Probably because she imagined I had access to the safe. But that wasn't the case. As I said, my wife was the only person with a key. She kept it on a chain around her neck, dangling between her breasts. And I had not had access to her breasts for a long time."

I ignored this. "So what happened?"

"Nola flattered me. She said: 'You're so clever. You'll find a way.' So I ended up agreeing. I told her I would try."

"Why?" I asked.

"Why? Because of love. As I said, she was only fifteen, but she told me about things that I had never known and that I probably will never know. Even if, truth be told, her affair with Harry made me want to throw up. I did it for her, not for him. And I asked her how she intended to deal with Chief Pratt. Because, proof or no proof, Chief Pratt now knew everything. She looked me in the eyes and said: 'I'm going to stop him from getting involved. I'm going to make him a criminal.' At the time I didn't understand what she meant. And then when Pratt was arrested this summer, I realized what she meant."

Wednesday, August 6, 1975

Without discussing it, both Nola and Robert took action the day after their conversation. Around 5 p.m., in a Concord pharmacy, Robert Quinn bought sleeping pills. At the same moment, in the police station, Nola was on her knees in Chief Pratt's office, attempting to protect Harry by turning Pratt into a criminal, setting off what would become for him a thirty-three-year downward spiral.

That night Tamara slept like a log. After dinner she was so tired that she went to bed without even removing her makeup. She collapsed in a heap on the bed and fell into a deep sleep. It happened so quickly that Robert briefly feared he might have put too strong a dose in her glass of water and accidentally killed her, but he was immediately reassured by the magnificent snores that escaped his wife's open mouth every seven seconds. He waited until after midnight before acting: He had to be sure that Jenny was asleep, and that no-one would see him in town. When the time came, he gave his wife a good shake to make sure she was definitely asleep. He was very happy when she didn't stir. For the first time, he felt powerful: The dragon, sprawled on her mattress, no longer frightened anyone. He unhooked the chain from around her neck and triumphantly took the key. Since he was down there anyway, he squeezed and fondled her breasts, but he noticed with regret that this had no effect on him whatsoever.

He left the house without making a noise, then borrowed his daughter's bicycle so as not to risk someone hearing his car. Pedaling through the night, the keys to Clark's and to the safe in his pocket, he felt a rising excitement at the prospect of breaking the rules. He no longer knew whether he was doing this to help Nola or to annoy his wife. And he felt so free on this bicycle, riding fast across town, that he decided to divorce Tamara. Jenny was now an adult; there was no longer any reason for him to stay with his wife. He'd had enough of that damn harpy; he wanted a new life. He deliberately took a few wrong turns in order to prolong this heady feeling. When he got to the main street, he walked his bike so he would have time to look around. The town was sleeping peacefully. There was no light and no noise. He leaned his bike against a wall, opened the door to Clark's, and crept inside, the restaurant illuminated only by streetlights whose glare filtered through the windows. He reached the office—the office he had never been allowed to enter without his wife's permission. Well, now he was the master. He violated its borders, he invaded its space; it became conquered territory. He turned on the flashlight he had brought and began by exploring the files on the shelves. He had been dreaming of searching through this place for years. What could his wife be hiding here? He grabbed various folders and skimmed their contents, surprising himself when he realized that he was looking for love letters. He thought his wife was probably cheating on him. How could she make do with only him? But all he found was purchase orders and balance sheets. So he moved on to the safe. It was made of steel and must have been at least three feet tall, mounted on a wooden pallet. He slid the key into the lock, turned it, and shivered as he heard the mechanism click into place. He pulled open the heavy door and pointed the flashlight beam inside. The safe consisted of four shelves. This was the first time he had seen it open; he was trembling with excitement.

On the first shelf he found financial documents: the latest bank statement, payment receipts, and employee pay slips.

On the second shelf he found a tin box containing Clark's change fund and another containing the small amount of cash necessary to pay suppliers.

On the third shelf he found a piece of wood that looked like a bear. He smiled. It was the first present he had given to Tamara from the first time they had really gone out together. He had carefully prepared for that moment for weeks beforehand, putting in extra hours at the gas station where he worked to pay for his studies so he could take his Tammy to one of the best restaurants in the area, Chez Jean-Claude, a French place where the lobster was supposedly to die for. He had studied the menu and worked out exactly how much it would cost him if she ordered the most expensive dishes; he had saved up until he had that much money, and then he had invited her. That night, when he picked her up from her parents' house and told her where they were going, she had begged him not to break the bank for her. 'Oh, Robert, you're so sweet. But it's too much—it really is,' she had said. And to persuade him to give up his plan, she had suggested they go to a little Italian restaurant in Concord that she had long been tempted by. They had eaten spaghetti, they had drunk Chianti and the house grappa, and, slightly intoxicated, they had gone to a nearby carnival. On the way home they had stopped by the ocean and waited for sunrise. Walking along the beach, he had found a piece of wood that resembled a bear and had given it to her when she held him tight in the first rays of dawn. She had said she would always keep it, and she had kissed him for the first time.

Continuing his exploration of the safe, Robert was touched to find, next to the piece of wood, a number of photographs of himself taken throughout the years. On the back of each Tamara had scribbled a few annotations, even the most recent ones. The latest was from April, when they had gone to a horse race. It was of Robert, binoculars to his eyes, narrating the action. On the back Tamara had written: *My Robert, still in love with life. I will love him until my dying breath.*

In addition to the photographs, there were mementos of their life together: their wedding invitation, Jenny's birth announcement, vacation snapshots, little things he had thought had been thrown away years ago: cheap gifts, a plastic brooch, a souvenir ballpoint pen, and those snake-shaped paperweights he had bought on a vacation in Canada and that had earned him nothing but an acerbic telling off: "For God's sake,

Bobbo, what were you thinking, buying such crap? What am I supposed to do with them?" And yet, here they were, kept like sacred objects in this safe. Robert began to think that what his wife kept hidden here was her heart. And he wondered why.

On the fourth shelf he found a thick, leather-bound notebook, which he opened: Tamara's journal. His wife kept a journal. He had never known. He opened it at random and read by flashlight:

January 1, 1975

Celebrated New Year's Eve at the Richardsons'.

Rating, 1 to 10: 5. Food wasn't great, and the Richardsons are boring people. I had never noticed that before. I think New Year's Eve is a good test to find out which of your friends are boring. Bobbo quickly saw that I was bored, and he tried to entertain me. He clowned around, telling jokes and pretending to make his crab talk. How the Richardsons laughed! Paul Richardson even got up from the table to note down one of Bobbo's jokes. He said he wanted to make sure he remembered it. As for me, all I managed to do was argue with Bobbo. In the car on the way home, I said terrible things. I said: "Nobody thinks your jokes are funny. They're in bad taste. You're pathetic. Who asked you to play the fool? You're an engineer in a big factory, aren't you? So talk about your job, show them you're someone serious and important. You're not in the circus, for God's sake!" He replied that Paul had laughed at his jokes, and I told him to shut up. I said I didn't want to hear him speak anymore.

I don't know why I have to be so nasty. I love him so much. He is so sweet and thoughtful. I don't know why I behave so badly with him. Afterward I feel guilty and I hate myself, and then I treat him even more badly.

But today is New Year's Day, so I am making a resolution to change. Well, I make this resolution every year and never keep it. Dr Ashcroft suggested I keep this journal. Maybe it'll help me keep my resolutions. Nobody knows about Dr Ashcroft. I would be so ashamed if anyone knew I was going to see a psychiatrist. People would say I was crazy. I'm not crazy. I'm suffering. I am suffering, but from what, I don't know. Dr Ashcroft says I have a tendency to destroy everything that's good for me. He says I have a fear of death and that this is perhaps connected. All I know is that I'm suffering. And that I love my Robert. He is all I love. What would I be without him?

Robert closed the journal, crying now. His wife had written what she had never been able to tell him. She loved him. She truly loved him. She loved only him. He thought that these were the most beautiful words he had ever read. He wiped his cheeks so his tears would not stain the pages, and kept reading. Poor Tamara, darling Tamara, suffering in silence. Why had she never told him about this Dr Ashcroft? If she was suffering, he wanted to suffer with her; that was why he had married her. Sweeping the last shelf with the flashlight's beam, he found Harry's note and was brought back to reality with a bump. He remembered his mission; he remembered that his wife was sprawled out on her bed, in a drug-induced sleep, and that he had to get rid of this piece of paper. He suddenly felt bad about what he was doing. He was about to give up the idea when it occurred to him that getting rid of this letter might make his wife less obsessed with Harry Quebert and more concerned with him. He was the one who mattered; she loved him. This was what finally pushed him to take the note and to leave Clark's in the silence of the night, having first made certain that he had left behind no trace of his trespass. He crossed the town on his bicycle and, in a quiet back alley, he used his lighter to set fire to Harry Quebert's words. He watched the piece of paper burn, turn brown, twist up in a flame that flared up and slowly disappeared. Soon nothing remained of it. He went home, returned the key to its habitual place between his wife's breasts, lay down next to her, and embraced her for a long time.

It took Tamara two days to realize that the note was no longer in the safe. She thought she was going crazy. She was certain she had put it in the safe, and yet it was not there. Nobody could have gotten into the safe: she kept the key with her, and there hadn't been a break-in. Had she mislaid it somewhere in the office? Had she unthinkingly stashed it away in another place? She spent hours searching the room, emptying and refilling folders, sorting through papers and filing them again . . . all in vain. That tiny piece of paper had mysteriously vanished.

Robert Quinn told me that when Nola disappeared a few weeks later, his wife took it very badly.

"She kept repeating that if she still had the note the police would be able to investigate Harry. And Chief Pratt told her that, without that piece of paper, he couldn't do anything. She said to me over and over again: 'It's Quebert, it's Quebert! I know it, you know it, we all know it. You saw that note as well as I did.'"

"Why didn't you tell the police what you knew?" I asked. "Why not say that Nola came to find you and that she told you about Harry? Wasn't that worth investigating?"

"I wanted to. I was torn. Could you turn off your recorder, Mr Goldman?"

"Of course."

I turned off the device and put it back in my bag.

He went on. "When Nola disappeared, I blamed myself. I regretted burning the piece of paper that linked her to Harry. I thought that, if they'd had that note, the police could have interrogated Harry, dug deeper into the whole thing. And that if he hadn't done anything wrong, he wouldn't have anything to fear. After all, if someone's innocent, he has nothing to worry about, does he? So, anyway, I felt bad. So I started writing anonymous letters, which I stuck to his door when I knew he was away."

"It was *you* who wrote those letters?"

"It was me. I'd prepared several of them, using my secretary's type-writer at the glove factory in Concord. 'I know what you've done with that 15-year-old girl. And soon the whole town will know.' I kept the letters in the glove compartment of my car. And each time I saw Harry in town, I drove to Goose Cove to leave a letter."

"But why?"

"To ease my conscience. My wife never stopped talking about how Harry was guilty, and it seemed plausible to me. I thought that if I scared him, he would end up confessing. That went on for a few months. And then I stopped."

"What made you stop?"

"The way he looked. After she disappeared, he looked so sad. He wasn't the same man anymore. I decided it couldn't have been him. So I finally gave up."

I couldn't believe what I had just heard. As a long shot, I asked him: "Tell me, Mr Quinn, it wasn't by any chance you who set fire to Goose Cove, was it?"

He smiled, almost amused by my question.

"No. You're a nice guy, Mr Goldman. I wouldn't do that. I don't know who did that, but whoever he is, he's sick."

We drained our beers.

"So, in fact," I said, "you didn't get divorced in the end. Did things get better with your wife? After you found all those mementos in the safe, I mean, and her diary?"

"Things got worse and worse, Mr Goldman. She never stopped nagging and scolding me, and she never told me she loved me. Never. In the months and then the years that followed, I would often drug her with sleeping pills so I could go read her journals and cry over our mementos, hoping that one day things would be better. Maybe that's what love is: hoping that one day things will be better."

I nodded. "Maybe."

*

In my suite at the hotel, I redoubled my efforts on the book. I wrote about how Nola Kellergan, fifteen years old, had done everything she could to protect Harry. The sacrifices she had made so he could stay in that house and write, untroubled. How she had gradually become both the muse and the keeper of his masterpiece. How she had managed to create a sort of bubble around him, allowing him to concentrate on his writing and to produce the greatest work of his life. And the more I wrote, the more I began to believe that Nola Kellergan might even have been that extraordinary woman of whom writers all over the world undoubtedly dream.

One afternoon Denise called me from New York, where she was typing up my words with uncommon devotion and efficiency, and said: "Marcus, I think I'm crying."

"Why?" I asked.

"Because of that young girl, that Nola. I think I love her too."

I smiled and said, "I think everyone loved her, Denise. Everyone."

Then, two days later—on August 3—I received a call from Gahalowood, who was beside himself with excitement.

"Hey, writer!" he bellowed. "I got the lab results. Jesus, you won't believe this. The writing on the manuscript really is Luther Caleb's! Without any doubt at all. We've got our man, Marcus. We've got our man!"

7

After Nola

"Cherish love, Marcus. Make it your greatest conquest, your sole ambition. After men, there will be other men. After books, there will be other books. After glory, there will be other glories. After money, there will be yet more money. But after love, Marcus, after love, there is nothing but the salt from tears."

Life after Nola was no longer life. Everyone said in the months that followed her disappearance, the town of Somerset sank slowly into depression, obsessed by the fear of a second abduction.

It was fall, and the leaves had changed color. But the town's children were no longer able to throw themselves with abandon into the huge piles of dead leaves swept to the sides of the streets; their parents watched them constantly, afraid. From now on they would wait with them before they caught the school bus and would be there again when the bus dropped them off in the afternoon. At 3.30 every afternoon, the sidewalks were lined with mothers, one in front of each house, forming a human fence along the empty avenues, impassive sentinels watching over the arrival of their progeny.

Children were no longer allowed to travel alone. The golden age when the streets were filled with happy, shouting kids was over: There were no more street hockey games on driveways, no more jump-rope contests, no more giant hopscotch courts drawn in chalk on asphalt; on the main street there were no longer bicycles scattered all over the sidewalk in front of the Hendorf family's general store, where you could buy a small bag of candy for a quarter. Soon the streets would take on the disturbing hush of a ghost town.

The front doors of all the houses were locked, and at nightfall the town's men, organized into citizen patrols, walked the streets to protect their neighborhoods and their families. Most of them carried baseball bats; a few had their shotguns. They said they would not hesitate to shoot if necessary.

Trust had been shattered. Anyone passing through—truck driver and deliveryman alike—was treated with suspicion and watched constantly. But the worst thing of all was the mistrust that grew among Somerset's residents. Neighbors, friends for twenty-five years, now spied on one another. And everyone wondered what everyone else had been doing early in the evening of August 30, 1975.

Police cars constantly patrolled the town's streets; if there were no police, people worried, but too many police made them frightened. And when a very recognizable black Ford, an unmarked state police car, parked in front of 245 Terrace Avenue, everyone wondered if it was Captain Rodik, come to deliver the bad news. The curtains in the Kellergan house were drawn for days, weeks, and then months. With David Kellergan no longer performing his duties, a substitute pastor was summoned from Manchester to take over the services at St James's.

Then came the late-October fog. The region was covered by thick, gray, damp clouds, and soon a cold rain fell day after day. At Goose Cove, Harry wasted away, alone. He had not been seen anywhere for two months. He spent his days locked away in his office, working at his typewriter, absorbed by the pile of handwritten pages that he was meticulously revising and typing up. He woke early and went through the motions, shaving and dressing every morning, even though he knew he would not leave his house or see anyone. He sat at his desk and got to work. He took a break only rarely, to brew more coffee; the rest of the time was spent typing, rereading, correcting, tearing up pages, and starting over.

The only thing that disturbed his solitude was Jenny. Every day after her shift was over, she came to see him, worried by his slow decline. She usually arrived about 6 p.m.; by the time she had made it from her car to the porch, she was already soaked by the rain. She brought him a basket filled with provisions from Clark's: chicken sandwiches, egg salad, macaroni and cheese that she kept warm in a metal dish, filled pastries that she had to hide from her customers to make sure there would be some left for Harry. She rang the doorbell.

Harry sprang from his chair. Nola! Darling Nola! He rushed to the door. There she was, standing before him, radiant and beautiful. They threw themselves at each other, and he took her in his arms. He swung her around him, around the world, and they kissed. Nola! Nola! Nola! They kissed again, and they danced. It was high summer; the sky was painted with the dazzling colors of sunset, and above them clouds of seagulls sang like nightingales. She smiled, she laughed, her face was the sun. There she was: He could hold her to him, touch her skin, caress her face, smell her scent, run his fingers through her hair. There she was, alive. They were both alive. "But where were you?" he asked, holding her hands. "I waited for you. I was so afraid! Everyone thought something bad must have happened to you. They say Mrs Cooper saw you covered in blood near Side Creek. There were police everywhere. They searched the forest. I thought something terrible had happened, and I was going crazy not knowing." She squeezed him tightly; she held him close to her and comforted him: "Don't worry, darling Harry. Nothing bad happened to me. I'm here. Look, here

I am! We are together, forever. Have you eaten? You must be hungry. Have you eaten?"

"Have you eaten? Harry? Harry? Are you O.K.?" Jenny asked the pale, emaciated ghost who answered the door.

The young woman's voice brought him back to reality. It was dark and cold outside, the rain was falling in torrents. Winter was almost here. The seagulls were long gone.

"Jenny?" he asked, his eyes wild. "Is that you?"

"Yes, it's me. I brought you some food. You have to eat. You don't look well at all."

He looked at her, wet and shivering. He let her in. She stayed for only a brief while: just the time it took to leave the basket in the kitchen and pick up the dishes she had left the day before. When she noticed that he had hardly touched the food she'd brought, she scolded him gently.

"Harry, you have to eat!"

"I forget sometimes," he replied.

"How can you forget to eat?"

"It's because of the book I'm writing. I live inside the book and forget everything else."

"It must be a wonderful book," she said.

"A wonderful book."

She didn't understand how a book could put someone in such a state. Each time she came, she hoped he would ask her to stay for dinner. She always brought enough for two people, and he never noticed. She stayed a few minutes, standing between the kitchen and the dining room, not knowing what to say. He always thought about asking her to stay for a while, but decided against it because he did not want to give her false hope. He knew he would never love anyone else. When the silence became embarrassing, he said, "Thank you," and opened the door to let her out.

She went home, disappointed and worried. Her father lit the fire in the living room and made her a hot chocolate with a marshmallow melting in it. They sat on the couch, facing the fireplace, and she told her father how depressed Harry seemed.

"Why is he so sad?" she asked. "You'd think he was dying."

"I don't know, sweetie," Robert Quinn replied.

He was afraid to go out. On the rare occasions when he left Goose Cove, he came back to find those horrible letters waiting for him. Someone was spying on him. Someone wanted to hurt him. Someone was watching out for his absences and then jamming an envelope into the frame of the door. And inside the envelope, always those same words:

> *I know what you've done with that 15-year-old girl.*
> *And soon the whole town will know.*

Who? Who could have a grudge against him? Who knew about him and Nola? Who now wanted to destroy him? It made him ill; each time he found a letter he felt feverish. He had headaches and felt anxious. Sometimes he vomited, and he suffered from insomnia. How could he prove his innocence? He started imagining worst-case scenarios: the horror of being locked in the high-security ward of a federal penitentiary until the end of his life, or of being strapped to a gurney and given a lethal injection. He gradually developed a fear of the police: the sight of a uniform or a police car was enough to put him in a nervous state. One day, coming out of the supermarket, he noticed a state police car in the parking lot, with an officer inside watching him. He forced himself to remain calm and increased his pace as he walked to his car, carrying his groceries. But then he heard someone calling. It was the policeman. He pretended not to hear. There was the sound of a door closing behind him: The policeman was getting out of his car. Harry heard the man's footsteps, the sounds made by his handcuffs, gun, and nightstick as they jingled on his belt. When he reached his car, he put the groceries in the trunk so he could get away more quickly. He was trembling, drenched in sweat, his vision blurred; he was in a total panic. *For God's sake, stay calm,* he told himself. *Get in your car and disappear. Do not go back to Goose Cove.* But he didn't have time to do anything: He felt a powerful hand grip his shoulder.

He had never been in a fight. He didn't know how to fight. What should he do? Should he push the policeman away, to give himself time to get into his car and speed out of the parking lot? Should he punch him? Grab his gun and shoot him? He turned around, ready for anything. And the policeman handed him a twenty-dollar bill.

"This fell out of your pocket, sir. I called you, but you didn't hear. Are you alright, sir? You look very pale."

"I'm fine," Harry replied. "I'm fine. I was . . . I was thinking about something and . . . Anyway, thank you. I . . . I should go."

The policeman gave him a friendly wave and returned to his car. Harry was shaking.

Following this episode, Harry joined a boxing class; he practiced assiduously. Eventually he decided to see someone. Having done some research, he contacted Dr Roger Ashcroft, in Concord, who was apparently one of the best psychiatrists in the region. They agreed to meet weekly, on Wednesday mornings, from 10.40 to 11.30. He didn't talk about the letters, he talked about Nola. Without ever mentioning her. But for the first time he was able to talk to someone about Nola. That did him a world of good. Ashcroft, sitting in his upholstered chair, listened attentively, his fingers drumming softly on a desk blotter whenever he launched into an interpretation.

"I think I see dead people," Harry said.

"So your friend is dead?" Ashcroft concluded.

"I don't know. That's what's driving me crazy."

"I don't think you're crazy, Mr Quebert."

"Sometimes I go to the beach and shout out her name. And when I don't have the strength to shout anymore, I sit on the sand and cry."

"I think you're going through a grieving process. Your rational, lucid, conscious self is battling another part of you that refuses to accept something that is, for it, unacceptable. When reality is unbearable, we try to turn it away. Perhaps I could prescribe you some relaxants to help you calm down."

"No, certainly not. I have to concentrate on my book."

"Tell me about your book, Mr Quebert."

"It's a love story. A beautiful love story."

"What is it about?"

"A love affair between two people that should never have happened."

"Is it about you and your friend?"

"Yes . . . I hate books."

"Why?"

"They cause me pain."

"It's time to stop. I'll see you again next week."

"Alright. Thank you, Doctor."

One day, from the parking lot, he saw Tamara Quinn coming out of the doctor's office.

The manuscript was finished in mid-November, on an afternoon so dark you could hardly tell whether it was day or night. He straightened the sheaf of pages and carefully reread the title he had written in capital letters on the first page:

THE ORIGIN OF EVIL
by Harry Quebert

He suddenly felt the need to tell someone, so he went to Clark's to see Jenny.

"I finished my book," he told her, feeling euphoric. "I came to Somerset to write it, and now I've done exactly that. It's finished. Finished!"

"That's wonderful," Jenny replied. "I'm sure it's a great book. What are you going to do now?"

"I'll go to New York for a while. To offer it to publishers."

He sent copies of the manuscript to five of the biggest publishers in New York. Less than a month later, the five publishers got back in touch with him, certain that the book was a masterpiece and bidding for the rights. This was the beginning of a new life. A few days before Christmas he signed a six-figure contract with one of the publishers. Fame and fortune were within his grasp.

He went back to Goose Cove on December 23, behind the wheel of a brand-new Chrysler Cordoba. He had been eager to spend Christmas in Somerset. In the doorframe he found another anonymous letter, evidently left there several days earlier. It was the last one he would ever receive.

The next day was devoted to the preparation of the evening meal: He roasted a gigantic turkey, sautéed some green beans in butter and some potatoes in oil, and made a chocolate cake. "Madame Butterfly" played on the stereo. He set the table for two, next to the Christmas tree. He did not notice Robert Quinn watching him through the steamed-up window and resolving, that day, not to leave any more letters.

After dinner Harry excused himself to the empty place that faced him and slipped away to his office for a moment. He returned with a large box.

"Is that for me?" Nola squealed.

"It wasn't easy to find, but I got there in the end," Harry said, placing the box on the floor.

Nola knelt next to the box. "What is it? What is it?" she said, lifting up the box's flaps, which were not sealed. A muzzle appeared, quickly followed by a little yellow head. "A puppy! It's a puppy! A dog the color of the sun . . . Oh, Harry, my darling! Thank you! Thank you!" She took the little dog out of the box and held it in her arms. It was a Labrador, no more than ten weeks old. "You'll be called Storm," she told the dog. "Storm! Storm! You're the dog I always dreamed of."

She put the puppy on the floor. Yapping, it began exploring its new home, while Nola hugged Harry.

"Thank you, Harry! I'm so happy. But I feel bad that I didn't get you a gift."

"All I want is your happiness, Nola."

He held her in his arms, but she seemed to slip away from him, and soon he could no longer feel her, no longer see her. He called her, but she did not reply. He found himself alone, standing in the middle of the dining room, hugging himself. At his feet the puppy had escaped from its box and was playing with his shoelaces.

The Origin of Evil was published in June 1976. It was a huge success, right from the start. Acclaimed by the critics, the prodigious Harry Quebert, thirty-five years old, was from that point on considered the greatest writer of his generation.

Two weeks before the book came out, already aware of the impact it was going to have, Harry's editor came all the way to Somerset to see him.

"Harry, what's this about your not wanting to come to New York?"

"I can't leave," Harry said. "I'm waiting for someone."

"You're waiting for someone? What are you talking about? The entire country is waiting to see you. You're going to be famous."

"I can't leave. I have a dog."

"Then let's take it with us. Don't worry: It'll have its own nanny, its own chef, someone to take it for walks, someone to groom it. Come on—pack your suitcase."

So Harry left Somerset for a nationwide book tour that lasted several months. All anyone talked about was him and his amazing novel. Jenny followed his success, on radio and television, from the kitchen at Clark's or from her bedroom. She bought every newspaper she could find and religiously kept every article about him. Each time she saw his book in a store, she bought it. She had more than ten copies, and she had read every one. Sometimes she wondered if he would come back for her. Whenever the mailman came, she hoped there would be a letter from Harry. Whenever the telephone rang, she hoped it would be him.

She waited all summer. Whenever she passed a car that looked like his, her heart beat faster.

She waited all fall. Whenever the door of Clark's opened, she imagined it was him, come to take her away. He was the love of her life. To occupy her mind while she waited, she remembered those glorious days when he would come to work at Table 17. Right there, close to where she stood, he had written that great masterpiece. If he wanted to continue living in Somerset, he could keep coming here every day; she would stay here to work as a waitress, for the pleasure of being near him. She would save that table for him, always. And, ignoring her mother's protests, she ordered, at her own expense, a metal plaque that she had screwed to the top of Table 17, engraved with the words:

IT WAS AT THIS TABLE, IN THE SUMMER OF 1975,
THAT HARRY QUEBERT WROTE HIS FAMOUS NOVEL,
"THE ORIGIN OF EVIL"

She celebrated her twenty-sixth birthday on October 13, 1976. Harry was in Philadelphia; she had read that in the newspaper. He had not been in touch at all since his departure. That evening Travis Dawn, who had been having Sunday lunch with the Quinns every week for the past year, got down on one knee—in the family living room, in front of her parents—and asked Jenny to marry him. And because she had no hope left, she accepted his proposal.

July 1985

Ten years on, the specter of Nola and her kidnapping had faded. In the streets of Somerset, life had long returned to normal: Children noisily played street hockey again, the jump-rope contests had restarted, and giant hopscotch courts had reappeared on the asphalt. On the main street, bicycles were once more blocking the storefront window of the Hendorf family store.

At Goose Cove, late one morning during the second week of July, Harry sat on the deck in the warm sun, correcting the proofs of his new novel; his dog, Storm, lay close by, asleep. A flock of seagulls passed overhead. He watched them as they swooped down and landed on the beach. Immediately he got up and went to the kitchen to look for the stale bread that he kept in a tin box emblazoned with the words SOUVENIR OF ROCKLAND, MAINE, then walked down to the beach so he could toss it to the birds. Storm followed in his footsteps, the dog walking painfully due to its arthritis. Harry sat on the sand to watch the birds, and Storm sat next to him. He petted the dog for a long time. "Poor old Storm," he said. "You can hardly walk now, can you? You're not a young pup anymore. I remember the day I bought you; it was just before Christmas, 1975 . . . You were just a tiny ball of fur, no bigger than my two fists."

Suddenly he heard someone calling him.

"Harry?"

On the deck of his house, a visitor was waving. Harry squinted and recognized Eric Rendall, the president of Burrows College in Massachusetts. The two men had met at a conference a year earlier, and they had kept in regular contact ever since.

"Eric? Is that you?"

"Yes."

"Don't move. I'm coming up."

A few moments later, Harry, with the old Labrador hobbling behind, joined Rendall on the deck.

"I tried to get hold of you," his friend explained, justifying his impromptu visit.

Harry smiled. "I rarely answer the telephone."

"Is this your new novel?" Rendall asked, spotting the pages scattered over the table.

"Yes. It's coming out this fall. I've been working on it for two years. I still have to reread the proofs, but . . . you know, I don't think anything I write will ever live up to *The Origin of Evil.*"

Rendall gave Harry a sympathetic look.

"Writers only really write one book in their life," he said.

Harry nodded in agreement and got his visitor some coffee. Then they sat at the table and Rendall explained the reason for his visit: "Harry, I came to see you because I remember your telling me you would like to teach at the college level. Well, there's a position available in the English department at Burrows. I know it's not Harvard, but we are a good school. If you're interested, the position is yours."

Harry turned toward the sun-colored dog and patted its neck. "You hear that, Storm?" he whispered. "I'm going to be a college professor."

6

The Barnaski Principle

"You see, Marcus, words are good, but sometimes they're not enough. There comes a time when some people don't want to hear you."

"So what should you do?"

"Grab them by the collar and shove your elbow into their throat. Hard."

"Why?"

"To throttle them. When words lose their power, you have to throw a few punches."

At the beginning of August 2008, in light of the new evidence uncovered by the investigation, the D.A. presented the judge with a new report concluding that Luther Caleb was guilty of the murders of Deborah Cooper and Nola Kellergan, whom he had kidnapped, beaten to death, and buried at Goose Cove. Upon reading this report, the judge summoned Harry for an urgent hearing, during which the charges against him were finally dropped. This latest development turned the case into the great soap opera of the summer: Harry Quebert, the star author whose past had caught up with him and who had fallen into disgrace, was cleared at last, having seen his career destroyed and having nearly been convicted of murder.

Luther Caleb achieved a posthumous infamy, with his personal history recounted all over the newspapers and the Internet and his name added to the pantheon of notorious American criminals. Soon the nation's attention was focused entirely on him. His past was ransacked, and the tabloid magazines told the story of his life, illustrated by old photographs purchased from friends and relatives: his early carefree years in Portland, his talent for painting, the horrific attack on him, and his descent into hell. The public was fascinated by his need to paint naked women, and psychiatrists were asked to provide explanations: Was this a well-known pathology? Could it have foretold the story's tragic ending? A leak from the authorities enabled the press to publish photographs of the painting found in Elijah Stern's house, paving the way for the most outrageous speculation. Everyone was left wondering why Stern, a powerful and respected man, should have allowed his disturbed employee to paint a nude fifteen-year-old girl.

Disapproval was directed at the D.A., whom certain people held responsible for having rushed to judgment, thus causing the Quebert fiasco. Some even believed that by signing the August report, the D.A. had signed off on his own career. He was saved in part by Gahalowood, who, having led the police investigation, fully accepted responsibility for it, holding a press conference to explain that he was the one who had arrested Harry Quebert, but that he was also the person who had freed him, and that this was neither a paradox nor a failure, but was in fact proof that the justice system was functioning correctly. "We did not wrongly imprison anyone," he told the clamoring reporters. "We had suspicions and we cleared them up. We acted consistently in both cases. That is the job of the police." And to explain why it had taken so many years to identify the culprit, Gahalowood mentioned his theory: Nola was the central piece of evidence toward which many others gravitated.

All of these had to be examined in order to discover her murderer. But that work had been possible only after her body had been found. "You say it took us thirty-three years to solve this murder," he told his audience, "but in fact it took us only two months. Prior to that there was no body, and therefore no murder. Just a girl who had disappeared."

The man left most confused by the situation was Benjamin Roth. One afternoon I bumped into him in the cosmetics aisle of one of Concord's big drugstores.

"It's crazy," he told me. "Yesterday I went to see Harry at his motel. He didn't even seem happy that the charges had been dropped."

"He's sad," I explained.

"Sad? We won, and he's sad?"

"He's sad because Nola is dead."

"But she's been dead for thirty-three years."

"But now she's really dead."

"I have no idea what you're talking about, Goldman."

"That doesn't surprise me."

"Anyway, I went to see him so I could make arrangements for the house. I've been talking to the insurance people, and they're going to pay for everything, but he has to get in touch with an architect and decide what he wants to do. But he seemed completely indifferent. All I managed to get out of him was: 'Take me there.' So we went to the house. It's still full of crap—did you know that? He left everything inside, furniture and other undamaged items. He says he no longer needs any of it. We stayed there over an hour. An hour to ruin my expensive shoes. I showed him what he could recover, especially the old furniture. I suggested he knock down one of the walls to extend the living room, and I also reminded him that we could sue the state for compensatory damages over this whole affair and that we could probably get a nice payoff. But he didn't even react. I offered to contact a moving company to take away everything that was undamaged and put it in storage. I told him he'd been lucky so far because it hadn't rained and no-one had stolen anything, but he told me there was no point. He even said it didn't bother him if anything was stolen, because at least that way the furniture would be of use to someone. Does any of this make sense to you?"

"Yes. The house is of no use to him now."

"Why not?"

"Because there's no longer anyone to wait for. Nola's dead."

Roth shrugged. "Basically," he said, "I was right all along. That Kellergan girl was a slut. The whole town had her, and Harry was just the butt of the joke, a sweet and slightly stupid romantic who shot himself in the foot by writing a love letter to her. Well, a whole book of love letters, in fact!"

He laughed heartily.

This was too much for me. With one hand, I grabbed him by the collar and smashed him against a wall, causing bottles of perfume to rain down and crash to the floor. Then I shoved my free forearm into his throat.

"Nola changed Harry's life!" I shouted. "She sacrificed herself for him. I will not let you go around telling everyone that she was a slut."

He tried to free himself, but he couldn't move. I heard him gasping. People crowded around, and security guards came running in our direction. Finally I let him go. His face was bright red like a tomato, his shirt rumpled.

"You . . . you . . . you're crazy, Goldman," he stammered. "You're insane! As crazy as Quebert. I could file a complaint against you for this, you know."

"Do what you want."

He stalked off angrily, and when he was a safe distance away, he yelled: "You were the one who said she was a slut, Goldman! It's in the pages you wrote. All of this is your fault!"

Roth was right about that last point, at least, and I was hoping my book would repair the damage caused by the publication of my notes. A month and a half remained before its official publication, and Roy Barnaski called me several times a day to share his enthusiasm about it.

"Everything's perfect!" he told me during one of our conversations. "Perfect timing. The D.A.'s report coming out now, all this commotion—it's an incredible stroke of luck, because three months from now it'll be the presidential election, and no-one will give a flying fuck about your book or this case. You know what information is, Goldman? It's a limitless flow in a limited space. The mass of information is exponential, but the time that each person gives it is very limited. The average person devotes—what—one hour a day to the news? Twenty minutes reading the free paper on the subway in the morning, maybe half an hour on the Internet at the office, and fifteen minutes of C.N.N. in the evening before switching to their favorite T.V. show. And yet there is an endless amount of material competing to fill this small space! So many terrible things are happening in the world, but most of them never get mentioned because there isn't time. The news can't cover Nola Kellergan *and* Sudan, there's not enough time. Life is about priorities."

"You're a cynical man, Roy," I said.

"No, I'm just a realist. You're a romantic dreamer, an idealist who would travel the world in search of inspiration. But you could write me a masterpiece on Sudan, and I wouldn't publish it. Because no-one gives a shit about Sudan! People couldn't care less. So, sure, you can label me a bastard if you like, but all I'm doing is responding to public demand. Everyone is washing their hands of Sudan—that's just how it is. All people care about right now is Harry Quebert and Nola Kellergan, and we have to take advantage of that. Two months from now they'll all be talking about the next president, and your book will no longer exist. But we'll have sold so many copies that you won't care because you'll be chilling out in your new house in the Bahamas."

There was no point arguing with him. Barnaski had a gift for commanding the media spotlight. Everyone was talking about my book already, and the more they talked, the more he made them talk by intensifying the advertising campaign. *The Harry Quebert Affair*: the two-million-dollar book, as the press was calling it. Because I now realized that the astronomical sum he had offered me, which had been widely publicized, was in fact an advertising investment: Instead of spending that money on conventional promotion, he had used it to attract public interest. He didn't even attempt to deny this when I asked him about it: According to him, all rules had been overturned by the new dominance of the Internet and social networks.

"Think how much it costs, Marcus, to buy advertising space in a New York subway car. A fortune. You pay a lot of money for a poster with a limited lifespan that will be seen by a limited number of people; in order to see it, people have to be in New York and take that particular subway line within a given time frame. Whereas now all you have to do is get people interested, one way or another, to create a buzz, to get them talking about you, and you can rely on those people to talk about you on social networks. In that way you access an advertising space that is free and limitless. People all over the world take responsibility, without even being aware of it, for advertising your product on a global scale. Isn't that incredible? Facebook users are just people wearing sandwich boards for free. It would be stupid not to use them."

"So that's what you've done?"

"By paying you two million dollars? Yes. Pay a guy an N.B.A. or N.H.L. salary to write a book, and you can be sure that everyone will be talking about him."

At Schmid & Hanson's headquarters in New York, tension was at its height. Entire teams had been mobilized to ensure the book's timely publication. A teleconference machine was sent to me via FedEx so I could participate from my hotel in all sorts of meetings that were taking place in Manhattan: meetings with the marketing team in charge of the book's promotion; with the design team in charge of creating the book's jacket; with the legal team in charge of studying all possible libel issues;

and, last, with a team of ghostwriters which Barnaski desperately wanted to palm off on me.

Conference Call Number Two: With the Ghostwriters

"The book has to be done in three weeks, Marcus," Barnaski told me for the umpteenth time. "After that we'll have two weeks to edit it, get it in type, and correct proofs, and then one week for printing. Which means we hit the bookstores in mid-September. Are you going to make that deadline?"

"Yes, Roy."

"We can come right away if you need us," shouted the head of the ghostwriting team, a man named Frank Lancaster. "We can be there in a matter of hours."

I heard all the others saying yes, they'd be there as soon as possible and it would be fantastic.

"What would be fantastic is if you'd let me do some work," I replied. "I'm writing this book on my own."

"But they're very good," Barnaski insisted. "Even you won't notice the difference!"

"Yup, even you won't notice the difference," Frank repeated. "Why would you choose to work when you don't have to?"

"Don't worry—I'll meet the deadline."

Conference Call Number Four: With the Marketing Team

"Mr Goldman," said Sandra from marketing, "we're going to need photographs—of you during the writing of the book, of Harry, of Somerset. And the notes you took while you were writing the book."

"Yes, all your notes!" Barnaski said.

"Yes ... Alright ... Why?"

"We want to publish a book about your book," Sandra explained. "Like a diary, with lots of illustrations. It'll be big: Everyone who buys your book will want the diary, and vice versa. You'll see."

I sighed. "Don't you think I have enough on my plate right now, without having to prepare a book on the book that I haven't even finished writing yet?"

"Not finished writing?" Barnaski yelled. "I'm sending you the ghost-writers now!"

"Don't send anyone! For God's sake just leave me alone so I can finish my book."

Conference Call Number Six: With the Ghostwriters

"We've written that Caleb cries when he buries the kid," Frank Lancaster told me.

"What do you mean, 'we've written'?"

"Yes, he buries the kid and he cries. The tears fall onto her grave, and the soil turns to mud. It's a really nice scene—you'll see."

"Jesus Christ! Did I ask you to write a nice scene about Caleb burying Nola?"

"Well . . . no . . . but Mr Barnaski said . . ."

"Barnaski? Hello? Roy, are you there? Hello?"

"Um . . . yes, Marcus, I'm here . . ."

"What is all this bullshit?"

"Don't get annoyed. I can't take the risk that the book won't be finished in time. So I asked them to go ahead, just in case. It's simply a precaution. If you don't like it, we won't use it. But just think—if you don't have time to finish it, this will be our lifeline."

Conference Call Number Ten: With the Legal Team

"Hello, Mr Goldman, this is Richardson, from the legal department. So we've been through everything here, and we feel you can use people's real names in your book. Stern, Pratt, Caleb. Everything you've written is in the D.A.'s report, which has been widely reported in the media. We're bulletproof—there's no risk at all. There is no invention, no defamation, only the facts."

"They say you can also add sex scenes and orgies in the form of fantasies or dreams," Barnaski added. "Isn't that so, Richardson?"

"Absolutely. I told you that before. As long as it's in a dream, you can put the sex into your book without risking a lawsuit."

"We need a bit more sex, Marcus," Barnaski said. "Frank was saying the other day that your book is very good, but she's fifteen years old, and Quebert was thirty something at the time. Let's heat things up a little! *Caliente*, as they say in Mexico."

"You're nuts," I told Barnaski.

"You're spoiling everything, Goldman," he said with a sigh. "No-one likes stories about goody-goodies."

Conference Call Number Twelve: With Roy Barnaski
"Hello, Roy?"

"Markie?"

"Mom?"

"Markie? Is that you? Who's Roy?"

"Shit, I dialed the wrong number."

"Wrong number? You call your mother, you say 'shit,' and then you say it's the wrong number?"

"That's not what I meant. It's just that I had to talk to Roy Barnaski and, without thinking, I dialed your number. My head's in the clouds at the moment."

"You call your mother because your head's in the clouds . . . this gets better! I give you life, and what do I get in return? Nothing."

"Sorry, Mom. Tell Dad hi from me. I'll call you back."

"Wait!"

"What?"

"So you can't even spare a minute for your poor mother? Your mother, who made you such a handsome and talented writer, doesn't even merit a few seconds of your time? Do you remember little Jeremy Johnson?"

"From elementary school? Yes. Why?"

"His mother was dead. Remember? Well, don't you think he would have liked to have been able to pick up the telephone and talk to his darling mommy who's in heaven with the angels? There is no telephone line to heaven, Markie, but there is a line to Montclair! Try to remember that from time to time."

"Jeremy Johnson? His mother wasn't dead! That's what he told people because she had so much hair on her face she looked like she had a beard, and everyone made fun of him about it. So he claimed his mother was dead and that woman was his nanny."

"What? The nanny with the beard was Jeremy's mother?"

"Yes, Mom."

I heard my mother calling my father. "Nelson, come here quickly! There's some *plotke* I absolutely have to tell you about. The bearded woman at the Johnsons' house—she was the mother! What do you mean, you knew? Why didn't you tell me?"

"Mom, I have to hang up now. I have a conference call."

"What's that?"

"It's a meeting that takes place on the telephone."

"Why don't we have conference calls?"

"Conference calls are for work, Mom."

"Who is that Roy you were talking about, my darling? Is it the naked man who was hiding in your room? You can tell me everything, you know. I'm prepared to hear anything. But why do you want to have conference calls with that dirty man?"

"Roy's my publisher. You know him. You met him in New York."

"You know, Markie, I had a talk with the rabbi about your sexual problems. He says that—"

"Mom, that's enough. I'm going to hang up now. Give Dad a hug from me."

Conference Call Number Thirteen: With the Design Team

They were engaged in a brainstorming session to create a jacket for the book.

"It could be a photograph of you," said Steven, the head designer.

"Or a photo of Nola," another designer suggested.

"A picture of Caleb would work, wouldn't it?" said a third person, to no-one in particular.

"What about a photo of the forest?" another voice said.

"Yes, something dark and frightening might work well," said Barnaski.

"How about something more understated?" I suggested. "A view of Somerset, with two shadows in the foreground that are not identifiable but that might be Harry and Nola, walking together along Shore Road."

"You have to be careful with understatement," Steven said. "Understatement is boring. And boring doesn't sell."

Conference Call Number Twenty-one: With the Legal, Design and Marketing Teams

I heard the voice of Richardson, from the legal department.

"Do you want doughnuts?"

"Huh?" I replied. "Me? No, thanks."

"He wasn't talking to you," said Steven, the head designer. "He was talking to Sandra from marketing."

Barnaski grew irritated. "Can you please stop eating and interrupting the discussion with offers of coffee and doughnuts? Are we having a party or making a bestseller?"

While my book was progressing, the investigation into Chief Pratt's murder was at a standstill. Gahalowood had commandeered several detectives from the criminal division, but they were getting nowhere. Not a clue, not a single usable lead. We had a long discussion about this in a bar on the edge of town where Gahalowood sometimes came to play pool.

"It's my hideaway," he told me as he handed me a cue stick so I could begin the next game. "I've been coming here quite often recently."

"It's not been easy, huh?"

"It's O.K. now. At least we've solved the Kellergan case—that's the most important thing. Even if it caused a bigger shitstorm than I'd anticipated. It's the D.A. who's taken the brunt of it, as always. Because he's elected."

"What about you?"

"The governor is happy, the chief of police is happy, so everyone is happy. Actually, my bosses are thinking about starting a unit for cold cases, and they want me to lead it."

"Cold cases? But wouldn't that be frustrating? When it comes down to it, you're just talking about a bunch of dead people."

"No, you're talking about a bunch of living people. In the case of Nola Kellergan, the father has the right to know what happened to his daughter, and Quebert was almost wrongfully put through a criminal trial. Justice has to be done, even if it happens years later."

"What about Caleb?" I asked.

"I think he's just a guy who lost control. You know, in this kind of case, it's usually either a moment of madness or a serial killer—and there weren't any similar cases to Nola's in the region in the two years that preceded her disappearance."

I nodded.

"The only thing that bothers me," Gahalowood said, "is Pratt. Who killed him? And why? That's still a big question mark, and I'm afraid we might never figure it out."

"You still think it might have been Stern?"

"All I have are suspicions. I told you my theory, but there are gray areas there in terms of his relationship with Luther. What was the link between them? And why didn't Stern mention that his car had disappeared? There's something strange there. Could he have been mixed up in this somehow? It's possible."

"Didn't you ask him?"

"Of course I did. He received me twice, and was perfectly nice. He said he felt better now that I knew about the painting. He told me he sometimes let Luther take the Monte Carlo for his own private use because the blue Mustang had a steering problem. I don't know whether that's true or not, but it's a plausible explanation. It's all perfectly plausible. I've been investigating Stern for a while now, and I haven't found anything. I also talked to Sylla Mitchell again, and asked her what had happened to her brother's blue Mustang. She said she had no idea; that car just disappeared. But I have nothing on Stern, nothing that might suggest he was involved in this."

"Why would a man like Stern let himself be at the whim of his chauffeur? Giving into his wishes, letting him borrow a car . . . There's something here I don't understand."

"Yeah, I have the same feeling."

I arranged the pool balls inside the triangle.

"My book should be finished in two weeks," I said.

"Already? You've written it quickly."

"Not really. You might hear people saying that it was written in two months, but really it took me two years."

He smiled.

I finished writing *The Harry Quebert Affair* toward the end of August, slightly ahead of schedule. It was time for me to return to New York, where Barnaski was getting ready to launch the book with a big media splash. By chance, I left Concord on the penultimate day of August. I made a stop that morning in Somerset so I could see Harry. As usual he was sitting in front of the door to his motel room.

"I'm going back to New York," I told him.

"So this is farewell."

"Don't make it sound so final. I'll be back soon. I'm going to restore your reputation, Harry. Give me a few months and you'll be the most respected writer in the country again."

"Why are you doing this, Marcus?"

"Because you made me what I am."

"So what? You feel you owe me? I made you a writer, but since I seem to no longer be one myself, as far as public opinion is concerned, you're trying to give me back what I gave you?"

"No, I'm defending you because I always believed in you. Always."

I handed him a package.

"What is it?" he asked.

"My book."

"I won't read it."

"I want your approval before I publish it. This book is your book."

"No, Marcus, it's yours. And that's the problem."

"What's the problem?"

"I'm sure it's a wonderful book."

"Why is that a problem?"

"It's complicated, Marcus. You'll understand one day."

There was a long silence.

"What are you going to do now?" I finally asked.

"I'm not going to stay here."

"What do you mean by here? This motel? New Hampshire?"

"I want to go to writers' heaven."

"Writers' heaven? What's that?"

"Writers' heaven is the place where you decide to rewrite your life the way you wish you had lived it. Because a writer's power, Marcus, is that he gets to decide the ending of the book. He has power over life and death; he has the power to change everything. Writers have more power in their fingertips than they imagine. All they have to do is close their eyes and they can change an entire lifetime. What might have happened on August 30, 1975, if—"

"You can't change the past, Harry. Don't go there."

"How can I not go there?"

I placed the package on the chair next to his and pretended to leave.

"Is it a good story?" he said.

"It's the story of a man who loved a young woman. She had so many dreams for them. She wanted them to live together, for him to become a great writer and a college professor, she wanted them to have a dog the color of the sun. But one day the young woman disappeared. She was never found. The man went back to the house to wait for her. He became a great writer, he became a college professor, and he had a dog the color of the sun. He did everything she had ever asked him to do, and he waited for her. He never loved anyone else. He waited faithfully for her return. But she never returned."

"Because she's dead!"

"Yes. But now this man can grieve."

"No, it's too late! He's sixty-seven years old!"

"It's never too late to love again."

I waved.

"I'll call you when I get to New York."

"Don't call me," Harry said. "It's better that way."

I went down the outside stairs to the parking lot. As I was about to get in my car, I heard him call out to me from the second-floor railing.

"Marcus, what's today's date?"

"August 30, Harry."

"And what time is it?"

"Nearly 11 a.m."

"Only eight hours!"

"Eight hours until what?"

"Until 7 p.m."

I didn't grasp his meaning at first: "What happens at 7 p.m.?"

"We're supposed to meet then, me and her—you know that. She'll come. Look, Marcus! Look where we are. We're in writers' heaven. All we have to do is write it, and everything could change."

August 30, 1975, in Writers' Heaven

She decided not to take Shore Road but to walk along the ocean. It was safer. Holding the manuscript tightly, she ran over shells and sand. She had almost passed Goose Cove. Another two miles to walk and she would reach the motel. She looked at her watch. It was just after six. Forty-five minutes from now, she would be there. At 7 p.m., as they had agreed. She kept walking and reached the edge of the Side Creek forest. She climbed from the beach to the woods over a series of rocks, then cautiously walked through the rows of trees, taking care not to tear her red dress in the undergrowth. Through the trees she saw a house in the distance. In the kitchen a woman was making an apple pie.

She reached Shore Road. Just before she exited the woods, a car sped past. It was Luther Caleb, returning to Concord. She arrived at the motel at exactly 7 p.m. She crossed the parking lot and climbed the outside stairs. Room 8 was on the second floor. She ran up the steps two by two and drummed triumphantly on the door.

Someone was knocking at the door. He quickly got up from the bed.

"Harry! Darling Harry!" she shouted when she saw him.

She jumped up and hugged him, covering his face with kisses. He lifted her up.

"Nola . . . you're here. You came! You came!"

She gave him a puzzled look. "Of course I came. What did you think I was going to do?"

"I must have nodded off, and I had a nightmare. I was in this room, and I was waiting for you. I waited for you, and you didn't come. I waited so long. And you never came."

She held him tightly.

"What a terrible dream! But I'm here now. I'm here, and I'll always be here."

They embraced for a long time. Then he gave her the flowers that had been soaking in the sink.

"Didn't you bring anything?" Harry asked when he noticed she did not have any luggage.

"Nothing. I wanted to be discreet. We can buy what we need on the way. But I brought your manuscript."

"I was looking for it everywhere!"

"I took it with me. I read it. I love it so much, Harry. It's a masterpiece." They hugged again, and then she said, "Let's go! Let's go now, as fast as we can!"

"Now?"

"Yes, I want to get far away from here. Please, Harry, I don't want to risk anyone finding us. Let's go right away."

Night was falling. It was August 30, 1975. Two figures left the motel room, ran down the stairs to the parking lot, and got into a black Chevrolet Monte Carlo. The car took Shore Road, heading north, and sped away, vanishing into the horizon. Soon only its shape could be seen. It became a black dot, then a tiny pinprick. For a moment longer you could just see the tiny point of red made by its taillights, and then it disappeared completely.

PART THREE

Writers' Heaven
(The Book's Publication)

5

The Girl Who Touched the Heart of America

"A new book, Marcus, is the start of a new life. It's also an act of great generosity: You are offering, to whoever wishes to discover it, a part of yourself. Some will love it, some will hate it. Some will worship you, others will despise you. Some will be jealous, others will be curious. But you're not writing it for them. You're writing it for all those who, in their daily lives, will enjoy a sweet moment because of Marcus Goldman. You may say that doesn't sound like much, but it's actually quite something. Some writers want to change the world. But who can really change the world?"

My book was the talk of the town. I could no longer walk the streets of Manhattan in peace. I could no longer go jogging without passersby recognizing me and calling out, "Look, it's Goldman! It's that writer!" Some even started running after me so they could ask me the questions that were gnawing at them: "Is it true what you say in your book? Did Harry Quebert really do that?" In the café in the West Village where I was a regular, certain customers felt free to sit at my table and talk to me.

"I'm reading your book right now, Mr Goldman. I can't put it down! The first one was good, of course, but this one . . . Did they really pay you two million bucks to write it? How old are you? I bet you're not even thirty. Twenty-eight! And you're already a multi-millionaire!" Even the doorman at my building, whose progress through my book I was able to note each time I came or went, cornered me for a long talk by the elevator once he had got to the end. "So that's what happened to Nola Kellergan? That poor girl! But how could it happen? How could such a thing be possible, Mr Goldman?"

From the day of its publication, *The Harry Quebert Affair* was the number one bestseller all over the country; it promised to be the best-selling book of the year. They were talking about it everywhere: on T.V., on the radio, in every newspaper, all over the Internet. The critics, who had been waiting to ambush me, ended up lavishing me with praise. They all said my new book was one for the ages.

Immediately after publication, I began a marathon promotional tour that took me to all four corners of the country in the space of only two weeks. Barnaski believed two weeks was all we had before everyone's attention turned full time toward the presidential election on November 4. Back in New York I had already appeared on numerous television shows, hopping from studio to studio at a frantic pace. Reporters swarmed my parents' house. To give my parents some peace, I bought them an R.V. so they could realize one of their oldest dreams: driving out to Chicago and then down Route 66 and out to California.

An article in the *New York Times* referred to Nola as "The Girl Who Touched the Heart of America," and this was how she was now known. So many people had been moved by her story—the letters I received all testified to this. Some literary experts claimed that *The Origin of Evil* could be read correctly only in conjunction with my book; they suggested a new approach in which Nola no longer represented an impossible love but the omnipotence of love. And so *The Origin of Evil*, which had been pulled from the shelves of practically every bookstore in the country four months earlier, now saw its sales soaring again. For Christmas, Barnaski was preparing a limited edition boxed set containing *The Origin of Evil* and *The Harry Quebert Affair*, along with an analysis of the text written by a certain Frank Lancaster.

I had not heard from Harry since I left him at the Sea Side Motel. I had tried to call him many times, but his cell phone was off, and when I called the motel and asked for Room 8, the telephone just rang and rang. In fact, I had no contact with Somerset at all, which was perhaps for the best; I had little desire to find out how the book was being received there. All I knew, because my publisher's legal department had told me, was that Elijah Stern was still desperately attempting to take Schmid & Hanson to court, claiming that the passages about him were defamatory, particularly those in which I wondered about his reasons for granting Luther's request to paint Nola nude and for not telling the police about the disappearance of his black Monte Carlo. I had called him before the book's publication to obtain his version of events, but he had not deigned to reply.

By the third week in October, the presidential election essentially took over the media, exactly as Barnaski had predicted. Requests for my time suddenly dwindled, and I breathed a sigh of relief. I had been through two very tough years: my first success, the writers' disease, and then, finally, this second book. I felt much calmer, and had a real desire to get away for a while. Since I did not wish to go alone, and wanted to thank Douglas for his support, I bought two tickets to the Bahamas. My plan was to surprise him one night when he came over to my apartment to watch a game with me. But, to my great dismay, he turned me down.

"That would have been cool," he said, "but I've got plans to take Kelly to the Caribbean then."

"Kelly? Are you still with her?"

"Yes, of course. Didn't you know? I'm going to ask her to marry me while we're on vacation."

"Wow, that's great! I'm really happy for you both."

I must have looked a little sad, because he said to me: "Marc, you have everything you could possibly want from life. It's time you found a girlfriend."

I nodded. "It's just that . . . it's been so long since I went on a date."

He smiled. "Don't worry about that."

It was this conversation that led us to the evening—October 23, 2008—when everything changed.

Douglas had arranged a date for me with Lydia Gloor, whose agent had told him she still had a crush on me. He had persuaded me to call her, and we agreed to meet at a bar in SoHo. At exactly 7 p.m. Douglas came by my apartment to offer me some moral support.

"You're not ready yet?" he said, noticing that I was shirtless when I opened the door.

"I can't decide which of these to wear," I said, holding up two options.

"Wear the blue one."

"Are you sure this isn't a mistake, Doug, going out with Lydia Gloor?"

"You're not going to marry her, Marc. You're just going to have a drink. You'll see if there's still a spark."

"And what do we do after we've had a drink?"

"I booked you a table at a cool Italian place not far from the bar. I'll text you the address."

I smiled. "What would I do without you?"

"That's what friends are for, isn't it?"

Just then my cell phone rang. I probably wouldn't have answered had I not seen that it was Gahalowood.

"Hello, Sergeant! It's good to hear from you."

"Good evening," he said, sounding unhappy. "I'm sorry to disturb you . . ."

"You're not disturbing me at all."

"Listen, writer, I think we have a very serious problem."

"What's going on?"

"It's about Nola Kellergan's mother."

"Louisa Kellergan? What about her?"

"Check your e-mail."

I went to my computer in the living room. Gahalowood's e-mail was waiting for me.

"What is it?" I asked, clicking on his message, which had a photograph attached. "You're beginning to worry me."

"Open the image. You remember you mentioned Alabama to me?"

"Of course I remember. That's where the Kellergans came from."

"We fucked up, Marcus. We completely forgot to look into Alabama. You even told me I should."

I clicked on the image. It was a photograph of a cemetery headstone with the following words engraved on it:

LOUISA KELLERGAN

1930–1969

BELOVED WIFE AND MOTHER

I stared at it, aghast.

"Oh, my God," I breathed. "What does this mean?"

"That Nola's mother died in 1969. Six years before her daughter's disappearance."

"Who sent you that photo?"

"A journalist in Concord. It'll be front-page news tomorrow, writer. Which means the whole country is gonna know that your book and our investigation are both wrong."

I didn't go out to dinner with Lydia Gloor that evening. Douglas got Barnaski out of a business meeting, Barnaski got Richardson from legal out of his house, and we had a particularly heated crisis meeting in a room at Schmid & Hanson. The photograph had actually come from a local newspaper near Jackson, Alabama. Barnaski had just spent two hours trying to persuade the editor of the *Concord Herald* not to publish this image on the front page of the next day's paper, but without success.

"Can you imagine what people are going to say when they find out your book is a pack of lies?" he yelled at me. "For God's sake, Goldman, didn't you check your facts?"

"I don't know. This is insane! Nola was beaten by her mother—Harry told me! I don't understand. Harry told me about the beatings and that waterboard torture."

"And what does Quebert say now?"

"I can't reach him. I tried calling him a dozen times tonight. But I haven't heard from him in two months."

"Keep trying. You have to get hold of him! Talk to someone who will answer! Find me some kind of explanation that I can give the journalists tomorrow morning when they all start calling."

At 10 p.m. I finally called Ernie Pinkas.

"But where did you get the idea that the mother was still alive?" he asked me.

"Nobody told me she was dead."

"But nobody told you she was alive!"

"Yes. Harry told me."

"Then he was screwing with you. David Kellergan came to Somerset alone with his daughter. The mother was never here."

"I don't understand! I feel like I'm going crazy. What will people think of me now?"

"They'll think you're a shit writer, Marcus. I have to tell you that nobody is very happy with you here. We've been watching you strut all over the newspapers and T.V. for a month now, all of us knowing that what you wrote was a pile of crap."

"Why didn't anyone warn me?"

"Warn you? To say what? To ask you if you had, by any chance, made a mistake by writing about a mother who was dead long before any of this happened?"

"What did she die of?" I asked.

"I have no idea."

"But what about the music? And the beatings? I have witnesses to back those things up."

"Witnesses to back up what? That the pastor played music full blast to drown out his daughter's sufferings? Yeah, we all suspected that. But in your book you say that Mr Kellergan hid in his garage while Mrs Kellergan beat the kid. The problem with that is that the mother never set foot in Somerset because she was dead before they moved here. So how can we believe anything else you say in the book? And you told me you were going to put my name in the Acknowledgments . . ."

"I did!"

"You wrote a whole bunch of names with 'E. Pinkas, Somerset' among them. I wanted my name in big letters. I wanted people to talk about me."

"What? But . . ."

He hung up on me. Barnaski glared at me. "Goldman, take the first plane to Concord tomorrow and sort this shit out."

"Roy, if I go to Somerset, they'll lynch me."

He forced a laugh and said, "Just be grateful that's all they'll do to you."

So was the Girl Who Touched the Heart of America also a product of the sick imagination of a writer starved of inspiration? How could such an important detail have been missed? The news story in the *Concord Herald* was now sowing serious doubt about the entire book.

On Friday morning, October 24, I took a flight to Manchester, where I arrived just after noon. I rented a car at the airport and drove straight to Concord, to the state police headquarters, where Gahalowood was waiting for me. He updated me on what he had managed to learn about the Kellergan family's past in Alabama.

"David and Louisa Kellergan were married in 1955," he told me.

"He was already the pastor of a flourishing congregation, and his wife helped him to grow it. Nola was born in 1960. Nothing noteworthy occurred in the years that followed. But one night in the summer of 1969, the house burned down. The girl was saved, but the mother died. A few weeks later the pastor left Jackson.

"A few weeks?" I said, surprised.

"Yes. And they moved to Somerset."

"But then why did Harry tell me that Nola was beaten by her mother?"

"It must have been her father."

"No! No!" I exclaimed. "Harry told me about her mother. It was the mother! I even have the recordings."

"Well, let's listen to them, then," Gahalowood said.

I had brought all my minidiscs with me. I spread them out over Gahalowood's desk and attempted to find the right one. I had labeled them carefully, by person and by date, but I still couldn't manage to locate the recording in question. Only when I emptied my bag did I find one last disc, undated, that I had missed. I put it in the recorder.

"That's strange," I said. "Why didn't I write the date on this disc?"

I pressed PLAY and heard my voice announce that it was Tuesday, July 1, 2008. I was recording a conversation with Harry in the prison visiting room.

"Is that why the two of you wanted to leave? I mean, when you arranged to elope, the night of August 30—why did you do that?"

"That was because something awful happened. Are you recording this?"

"Yes."

"I'm going to tell you about a very serious incident, so that you'll understand. But no-one else can know about it."

"You can trust me."

"You know, for our week on Martha's Vineyard, instead of saying

she was with a friend, Nola had simply run away. She left without saying a word to anyone. When I saw her again, the day after our return, she was terribly upset. She told me her mother had beaten her, and indeed her body was covered in bruises. That day, she told me her mother often punished her for nothing. That she hit her with a metal ruler, and also did a really terrible thing: She filled a bowl with water, took her daughter by her hair, and forced her head underwater. Just like they do to terrorist suspects. She said it was to deliver her."

"Deliver her?"

"Deliver her from evil. A kind of baptism, I imagine. Jesus in the Jordan River, or something like that. At first, I couldn't believe it, but the evidence was there. So I asked her why her father didn't intervene, and she said he locked himself in the garage and played music very loud whenever her mother punished her. He didn't want to hear, she said. Nola couldn't take it anymore—she'd had enough. I wanted to go see the Kellergans, to deal with this problem, to put an end to it, but Nola begged me not to. She told me she would get in terrible trouble, that her parents would move away, and that we would never see each other again. But still, this couldn't be allowed to continue. So, toward the end of August—around the twentieth—we decided we had to leave. Soon. And secretly, of course. We were going to go to British Columbia, maybe, and live in a cabin. Have a simple life by the edge of a lake. Nobody would ever have known."

"So that's why you decided to elope?"

"Yes."

"But why don't you want anyone to know this?"

"That's only the beginning of the story. Soon afterward, I made a terrible discovery about Nola's mother—"

"Time's up." Another voice—the guard, interrupting.

"Let's finish this conversation next time, Marcus. But in the meantime, keep it to yourself."

"So what did he discover about Nola's mother?" Gahalowood asked impatiently.

"I don't remember," I replied, frowning, as I searched through the other minidiscs.

Suddenly I felt myself go pale and stopped searching. "Oh, God, I don't believe it!"

"What, writer?"

"That was the last recording of Harry. That's why there's no date on the disc—I'd completely forgotten it. We never finished that conversation. Because after that there were the revelations about Pratt, and then Harry no longer wanted to be recorded, so I continued my interviews by taking notes. And then there was the leak of my notes to the press, and Harry got angry at me. Oh, shit, how could I have been such an idiot?"

"We have to talk to Harry," Gahalowood said, grabbing his coat. "We need to know what he discovered about Louisa Kellergan."

We left for the Sea Side Motel.

To our surprise, the door to Room 8 was opened not by Harry but by a tall blond woman. We went to see the front-desk clerk, who told us: "There hasn't been any Harry Quebert here recently."

"That's impossible," I said. "He was here for weeks."

At Gahalowood's request, the clerk looked through the register for the past six months. But he remained categorical: "No Harry Quebert."

"But I saw him here myself!" I said, struggling to conceal my irritation. "A tall guy with messy gray hair."

"Oh, him! Yes, he was here a lot. He often hung around the parking lot. But he never had a room here."

"He had Room 8!" I shouted. "I know he did. I often saw him sitting in front of the door."

"That's right—he sat in front of it. I kept asking him to leave, but each time I did, he gave me a hundred-dollar bill! At that rate I figured he could stay there as long as he liked. He said being here brought him good memories."

"When was the last time you saw him?" Gahalowood asked.

"Jeez . . . it must've been quite a few weeks ago. All I remember is that the day he left he gave me another hundred-dollar bill so that if someone called Room 8, I would pretend to transfer the call and let it ring indefinitely. He seemed in a big rush. This was just after the argument—"

"What argument?" Gahalowood demanded. "What are you talking about?"

"Well, your friend had an argument with some guy. A little old guy who came here in a car to bawl him out. It was pretty lively. They were yelling at each other. I was about to intervene when the old guy finally got in his car and left. That was when your friend decided to leave. I would have told him to leave anyway, though; I don't like it when people make noise like that. The other guests complain, and it can cause me trouble with my boss."

"But what was the argument about?"

"About a letter, I think. 'It was you!' the old guy kept yelling at your friend."

"A letter? What letter?"

"How should I know?"

"Alright. So what happened after that?"

"The old guy left, and your friend got out of here in no time."

"Would you recognize him?" Gahalowood asked.

"The old guy? No, I don't think so. But you could ask your colleagues. Because he came back. My guess was that he wanted to bump off your friend. I know all about police investigations; I watch all the cop shows on T.V. Your friend had already cleared out, but I had the feeling something fishy was going on, so I called the police. Two state troopers got here pretty quickly and talked to the guy. But they let him go. They said it was nothing."

Gahalowood called the station right away to ask them to retrieve the identity of the person recently interviewed at the Sea Side Motel by the highway police.

"They're going to call me back as soon as they have the information," he told me as he hung up.

I felt lost. Running my hand through my hair, I said: "This is insane! Insane!"

The clerk suddenly gave me a strange look and asked: "Are you Mr Goldman?"

"Yes, why?"

"Because your friend left an envelope for you. He said a young guy would come to look for him and that he would undoubtedly say, 'This is insane! This is insane!' He said that if that guy came to the motel, I had to give him this."

He handed me a manila envelope, inside of which was a key.

"A key?" Gahalowood said. "Nothing else?"

"Nothing."

"But what's the key to?"

I carefully studied the key. And then I recognized it: "The gym locker in Montburry!"

Twenty minutes later we were in the locker room. Inside Locker 201 there was a bound sheaf of papers, accompanied by a handwritten letter.

Dear Marcus,

If you're reading this, it's because there is a shitstorm gathering around your book and you're looking for answers.

This may interest you. This book is the truth.

Harry

The sheaf of papers was a slim typewritten manuscript bearing the title:

THE SEAGULLS OF SOMERSET
by Harry L. Quebert

"What's this about?" Gahalowood asked me.

"I have no idea. It seems to be an unpublished book of Harry's."

"The paper's old," Gahalowood noted, carefully inspecting the pages.

I skimmed the text.

"Nola used to talk about seagulls," I said. "Harry told me she loved them. There must be a connection."

"But why did he say it was the truth? Is this a story about what happened in 1975?"

"I don't know."

We decided to postpone reading the manuscript until later, and to first go to Somerset. I was not greeted warmly. In front of Clark's, Jenny—furious about the way I had described her mother and refusing to believe that her father was the author of the anonymous letters—gave me a public dressing-down. Others, passing by, chimed in and told me to get out of town.

The only person who deigned to speak with us was Nancy Hattaway, whom we went to see in her store.

"I don't understand," Nancy told me. "I never said anything about Nola's mother."

"But you did tell me about the Nola's bruises. And that time when Nola had run away for a week and they tried to make you believe she was sick."

"But that was just her father. He was the one who refused to let me in the house when Nola disappeared that week in July. I never mentioned her mother to you at all."

"You told me how she had been beaten on her breasts with a metal ruler. Don't you remember?"

"Of course, yes. But I never said it was her mother who beat her."

"I recorded you! It was June 26. I have the disc with me. Look—the date is on it."

I pressed PLAY:

"I'm surprised by your comments about Mr Kellergan. I met him a few days ago and he seemed like quite a gentle man."

"He can come across that way. In public, at least. He'd been recruited to save St James's, which had fallen into neglect, after apparently performing miracles in Alabama. And it's true that, soon after he took it over, the church was full every Sunday. But apart from that, no-one really knows what went on in the Kellergan house."

"What do you mean?"

"Nola used to get beaten."

"What?"

"Yes, she was severely beaten. And I remember one terrible incident, Mr Goldman. It was in early summer. That was the first time I saw those kinds of marks on Nola's body. We were walking to Grand Beach to go swimming, when out of the blue she asked me if she was 'a wicked girl.' She told me that she was bullied at home, that she was called wicked. I asked her why, and she mentioned events in Alabama, but she wouldn't say any more. She seemed sad; I thought it was because of a boy. There was this guy Cody, a junior who was always hanging around her. Later, on the beach, when she got undressed, I saw she had terrible bruises on her breasts. I asked her what they were, and guess what she replied: 'It was Mom. She hit me on Saturday.' Obviously I was completely shocked by this. I thought I must have misheard her. But she went on: 'It's true. She's the one who says I'm a wicked girl.' Nola seemed desperate, so I didn't argue with her. After Grand Beach we went home, and I gave her ointment to rub onto her breasts. I told her she should talk to someone about her mother. Like the nurse at the high school, for example. But Nola told me she didn't want to talk about it anymore."

"There!" I shouted, pausing the recorder. "You see? You talk about the mother."

"No," Nancy replied. "I told you how shocked I was when Nola mentioned her mother. I was trying to explain that there was something strange going on at the Kellergans' house. I was absolutely sure you already knew her mother was dead."

"But I didn't know anything! I mean, I knew her mother was dead, but I thought she must have died after her daughter disappeared. I even remember David Kellergan showing me a photograph of his wife the first time I went to see him. I remember being surprised by how friendly he was. And I remember asking him something like: 'What about your wife?' And he replied: 'She died a long time ago.'"

"Now that I've heard the recording, I can understand how you got the wrong idea. It's a terrible misunderstanding, Mr Goldman. I'm sorry about that."

I pressed PLAY again:

". . . Like the nurse at the high school, for example. But Nola told me she didn't want to talk about it anymore."
"What happened in Alabama?"
"I have no idea. I never found out. Nola never told me."
"Was it connected to their moving here?"
"I don't know. I'd like to help you, but I just don't know."

"It's all my fault, Ms Hattaway," I said. "After that, I forgot about Alabama."

"So it was her father who used to beat her?" Gahalowood asked, puzzled.

Nancy thought about this for a moment. She seemed a little confused. Finally she answered: "Yes. Or no. Oh, I don't know. There were those marks on her body. When I asked her what happened, she told me she was punished at home."

"Punished for what?"

"That was all she said. But she never said it was her father who beat her. I just don't know. My mother saw bruises on her body one day at the beach. And then there was that deafening music that the father used to play all the time. People suspected that Mr Kellergan beat his daughter, but nobody dared say anything. He was our pastor, after all."

After we left Nancy Hattaway's store, Gahalowood and I sat on a bench outside for a long time in silence. I was in despair.

"Just a stupid misunderstanding," I said finally. "All-this because of a stupid fucking misunderstanding! How could I have been such an idiot?"

"Calm down, writer. Don't be so hard on yourself. We were all fooled. We were so excited by what we were discovering that we didn't see what was clearly in front of us. It's just a psychological block—everyone gets them."

Just then his cell phone rang. It was the state police returning his call.

"They found the name of the old guy from the motel," he whispered to me while waiting to hear the news.

Then a strange expression appeared on his face. He removed the receiver from his ear and said:

"It was David Kellergan."

The never-ending music reverberated from 245 Terrace Avenue. Evidently Mr Kellergan was home.

"We have to find out what he wanted from Harry," Gahalowood said to me as we got out of the car. "But please, writer, let me do the talking!"

When interviewing Mr Kellergan at the Sea Side Motel, the state troopers had found a shotgun in his car. He did, however, possess a license for it. He had explained that he was on his way to the shooting range and had stopped at the motel restaurant for coffee. The troopers, having no reason to hold him or charge him, had let him go.

"Pry it out of him, Sergeant," I said as we walked down the driveway to the house. "I'm curious to know what that letter was about. Kellergan told me he barely knew Harry. You think he lied?"

"That's what we're going to find out."

David Kellergan must have seen us arriving, because he opened the door before we even rang the bell. He was holding his shotgun. He looked mad as hell. I got the distinct impression that he wanted to kill me. "You've desecrated the memory of my wife and my daughter!" he screamed at me. "You bastard! You son of a bitch!" Gahalowood tried to calm him down. He asked him to put his shotgun away, while explaining that we were there so we could work out what actually happened to Nola. Neighbors, alerted by the noise, rushed over to see what was going on. Soon there was a crowd of onlookers in front of the house while David Kellergan continued to yell and Gahalowood signaled to me that we should move away slowly. Two Somerset police cars arrived, sirens on. Travis Dawn got out of one, visibly unhappy to see me. "Don't you think you've already caused enough trouble in this town?" he said. Then he asked Gahalowood if there was a good reason for the state police to be in Somerset without giving him prior notice. Because I knew we were running out of time, I shouted at David Kellergan:

"So you turned the music up loud and you had a ball, didn't you, Reverend?"

He made a threatening motion with his shotgun.

"I never raised a hand to my daughter! She was never beaten. You're full of shit, Goldman! I'm going to hire a lawyer, and I'm going to take you to court."

"Oh yeah? So how come you haven't already done that? Why aren't we in court now? Maybe you don't want people looking into your past? What happened in Alabama?"

He spat in my direction.

"People like you would never understand, Goldman."

"What happened with you and Harry Quebert at the Sea Side Motel? What are you hiding from us?"

Just then Travis started yelling too, threatening Gahalowood that he would inform his superiors, and we had to leave.

We drove in silence toward Concord. Finally Gahalowood said, "What are we missing, writer? I have a feeling it's something we've been looking at the whole time but we've somehow failed to see."

"We now know that Harry was aware of something about Nola's mother that he didn't tell me."

"And we can assume that Mr Kellergan knows that Harry knows. But knows what, for God's sake?"

The press was having a field day.

New development in the Harry Quebert case: inconsistencies discovered in Marcus Goldman's account call into question the credibility of his book, which was acclaimed by critics and presented by publisher Roy Barnaski as an accurate depiction of the events leading up to the murder of Nola Kellergan in 1975.

Knowing I could not return to New York until I had cleared up this case, I took refuge in my suite at the hotel in Concord where I had stayed over the summer. The only person who knew where I was was Denise; I had told her so she could keep me informed of events in New York and the latest developments regarding the ghost of Nola's mother.

That evening, Gahalowood invited me to dinner at his house. His daughters were volunteering for the Obama campaign, and they dominated the conversation. They gave me bumper stickers for my car. Later, as I was helping wash the dishes, Helen mentioned that I looked upset.

"I don't understand what I did wrong," I explained. "How could I have messed up this badly?"

"There must be a reason, Marcus. You know, Perry has great faith in you. He thinks you're an exceptional person. I've known him for thirty years, and I've never heard him use that word about anyone. I'm sure you haven't messed up, and that there's a rational explanation for all this."

That night Gahalowood and I stayed up late in his office, reading the manuscript that Harry had left me. The unpublished novel *The Seagulls of Somerset* turned out to be a wonderful story about Harry and Nola. The manuscript was undated, but I guessed it must have been written after *The Origin of Evil*. While the latter was the story of an impossible love affair that was never consummated, in *The Seagulls of Somerset*, Harry recounted how Nola had inspired him, how she had always believed in him and encouraged him, helping him to become the great writer he was. But at the end of the book, Nola did not die; a few months after his success, the central protagonist, named Harry, goes to Canada, where Nola is waiting for him in a lakeside cabin.

At 2 a.m. Gahalowood made us coffee and asked me: "So what do you think he's trying to tell us with this book?"

"He's imagining his life if Nola hadn't died," I said. "This book is writers' heaven."

"Writers' heaven? What's that?"

"It's when the power of writing turns against you. You no longer know if your characters exist only in your head or if they are truly alive."

"And how does that help us?"

"I have no idea. It doesn't. It's a very good book, and yet he never published it. Why did he keep it at the bottom of a drawer?"

Gahalowood shrugged. "Maybe he didn't dare publish it because it was about a girl who had disappeared."

"Maybe. But *The Origin of Evil* was about Nola too, and that didn't stop him from offering it to publishers. And why did he write to me: 'This book is the truth'? The truth about what? Nola? What does he mean? That Nola never died and is living in a cabin somewhere?"

"That would make no sense at all," said Gahalowood. "The forensics tests were unequivocal: It was her skeleton we found."

"So . . . what then?"

"So we haven't gotten any closer, writer."

The next morning Denise called to inform me that a woman had been looking for me, and Schmid & Hanson had given her my office number.

"She wanted to talk to you," Denise explained. "She said it was important."

"What was it about?"

"She said she had gone to school with Nola Kellergan in Somerset, and that Nola had talked to her about her mother."

Cambridge, Massachusetts, Saturday, October 25, 2008

She was in the 1975 Somerset High School yearbook, listed as Stephanie Hendorf; only two photographs separated her from Nola. She was one of the students Ernie Pinkas had been unable to find. Having married a man of Polish origin, she was now named Stephanie Larjinjiak and lived in an opulent house in Cambridge, Massachusetts. That was where Gahalowood and I met with her. She was forty-eight, the same age Nola would have been now had she lived. She was pretty, twice married, and the mother of three children, and she had taught art history at Harvard and now ran her own art gallery. Growing up in Somerset, she had been in the same year in school as Nola, Nancy Hattaway, and a few other people I had met during my investigation. Listening to her tell the story of her life, I thought of her as a survivor. On the one hand there was Nola, murdered at the age of fifteen, and on the other there was Stephanie, who had lived and had a family and a career.

A few old photographs were scattered on the coffee table in her living room.

"I've been following the case from the beginning," she told us. "I remember the day Nola disappeared; I remember it all—just like all the girls my age who lived in Somerset then, I imagine. So when her body was found and Harry Quebert was arrested, I obviously felt very involved. What a story. I really liked your book, Mr Goldman. You described Nola so well. I felt like I'd got her back a little bit, thanks to you. Is it true they're going to make a movie?"

"Warner Brothers wants to buy the rights," I said.

She showed us the photographs: they were from a birthday party in 1973.

"Nola and I were very close," she said. "She was a wonderful girl. Everyone loved her in Somerset. Probably because people were moved by the image she and her father conveyed: the kind pastor, a widower, and his devoted daughter, always smiling, never complaining. I remember whenever I would act willfully, my mother would say: 'Why can't you be more like Nola? That poor girl—the good Lord took her mother, and yet she is still pleasant and appreciative.'"

"My God, how could I not have realized that her mother was dead?" I said. "And you say you liked my book? You should have been thinking what a pathetic excuse for a writer I was!"

"No, not at all. Quite the opposite, in fact. I even thought you had done it deliberately. Because I experienced the same thing with Nola."

"Tell me about that."

"One day something very strange happened, something that made me want to keep my distance from her."

March 1973

Stephanie Hendorf's parents ran the general store on the main street in Somerset. Sometimes Stephanie took Nola there after school, and the two of them would secretly stuff themselves with candy in the storeroom. That is what they were doing on this particular afternoon: Hidden behind bags of flour, they were gobbling so much candy that they got stomachaches, laughing with their hands over their mouths so no-one would hear them. But suddenly Stephanie noticed that there was something wrong with Nola. Her expression had changed; she was no longer listening.

"Nola? You O.K.?" she asked.

No reply. Stephanie repeated her question, and finally Nola said: "I ... I have to go home."

"Already? Why?"

"Mom wants me to go home."

Stephanie thought she must have misheard. "Your mother?"

Nola stood up in a panic. "I have to go home!" she repeated.

"But, Nola ... your mother is dead!"

Nola rushed toward the storeroom door, and when Stephanie attempted to hold her back, she turned around and shoved her.

"My mother!" she screamed, terrified. "You don't know what she'll do to me. When I'm wicked, I get punished."

And she ran away.

Stephanie was speechless. That evening she told her mother what had happened, but Mrs Hendorf didn't believe her. She stroked her hair tenderly.

"I don't know where you come up with these stories, darling. Come on now, stop being silly and go wash your hands—it's time for dinner. Your father's been working all day and he's hungry."

The next day in school, Nola seemed fine, as if nothing had happened. Stephanie did not dare say anything. But she kept worrying, so about ten days later she spoke directly to Nola's father about what had happened. She went to see him in his parish office, where he welcomed her very kindly, as always. He offered her a glass of lemonade, then listened attentively, thinking she must have come to see him as her pastor. But when she told him what she had witnessed, he did not believe her either.

"You must have misheard," he said.

"I know it sounds crazy, Reverend. But I swear it's true."

"But it makes no sense. Why would Nola come out with such garbage? Don't you know her mother is dead? Are you trying to hurt us?"

"No, but . . ."

David Kellergan wanted to end the conversation, but Stephanie persisted. Suddenly the pastor's face changed. She had never seen him like that before. The friendly minister vanished, and a somber-faced, frightening man took his place.

"I don't want you to mention this ever again!" he told her. "Not to me or to anyone else—do you hear me? If you say anything, I'll tell your parents that you're a little liar. And I will tell them that I caught you stealing from the church. I'll tell them you stole fifty dollars from me. You don't want to get in trouble, do you? So be a good girl."

Stephanie went silent. She fiddled with the photographs for a moment, before turning toward me.

"So I never spoke about this again," she said. "But I never forgot it either. Over time I convinced myself that I must have misheard, misunderstood, and that it was really nothing. And then your book came out, and I found her mother alive and abusing her. I can't tell you how that affected me. You have an incredible talent, Mr Goldman. When the newspapers started saying that what you wrote was false, I decided I had to contact you. Because I know you're telling the truth."

"But how can it be the truth?" I asked. "The mother had been dead for years."

"I know that. But I also know you're right."

"Do you think Nola was beaten by her father?"

"Well, that's what everyone thought. At school people noticed her bruises. But who would accuse our pastor of such a thing? In Somerset in 1975, you didn't get mixed up in other people's business. That was a different time."

"Is there anything else you can tell me?" I asked. "About Nola or what you read in the book?"

She thought for a moment. "No. Except that . . . it's almost funny to discover after all these years that it was Harry Quebert who Nola was in love with."

"What do you mean?"

"Well, I was such a naive little kid, you know. I didn't see Nola as much after that incident. But the summer she disappeared, I bumped into her quite often. During that summer I spent a lot of time working in my parents' store, which was across from the post office. And I kept seeing Nola there. She went to mail letters. I know that because I kept asking her who she was writing to, and she didn't want to say. One day she finally spilled the beans. She told me she was madly in love with someone, and was corresponding with him. She never told me who it was, though. I thought it must be Cody, this boy from our high school who was on the basketball team. I never managed to see the name on the envelope, but one time I did notice that the address was in Somerset. I wondered why she was bothering to mail letters to someone in Somerset when she lived there herself."

When we left Stephanie Larjinjiak's house, Gahalowood looked at me with a puzzled expression. "What's going on, writer?"

"I was about to ask you the same question. What do you think we should do now?"

"What we should have done a long time ago: go to Jackson, Alabama. You asked the right question at the beginning: What happened in Alabama?"

4

Sweet Home Alabama

"When you get to the end of the book, Marcus, give your reader a last-minute twist."

"Why?"

"Because you have to keep them on tenterhooks until the end. It's like when you're playing cards: You have to hold a few trump cards for the final part of the game."

Jackson, Alabama, October 28, 2008

So we went to Alabama.

Upon arriving at the airport in Mobile, we were met by a young state trooper, Philip Thomas, whom Gahalowood had contacted a few days earlier. He was standing in the arrivals lounge, ramrod straight in his uniform, eyes shaded by his cap. He greeted Gahalowood with deference, then, seeing me, he lifted his cap slightly.

"Haven't I seen you somewhere before?" he asked me. "On television?"

"Maybe," I replied.

"I'll help you out," Gahalowood said. "It's his book that's at center of all this fuss. Watch out for him. My life was perfectly calm and peaceful until I met him."

At Gahalowood's request, Officer Thomas had prepared a slim file on the Kellergans, which we looked through in a restaurant close to the airport.

"David J. Kellergan was born in Montgomery in 1923," Thomas recited. "He studied theology before becoming a minister and moving to Jackson to take over at the Mount Pleasant parish. He married Louisa Bonneville in 1955. They lived in a quiet neighborhood in the northern part of town. In 1960 Louisa Kellergan gave birth to a daughter, Nola. There's nothing more to say. They were just a peaceful, God-fearing Alabama family. Until the tragedy, in 1969."

"What tragedy?" asked Gahalowood.

"There was a fire. One night the house burned down, and Louisa Kellergan died."

Thomas's file included newspaper clippings from the time.

FATAL FIRE ON LOWER STREET

A woman died last night in a house fire on Lower Street. Firefighters say a lighted candle may have caused the tragedy. The house was completely destroyed. The deceased was the wife of a local pastor.

An extract from the police report indicated that on the night of August 30, 1969, around one in the morning, while David Kellergan was at the bedside of a dying parishioner, Louisa and Nola slept as the house burned. Coming back to the house, the pastor noticed smoke pouring from it and rushed inside. The second floor was already on fire. Nevertheless he managed to reach his daughter's room; he found her in bed, half-conscious. He carried her out to the yard, then wanted to go back inside to find his wife, but by then the fire had reached the staircase. Neighbors rushed over, alerted by screaming, but they were powerless to intervene. When the firefighters arrived, the whole second floor was ablaze: Flames burst through the windows and consumed the roof. Louisa Kellergan was found dead, asphyxiated. The police report concluded that a lighted candle had probably set fire to the curtains, before the fire spread quickly through the rest of the house. Mr Kellergan stated that his wife often lit a scented candle on her chest of drawers before going to bed.

"The date!" I gasped as I read the report. "Look at the date of the fire, Sergeant!"

"My God. August 30, 1969."

"The officer in charge of the investigation had his doubts about the father for a long time," Thomas said.

"How do you know?"

"I talked to him. His name is Edward Emerson. He's retired now. He spends his days working on his boat, in front of his house."

"Could we arrange to see him?" Gahalowood asked.

"I've already done that. He's expecting us at 3 p.m."

The retired detective Edward Emerson stood in front of his house, calmly sanding the hull of a wooden dinghy. The sky was threatening rain, so he raised his garage door so we could stand under it. He invited us to dig into the pack of beers that lay on the ground, and talked to us without interrupting his work, although he made it clear that we had his full attention. He told us about the fire, repeating what we had learned from reading the police report, without adding many more details.

"It was strange, that fire," he said in conclusion.

"Why do you say that?" I asked.

"We thought for a long time that David Kellergan started the fire intentionally to kill his wife. There's no evidence for his version of events: As if by a miracle, he arrives in time to save his daughter but just too late to save his wife. It was tempting to conclude that he started the fire himself. Particularly when he cleared out of town a few weeks later. The house burns down, his wife dies, and he disappears. There was something fishy about it, but we had no evidence against him at all."

"It's the same scenario with the disappearance of his daughter," Gahalowood observed. "In 1975 Nola disappeared. She was probably murdered, but there was no evidence to prove it irrefutably."

"What are you thinking, Sergeant?" I asked. "You think David Kellergan could have killed his wife and then his daughter? You think we got the wrong man?"

"If that's true, it will be a disaster," Gahalowood replied. "Who could we question here, Detective?"

"It's difficult to say. You could pay a visit to Mount Pleasant Church. They might have a register of parishioners; some of them will have known David Kellergan. But thirty-nine years after the event . . . It's going to be time-consuming to find them."

"We don't have any time," Gahalowood said bleakly.

"I know David Kellergan was quite close to some religious nuts who live on a commune an hour from here," Emerson said. "That's where he and his daughter stayed after the fire. I know that because I had to go there when I needed to talk to him for my investigation. He lived there until he left the state. Ask to speak to Pastor Lewis, if he's still there. He's their guru-type guy."

The Pastor Lewis mentioned by Emerson was the leader of the Community of the New Church of the Savior. We went to see him the next morning. Officer Thomas came to fetch us from the local Holiday Inn, where we had taken two rooms—one paid for by the state of New Hampshire, the other by me—and took us to a vast property, most of which consisted of farmland. Having gotten lost on a road bordered by cornfields, we came across a guy on a tractor who led us to a group of houses and pointed out where the pastor lived.

We were given a friendly welcome by an overweight woman. She left us in an office where, a few minutes later, Pastor Lewis joined us. I knew he had to be in his nineties, but he looked about twenty years younger than that. He seemed like a nice enough guy—very different from Emerson's description.

"Police?" he asked, shaking hands with each of us.

"State police of New Hampshire and Alabama," Gahalowood replied. "We're investigating the death of Nola Kellergan."

"Seems like that's all anyone talks about lately."

While he shook my hand, he stared at me for a moment and said, "Hang on, aren't you . . ."

"Yes, it's him," replied a clearly irritated Gahalowood.

"So . . . what can I do for you, gentlemen?"

Gahalowood began the interrogation.

"Pastor Lewis, unless I'm mistaken, you knew Nola Kellergan."

"Yes. Well, it was really her parents I knew. Lovely people. Very close to our community."

"What is 'your community'?"

"We're Pentecostals, Sergeant. Nothing more than that. We have Christian ideals, and we share them. Yes, I know some people say we're a sect. We're visited by welfare services twice a year so they can check that our children are properly educated, well fed, and not mistreated. They also come to see if we have weapons or if we're white supremacists. It's becoming ridiculous. All our children go to the local high school; I have never held a rifle in my life; and I am actively involved in Barack Obama's election campaign. So what would you like to know?"

"What happened in 1969," Gahalowood said.

"*Apollo 11* landed on the moon," Lewis replied. "An important victory for America in its ongoing struggle with the Soviets."

"You know perfectly well what we're talking about. The fire at the Kellergans' house. What really happened? How did Louisa Kellergan die?"

Although I had not spoken a single word, Lewis stared at me for a long time and then spoke directly to me.

"I've seen you on T.V. a lot lately, Mr Goldman. I think you're a good writer, but how did you mess up so badly about Louisa? I imagine that's why you're here, isn't it? Your book's been discredited, and—let's call a spade a spade—I imagine you're shitting your pants. Am I right? What are you looking for here? Something to back up your lies?"

"The truth," I said.

He smiled sadly.

"The truth? But which one, Mr Goldman? God's truth or man's truth?"

"Yours. What is your truth about the death of Louisa Kellergan? Did David Kellergan kill his wife?"

Pastor Lewis got up from his chair and went to close the door to his office, which had been left ajar. He then stood by the window and looked outside. This scene immediately reminded me of our visit to Chief Pratt. Gahalowood indicated to me that he would take over the interrogation.

"David was such a good man," Lewis finally said with a sigh.

"Was?" said Gahalowood.

"I haven't seen him in thirty-nine years."

"Did he beat his daughter?"

"No! No, he was a man with a pure heart. A man of faith. When he arrived in Jackson, Mount Pleasant Church was always empty. Six months later it was full every Sunday morning. He could never have caused the slightest harm to his wife or to his daughter."

"So who were they?" Gahalowood asked gently. "Who were the Kellergans?"

Pastor Lewis called his wife. He asked her to make tea with honey for everyone. He came back and sat in his chair, then looked at each of us in turn. His expression was tender and his voice warm.

"Close your eyes, gentlemen," he told us. "Close your eyes. It is 1953, and we are in Jackson, Alabama."

One day in early 1953, a young pastor from Montgomery entered run-down Mount Pleasant Church, in the center of Jackson. It was a stormy day. Rain was pouring from the sky, and a violent wind was uprooting trees. A newspaper vendor cowered beneath a store window's canopy as his wares flew through the air; passersby ran for cover.

The pastor pushed open the church door, which banged shut behind him. Inside, it was dark and extremely cold. He walked slowly up the aisle. Rain came in through holes in the roof, forming puddles on the floor. The place was deserted; there were no believers there, not the slightest sign of habitation. There were no altar candles, only a few wax stubs. He moved toward the altar. Then, seeing the pulpit, he placed his foot on the first step of the wooden staircase, ready to climb it.

"Don't do that!"

The voice, bursting from the void, made him jump. He turned around and saw a short, plump man emerge from the darkness.

"Don't do that," he repeated. "The stairs are worm-eaten. You could break your neck. Are you the Reverend David Kellergan?"

"Yes," replied Kellergan, feeling ill at ease.

"Welcome to your new parish, Reverend. I'm Pastor Jeremy Lewis; I run the Community of the New Church of the Savior. I was asked to look after this congregation when your predecessor left. It's all yours now."

The two men shook hands warmly. Kellergan shivered.

"You must be freezing!" Lewis said. "Come with me—there's a coffee shop on the corner."

That was how Jeremy Lewis first met David Kellergan. Sitting in the coffee shop, they waited for the storm to pass.

"I'd heard that Mount Pleasant wasn't doing well," Kellergan said, somewhat disconcerted, "but I have to admit I wasn't expecting that."

"Yes. I won't hide the fact that you're about to take over a parish in a pitiful state. The parishioners no longer attend services or make donations. The building is in disrepair. There's a lot of work to do. I hope you're not discouraged."

"It would take a lot more than that to discourage me, Pastor Lewis."

Lewis smiled, already under the spell of his charismatic colleague.

"Are you married?" he asked.

"No, I'm still single."

The new pastor spent six months visiting every household in the parish, introducing himself and persuading people to return to church on Sunday mornings. He raised funds for a new roof and, because he had not served in Korea, took part in the war effort by setting up a program to help veterans find jobs. Then some volunteers helped to refurbish the parish hall. Little by little, community spirit returned; Mount Pleasant Church regained its luster; and David Kellergan was soon considered a rising star in Jackson. Local bigwigs and members of the congregation saw a future for him in politics. A position in local government seemed his for the taking, and perhaps afterward a statewide one. Who knew—he might even be a senator.

One night in late 1953, David Kellergan went to eat dinner at a small restaurant close to the church. He sat at the counter, as he often did. Next to him a young woman he hadn't noticed turned around and smiled as if she recognized him.

"Hello, Reverend," she said.

He smiled back somewhat awkwardly.

"Excuse me, ma'am, but do we know each other?"

She laughed, throwing back her blond hair.

"I'm a member of your congregation. My name is Louisa. Louisa Bonneville."

Embarrassed at his failure to recognize her, he blushed, and she laughed even harder. He lit a cigarette in an effort to compose himself.

"Could I have one?" she asked.

He handed her the pack.

"You won't tell anyone I smoke, will you, Reverend?" Louisa said.

He smiled. "I promise."

Louisa was the daughter of a prominent member of the congregation. She and David began dating. Everyone thought they made a wonderful couple. They were married in the summer of 1955. Both of them were so happy. They wanted lots of children, at least six—three boys and three girls, cheerful, laughing children who would bring life into the house on Lower Street, where the Kellergans had just moved. But Louisa was having trouble getting pregnant. She consulted several specialists, unsuccessfully at first. Finally, in the late summer of 1959, her doctor gave her the good news: She was going to have a baby.

On April 12, 1960, Louisa Kellergan gave birth to her first and only child.

"It's a girl," the doctor told David Kellergan, who had been pacing the hospital corridor.

"A girl!" Kellergan exclaimed, his face beaming.

He rushed to join his wife, who was holding the newborn in her arms. They hugged and looked at the baby, whose eyes were still closed. You could already see she would have blond hair like her mother.

"What do you think of the name Nola?" Louisa asked her husband.

The pastor thought this was a very pretty name.

"Welcome, Nola," he said to his daughter.

In the years that followed, the Kellergans were often held up as a model family: the goodness of the father, the sweetness of the mother and their beautiful little daughter. David Kellergan threw himself into his work. He was full of ideas and always enjoyed the support of his wife. On Sundays in summer they would regularly picnic at the Community of the New Church of the Savior; David Kellergan had been close friends with its pastor, Jeremy Lewis, since they first met on that stormy day almost ten years earlier.

"I've never met anyone who seemed happier than the Kellergans," Pastor Lewis said. "David and Louisa were madly in love. It was incredible, as if the Lord Himself had made them just so they could love each other. And they were excellent parents. Nola was an extraordinary little girl, lively and gorgeous. It was the kind of family that made you want to have children and gave you undying hope in humanity. It was wonderful to see."

"But it all went wrong," Gahalowood prompted.

"Yes."

"How?"

There was a long silence. The pastor grimaced in discomfort. He got up and walked restlessly around the room.

"Why do we have to talk about all that?" he asked. "It was so long ago . . ."

"Reverend Lewis, what happened in 1969?"

The pastor turned toward a large cross on the wall and said: "We exorcized her. But it didn't go as planned."

"What?" Gahalowood said, taken aback. "What are you talking about?"

"The little girl . . . little Nola. We exorcized her. But it was a disaster. I think there was just too much evil in her."

"Please explain what you mean."

"The fire . . . the night of the fire. It's true that David Kellergan went to see a dying parishioner and that when he got back at 1 a.m. he found the house in flames, but—I don't know how to say this—things didn't happen quite the way David Kellergan told the police."

August 30, 1969

In a deep sleep, Jeremy Lewis did not hear the doorbell ring. His wife, Matilda, answered the door and then came to wake him. It was 4 a.m.

"Jeremy, wake up!" she said, her eyes bright with tears. "Something terrible has happened. David Kellergan is here . . . There was a fire. Louisa is . . . she's dead!"

Lewis leaped out of bed. He found the pastor in the living room, weeping and wild-eyed with grief. His daughter was with him. Matilda escorted Nola to the spare bedroom so she could sleep.

"My God! David, what happened?" Lewis asked.

"There was a fire. The house burned down. Louisa is dead. She's dead!"

David Kellergan could no longer contain himself. Slumped in a chair, he let the tears roll down his cheeks. His whole body trembled. Jeremy Lewis gave him a large glass of whiskey.

"And Nola? Is she alright?" he asked.

"Yes, thank God. The doctors examined her. She escaped without a scratch."

Jeremy Lewis's eyes welled up with tears.

"My God . . . David, what a tragedy. What an awful tragedy!"

He put his hands on his friend's shoulders to comfort him.

"I don't understand what happened, Jeremy. I had gone to see a member of the congregation who was dying. When I got back, the house was on fire. The flames were enormous."

"Was it you who saved Nola?"

"Jeremy . . . I have to tell you something."

"What is it? You can tell me anything, David—you know that."

"Jeremy . . . when I got home, there were those flames. The entire second floor was on fire. I wanted to go upstairs to save Louisa, but the staircase was already ablaze. I couldn't do anything. Nothing!"

"Heavens above! And Nola?"

David Kellergan choked.

"I told the police that I went upstairs and carried Nola from the house, but that I couldn't go back for my wife . . ."

"And that's not true?"

"No, Jeremy. When I got home, the house was burning. And Nola . . . Nola was on the porch, singing."

The next morning David Kellergan went to see his daughter alone in the spare bedroom of Jeremy Lewis's house. First of all he wanted to explain to her that her mother was dead.

"Sweetie," he said, "do you remember last night? There was a fire— you remember?"

"Yes."

"Something very serious happened. Something very serious and very sad that's going to make you upset. Mommy was in her bedroom when the fire started, and she wasn't able to get out of the house."

"Yes, I know. Mommy is dead," said Nola. "She was wicked. So I set fire to her bedroom."

"What? What did you say?"

"I went into her room. She was asleep. I thought she looked wicked. Wicked Mommy! Wicked! I wanted her to die. So I picked up the box of matches on her chest of drawers and I set fire to the curtains."

Nola smiled at her father, who asked her to repeat what she had said. Nola repeated it. David Kellergan heard the floorboards creak, and he turned around. Pastor Lewis, who had come to look in on Nola, had overheard their conversation.

They went into the office and closed the door.

"Nola set fire to your house? Nola killed her mother?" Lewis said in disbelief.

"Shh. Not so loud, Jeremy! She . . . she . . . says she set fire to the house, but . . . God, surely that can't be true!"

"Does Nola have demons?" Lewis asked.

"Demons? No, no! It's true that her mother and I sometimes noticed that she acted a little strangely, but it was never anything really bad."

"Nola killed her mother, David. Do you realize how serious this is?"

David Kellergan was trembling and felt sick to his stomach. Jeremy Lewis gave him a wastepaper basket so he could throw up.

"Don't tell the police, Jeremy! Please, I'm begging you."

"But this is serious, David."

"Don't say anything! Please, in the name of God, don't say anything. If the police find out about this, Nola could end up in a reformatory or God knows what. She's only nine years old . . ."

"Then we have to cure her," Lewis said. "Nola is possessed by the Devil. She has to be cured."

"No, Jeremy! Not that!"

"I have to exorcize her, David. It's the only way to deliver her from evil."

"I exorcized her," Pastor Lewis told us. "For several days we attempted to force the demon from her body."

I shook my head in disgust.

Lewis looked at me intently. "Why are you so skeptical? Nola was not Nola: The Devil had taken possession of her body."

"What did you do to her?" Gahalowood asked roughly.

"Normally prayers are enough, Sergeant."

"Let me guess: They weren't enough in this case."

"The Devil was strong. So we submerged her head in a tub of holy water to finish him off."

"The waterboard torture," I said.

"But that wasn't enough either. So to bring down the Devil and force him to abandon Nola's body, we beat her."

"You beat a little girl?" Gahalowood shouted.

"No, not the little girl—the Devil!"

"You're crazy, Lewis."

"We had to liberate her! And we thought we had succeeded. But Nola started having some . . . problems. She and her father stayed with us for a while, and she became uncontrollable. She started seeing her mother."

"You mean Nola was hallucinating?" Gahalowood asked.

"Worse than that. She developed a sort of split personality. She would become her mother, and she would punish herself for what she had done. One day I found her screaming in the bathroom. She had filled the bathtub and was grabbing herself by her hair and shoving her own head into the cold water. It couldn't go on like that. So David decided to move away. Far away. He said he had to leave Jackson, leave Alabama. He thought the distance, coupled with time, would help Nola to get better. Then I heard that St James's in Somerset was looking for a new pastor, and David did not hesitate for a second. That was how he came to move to New Hampshire."

3

Election Day

"Your life will be punctuated by a succession of major events. Mention them in your books, Marcus. Because if the books turn out to be bad, they will at least have the merit of recording a few pages of history."

Extract from the Concord Herald, *November 5, 2008*

BARACK OBAMA ELECTED 44TH PRESIDENT OF THE UNITED STATES

Democratic nominee Barack Obama has won the presidential election against Republican nominee John McCain, and becomes the 44th President of the United States. New Hampshire, which voted for John Kerry in 2004 [...]

November 5, 2008

The day after the election, New York was in a state of jubilation. People celebrated Obama's victory in the streets until late at night. I watched the festivities on television in my office, where I had been living for three days.

That morning Denise arrived at the office at 8 a.m., carrying an Obama sweatshirt, an Obama pin, an Obama cup, and a pack of Obama bumper stickers. "Oh, here you are, Marcus!" she said as she passed my door and saw the lights on. "Did you go out last night? What a victory, huh? I brought you some bumper stickers as mementos." While she talked to me, she placed her Obama paraphernalia on her desk, turned on the coffee maker, and unplugged the answering machine, then entered my office. When she saw the state the room was in, she stared wide-eyed and cried out: "My God, Marcus, what the hell happened here?"

I was sitting in my chair and looking at one of the walls, which I had spent half the night covering with my notes and diagrams from the investigation. I had listened to the recordings of Harry, Nancy Hattaway, and Robert Quinn over and over again.

"There's some aspect of this case that I just don't understand," I said. "It's driving me crazy."

"Were you here all night?"

"Yes."

"Oh, Marcus. And I thought you must be out somewhere enjoying yourself. How long is it since you last had any fun? Are you worrying about your book?"

"I'm worrying about what I discovered last week."

"What's that?"

"I'm not sure—that's the problem. Denise, what do you do when you discover that someone you have always admired has betrayed you and lied to you?"

She thought for a moment, and then said: "It happened to me. With my first husband. I found him in bed with my best friend."

"What did you do?"

"Nothing. I didn't say anything. I didn't do anything. It was in the Hamptons. We'd gone for the weekend to an oceanfront hotel with my best friend and her husband. On Saturday evening I went for a walk on the beach. Alone, because my husband had told me he was tired. I came back much earlier than I'd intended to: Walking on my own turned out not to be much fun. I went up to our room, opened the door with my key card, and there they were in bed. He was on top of her, my best friend. It's funny . . . with those key cards you can enter a room without making any noise. They didn't see me or hear me. I watched them for a few moments—watched my husband shaking his butt like crazy to make her moan like a little dog—and then I silently left the room, went to vomit in the lobby bathroom, and started off on my walk again. I came back an hour later: My husband was at the hotel bar, drinking gin and having a good laugh with my best friend's husband. I didn't say anything. We all ate dinner together. I pretended nothing had happened. That night he slept like a log; he told me it was exhausting, doing nothing. I didn't say anything. I didn't say anything for six months."

"And in the end you asked for a divorce . . . ?"

"No. He left me for her."

"Do you regret not doing anything?"

"Every day."

"So I should do something. Is that what you mean?"

"Yes. Do something, Marcus. Don't be a pathetic dope like I was."

I smiled.

"You're definitely not a dope, Denise."

"Marcus, what happened last week? What did you discover?"

Five days earlier

On October 31, Dr Gideon Alkanor, one of the most respected child psychiatrists on the East Coast and a man Gahalowood knew well, confirmed what now seemed obvious: Nola had been suffering from serious psychological problems.

The day after our return from Jackson, Gahalowood and I drove down to Boston, where Alkanor met us in his office at Children's Hospital. On the basis of the evidence that had been sent to him the day before, he believed it was possible to diagnose infantile psychosis.

"So what does that mean in layman's terms?" Gahalowood asked impatiently.

Alkanor took off his glasses and slowly cleaned the lenses while he considered what he would say. Finally he turned toward me.

"It means that I think you are right, Mr Goldman. I read your book a few weeks ago. Considering what you describe and the evidence that Perry has provided me with, I would say that Nola sometimes lost her grip on reality. It was probably during one of those fits that she set fire to her mother's bedroom. That night of August 30, 1969, Nola had a skewed view of reality: She wanted to kill her mother, but for her, at that particular moment, killing meant nothing. She performed an act without any understanding of its significance. On top of that first traumatic incident, there was also the exorcism, the memory of which could easily trigger the split-personality fits in which Nola becomes the mother she killed. And that's where it gets complicated. When Nola lost touch with reality, the memory of her mother and what she did to her came back to haunt her."

For a moment I was stunned. "So you mean she—"

Alkanor nodded before I could finish, and said: "Nola beat herself during these breakdowns."

"But what could set off these fits?" Gahalowood asked.

"Probably major emotional upheavals: stress, sadness, and so on. What you describe in your book, Mr Goldman: the meeting with Harry Quebert, where she falls head over heels in love, then his rejection of her, which leads to her suicide attempt. I would say that's almost a classic pattern. When her emotions snowballed, her psychological defenses broke down. And when that happened, she saw her mother again, come back to punish her for what she'd done."

*

All that time Nola and her mother had been the same person. We now needed David Kellergan's confirmation, so on November 1, Gahalowood and I went to 245 Terrace Avenue, along with Travis Dawn, whom we had informed of what we had discovered in Alabama, and whose presence Gahalowood had requested in order to reassure David Kellergan.

When he found us standing at his door, he immediately told us: "I have nothing to say to you. Not to you or to anyone."

"I'm the one with things to say," Gahalowood calmly explained. "I know what happened in Alabama in August 1969. I know about the fire, I know everything."

"You don't know anything."

"You should listen to them," Travis said. "Let us in, David. It would be better to talk about this inside."

Finally David Kellergan let us in and led us to the kitchen. He poured himself coffee, not offering us any, and sat at the table. Gahalowood and Travis sat opposite him, and I remained standing, farther back.

"So what do you want?" Kellergan demanded.

"I went to Jackson," Gahalowood replied. "I talked to Jeremy Lewis. I know what Nola did."

"Shut your mouth!"

"She was suffering from infantile psychosis. She had schizophrenic episodes. On August 30, 1969, she set fire to her mother's room."

"No!" David Kellergan yelled. "You're lying!"

"You found Nola on the porch that night. She was singing. You finally understood what had happened. You exorcized her. You thought you were helping her. But it was a disaster. She began having split-personality episodes in which she would attempt to punish herself. So you went far away from Alabama. You moved north, hoping to leave your ghosts behind. But the ghost of your wife pursued you, because she still haunted Nola's mind."

A tear rolled down Kellergan's cheek.

"She would have fits sometimes," he said hoarsely. "There was nothing I could do. She beat herself. She was the daughter and the mother. She hit herself, and she begged herself to stop."

"So you blasted music and locked yourself in the garage because you couldn't bear to watch, to hear."

"Yes! Yes! It was unbearable! I didn't know what to do. My daughter, my sweet daughter, she was so sick."

He began to sob. Travis looked on, horrified by what he was hearing.

"Why didn't you get her professional help?" Gahalowood asked.

"I was afraid they would take her away from me. That they would lock her up. And then, over time, there were fewer fits. I even thought, for a few years, that her memory of the fire was fading; I thought it was possible that her fits would stop altogether one day. She was getting better and better. Until the summer of 1975. Suddenly, and I had no idea why, she started having these violent fits again."

"Because of Harry," Gahalowood said. "The meeting with Harry was emotionally overwhelming for her."

"That was a terrible summer," Kellergan said. "I could sense the fits coming. I could almost predict them. It was so horrible. She hit herself with a metal ruler on her breasts and her fingers. She filled a tub with water and shoved her head into it while begging her mother to stop. And her mother, in Nola's voice, would yell the most hideous things."

"The water-torture—you put her through that during the exorcism?"

"Jeremy Lewis swore it was the only solution. I'd heard that Lewis performed exorcisms, but he and I had never discussed it. And then suddenly he was saying that the Devil had taken possession of Nola's body and he had to liberate her. I only agreed to it so he wouldn't turn her in. Jeremy was a madman, but what else could I do? I had no choice—she could have gone to jail!"

"Tell us about Nola's running away from home," Gahalowood said.

"She sometimes ran away. She was gone for a whole week once. It was at the end of July, 1975. What should I have done? Call the police? And tell them what? That my daughter was going insane? I decided to wait until the end of the week before alerting the police. For a week I searched everywhere, day and night. And then she came back."

"And what happened on August 30 of that year?"

"She had a very bad fit. I had never seen her in a state like that before. I tried to calm her, but nothing worked. So I hid out in the garage and worked on that damn motorcycle. I turned the music up as loud as possible. I stayed there for most of the afternoon. You know the rest: When I went to look for her again, she wasn't there. I went out to look around the neighborhood, and then I heard that a girl had been seen, covered in blood, near Side Creek. I realized the situation was serious."

"What did you think had happened?"

"To be honest, I first assumed that Nola had run away and that the blood was from the beatings she had given herself. I thought Deborah Cooper had perhaps seen Nola in the middle of one of her fits. It was August 30, after all: the anniversary of the fire."

"Had she suffered fits before on that date?"

"No."

"So what could have triggered such a violent fit?"

David Kellergan hesitated for a moment before replying. Travis Dawn realized he needed encouragement.

"If you know something, David, you have to tell us. It's very important. Do it for Nola."

"When I went into her room that day, and she wasn't there, I found an envelope on her bed. It was opened, her name was on it, and inside was a letter. I think that letter caused the fit. It was a break-up letter."

"A letter?" Travis exclaimed. "You never told us about that letter!"

"Because it was written by a man who, judging from the way he wrote, was clearly too old to be going out with my daughter. What else could I have done? Should I have let the whole town think that Nola was a slut? I was sure the police were going to find her and bring her home. And that I would be able to cure her for good."

"And who was the author of the letter?" Gahalowood asked.

"Harry Quebert."

We were all struck dumb. Kellergan stood up and left the room for a while before returning with a shoebox full of letters.

"I found these after her disappearance, hidden in her room, under a loose floorboard. Nola had been corresponding with Harry Quebert."

Gahalowood picked a letter at random and quickly read it. "How do you know it was Harry Quebert?" he asked. "These letters aren't signed."

"Because . . . because these letters are in his book."

I rummaged through the box. The old man was right: The letters were those in *The Origin of Evil.* They were all there: the letters about the two of them, the letters to her at Charlotte's Hill. They were written in the same clear, perfect prose as the letters from the manuscript. I was almost frightened.

"And this is the last letter," said Mr Kellergan, handing an envelope to Gahalowood.

He read it, then gave it to me.

My darling,

This is my final letter. These are my last words. I am writing you to say goodbye.

From today on there will be no more "us."

Lovers separate and never find each other again, and that is how love stories end.

I will miss you, my darling. I will miss you so much.

I am crying. Inside, I am burning.

We will never see each other again. I will miss you so much. I hope you will be happy.

You and me: that was a dream, I think. And now we must wake up.

I will miss you all my life.

Goodbye. I love you as I will never love anyone again.

"It's the same as the letter on the last page of *The Origin of Evil*," Kellergan told us.

I nodded. I recognized it. I was dumbfounded.

"How long have you known that Harry and Nola were corresponding?" Gahalowood asked him.

"I realized it only a few weeks ago. I saw *The Origin of Evil* in the supermarket. It had just gone back on sale. I bought a copy. I don't know why. I needed to read that book, so I could try to understand. I quickly began to feel I'd already read some of those sentences before. Strange how memory works. I thought about it for a while, and then it suddenly came to me: These were the letters I had found hidden in Nola's room. I had not even touched them in all these years, but somehow they had remained engraved in my memory. I took out the shoebox and reread them, and that was when I understood. That damn letter made my daughter crazy with grief, Sergeant. Luther Caleb might have killed Nola, but to my mind Quebert is just as guilty. Were it not for that fit, she might never have run away from home and bumped into Caleb."

"So that's why you went to see Harry at his motel," Gahalowood said.

"Yes. For thirty-three years I had wondered who had written those letters. And all that time, the answer had been sitting in every bookstore in America. I went to the Sea Side Motel, and we had an argument. I was so angry that I came back here to get my shotgun, but when I got back to the motel he had disappeared. I think I would have killed him. He knew how fragile she was, and he pushed her to the edge."

"What?" I gasped. "What do you mean, *he knew*?"

"He knew everything about Nola! Everything!" shouted David Kellergan.

"You mean Harry knew about her psychotic episodes?"

"Yes. I knew Nola sometimes went to his house with the typewriter. I didn't know about the rest, obviously. I even thought it was good for her that she knew a writer. It was summer vacation, and this was keeping her busy. Until that damn writer came to pick a fight with me because he thought my wife was beating Nola."

"Harry came to see you that summer?"

"Yes. In the middle of August. Just before she disappeared."

August 15, 1975

It was midafternoon. From his office window the Reverend David Kellergan noticed a black Chevrolet pulling into the church parking lot. He watched as Harry Quebert got out of the car and walked quickly toward the main entrance of the church. He wondered what was behind his visit: Harry had never been to church since his arrival in Somerset. He heard knocking at the front door, then footsteps in the corridor, and then he saw Harry in the office doorway.

"Hello, Harry," he said. "What a pleasant surprise."

"Hello, Reverend. Am I disturbing you?"

"Not in the least. Please, come in."

Harry entered, closing the door behind him.

"Is everything alright?" the pastor asked. "You look unhappy."

"I came to talk to you about Nola . . ."

"Oh yes, I've been meaning to thank you. I know she often goes to see you, and she always seems very happy when she comes back. I hope she hasn't been bothering you. Thanks to you, she hasn't been bored at all this summer."

Harry's expression did not change.

"She came this morning," he said. "She was in tears. She told me all about your wife . . ."

The minister went pale.

"My wife? What did she say?"

"That your wife beats her! That she shoves her head in a tub of ice-cold water!"

"Harry, I—"

"It's over, Reverend. I know everything."

"It's more complicated than that . . . I—"

"More complicated? Are you going to try to convince me that there's a good reason why she is beaten like that? I'm going to call the cops, Reverend. I'm going to tell them everything."

"No, Harry . . . you can't—"

"Oh yes, I can. What do you think? That I wouldn't dare denounce you because you're a man of the cloth? You're nothing as far as I'm concerned! What kind of man lets his wife beat his daughter?"

"Harry, please, listen to me. I think there's been a terrible misunderstanding. We need to speak about this calmly."

"I don't know what Nola had told Harry," Kellergan explained to us. "He was not the first person who had suspected that there was something strange going on. But until Harry got involved, I only had to deal with Nola's friends, and it was easy to evade children's questions. This was different. So I had to admit to him that Nola's mother existed only in her head. I begged him not to talk to anyone about it, but then he started sticking his nose into what was not his business, telling me what to do with my own daughter. He wanted me to get her professional help! I told him to get lost . . . And then, two weeks later, she disappeared."

"And after that, you avoided Harry for the next thirty-three years," I said. "Because you were the only people who knew Nola's secret."

"She was my only child—don't you see? I wanted people to have a good memory of her; I didn't want them to think she was crazy. And anyway she wasn't crazy! Just fragile. And if the police had known the truth about her fits, they would never have searched so hard for her. They would just have said she was crazy and that she'd run away from home."

Gahalowood turned to me. "What are we to make of this, writer?"

"It means that Harry lied to us. He wasn't waiting for her at the motel. He wanted to break up with her. He knew all along that he was going to break up with Nola. He never intended to elope with her. On August 30, 1975, she received a final letter from Harry, telling her he had left without her."

Following this meeting with David Kellergan, Gahalowood and I returned to the state police headquarters in Concord to compare the letter with the final page of the manuscript that had been buried with Nola: They were identical.

"He planned it all!" I shouted. "He knew he was going to leave her. He knew from the beginning."

Gahalowood nodded. "When she suggested they run away, he knew he wouldn't go with her. He couldn't imagine being stuck with a fifteen-year-old girl."

"But she read the manuscript," I pointed out.

"Of course, but she thought it was a novel. She didn't realize Harry was writing the truth about their love affair, and that the ending was already written: Harry didn't want her. Stephanie Larjinjiak told us they were corresponding and that Nola waited for the mailman to come each day. On Saturday morning, the day she disappeared, the day she imagined she was going to leave for a happier life with the man of her dreams, she waits by the mailbox for the last time. She wants to make sure there is not one final, forgotten letter that might compromise their elopement by revealing important information. Instead she finds that note from him, telling her it's over."

Gahalowood examined the envelope that contained the final letter.

"There's an address on the envelope, but no stamp or postmark," he said. "It must have been dropped directly into the mailbox."

"By Harry, you mean?"

"Yes. He probably left it there at night, before going away. I would guess he did it at the last minute, on the Friday night. So that she wouldn't come to the motel. So she would understand they wouldn't be meeting. On Saturday, when she finds his note, she goes back into the house in a rage, she breaks down, she has a terrible fit, and begins punishing herself. Her father panics and locks himself in his garage again. When she comes to again, Nola makes the connection with the manuscript. She wants an explanation. She takes the manuscript and starts walking to the motel. She hopes it isn't true, she hopes Harry will be there. But on the way she runs into Luther. And it all goes wrong."

"But then why would Harry go back to Somerset the day after her disappearance?"

"He finds out Nola has disappeared. He'd left her that letter: He panics. I'm sure he's worried about her, and probably feels guilty, but more than anything I imagine he's scared that other people will get their hands on that letter, or on the manuscript, and that he'll get in trouble. He would rather be in Somerset so he can see how the situation develops, and perhaps also so he can recover any evidence he thinks might be compromising."

We had to find Harry. It was essential that I talk to him. Why had he told me that he was waiting for Nola when in reality he had written her a farewell letter? Gahalowood carried out a remote search for Harry, using credit card and telephone records. But his credit card had not been used, and his cell phone was evidently turned off. By examining the border patrol records, we discovered that he had crossed into Canada at Derby Line, Vermont.

"So he's gone to Canada," Gahalowood said. "Why Canada?"

"He thinks it's writers' heaven," I said. "In the manuscript he left for me, *The Seagulls of Somerset*, he ends up there with Nola."

"Yes, but that's a work of fiction. Not only is Nola dead, but it seems like he never even intended to elope with her. And yet he leaves you this manuscript, in which he and Nola end up in Canada. So where is the truth?"

"I don't understand anything!" I said. "Why the hell has he run away?"

"Because he has something to hide. But we don't know what, exactly."

That evening I told Gahalowood I was catching a flight to New York the next day.

"What the hell . . . ? You're going back to New York? Are you crazy, writer? We've almost nailed this!"

I smiled. "I'm not abandoning you, Sergeant. But it's time."

"Time for what?"

"Time to vote. America has an appointment with history."

At noon on November 5, 2008, while New York was still celebrating the election of the first black president in American history, I had a lunch meeting with Barnaski at the Pierre Hotel. The Democratic victory had put him in a good mood: "I love black people!" he told me. "I love them. If you get invited to the White House, take me with you. Anyway, what's your important news?"

I told him what I had discovered about Nola and the diagnosis of infantile psychosis, and his face lit up.

"So those scenes where you describe Nola being abused by her mother—she was doing it herself?"

"Yes."

"That's terrific!" he roared over the noise of restaurant. "Your book is the pioneer of a new genre! The reader is implicated in the insanity because the character of the mother exists without actually existing. You're a genius, Goldman! A genius!"

"No, I just got it wrong. I let Harry pull the wool over my eyes."

"Harry knew about this?"

"Yes. And now he's disappeared off the face of the earth."

"What do you mean?"

"He's nowhere to be found. Apparently he crossed the border into Canada. The only clues he left me are a cryptic message and an unpublished manuscript about Nola."

"Do you own the rights?"

"I'm sorry?"

"Do you own the rights to the unpublished manuscript? I'll buy them from you!"

"Goddamn it, Roy. You're completely missing the point!"

"I beg your pardon. I was only asking."

"There's something we're missing here. Something I haven't understood yet. This whole story of infantile psychosis, Harry disappearing. There's a piece of the puzzle missing, I know, but I can't think what it could be."

"You need to calm down, Marcus. Believe me, getting anxious about this is not going to help. Go see Dr Freud and ask him for some pills to help you relax. For my part I'm going to contact the media. We'll put together a press release about the kid's illness; we'll make out that we knew all about it from the beginning, and that the truth was your big surprise, a way of demonstrating that the truth is not always what it seems. All those who panned you will have egg on their faces, and people will say you're a creative genius. And of course everyone will be talking about your book again, and sales will surge. Because, with a story like this, even those who had no intention of buying the book won't be able to resist. They'll be burning with curiosity to see how you represented the mother. Goldman, you're a genius. Lunch is on me!"

I frowned. "I'm not convinced, Roy. I'd like some time to dig more deeply into this."

"But you're never convinced, Marcus! We don't have time to 'dig more deeply,' as you put it. You're a poet: You think the passing of time has meaning. But the passing of time is either money earned or money lost. And I'm a big supporter of the former. Nevertheless, as you are probably aware, we now have a handsome, black, and very popular new president, and by my reckoning we will be hearing all about him—and nothing but him—for at least the next week. So there's no point in our trying to communicate with the media about anything else. The best we could hope for is a paragraph at the bottom of page seven. So

I'll give you a week to get this worked out. Unless, of course, some southerners in pointy hats pick off our new president, which would keep us from getting front-page coverage for about a month. Yup, at least a month if that happens. My God, what a disaster that would be: A month from now we'd be into Christmas, and no-one would pay any attention to our story! So anyway, a week from today we'll feed the media the story of infantile psychosis. Newspaper supplements and all that jazz. If I had more time I'd rush out a book for parents. You know the kind I mean: *Detecting Infantile Psychosis: How to Prevent Your Child from Becoming the Next Nola Kellergan and Setting Fire to You in Your Sleep.* Now *that* would be a bestseller! But anyway, we don't have time."

So I had only one week before Barnaski would tell all. One week to try to understand what still eluded me. Four days passed, four fruitless days. I called Gahalowood constantly, but the investigation appeared to be at a standstill. Then on the night of the fifth day, November 10, something happened that would change the whole ballgame. It was just after midnight. During a routine patrol, Police Officer Dean Forsyth began chasing a car on the Montburry–Somerset road, having seen it run a red light at far above the speed limit. This might easily have led to nothing more than a ticket if the suspicious behavior of the driver—who seemed highly agitated and was sweating profusely—hadn't caught the officer's attention.

"Where are you coming from, sir?" Officer Forsyth asked.

"Montburry."

"What were you doing there?"

"I was . . . I was with friends."

"Their names, please?"

Seeing the glimmer of panic in the driver's eyes as he hesitated over his answer, Officer Forsyth shone his flashlight on the man's face and noticed a scratch on his cheek.

"What happened to your face?"

"It was a low branch on a tree. I didn't see it."

The officer was unconvinced.

"Why were you driving so fast?"

"I . . . I'm sorry. I was in a rush. You're right, I shouldn't have—"

"Have you been drinking, sir?"

"No."

"Would you mind stepping out of the vehicle? "

A Breathalyzer test was negative, and everything seemed to be in order; the officer didn't see any empty medicine bottles or similar junk that was usually strewn across the backseats of cars belonging to drug addicts. And yet he had a hunch. Something in this man's behavior—the way he was too nervous and yet too calm at the same time—made him want to investigate further. And then he noticed, as the man climbed back into the car, what had hitherto escaped his attention: his hands were dirty, his pants soaked, and his shoes covered in mud.

"Please get out of your vehicle, sir," Forsyth ordered.

"What? But . . . why?" the driver stammered.

"Do what I say, sir. Get out of your vehicle."

The man stalled. Irritated, Officer Forsyth decided to use force to get him out and to arrest him for disobeying a police officer. He took him to the station, where he personally took care of the regulation photographs and electronic fingerprinting. He was perplexed for a moment by the information that appeared on his computer screen. Then, even though it was 1.30 a.m., he picked up the telephone, deciding that the discovery he had made was sufficiently important to wake Sergeant Perry Gahalowood of the state police criminal division.

Three hours later, at about 4.30 a.m., I, in turn, was awakened by a telephone call.

"Writer? It's Gahalowood. Where are you?"

"Sergeant?" I replied, still half comatose. "I'm in bed, in New York. Where else would I be at 4.30 in the morning? What's going on?"

"We've caught our firebug," he said.

"Sorry?"

"The arsonist who set fire to Harry's house. He was arrested tonight."

"Oh. Who is it?"

"Are you sitting down?"

"I'm lying down."

"Good. Because you're in for a shock."

2

Endgame

"Sometimes you'll feel discouraged, Marcus. That's normal. I told you that writing was like boxing, but it's also like running. That's why I keep sending you out to pound the pavement: If you have the moral courage to run a long way, in the rain, in the cold, if you have the strength to keep going until the end, to give it all you have and to reach your goal, then you're capable of writing a book. Never let fear or fatigue stop you. On the contrary: You should use them to help you keep going."

I caught a flight to Manchester that morning, stunned by what I had just discovered. I landed at 1 p.m., and forty-five minutes later I was at police headquarters in Concord. Gahalowood came to meet me in reception.

"Quinn!" I repeated, when I saw him, still unable to believe it. "Robert Quinn set fire to the house? So he sent me all those messages too?"

"Yes, writer. His fingerprints were on the gas can."

"But why?"

"I wish I knew. He hasn't said a word. He's refusing to talk."

Gahalowood led me into his office and offered me coffee. He explained that the criminal division had searched the Quinns' house that morning.

"What did they find?"

"Nothing. Nothing at all."

"What about his wife? What did she have to say?"

"That's a strange one. We got there at 7.30 a.m. Impossible to wake her up. She was sleeping like a log. She hadn't even noticed her husband's absence."

"He drugs her," I explained.

"He *drugs* her?"

"Quinn gives his wife sleeping pills when he wants some peace. He probably did that last night so she wouldn't suspect anything. But suspect what? What was he doing in the middle of the night? And why was he covered in mud? Was he burying something?"

"That's exactly what we need to find out. But without a confession, I can't really make anything stick."

"What about the gas can?"

"His lawyer is already claiming that Quinn found it on the beach. That he went for a walk, saw the gas can, picked it up, and threw it in the bushes. We need more evidence. Otherwise his lawyer will have no problem taking our case apart."

"Who's his lawyer?"

"You won't believe this . . ."

"Tell me."

"Benjamin Roth."

I sighed.

"So you think Quinn killed Nola Kellergan."

"Well, it's a possibility."

"Let me talk to him."

"No way."

At that moment a man entered the office without knocking, and

Gahalowood immediately stood at attention. It was Dennis Lansdane, the state police chief. He looked to be at the end of his tether.

"I've spent the morning on the phone with the governor, a bunch of reporters, and that goddamn lawyer Roth."

"Reporters? About what?"

"The guy you arrested last night."

"Yes, sir. I think this is an important lead."

The chief placed a friendly hand on Gahalowood's shoulder. "Perry, we can't go on like this."

"What do you mean?"

"This case is never-ending. Let's get serious, Perry. You change perps as often as you change shirts. Roth says he's going to make a stink about this. The governor wants it over with. It's time to close this case."

"But, Chief, we have new evidence! The death of Nola's mother, the arrest of Robert Quinn. We're close to finding something."

"First it was Quebert, then it was Caleb. Now it's Nola's father, or this Quinn guy, or Stern, or God knows who else. What evidence do we have against the father? Nothing. Stern? Nothing. Robert Quinn? Nothing."

"There's that gas can—"

"Roth says he would have no problem convincing a judge of Quinn's innocence. Do you intend to formally charge him?"

"Of course."

"Then you'll lose, Perry. Again. You're a good cop, Perry. Probably the best we have. But sometimes you have to know when to give up."

"But, Chief—"

"Don't throw your career away, Perry. As a gesture of friendship, I'm not going to insult you by forcing you off the case immediately. At 5 p.m. tomorrow, you will come to my office and tell me officially that the Kellergan case is closed. That gives you twenty-four hours to tell your colleagues that you're giving up and to save face. Take the rest of the week off, and go somewhere nice with your family for the weekend. You deserve it."

"Chief, I—"

"You have to know when to give up, Perry. See you tomorrow."

Lansdane left the office, and Gahalowood slumped back into his chair. As if that were not enough, I got a call on my cell from Barnaski.

"Hi there, Goldman," he said cheerfully. "Tomorrow it'll be one week, as I'm sure you're aware."

"What'll be one week, Roy?"

"The deadline I gave you before telling the press about the latest developments. Surely you didn't forget? I assume you haven't found anything."

"Listen, we have a lead, Roy. It would be great if you could postpone your press conference."

"Oh, for God's sake . . . You always have a lead, Goldman. But it never actually leads anywhere! Come on now—it's time you stopped this bullshit. I've arranged a press conference for 5 p.m. tomorrow. I expect you to be there."

"That's impossible. I'm in New Hampshire."

"Goldman, you're the one they want to see! I need you."

"Sorry, Roy."

I hung up.

"Who was it?" Gahalowood asked.

"Barnaski, my publisher. He wants to give a press conference tomorrow afternoon about Nola's illness. He's going to claim my book is a work of genius because it takes you inside a fifteen-year-old girl's split personality."

"So, by 5 p.m. tomorrow, we will have officially fucked up."

Gahalowood still had twenty-four hours; we had to do something. He suggested we go to Somerset to talk to Tamara and Jenny, to see if we could learn more about Robert.

On the way, he called Travis to inform him of our arrival. We found him in front of the Quinns' house. He looked incredulous.

"So they were really Robert's fingerprints on that gas can?" he asked.

"Yes," Gahalowood said.

"My God, I can't believe it! Why would he do such a thing?"

"I have no idea—"

"Do you ... you don't think he could be involved in Nola's murder?"

"At this point I wouldn't rule anything out. How are Jenny and Tamara?"

"Not good. They're in shock. So am I. This is a nightmare!" He sat dejectedly on the hood of his car. "I haven't been able to stop thinking about it all morning ... This case is bringing back so many memories."

"What kind of memories?" Gahalowood said.

"Robert Quinn took a very keen interest in the investigation. Back then, I was seeing a lot of Jenny, having lunch with the Quinns every Sunday. He was always talking to me about the case."

"I thought it was his wife who was always talking about it."

"At the table, yes. But as soon as I arrived, Robert would give me a beer on the porch and pump me for information. Did we have a suspect? Were there any leads? After lunch he would accompany me to my car and we would talk some more. I sometimes had trouble getting rid of him."

"Are you suggesting that—"

"I'm not suggesting anything. But ..."

He reached into his jacket pocket and pulled out a photograph.

"This morning I found this in a family album that Jenny keeps at our house."

The photograph showed Robert Quinn standing next to a black Chevrolet Monte Carlo, in front of Clark's. On the back were the words *Somerset, August 1975*.

"What does this mean?" Gahalowood demanded.

"I asked Jenny about it. She told me her father wanted to buy a new car that summer, but he wasn't sure what model to get. He approached some local dealerships for test drives, and for several weekends he was able to try out different models."

"Including a black Monte Carlo?" Gahalowood said.

"Including a black Monte Carlo," Travis said.

"You mean it's possible that the day Nola disappeared, Robert Quinn was driving this car?"

"Yes."

Gahalowood ran his hand over his head. He asked to keep the photograph.

"Travis," I said, "we have to talk with Tamara and Jenny. Are they inside?"

"Yes, of course. Come in. They're in the living room."

Tamara and Jenny were prostrate on a couch. We spent over an hour trying to get them to speak, but they were in such a state of shock that they were unable to say anything coherent. Finally, between sobs, Tamara managed to describe the previous evening. She and Robert had eaten dinner early, then they had watched television.

"Did you notice anything strange about the way your husband was acting?" Gahalowood asked.

"No . . . Well, yes, he did seem very eager for me to drink a cup of tea. I didn't want to, but he kept repeating: 'Drink, honey bunny, drink. It's a diuretic tea—it'll do you good.' In the end I drank that stupid tea and fell asleep on the couch."

"What time was that?"

"Around eleven, I would guess."

"And afterward?"

"I don't remember anything afterward. I slept like a log. When I woke up it was 7.30 a.m. I was still on the couch and there were policemen knocking on the door."

"Mrs Quinn, is it true that your husband was thinking about buying a Chevrolet Monte Carlo in the summer of 1975?" Gahalowood asked.

"I . . . I don't know. Yes, maybe, but you don't think he could have harmed the girl, do you? Was it him?"

With these words she rushed to the bathroom.

The discussion wasn't going anywhere, and we left without having learned anything new. Time was running out. In the car, I suggested to Gahalowood that we confront Robert with the photograph of the black Monte Carlo, which constituted damning evidence against him.

"It wouldn't do any good," he replied. "Roth knows Lansdane is about to crack. He's probably advised Quinn to play for time. Quinn won't talk. And we'll take the fall. Tomorrow at five the investigation will be closed; your friend Barnaski will do his thing for the national television cameras; Robert Quinn will be free; and we will be the laughingstock of America."

"Unless—"

"Unless there's a miracle, writer. Unless we figure out what Quinn was in such a rush to do last night. His wife said she fell asleep at 11 p.m. He was arrested just after midnight. So he only had an hour. We know wherever he went, it must have been local. But where?"

Gahalowood thought there was only one thing we could do: go to the place where Robert Quinn had been arrested and attempt to retrace his steps. He even persuaded Officer Forsyth, on his day off, to meet us and show us the arrest spot. An hour later we met him on the outskirts of Somerset, and he led us to a spot on the Montburry road.

"It was here," he said.

The road was straight, with thick vegetation on both sides. That did not help us much.

"What happened, exactly?" Gahalowood asked.

"I was coming from Montburry, routine patrol, when suddenly this car came hurtling out in front of me."

"Hurtling out from where?"

"An intersection about half a mile from here."

"Which one?"

"I'm not sure which road it crosses, but it's definitely an intersection, with a traffic light. I know it has a traffic light because it's the only one on this stretch of road."

"The traffic light down there?" Gahalowood asked, pointing into the distance.

"That's right," Forsyth said.

Suddenly a lightbulb came on in my head. "That's the road to the lake!" I shouted.

"What lake?" Gahalowood asked.

"It's the intersection with the road that leads to the Montburry lake."

We drove to the intersection and took the road to the lake. After three hundred feet we came to a parking lot. The lakefront was in a terrible state; the recent fall storms had turned it to mud.

Wednesday, November 12, 2008, 8 a.m.

A line of police vehicles arrived at the lake's parking lot. Gahalowood and I stayed in his car a little longer. As the van bringing the police diving team turned up, I asked: "Are you sure about this, Sergeant?"

"No. But what choice do we have?"

This was our last roll of the dice; we were in an endgame. Robert Quinn had undoubtedly come here. He had slogged through the mud to reach the edge of the lake and thrown something into the water. That, at least, was our theory.

We got out of the car and went to see the divers, who were getting ready to go in. The team leader gave his men a few instructions and then had a discussion with Gahalowood.

"So what are we looking for, Sergeant?"

"Everything. Anything. Documents, a gun, I have no idea. Anything that might be linked to the Kellergan case."

"You realize this lake is a dumping ground? If you could be a little more precise . . ."

"I think whatever we're looking for is obvious enough that your guys will recognize it if they see it. But I don't know what it is yet."

"And whereabouts in the lake, sir?"

"Near the shore. No farther than a stone's throw from the edge. I would focus on the opposite side of the lake. Our suspect was covered in mud, and he had a scratch on his face, probably caused by a low branch. He undoubtedly wanted to hide whatever it was where no-one would want to go look for it. So I would guess he went to the opposite bank, which is surrounded by brambles and bushes."

The search began. We stood at the edge of the lake, close to the parking lot, and watched the divers disappear into the water. It was ice-cold. The first hour passed uneventfully. We stayed close to the diving team's leader, listening to the few radio communications.

At 9.30 Lansdane called Gahalowood to read him the riot act. He shouted so loud that I was able to hear their conversation through the sergeant's cell phone.

"Tell me this is a joke, Perry!"

"What, Chief?"

"You've got a team of divers out there?"

"Yes, sir."

"Are you completely crazy? You're screwing up your career. I could suspend you for something like this! I'm having a press conference at five o'clock. You will be there. You will announce that the investigation is over. You can clear up the mess you've created. I'm not covering for you anymore, Perry. I've had enough of this shit."

"Very good, sir."

He hung up. We stood in silence.

Another hour passed fruitlessly. In spite of the cold, Gahalowood and I remained in the same spot. Finally I said: "Sergeant, if—"

"Shut up, writer. Please. Don't say a word. I don't want to hear your questions or your doubts."

We kept waiting. Suddenly the chief diver's radio crackled to life. Something was happening. Divers resurfaced. There was a rush of excitement.

"What's happening?" Gahalowood asked the chief diver.

"They found it! They found it!"

"Found what?"

About forty feet from the edge of the lake, buried in the mud, the divers had discovered a Colt .38 and a gold necklace with the name NOLA engraved on it.

At noon that day, standing behind the one-way mirror of an interview room in the state police headquarters, I watched Robert Quinn confess, after Gahalowood had placed the gun and the necklace in front of him.

"So this is what you were doing last night?" he said, almost gently. "Getting rid of compromising evidence?"

"How . . . how did you find them?"

"This is it, Mr Quinn. Game over for you. The black Monte Carlo was yours, wasn't it? An unlisted dealership car. No-one would have been able to connect you with it if you hadn't been stupid enough to get yourself photographed next to it."

"I . . ."

"But why? Why did you kill that girl? And that poor woman?"

"I don't know. I think I wasn't myself. It was just an accident, really."

"What happened?"

"Nola was walking by the side of the road, and I offered her a ride. She agreed, and got in. And then . . . I felt so alone. I wanted to stroke her hair . . . She ran into the forest. I had to catch her so I could ask her not to tell anyone. And then, she went to Deborah Cooper's house. I had no choice. They would have talked otherwise. It was . . . it was a moment of madness!"

And he broke down.

When he left the interview room, Gahalowood telephoned Travis to let him know that Robert Quinn had signed a full confession.

"There'll be a press conference at 5 p.m.," he told him. "I didn't want you to find out from the television."

"Thank you, Sergeant. I . . . what should I tell my wife?"

"I don't know—I'm sorry. But tell her soon. The news will spread quickly."

"I'll do that."

"Chief Dawn, could you maybe come to Concord to clear up a few things about Robert Quinn? I'd prefer not to inflict that on your wife or your mother-in-law."

"Of course. I'm on duty at the moment. There's been a car accident, and they're waiting for me. And I have to talk to Jenny. But I could come this evening or tomorrow."

"Tomorrow would be fine. There's no rush now."

Gahalowood hung up. He seemed calm and happy.

"And now?" I asked.

"Now we're going to get a bite to eat. I think we deserve it."

We had lunch at the police cafeteria. Gahalowood looked thoughtful: He didn't touch his food. He had kept the case file with him, on the table, and for fifteen minutes he stared at the photograph of Robert and the black Monte Carlo.

"What's bugging you, Sergeant?"

"Nothing. I'm just wondering why Quinn had a gun with him. He told us he saw the girl by chance as he was driving. But either it was all premeditated, the car and the gun, or he did meet Nola by chance. And if it was by chance, I wonder why he had a gun on him and where he got it."

"You think it was premeditated, but he didn't want to confess that?"

"It's possible."

He looked at the photograph again, holding it close to his face to examine the details. Suddenly his expression changed.

"What's up, Sergeant?" I asked.

"The headline . . ."

I went over to his side of the table. He pointed to a newspaper vendor in the background, next to Clark's. If you looked closely, it was just possible to make out the headline:

"Richard Nixon resigned in August 1974!" Gahalowood said. "This photograph could not have been taken in August 1975."

"So who put that date on the back of the photo?"

"I don't know. But this means Robert Quinn's lying to us. He didn't kill anyone!"

Gahalowood ran out of the cafeteria and down the main staircase. I followed him through the building's hallways until we reached the detention cells. He asked to see Robert Quinn immediately.

"Who are you protecting?" Gahalowood yelled when he saw Quinn behind the bars of his cell. "You didn't test drive a black Monte Carlo in August 1975! You're protecting someone and I want to know who! Your wife? Your daughter?"

Robert's face was a mask of despair. Without moving from the small padded bench, he muttered: "Jenny. I'm protecting Jenny."

"Jenny?" Gahalowood repeated incredulously. "Your daughter was the one who . . ."

He took out his cell phone.

"Who are you calling?" I asked him.

"Travis Dawn. I don't want him to tell his wife. If she knows her father has confessed, she'll panic and make a run for it."

Travis did not answer his cell phone. Gahalowood contacted the Somerset police station so they could get him on the car radio.

"This is Sergeant Gahalowood, New Hampshire State Police," he said. "I need to talk to Chief Dawn right away."

"Chief Dawn? Call him on his cell phone. He's not on duty today."

"What? I called him earlier, and he told me he was investigating a car accident."

"That's impossible, Sergeant. I'm telling you—he's not on duty today."

Gahalowood hung up, a look of shock on his face, and immediately sent out a general alert.

Travis and Jenny Dawn were arrested a few hours later at Boston's Logan Airport, where they were about to catch a flight to Caracas.

It was late at night when Gahalowood and I left the headquarters in Concord. A pack of reporters was waiting by the building's entrance and they swarmed around us as we walked out. We cut a path through them without making a single comment and dived into Gahalowood's car. He drove in silence.

"Where are we going, Sergeant?"

"I don't know."

"What do cops usually do at times like this?"

"They drink. What about writers?"

"They drink."

So he drove us to his favorite bar on the outskirts of Concord. We sat at the bar and ordered double whiskeys. On the television screen behind us, the headline scrolled in a loop across the news ticker:

SOMERSET POLICE OFFICER CONFESSES TO MURDER
OF NOLA KELLERGAN

1

The Truth about the Harry Quebert Affair

"The last chapter of a book, Marcus, should always be the best."

New York City, Thursday, December 18, 2008
One Month After the Discovery of the Truth

It was the last time I saw him.

It was 9 p.m., and I was at home listening to my minidiscs when the doorbell rang. I opened the door, and we looked at each other for a long time in silence. Finally he said: "Good evening, Marcus."

After a second's hesitation I replied: "I thought you were dead."

He nodded. "I'm just a ghost now."

"Do you want some coffee?"

"I'd love some. Are you alone?"

"Yes."

"You shouldn't be alone."

"Come in, Harry."

I went into the kitchen, and he waited in the living room, playing nervously with the framed photographs on my bookshelves. When I came back with the coffeepot and cups, he was looking at one of him and me, from my graduation day at Burrows.

"This is the first time I've been to your place," he said.

"The spare bedroom is ready for you. It has been for several weeks."

"You knew I'd come?"

"Yes."

"You know me well, Marcus."

"Friends know each other."

He smiled sadly.

"Thank you for your hospitality, Marcus, but I won't stay."

"So why did you come?"

"To say goodbye."

I tried not to let my distress show, and filled the cups.

"I won't have any friends at all if you leave me," I said.

"Don't say that. You were more than a friend. I loved you like a son."

"And I loved you like a father."

"In spite of the truth?"

"The truth does not change how you feel about someone. That's the great tragedy of love."

"You're right," Harry said. "So you know everything, huh?"

"Yes."

"How did you know?"

"I worked it out in the end."

"You were the only one who could have found me out."

"So that was what you were talking about, in the motel parking lot. When you said that nothing would ever be the same between us. You knew I would discover the truth."

"Yes."

"How could you, Harry?"

"I don't know . . ."

"I have the video recordings of the interrogations. Do you want to see them?"

"Yes, please."

He sat on the couch. I inserted a D.V.D. into the machine and pressed PLAY. Jenny appeared on the screen. She was looking straight into the camera, in a room at the New Hampshire State Police headquarters. She was crying.

Extract from the Interrogation of Jenny Q. Dawn

Sergeant P. Gahalowood: Mrs Dawn, how long have you known?

Jenny Q. Dawn (sobbing): I . . . I never suspected a thing. Never! Not until the day Nola's body was found at Goose Cove. The whole town was in a frenzy. Clark's was full of people: customers, journalists asking questions. It was hell. I started feeling sick, so I went home earlier than usual. There was a car I didn't recognize in our driveway. I went inside the house, and I could hear voices. I realized it was Chief Pratt, and that he was arguing with Travis. They didn't hear me.

June 12, 2008

"Calm down, Travis!" Pratt thundered. "No-one will suspect—just wait and see."

"How can you be so sure?"

"Quebert's going to get blamed for it. The body's on his property. Everyone's accusing him already."

"And what if he's found not guilty?"

"He won't be. We can't ever talk about this again—do you understand?"

Jenny heard footsteps and hid in the living room. She saw Chief Pratt leave the house. When she heard his car engine, she rushed into the kitchen, where she found her husband, a horrified expression on his face.

"What's going on, Travis? What are you hiding from me? Tell me the truth about Nola!"

Jenny Q. Dawn: That was when Travis told me. He showed me the necklace. He said he'd kept it so he would never forget what he'd done. I took it and said I was going to take care of everything. I wanted to protect my husband, our marriage. I was always alone, Sergeant. I don't have any kids. Travis is all I have. I didn't want to risk losing him. I was hopeful that the investigation would be over quickly and that Harry would be accused. But then Marcus Goldman started stirring up the past because he was sure Harry was innocent. He was right, but I couldn't let him do it. I couldn't let him discover the truth. So I decided to send him those messages. I set fire to that damn Corvette. But he ignored my warnings. So I decided to set fire to the house.

Extract from the Interrogation of Robert Quinn

Sergeant P. Gahalowood: Why did you do that?

Robert Quinn: For my daughter. She looked so worried after Nola's body was discovered and everyone in town was talking about it. Her behavior was odd, and she seemed preoccupied. She would leave Clark's for no reason. The day Goldman's notes were published in the newspapers, she went into a rage. It was almost frightening. Then when I was coming out of the employees' bathroom, I saw her sneaking out the back door. I decided to follow her.

Thursday, July 10, 2008

She parked on the forest path and quickly got out of the car, carrying a gas can and a can of spray paint. She was wearing gardening gloves so as not to leave fingerprints. He followed her cautiously, from a long way behind. By the time he got through the trees, she had already left a message on the Range Rover and was pouring gasoline on the porch.

"Jenny! Stop!" her father yelled.

She hurriedly lit a match and threw it to the ground. The front door went up in flames. She was surprised by the intensity of the flames and had to walk back about ten feet, with her hands over her face. Her father grabbed her by the shoulders.

"Jenny! This is crazy!"

"You don't understand, Dad! What are you doing here? Go away, go away!"

He took the gas can from her hands.

"Run!" he ordered her. "Run before they catch you!"

She disappeared into the forest and got back in her car. He had to get rid of the gas can, but he was panicking and couldn't think straight. In the end he ran down to the beach and hid it in the bushes.

Extract from the Interrogation of Jenny Q. Dawn

Sergeant P. Gahalowood: And after that?

Jenny Q. Dawn: I begged my father not to get involved in all this. I didn't want him to get in trouble.

Sergeant P. Gahalowood: But he already was. So what did you do?

Jenny Q. Dawn: The pressure was mounting on Chief Pratt after he'd confessed to forcing Nola to go down on him. He'd been so confident before, but now he was close to cracking. He would have told them everything. We had to get rid of him. And get hold of the gun.

Sergeant P. Gahalowood: He'd kept the gun, damn it.

Jenny Q. Dawn: Yes. It was his service pistol. He was never without it.

Extract from the interrogation of Travis S. Dawn

Travis S. Dawn: I will never forgive myself for what I did, Sergeant. It's haunted me now for thirty-three years.

Sergeant P. Gahalowood: What I don't understand is that you're a cop, and yet you kept that necklace, which was a damning piece of evidence.

Travis S. Dawn: I couldn't get rid of it. That necklace was my punishment. It reminded me of the past. Ever since August 30, 1975, not a day has passed that I haven't shut myself away somewhere to look at that necklace. And anyway, it seemed so unlikely that anyone would ever find it.

Sergeant P. Gahalowood: Tell me about Pratt.

Travis S. Dawn: He was going to talk. He'd been terrified ever since you found out about him and Nola. He phoned me one day: He wanted to see me. We met on a beach. He said he was going to tell all, that he was going to make a deal with the D.A. and that I should do the same because the truth would come out in the end. That night I went to see him at his motel. I tried to reason with him. But he wasn't having it. He showed me his old Colt .38, which he kept in a drawer in his nightstand. He said he was going to give it to you the next day. He was going to talk, Sergeant. So I waited for him to turn his back on me and I hit him with my nightstick. I picked up the Colt and got the hell out of there.

Sergeant P. Gahalowood: A nightstick? The same as for Nola.

Travis S. Dawn: Yes.

Sergeant P. Gahalowood: The same one?

Travis S. Dawn: Yes.

Sergeant P. Gahalowood: Where is it?

Travis S. Dawn: It's my service club. That's what Pratt and I decided back then: He said the best way of hiding the murder weapons was to leave them in clear view of everyone. The Colt and the nightstick that we wore on our belts as we searched for Nola were the murder weapons.

Sergeant P. Gahalowood: So why did you get rid of it in the end? And how did Robert Quinn end up in possession of the Colt and the necklace?

Travis S. Dawn: Jenny pressured me into it, and I gave in. She hadn't been able to sleep since Pratt's death. She was at her wits' end. She said we shouldn't keep them at home, that if the investi-gation into Pratt's murder turned to us, we were screwed. I wanted to throw them in the middle of the ocean, where no one would ever find them. But Jenny panicked, and she made the first move without consulting me. She asked her father to take care of it.

Sergeant P. Gahalowood: Why her father?

Travis S. Dawn: I don't think she trusted me. I hadn't managed to get rid of the necklace in thirty-three years, so she was afraid I wouldn't go through with it. She's always had absolute faith in her father. She thought he was the only person who could help her. And of course, no-one would suspect him—kind old Robert Quinn.

November 10, 2008

Jenny burst into her parents' house. She knew her father would be alone.

"Dad!" she cried. "Dad, I need your help!"

"Jenny? What's the matter?"

"No questions. I need you to get rid of this."

She handed him a plastic bag.

"What is it?"

"Don't ask. Don't open it. This is serious. You're the only one who can help me. I need you to throw this someplace where no-one will ever look for it."

"Are you in trouble?"

"Yes. I think so."

"Alright, I'll do it, darling. Don't worry. I'll do everything I can to protect you."

"Whatever you do, don't open that bag, Dad. Just get rid of it."

But as soon as his daughter had left, Robert opened the bag. Shocked by what he saw, and fearing that his daughter was guilty of murder, he decided that as soon as night fell he would throw the bag's contents into Montburry Lake.

Extract from the Interrogation of Travis S. Dawn

Travis S. Dawn: When I learned that my father-in-law had been arrested, I knew the game was up. I knew I had to do something. I decided I had to let him take the blame. At least for a while. I knew he would want to protect his daughter, that he would give us a day or two: enough time for us to reach a country with no extradition treaty. I went in search of evidence I could use against Robert. I looked through Jenny's family albums, hoping I could find a photograph of Robert and Nola so I could write something compromising on the back. But then I found that picture of him and the black Monte Carlo. I couldn't believe my luck! I wrote the date, August 1975, in ballpoint pen, and when the time was right, I gave it to you.

Sergeant P. Gahalowood: Chief Dawn, it's time to tell us what really happened on August 30, 1975 . . .

*

"Turn it off, Marcus!" Harry shouted. "I'm begging you, turn it off. I can't bear to hear that."

I pressed the power button on the remote and the screen went black. Harry was crying. He got up from the couch and stood by the window. Outside, large snowflakes were falling. The city, all lit up, was beautiful.

"I'm sorry, Harry."

"New York's an amazing place," he whispered. "I often wonder what my life would have been like if I'd stayed here instead of going to Somerset."

"You would never have found love," I said.

He stared out into the night. "How did you work it out, Marcus?"

"Work what out? That you didn't write *The Origin of Evil*? It was just after Travis Dawn was arrested. The press was all over the case again, and a day or two later I received a call from Elijah Stern. He said he desperately needed to see me."

Friday, November 14, 2008
Elijah Stern's estate, near Concord, New Hampshire

Elijah Stern received me in his office.

"Thank you for coming, Mr Goldman."

"I was surprised by your call, Mr Stern. I thought you didn't like me very much."

"You're a talented young man. Is it true what they say in the papers, about Travis Dawn?"

"Yes, sir."

"It's so awful . . ."

I nodded, then said, "I was wrong all along about Caleb. I regret that."

"But if I understand correctly, it was your tenacity that finally enabled the police to solve the case. That policeman keeps praising you to the skies. Gahalowood is his name, isn't it?"

"I asked my publisher to withdraw *The Harry Quebert Affair* from sale."

"I'm glad to hear that. Are you going to write a corrected version?"

"Probably. I don't know what it will be like yet, but justice will be done. I fought to clear Quebert's name, and I will fight to clear Caleb's too."

He smiled.

"Actually, Mr Goldman, that's why I asked you here. I have to tell you the truth. And perhaps you will understand why I don't blame you for having thought Luther was guilty these past few months: I myself spent thirty-three years convinced that Luther had killed Nola Kellergan."

"Never a doubt?"

"I was always sure of it. One hundred per cent."

"Why didn't you ever say anything to the police?"

"I didn't want to kill Luther a second time."

"I don't understand what you mean, Mr Stern."

"Luther was obsessed with Nola. He spent his time in Somerset, watching her."

"I know. I know you found him at Goose Cove. You told Sergeant Gahalowood about it."

"But I think you underestimate the scale of Luther's obsession. That August, in 1975, he spent his days at Goose Cove, hidden in the woods, spying on Harry and Nola as they walked on the beach or sat on the deck, wherever they went. Everywhere! He was going completely crazy. He knew everything about them. Everything! He told me about it all the time. Day after day he would describe what they had done, what they had said. He told me their whole story: how they met on the beach, that they were working on a book, that they had been away together for a week. He knew it all. Gradually I understood that he was living a love affair through them. The love he could not experience himself, because of his repulsive physical appearance, he experienced vicariously. So much so that I hardly ever saw him at all most days. I ended up having to drive myself to all my meetings!"

"Excuse me for interrupting, Mr Stern, but there's something I don't understand: Why didn't you just fire him? I mean, it seems insane to me. It's as if you were obeying your own employee, the way you let him paint Nola or the way you let him spend all his time in Somerset. I realize this is a personal question, but what was there between the two of you? Were you—"

"In a relationship? No."

"So what was behind the strange dynamic between you? You're a powerful man. You don't seem the type to let people walk all over you. And yet—"

"Because I was in his debt. I . . . I . . . Just let me finish, and you'll soon understand. So Luther was obsessed with Harry and Nola. And, little by little things began to degenerate. One day he came back, and he was badly beaten up. He told me that a cop in Somerset had attacked him because he'd been hanging around, and that a waitress at Clark's had even filed a complaint against him. The whole thing was a mess. I told him I didn't want him to go to Somerset anymore. I said I wanted him to take some time off; go away for a while; visit his family in Maine, maybe; go anywhere, really. I said I would pay for it all."

"But he refused," I said.

"Not only did he refuse, he even asked me to lend him a car. He said his blue Mustang was now too easily recognizable. I turned him down, of course. I told him enough was enough. And then he started screaming: 'You don't understand, Eli! They're going to leave! In ten days they'll be gone and they'll never come back! Never! They made the decision on the beach! They decided to leave on the thirtieth! On the thirtieth they'll leave forever. I just want to be able to say goodbye to Nola. These are my last days with her. You can't deprive me of her when I already know I'm going to lose her.' I didn't give in. I kept an eye on him. And then it was August 29. That day I looked everywhere for him. He was nowhere to be found, although his Mustang was parked in its usual place. Finally one of my employees spilled the beans and told me that Luther had left in one of my cars, a black Monte Carlo. Luther had said that I'd given my approval, and because everyone knew I let him do what he wanted, no-one questioned him. That made me mad. I immediately went to search his room. I found that portrait of Nola, which made me want to throw up, and then, in a box under his bed, I found all those letters, letters he had stolen . . . letters from Nola to Harry that he must have taken from Harry's mailbox. So I waited for him, and when he came back, late that evening, we had a terrible argument."

Stern went silent and stared into space.

"What happened?" I asked.

"I . . . I wanted him to stop going there, you see. I wanted his obsession with Nola to end. But he wouldn't listen to me! He said it was stronger than ever between him and Nola, that no-one could prevent their being together. I lost my temper. We grappled with each other, and I hit him. I grabbed him by the collar, I yelled, and I hit him. I called him a fucking redneck. He was lying on the ground. He put his hand to his nose, which was bleeding. I was frozen to the spot. And he said . . . he said to me . . ."

Stern could no longer speak. His face crumpled.

"Mr Stern," I said, not wishing him to lose the thread of his story, "what did he say?"

"He said to me: 'It was you!' He yelled: 'It was you! It was you!' I was in shock. I couldn't move. He went to get a few things from his room, and he fled in the Monte Carlo before I could react. He had . . . he had recognized my voice."

Stern was crying now. His fists were clenched.

"He'd recognized your voice?" I repeated.

"There . . . there had been a time in my life when I used to meet up with some old Harvard friends. A sort of stupid fraternity. We would go to Maine for the weekend and stay in expensive hotels, drinking, eating lobster. We liked fighting. We liked beating up poor people. We said that people from Maine were rednecks and it was our mission on earth to beat them up. We were in our twenties, we were rich kids. We were arrogant and somewhat racist, we were miserable and violent. We had invented a game, the Field Goal, which consisted of kicking our victims in the head as if we were kicking a football. One day in 1964 we were up near Portland, very drunk. We drove past a young guy walking along the road. I was driving . . . I stopped and suggested we have a little fun . . ."

"You were Caleb's attacker?"

"Yes! Yes!" he exploded. "I have never forgiven myself! We woke up the next morning in our luxury hotel suite with massive hangovers. The attack was in all the papers: The boy was in a coma. The police were looking for us; we had been nicknamed the Field Goals Gang. We decided we would never talk about it again, that we would expunge that night from our memories. But I was haunted by it. In the days and months that followed, it was all I could think of. It was making me ill. I started going to Portland to find out what had happened to that kid we had battered. Two years had passed when, one day, unable to take it anymore, I decided to give him a job, a chance to get over it. I put a nail in my tire, I asked him to help me fix it, and I hired him as my chauffeur. I gave him everything he wanted. I made an artist's studio for him on the house's veranda; I gave him money; I gave him a car; but none of it was enough to release me from my guilt. I always wanted to do more for him. I had ruined his career as an artist, so I funded every exhibition I could, and I often let him spend whole days painting. And then he started saying he felt lonely, that nobody wanted him. He said the only thing he could do with a woman was paint her. He wanted to paint blondes; he said they reminded him of the girl he had been intending to marry before the attack. So I hired carloads of blond prostitutes to pose for him. But then one day in Somerset he met Nola. And he fell in love with her. He said it was the first time he had loved anyone since his fiancée. And then Harry turned up, a brilliant writer and a handsome man. The man Luther wanted to be. And Nola fell in love with Harry. So Luther decided that he also wanted to be Harry. What was I supposed to do? I had stolen his life, I had taken everything from him. Who was I to stop his loving someone?"

"So all of that was to relieve your sense of guilt?"

"Call it what you want."

"So August 29 . . . what happened next?"

"When Luther realized that I was the one who . . . He packed his suitcase and drove away in the black Monte Carlo. I immediately set off in pursuit. I wanted to explain to him. I wanted him to forgive me. But I couldn't find him anywhere. I searched all day for him and part of the night too, but nothing. I was so angry with myself. I hoped he would soon be his old self again. But the next night the radio announced the disappearance of Nola Kellergan. The suspect was driving a black Monte Carlo. You can imagine what I thought. I decided never to speak about it to anyone at all, so that Luther would never be suspected. Or perhaps because, when it came down to it, I was just as guilty as Luther was. That was why I was so upset with you for dredging up the past. But it's thanks to you that I've finally learned that Luther didn't kill Nola. I feel as if I, too, were suddenly found not guilty of her murder. You've eased my conscience, Mr Goldman."

"And the Mustang?"

"It's in my garage, under a tarp. I've been hiding it in my garage for thirty-three years."

"What about the letters?"

"I kept those too."

"I would like to see them, if I could."

Stern removed a picture from the wall, revealing a safe that he then opened. He took out a shoebox filled with letters. I recognized the first one right away: It was the letter with which *The Origin of Evil* began, the one from July 5, 1975, so full of sadness, the one that Nola had written to Harry when he had rejected her and she had learned that he was with

Jenny on the night of July 4. That day she had left him an envelope containing the letter and two photographs taken in Rockland. One showed a flock of seagulls; the other was of the two of them during their picnic.

"How the hell did Luther get all of these?" I asked.

"I don't know," Stern said. "But it wouldn't surprise me if he had gone into Harry's house."

I thought about it: He could easily have stolen these letters when Harry was away from Somerset. But why had Harry never told me that those letters had disappeared? I asked to borrow the box, and Stern let me. I was suddenly overcome by doubt.

As he looked out at the skyline and listened to my story, Harry wept silently.

"When I saw those letters, something shifted in my mind," I told him. "I thought again about your book, the one you left in the gym locker: *The Seagulls of Somerset.* And I realized something I had somehow completely missed up to that point: There are no seagulls in *The Origin of Evil.* How did I not see that before? Not a single seagull! And you had sworn to her that you would put seagulls in your book! That was when I understood that you didn't write *The Origin of Evil.* The book you wrote in the summer of 1975 was *The Seagulls of Somerset.* That was the book you wrote and that Nola typed up for you. This was confirmed for me when I asked Gahalowood to make a comparison between the handwriting in the letters that Nola received and the message on the manuscript found with Nola's body. When he told me it was the same handwriting, I realized how you had used me when you asked me to burn your handwritten manuscript. Because it wasn't your writing. You didn't write the book that made you famous! You stole it from Luther!"

"That's enough, Marcus!"

"Am I wrong? You stole a book! What greater crime could a writer commit? *The Origin of Evil*—that's why you gave the book that title. And I couldn't understand why such a beautiful book should have such a dark title. But the title has nothing to do with the book; it has to do with you. You always told me that a book is not a relationship between words; it's a relationship between people. That book is the origin of evil that has gnawed at you ever since: the evil of remorse and imposture."

"Stop, Marcus! Shut up now!"

He continued to cry.

"One day," I went on, "Nola left an envelope in the front door of your house. It was July 5, 1975. An envelope containing photographs of seagulls and a letter written on her favorite paper, in which she mentions Rockland and says she will never forget you. It was during that time when you were forcing yourself not to see her anymore. But that letter never reached you because Luther, who was spying on you, took it as soon as Nola went away. That was how, from that day on, he began writing to Nola. He replied to that letter, pretending to be you. She replied, thinking she was writing to you, but he intercepted all her letters in your mailbox before you ever saw them. And he replied again and again, always pretending to be you. That was why he hung around outside your house. Nola thought she was corresponding with you, and that correspondence became *The Origin of Evil*. But, Harry, how *could* you? How could you *do* such a thing?"

"I panicked, Marcus. That summer I was struggling so badly to write. I didn't think I would ever manage it. I wrote *The Seagulls of Somerset*, but I thought it was terrible. Nola told me she loved it, but nothing could convince me. I went into fits of rage. She typed up my handwritten pages; I reread them, and I tore up everything. She begged me to stop. She said, 'Don't do that. You're such a brilliant writer. Please, finish the book. Darling Harry, I won't be able to bear it if you don't finish it!' But I didn't believe in it. I thought I would never become a writer. And then one day Luther Caleb rang my doorbell. He said he didn't know whom to ask, so he had come to me: He had written a book, and he wondered if it was worth sending to a publisher. You see, Marcus, he thought I was a famous New York writer and that I could help him."

August 20, 1975

Harry did not conceal his surprise when he opened the door.

"Luther?"

"Hel . . . Hello vere, Harry."

There was an embarrassed silence.

"What can I do for you, Luther?"

"I've come to fee you for a perfonal reavon. I need fome advife."

"Advice? Alright. Do you want to come in?"

"Fank you."

The two men sat in the living room. Luther was nervous. He had brought a package with him, and he held it close to his body.

"So, Luther, what's the matter?"

"I . . . I've written a book. It'f a love ftory."

"Really?"

"Yef. I don't know if it'f any good, vough. I mean, how do you know if a book iv good enough to be published?"

"I don't know. But if you think you've done your best . . . do you have it with you?"

"Yef, but it'f a handwritten manufcript," Luther said apologeticaily. "I juft realived. I have a typewritten version, but I picked up ve wrong package when I left ve houfe. Should I go and get it and come by later?"

"No, show it to me anyway."

"It'f juft vat . . ."

"Come on, don't be shy. I'm sure it's readable."

Luther handed him the package. Harry took out the pages and read a few of them, staggered by the quality of the writing.

"Is this your writing?"

"Yef."

"It's unbelievable. It's like you . . . I mean . . . It's beautifully written. How do you do it?"

"I don't know. Vat'f juft how my writing iv."

"Would you let me keep this, so I can read it? I'll give you my honest opinion."

"Really?"

"Of course."

Luther readily agreed, and he left. But he did not leave Goose Cove. Instead he hid in the bushes and waited for Nola, as he always did. She arrived soon afterward, happy in the knowledge that she and Harry would soon be going away together. She did not notice the crouching figure in the bushes. She entered the house through the front door, without ringing the doorbell, as she always did now.

"Harry, darling!" she called out.

There was no reply. The house seemed empty. She called out again. Silence. She checked the dining room and the living room but couldn't find him. He wasn't in his office, or on the deck. She went down the stairs to the beach and called his name. Maybe he'd gone swimming? He did that sometimes when he'd been working too hard. But there was no-one on the beach. She began to panic: Where could he be? She went back to the house, called his name again. Nothing. She checked all the rooms on the first floor again, then went upstairs. Opening the door to his bedroom, she found him sitting on his bed, reading a stack of papers.

"Harry? Were you here all along? I've spent the last ten minutes looking all over for you."

Her voice had startled him.

"Sorry, Nola, I was reading. I didn't hear you."

He got up, reordered the papers in his hands, and put them in his bureau.

She smiled. "So what was so fascinating that you didn't hear me yelling your name all over the house?"

"Nothing important."

"Is it the next part of your novel? Show me!"

"No, it's nothing important. I'll show you some other time."

She looked at him curiously. "Are you sure everything's O.K., Harry?"

He laughed. "Everything's fine, Nola."

They went out to the beach. She wanted to see the seagulls. She opened her arms wide as if they were wings, and ran in wide circles on the sand.

"I'd love to be able to fly, Harry! Only ten days! In ten days we'll fly away together! We'll leave this miserable town forever!"

Neither Harry nor Nola had any idea that Luther Caleb was watching them from the trees above the rocks. He waited until they had gone back into the house before emerging from his hiding place. Then he ran along the path from Goose Cove until he reached his Mustang. He drove to Somerset and left his car in front of Clark's. He rushed inside; he needed to speak to Jenny. Someone had to know. He had a bad feeling about this. But Jenny didn't want to see him.

"Luther? You shouldn't be here," she said when he appeared at the counter.

"Jenny . . . I'm forry for ve over morning. I wav wrong to grab your arm ve way I did."

"I have a bruise . . ."

"I'm forry."

"You have to leave now."

"No, wait . . ."

"I've filed a complaint against you, Luther. Travis says that if you come back to town, I should call him—and you'll have to deal with the police. You really ought to leave before he sees you here."

He looked upset. "You filed a complaint againft me?"

"Yes. You really scared me the other day . . ."

"But I have to fpeak to you about fomefing important."

"Nothing is important, Luther. Please go away . . ."

"It'f about Harry Quebert."

"Harry?"

"Yef. Tell me what you fink about Harry Quebert."

"Why are you asking me about him?"

"Do you truft him?"

"Trust him? Yes, of course. Why are you asking me that?"

"I have to tell you fomefing . . ."

"Tell me something? What?"

Just as Luther was about to reply, a police car appeared outside Clark's.

"It's Travis!" Jenny said. "Run, Luther, run! I don't want you to get in trouble."

"It's very simple," Harry told me. "It was the most beautiful book I had ever read. And I didn't even know it had been written for Nola! Her name didn't appear in it. It was an extraordinary love story. I never saw Caleb again. I never got the chance to give him back his manuscript. Because so many things happened, as you know. A month later I found out that he had been killed in a car accident. And I still had the original manuscript of what I knew was a masterpiece. I made the decision to claim it as my own. So my whole career is based on a lie. But how could I imagine how successful that book would be? That success gnawed at me my whole life. My whole life! And then, thirty-three years later, the police find Nola and the typewritten version of that manuscript in my yard. In my yard! And at that moment, I was so afraid of losing everything I had, that I told them I had written that book for her."

"Because you were afraid of losing everything? You chose to be accused of murder rather than reveal the truth about the manuscript?"

"Yes! Yes! Because my whole life is a lie, Marcus!"

"So Nola never took that copy from you. You said that to ensure that no-one would suspect you weren't the author."

"Yes. But I've always wondered where she got the copy she had with her."

"Luther had left it in her mailbox," I said.

"In her mailbox?"

"Luther knew you were going to elope with Nola; he'd heard you talking on the beach. He knew that Nola was going without him, so that was how he ended his book: with the heroine's departure. He wrote her a final letter, a letter in which he wishes her a good life. And that letter was in the handwritten manuscript that he gave you. Luther knew everything. But then on the day of your departure, probably during the night of August 29 or early in the morning of August 30, he felt the need to tie up loose ends: He wanted to conclude his story with Nola the same way his book concluded. So he left a final letter in the Kellergans' mailbox. Or, rather, a final package. The goodbye letter and the typescript of his book, so that she would know how much he loved her. And since he knew he would never see her again, he wrote on the cover: *Goodbye, darling Nola.* He undoubtedly stayed there until morning, as he always did, to make sure she was the one who took the package from the mailbox. But when she found the letter and the typescript, Nola thought they were from you. She thought you weren't coming. She had another breakdown. She lost her mind."

Harry put his hands to his chest, and collapsed.

"Tell me, Marcus! Tell me, in your own words. I want to hear it from you. Your words are always so well chosen. Tell me what happened on August 30, 1975!"

August 30, 1975

One day in late August, a fifteen-year-old girl was murdered in Somerset. Her name was Nola Kellergan. Every account of her you hear will describe her as being full of life and dreams.

It is difficult to pin down the causes of her death that day. Perhaps, ultimately, everything began years before. During the 1960s, when her parents failed to notice the sickness that had taken hold of their child. One night in 1964, perhaps, when a young man was permanently disfigured by a gang of drunken thugs. Or in the years that followed, when one of those thugs attempted to assuage his guilt by secretly getting close to his victim. That night in 1969, when a father decided to keep quiet about his daughter's secret. Or perhaps everything began one afternoon in June 1975, when a writer named Harry Quebert met her and they fell in love.

This is the story of parents who did not wish to see the truth about their child.

This is the story of a rich young man who, acting thuggishly in his youth, destroyed the dreams of another young man, and was forever haunted by what he had done.

This is the story of a man who dreamed of becoming a great writer, and who was slowly consumed by his ambition.

At dawn on August 30, 1975, a car pulled up in front of 245 Terrace Avenue. Luther Caleb wanted to say goodbye to Nola Kellergan. His head was all over the place. He no longer knew whether they had really loved each other or whether he had merely dreamed it; he no longer knew whether they had really written all those letters. But he knew that Harry Quebert and Nola were planning to elope that day. Luther wanted to leave New Hampshire too, and go far, far away from Elijah Stern. His thoughts were all mixed up: The man who had given him back his will to live was the same man who had taken it from him in the first place. It was a nightmare. The only thing that mattered to him at that moment was the end of his love affair. He had to give Nola the last letter. He had written it ten days ago: the day he heard Harry and Nola talk about leaving Somerset on August 30. He had rushed to finish his book, and had even given the handwritten version to Harry; he wanted to know if it was worth publishing. But nothing was worth anything right now. He had even decided not to bother getting his manuscript back. He had kept a typewritten copy, and he'd had it nicely bound, for Nola. That Saturday, August 30, he would leave it in the Kellergans' mailbox, so that Nola would have something to remember him by, along with the final letter that would bring an end to their affair. What title should he give the book? He didn't know. There would never be a published book, so why bother with a title? Instead he wrote a dedication on the cover, as a way of wishing Nola good luck for the future: *Goodbye, darling Nola.*

He sat in his car and waited for the sun to rise. Then he waited for Nola to come out. He just wanted to make sure she was the one who found the manuscript. Ever since they had started writing to each other, she was always the one who came out to check the mailbox. He waited, hiding himself as best he could: No-one must see him here, particularly that brute Travis Dawn, because if he did he would beat him up. And Luther had taken more than his fair share of beatings already.

At 11 a.m. she finally came out. As always she looked around before walking to the mailbox. She was gorgeous. She was wearing a beautiful red dress. She hurried to the mailbox and smiled when she saw the envelope and the package. She quickly read the letter, and then staggered as if she had been punched. Sobbing, she ran back to the house. They would not be leaving together, after all; Harry would not be waiting for her at the motel. His last letter was a letter of farewell.

She shut herself in her room and collapsed on the bed. Why was he rejecting her? Why had he made her believe they would love each other forever? She skimmed the manuscript. What was this book? He had never mentioned it to her. Her tears ran down onto the pages. Their letters were here, all of them, including the one she had gotten today. So he had lied to her from the beginning. He had never intended to elope with her. She was crying so hard that her head hurt. It hurt so much that she wanted to die.

The door to her room opened softly. Her father had heard her crying.

"What's wrong, Nola?"

"Nothing, Dad."

"Don't lie to me. I can see something is wrong . . ."

"Oh, Dad, I'm so sad. So sad!"

She hugged her father tightly.

"Let go of her!" yelled Louisa Kellergan suddenly. "She doesn't deserve love! Let go of her, David!"

"Stop, Nola. Don't start with this again . . ."

"Shut your mouth, David! You're pathetic. You're incapable of doing what needs to be done. Now I have to do it myself."

"Nola, for God's sake! Calm down, calm down! I'm not going to let you hurt yourself again."

"Leave us alone, David!" Louisa screamed, shoving her husband away.

He stepped back into the hallway, feeling powerless.

"Come here, Nola!" her mother yelled. "Come here! Come and get what's coming to you."

The door slammed shut. David Kellergan, paralyzed by shock, could only listen to what was happening through the bedroom wall.

"No, Mom, please! Stop! Stop!"

"Take that! This is what happens to girls who kill their mother!"

David Kellergan ran to the garage, where he turned on his stereo, the volume cranked up as high as it would go.

All day long the music blasted from the house. Neighbors glared through their windows. Some of them looked at one another knowingly: They knew what happened at the Kellergans' house whenever the loud music came on.

Luther had not moved. Still sitting at the wheel of his Chevrolet, hidden among the line of parked cars, he never took his eyes off the house. Why had she started crying? Didn't she like his letter? He had put so much care into what he wrote. He had written her a love story; love should not make you cry.

He waited there until 6 p.m. He no longer knew whether he should wait for her to reappear or whether he should ring the doorbell. That was when he noticed her in the yard: She had climbed out of her bedroom window. She looked down the street to make sure she wasn't seen and then began walking along the sidewalk. She was carrying a leather shoulder bag. Soon she began to run. Luther started the engine.

The black Chevrolet pulled up alongside her.

"Luther?" said Nola.

"Don't cry. I juft came to fay vat you shouldn't cry."

"Oh, Luther, something so sad has happened to me. Can you give me a ride?"

"Where are you going?"

"Far away."

She dived into the passenger seat without even waiting for Luther's reply.

"Drive, Luther! I have to go to the Sea Side Motel. I can't believe he doesn't love me! We loved each other like no couple has ever loved before."

Luther obeyed. But neither he nor Nola had noticed the police car at the intersection. Travis Dawn had just been to the Quinns' house for the umpteenth time, waiting for Jenny to be alone so he could her give her the wild roses he had picked. Incredulous, he watched Nola get into a car he didn't recognize, with Luther at the wheel. He watched the Chevrolet pull away, waiting a bit before he followed. He had to keep the car in sight, but he couldn't get too close. He wanted to know why Luther spent so much time in Somerset. Was he spying on Jenny? Why had he picked up Nola? Travis grabbed his car radio. He was going to call for backup so he could be sure of catching Luther if the arrest took a turn for the worse. But then he changed his mind: He did not want the encumbrance of a colleague; he wanted to deal with this his way. Somerset was a peaceful place, and he intended to keep it that way. He was going to teach that guy a lesson he would never forget. This would be the last time Luther Caleb would set foot in Travis's town. And once again he wondered how on earth Jenny could have fallen in love with that monster.

"*You* wrote those letters?" Nola shrieked inside the car when she had heard Luther's explanation.

"Yef . . ."

She wiped her tears with the back of her hand.

"Luther, you're crazy! You can't steal people's mail. What you did is very wicked."

He lowered his head in shame.

"I'm forry. I felt fo lonely . . ."

She placed a friendly hand on his powerful shoulder.

"Alright, never mind, Luther. It doesn't matter. And this means that Harry *is* waiting for me! He's waiting for me! We *are* going away together!"

This thought was enough to light up her face.

"You're fo lucky, Nola. You and Harry love each over. Vat meanv you will never be lonely."

They were now driving along Shore Road. They passed the entrance to Goose Cove.

"Goodbye, Goose Cove!" Nola said gaily. "That house is the only place in this town with happy memories for me."

She laughed for no reason. And Luther smiled in response. He and Nola were parting, but at least they were parting on good terms. Suddenly they heard a police siren behind them. They were close to the forest now, and it was here that Travis had decided to intercept Luther and give him what he deserved. No-one would see them in the woods.

"It'f Travif," Luther groaned. "If he catchev uv, we're fcrewed."

Nola started to panic.

"Not the police! Oh, Luther, please, do something!"

The Chevrolet accelerated. It was a powerful car. Cursing, Travis grabbed his handset and ordered Luther through the car megaphone to pull over.

"Don't stop!" Nola begged. "Speed up! Speed up!"

Luther pressed down harder on the accelerator. After Goose Cove, Shore Road went through a series of bends: Luther took them at high speed and increased the gap between him and the police car. The sound of the siren was fading.

"He'v going to call for backup," Luther said.

"If he catches us, I'll never be able to leave with Harry!"

"Ven let'f efcape into ve foreft. Ve foreft iv maffive—no-one will find uv vere. You can reach ve Fea Fide Motel from vere. If vey catch me, Nola, I won't fay a word. I won't tell vem you were wiv me. Vat way you can ftill efcape wiv Harry."

"Oh, Luther . . ."

"Promif me you'll keep my book! Promif you'll keep it av a fouvenir of me."

"I promise."

At these words Luther slammed on the brakes, and the car disappeared into the undergrowth at the edge of the forest before stopping behind a copse of thick brambles. They got out as fast as they could.

"Run!" Luther told her. "Run, Nola!"

They pushed through some thorny bushes. Nola's dress was torn, and her face was covered with scratches.

Travis swore. He could no longer see the black Chevrolet. He sped up again but did not notice the vehicle hidden behind the brambles. He proceeded straight along Shore Road.

They ran through the forest. Nola went first, with Luther behind, as he found it more difficult to duck under the low branches.

"Run, Nola!" he shouted. "Don't ftop!"

Without realizing it, they had reached the edge of the forest. They were close to Side Creek Lane.

From her kitchen window Deborah Cooper looked out at the woods. Then she thought she saw something. She watched more carefully and glimpsed a girl running very fast, pursued by a man. She rushed to the telephone and dialed 911.

Travis had just stopped by the roadside when he received the call from the police station: A young girl had been seen near Side Creek Lane, apparently pursued by a man. The officer acknowledged the call and immediately made a U-turn. Siren screaming and blue lights flashing, he headed toward Side Creek Lane. After half a mile his attention was caught by a bright reflection: a windshield! It was the black Chevrolet, concealed in the bushes. He stopped close to the vehicle, firearm at the ready. The car was empty. He went back to his car and drove to Deborah Cooper's house.

They stopped close to the beach to catch their breath.

"You think it's O.K.?" Nola said.

Luther listened: He couldn't hear anything.

"We fould wait here for a while," he said. "Ve foreft iv a good plafe to hide."

Nola's heart was pounding. She thought of Harry. She thought of her mother. She missed her mother.

"A girl in a red dress," Deborah Cooper explained to Officer Dawn. "She was running toward the beach. A man was following her. I couldn't see him clearly. But he looked quite big."

"That's them," he said. "Can I use your telephone?"

"Of course."

Travis called Chief Pratt at home.

"Chief, I'm sorry to disturb you on your day off, but there's something strange going on here. I saw Luther Caleb in Somerset—"

"Again?"

"Yes. But this time Nola Kellergan got in his car. I tried to catch him, but he lost me. He went into the woods, with Nola. I'm afraid he might hurt her, Chief. The forest is dense. I can't catch him on my own."

"You were right to call. I'm on my way."

*

"We'll go to Canada. I like Canada. We'll live in a pretty house, by a lake. We'll be so happy."

Luther smiled. Sitting on a fallen tree, he listened to Nola's hopes and dreams.

"Vat foundv wonderful," he said.

"Yes . . . what time is it?"

"It'f nearly fikf forty-five."

"Then I have to get going. I'm meeting Harry at seven, in Room 8. I don't think we have anything to worry about now anyway."

But at that very moment they heard a noise. And then voices.

"It's the police!" Nola said, almost hysterical.

Chief Pratt and Travis searched the forest; they walked along its edge, close to the beach. They moved through the trees, nightsticks at the ready.

"You go, Nola," Luther said. "You go, and I'll ftay here."

"No, I can't leave you!"

"Go now, for God'v fake! Go! You'll have time to get to ve motel. You'll fee Harry vere, and everyfing will be good. Go quickly. Run av faft av you can. Run away and be happy."

"Luther, I—"

"Goodbye, Nola. I hope you love my book ve way I wanted you to love me."

Weeping, she waved to him and disappeared into the trees.

The two policemen advanced quickly. After a few hundred yards they saw a figure ahead of them.

"It's Luther!" Travis yelled. "It's him!"

He was sitting on the tree stump. He had not moved. Travis rushed at him, grabbing him by the collar.

"Where's the girl?" he shouted, shaking him.

"What girl?" Luther asked.

He tried to work out how long it would take Nola to reach the motel.

"Where's Nola? What did you do with her?" Travis demanded.

When Luther did not reply, Chief Pratt, approaching from behind, grabbed his leg and smashed the nightstick into his knee.

Nola heard a scream. She stopped dead and shuddered. They had found Luther. They were beating him. She hesitated for a fraction of a second: She should go back and show herself to the police officers. It would be awful if Luther got into trouble because of her. She wanted to return to the tree stump, but then she felt a strong hand on her shoulder. She turned around and gasped.

"Mom?" she said.

Luther was lying on the ground and groaning, both his kneecaps broken. Travis and Pratt took turns kicking him and hitting him with their nightsticks.

"What did you do to Nola?" Travis yelled. "Did you hurt her? Did you? You're a fucking pervert, aren't you? You had to hurt her, didn't you?"

Luther howled under the repeated blows, begging the policemen to stop.

"Mom?"

Louisa Kellergan smiled tenderly at her daughter.

"What are you doing here, my love?"

"I'm running away."

"Why?"

"Because I want to be with Harry. I love him so much."

"You shouldn't leave your father on his own. Your father will be lonely without you. You can't leave like that . . ."

"Mom . . . Mom, I'm sorry for what I did to you."

"I forgive you, my darling. But you should stop hurting yourself now."

"Alright."

"Do you promise?"

"I promise, Mom. What should I do now?"

"Go home to your father. He needs you."

"But what about Harry? I don't want to lose him."

"You won't lose him. He'll wait for you."

"Really?"

"Yes. He'll wait his whole life for you."

Nola heard more screams. Luther! She ran as fast as she could toward the stump, yelling at the top of her voice for them to stop beating him. She burst into the clearing. Luther was lying on the ground, dead. Chief Pratt and Officer Dawn were staring wild-eyed at the corpse. There was blood everywhere.

"What have you done?" Nola screamed.

"Nola?" Pratt said. "But—"

"You killed Luther!"

She threw herself at Chief Pratt, who slapped her in the face. Blood poured from her nose. She shook with fear.

"Sorry, Nola. I . . . I didn't mean to hurt you," Pratt stammered.

She recoiled.

"You . . . you killed Luther!"

"Wait, Nola!"

She fled. Travis tried to grab her, but was left with nothing but a handful of blond hair.

"Catch her, for God's sake!" Pratt yelled at Travis. "Catch her!"

She ran through the forest, scratching her cheeks on low branches, and finally emerging from the last line of trees. A house. She saw a house. She ran toward the kitchen door. Her nose was still bleeding. There was blood all over her face. Deborah Cooper opened the door, her face a mask of terror, and let her in.

"Help me," Nola whimpered. "Call for help."

Deborah rushed once more to the telephone to call the police.

Nola felt a hand over her mouth. Travis lifted her up with a single powerful motion. She fought, but he was too strong. Before he could get her out of the house Deborah Cooper came back into the living room. She cried out in terror.

"Don't worry, ma'am," Travis said. "I'm a police officer. Everything is under control."

"Help!" Nola screamed, attempting to escape his grip. "They killed a man! These policemen are murderers! There's a man dead in the forest!"

The next few moments felt like an eternity. Deborah Cooper and Travis stared at each other in silence. She did not dare run to the telephone; he did not dare run away. Then there was a gunshot, and Deborah Cooper crumpled to the floor. Chief Pratt had shot her with his service pistol.

"Are you crazy?" Travis shouted. "What the fuck! Why did you do that?"

"We had no choice, Travis. You know what would have happened to us if she had talked . . ."

Travis was trembling. "What now?" he asked.

"I don't know."

Nola, who was terrified, gathered up her strength and took advantage of their indecision to break free of Travis's grip. Before Chief Pratt had time to react, she had climbed through the kitchen window and was running down the steps. But she lost her balance and fell. She got right back up, but by then the chief was holding her by her hair. She screamed and bit his hand. The chief loosened his grip, but she didn't have time to run away. Travis hit her on the back of her head with his nightstick. She collapsed to the ground. He recoiled in horror. There was blood everywhere. She was dead.

Travis remained crouched over the body for a moment. He wanted to throw up. Pratt was shaking. The sound of birdsong reached them from the woods.

"What have we done, Chief?" whispered Travis, eyes glinting.

"Stay calm, Travis. Stay calm. Panicking is not going to help."

"Yes, Chief."

"We have to get rid of Caleb and Nola. We could get the death penalty for this, you know."

"Yes, Chief. What about Mrs Cooper?"

"We'll make it look like she was killed by a robber. You need to do exactly what I tell you."

Travis was crying now.

"Yes, Chief. I'll do what I have to."

"You told me you saw Caleb's car near Shore Road?"

"Yes. The keys are in the ignition."

"Good. We're going to put his body in the car. And you're going to get rid of it, O.K.?"

"Yes."

"As soon as you're gone, I'll call for backup, so nobody suspects. We'll have to act fast. By the time the reinforcements arrive, you'll be long gone. In the crush of people, no-one will notice your absence."

"Yes. But, Chief . . . I think Mrs Cooper called 911 again."

"Fuck! We have to get going then!"

They dragged Luther's and Nola's bodies to the Chevrolet. Then Pratt ran through the forest back toward Deborah Cooper's house and his police car. He used his car radio to say he'd found Deborah Cooper shot dead.

Travis got behind the wheel of the Chevrolet and started the engine. As he was emerging from the bushes, he passed a sheriff's patrol car that had been dispatched after Deborah Cooper's second phone call.

Pratt was talking to the station when he heard a police siren close by. The radio announced a chase on Shore Road between a sheriff's car and a black Chevrolet Monte Carlo spotted coming out near Side Creek Lane. Chief Pratt told them he would join the chase immediately. He started up his vehicle, turned on the siren, and drove along the parallel forest path. When he came out on Shore Road, he just avoided crashing into Travis. Their eyes met for a moment: Both men were terrified.

During the chase, Travis managed to make the sheriff's car swerve off the road. He then took Shore Road back southward and turned off at Goose Cove. Pratt followed close behind, pretending to pursue him. He gave false positions on the car radio, claiming he was on the Montburry road. He turned off his siren, pulled in to the Goose Cove path, and met up with Travis in front of the house. The two men got out of their cars, both feeling desperate.

"Are you crazy? Why the hell did you stop here?" Pratt demanded.

"Quebert's not here," Travis said. "He'll be out of town for a while. He told Jenny Quinn, and she told me."

"I asked for roadblocks on every road. I had to."

"Shit! Shit!" Travis hissed. "We're trapped! So what do we do now?"

Pratt looked around. He noticed the empty garage. "Leave the car in there, lock the garage door, and get back to Side Creek Lane as fast as you can along the beach. Pretend to search Mrs Cooper's house. I'll join the chase again. We can get rid of the bodies tonight. Do you have a jacket in your car?"

"Yes."

"Put it on. You're covered in blood."

Fifteen minutes later, while Pratt was passing backup patrols near Montburry, Travis—wearing a rain jacket, and surrounded by colleagues who had come from all over the state—was sealing off the area around Side Creek Lane, where Deborah Cooper's body had just been found.

In the middle of the night, Travis and Pratt went back to Goose Cove. They buried Nola about sixty feet from the house. Pratt had already defined the search area with Captain Rodik from the state police.

He knew that Goose Cove was not included, so nobody would come here to look for Nola. They buried her with her leather shoulder bag, without even looking inside to see what was in it.

When the hole had been filled in, Travis took the black Chevrolet and drove down Shore Road, with Luther's corpse in the trunk. He entered Massachusetts. On the way, he had to pass through two police roadblocks.

"Can I see your papers please, sir?" the cops said each time, nervously eyeing the car.

And each time Travis showed them his badge.

"Somerset police, guys. I'm trying to find our man too."

The policemen respectfully waved their colleague through, wishing him good luck.

He drove until he reached a small coastal town that he knew well. Sagamore. He took the ocean road, the one that runs back north toward Ellisville Harbor. The parking area was empty. The view from here was beautiful in the daytime; he had often thought of bringing Jenny here for a romantic vacation. He stopped the car, put Luther's body in the driver's seat, and poured alcohol down his throat. Then he put the car in neutral and pushed it. It rolled slowly down the little grassy slope, before hurtling over the edge and disappearing into the void amid a crash of metal.

He walked back down the road for a few hundred yards. A car was waiting on the shoulder. He got in the passenger seat. He was sweating and covered in blood.

"It's done," he told Pratt, who sat behind the wheel.

The chief started the car.

"We must never talk about what happened, Travis. And when they find the car, I'll just keep it quiet. The only way we can be sure to get away with this is to never arrest anyone. You understand?"

Travis nodded. He slid his hand into his pocket and fingered the necklace he had secretly taken from around Nola's neck before they buried her. A pretty gold necklace with the name NOLA engraved on it.

Harry had sat back down on the couch.

"So they killed Nola, Luther, and Mrs Cooper."

"Yes. And they arranged it so that the investigation would never lead anywhere. So, Harry, you knew that Nola had psychotic episodes, didn't you? You talked about it with David Kellergan . . ."

"I didn't know about the fire. But I discovered that Nola was mentally fragile when I went to the Kellergans' house to confront them about the physical abuse. I had promised Nola I would not go to see her parents, but I felt I couldn't just let it continue. That was when I realized that Nola's father was the only parent still alive, that he had been a widower for six years, and that the situation was way beyond him. He refused to face facts. I had to take Nola far from Somerset so she could receive the treatment she needed."

"So that was why you were running away? To get Nola help?"

"That had become the reason, for me. I would have taken her to a good doctor, and she would have been treated. She was an amazing girl, Marcus. She would have helped me become a great writer, and I would have helped her be happy and sane. She was my guide and my inspiration. She has guided me throughout my life. You know that, don't you? You know that better than anyone."

"Yes, Harry. But why didn't you tell me?"

"I wanted to. I would have, if it hadn't been for those leaks from your book. I thought you had betrayed my trust. I was angry with you. I think I wanted your book to be a failure; I knew that no-one would take you seriously if you made a mistake like that about Nola's mother. Yes, that's what it was: I wanted your second book to be a failure. As mine was."

We were silent for a moment.

"I regret it," Harry finally added. "I regret everything. You must be so disappointed in me."

"No."

"I know you are. You put so much faith in me. And I built my life on a lie!"

"I've always admired you for who you are, Harry. It doesn't really matter to me whether you wrote that book or not. It was you—the man you are—who taught me so much about life. And no-one can take that away."

"No—you'll never see me the same way anymore. And you know it. I'm just a fraud. An impostor! That was why I said we could no longer be friends. It's all over. You're becoming a great writer, and I'm no longer anything at all. You're a real writer; I have never been one. You struggled to write your book, you struggled to rediscover inspiration, you overcame all the hurdles. And when I was in the same situation as you, I cheated."

"Harry, I—"

"That's life, Marcus. And you know I'm right. You could never look me in the eyes anymore. And I could never look at you without feeling an overwhelming, destructive jealousy—because you succeeded where I failed."

He held me close to him.

"Harry," I whispered, "I don't want to lose you."

"You'll be fine without me. You've become a great man, a great writer. You'll be absolutely fine—I know you will. Our paths are taking different directions now. We have different destinies. It was never my destiny to become a great writer. I tried to change my destiny—I stole a book, I lied for thirty-three years. But destiny is invincible: It always triumphs in the end."

"Harry—"

"Your destiny was always to be a writer, Marcus. I knew that from the beginning. And I also knew that this moment would arrive."

"You'll always be my friend."

"Finish your book. The book about me—you have to finish it. You know the truth, and now you need to tell it to the world. The truth will set us all free. Write the truth about the Harry Quebert affair. Free me from the evil that has plagued me for thirty-three years. This is the last thing I'll ask of you."

"But how? I can't erase the past."

"No, but you can change the present. That's a writer's power. Writers' heaven, remember? I know you'll find a way to do it."

"Harry, I owe you everything! You made me the man I am now."

"That's just an illusion. I didn't do anything. You did it on your own."

"No, that's not true! I followed your advice. I followed your thirty-one rules. That's how I wrote my first book. And the next one. And it's how I'll write all the others that will come after. Your thirty-one rules, Harry—don't you remember?"

He smiled sadly. "Of course I remember."

Burrows, Christmas 1999

"Happy Holidays, Marcus!"

"You got me a gift? Thank you, Harry. What is it?"

"Open it. It's a minidisc recorder. The latest technological gizmo, apparently. You spend all your time taking notes on what I say, but then you lose the notes and I have to repeat it all. I figured with this you can just record everything."

"That's a great idea. Let's do it."

"Do what?"

"Give me your first piece of advice. I'm going to record it all."

"Oh, O.K. What kind of advice?"

"I don't know . . . Rules for writers. And for boxers. And for human beings."

"Ha-ha. Alright. How many do you want?"

"At least a hundred!"

"A hundred? I'm going to give you thirty-one rules. But I'll give them to you over the years, not all at the same time."

"Why thirty-one?"

"Because thirty-one is an important age. Your teenage years mold you as an adolescent. Your twenties mold you as an adult. Your thirties will make you a man, or not. And when you reach thirty-one, you begin that phase. How do you imagine yourself at thirty-one?"

"Like you."

"Don't be silly. Turn on your recorder. I'm going to give you the rules in descending order. Rule number thirty-one: This one will be advice about books. So, rule thirty-one: The first chapter, Marcus, is essential. If the readers don't like it, they won't read the rest of your book. How do you plan to begin yours?"

"I don't know, Harry. Do you think I'll ever be able to do it?"

"Do what?"

"Write a book."

"I'm certain you will."

He looked at me steadily and smiled.

"You're not even thirty, Marcus. And you've done it: you've become a magnificent man. Being Marcus the Magnificent was an achievement of sorts, but becoming a magnificent man is the crowning glory of a long and wonderful battle with yourself. I'm very proud of you."

He put his coat back on and wound his scarf around his neck.

"Where are you going?" I said.

"I have to leave now."

"Don't leave! Stay!"

"I can't . . ."

"Stay, Harry! Stay a little longer."

"I can't. Goodbye, Marcus. I'm so glad you came into my life."

"Where are you going?"

"I have to wait for Nola somewhere."

He embraced me.

"Find love, Marcus. Love gives life its meaning. You're stronger when you love. You're bigger. You go further."

"Harry! Please don't leave!"

"Goodbye, Marcus."

He left. He did not close the door behind him, and I left it open for a long time afterward. That was the last time I saw my master and my friend, Harry Quebert.

May 2002, finals of the university boxing championship

"Marcus, are you ready? You go in the ring in three minutes."

"I'm scared, Harry."

"I'm sure you are. But that's good: You can't win unless you're scared. Don't forget: Boxing is like writing a book. You remember? Chapter one, chapter two . . ."

"Yes. Jab in the first, hook in the second . . ."

"Exactly, champ. Are you ready? You're in the finals, Marcus! The finals! Not so long ago you were still fighting against heavy bags, and now you're in the finals. Can you hear the loudspeaker? 'Marcus Goldman and his coach, Harry Quebert, from Burrows College.' That's us! Let's go!"

"Wait, Harry . . ."

"What?"

"I have a gift for you."

"A gift? Now?"

"Absolutely. I want you to have it before the match. It's in my bag. Take it. I can't give it to you with these gloves on."

"It's a C.D.?"

"Yes, a compilation. Your thirty-one most important statements. About boxing, about life, about books."

"Thank you, Marcus. I'm touched. Now, are you ready to fight?"

"I sure am."

"Let's go, then."

"Hang on—there's still one thing I'm wondering . . ."

"Marcus, they're waiting for us!"

"But this is important. I've listened to all our recordings, and you never answered me about one thing."

"Alright. What is it?"

"How do you know when a book is finished?"

"Books are like life, Marcus. They never really end."

EPILOGUE

October 2009
(one year after the book's publication)

"A good book, Marcus, is judged not by its last words but by the cumulative effect of all the words that have preceded them. About half a second after finishing your book, after reading the very last word, the reader should be overwhelmed by a particular feeling. For a moment he should think only of what he has just read; he should look at the cover and smile a little sadly because he is already missing all the characters. A good book, Marcus, is a book you are sorry to have finished."

The beach at Goose Cove, October 17, 2010

"Rumor has it you have a new book, writer."

"That's true."

I was sitting next to Gahalowood, facing the ocean. We were drinking beer. The sun was going down.

"To the latest success of the talented Marcus Goldman!" Gahalowood declared. "What's it about?"

"I'm sure you'll read it. You're in it, after all."

"Really? Can I take a look now?"

"No chance, Sergeant."

"Well, if it's bad I'll expect a refund."

"Goldman doesn't offer refunds anymore, Sergeant."

He laughed.

"Tell me, writer, what gave you the idea of rebuilding this house and turning it into a retreat for young writers?"

"I don't know. It just came to me."

"The Harry Quebert House for Writers. It's got a nice ring to it. You writers have a great life, you know. Coming here to look at the ocean and write books . . . I'd like a job like that. Have you seen today's *New York Times*?"

"No."

He took a newspaper clipping from his pocket and unfolded it, then read out loud: "The Seagulls of Somerset *is a must-read new novel. Luther Caleb, wrongly accused of murdering Nola Kellergan, was a brilliant writer whose talent was never discovered during his lifetime. Schmid & Hanson do honor to his memory by publishing a posthumous edition of the scintillating novel he wrote about the relationship between Nola Kellergan and Harry Quebert. This wonderful novel tells how Harry Quebert was inspired by his love for Nola Kellergan to write* The Origin of Evil."

He stopped reading and laughed.

"What's funny, Sergeant?" I asked.

"Nothing. You're just brilliant, Goldman. Brilliant!"

"The police are not the only ones who can dispense justice, Sergeant."

We finished our beers.

"I'm going back to New York tomorrow," I said.

He nodded. "Drop by from time to time, writer. Just to say hi. It would make my wife happy."

"I'd love to."

"Oh, you never told me—what's the title of your new book?"

"*The Truth about the Harry Quebert Affair.*"

He looked thoughtful. We walked back to our cars. A flock of seagulls crossed the sky; we watched them for a moment. Then Gahalowood asked: "So what are you going to do now, writer?"

"One day Harry said to me: 'You must give meaning to your life. Two things can make life meaningful: books and love.' Thanks to Harry I already have books. Now I am setting off in search of love."

BURROWS COLLEGE

congratulates

Marcus P. GOLDMAN

Winner of the
University Boxing Championship 2002

And his trainer:

Harry L. Quebert

ACKNOWLEDGMENTS

My heartfelt thanks to Ernie Pinkas, of Somerset, New Hampshire, for the valuable help he gave me.

Also to Sergeant Perry Gahalowood (New Hampshire state police) and Officer Philip Thomas (Alabama state police highway patrol).

Last, special thanks to my assistant, Denise, without whom I would not have been able to finish this book.

TABLE OF CONTENTS

The Day of the Disappearance (Saturday, August 30, 1975)

PROLOGUE
October 2008 (thirty-three years after the disappearance)

PART ONE
WRITERS' DISEASE
(eight months before the book's publication)

31. In the Caverns of Memory
30. Marcus the Magnificent
29. Is it Possible to Fall in Love with a Fifteen-Year-Old Girl?
28. The Importance of Knowing How to Fall
      (Burrows University, Massachusetts, 1998–2002)
27. Where the Hydrangeas Were Planted
26. N-O-L-A
      (Aurora, New Hampshire, Saturday, June 14, 1975)
25. About Nola
24. Memories of Independence Day
23. Those Who Knew Her Well
22. Police Investigation
21. On the Difficulties of Love
20. The Day of the Garden Party
19. The Harry Quebert Affair
18. Martha's Vineyard
      (Massachusetts, late July, 1975)
17. Escape Attempt
16. *The Origin of Evil*
      (Aurora, New Hampshire, August 11–20, 1975)
15. Before the Storm

PART TWO
WRITERS' CURE
(writing the book)

14. August 30, 1975
13. The Storm
12. The Man Who Painted Pictures
11. Waiting for Nola
10. In Search of a Fifteen-Year-Old Girl
    (Aurora, New Hampshire, September 1–18, 1975)
9. A Black Monte Carlo
8. The Identity of Anonymous
7. After Nola
6. The Barnaski Principle

PART THREE
WRITERS' PARADISE
(the book's publication)

5. The Girl Who Touched the Heart of America
4. Sweet Home, Alabama
3. Election Day
2. Endgame
1. The Truth about the Harry Quebert Affair

EPILOGUE
October 2009 (one year after the book's publication)

Acknowledgments

JOËL DICKER was born in Geneva in 1985. *The Truth about the Harry Quebert Affair* was shortlisted for the Prix Goncourt and won the Grand Prix du Roman de l'Académie Française and the Prix Goncourt des Lycéens. It has sold more than two million copies across Europe.

SAM TAYLOR's translated works include Laurent Binet's award-winning novel *HHhH*. His own novels have been translated into ten languages.